Rolling Thunder

Rolling Thunder

Mickey Minner

P.D. Publishing, Inc.
Clayton, North Carolina

ISBN-13: 978-1-933720-36-4
ISBN-10: 1-933720-36-0

9 8 7 6 5 4 3 2 1

Cover photo by Mickey Minner
Cover design by Barb Coles
Edited by: Day Petersen/Medora MacDougall

Published by:

P.D. Publishing, Inc.
P.O. Box 70
Clayton, NC 27528

http://www.pdpublishing.com

Acknowledgements

I would like to thank the readers who take time from their busy lives to read my stories and write me with words of encouragement. And the members of my discussion group who generously support my writing yet keep my feet firmly rooted to the ground.

I would also like to thank Linda and Barb at PD Publishing for the enthusiastic support of my writing. Theresa Harris, Day Petersen, and Medora MacDougall for their editing expertise and guiding me through the process, and Jo Fothergill for being my rock during some stressful months.

The Sweetwater Saga stories are dedicated to my Grandfather, Charley F. Stetler, who inspired my love for the old west — a love that has never faded and continues to grow.

To my Grandmother, Edith M. Stetler, who always said I should be a writer.

To my parents, Bob and Madelyn Minner, who even when they didn't understand never stopped loving me.

CHAPTER ONE

Jesse Branson strode across the ranch yard through the late afternoon shadows. Her shoulder-length auburn hair, once tied neatly back into a ponytail, had come loose as she completed her chores, and now a warm breeze blew wisps of hair about her tanned face. A pail of warm milk swinging easily at the end of a sinewy arm, Jesse walked effortlessly, her long legs making short work of the distance between barn and cabin. With her work done, she was looking forward to spending the evening with her lover and daughter.

"Darlin'?" Jesse called into the cabin as she pushed the door open. "Brought some fresh milk for KC." She stepped inside, surprised to find the cabin dark lit only by the glowing embers in the fireplace. "Jennifer?" She set the milk pail on a table under the window to her left. "Ya can't have gone too far," she said as she surveyed the deserted room.

The plain log cabin had a fireplace at each end and a door in the middle of each long side. Between the doors and end walls, windows had been cut into the logs to allow sunlight into what would have otherwise been a rather dark interior.

Jesse smiled. How different the simple cabin seemed since Jennifer had come to live with her. Gone were the rickety chairs and table under the window, replaced by a much studier set. Neatly arranged dishes and cooking pots were stacked on newly made shelves attached to the logs, and foodstuffs — once left in boxes until needed — were arranged in an orderly fashion on more shelves.

At the opposite end of the cabin, the head of the bed remained in its original location — pushed up against a window — but new blankets had replaced the tattered quilts Jesse had inherited from the ranch's previous owner. The bookcase she had made still occupied the space under the opposite window, only now it held many more books, as Jennifer was also a devoted reader. The dresser, which she had rarely used, now held the carefully folded dresses Jennifer wore when teaching school and extra clothing and diapers for the baby.

The cabin definitely had a different feel to it. It was no longer just the place Jesse came back to after a long day of working on the ranch or in town at the boarding house she owned. The cabin was now a home she shared with the woman she loved and the baby they were raising as their own.

Smiling, Jesse walked toward the door at the back of the cabin.

Sitting outside on the wooden steps, Jennifer Kensington could hear the rancher's boot heels striking the floor planks as she moved about the cabin. She knew her lover would soon come looking for her.

"Your mommy is back," Jennifer told the baby in her arms. Sleepy eyes opened wide in response, and the baby's feet kicked excitedly. "You love her, too, don't you?" she said to the smiling baby.

"Everything all right, darlin'?" Jesse asked as she walked out of the cabin and sat on the rough steps beside Jennifer.

"Yes."

"Then what're you doin' sittin' out here?"

"Thinking."

There was a hint of sadness in Jennifer's voice, and it concerned Jesse more than a little. "About?"

"KC's been waiting for you to sing her to sleep." Jennifer laid the baby in Jesse's waiting arms.

"Seems to me, she's mostly asleep already. Ain't ya, Sunshine?" Jesse lifted the baby to her face, rubbing her nose against KC's and laughing when the baby giggled. Every time she held KC, the infant they had discovered under a burned and ransacked Conestoga wagon, she was amazed by how much the child looked like Jennifer, sharing the same ginger-colored hair and blue eyes. "I love you, KC. You have sweet dreams tonight." She kissed the baby's forehead, then cradled KC in her arms, rocking and softly singing a favorite lullaby. Before long, the baby was sound asleep.

Jennifer reached over to make sure the blanket was tucked snugly around KC, protecting her from the cooling air.

"Want to talk about it?"

Jennifer leaned against Jesse's shoulder. "I'm not sure."

Shifting the baby to one arm, Jesse wrapped the other around Jennifer. The women sat watching the sun slowly drop in the west, changing the blue sky to a mosaic of reds and oranges.

"I was thinking about how much my life has changed in the past few months," Jennifer began quietly. "It seems like only yesterday I was talking Matt into buying me a train ticket to Denver so I could live the life I've always dreamed of."

"And what is the life you dreamed of?"

"To prove I was more than just my father's chattel, good only for marrying off in some business arrangement. That I was smart and capable and could do something useful."

"I'd say you prove that every day at the schoolhouse," Jesse assured Sweetwater's schoolteacher. "And every day you take care of this baby and me." When Jennifer remained quiet, Jesse posed a question straight on. "Are you happy, darlin'? Being here, being with me?"

Jennifer sat up to look at her lover. The questions, and the doubt behind them, had caught her completely off guard. "Yes. Why would you ask that?" The rancher's body tensed. "Do you think I'm not?"

"To be honest, darlin', you've been... Well, I wasn't sure. I mean, ever since we got back from Bannack, you've been kind of quiet. I just...I just thought that maybe you might be..."

"Having second thoughts?"

"Yeah. Somethin' like that."

"I'm not. I'm happier now than I've ever been. I'm happier than I ever thought I could be." Jennifer snuggled into the circle of Jesse's arm.

"Good." Jesse relaxed and laid her head against Jennifer's. "'Cause I don't know what I'd do if you weren't."

"I love you, Jesse. And I can't think of any place I would rather be than with you."

"But?"

"But you have to admit that since I arrived in Sweetwater, our lives have been...well, unusual to say the least. First, you got arrested for cattle rustling and almost got hanged. We barely got you out of that and then you got shot. When all of that mess got settled, we rode to Bannack and along the way found KC's parents murdered. The reverend in Bannack tried to take KC away from us, and the sheriff tried to have us killed. And in the middle of all that — we fall in love, you propose, and we decide to raise KC as our own daughter."

"When you put it like that, it does seem to have been a tad more than most folks are used to havin' happen." Jesse grinned as Jennifer playfully poked her in the side. "But you have to admit, there were good things along with the bad. We found each other and we found KC."

"Those are wonderful, sweetheart, but are you sure that getting married is the right thing to do?"

"I thought you wanted to get married. Wasn't that part of your dream, too?"

"Yes. But I just expected I'd meet a—"

"Man?"

Jennifer sighed. "Yes. But Jesse, I didn't know anything else. I never knew two women could fall in love. In fact, I didn't know very much about love at all, except what my mother and father had, and I was sure that wasn't anything I wanted."

"How do you feel about loving me, darlin', lovin' a woman?"

"I don't think anyone else could make me as happy as you do, Jesse, man or woman. But are you sure two women can get married?"

"Billie said there ain't no law saying we can't."

"I'm...I don't know if I want to do it in town. I mean, in front of the whole town. Can't we ask Mayor Perkins to perform the ceremony here? We can have Bette Mae and Ed and Billie come out to the ranch."

Jesse mulled over Jennifer's suggestion. Although she thought she understood how Jennifer felt, she was sure she knew her own feelings. "Do you love me?"

"More than anything."

"Enough to want to be my wife?"

"Yes."

"I love you, too, darlin', and I want everyone to know just how much. But if you don't want us to get married in town, we won't. It doesn't matter to me where we do it, just as long as we do."

"Then," Jennifer sat up, turning to face Jesse, "let's get married."

"That's my girl." Jesse beamed at her lover. "What do ya say we put KC to bed and I'll show you just how happy you make me?" She tried to pull Jennifer back to her, intending to kiss her.

Jennifer stood. "First, you need a bath." Laughing at the pout forming on Jesse's face, she added, "I'll scrub your back."

"How about you joining me and I'll scrub yours?"

"How could I possibly turn down such an offer?"

"You can't." Jesse stood. Reaching for Jennifer's hand, she entwined their fingers. Gently tugging Jennifer to her, she pressed her lips against her lover's. "I love you."

"I love you more."

"So's yer goin' through with it?" Bette Mae asked after Jesse told her of her talk with Jennifer the night before.

"Is there some reason we shouldn't?"

The women were in Jesse's office in the Silver Slipper, the rooming house and saloon Jesse owned in Sweetwater and Bette Mae ran for her. The older woman was more a friend than an employee. KC was sitting in Bette Mae's lap, happily playing with the little toy horse Jesse had bought for her during their stay in Bannack. Every few minutes she would look toward the office door, hoping to see her momma returning from her walk to the schoolhouse.

"Now don' go gettin' yer feathers all ruffled up," Bette Mae said to calm the rancher. "But ya knows there's folks in the valley tha' won' take kindly ta two of the prettiest girls about these parts gettin' hitched to each other. Sure ya shouldn't jus' keep things the ways they are?"

"What difference does it make if we just live together or we get married? Either way, we ain't gonna be allowin' any lonesome cowpoke to come callin'."

Bette Mae had to think on Jesse's answer for a minute. "Guess that makes sense. But them lonesome cowpokes still ain't gonna take kindly to you two marryin'. There's damn few marryin' women in this valley as it is, especially since ya sent the workin' girls packin' when ya took over the Slipper. Not that I'm complainin' 'bout that." She and the other girls who had stayed to work in the Slipper as cooks, maids, and bartender had been more than happy to give up their previous livelihoods. The ones that hadn't been happy with the changes were provided a one-way stage ticket out of Sweetwater, courtesy of Jesse.

"Reckon they'll just have to get used to it."

"Who will have to get used to what?" Jennifer asked as she entered the office. She didn't need to see the scowl on her lover's face to know she wasn't happy about something.

"Bette Mae seems to think the cowboys in the valley will be upset if we get married." Jesse stood to greet her lover with a welcoming hug and kiss. "Someone has been missin' ya, darlin'."

"I've been missing her, too." Jennifer looked over the rancher's shoulder at their daughter who was reaching out for her. "Give your mommy a minute to hug me, sweetie," she told KC, "then I'll come get you."

"Everything all right at the schoolhouse?"

"Yes. I really wasn't expecting it not to be, but I guess I just needed to check it out for myself." The school term had ended several weeks earlier. With their trip to Bannack and being so busy with KC since returning, she had not had a chance to visit the one-room building before now.

"Just had to make sure it was still there, didn't ya?" Jesse teased, but she could understand how Jennifer felt. After winning the Silver Slipper in a poker game, more than once she had found herself just standing in the middle of Sweetwater's only street, staring at the two-story building as if to assure herself that she wasn't dreaming her good luck.

"Something like that." Jennifer smiled, kissing Jesse once more before gently pushing out of her arms to go to KC. "Have you been a good girl?" she asked as she sat beside Bette Mae on the couch and lifted the baby into her arms.

"She's been a right angel," Bette Mae said. She frowned at Jesse. "More than I can say for that one."

"Okay, what is this about the cowboys in the valley?"

"Bette Mae thinks that if I marry you, it'll dash their hopes," Jesse leaned against the front edge of her desk, grinning at the frowning woman, "and hearts."

"I never thought of that." Jennifer leaned back and held KC firmly as the baby stood in her lap, testing the strength of her legs. "Maybe getting married isn't a good idea. I don't want to upset anyone."

Jesse was frustrated with Jennifer's backsliding and upset that Bette Mae was causing it. "Darlin', do you plan on courtin' any of them cowboys?"

"Of course not."

"You plannin' on getting' hitched to any of 'em?"

"Don't be silly."

"Then they're gonna be upset anyway. Us gettin' married shouldn't make that much of a difference."

Jennifer looked at Bette Mae, who shrugged. "Much as it pains me to say so, she does have a point," Bette Mae said. "I jus' think ya should figure on some not takin' too kindly to it happenin'."

"Sweetheart?"

Jesse pushed off the desk. There wasn't enough room on the couch for her to sit beside Jennifer so she knelt in front of her instead. "Darlin', the boys around here didn't like me when I showed up in town with the deed to the Slipper in my pocket. And they didn't like me for clearing out the gamblers and the working girls. They didn't take too kindly to me buying the ranch and startin' a cattle herd. I didn't care what they thought then, and I don't care what they think about me loving you. All I care is that you love me."

"I do love you."

"So do we get married or not?"

Jennifer smiled. "We do."

"It's 'bout time ya made up yer minds," Bette Mae declared gleefully. "I was beginnin' ta think ya'd never get around to it."

Jesse shot Bette Mae a glare, only to catch the twinkle in her eyes. "You was saying all that just to make sure we knew what we were doing," she accused.

"Best ya thinks 'bout it afore than after, when the tittle-tattle gets a-started."

"Anyone says anything and I'll—"

"Jesse," Jennifer placed her hand against her lover's cheek, "promise me you won't do anything. No matter what anyone says."

Jesse leaned into Jennifer's caress. "I can't promise that, darlin'. You'll be my wife, and I won't let anyone say or do anything that hurts you. Or KC." She looked into her lover's eyes. "Don't ask me to." She was pleased when Jennifer nodded.

"Seein' yers down on yers knees anyway, ya goin' ta ask her to marry ya, right and proper?"

"I thought I already had."

"Never hurts ta make sure she knows how ya feel."

Jesse turned back to Jennifer. "Marry me?"

"Yes."

Jesse looked up at the grinning Bette Mae. "Happy?"

"I don' have time to be happy right now." Bette Mae leapt up from the couch, the movement so unexpected that both Jesse and Jennifer jumped in surprise. "I gots me a weddin' ta plan."

"Wait a minute," Jesse called after the woman scurrying toward the office door. "Don't you want to hear..."

"You might as well give up on her." Jennifer laughed. "I don't think we'll be getting much say in *our* wedding plans."

Jesse took Bette Mae's place on the couch. "I'll talk to her."

"Don't."

"No?"

Jennifer scooted over to lean against Jesse. "Don't spoil her fun, sweetheart. I think our wedding may mean more to her than we know."

Remembering the reason behind their recent trip to Bannack, Jesse had to wonder if Bette Mae might be thinking about a lost love, a woman who had married a no-account man and paid for that mistake with her life. "You think she probably wanted the chance to ask Elizabeth about marryin'?"

"Yes." Jennifer sighed. "I'm glad we found each other before we ended up like Elizabeth."

Bette Mae strode back into the office and stood with her hands on her ample hips. "Well, what are ya waitin' for? This here's yer weddin', so's yas might want ta come on out and help us plan it."

"We're coming, Bette Mae." Jesse laughed as the woman tapped her foot impatiently. "But first KC needs her britches changed and a feeding, or she'll be wailing loud enough to raise the roof."

"I can do that," Jennifer offered.

Jesse took the baby. "No, you go on with Bette Mae. I'm pretty sure you know a lot more about planning weddings than I do."

"Ain't tha' the truth," Bette Mae said with a chuckle.

"Don't be long," Jennifer said as she followed Bette Mae out of the room.

"I won't." Jesse reached for the canvas bag on the floor beside the couch that held clean diapers for the baby. "I'm not sure what kind of wedding Bette Mae is goin' ta be fixin' for us, KC," she told the baby as she laid her down on the couch. "But as long as your momma and you are there, that's all I need."

KC smiled and wrapped her fingers around Jesse's much larger one. She pulled the finger to her mouth and sucked on it. "I know you're hungry, Sunshine. Let's get your britches changed, then I bet we can find some milk in Bette Mae's kitchen.

CHAPTER TWO

The days leading up to the wedding were full of activity. Bette Mae closed the Silver Slipper so the dining room could be converted into a wedding chapel. The saloon was cleared of the gaming tables to provide a dance floor for the after-ceremony festivities. The wedding was to be the biggest social event ever in the small community. Word was sent out to everyone in the valley, and not much else was being talked about. Despite Bette Mae's concerns, folks were breaking out their best clothes and shining up their boots and belt buckles. Jesse and Jennifer spent the days at the ranch, happy to leave Bette Mae in charge of the wedding plans.

"Jesse?" Jennifer settled KC on a blanket in the shade of the cabin's porch, then sat beside the baby. "Why won't you tell me what you're going to wear at the wedding?"

The topic of Jesse's clothing had become an obsession for Jennifer. While Jesse knew what she was wearing, the rancher had been very secretive about her own outfit.

Jesse chuckled as she continued cutting lengths of wood. After putting the finishing touches on a crib for the baby, she had begun work on a much-needed high chair. The women realized it would be better for KC to sit on her own when eating than to continue being fed while one of them held her.

"I told you not to worry about it. I've got the perfect thing."

Jennifer kept her eyes on KC, who was rocking on all fours. "But it's not fair, you've seen my dress." A wedding dress had been a surprise purchase during their stay in Bannack.

"True." Jesse finished cutting another chair leg. "But I haven't seen you in it, darlin'."

"You're not going to tell me, are you?"

Jesse grinned. "Nope." Jennifer frowned, and Jesse put down her saw and crossed to the porch. "Only have one more day to wait, darlin'." Claiming the spot next to Jennifer, Jesse wrapped an arm around her lover's waist and pulled her close. "I love you," she whispered as she leaned in for a gentle kiss.

While they spent the next several moments enjoying each other's lips, Jennifer's hand found its way under Jesse's shirt, and she caressed the strong back, slick with sweat. Jesse pulled Jennifer closer, slipping a hand inside her shirt where it quickly found a breast to squeeze. Just when Jesse was going to lay Jennifer down onto the porch so they could explore each other further, a small hand smacked her leg, and she heard KC talking to her in baby gibberish. Jennifer laughed as Jesse pulled back in frustration to glare at the child.

A big grin on her face, KC reached up to Jesse, wanting to join her favorite playmate.

Lifting the baby into her lap, Jesse said seriously, "Seems I'm goin' have to teach you not to interrupt when I'm kissin' your momma, Sunshine."

Leaning against Jesse's shoulder, Jennifer tickled KC. "Seems someone has gotten over her fear of doing that in front of the baby."

"Figured if we were goin' to have her around all the time, she'd just have to get used to it." Jesse helped the baby climb up her body to wrap tiny arms around her neck. The baby looked the rancher straight in the eye, setting off on a long tirade of baby gibberish. "I do believe she has your argumentative streak," Jesse teased.

Jennifer poked Jesse in the side. "Wonder what she's telling you."

"Probably that I should wait until she takes her nap before I try to kiss her momma." Jesse kissed the baby. "Ain't that right, Sunshine?"

"Sweetheart, don't talk that way in front of her," Jennifer scolded.

"What? I shouldn't say kiss?"

"No. Don't say ain't. It isn't proper."

"Uh, oh, Sunshine," Jesse told the baby. "Looks like you and me are in trouble with your momma. She's gonna want us to be nice and proper ladies." Placing her mouth next to the KC's ear, Jesse whispered loudly enough for Jennifer to hear, "But it *ain't* gonna happen, is it?"

The baby giggled at the warm breath tickling the side of her face.

Jennifer scowled at her smirking lover and rolled her eyes. "Oh, bother."

The morning of the wedding dawned bright and clear. Jesse, Jennifer, and KC arrived in town early to enjoy breakfast with Bette Mae and the other employees of the Slipper who had worked tirelessly to prepare for the wedding. After breakfast, Jennifer and KC went upstairs to dress. Left alone, Jesse disappeared into her office.

Sitting at her desk, she smiled as she thought about the impending ceremony. She was happy, but happy really wasn't enough of a word to describe her feelings. It was more a sense of peace. Yes, that was it. She was at peace with her life, her lover, and her child. She was indeed the happiest woman on earth. Except, maybe, for the ginger-haired beauty she was about to marry.

Best get this show on the road, Jesse thought. She leaned down and opened the bottom drawer of her desk, carefully removing a box with a string tied around it. "Never did understand why I felt I had to buy this, but guess it makes sense now." She stood, carrying the box from the room.

Jennifer stood beside the bed where her wedding dress was laid out.

"It's a beautiful dress, Miss Jennifer," Ruthie said. The young woman worked at the Slipper, and Jennifer had discovered soon after arriving in Sweetwater that Ruthie was a skilled seamstress.

"Thank you, Ruthie. I appreciate you altering it to fit me better."

"Seems ta me, tha' dressmaker in Bannack shoulda done tha' for ya," Bette Mae groused.

"You're probably right. But by the time Jesse surprised me by buying it, we'd already been in the store for a couple of hours. I just didn't want to spend any more time with that woman; she gave me a funny feeling." Jennifer stood still while Bette Mae and Ruthie raised the dress over her head and then slipped it down her body to rest on her shoulders.

"Wha' kinda feelin'?" Bette Mae asked when Jennifer's head reappeared.

"Oh, it's probably nothing." Jennifer straightened the dress around her hips. "I just think she knew me from before."

"Thinkin' she might bring ya trouble?"

"I hope not." Jennifer smiled at KC who was sitting on the bed, jabbering and pointing at her. "You like my dress, sweetie? Your mommy has good taste, doesn't she?"

"Surprisin', ain't it?" Bette Mae laughed, bending over to lift KC into her arms. "Your momma is awful pretty, ain't she?" she asked the baby.

Jennifer shook her head, laughing. Trying to teach the giggling child proper grammar was going to be a difficult task, but that truly didn't bother her. She was much too happy at seeing the love surrounding KC, a love she had seldom felt as a child.

"Go on, child," Bette Mae commanded. "Take a look at yerself."

As Ruthie finished buttoning up the back of the dress, Jennifer stood in front of the full-length mirror. Though the dress was a simple design of linen and lace, she thought she had never seen one more exquisite. Of course, the fact that it had been purchased for her by Jesse probably had a lot to do with that. "It is beautiful, isn't it?" she breathed.

"It surely is. And so is you." Bette Mae smiled at the schoolteacher admiring her reflection. "Ruthie, ya stay here and help Jennifer with her hair while I go see what our Jesse is up ta."

"Tell her I love her," Jennifer said.

"Oh, lordy, I'm sure she knows that by now. But I'll tell her. Now give this young 'un a kiss so we can go."

Jennifer kissed KC on the cheek. "Be a good girl."

"She's an angel. Ain't ya, honey?" Bette Mae chucked the baby under the chin as they left the room.

Jennifer chuckled. "We'll see if she still thinks that once KC starts walking and talking."

Bette Mae walked into the room Jesse was using to dress. "I'll be. Is that really yer mommy?" she teasingly directed at the baby.

"Stop that," Jesse scolded playfully. "Come here, Sunshine." She lifted the baby from Bette Mae's arms. "What do you think? Will Jennifer like it?" she asked with belated worry.

"I'd say that she'll be mighty surprised." Bette Mae sat down on the bed.

"Is that a yes or a no?" Jesse asked, tickling KC and making the baby laugh.

"Quit worryin', will ya?" Bette Mae shook her head. "She'll think ya is the handsomest dude in the territory."

Jesse grinned at her friend. "Why do I put up with you?"

"Tha's a good question. When ya figure it out, let me know." Bette Mae reached out her arms. "Now give me the young 'un, and let me get a good look at ya."

Jesse did as requested and stood for Bette Mae's inspection. She was wearing a suit of soft buckskin. Short fringe hung from the shoulders of the jacket and the lapels were beautifully beaded in geometric designs of Indian origin. The beaded design continued in a strip down the outside of the pant legs. Under the jacket, she wore a linen shirt that matched the color of the buckskin. Her boots were polished to such a high shine that Bette Mae could see herself in them, and her auburn hair was pulled back into a simple but neat ponytail.

"Lordy, that is mighty pretty. Where ya been hiding it?"

"In my desk. Saw it in a store window in Denver; something made me buy it. Never could understand the need until the wedding came up." She smiled as she ran her hands down the front of the soft jacket.

"I'd say that was a fine decision. Yep, it surely was." Bette Mae nodded her approval. "Won't be long now, ya ain't gettin' cold feet?"

"Nope. Wish it was time, I can't wait to see Jennifer."

"Oh, that reminds me — she wanted me to tell ya she loves ya." Bette Mae chuckled. "I'd say if she didn', this day would surely be a waste of lots of folks' time. Let's get my little angel dressed so ya can git downstairs."

Bette Mae had offered to take care of KC during the ceremony and for the wedding night, but after thinking about it, Jesse and Jennifer decided the wedding was more than just the joining of their lives. It would also join KC's with theirs. Ruthie had made a smaller version of Jennifer's wedding dress for KC to wear while Jesse held her during the ceremony. And she would return home with her mothers afterward so the three could start their life as a real family.

Once the baby had been dressed, Bette Mae asked, "Ready?"

"Yes." Jesse lifted KC to her face and nuzzled her forehead. "Let's go marry your momma."

"Go on then." Bette Mae turned to go.

"Wait." Jesse stopped her, wrapping an arm around Bette Mae's shoulders and hugging her tightly. "Thank you."

Tears in her eyes, Bette Mae asked, "What for?"

"For being my friend, for accepting Jennifer and me. For being you. I can't tell you how much it means to have you stand with me today."

"Hush, you." Bette Mae pulled a hankie from her sleeve and wiped at her tears. "Where else would I be on such a day?" She returned the hug. "Ya know I love ya like ya was my own, don'cha?"

"I love you too." Jesse's eyes were brimming.

"Now stop that." Bette Mae grinned tearfully at the rancher. "Can't have ya gettin' hitched all puffy eyed. Go on, git downstairs and I'll go check on that beautiful woman waitin' to join ya."

Jesse carried KC down the back stairs that led directly to the kitchen and found Sweetwater's sheriff, her friend and best man, Billie Monroe, waiting for her.

Billie whistled when he saw her. "Gosh, don't you look pretty?"

"Knock it off, Billie. It ain't like you've never seen me before."

"You? I was talking to little KC here." Billie smiled at his friend. "You do look mighty pretty yourself, though, Jesse."

"Thanks, I think." Jesse could hear people talking and laughing in the converted dining room. "Sounds like quite a few showed up."

"Heck, Jesse, the whole valley is out there. And all in their Sunday best, too. Even Butler and his cowboys showed up, with their boots shined."

"Whoa." Jesse was staggered by the news. She knew Bette Mae had invited everybody, but she'd never expected them all to come.

"Ya got a lot of friends in the valley, Jesse," Billie assured her. "And everyone loves Jennifer."

"It's kinda overwhelming," Jesse said nervously.

Ed Granger, dressed in his best suit and with his hair slicked back, tapped on the door to Jennifer's dressing room. "Are you ready for me?"

"Come on in, Ed," Jennifer called out.

The big man opened the door and stopped short. "My goodness, Jennifer, you look beautiful." After taking a few moments to appreciate the young woman in her wedding dress, Ed crossed the floor to where she was standing. "Ready to get married?"

"I think so." Jennifer licked her lips nervously. The big man who had agreed to give her away had befriended Jennifer immediately upon her arrival in Sweetwater, and she had come to think of the large, good-natured man as the father she had always wanted.

"Well, then, let's not keep Jesse waiting. Don't want her thinking you changed your mind."

"Oh, no." Jennifer giggled. "We definitely don't want her thinking that."

Ed offered his arm; Jennifer cheerfully took it and was escorted from the room.

Joined by Bette Mae, Billie led Jesse through the kitchen door and into the temporary wedding chapel. Oohs and ahs rippled through the seated citizenry of Sweetwater as Jesse entered, and she blushed. KC sat quietly in Jesse's arms, looking around curiously.

Mayor Perkins stood at the front of the crowd, smiling when the threesome joined him. They all turned to look at the main stairway leading from the boarding rooms upstairs. A hush fell over the room while everyone waited for Jennifer to appear. Ed preceded Jennifer down the narrow stairs, then stood aside, allowing her to be seen. Jesse gasped and her heart almost stopped.

Jennifer turned to face Jesse and couldn't believe her eyes. *Now I know why she wouldn't let me see what she was wearing; she's gorgeous.* She thought her heart would burst with the love she felt. Smiling at the woman who would soon be her wife, she mouthed the words *"I love you."*

Jesse returned the smile and the sentiment.

The wedding ceremony ended to loud applause and good-natured shouts of congratulations. Jesse and Jennifer received the good wishes of the attendees and, in turn, thanked them for coming. The party was in full swing with Jesse holding KC and leading Jennifer around the dance floor to the music led by Ed's fiddle. Those not dancing were enjoying drinks on the house or eating from the over-flowing platters of food Bette Mae had spent the last few days preparing. The town of Sweetwater was well into the celebration when the door to the Slipper burst open.

Hank, the stage driver, looked surprised at the festivities. "So this is where everyone disappeared to," he said to the crowded room.

"What's up, Hank?" Billie asked.

"Got a telegram to deliver. Woulda left it at the stage office, but it says it needs to be hand delivered soon as I get to town."

"Everyone is here. Who's it for?"

"Jennifer Kensington."

Jennifer's heart clenched. It couldn't be for her. No one knew she was in Sweetwater. *Please,* she thought, *please don't let it be.* Hesitantly, she stepped forward, holding out her hand.

"You Jennifer Kensington?" Hank asked.

"I was. I'm Jennifer Branson now."

Jesse was startled by the declaration. They hadn't discussed the use of names after the wedding. Jesse had assumed Jennifer would want to keep her own surname. She smiled at the knowledge that her bride had thought differently. Oh, how she loved the woman.

Hank handed Jennifer the telegram. As Jennifer read the paper, her hands start to shake, and tears welled up in her eyes.

"Darlin', what's wrong?" Jesse asked in alarm.

"My father's coming to take me back. And he's bringing my fiancé with him."

For that instant, Jesse's heart stopped beating.

CHAPTER THREE

The telegram's arrival immediately put a damper on the festive wedding activities. As word of its message spread through the celebrating citizens of Sweetwater, many who did not know what to say to the upset women simply made a quiet exit.

At Bette Mae's urging, Jesse took Jennifer and KC home and, after tucking the sleeping baby in her crib, Jesse held her wife while she cried. It was almost dawn before sleep claimed them.

Jennifer awakened to find Jesse and KC playing on the cabin's floor.

"Come on, Sunshine," Jesse quietly encouraged the baby crawling tentatively toward her open arms.

KC reached out once more with her arm and pulled herself forward. Her body pressed against the inside of Jesse's thigh as she wobbled on shaky arms and legs.

Jesse gathered the child into her arms. "You're gettin' the hang of it." Jesse kissed the grinning baby before swinging her up to Jennifer, who was now standing behind her.

"I love you, sweetie." Jennifer wrapped her arms around the baby and kissed her. Placing KC back on the floor, she watched as the baby picked up her favorite toy and began playing with it. Tears filled Jennifer's eyes.

Seeing her wife's unhappiness, Jesse stood and wrapped her arms around Jennifer. "It's going to be okay, darlin'," she said soothingly. "I promise. You belong here now, with your family. No one is going to change that."

"I'm so afraid, Jesse," Jennifer whispered. "You don't know what he's like, especially if he thinks someone has crossed him. He might try to hurt you," she cried in terror.

"He's not going to do anything, darlin'." Gentle fingers brushed the tears from Jennifer's cheeks. "Once he sees that you have a family here, he'll go home and leave you be." Jesse hoped the words would comfort her wife, even though she didn't believe them herself.

KC looked up at her mothers, frowning at their sad faces. Dropping back onto her hands from her sitting position, she shakily crawled to where the women stood. Plopping down on Jesse's booted foot, KC tried to pull herself upright using the rancher's pant leg.

"Hey, Sunshine." Jesse reached down to steady the baby. "Did you come to cheer up your momma?" Jesse smiled at Jennifer. "She doesn't like to see you sad, darlin'."

"I know." Jennifer dried her eyes with her sleeve. "Come on, sweetie." She bent down to pick up KC. "Help me get dressed. Then I bet we can get mommy to take us for a ride to see the cows you like so much."

Jesse nodded happily.

"All done," Jesse said as she set her finished project on the table.

On their ride, Jesse had noticed how hard it was to hold the growing infant. She decided they needed a way to carry KC that was safer for the baby. Back at the ranch, she had taken a piece of deer hide and set to work making it into a carry sack for KC. Openings were cut for the baby's legs to drop through, and shoulder straps were fashioned that would provide a way to carry the sack on their backs. Jesse sewed the pieces of the sack together with strong rawhide cords. Now the carry sack was ready for testing.

"Think she'll sit in it?" Jennifer asked, carrying KC from the bed where she had changed her wet britches.

"Only one way to find out," Jesse said. "Let's try it."

Jennifer held KC on the edge of the table while Jesse carefully slipped KC's legs through the openings and then pulled the sack up around the baby. It stopped at her shoulders, allowing the baby some freedom of movement. Jesse lifted the baby and sack and held the contrivance for Jennifer to slip her arms through the holding straps.

With the sack settled on her back, Jennifer twisted her head to look at KC who was peering over her shoulder. "How's that, sweetie?" Jennifer asked the smiling baby. "Think you'd like to sit back there when we go for rides?" KC bounced in the sack, giggling happily.

"Hold on there, Sunshine." Jesse reached out to steady the baby. "You have to sit still. Don't want you falling out."

The baby stilled and looked at her mommy. Jesse couldn't help laughing at the pitiful look on KC's face. "If you promise not to bounce around, we'll go for a ride tomorrow." She leaned forward to kiss the baby.

"It's almost time for supper," Jennifer said. "Why don't we spread a blanket out back? It should be a nice evening."

Jesse removed KC and the sack from Jennifer's back. "Sounds good to me."

"We need more milk."

Jesse sat KC on the blanket they kept on the floor for her to play on. "I'll see what the cow can give. Need any help?"

"No. I'm just going to throw something together."

"I'll be right back." Jesse pulled Jennifer into her arms and kissed her.

The casual peck quickly flared into something much more as the women pressed their mouths and bodies together.

After several moments, Jesse pulled back but kept her arms tight around Jennifer. "I love you," she whispered, resting her forehead against Jennifer's.

"I love you, too." Jennifer wanted to take Jesse to their bed and show her how much, but the sound of the baby playing reminded her that there was now someone else in their life. "You'd better go."

"Drat," Jesse playfully protested before stealing one more kiss. "Be good, Sunshine." She reached down and ruffled KC's soft hair as she walked by the baby on her way to the cabin door.

Humming as she prepared the food for their picnic, Jennifer smiled to herself, thinking about what she and Jesse would do after KC went to sleep.

The next morning, both Jesse and Jennifer were still asleep when KC woke. She rolled onto her stomach and pushed herself up onto all fours before plopping into a sitting position. Looking around the room, she didn't see her mothers moving about the cabin. She was about to wail when she spotted the women cuddled together in the large bed next to her crib.

Jesse felt someone watching her. She knew it was later than they normally woke, but Jennifer had kept them busy until the early hours of the morning. She wanted to ignore the feeling of being watched, but she couldn't. Slowly lifting one droopy eyelid, she saw KC watching her. As soon as KC saw she was awake, the baby reached out for her.

Jesse wiggled her fingers at the baby and was rewarded by a return waggle of baby fingers. Chuckling, Jesse tried to slip out of the bed but had to stop when she discovered Jennifer had her wrapped up in a tangle of arms and legs. "Darlin'," Jesse whispered, "you've got to let me go."

"Don't want to," a sleepy voice answered. Jennifer tightened her hold and kissed Jesse's bare shoulder. Her lips continued on a path that would eventually lead to a bare breast.

"KC is awake." When Jennifer's mouth continued its mission, Jesse added, "She's watching us."

Jennifer's lips halted. "She's what?" she mumbled against Jesse skin.

"Watching us."

"Think she'd go back to sleep if we asked her to?"

"Nope." Jesse rolled Jennifer onto her back and stretched her body out on top of her lover's. After kissing Jennifer soundly, she said, "Besides, after what you did to me last night, I'm too exhausted to start all over this morning."

Jennifer looked up at Jesse. "Then how about we just lay in bed all day, beautiful?"

Jesse pretended to be shocked by the suggestion. "Jennifer Kensington, is that any way for a proper young woman to behave?"

"Branson," Jennifer said seriously. "I'm no longer a Kensington."

Jesse slipped off Jennifer to lie at her side. "Darlin', I know you said that the other night, but is it really what you want?"

Confused and hurt, Jennifer asked, "Don't you want me to have your name?"

"It would make me the proudest woman in the territory," Jesse assured her new wife. "But giving up your father's name..."

"I'm not giving up much, Jesse. I would rather be known as a Branson than a Kensington. It's who I am now."

Hearing the resolve in her lover's voice, Jesse leaned down and softly kissed Jennifer. "Then, *Mrs. Branson*, what say we get up and spend the day with our daughter?"

"I'd like that, Mrs. Branson."

Billie pulled up to the Silver Slipper in a buggy he had polished until it sparkled in the late morning sun. The matching team of black horses had also received special attention that morning, their coats shining under the recently burnished and oiled harnesses. Billie was wearing his Sunday suit, complete with tie; his hat had been brushed free of all dust and dirt, and the shine on his boots matched that of the buggy.

Ruthie thought Billie looked adorable as he nervously climbed the steps to join her on the porch of the Slipper.

"Miss Ruth, are you ready?" Billie asked, leg twitching beneath his pressed trousers.

"Yes. I took the liberty of preparing a picnic basket." Ruthie bent to lift the large basket at her feet. She knew the sheriff had a healthy appetite so she had packed a lot of food.

"I'll get that." He quickly reached down and picked up the basket, thankful she had thought of bringing food. So focused was he on making sure the buggy was prepared properly, he had completely forgotten they probably would get hungry sometime during the day. He shyly offered Ruthie his arm. "Shall we?"

Ruthie timidly laid her arm across his, allowing Billie to lead her across the porch and down the stairs. She felt a jolt when his strong hands gently grasped her waist as he helped her step up into the buggy. Her skin tingled even after he released her to walk around the horse team and climb up into the seat.

With a flick of his wrist, the reins snapped against the horses' rumps, nudging them into motion. The couple set off for a nearby lake, on this, their first official date.

At first conversation was uneasy, but they soon relaxed as they discovered they truly liked each other's company. By the time the lake came into view, they were laughing and joking as if they were old friends.

Billie pulled the team to a stop near the water's edge. He helped Ruthie down from the buggy and lifted the food basket out, setting it down on a small patch of sand along the stone-littered shoreline. Normally this part of the shore would be underwater, but because the summer had been dry the water level was down considerably.

"I'll just tie the team to that tree," he said.

A few feet from shore and surrounded by water lay a tree that had fallen during some storm, tipping into the lake. What would have been its canopy rested in deeper water, and the twisted, gnarled root system lay in the shallows. Billie planned to tie the team to the closest end, giving the horses access to the water. Between the shore and tree were several large rocks he figured he could use as stepping-stones to reach the stump without getting his boots wet. What he hadn't figured on was a thin, slick layer of moss covering the stones that were usually submerged.

As Ruthie watched, Billie gingerly stepped onto a stone. When it didn't rock or move, he warily tested a second. He balanced on both rocks, testing their steadiness. When neither stone moved under his weight, he became overly confident. Not paying close enough attention to the placement of his feet, he missed seeing a small rock half buried under the large stone he was about to step on. As his foot came in contact with the stone, it shifted and threw him off balance. Instinctively, he tightened his grip on the reins clutched in his hand, causing the horses to rear. He quickly tried to shift his weight back onto his other leg, but it was too late. His boots lost their grip on the slippery stones, and his feet flew out from under him as his arms flailed uselessly in the air. Before Ruthie could do anything to help, Billie fell backward, splashing into the cold lake.

He landed in a patch of mud and not on one of the hard stones he had been trying to navigate. Not quite sure what to do, he stayed where he had fallen. He was certain that his unintentionally amusing performance would ruin any chance he had with the pretty girl standing a few feet away. His boots were full of water, his Sunday suit was waterlogged, and he had a nasty feeling that the muck on the lake bottom was starting to seep though the material. His hat, knocked from his head, was floating off toward the deep end of the lake. Water from his drenched hair ran down his face, dripping off his nose and chin. Humiliated, he looked to the shore.

Ruthie was mortified. Billie looked like a drowned rat. A very cute drowned rat but a drowned rat, nonetheless. She met his eyes.

What Billie saw on Ruthie's face surprised him; she looked concerned, not amused. Maybe a little amused, but mostly concerned. His lips twitched when he considered that he probably looked pretty silly sitting in the muddy water.

Relieved to see that Billie appeared uninjured, Ruthie felt her lips twitching as well.

Soon both Billie and Ruthie were laughing so hard that Billie ending up sitting in the lake for some time. Through it all he had managed to keep a firm grasp on the reins, and before sloshing his way back to shore, he tied them to the tree.

"Wasn't how I was expectin' to impress you today," Billie said, shaking off water as he returned to dry land, the liquid bubbling over the tops of his boots. He took care not to spray any muck on Ruthie as he removed his sodden jacket.

"Billie, you don't need to impress me." Ruthie rummaged around in the picnic basket and pulled out a couple of small towels. "Here. You can use these to wipe your head dry." She handed them to the drenched suitor. "Why don't you pull off those boots? Might as well take off your shirt, too."

Billie looked aghast. "Miss Ruth!"

"Doubt you have anything I haven't seen before," Ruthie told him.

"Even so, I'll keep me shirt on. Ain't fittin' to be undressed in front of a lady."

Ruthie smiled. It was the first time a man had ever taken her feelings into consideration. "Haven't been called that too often," she said shyly.

Billie was laying his jacket out on a rock to dry in the summer sun. "Well, you are a lady and that's how I aim to treat you." He sat on another rock and began tugging off his boots, holding them upside down to empty out the water. He removed his socks and placed them beside the jacket, then stood. "Now, how about some lunch? I'm always hungry after I swim."

"Seems to me," Ruthie giggled, reaching for the lunch basket, "you did a lot more splashing than swimming."

"Still made me hungry."

"How much further?" Martin Kensington demanded of the carriage driver.

"'Nother day," Cliff Ducane answered.

Kensington was incensed. "You're not suggesting that my wife spend another night sleeping on the ground in this godforsaken country? Push the horses. I want to be in Sweetwater by nightfall."

The autocratic Kensington had surprised Cliff Ducane by striding into his livery and demanding his best team of horses and a driver to provide transportation to Sweetwater. Not blinking at the cost of the unusual request, he had pulled out a wallet and handed Ducane payment in full, then demanded that they leave immediately.

Kensington had hired the carriage because he thought it would be a faster way to travel than by stagecoach. Unfortunately, the Easterner hadn't considered that the stage exchanged horse teams at regular intervals, thereby allowing the coach drivers to push their teams harder over the rough roads. Ducane's pride and joy, a team of four matching chestnuts, needed to travel more slowly and rest more frequently, and the trip from Denver had stretched into yet another day.

Ducane turned to look at his three passengers. Kensington, an older man, looked to have done some hard work in his younger days. Andrew Barrish, an obnoxious young man barely into his twenties, carried himself with much more authority than Ducane figured he had earned. And Mrs. Kensington, a small, demure woman who, in contrast to her husband and young Barrish, seldom spoke but always took time to thank Ducane for his efforts. He felt sorry for the woman who was generally ignored by her husband and the young man.

The trip from Denver had been filled with complaints and demands from Kensington and Barrish, and Ducane quickly figured out that he would never make them happy so he had given up trying. On the other hand, he did what he could to make the woman as comfortable as possible. Glaring at the men, Ducane wondered who in Sweetwater was unlucky enough to soon be suffering Kensington's tirades. Although he would love to see Sweetwater by nightfall and be rid of his rude passengers, Ducane knew the horses were tired, and he wasn't going to push them any harder. "Ain't gonna happen. Horses are goin' as fast as they can."

"Mr. Kensington said to push them," Barrish demanded.

"That may be how you git folks to do somethin' in the East, but out here that won't git ya nothin'. Can't make the distance to Sweetwater any shorter by drivin' the horses harder, so I suggests you sit back and enjoy the ride. We'll get to Sweetwater sometime t'morrow." Ducane spat tobacco juice over the side of the carriage. "'Scuse me, ma'am." He nodded to the woman before turning back around.

CHAPTER FOUR

Bette Mae was surprised to see Jesse and Jennifer entering the Silver Slipper's dining room so soon after their interrupted wedding celebration.

"Goodness me." The older woman rushed to give Jennifer a big hug. "How are ya doin'?"

"I'm fine, Bette Mae." Jennifer smiled, but her eyes told another story.

"Come on." Bette Mae pulled a chair out from one of the tables. "Sit down and let me git ya sum breakfast. Bet ya could use a cup of coffee, too."

Jennifer sat as instructed. "That sounds wonderful. I'm afraid poor Jesse had to do some of the cooking the past few days."

"Well, then," Bette Mae winked at the schoolteacher, "you must be starving." When Jesse started to protest, her friend cut her off. "Hush, I've eaten some of yer cookin' and I must say it can be lackin'."

"That's not fair." Jesse dropped down in a chair next to Jennifer, sitting KC on the edge of the table. "You like my cooking, don't you, Sunshine?" she asked the baby. KC giggled, wrinkling up her nose and sticking her tongue out.

Bette Mae laughed. "Looks like she's got yer smarts." She winked at Jennifer a second time before she headed to the kitchen.

Jennifer laughed as Jesse pouted. "Oh, honey," she reached over to take Jesse's hand, "she's just a baby. She doesn't know what she's doing. And if you hadn't been teaching her to do that..." Jesse yanked her hand out of Jennifer's reach, and Jennifer chuckled. "KC, tell mommy you love her."

Jesse hugged the baby tight, whispering into her ear, "I love you, too, Sunshine."

KC giggled, as she always did when Jesse's warm breath tickled her.

Jennifer smiled at her wife. "All better?"

"Yep." Jesse smiled back and reached out a hand which Jennifer instantly accepted.

"Here ya go." Bette Mae slid a plate filled with eggs, bacon, biscuits, gravy, and toast in front of each woman. She returned to the kitchen to reappear moments later with a fresh pot of coffee. After filling their cups, she set the pot on the table. "Whilst ya eat, let me visit with my little angel." She lifted the baby from Jesse's arms and sat at the table with KC in her lap.

Comfortable in Bette Mae's lap, KC started waving her arms and talking her baby gibberish.

After breakfast, Jesse and Jennifer walked down Sweetwater's only street to the wood building next to Ed's general store, which housed the offices of the mayor, newspaper, and sheriff.

Jesse called a greeting as she carried KC into the office. "Morning, Billie."

"Morning, Jesse. Jennifer." The sheriff rose from behind his desk. "Morning, Miss KC." He smiled at the baby. Scooting the chair he had just vacated to the front of his desk, he gestured for Jennifer to sit. Jesse sat in the only other chair in the room, while the sheriff perched on the edge of his desk.

"What's up, Billie?" Jesse asked. "Bette Mae said you wanted to talk to us."

"Thought you might like to know I heard back from Virginia City." The sheriff had written to the territorial authorities about the Bannack sheriff and his dealings with the women.

"Are they going to do something about Sheriff Logan?" Jennifer asked.

"Yep." Billie picked up a piece of paper from his desk. "Citizens in Virginia City formed a vigilante committee to take care of the bandits in the territory. After Virginia and Nevada Cities, Bannack is their first stop. They figure to deal with Logan in the next few days; they already caught a couple members of the gang in Virginia City."

"What will they do with Logan?" Jennifer asked.

"Probably same thing they did with the two in Virginia City."

"What was that?"

"Hanged 'em."

Jennifer gasped. "Without a trial?"

"That's vigilante justice, darlin'," Jesse told her wife. "Ain't time to wait for the circuit judge."

"Besides," Billie added, "best to hang 'em and be done with it."

"But what if they hang an innocent man?"

"Ones they hang are guilty of more than just one crime. So even if they don't belong to Logan's group, they've sure been livin' on the wrong side of the law. Ain't what you'd call 'honest' citizens that the vigilantes go lookin' for," Billie explained. "Don't worry, Jennifer. If the vigilantes decide to hang 'em, you can be sure they deserve it. Ones they don't feel like hanging will be told to clear out of Montana."

"Doesn't seem right," Jennifer argued. "Every man is entitled to a fair hearing."

"Sometimes you have to take the law into your own hands," Jesse said softly. "May not seem right, but it has to be done. Once the territory is cleaned up, it'll be safer for everyone."

Jennifer sat quietly, thinking. The West was much different than she had expected. She'd never heard of people taking the law into their own hands back East, but then they didn't have bandit gangs being led by the sheriff, either. Maybe vigilante law *was* necessary to make the territory more safe for everyone.

"So what brings you into town today?" Billie was asking Jesse.

"Thought we should let Bette Mae know we were all right. Things got a little confused the other night."

"Shame to ruin your party like that." The sheriff shook his head, then smiled. "But it was a right nice weddin'."

"Thanks, Billie. Guess yours will be next, from what I hear." Jesse grinned at her friend. "You and Ruthie set a date yet?"

"Oh hell, Jesse, I haven't even kissed her yet."

Jesse laughed. "What're you waiting for?"

"I get so nervous, I'm afraid I'll make a fool out of myself," he admitted reluctantly.

"You love her?" Jesse asked.

"Yes."

"Then you should just get on and kiss her; can't ask her to marry ya until you do. Believe me, once you kiss her you'll be glad you did." Jesse beamed at Jennifer. "I know I am."

Jennifer looked at the woman who had become her whole life. Would it be possible to love her any more than this? No. Could she ever live without her? Never.

After talking with Billie, the women returned to Jesse's office at the Slipper so KC could take a nap. Jennifer rocked the baby while Jesse tried to catch up on paperwork. "Sweetheart, why don't you let me do that?" Jennifer offered as a frustrated Jesse toiled over the Slipper's bookkeeping.

Jesse grumbled as she tried to get columns of numbers to balance. "You have plenty to do with your teaching and taking care of me and KC." She scratched out a number and tried again.

Laying the sleeping baby on the couch, Jennifer went over to the desk and placed her hand on top of the rancher's. "Jesse, I want to help. You know you'd rather be working at the ranch than doing this, so why don't you let me take care of it?"

Jesse tossed down her pencil to pull Jennifer into her lap. "Darlin', whether you do the books or I do, we still need to spend time in town. Unless you're suggestin' you come to town without me." Jesse stuck out her lower lip in a pout.

"No, silly." Jennifer kissed the offended lip. "Why can't we take this out to the ranch and do it there?"

Cocking her head to one side, Jesse looked at the papers and ledgers spread over her desk. She thought for a moment. "Guess there really isn't a reason we can't. But," she looked at Jennifer, "are you sure you want to do this? I mean with your teachin' and all, won't you be too busy?"

"I'm not teaching right now. And when school starts again, I'll have plenty of time in the afternoons while you're out playing with your cows."

"Mooooo." Jesse did her best impression. "Okay, if you're sure." She kissed Jennifer.

"Yes, I'm sure." Jennifer sighed as Jesse pulled back. "Think you can do that again," she asked, leaning back toward Jesse's lips.

"Yep." Jesse nodded, then, giving her wife a little laugh, she added, "Mooooooooooo." A soft moooooo was heard in response.

"What was that?" Jennifer asked.

"Wasn't me."

"Mooooo." The sound came again.

Jesse smiled at Jennifer. "You thinkin' what I'm thinkin'?"

The women peeked over the edge of the desk at the couch. KC, sitting up and wide-awake, smiled at her mothers.

"Mooooo?" Jesse called out.

KC responded. "Mooooo."

"Wouldn't have thought that would be her first word, but I guess it'll do." Jesse laughed. "Mooooo."

"Mooooo."

Jennifer shook her head in amusement as Jesse and KC continued to exchange cow calls.

Ducane pulled the carriage to a stop in front of Sweetwater's stage depot, more than happy to finally be rid of his passengers. "Here you are, Mr. Kensington." Ducane tied the reins around the brake handle. "Sweetwater."

"This is Sweetwater?" Barrish snorted as he stood in the carriage to survey the few buildings that made up the town. "Why would your daughter have chosen *this* place to live?"

Martin Kensington remained seated. "I've told you before, she didn't come out here of her own free will. Why are you dropping us here?" he snapped at Ducane. "There must be a more suitable place in town for us to stay."

Frustrated that he couldn't seem to get rid of his passengers, Ducane turned back to face Kensington. "Let me check inside, maybe the depot operator can suggest a place. But, by the looks of this town, I wouldn't count on too much." He quickly disappeared inside the old adobe building before anything more could be said.

"Dammit, Kensington." Barrish couldn't believe he had traveled the width of the country to end up in such a miserable little town. "If this turns out to be a wild goose hunt, my father will hear of your—"

Kensington's eyes narrowed as he snapped at the fuming young man, "My daughter is here." Before Barrish could say more, Ducane reappeared.

"Says you can get rooms at the Silver Slipper. Sweetwater ain't got no hotel."

Barrish grunted. "Of course it doesn't."

"Fine," Kensington barked. "Take us there."

Ducane climbed back up into his seat and set the horses in motion before Barrish had settled in his seat. The young man was thrown toward the back of the carriage and almost landed in Kensington's lap before regaining his footing.

"Damn fool," Barrish swore.

Ducane smirked and spat over the side of the buggy. "Tenderfoot."

A few moments later, Ducane stopped the carriage in front of the Silver Slipper at the edge of town. The two-story wooden structure with a wide wrap-around covered porch was the largest building in Sweetwater.

Kensington and Barrish climbed down from the carriage and quickly made their way up the steps to the porch.

Ducane helped Mrs. Kensington out of the carriage while her husband and the young man disappeared inside. When she followed the men, Ducane removed their luggage and tossed it up onto the porch. Not wanting to waste another moment, he quickly climbed back into the driver's seat and urged the horses into motion and toward the stables. As far as he was concerned, his business with Martin Kensington was finished.

"Ready?" Jesse asked as she finished changing KC's britches.

"Yes," Jennifer said as Jesse lifted the baby up. "Let's take our little 'moo' girl home."

KC giggled. "Moooo."

"I think we've created a monster." Jesse tickled the baby.

Jennifer laughed as she walked toward the office door. "Let's hope she learns another word soon." She stepped into the dining area and noticed two men talking to Bette Mae. A familiar-looking woman was standing off to the side and looking around the room with curiosity.

"Mother?" Jennifer asked hesitantly.

The woman turned. The young woman who had addressed her bore the features of her daughter but was dressed in a pair of men's denim pants, a flannel shirt, and boots. Her hair was tucked up into the type of hat worn by most men in the West, and her skin was deeply tanned from exposure to the harsh sun. If this was her daughter, she had changed greatly.

"Jennifer?"

The knot in Jennifer's throat was so thick she could barely get the words out. "What are you doing here?"

The larger of the two men spun around at the sound of his daughter's voice. "Jennifer Kensington, is that any way to address your mother? Why are you dressed like that? I informed you that I was bringing your fiancé with me. Go put on some proper clothing, then you can tell me who forced you to come to this godforsaken country. I'll deal with them before we leave for home."

Jennifer flinched at the sound and sight of her father, but she was determined to tell him right away she would not be returning to the East with him. "Father, I came here because I wanted to. And I plan to stay here. Sweetwater is my home now and my family's."

"Family?" Barrish spoke for the first time. "You mean to say that you are married?"

"Yes." Jennifer wondered if the gangly young man was the fiancé. "Jesse and I were married a few days ago."

"Rubbish," Kensington barked. "What husband would allow his wife to dress in such an unwomanly manner?"

"I would." Jesse walked out of her office and stood beside Jennifer, wrapping an arm around her wife's waist.

"Father, this is Jesse." Jennifer took the baby from Jesse, adding proudly, "And this is our daughter, KC."

"A woman?" the older Kensington sputtered. "You're married to a woman? Impossible."

"Actually," Bette Mae told the angry man, "they was married right here in this very room with the whole town watchin'. Right pretty ceremony it was, too."

"What is this, Kensington? You don't expect me to marry her now, do you?"

"Shut up, Barrish." Kensington stormed across the room toward Jennifer. Jesse quickly positioned herself between her wife and father-in-law. "Get out of my way," Kensington demanded, raising a hand to Jesse. Looking past Jesse to Jennifer, he commanded, "You'll come with me. *Now.*"

"Jennifer is not going anywhere," Jesse said, her voice hard as she faced down the larger Kensington.

Kensington's hand formed into a fist and started forward toward Jesse's face. "Then I'll just have to—"

"I wouldn't if I were you," Billie said as he rushed through the Slipper's front door, accompanied by Ruthie. Bette Mae had sent the girl to fetch the sheriff when she realized Jennifer's parents had arrived at the Slipper.

"Stay out of this, whoever the hell you are," Kensington told Billie.

"I'm the sheriff," Billie maneuvered himself between Jesse and Kensington, "and I'm telling you to back off."

Kensington looked at the sheriff, his badge in clear sight. "My daughter has obviously been forced to stay here against her will by this...this..." He glared at Jesse. "I'm here to take her home."

"Since the day Jennifer arrived in Sweetwater, I haven't seen her do anything she didn't want to do," Billie answered calmly.

"She claims to be married to this woman!" Kensington bellowed. "You can't tell me you think my daughter would willingly do that."

Billie smiled. "She looked pretty willing to me."

"Father, if you would just listen—"

"NOOOOO!" Kensington shouted.

Scared by the loud shouting, KC scrunched her face up as an eruption built inside her little body. Her frightened wail shocked everyone in the room and froze them in place.

After KC's cries interrupted the impending melee, Bette Mae immediately took control. She quickly ushered Jesse and Jennifer back into Jesse's office and, with Billie's help, directed Kensington and Barrish to rooms upstairs.

A light tapping on the office door drew Jesse's attention. She cautiously approached the door and pulled it open to find Mrs. Kensington standing outside. Though shorter than Jennifer and with hair graying at the temples, Jesse easily recognized the resemblance between this woman and her wife. As Jesse studied her, the woman stood quietly waiting for Jesse to make the next move.

"Mrs. Kensington," Jesse finally acknowledged.

Jennifer's mother smiled timidly. "I would like to speak with my daughter."

Jesse looked into the room where Jennifer was pacing, trying to calm KC and herself. She waited for Jennifer to make the decision. Jennifer nodded uncertainly, and Jesse stepped aside, allowing the woman to enter the room. "I can wait outside," she said, more to Jennifer than Mrs. Kensington.

"No." Jennifer shook her head. "I want you to stay."

Jesse closed the door, and Mrs. Kensington walked slowly across the room, stopping several steps from where Jennifer paced with an agitated KC still whimpering in her arms.

"I'm sorry, Jennifer."

"Why did you come, Mother?" Jennifer relinquished the baby when KC reached for Jesse, who had come to stand beside them. KC snuggled into Jesse's shoulder, guardedly watching the unfamiliar woman.

"I wanted to see you. It was such a shock to find you had left without even a note to explain. I was so afraid. I..." She hesitated. "I wanted to make sure you were all right."

"And Father? He obviously wasn't concerned about my well-being since he managed to arrange for a fiancé for me," Jennifer said bitterly.

"No, you're wrong." Jennifer's mother sighed. "Your father was very concerned, Jennifer. He has spent every day trying to find out what happened to you. He talked to everyone in town. He paid for advertisements in newspapers up and down the Coast. He even offered a reward to anyone with information about you. He was so relieved when he finally received word telling him you were here. He immediately made plans to come after you."

"I'm not going back."

"But your family," her mother protested.

"Jesse is my family. And KC."

The older woman looked first at her daughter and then at the woman standing beside her. "I don't understand."

"You don't have to understand, it's the way it is. This is my home now."

"What about Mr. Barrish? You're father has gone to great trouble—"

"Is that the name of my 'fiancé'? Oh, Mother, why do you accept everything Father says and does? Is that really the life you want for me — married off to some man I know nothing about and have no feelings for? I love Jesse. I'm happy here. Why can't you understand that?"

"Your father is a good man, Jennifer. He has always done what he thinks is best for you. I don't know why you can't see that."

Jennifer realized it was senseless to explain; her mother could never understand, would never even try to understand. She felt Jesse's arm wrap around her shoulders, and she leaned against her. "This is your granddaughter, Mother. Aren't you even going to acknowledge her?" Jennifer smiled at KC who was contentedly playing with the toy horse that she had discovered in Jesse's pocket.

"My granddaughter? But how can that be? How could you..." Mrs. Kensington looked at the baby in Jesse's arms. As a thought occurred to her, a hand flew up to her mouth in shock. "Jennifer, you aren't telling me that you had a child out of wedlock!"

"No, Mother." Jennifer sighed. "KC's parents were killed, and Jesse and I decided to raise her as our own. She is our daughter now."

"But you can't possibly expect your father to support this child."

"No. I don't expect Father to support KC." Jennifer's initial disbelief at her mother's words was quickly turning to anger. "Jesse and I don't need anything from Father, except to be left alone." She felt Jesse's embrace tighten. "I think you should go, Mother. We need to get KC home."

"Home? You don't live here?"

"Jesse has a ranch outside of town. We live there."

"Is that safe? Jennifer, your father might not approve of such arrangements."

"I don't care. Father doesn't care a whit about me except for what he can gain by marrying me off in some business arrangement. He has never cared about me. Jesse does." Turning to look into her lover's eyes, Jennifer whispered, "Take us home, sweetheart."

Mrs. Kensington walked stiffly across the office. When she reached the door, she paused and turned to her daughter. "I love you, Jennifer. So does your father." Then she left the room.

"Well?" Martin Kensington asked as soon as his wife entered. He had been waiting impatiently in the room Bette Mae had provided them.

"I'm sorry, dear," Mrs. Kensington told her husband nervously. "She says her family is here, and she is staying."

"Like hell she is!" Kensington strode to the window, fuming as he looked out over the handful of ramshackle buildings that made up the town of Sweetwater. He saw two horses slowly walking away from the Slipper and recognized his daughter as one of the riders. "What power does that woman hold over her?" he wondered aloud as he watched them ride out of town.

"I don't know."

"I'm going to find out. I won't leave this town without my daughter."

"Are you sure about this?"

Turning to glare at his wife, Kensington asked, "Are you questioning me?"

"No, dear," she quickly assured her husband. "It's just that she seems so determined that this is the right place for her."

"She's a silly girl. How could she possibly know what's right for her? She'll return with us and marry Barrish, as arranged."

CHAPTER FIVE

Late the next morning, Jesse heard a horse approaching the cabin. Grabbing her rifle, she went out on the porch to see Billie Monroe riding up.

"Mornin', Billie."

The sheriff noted the rifle resting in Jesse's arms. Knowing what Jesse and Jennifer had already gone through to protect each other, Billie was sure that Jesse would not hesitate to use the rifle if the need arose. "Mornin'."

"What brings you out this morning, Billie?"

"Your father-in-law. He's been raising a ruckus in town."

"Might as well get down and come in. KC's having a bath." Jesse turned to re-enter the cabin and inform Jennifer of their guest.

KC was happily splashing in the tub, her giggles filling the cabin.

"Mite early in the day for a bath, ain't it?" Billie asked when he walked inside.

Jennifer laughed. "Not when you find the only mud hole in the territory to play in." She had been out tending the garden when KC crawled to the water bucket. In an attempt to pull herself upright, the baby had knocked the bucket over, spilling its contents. The resultant mud puddle had immediately become her playground. By the time Jennifer saw what the baby was up to, KC was covered from head to toe in thick Montana mud.

"Coffee, Billie?" Jesse asked as she filled a cup.

"Thanks."

She carried the cup to Billie and handed another to Jennifer, then lifted KC from the tub to dry her off. KC tried to wriggle out of Jesse's grasp and ended up hanging upside down, held securely by one of Jesse's strong hands.

"Come on, Sunshine." Jesse playfully swatted the dangling child on her bare bottom. "Let's get you dressed so we can hear what Uncle Billie has to say."

"Why don't you sit, Billie?" Jennifer took a seat at the table under the window, offering the lawman the other chair.

"Thanks."

Moments later, Jesse rejoined Jennifer and Billie. KC was set on the floor to play with her toy horse, and Jesse pulled a box from under the kitchen table to sit on.

"She sure likes that pony." Billie smiled, watching the baby play. "Say, KC, does that pony have a name?"

Looking up when she heard her name, KC smiled at the sheriff and held up her toy. "Baze."

Jennifer and Jesse both stared at the baby, huge smiles spreading across their faces. "Blaze," Jennifer corrected.

"Baze." KC hugged the toy horse to her chest. "Baze."

"Guess she's got the important stuff down," Jesse stated. When Billie looked at her in confusion, Jesse explained, "Cows and horses. What else does she need to know?"

Jennifer laughed at the baffled expression on the sheriff's face. "I don't suppose this is a social call, Billie."

"I thought you might want to know what your pa has been doin' in town."

"I can just imagine."

"He came to me first thing this morning wantin' me to declare your marriage illegal. I told him there weren't no law against it in the territory. Then he went to see Mayor Perkins, offered him a reward to do it. I think Miles might have accepted if Mrs. Perkins hadn't chased him out of the house with a broom. Then she gave your father a lecture on what a wonderful schoolteacher you are and how much you've done for her children."

"It doesn't matter if he does have the marriage annulled; I'm not going back with him."

"I know," Billie said. "But he's telling everyone that he's not leaving Sweetwater without you. And that Barrish fellow has been talkin' up that your relationship is unnatural, that you need to be taken back and re-taught to be a proper lady. Anyway, I just wanted to come out and tell you that it might be a good idea to stay out of town for a few days."

"It won't make any difference, Billie. If we don't go to town, he'll just come out here. At least in town, we have friends around to help us."

"That's true. Bette Mae has got the girls keepin' an eye on your pa and Barrish."

"Is there any way to force him to leave Sweetwater?"

"Wish there was, Jesse. But less'n he does somethin' illegal, ain't much I can do but keep a watch on him."

"Guess we'll just have to go in and try to talk to him," Jesse told Jennifer. "Maybe he'll listen."

"No, sweetheart." Jennifer shook her head. "He won't."

"What do you want to do?"

"Take KC and go south, back over the pass, and get lost in the mountains where he'll never be able to find us." Jennifer sighed at the impossibility of the thought. "But we can't."

"Yes, we can," Jesse told her solemnly.

Jennifer knew if she asked, Jesse would take her to hide in the mountains, but that wasn't the life she wanted for her family. "No, sweetheart. This is our home, and this is where I want us to be." Jesse smiled and Jennifer smiled back. "Let's go into town and try to talk to him."

Jesse reached out and took Jennifer's hands into her own. "Are you sure?"

Jennifer squeezed Jesse's hands. "Yes."

"All right. Guess we'll ride back into town with you, Billie."

Bette Mae and Mrs. Kensington were sitting at a table in the Silver Slipper when Jesse and Jennifer returned. As soon as KC saw Bette Mae, she started jabbering, but when she spied Jennifer's mother, she instantly quieted, wrapping her arms around Jesse's neck.

"It's okay, Sunshine, I won't let anyone hurt you or your momma." Jesse rubbed the baby's back in comfort.

"Hello, Bette Mae," Jennifer soberly greeted her friend. "Is my father here?"

"He and tha' young fella hired some horses at the livery. Said they was goin' for a ride."

"Where on earth would they be riding to around here?"

"Don' know. Didn' say," Bette Mae said, looking at Mrs. Kensington to provide the answers.

When she remained silent, Jennifer asked, "Mother, do you know?"

"Your father did not mention his plans to me."

"No, I guess he wouldn't. We'll be in Jesse's office. Would you ask him to join us when they return?" Jennifer didn't wait for a response before walking away.

Bette Mae stood and moved closer to Jesse. Whispering, she asked, "Is she all right?"

"Yes. But she'll be better when all of this is settled."

KC reached out to play with Bette Mae's hair and giggled when the woman tickled her tummy. "I'll bring some hot coffee in for ya. And some fresh milk for you, little angel," she told the baby.

"Don't think you would have said that earlier today," Jesse said. "Made herself a mud puddle to play in."

"Ain't you the clever one." Bette Mae tickled the baby again, winking at Jesse.

"Unh, huh." Jesse smirked.

"Go on. Git in there with your bride. She needs ya now."

"Thanks, Bette Mae." Jesse nodded, being quick to follow her instructions.

It was dusk when Kensington and Barrish returned to the Silver Slipper. After tying their horses to the hitching rail, they climbed the steps to the wide porch.

"This is a waste of my time," Barrish grumbled. "We've been all over this valley, and there's not one man willing to help us."

"It doesn't matter," Kensington growled. "We'll do it ourselves if we have to."

"Sheriff says their marriage is legal. If that's so, how can she marry me?"

"No one back East will know. You marry her and keep your mouth shut."

"I'm not sure I want to anymore," the young man objected. "She's been living with that woman as if they were married. If they've been sharing a bed, she's spoiled. Not exactly the wife you promised."

"She's not spoiled; she hasn't slept with a man. I said you'd be her first, and you will. Just do what I say and you'll be attending your own wedding soon enough. What you do after that isn't my concern."

Mrs. Kensington was sitting in one of the large overstuffed chairs placed to the side of the Slipper's dining room, next to the wall of bookcases overflowing with the books which Bette Mae had told her were received in regular shipments from a book peddler. Not having thought that anyone out West would take the time for such diversions, she'd been surprised to find the large library funded by Jesse. She looked up when her husband and Barrish entered.

Bette Mae appeared from the kitchen and approached the two men. "Miss Jennifer asked ya to join her in the office." She pointed to the office door in an alcove under the stairs leading up to the boarding rooms.

Without a word, Kensington, followed by Barrish, walked to the door and entered without knocking. Jesse was sitting on the floor playing with KC while Jennifer worked on the Slipper's books, trying to keep her mind busy. All three looked up when the office door opened.

As her father strode into the room, Jennifer said, "It's customary to knock, Father."

"I was told you wanted us to join you." Kensington looked at the papers spread out on the desk. "You work for her, too?"

"No." Jennifer closed the ledgers. "I'm helping her, as any good wife would do. Jesse owns the Silver Slipper."

Barrish laughed. "Married to the owner of a saloon filled with ex-whores. It just keeps getting better."

Ignoring his insult, Jennifer said to the young man, "I would like to talk to my father, *alone*."

"I think that would be a good idea," Kensington agreed. He looked at Jesse. "Leave us. And take that brat with you."

"Jesse stays, Father. And that brat, as you call her, is *your* grandchild."

KC crawled to Jesse and climbed into her arms. Jesse comforted the displeased baby. "It's okay, Sunshine. They won't be here long."

"I understand you didn't give birth to her, therefore she's not my grandchild. And if *that* woman stays, so does Barrish. After all, he is your fiancé and has every right to be here."

"Father, I cannot have a fiancé when I'm already married. I don't even know this man."

"You will. Young Barrish comes from an upstanding family. He'll be a fine asset to our family."

Holding KC, Jesse rose from the floor and crossed the room to sit on the edge of her desk next to Jennifer. "Mr. Kensington," she addressed her father-in-law, "you may not approve of our marriage or of Jennifer living in Sweetwater, but the fact is that whether you approve or not, there isn't anything you can do about either matter."

Ignoring Jesse, Kensington glared at Jennifer. "Had I known what trouble this town would be, I would have brought your brothers with me. Be that as it may, you will return with me. We will leave in the morning." Kensington turned to leave. Stopping at the office door, he added, "That *child* will not be coming." Barrish followed the older man from the room.

"I knew he wouldn't listen," Jennifer groaned, dropping her head into her hands.

Jesse reached over to rub Jennifer's neck. She could feel the tight muscles bunching under the delicate skin. "Maybe by tomorrow, he'll feel different."

"No, he won't. Once his mind is made up, he never changes it."

"Let's go home, darlin'." Jesse smiled sadly at Jennifer. "You'll feel better once we're back at the ranch."

"I think we should stay in town tonight." Jennifer sat up to let the baby climb into her lap. "I don't trust him, and out at the ranch we'd be alone."

Jesse was not at all sure that staying in town would be safer. "I don't know, darlin'. Won't it be a little uncomfortable with them bein' so close? I mean, there ain't much space between rooms upstairs."

"Can we stay here?"

"Here? In the office?"

"Yes."

"Darlin', there's no bed in here."

Jennifer was afraid that her father was up to something, and, as unpleasant as sleeping on the hard floor would be, she knew that staying in town and close to their friends was much more important than returning to the comfort of the isolated ranch. Even if that was exactly what she desperately wanted to do, go back to the ranch with Jesse and KC and forget about her father and young Barrish. "We can spread blankets on the floor and sleep there. Please."

"I'll ask Bette Mae to get some blankets and pillows. And I'll see if there's a cowboy in the saloon that can be talked into riding out to the ranch and tending to the milk cow." Jesse bent to kiss Jennifer. "I love you."

"I love you, too."

Kensington was pulling on his boots. Awakened by her husband's furtive activities, Mrs. Kensington whispered from the bed, "Where are you going?"

"Go back to sleep."

She doubted he had slept at all. For hours after his confrontation with Jennifer, he had ranted about how he would never allow her to remain in Sweetwater, especially not with the rancher he blamed for her insolence. She was afraid that now he might be meaning to carry out his threats against their daughter. "What are you going to do?"

"Go back to sleep. Barrish and I have business to attend to." Kensington stepped to the door, pulling on his coat.

"It's after midnight. What business could you possibly have at this hour?"

"Don't question me," Kensington hissed. "Go back to sleep."

He exited the room, noisily pulling the door shut behind him. Barrish was waiting in the hall. "Let's go." Kensington moved past the younger man and down the hallway to the stairs.

The pair descended the stairs, then quietly made their way through the deserted room to Jesse's office. Easing open the door, they found the room dark except for a single lamp burning low on Jesse's desk. By its light, they spotted Jennifer and KC sleeping in the makeshift bed on the floor.

"Where's the other one?" Barrish whispered.

"Right here," Jesse said from behind the door. She had been awakened by hearing their footsteps from upstairs and was waiting for them.

Kensington and Barrish whirled to see Jesse standing behind them, a pistol held steadily in her hand.

"It's a little late for a social call."

Jennifer woke at the sound of voices. "What's going on?"

"Seems your father believes in uninvited late night visits." Jesse's eyes never left the two men. "I'll ask you *gentlemen* to return to your rooms. Tomorrow you'll leave Sweetwater and never bother Jennifer again."

"I'll not let you ruin my plans!" Kensington shouted, waking the baby.

Moving faster than Jesse would have imagined the big man was capable of, Kensington swung a fist at the side of her head. She staggered, knocked back a half step by the fierceness of the blow. Before she could recover, Barrish joined the attack, slapping the gun out of her hand. Jesse was taken by surprise by the sudden violent attack. After absorbing the first blows, she fought back, striking out at the men, not caring where her blows landed just as long as they did.

Jennifer leapt up from the floor. She had seen the pistol skitter across the floor, and she bolted toward it. Before she could reach the gun, Barrish intercepted her. Wrapping her in a bear hug, he determinedly pulled her struggling from the room.

Left with only Kensington to fight and spurred on by screams from Jennifer and KC, Jesse redoubled her efforts. But he was too big for her; his size and powerful blows soon had her at a disadvantage. Driven to her knees and too exhausted to stop him, Jesse could do nothing when Kensington picked up the pistol and turned it on her. She raised her arms over her head to ward off his attack, but he pushed them aside and slammed the pistol barrel down on her skull. Stunned by the crushing blow, the rancher crumpled to the floor.

"*Jesse!*" Jennifer screamed, but there was no response.

In her room at the back of the kitchen, Bette Mae bolted from her bed. As she ran into the dining room, she saw Jennifer being dragged outside. Chasing after her, Bette Mae ran onto the porch just in time to see Barrish yanking Jennifer onto his horse, forcing her to sit in front of him.

"Stop!" Bette Mae shouted.

Ignoring the screams, Kensington mounted, and the men kicked their horses into a gallop.

Helplessly watching as horses and riders disappeared, Bette Mae heard Jennifer cry out, "Jesse, I love you."

Ruthie and Sally, the Slipper's bartender, ran out onto the porch. "Go get Billie," Bette Mae told Ruthie, who was quickly off and running for the sheriff's office. "Come on," she said to Sally as she turned to go back inside the Slipper. They found Jesse unconscious on the floor of her office. KC had crawled to the injured woman and was huddled against her mother's still form, her body shaking as she cried for her mothers. "Lord have mercy on those men when Jesse finds them," Bette Mae muttered, kneeling to attend to Jesse and the baby.

CHAPTER SIX

Jesse's eyelids fluttered. She could sense people moving around her, but she couldn't remember where she was or how she got there. Then her brain registered KC's frightened cries and she was instantly awake, trying to sit up. Groaning, she grabbed her throbbing head.

"Hold on there." Bette Mae clutched Jesse's hand and pressed it down to her side. "Let me git the bandage on tha' cut afore ya start pokin' around."

When KC saw that her mother was awake, her sobs subsided, but she stubbornly clung to Jesse's chest, where she had climbed while Bette Mae worked on her mother's injuries.

The older woman positioned Jesse's hands on the baby's back to help calm her. "Yer mommy is goin' ta be jus' fine, little angel." Bette Mae patted the baby's wet cheek. "You lay there and don' let her try to sit up again."

Jesse carefully opened her eyes. "Jennifer?"

"They took her," Bette Mae said.

Fear lending her strength, Jesse struggled upright. "I've got to—"

Placing a hand on Jesse's shoulder, the older woman held her down. "I know ya do, but ya can't do nothin' 'til mornin'. She was fine when they left, kickin' and screamin' the whole way. Don' worry, she'll be waitin' for ya."

"Damn!" Jesse hoped Bette Mae was right. "Why couldn't he just have let her be?"

"Men like that, don' take no for an answer." Bette Mae finished binding the gash on Jesse's temple. "Ya rest and comfort yer baby; she needs ya." Bette Mae rose from the floor. "I'll see if Sally got the coffee started."

Jesse pulled KC to her, tenderly kissing the distraught child. "Don't worry, Sunshine, we'll find your momma and bring her home." Jesse rubbed the baby's back, pleased to hear her whimpers subside. As the cobwebs cleared from her head, Jesse became aware of a shuffling of feet nearby. She rolled her head to discover the source of the noise and saw Billie and Ruthie sitting on the couch.

Billie nodded when he saw her looking at them. "How ya feeling?"

Jesse managed a half smile. "Why's it always got to be my head that gets hit?"

"Probably 'cause that's your hardest part," Bette Mae said, coming back into the room carrying a tray loaded with coffeepot and cups. "Good, my little angel stopped cryin'. I was afraid she'd burst somethin', she was going on so."

Jesse kissed the top of KC's head. "She's seen an awful lot of hurt in her short life, Bette Mae."

"That she has, but she's got a lotta love in it now. And that'll go a long way to erasin' the hurt."

"I sure hope so."

"Want me to take her?" Bette Mae asked.

"Better leave her be for now." Jesse could still feel the baby's body trembling. "Billie, I'm leaving at first light."

"I know. I'm goin' with ya." The sheriff accepted a cup of steaming coffee. "Figure they'll head back to Denver. Already sent a rider with a telegram for the Denver sheriff. He should get it in plenty of time to stop them."

Jesse considered her father-in-law's options. "No," she decided. "I don't think Kensington will chance going to Denver."

"But that's the closest place to catch a train."

"I know. But he's smart. He'll head east, hoping we go to Denver."

"I don't know, Jesse."

"Doesn't matter. Soon as I pick up their trail, I'll know for sure." Lying on the hard floor with the baby on her chest was beginning to be extremely uncomfortable for the injured woman. "Reckon you can help me up to somethin' a little softer?"

It was awkward because KC refused to release her hold on Jesse, but Bette Mae and Billie managed to get Jesse up and help her to the couch. Ruthie pushed a couple of pillows to one end, and Jesse gingerly propped herself up against them.

"That feels better," she sighed, settling back against the pillows. KC snuggled against her, making smacking noises with her lips. "Hungry, Sunshine? I bet Bette Mae has something for you."

"I sure do, little angel," Bette Mae handed Jesse a bottle of warmed milk. "This should feel real good in yer tummy. And I've got some nice warm oatmeal cooking in the kitchen. Bet ya'd like some of that, too."

Jesse shifted KC into a more suitable position for her to drink and offered her the milk. The baby wrapped both hands around the bottle, pulling it to her mouth. A tapping at the office door drew the attention away from KC. Turning, they saw Mrs. Kensington standing in the doorway.

Jennifer's mother hesitated before speaking. "What has he done?"

Jesse glared at the woman, then grudgingly answered, "He took Jennifer."

"No," Mrs. Kensington gasped, slumping against the doorframe. "I didn't think he would go this far."

"What did you think he was going to do?" She kept her voice calm, so as not to upset KC. "Did you really think he would travel across the country to just shake my hand and wish us a happy marriage? After all the years that he treated Jennifer like nothing more than a business proposition, how could you have expected anything less than what he has done?"

"I...I don't..." Mrs. Kensington stopped. What had she expected? Certainly not for her husband to assault this woman and kidnap his own daughter. Then why had she insisted on accompanying him? He had not wanted her to come. Had she been afraid that this very thing would happen? She didn't have the answers. "I'm sorry," she said dejectedly, turning to retreat from the room where she obviously wasn't welcome.

Watching the woman struggle with her thoughts, Jesse realized that she was as much a victim of her husband as Jennifer was. That softened her toward her mother-in-law. "Might as well come in and have a cup of Bette Mae's coffee."

"Come on." Bette Mae waved the woman into the room. "Sit," she said, pulling the chair out from behind the desk.

Secure in her mother's arms and exhausted from the night's activities, KC fell asleep before she finished her bottle.

"Let me wash her face and get her fixed up with some fresh britches," Bette Mae offered, carefully lifting the baby from Jesse. "Little angel done tuckered herself out with all that cryin'."

Jesse watched Bette Mae carry the sleeping baby across the room. "How long until dawn, Billie?" she asked, having lost track of time while she had been unconscious.

"Less than two hours."

"Dusty and Blaze are at the livery."

"I know. They'll be saddled and ready with the others." Jesse looked at him quizzically, and he explained, "Whole town knows, Jesse. You won't be ridin' alone."

Overcoming her apprehension that they would reject her out of hand, Mrs. Kensington said timidly, "I'd like to come."

Jesse studied Jennifer's mother. As much as she didn't want to, she had to admit that the woman seemed genuinely shocked by her husband's actions. The eyes looking back at her were full of concern for the daughter that she obviously loved. And there was more just below the surface. But what? Determination? Resolve? Strength?

"All right. But we'll be riding fast, and I'm not stopping until I find Jennifer. We won't slow down if you can't keep up."

"Thank you." Mary Kensington rose from the chair and quickly left the room to get ready for the journey.

"Think she can ride?" Billie asked.

"Don't know." Jesse looked up as Bette Mae returned KC to her. "Don't care." She smiled sadly as the sleeping baby snuggled against her chest.

The morning's cloudless sky predicted another hot day as the pair of horses carried their riders across the broken, rocky ground. Leaving behind the rolling open valleys, the road climbed up the western slope of the Rocky Mountains, alternately passing through stretches of thick forest and open hillsides covered in sagebrush and littered with boulders.

Jennifer had kept up an endless string of protests since the trio had galloped away from Sweetwater, and she saw no reason to stop just because the sun was coming up. "You stupid fool!" she shouted at her father riding several feet away. "Jesse will come after me."

Kensington ignored his daughter's comments, pushing his horse faster. They would have to stop soon to rest the tired animals, but he wanted to cover as much ground as possible before then. Once the sun rose fully, the rocks surrounding them would soak up the heat and make the already uncomfortable ride unbearable.

Barrish had his arms wrapped in a death grip around Jennifer, preventing her from leaping off the galloping horse. Dangerous and foolhardy as it was, she had attempted just that more than once, and he didn't want her trying again.

Jennifer beat her fists against his arms and elbowed him in the chest and stomach trying to break his grasp. His body aching from her blows, he growled, "Stop it or I'll tie you to the saddle."

"Ha. I'd like to see you try." Jennifer continued her assault. "When Jesse catches up with us, you'd better hope she's in a good mood," Jennifer taunted.

Barrish laughed. "Like that woman could do anything to me."

"Oh, you'd be surprised what Jesse can do."

Deciding to try a different means of escape, Jennifer went limp. As soon as Barrish's grip relaxed in response, she pushed against the saddle with all her might and leaned away from him. It worked. She fell to the ground and rolled away from the horse. The shock of hitting the hard ground was more than she had anticipated, and she was too stunned to scramble to her feet. As she did finally manage to stand on shaky legs, she heard the sound of hoofbeats rushing up behind her. An instant later something struck her in the back, and she was knocked to the ground. Before she could regain her footing, her father dismounted and dragged her upright.

"If I have to, I'll hogtie you and drag you all the way back home," he told her. "I don't want you to mention that bitch again. Do you understand?"

Jennifer smiled at the man who meant less and less to her as each minute passed. "Oh, I understand. I understand that *Jesse*," she said pointedly, "will come after me. And when she does, I *understand* that you'll regret you ever came to Montana." Her father raised his hand to deliver a blow, but Jennifer defiantly stood her ground. "Go ahead. You've wanted to hit me for years. But proper gentlemen don't slap women, do they, Father?" she asked bitterly.

Kensington glared at her for several moments, hand frozen in the air, ready to strike. "Put this on." He removed his coat and threw it at Jennifer, who was dressed only in the borrowed nightshirt she had worn to bed the previous evening. "Tie her up," he ordered Barrish, then stomped off.

"You should show your father more respect," Barrish said, approaching Jennifer with a piece of rope.

"I have no father," Jennifer replied angrily. Realizing the truth in her words, she sighed. "I never have."

The sky had barely begun to lighten when Jesse mounted Dusty; KC sat in the carry sack on her back. Bette Mae, refusing to stay behind, was mounted on Blaze. Billie, Ed Granger, and newspaper editor Thaddeus Newby all sat on their own horses, while Mrs. Kensington was atop a horse rented from the livery. The remaining citizens of Sweetwater seeing them off were grouped around the horses or stood on the steps and porch of the Silver Slipper.

Mayor Perkins spoke for the town. "You bring Jennifer home, Jesse. And don't worry about the Slipper or your ranch. We'll see to them."

Jesse looked around at the many concerned faces. She was humbled at knowing that most of the town had turned out to show their support.

"I will, and thank you. Thanks to all of you." Jesse nodded at the crowd. "Now, Jennifer will be expecting me," she flicked Dusty's reins, "and I don't mean to keep her waiting."

Shouts of encouragement and wishes for good luck followed them as the riders rode away. When the dust settled, the citizens of Sweetwater went back to their regular morning business, but their thoughts remained with the rancher and the missing schoolteacher.

It was midday, and they had stopped to rest the horses at a small lake. "When we marry..." Barrish began.

"We'll never marry." Jennifer looked at the fiancé her father had arranged for her. "I'm already married to Jesse."

"It's not right," Barrish said with a look of disgust.

"Neither is kidnapping." Jennifer rose from the small boulder upon which she had been sitting. "Nor beating up women."

"Where do you think you're going?" Barrish asked as she walked toward the water.

"Nowhere." She had promised not to attempt another escape if her hands were left untied, deciding instead to delay her father in other ways in order to give Jesse time to catch up. Jennifer knew Jesse would come after her, but she was worried about her wife's injury from the hard blow to her head. She hoped Jesse was okay. And little KC, the baby had sounded so scared. Jennifer stood at the edge of the lake, wrapping herself in her arms as her shoulders shook with silent tears for her family.

After several minutes, Jennifer turned to face Barrish and surveyed her would-be fiancé. He wasn't bad looking, *if* she had been interested. He stood about the same height as herself but had a thin, almost scrawny build. Jennifer guessed him to be in his mid-twenties, yet it appeared that he had little need to shave regularly. His eyes were deep green, and she was surprised to see a depth of emotion in them. She wondered if there was any hope of making him realize the senselessness of her father's conduct. "You know, even if you get me back East, I'll just run away again."

"Why? Why would you prefer...*her* over a man?"

"Because I love her." Jennifer shook her head; maybe her instincts were wrong when it came to young Barrish. "Tell me, Barrish...What is your given name? I'm sorry, I've forgotten it, if I ever knew. Considering that we were never properly introduced, I guess it's to be expected."

"Andrew."

"Tell me, Andrew, what does my father get by our marrying?"

"What do you mean?"

"I'm not stupid, and I don't think you are either. My father doesn't do anything unless it's going to bring him financial gain. So, what does it profit him if we were to marry?"

"Your father needs backing to expand his shipping business. My father owns a bank."

"What? He isn't making enough money now?" Jennifer scoffed. "Father could already buy and sell half the town if he had a mind to. Why does he need to expand?"

"So your brothers will be taken care of when I pass the company on to them," Kensington supplied, returning from the knoll where he had been watching for any sign of their followers.

"And what about me, Father? Am I to benefit by any of this?"

"Of course you are," Kensington said, as if he couldn't understand why she would ask the question. "You will be married to a man who will see to your needs."

"But I don't love him!" Jennifer screamed in frustration. "I don't even know him."

"Don't use that tone with me." Kensington glared at Jennifer. "Get the horses," he commanded Barrish. He turned back to his daughter. "The only thing you need to know about him is that I want him for your husband. As for love — your mother and I don't share that, why should you?"

It took a few minutes for Barrish to collect the horses that had wandered away in search of edible vegetation. He led them back to where the Kensingtons were facing off.

"Let's go." Kensington mounted.

Jennifer mounted Barrish's horse. Waiting for him to mount behind her, she looked back the way they had come and sent a silent message to Jesse, *"Hurry, my love."*

At noon, Jesse called a halt at a small stream. Having pushed the horses since leaving Sweetwater, both animals and riders needed to rest. After everyone dismounted, Jesse and Billie took charge of the reins and led the horses down a muddy embankment to the water.

"What're you lookin' at?" Billie asked as Jesse stared intently across the shallow water.

The stream was no more than fifteen feet wide, and the muddy banks made it easy for Jesse to spot tracks along the opposite side. "Two horses passed here during the night." Jesse's eyes scanned the opposite stream bank. "Crossed here and came out over there. One is carrying more of a load than the other."

Billie clapped Jesse's shoulder. "It could be them."

Jesse nodded absently, straining her eyes to look into the distance as if it were possible to see Jennifer out there. "I'm coming, darlin'," she whispered. KC's fussing drew Jesse's attention to her daughter. She carefully slipped the carry sack off her shoulders as she walked back to the others.

KC sleepily looked at her mother and smiled. She looked around for her other mother, sniffling when she couldn't see Jennifer.

"Hey, Sunshine." Jesse held KC close, nuzzling the soft downy head with her cheek. "I miss her, too. But we'll find her, okay?"

"Otay," KC said in a tiny voice.

Jesse smiled at her daughter's use of the new word. "Good girl; your momma will be proud. Let's get your britches changed and get you something to eat." KC leaned in to Jesse, placing a wet kiss on her nose. Jesse laughed, wiping baby slobber off her nose. "I love you, too." She sat KC on the ground while she retrieved her saddlebag, turning back just in time to see KC start to crawl away. "No, you don't." Jesse grabbed a sock-covered foot and pulled KC back. "No exploring 'til you get fresh pants." Jesse tickled the scowling baby and got the laugh she hoped for. "That's better. Now hold still."

KC giggled. "Otay."

Mrs. Kensington came over to stand next to Jesse and KC. Watching curiously as Jesse took care of the child's needs, she was struck with the similarities between KC and her own daughter at the same age. "If I didn't know better, I'd say that she was Jennifer's child," she told Jesse.

"She is." Jesse noted KC's frown. "It's all right, Sunshine." She finished diapering the baby. "She's not going to hurt you." She left KC on the ground to play. Mrs. Kensington said nothing as Jesse carried her saddlebags to a log and sat down. KC crawled to the log and pulled herself upright using Jesse's pant leg. Grasping on to the rough bark, the baby inched along the length of the log.

"Bet that feels good after sitting so long," Jesse said, keeping a close watch on the unsteady progress. Lifting her saddlebag into her lap, she pulled a cloth napkin from the bag and spread it out on the log, unwrapping some biscuits.

KC immediately moved toward her mother to reach for the soft biscuits. Jesse tore a small piece from one and handed it to KC, who shoved it in her mouth. Losing her grip on the log, KC dropped to the ground. With a mouth full of biscuit, she reached up a dirty hand to ask for more.

Jesse chuckled at the baby's bulging cheeks. "Small bites, Sunshine, just like Momma taught you." KC pulled the piece from her mouth and studied it before returning it to her mouth.

"Good girl." Jesse smiled at the baby, who responded with a biscuit-filled smile. Jesse took a bite of biscuit.

"I would never hurt that child," Mrs. Kensington said from where she stood watching.

Without taking her eyes of the baby, Jesse said, "You already have. You've hurt her momma." She tore off another piece of biscuit, handing it to KC as she addressed Mrs. Kensington. "You'd better get something to eat. We'll be leaving soon."

Bette Mae listened quietly to the exchange between the two women and saw the anguish in the older woman's eyes at Jesse's words. *Maybe this one still has a heart.*

The afternoon shadows lengthened into evening. Kensington and Barrish continued to push the horses, so Jennifer needed to do something to slow them down. Every idea she had came up with proved to be less successful than the last. Hoping to see something that would help accomplish her goal, she looked around, but the landscape offered no solutions. Then inspiration struck. "Get your hands off me." Jennifer swung an elbow backward, connecting with Barrish's jaw.

Barrish rubbed his injured face, confused by the sudden movement. "What?"

"I said, keep your hands to yourself!" Jennifer shouted to be sure her father, riding several feet ahead of them, heard. She smirked when her father slowed his horse. "We're not married yet, and you can't take those liberties with me."

"What's going on?" Kensington asked as Barrish's horse came even with his own.

"I don't know," Barrish yelped as he fended off another elbow from Jennifer.

"He touched me," Jennifer said indignantly.

"Of course I'm touching you." Barrish tried to pin Jennifer's arms to her sides. "I've got to hold you on the horse, don't I?"

"Jennifer, quit playing these games," Kensington threatened.

"Father, he touched my...my...my breast," she cried, as she clutched her arms across her chest as if to protect herself.

Kensington pulled his horse to a stop, glaring at Barrish. Jennifer knew her father believed that a man did not touch a woman until they were married. She thought it ironic that he didn't seem to see kidnapping and assaulting women as taboo.

"I did no such thing, Mr. Kensington," Barrish said in defense of himself. "My hands have never left her waist."

Jennifer added what fuel she could to the fire. "What about the time you rubbed my thigh?"

"Get down," Kensington ordered as he swung down from his horse. Jennifer quickly swung a leg over the horse's neck and dropped to the ground. Barrish followed more slowly. Kensington barked at the young man, "Have you touched my daughter?"

"No, sir." Barrish vehemently waggled his head from side to side. "As a man of honor, I tell you, I have not."

"Ha," Jennifer cried. "You have."

Kensington looked from his bullheaded daughter to the nervous young man quaking before him.

Seeing her father's hesitation, Jennifer pleaded, "Father, I'm your daughter. You must protect me against the inappropriate actions of this man. He should not dishonor me this way. He should not dishonor *you* this way."

Kensington pushed Jennifer aside as he stepped toward Barrish. Before the young man could react, a fist exploded against his chin. Barrish dropped to ground like a sack of rocks.

Jennifer screamed and rushed to Barrish's side. "How could you, Father! He is my intended." Jennifer knelt beside Barrish and patted him on the cheek, trying to revive him. "How am I to marry him now?"

Confused by his daughter's reaction, Kensington stood unmoving. He watched mystified as Jennifer tried to help the very same man she had spent the past days insisting she had no interest in.

"Come on." Kensington reached down and grabbed Jennifer's arm. "Leave him. We need to keep going."

"Leave him?" Jennifer pulled her arm from her father's grasp. "Leave him? I will not. Are we not to be married? How can you possibly suggest that he be left here?"

"Damn it, girl." Kensington was bewildered and annoyed. He looked up at the sky; it was more dark than light. "All right. We'll stay here until he wakes up, then we'll go."

Jennifer simply nodded, but inside she was doing somersaults. It had worked. As her father led the horses to a nearby spring partially encircled by a grove of trees, she pushed herself up from the ground. Barrish's head, which had been resting in her lap, dropped to the ground, landing with a clunk.

"Marry you?" Jennifer mocked the unconscious man. "When pigs fly." She dusted off her hands before joining her father.

"It's late, Jesse," Billie commented as the sun disappeared from the sky.

She looked at the sheriff and then at the sky. So concentrated on catching up to Jennifer was she that she hadn't noticed the growing darkness. Jesse would have kept riding into the night, but she knew her daughter was tired and the horses need resting. "You're right. Let's set camp."

It didn't take long for a fire to be started and bedrolls to be laid out. Bette Mae busied herself with making supper and Mrs. Kensington volunteered to help her. Thaddeus collected firewood while Ed and Billie took care of the horses. Jesse saw to KC's needs. The baby had not complained all day, seeming to understand the importance of their quest. After providing her with fresh britches and dressing her for bed, Jesse sat KC on her bedroll.

"Baze?" KC asked for the toy horse.

Jesse pulled it from her pocket. "You stay here and be good; I'm goin' to take care of Blaze and Dusty."

"Otay."

"I'll keep my eye on my little angel," Bette Mae said as she stirred the contents of a pot heating over the fire.

After Jesse walked away, Mrs. Kensington said, "She loves that baby very much."

"Tha' she does." Bette Mae added fixings to the boiling water.

"Even though it's not hers."

"Tha' baby is hers jus' as if she'd gave birth ta her herself," Bette Mae told the woman. "Why, I've never seen two people love a child as much as Jesse and Jennifer love my little angel."

"But how can Jennifer love a child that doesn't belong to her?"

Bette Mae slammed the lid down on the pot and angrily turned a fierce look on the other woman. "Don' belong ta her? Tha' baby may not have their blood, but she shares somethin' much mor' important." When Mrs. Kensington remained silent, Bette Mae said, "Their hearts. The little angel there is part of their hearts. A big part. A very big part." Scowling, Bette Mae lifted the lid and stirred the stew.

Mrs. Kensington turned to watch the child playing happily with her toy.

After dinner, Jesse sat on her bedroll, rocking KC and softly humming a lullaby as the baby drifted to sleep. Jesse continued to hold the baby even after she had nodded off; KC was her connection to Jennifer, and she didn't want to let go. "We're coming, darlin'," she whispered.

Mrs. Kensington sat on her own bedroll, watching the interaction intently. "Who were you talking to?" she asked softly.

Looking up to meet the eyes that were so much like her wife's, Jesse answered, "Jennifer."

"You care very much for my daughter." It was a statement, not a question.

"Yes."

"Yet you try to stop her from returning to her home."

"Her home is in Sweetwater, with me and KC."

"But you can't give her what her marriage to Mr. Barrish will."

Jesse thought for a moment. What could she say to make this woman understand? "I'm surprised that you ride as well as you do," she finally said. She had indeed been surprised when Mrs. Kensington not only knew how to ride, but had proven to be an accomplished rider. "I wouldn't think your husband would think such an activity to be proper for a woman."

Mrs. Kensington laughed sadly. "There are a number of activities I enjoyed before my marriage that my husband deemed improper. I learned to ride as a child and continued to ride right up to the day I married."

"Then you stopped?"

"Yes."

"Why?"

Mary Kensington sighed. "It was expected of me."

"Why did you marry him?"

"I had no choice. My father made an agreement with his father."

"Did you want to marry him?"

"As I said, I had no choice."

"Did you want to?" Jesse persisted.

In a voice so quiet it was almost inaudible, Mrs. Kensington answered, "No."

"Yet you would allow Jennifer to suffer the same fate?"

Mrs. Kensington stretched out on her bedroll, pulling the blanket around her to ward off the night's chill. She turned on her side, hiding the tears that fell.

Just when Jesse figured she wouldn't get an answer to her question, she heard a whispered response. "No, that's not what I want."

Jesse laid back on her bedroll, carefully placing a sleeping KC on her chest and tucking her blanket around the baby. Looking up into the sky, she searched for the star that she and Jennifer always wished upon when they were out at night. Locating the celestial body, Jesse smiled. "I love you, my darlin'. Be safe."

Jennifer pulled the coat tight around her. The nightshirt she had been wearing when she was dragged out of the Slipper did little to protect her against the cold. And the coat her father had given her wasn't long enough to cover her legs. She lay on her back and tried not to think of how miserable she felt. Looking up into the star-filled sky, Jennifer spied the star that was special to her and Jesse. Her smile was born of hope and faith. "I love you, sweetheart. Take care of our baby."

CHAPTER SEVEN

A full moon lit the travelers' way. The road they were following wasn't much more than two ruts, and without the moonlight it would have been almost impossible to follow. They had crested the divide less than an hour before and were riding down the eastern slope of the Rocky Mountain range. Kensington had awakened Jennifer as soon as Barrish regained consciousness. She was mounted on her father's horse to avoid any further improprieties from the young man. Looking up into the sky, Jennifer watched as a shooting star flew overhead. She smiled. Jesse was coming.

"Where are we going?" Jennifer asked, hoping that if she could get her father to talk he would slow their pace.

"Bozeman."

"Why there? That puts you further away from Denver and the train."

"More than one place to catch a train," Kensington grumbled, unhappy with the endless string of questions from his daughter, a trait she had exhibited as soon as she had learned to talk. Back then, he had found the practice more amusing than annoying.

"How did you know?"

"Know what?"

"Where to find me."

"Telegram from Bannack. Someone saw you there."

The dressmaker, Jennifer told herself. Of course. No wonder she'd felt uncomfortable in the dress shop.

"Did you think I wouldn't find you?"

"I was hoping."

"You have an obligation to your family, Jennifer. I raised you, fed you, clothed you; you owe me."

Shaking her head, Jennifer gave a sad laugh. "I owe myself, Father. I deserve a better future than what you have planned for me."

Kensington groaned, annoyed with his daughter's defiance. "You've been trouble ever since you learned to talk. Always asking questions, always wanting to do the same as your brothers, even trying to get your mother to question my authority. Nothing but trouble."

"I am a person, Father, with my own needs, my own feelings. I just want to express them. I want to see what I can accomplish. Why can't you understand?"

"Nonsense."

Jennifer recalled a childhood filled with lonely days as she tried to follow her dreams within the confines of her father's strict rules. She'd finally broken free, and she wasn't about to return to that life. "I ran away because I knew that I would never be allowed to be myself. You made me feel unworthy, Father. You almost made me too afraid to even try to change that, but I did. I found a way to feel important in Sweetwater." Kensington grunted his displeasure, but Jennifer was undeterred.

"Do you know that I'm a schoolteacher, Father? I'll have fifteen students in my class when the new term begins, and I've already made a difference for many of them. They're learning because I teach them, just like Jesse has taught me so much at the ranch. She taught me to ride and how to use the different tools. We built furniture for our home and fixed the cabin's roof and planted a garden. We did it together, Father. She never tells me I can't do something. Instead she encourages me to try."

"Not proper for a woman to do men's work," Kensington said. "Once you're back East and married, you'll see that."

"You won't get me back, Father. Jesse will make sure of that."

"You can't win, Jennifer," Kensington snapped. "Don't try."

"You are the one who will lose," Jennifer sadly told her father. "And this time you'll lose more than just me."

"Rubbish. Nothing but more of your silly nonsense," Kensington grunted as he kicked his horse into a canter.

"It's okay, Sunshine." Jesse was rocking KC, who had awakened screaming. "It was just a bad dream."

"Here's some milk." Bette Mae handed a bottle to Jesse. "It's the last 'til we find us a milk cow."

"Thanks." Jesse offered the bottle to the baby. KC quickly gulped a few mouthfuls and hiccupped. "Slow down. It's not going anywhere." Jesse looked around the camp and saw that KC's cries had awakened the others. "Might as well get breakfast going, Bette Mae."

"Alrighty." Bette Mae ambled to the fire ring and stirred the embers into flame. "Won' take but a minute or two to fix some coffee."

"I'll get the horses saddled." Billie carried his bedroll toward the picketed ponies, stopping for a moment to tickle KC on the foot. Getting a giggle from the baby, Billie smiled. "Don't much care for bad dreams myself," he confided to KC.

Ed rose from his bedroll. "I'll give you a hand, Billie. I gotta say, Jesse," Ed grinned at the rancher, "that little bitty thing can sure make some racket."

Thaddeus was rolling up his bedroll. "Must take after her other mom in that."

"Better not let Jennifer hear you say that." Billie laughed and the others joined him.

KC looked up at her mother and smiled. "You think that's funny, do you," Jesse tickled the giggling baby. The mood in the camp lightened for a few minutes.

"Come on, boys." Bette Mae beat a spoon against the coffeepot. "Get it while it's hot."

Breakfast wasn't more than cold biscuits and hot coffee, but no one seemed to mind. Jesse took care of KC before eating the portion Bette Mae had set aside for her. As soon as their plates were empty, they broke camp. If they made good time, they would cross the pass before noon and be well on the way to Bozeman by nightfall.

Jesse carefully dropped KC into the carry sack and made sure she was comfortable before slipping it onto her shoulders. "Won't be long now, Sunshine. Your momma isn't that far ahead of us. I bet we find her by tonight," Jesse said as she mounted Dusty.

"Otay," KC said. She didn't understand the words, but it sure seemed to make her mommy happy to say it.

The ride down the eastern side of the divide was steep, and the path was full of switchbacks to accommodate the wagons that normally traveled it. Frustrated with the seeming lack of progress, Kensington impatiently left the road, guiding his horse in a more direct route down the slope. Barrish followed, but not without complaint.

"Damn it, Kensington," the young man shouted, "is it really necessary to ride the horses into the ground?"

"Would you prefer that bitch catch us?" Kensington shouted back.

"What will it matter if the horses give out? We won't be able to outrun her without them."

"Jesse will catch you either way," Jennifer taunted.

"You'd better hope she doesn't."

"Or what, Father?" Jennifer had had enough of his threats. "Will you add murder to your list of crimes? How do you think your business associates will feel about that?"

"What happens out here will never be known back East." Kensington held tight to Jennifer as his horse jumped a small creek.

"How will you keep it a secret? If you force me to go back with you, I'll make sure everyone knows what you've done."

"My father will not appreciate you involving him in murder, Kensington. Kidnapping is bad enough." Barrish pulled his horse to a stop at the creek.

"No one will know!" Kensington bellowed.

"You heard her." Barrish dismounted. He was tired and sore and hungry, and if Kensington wanted to ride on without him, so be it. "She'll know."

Kensington looked back and saw Barrish standing next to the creek, his horse drinking its fill of the cold water. Yanking his horse around, Kensington rode back. "Get on your horse. We don't have time to stop."

"I'm stopping. I'm tired. My horse is tired. If you want to go on, go." Barrish sat on a log bridging the small creek. "This makes no sense. We can't force her to go back, marry me, and live happily ever after. I say we leave her here. Let that Branson woman have her."

"She's going back," Kensington growled. "Now get on your horse."

Disregarding the older man's anger, Barrish shook his head. "It's over."

"It's over when I say it's over." Kensington's horse dropped its head to drink from the creek. The sudden movement caused him to relax his hold on Jennifer, and she quickly slipped off the horse.

"He's right, Father. Leave me here. Go on to Bozeman and then home. I'll make sure no one follows you."

Kensington could barely contain his rage "I'll not have either of you ruining my plans. You'll be married; I'll get my money."

"Dammit, Father!" Jennifer shouted. "Can't you see this is wrong? There is no way for this to end the way you want it to. And what's wrong with you?" She turned on Barrish. "Why are you just standing there and allowing this to happen?"

Barrish looked at Jennifer with new eyes. She certainly had every right to be furious. She had been kidnapped and forced from the place she called home and from people who loved her and whom she loved. Dressed only in a coat and nightshirt, her bare legs were dirty and covered in cuts and scratches, and he knew she must be as cold and hungry as he was. He saw the grim determination in her eyes and knew that, no matter what her father had planned, Jennifer would somehow find a way to reunite with the woman and child she considered to be her family.

"I won't tell you again, Barrish, get on your horse."

"Or what? You can't kill everyone, Kensington." The young man sighed, his decision finally made. "I'm sorry, Jennifer. I never should have agreed to this. And when I get back home, I'll tell my father what happened out here. He won't hold us to this arrangement."

In her gratitude, Jennifer could have kissed the young man, but knew that a simple, "Thank you," was the better response.

"I don't care what you say." Kensington reached down to pull Jennifer back onto his horse. "Your father and I have an agreement, and I will see it carried out."

Jennifer deftly avoided her father's grasp. "Andrew is right; it's over."

Twisting in the saddle, Kensington opened the saddlebag. He reached inside and pulled out the pistol he had taken from Jesse. "Get on your horse," he said as he leveled the gun at Barrish.

Jennifer stepped in front of the young man. "Don't, Father!"

"Then get on the horse. *Now!*"

Barrish stood, took the few steps to where his horse grazed on a grassy patch of ground, and mounted. Reaching down, he offered a hand to Jennifer.

Without hesitating, she took the extended hand and was pulled up into the saddle. She knew that Barrish had become less of a threat than her father. Maybe between the two of them, they could escape from the man determined to take her away from her family.

Jesse's party had stopped to rest. KC was sitting on the ground, playing with her toy horse. She looked around for her mother and couldn't find her. Panicked, she began to cry.

Mrs. Kensington heard the baby's whimpers and turned to see KC with tears streaming down her face. She walked to the baby, slowly sitting down next to her. "It's all right, KC."

KC looked uncertainly at the woman who seemed to always upset her mothers. But right now she was smiling, reminding the baby of her missing momma.

Mrs. Kensington tentatively reached out to reassure the baby. When KC didn't protest, she cautiously rubbed the child's back. "Don't cry, honey. I promise, your mommy will be right back."

KC dropped to all fours, crawling closer to the woman, then looking up. After a few moments she crawled into the older woman's lap, allowing herself to be gently rocked.

Jesse returned from the bushes as KC crawled into Mrs. Kensington's lap. She took a step toward them, but Bette Mae's hand on her arm stopped her.

"Give 'em a minute, Jesse," Bette Mae said softly. She had been keeping an eye on the baby and knew she was in no danger. "I think they both need it."

Jesse stood quietly watching her mother-in-law carefully cradling KC, who had calmed in the woman's arms. After several minutes, KC remembered her neglected toy and pointed to the ground where she had left it.

Mrs. Kensington bent forward and picked up the little pony, then handed it to KC. "Is this your pretty horse?"

Once the toy was securely in her hand, KC held it up, proudly announcing, "Baze."

"That's the name of Jennifer's horse, isn't it?" Mrs. Kensington asked absently.

Jesse knelt beside Mrs. Kensington and KC. "Yes."

"See, I told you your mommy would be right back," Mrs. Kensington told KC as she moved to hand the baby to Jesse.

Shaking her head, Jesse said, "She's happy, let her be."

Tears filling her eyes, Mrs. Kensington nodded. "Thank you."

"It's what Jennifer would want," Jesse said with a shrug. "Her one regret about leaving your home was that she might never see you again. She loves you. She would want you to know and love her family as much as she does."

"I don't know if I can."

"I think you can." Jesse smiled. "If you want to."

Kensington's insistence that they continue to push the horses had finally resulted in a draining of all their energy. They had slowed to a walk and were having trouble maintaining even that pace. At mid-afternoon, with Bozeman in sight in the distance, Kensington was forced to call a halt so the exhausted animals could rest. He stopped at the edge of a boulder field where a small pond bubbled up from a natural spring. As the horses drank, Jennifer and Barrish sat in the shade of a large boulder under the watchful eye of their captor.

Jennifer looked at the father she no longer knew and questioned whether she ever really had. Even after all that had happened since his arrival in Sweetwater, he still believed he could take her back without incurring any consequences. All she could hope for now was that Jesse would catch up before they reached Bozeman and her father arranged faster transportation to the East. "What do you plan to tell people in Bozeman?" she asked.

"Nothing," Kensington scanned the route they had just traveled. He was sure that Jesse wasn't too far behind them, and being forced to stop could give her the time she needed to catch them.

Barrish picked up the questioning. "You can't ride in there holding a gun on us without questions being asked."

"Then I'll tell them the truth," Kensington told the pair. "She's my daughter, who ran away from home. She's been promised in marriage, and I have a right to take her back."

"What about me?" Barrish asked.

"You're her fiancé. You're helping me return her home."

"With a gun in my back?"

Kensington glared at the young man. He had thought Barrish would make a good husband for his daughter, now he wasn't so sure. The boy was beginning to ask as many questions as Jennifer, a trait unacceptable in a suitable son-in-law.

Jennifer sighed. She was tired. Tired from the ride and tired from her father's inability to see her as anything more than a bargaining chip. "The people in Bozeman won't believe you, not with us telling them the truth."

"We won't be there any longer than it takes to catch the next stage out of town. You won't have time to tell them anything."

Laughing, Jennifer asked, "Do you plan on me traveling all the way back East dressed like this?" She opened the coat and showed her father the dirty, tattered nightshirt that clung to her otherwise naked body. "I think my attire might raise a few questions, don't you?"

Turning back to watch for any sign of the riders behind them, Kensington chose to ignore the questions. Jennifer was right, though. She would need proper clothing, and he would have to think of something to tell the people they encountered in Bozeman. But there would be time for that when they reached town. Right now, he was only concerned with avoiding the woman on his trail. He grabbed the reins of his horse. "Let's go."

After mounting, Barrish guided the horse carrying him and Jennifer into the boulder field.

It was the last major obstacle before they entered the valley; Bozeman sat nestled in its center. The horses would have to slowly pick their way around the rocks, and Jennifer made a silent wish that the delay would be all Jesse needed.

As his horse entered the boulder field, Kensington looked back over his shoulder and saw riders rapidly approaching. "Get moving." He rode up next to Barrish and Jennifer. "They're coming."

Jennifer's heart leapt into her throat. She tried to look for Jesse, but with Barrish riding behind her, she was unable to see anything.

"Move." Kensington slapped the rump of their horse, and the animal bounded forward.

Mrs. Kensington was riding close to Dusty. Since their last stop, she had been thinking about Jesse, the woman that her daughter had declared she loved. And about the obvious love Jesse held for Jennifer. Looking over, she saw KC watching her. She smiled at the baby safely tucked into the carry pack on Jesse's back.

KC smiled back, lifted a small hand, and held it up. Tiny fingers opened and closed in an awkward baby wave. KC giggled when Mrs. Kensington returned the gesture.

Looking over her shoulder, Jesse caught the interaction between KC and Jennifer's mother. She slowed Dusty's pace just enough for the other horse to catch up.

"How far ahead are they?" Mrs. Kensington asked as they rode side by side.

"Couple of hours, maybe less." Jesse nudged Dusty back to her original speed. Mrs. Kensington urged her horse to keep pace. "Will we catch them today?"

"I'm planning on it."

"You could move faster if you weren't carrying KC," the woman said, telling Jesse what she already knew. When Jesse didn't answer, she offered, "Why don't you let me carry her?"

"Thanks, but—"

"Please." Mrs. Kensington reached out and put a hand on the rancher's arm. "I want you to find Jennifer."

Jesse pulled Dusty to a stop, then turned to the other woman. "I'm taking her home with us."

Mrs. Kensington nodded. "I expect that's what she'll want. Please," she held out her arms, "let me take the baby. You go ahead and find her momma."

Jesse looked at the woman, then into the distance where Jennifer was to be found. She turned her head to see what KC was doing. The baby was sitting quietly, smiling at her grandmother. Slipping the straps from her shoulders, Jesse held the pack so she could kiss KC. "Be a good girl," she told the baby as she helped Mrs. Kensington settle the carry sack on her back. "I'm going to go get your momma." Jesse expected KC to protest the exchange and was surprised when the baby just smiled at her. "I love you, KC." She cupped the baby's face and held it for a moment. "I promise, I'll bring Momma back."

"Otay." KC waved at Jesse as she rode away.

Free of the responsibility of carrying KC, Jesse urged Dusty into a gallop and was charging out of the foothills and into the valley. Bozeman was less than a few hours ride in the distance, and Jesse knew that Jennifer had to be somewhere in between. She was determined to find her wife as quickly as possible.

Billie urged his horse forward, racing to catch up with Jesse. It was a struggle, since Dusty was one of the fastest horses in the territory, but Billie was not about to let his friend go up against Kensington alone.

The two horses and their riders sped across the terrain of gently rolling hills, stopping for nothing as they leapt the smaller creeks and splashed through the larger ones. Ravines and gullies did not deter them from their path as they rode the most direct route to Bozeman. The closer they got to the town, the more the valley floor flattened, and the horses flew across the miles.

Mrs. Kensington, Bette Mae, Ed, and Thaddeus followed as quickly as they could. From an ever-widening distance, they watched as Jesse and Billie raced toward Bozeman.

"That was a mighty nice thin' ya done," Bette Mae said, riding alongside Jennifer's mother.

"We should never have come here," Mrs. Kensington answered sadly. "Jennifer would have been much better off."

"Now, ya is plain wrong there," Bette Mae told her. "Once this is all over, Jennifer is goin' ta be real happy tha' yer here. But yer husband, tha's gonna be a different matter."

"I never should have let him treat Jennifer the way he did." Mrs. Kensington reached up and grasped the tiny hand stretched over her shoulder, gently rubbing the soft skin. "Do you think she'll ever forgive me?"

"Lordy." Bette Mae chuckled. "She done forgave you years ago."

Mrs. Kensington gave Bette Mae a curious look. "I don't understand."

"Jennifer told me about her family back East. Said that 'cep' for you, she was pretty much ignored by the bunch of 'em. She's got almost no memories 'bout her brothers and only bad ones 'bout her poppa, but she's got plenty of real happy ones 'bout you. She knows ya couldn' done nothin' different. Yer husband jus' don' see much good in women, 'cept ta have his babies and cook his meals. Otherwise, he jus' don' need 'em. And Jennifer don' need him, neither." Bette Mae smiled at her companion. "But you and Jennifer are different. She needs her momma, and I'm thinkin' her momma needs her."

Mrs. Kensington stared at Bette Mae. She wondered how a woman who seemed to be uneducated could be so smart. Ultimately she decided it really didn't matter. What Bette Mae said was true. She did need Jennifer. And she was going to do whatever she could to mend the fences between herself and her daughter once this mess her husband had caused was over.

"Let's go find your mothers," Mrs. Kensington told KC as she glanced back over her shoulder at the baby.

Moments later, four more horses were galloping in pursuit of Jesse and Jennifer.

Billie pointed. "Look."

"I see them."

They had ridden over the top of a small hill. In the distance, Jesse made out the movement of two horses and their riders as they were entering a field of boulders. Another movement caught Jesse's sharp eyes. She swore as she pushed Dusty to run even faster.

Crouched, hidden in the rocks, her body coiled tightly as she patiently waited. Her ears were laid flat against her head, an indication of her intentions. Her prey was almost in position. She tensed her powerful leg muscles. Pouncing from her rocky hiding place and ignoring the screams of her victim, she sank deep, piercing claws into soft flesh. Her mouth opened wide, allowing her to force razor sharp teeth down into her victim's neck.

The horse Jennifer rode suddenly whinnied in fear and shied away from the nearby boulders. Seconds later, Barrish screamed in agony as the cougar landed on his back, knocking him to the ground. Jennifer was stunned when, in a blur of motion, Andrew was swept off the horse.

Rolling in an attempt to loosen the cat's hold, Barrish felt white-hot, searing pain shoot through his body, the cat's fangs and claws causing major damage as they sank deeper into his bone and muscle.

"Do something," Jennifer yelled at her father as she dropped to the ground. Picking up a broken branch, she ran to Barrish's aid.

The mountain lion held fast as the young man fought to free himself. Concentrating on her victim, the cat did not attend to the woman approaching until the branch struck her across the back. She turned, her victim's head still held firmly in her jaws, and growled at her attacker.

Kensington's horse was bucking and twisting in an attempt to get away from the mountain lion. When the other horse, now rider-less, ran past making its escape, Kensington's horse followed, carrying its rider with it.

Jennifer raised the branch for a second attack. The cat snarled but refused to let go of Barrish. Jennifer swung the branch down on the massive head this time. The cat released Barrish's neck. Displaying its bloodied fangs, it hissed a warning at the woman.

Exerting all of his strength, Kensington gained control of his horse and turned it back to the boulder field. As he approached, the mountain lion growled and, again, the horse reared. This time Kensington was thrown to the ground, and his horse galloped as fast as it could away from the danger. Kensington heard the cat growl again and looked up in time to see Jennifer swinging a branch, bringing the branch down on the head of the snarling animal. As she made contact, the cat swiped a large paw out in her direction. It connected, sharp claws raking down the length of her leg as Jennifer screamed in pain. The cat uncoiled its strong muscles to leap at the injured prey.

Jennifer looked up to see the cat, claws and fangs bared, springing toward her. Cat and woman crashed to the ground, where they lay motionless.

Jesse rode hard toward the boulder field and Jennifer. She saw the mountain lion leap from its hiding place and land on Barrish and was relieved to see Jennifer still on the horse when Barrish and the cat fell to the ground. Scant moments later, her heart stopped when Jennifer slipped off the horse, picked up a broken branch, and charged the large cat. She watched in horror as Jennifer struck the cat, then saw the cat whirl at her lover as she brought the branch down for a second time.

Without breaking Dusty's stride, Jesse pulled her rifle from the scabbard on the saddle and drew a bead on the animal. Just as she was about to pull the trigger, Kensington and his horse rode between her and her target. Jesse heard her lover's scream as the cat's sharp claws slashed into her flesh.

"Get out of the way!" Jesse yelled. She saw Kensington's horse rear and unseat its rider. As soon as she had a clear shot, Jesse fired, just as the cat sprang at Jennifer. She quickly fired a second shot.

Midway in its leap, the bullet pierced the cat's neck, slicing through an artery. Her momentum carried her toward her prey as a second bullet penetrated her chest, ripping through her lungs and heart. She was dead instantaneously.

When she saw the cat hit Jennifer and take her to the ground, Jesse screamed her lover's name. Charging forward, Dusty carried Jesse to the bloody site. The rancher dove from Dusty's back as the horse neared the spot where Jennifer and the cat lay together on the ground. Not caring if the cat was still alive, Jesse balled her fists in the large animal's coat and slung the carcass aside. Jennifer groaned in pain as the heavy weight of the cat was removed.

"I'm here, darlin'." Jesse fell to the ground beside her. "I'm here."

"I knew you'd come." Jennifer managed a weak smile, then blessedly lost consciousness.

CHAPTER EIGHT

Billie reached them moments later. He dropped to the ground beside Jesse, who was frantically trying to stem the flow of her lover's blood. "We've got to stop the bleeding!"

Kensington stumbled up to the group. "Get away from her or I'll..." He pointed the pistol he still carried.

Billie jumped up and yanked the gun from the old man's grasp. "You ain't doin' nothin'."

"I won't let her spoil my plans!" Kensington shouted.

"She won't." Billie's anger boiled over and without warning, he slammed a fist into Kensington's face, knocking him to the ground. "But I will." He pulled a rope off his saddle and tied the stunned man's hands. "Now shut your mouth while we try to save your daughter's life."

Jesse and Billie were crouched over Jennifer when the others rode up. Mrs. Kensington gasped at the sight of Jennifer covered in blood. She quickly dismounted and approached her daughter.

Bette Mae stopped her. "Don' let the little one see this," she said, reaching under her dress to rip off the bottom of her petticoat. Tearing it into strips, she knelt beside Jennifer.

Jesse's hands were slippery with blood as she desperately tried to compress the sides of the wounds and stanch the loss of blood.

"Here." Bette Mae wrapped one of the bandages around Jennifer's thigh. "Hold this as tight as you can. It'll slow the bleeding."

Unable to think, Jesse did as she was told.

Bette Mae went to work. "Ed, gather up all of the canteens. I need whatever water we have to clean out these gashes." She swabbed away as much of the dirt and blood as possible, then wrapped the rest of the bandages around Jennifer's leg, tightening the wrappings as much as she dared.

KC sensed something was wrong and that it involved her mothers. She tried to free herself of the carry sack, beating her arms and legs against her grandmother's back.

Seeing the baby's distress, Thaddeus removed her from the carry sack. "Hey, now," he spoke calmly to KC as he lifted her free, "your momma is going to be okay."

Mrs. Kensington turned to retake charge of KC, but Thaddeus shook his head. "Go on. Jennifer needs you." Wasting no time, the distraught mother rushed to her daughter's side.

Ed approached the body of young Barrish. He was lying face down and hadn't moved since they had arrived at the scene of the attack. As he rolled the young man over, Ed could tell that he was dead, so he rolled the body back face down. There was no reason for the women to see the boy's injuries, he reasoned. Pulling a blanket from his saddle, he covered the body.

"That should hold the leg until we get her to the doctor in Bozeman," Bette Mae was telling Jesse and Mrs. Kensington.

Jesse bent down and softly kissed Jennifer's lips. She started to lift her lover in arms, but, with her own body shaking violently with her fear, it was difficult.

Ed put a restraining hand on Jesse's arm. "Get on your horse. I'll pass her up to you."

Jesse looked up at the large man, trying to comprehend his words.

"Go on." Ed nudged Jesse toward Dusty. "You get up there, and I'll hand her up." Jesse slowly nodded. She pulled herself up into Dusty's saddle and waited. Ed gently lifted

Jennifer from the ground and eased her into the rancher's arms. "She'll be fine once you get her to the doc's," he said, hoping his words would prove true.

With Jennifer secure in her arms, Jesse looked around at the others. Mrs. Kensington was impatiently waiting as Thaddeus put the baby back into the carry sack she still wore. With the baby once again safely on her back, she mounted her horse and joined Jesse.

"Let's go."

That was all Jesse needed to hear. She urged Dusty forward, and the two women started for Bozeman. Bette Mae mounted Blaze and quickly rode after them.

"Should we go with 'em?" Billie asked.

"They don't need us underfoot," Ed said. "Best we stay and finish up here."

After the women left, Thaddeus jerked his head toward Barrish. "What about him?"

"He's dead," Ed replied.

"Dead?" Kensington looked at the covered body of the young man who was nothing more than a business deal to him.

Billie pulled Kensington to his feet. "Guess you'll have some trouble explainin' that to his poppa, won't you?"

"He can't be dead," Kensington replied absently.

Billie motioned to Thaddeus. "You'll have to ride with Ed. Their horses are long gone."

"All right." Thaddeus held his horse's reins while Kensington was helped into the saddle.

"Hang on." Ed walked over to the base of a boulder where the mountain lion lay crumpled in a heap where Jesse had tossed it.

"It still alive?" Billie asked.

"Nope." Ed poked the body with his boot, then reached down and lifted it off the ground.

"What you plannin' to do, Ed?"

"If I know Jesse," Ed hefted the body skyward until it came to rest on a small ledge, out of the reach of most scavengers, "she'll be wantin' this."

"Doubt she'll want it if anythin' happens to—"

"It won't." Ed glared at Thaddeus. "It'd kill Jesse if it did."

Thaddeus nodded, knowing the big man was right. But it was out of their hands.

Billie finished wrapping the body of the dead boy in the blanket, then tossed the bundle over the back of his saddle before mounting. Taking control of the reins of the horse Kensington rode, he said, "Let's get going."

As soon as Ed and Thaddeus were mounted, the men headed for Bozeman.

"I want that bitch arrested," Kensington told Billie as they left.

"Only one being arrested is you," Billie told the arrogant man.

"After what she's done to my daughter?" Kensington protested.

"What *she's* done." Billie laughed humorlessly. "Do you care at all, Kensington, that Jennifer may not live after what that cat did to her? And all because of you."

Before the man could answer, Billie set his horse into a gallop, pulling Kensington's mount behind him.

Kensington could do no more than hang on to the saddle horn and hope he wouldn't be thrown from the horse before they reached Bozeman.

Jesse, Bette Mae, and Mrs. Kensington pulled their horses to a stop in front of a small building. A shingle hanging over the porch identified it as the office of K. Fitzgerald, M.D. Jesse immediately slipped from the saddle, with Jennifer carefully cradled in her arms. By the time she reached the office door, Mrs. Kensington and Bette Mae were pushing the door open. The women rushed inside.

Looking up from his desk, the doctor immediately assessed the severity of Jennifer's injuries. "Bring her back here," he told the women as he led the way into a back room.

Jesse followed and tenderly laid Jennifer down on the examination table while the doctor poured clean water into a bowl.

"What happened?"

"Mountain lion," Jesse said as she brushed Jennifer's sweat-soaked hair from her face. Jennifer moaned in pain. "It's goin' ta be okay," Jesse whispered, looking to the doctor for verification of the truth of her words.

"Let's have a look." Fitzgerald began removing the bandages from Jennifer's leg. "She'll lose the leg," he said, grimacing as he examined the damage done by the cat's claws.

"No." Jesse reached across Jennifer's body and grabbed the doctor's arm. "She's too young."

"It's either that or she'll die."

"She can't," Jesse sobbed. "I can't lose her. I can't."

Fitzgerald looked into determined eyes, then at the injured woman. "I can't guarantee it won't get infected, what with all the dirt and muck in these wounds. If you want her to have a chance, I recommend taking the leg off."

Jesse tearfully leaned down close to Jennifer. "I'm sorry, darlin'. I'm so sorry," she whispered.

Marie Kensington laid a hand on Jesse's shoulder, and, with her other hand, she pried Jesse's grip from the doctor. "Jesse's right, Doctor. My daughter is too young to lose her leg."

He drew himself up to his full height. "Ma'am—"

"One thing I know about my Jennifer is that she has a lot to live for, and she'll fight anybody and *anything* to make sure she does. Try to save the leg. It's what she'd want."

"Best ya wait in the other room whilst the Doc and I fix up Jennifer." Bette Mae motioned for Mrs. Kensington to take Jesse out of the examination room.

When Jesse protested, Mrs. Kensington gently pulled her from Jennifer's side. "Come on, we'll only be in the way here. Besides I don't think you want KC watching this."

Jesse had forgotten about her daughter sitting quietly in the carry sack on the other woman's back. "All right." Before she was led away, she leaned down and kissed Jennifer's forehead. "Please don't leave us, darlin'. We love you." Tears welled in her eyes as she allowed Mrs. Kensington to guide her out of the room.

"Alrighty, Doc," Bette Mae rolled up her sleeves, "let's get her fixed up. I don' want to be tellin' Jesse any bad news. I don' think she could handle it."

"They friends?" Fitzgerald asked as he worked.

"Married," Bette Mae said.

"Hmm."

When Billie, Thaddeus, and Ed reached Bozeman, they rode directly to the sheriff's office with their prisoner and informed the lawman of the circumstances that brought them to Bozeman. "I need you to hold him until we sort all this out," Billie told the Bozeman sheriff.

"What're you planning to charge him with?" Sheriff Carson asked as he shoved Kensington into a small cell.

"Kidnappin' and assault, to start."

The lawman placed the ring of keys on a hook near his desk. "That should be good enough for the judge, for now. You goin' to the doc's?"

"Yeah," Billie answered. "We'll be with Jesse; I'll come back and sign the papers soon as I can."

"Wait," Kensington shouted from his cell. "You can't keep me here; I need to send some telegrams. I have business to attend to."

Shaking his head, Billie followed Ed and Thaddeus from the jail. They hurried to the doctor's office located a short distance away. Entering the squat, brick, one-story building, the men found Jesse slumped in a chair, white as a ghost and trembling as she held KC.

Mrs. Kensington looked up as the men entered, shaking her head in answer to their unspoken questions. "Bette Mae and the doctor are with her." KC whimpered, making smacking sounds with her mouth. "She's hungry, Jesse," Mrs. Kensington said. "I'll go see if I can find some milk."

"I'll go," Ed volunteered. "I know some of the shopkeepers. Won't take me long to round up something."

Mrs. Kensington smiled at the big man. She had not really wanted to leave the office until she knew how Jennifer was. "Thank you."

Jesse looked at the baby and started to cry. She looked so much like Jennifer. KC pulled herself upright using Jesse's shirt. Standing in Jesse's lap, the baby stretched her arms around Jesse's neck and placed a wet kiss on her mother's cheek. Jesse smiled tearfully at the baby, "I love you too, Sunshine." She returned the baby's hug, holding her tight to her chest. Jennifer would be all right; she had to be. KC needed her momma. "I need her, too," she sobbed softly.

Taking note of Jesse's emotional state, Billie whispered to Mrs. Kensington, "We'll wait outside. Let us know as soon as you hear anything."

Mrs. Kensington nodded, then pulled her chair close to Jesse and wrapped the bereft woman in her arms. "She'll be fine. She loves you too much to give up."

Jesse allowed herself to seek comfort in the older woman's embrace. After some time, her tears slowed and she wiped her eyes with her sleeves. "Thank you," Jesse told Jennifer's mother. "I guess it all caught up with me."

KC, still clinging to Jesse's neck, sniffled along with her mother. "Hey, Sunshine," Jesse kissed the baby, "just 'cause your silly mommy is crying doesn't mean you have to." Jesse tickled the baby and was rewarded with a giggle. "That's better. Don't want your momma waking up and finding us all teary eyed, do we?" She tickled the baby again.

Ed re-entered the office with a couple of bottles of fresh cow's milk and a handful of crackers. "This should keep her happy for a while," he said as he set the food on the doctor's desk.

"Moooo." KC reached for the bottle Ed was handing to Jesse.

"Here you go." Jesse kept hold of the bottle as KC pulled it to her mouth. She drank thirstily as she dropped to sit in Jesse's lap and lean back against her mommy's chest. "Thanks, Ed."

"Any word?"

"Not yet."

"You let us know if you need anything else. We're right outside," he said as he turned to leave.

"Ed," Jesse called, "tell Billie and Thaddeus to come in. We might as well wait together."

"You sure, Jesse?"

"Yes. I'd kinda like to have you guys around."

Ed smiled. "We'd kinda like that, too."

Moments later, Billie and Thaddeus joined them, and their vigil continued.

"That's all I can do." Doctor Fitzgerald was washing his hands. "The rest is up to her."

The claws had left one long, deep gash from Jennifer's hip to just below her knee and several shorter gashes along the length of her leg. It had taken most of the rest of the afternoon for the doctor, with Bette Mae's help, to clean the wounds and stitch Jennifer's leg together. Finished cleaning up, the doctor went into the outer office. Jesse stood as soon as he appeared even though KC slept in her arms.

"Doctor?" she asked breathlessly.

"She's alive."

Jesse released the breath she was holding. "Thank you."

"Don't thank me yet."

"But she'll be okay, won't she?"

"I'm not going to lie to you. Even if she survives the next several hours, she'll still have a long battle ahead. She's lost a lot of blood, and there's a good chance of infection. Even if she manages to get past that, she may never walk again. There was a lot of damage to her muscles and nerves. I can't do anything for that."

"What can I do?" Jesse asked.

"Wait. It's up to her now."

"Can we see her?" Mrs. Kensington asked.

"Yes, for a few minutes. She needs rest now, and lots of it."

Jesse was at Jennifer's side before the doctor finished speaking. She was shocked to see how pale her wife looked, her skin clammy despite the blankets that covered her. Shifting KC to one arm, Jesse cupped a hand against her wife's face to gently caress it. "I'm here, darlin'." She bent down and kissed Jennifer. "So is KC. We'll be right here when you wake up."

Mrs. Kensington paused at the doorway, allowing Jesse to have a few moments with Jennifer before joining her at the bed.

"She looks so pale," Jesse said.

"She'll be all right, Jesse." She ran a hand through her daughter's matted hair.

Jesse reached under the blankets and took Jennifer's hand into her own.

Knowing that Jesse would not leave Jennifer's side until the injured woman awakened, Bette Mae carried a chair into the room. "Here ya go." She set the chair next to the bed. "Why don' ya let me take my little angel while ya wait with Jennifer."

Jesse slumped into the chair. She had had very little sleep over the past few days, and the added stress of Jennifer's injuries had her about ready to collapse. "Thanks, but I think it's best KC stay with me. Jennifer will want to see her as soon as she wakes up."

Fitzgerald bustled back into the room and checked his patient's pulse. Lifting the blankets, he examined the stitches for any sign of bleeding. "She's going to need plenty of rest, and this isn't the best table to be doing it on," he told the women. "You know anyone in town that can provide her a bed?"

Jesse thought of her parents, then rejected the idea. After they refused any contact with her, she couldn't expect them to provide a bed for Jennifer. "No," she replied. "Guess we could get a room at the hotel."

"You could." The doctor replaced the blankets, making sure Jennifer was completely covered. "But I was thinking of someplace a little quieter than a hotel. Guess you'll be staying here, then."

"Guess we will," Jesse muttered. Her eyes never leaving her unconscious wife, she didn't see Bette Mae slip out of the room.

"Are you going to let me out of here?" Kensington bellowed.

"Nope." Sheriff Carson was leaning back in his chair, his feet resting on his desk. For the last several hours, he had been listening to Kensington order him to unlock the door to the cell and release him. It amazed him that the man had never once asked about his daughter, even though he knew she was at the doc's office fighting for her life.

"Look, I need to send a telegram to Andrew's father. He needs to know how that contemptible woman's actions led to his death," Kensington repeated.

"Seems to me," Carson took a swallow of coffee from the cup he held, "you had a lot more to do with that than anyone else."

"Me?" Kensington looked at the sheriff. "I had nothing to do with Barrish's death. If that goddamn woman hadn't been chasing us—"

"Enough." He had heard Kensington curse Jesse many times over the past hours. He finished his coffee and set the cup on his desk before standing and walking to the cell where Kensington paced. "I'd say you're gonna have a lot of explaining to do, especially to that boy's family. But for now, I've heard all I care to from you. The hotel will send over your supper around eight. Until then, sit down and shut your mouth."

Kensington watched the sheriff slam the heavy door between his office and the prisoners' cells. Once the door was shut, the room was left in almost complete darkness, the only light being let in by small barred windows in each cell. Having nothing else to do, he surveyed the room. The cell was one of four, but he was the only prisoner. The only furnishings were a cot with a rough and lumpy mattress and a bucket in the corner that served an obvious purpose.

He walked to the cot and sat. He had to think. With Barrish dead, his strategy for financing the company's expansion had fallen apart. He needed a new idea. How could his carefully thought out plan have ended so badly? The answer came out as a curse. "Damn you, Jesse Branson! Damn you to Hell fire!"

Stanley and Marie Branson were surprised when just before dark a woman knocked on the door to their small house. After hearing Bette Mae's story, Stanley accompanied her back to the doctor's office. Inside, Bette Mae directed him to the back room where Jesse waited beside her wife's bed.

Used to people coming in and out of the room, Jesse didn't take notice when the door opened and someone entered. Her focus was on Jennifer.

Stanley Branson stood at the door and took in the scene. His daughter sat in a chair, a sleeping child in one arm and her other hand clutching the hand of the woman lying on the examination table. He slowly closed the distance between him and his daughter.

"Jesse."

At the familiar voice, Jesse turned. "Poppa?"

Stanley placed a large, callused hand on his daughter's shoulder and squeezed gently. "Your momma's fixin' up a bed for her."

Tears sprang to Jesse's eyes. "How'd you know?"

"Your friend paid us a visit." He cast an appraising eye over Jesse. "Looks like you could use a bed yourself."

"I can't sleep, Poppa." Tears streamed down Jesse's cheeks. "Not until I know she's okay."

"Come on, then." Stanley carefully lifted Jennifer from the table, making sure the blanket was wrapped securely around her. "Your momma's waitin' for us." He looked at the baby. "That your young 'un?" When Jesse nodded, a faint grin curved his lips. "Best not keep your momma waitin'. She'll be wantin' to meet the tyke."

Jesse rose from the chair. She was exhausted, and her shaky legs proved it.

"Hold on, there." Bette Mae, having entered in Stanley's wake, rushed to Jesse's side and wrapped an arm around Jesse's waist. Once Jesse steadied, she said, "Now, let me take my little angel. Ya can barely hold yerself up." Bette Mae carefully lifted the sleeping child from Jesse's arms. Holding the baby in one arm, she kept her other around Jesse as they followed Stanley from the room.

Jennifer was laid in the bed belonging to Jesse's parents. Seeing that the injured woman lacked for proper bedclothes, Marie Branson pulled a nightshirt from a chest of drawers. "Help me get this over her head," she told Jesse. "She'll be more comfortable."

Jesse bent to slip an arm around Jennifer's shoulders. In her exhaustion, she barely managed to hold her lover off the bed as her mother carefully pulled Jennifer's arms through the sleeves. Jennifer groaned as the nightshirt was eased down her body.

"I'm sorry, darlin'." Jesse caressed Jennifer's cheek. "I'm so sorry."

"Now," Marie finished carefully tucking the blankets around Jennifer, "you get out of them clothes and put this on." She pulled a second nightshirt from a chest of drawers and tossed it onto the end of the bed. "You need some sleep."

"I can't leave her," Jesse protested.

"Don't expect you to. Get out of them clothes and crawl in with her. Probably the best thing for both of ya."

Jesse stared at her mother. Had she heard right?

"Go on. Quit gawking and do what you're told." Marie crossed the room to a cradle in the corner. KC slept in the same bed her mother had once occupied. "She's a tiny one, ain't she?"

Jesse was pulling off her dirty boots. "She'll grow."

"Reckon she will, if she eats like you." Marie chuckled as she watched her grandchild sleep. "KC is a funny name for a baby."

"Jennifer named her after her real folks, Kenneth and Catherine."

Marie lifted the cradle and carried it across the room. "Baby should be near her mommas," she said, setting it alongside the bed.

Jesse pulled the nightshirt on, the clean material feeling strange against her dirty skin. She could use a bath but was too tired to even think about preparing one.

"Go on, now. Get into bed."

"Momma," Jesse said as she moved to the bed. "I want to thank you."

"We're family. Couldn't do no less."

"But—"

"Go on," Marie admonished. "We can talk later."

"Thank you," Jesse said, her voice cracking.

Her mother paused as she turned to leave but said nothing. Moments later, Jesse and her family were alone in the room.

Jesse checked on KC before carefully rolling over next to Jennifer. She lay on the side opposite to the injured leg, which was propped up on pillows. Cautiously, she scooted as close as she dared to her wife.

Jennifer seemed to sense her closeness and reached out for her. Jesse captured Jennifer's hand, pulling it to her chest. "I'm here, darlin'," she whispered. "I'll always be here." She pressed her forehead against Jennifer's shoulder and was soon asleep. It was several hours before any sound but gentle snoring was heard in the room.

CHAPTER NINE

The next morning, Bette Mae was bustling about the kitchen of the Branson house. She had taken over cooking duties, refusing help from Jesse and Jennifer's mothers. When Billie went to check on his prisoner, Bette Mae sent Ed and Thaddeus out to buy food, knowing that Jesse would not want to impose on her parents' hospitality. She also directed the men to arrange for rooms at one of the hotels for the next several days, the house being too small for all of them to stay there.

"It's very kind of you to take us in." Mary Kensington was sitting with the Bransons at the kitchen table.

"Jesse's our daughter. Can't turn our back to her when she's in need," Stanley said.

"I'm sorry I didn't do the same for Jennifer."

Marie Branson had spent the better part of the night listening to the series of events that had brought her daughter back into their lives. "From what you've told me, it sounds to me like your husband is a determined man."

"Ha. That's a mighty fine way of sayin' he's crazier than a five-legged dog," Bette Mae interjected as she set a fresh pot of coffee on the table. The aroma of fresh biscuits baking in the oven filled the air.

"Shouldn't talk about the man like that," Mr. Branson said. "He was doing what he thought best."

"No." Mary shook her head. "Bette Mae is right. My husband was wrong. Jennifer was following her dreams. We should have encouraged her, not tried to destroy the life she's made for herself. We should have never come. If I'm lucky, I'll get the chance to make amends. I just hope it's not too late."

"Sometimes you don't know until it is too late." Stanley pushed up off of his chair, and his tread was heavy as he left the room.

His wife's eyes followed his departure. She hoped it wasn't too late for him and Jesse.

"He's a proud man," Bette Mae observed.

"Yes," Marie Branson agreed, "sometimes too proud."

The women drank their coffee in silence.

"That should keep him here a while," Billie said as he finished signing papers charging Martin Kensington with numerous crimes.

Kensington's shouting could be heard through the closed door, and Sheriff Carson laughed. "Think we can charge him with being a blowhard?"

"Don't think the judge will question it after he has a chance to listen to him." Billie handed over the signed papers.

"Probably not." The papers were tucked safely into a desk drawer. "What do you plan to do about the boy?"

"Stopped at the telegraph office coming over here; told them to send any response to your office. My guess is that we'll be sending the body back East."

"Body at the undertaker's?"

"Yeah."

"I'll take care of it."

"Thanks."

"You going back to the doc's?"

"No. Jesse's folks have a house a couple of streets over. They took Jennifer there. I'll be there or at the hotel."

Remembering that his prisoner had referred to Jesse by name and wondering why he hadn't recognized it before, he asked, "Say, is that Stanley and Marie Branson's daughter?"

"Yep."

"Damn." The sheriff sat back in his chair. "I haven't seen Jesse since her folks lost their ranch. She disappeared right about that time. Her folks don't ever mention her. I just figured they had some sort of falling out, you know, a family thing."

"Don't know, I never asked. Jesse don't talk much about her life before she came to Sweetwater."

"Sometimes that's for the best."

"Yep." Billie stood. "Best be gettin' back."

"All right. I'll let you know if I hear anything."

By the time Jesse woke, night had fallen. She was lying on her side, tucked up against Jennifer with an arm wrapped around her wife's waist. Disoriented, she tried to figure out why they were sleeping in a strange room and a strange bed. When Jennifer moaned in her sleep, Jesse immediately remembered.

"Darlin'," she murmured, hoping Jennifer was awake. Receiving no answer, she pushed up on her elbow to get a look at the woman beside her. The movement of the mattress disturbed the injured woman, and she moaned again. "I'm sorry, darlin'." Jesse reached up to caress Jennifer's cheek, panicking when her fingers brushed against skin that felt hot to her touch. "Jennifer!"

Bette Mae was climbing the stairs to see if anyone in the room was awake when she heard Jesse's cry. She hastened her steps and pushed the bedroom door open without knocking; the oil lamp she carried cast an eerie glow about the room. Jesse was sitting rigidly beside her feverish wife, fear on her ashen face. "Wha's wrong?"

"She's burning up."

"Let me see." Bette Mae set the lamp on a table beside the bed and bent over Jennifer.

"Everything all right?" Marie Branson asked from the doorway, having also heard Jesse's cry.

"Send for the doc," Bette Mae said without turning around. "And tell him to hurry. Fever's set in." As Marie hurried to fetch Doctor Fitzgerald, Bette Mae moved across the room to the pitcher and bowl that sat on top of the dresser. She poured the contents of the pitcher into the bowl, then soaked a towel in the cool water. Wringing it out, she carried the towel back to the bed and pressed it on Jennifer's forehead. As the rancher moved to get closer, Jennifer moaned again. "Ya best git out of bed, Jesse. All the bouncin' ye're doin' is causin' her pain."

Mary Kensington rushed into the room as Jesse scrambled off the bed. "Your mother told me what was going on. What can I do to help?"

"Baby needs carin' for." Bette Mae could hear KC whimpering in the cradle. "Jesse ain't of a mind ta see ta her jus' now." Concerned for her wife, Jesse was standing helplessly as a flurry of activity swirled around her. Bette Mae shot a pointed look at Jennifer's mother, standing anxiously beside the bed. "And she don' need to be seein' what we're 'bout ta do."

KC's grandmother took Bette Mae's hint and quickly went around to the cradle to remove the baby from the room. "Let's go get you some fresh britches, and I'll bet you're hungry." Filled with fear for her daughter, Mary nevertheless cuddled the baby who began to wail.

"Tell Marie to send up more clean towels and hot water," Bette Mae told Mary as she left. "Lots of hot water; we need to clean those gashes again."

Bette Mae threw off the blankets and started unwrapping the dressings from Jennifer's leg. Marie reappeared with towels and rags and a bucket of fresh water. Dropping most of her load in a chair pushed into a corner of the room, she carried the bucket around the bed and set it on the floor. Drenching a towel in the cold water, she used it to replace the one on Jennifer's head.

Moments later, Stanley entered the room carrying two large pots of steaming water. He hung them on the hook over the hearth and quickly stoked the fire to keep the water hot.

Doctor Fitzgerald rushed into the room, his medicine bag in one hand and his jacket in the other. The jacket was tossed aside as he hurried to his patient.

"Fever," Bette Mae said succinctly.

"Damn." The doctor laid his hand against Jennifer's neck. "Pulse is strong. Let's see what we've got." He jostled Bette Mae as he changed positions with her in the crowded room. "Everybody out, I need room to work."

Marie grasped Jesse's arm. "Come on, we can wait outside."

Jesse shook her head. "I can't leave her."

"Come on," her mother said gently. "We'll be right outside the door, honey. You can't do anything in here but get in the way."

Jesse allowed herself to be guided out of the room, but she refused to go any further than the doorway. Knowing it would be useless to argue, Marie stood beside her daughter, watching the concerted efforts taking place inside the room.

"These wounds look good," Fitzgerald murmured as he methodically examined the many lacerations and cuts.

"Here it is." Bette Mae carefully removed a section of bandage. "I can smell the infection."

As the bandage came off it revealed a gash several inches long just above the knee. The skin around the wound was bright red and hot to the touch.

"Must have missed something." The doctor spread the sides of the wound apart to get a better look at what was causing the putrefaction.

"Ugh." Bette Mae grunted at the greenish yellow pus that oozed from the opening.

"Soak pieces of rag in one of those pots and bring it here," the doctor instructed, and Bette Mae rushed to the fireplace, returning moments later with the pot.

The doctor pulled forceps from his bag to use in retrieving the pieces of cloth from the boiling water. "Spread the sides as far apart as you can," he told Bette Mae. "I need to see what's inside there."

Placing a strip of hot cloth inside the gash, Fitzgerald swabbed the infection from Jennifer's body. As Jennifer's brain registered the scalding heat, she writhed and thrashed about on the bed. "Hold her still!" the doctor yelled over the cries of agony.

Jesse ran into the room, grabbed the doctor by the shoulders, and threw him across the room. "What the hell are you doin' to her!" she screamed.

"Jesse," Bette Mae shouted, "he's got ta clean out the infection."

The frantic wife spun around, growling, "He's hurting her."

"I know." Bette Mae glared back. "But it'll hurt her lots worse if'n he don't lick this infection. If ya wan' ta somethin', get over here and hold Jennifer so's she don' thrash about. And I'd be hurryin' if'n I was you."

Jesse hesitated only a moment before she moved to the head of the bed and crawled onto it, pulling Jennifer into her lap. Tears streaming down her face, she took a firm hold on her wife. "I'm so sorry, darlin'," she cooed as the doctor renewed his efforts to purge the infection from Jennifer's leg. "I'm so sorry."

For several minutes, Doctor Fitzgerald worked the hot bits of cloth around inside the inflamed, trench-like wound, removing as much of the contamination as he could.

After tossing away the last piece of soiled material, he studied the leg. Frowning, he turned to Bette Mae. "I don't think we got it all. Damn claw must have twisted inside her, there's no telling how deep it might have gone."

"What're ya sayin', doc?" Bette Mae asked.

Jesse clutched Jennifer to her chest. The schoolteacher, having succumbed to the pain, lay motionless in her arms.

"I need to remove the leg."

"No." Bette Mae shook her head. "Ya don' have ta cut off the leg."

"She'll die if I don't!"

"Saw me plenty of wounds like this," Bette Mae told the disbelieving man. "Jus' need to cut away the bad stuff."

"What are you talking about?" The doctor reached for his bag and the surgical saw inside. "The leg has to come off."

"Won' hurt to try my way first." Bette Mae looked at Jesse. "If'n it don't work, then..."

"Do it," Jesse grunted. "Do whatever you have to do. Just bring her back to me."

"Don' you be worryin' 'bout that." Bette Mae nodded with determination. "We'll fix her up good for ya, Jesse."

"I won't be a party to this," the doctor said. "If you refuse to let me remove her leg, I can't be responsible for causing her death."

Marie stepped back into the room. "What can I do, Bette Mae?"

"I need the sharpest knife you have."

"Use the one in my boot," Jesse directed.

"Stick it in the fire until it burns red," Bette Mae ordered.

With a loud "humppft", Doctor Fitzgerald picked up his medicine bag and jacket and stormed out of the room. Bette Mae patted Jesse on the leg. "Let's git this little one fixed up."

With Jesse holding Jennifer still, and Marie assisting, Bette Mae made quick work of cutting the infected tissue away from the injury. "There," she said as she straightened. "Don't know how tha' will effect her bein' able ta dance with ya, Jesse, but had to get rid of the bad parts."

"Don't care," Jesse sobbed. "I just want her."

"You'll have her." Bette Mae tenderly squeezed her friend's shoulder. "I promise ya, Jesse."

Jesse looked into her eyes and saw she meant what she said. "Thank you."

Bette Mae smiled. "Let's get her laid back down so's she can rest; she must be a mite uncomfortable all twisted up like that. Ya probably could use some rest, too. And I'm pretty sure there's someone downstairs that is missin' her mommy right 'bout now."

In her concern for her wife, Jesse had temporarily forgotten about KC. Her tears starting falling again as she caught the sound of the baby's frantic wails downstairs.

"Don' ya be frettin' 'bout it now," Bette Mae said; supporting Jennifer while Jesse crawled off the bed. "She'll be fine once she's back in yer arms."

"I'll tell Mary to bring her up." Marie hugged Jesse and then went downstairs.

Jesse didn't have to wait long before Mary appeared with KC. The baby literally leapt into the rancher's arms, wrapping her arms around her mommy's neck and clinging on for dear life.

"It's okay, Sunshine." Jesse rubbed the baby's back, attempting to comfort her. "I'm sorry you had to go downstairs, but I bet your grandma took real good care of you. Did she feed you?" When KC tearfully nodded, Jesse said solemnly, "Now how about we stop our crying, Sunshine? Momma's sick and we have to be real quiet so she can sleep, okay?"

KC lifted her head off Jesse's shoulder to look at Jennifer. She turned back and whispered in her mommy's ear, "Otay."

"That's my girl." Jesse kissed the baby's face. "What say we lay down with Momma and let her know how much we love her? You think she'd like that?" KC's little head rapidly bobbed up and down.

As Marie and Bette Mae gathered up the soiled linens and the dirty basin, Mary helped Jesse and KC get settled on the bed without disturbing Jennifer any more than was unavoidable. When she finished tucking the blankets in around the family, Mary knelt at the side of the bed beside her daughter. "I love you, Jennifer," she whispered, kissing the pale face. "When this is over, I'm going to prove that to you."

Jesse nodded at her mother-in-law. "Reckon she'd like that."

"So would I." Mary's gaze never left her daughter. "So would I." As she kept watch, first Jesse and then KC fell asleep. At length, she rose to go.

Marie followed the other women from the room, pausing for a moment to observe her daughter. *How much I've missed*, she thought.

Night gave way to day, and still the women slept. Early in the morning, a fussy KC was quietly removed from the room and taken downstairs where she was fed and kept entertained by Bette Mae, Billie, Ed, Thaddeus, and her assortment of grandparents.

Bette Mae, keeping an hourly vigil on Jennifer, was relieved to feel the schoolteacher's skin cool to the touch when she checked on her shortly after midday. She happily reported the news to the others.

When the baby tired in the afternoon, Bette Mae rocked her to sleep, then carried her back into her mothers' room and placed her in the cradle. Once Bette Mae had pulled the door closed, KC pushed herself up into a sitting position. Looking for her mothers, she smiled upon seeing them cuddled under the blankets on the bed.

As the shadows lengthened with the coming of another evening, KC awoke and immediately checked to make sure her mothers still slept on the bed. Her cradle had been pushed against the bed, and the baby used the blankets to pull herself up to stand unsteadily. Using what foot and handholds she could find, KC climbed onto the bed and crawled to her mothers. Jesse was lying on her side, an arm draped across Jennifer's waist. KC pulled herself upright against her back and peeked over.

Jennifer had awakened some time earlier. Her first attempt at moving had resulted in excruciating pain exploding the length of her injured leg, and she had quickly decided that wasn't something she wanted to try again. She lay stock-still until the pain subsided and she could relax back against the mattress. Feeling Jesse beside her, Jennifer rolled her head to look at the woman she loved. She was shocked to see the drawn features, the brow creased in worry even as she slept. Her gaze shifted at the sound of movement behind Jesse, and her eyes focused on KC.

So intent was the baby on her objective that she didn't realize she was being observed and was surprised to look up and see her momma smiling at her. Thrilled at finding Jennifer awake, KC slapped her hands on Jesse's side, trying to gain leverage to climb over. "Momma," the baby cried excitedly. "Momma."

Jesse woke at the feel of KC pressing against her, the baby's hands smacking her arm. "Hush, Sunshine. You'll wake up Momma." Jesse reached for the baby to quiet her.

KC pointed. "Momma." She struggled to reach Jennifer.

Jesse turned to look. "Darlin'," she gasped when she saw Jennifer was awake. "Oh, baby, you're awake." Seeing the tears flowing down her wife's cheeks, Jesse feared that her motion was causing Jennifer pain. "Oh, darlin', I'm so sorry. I'll get off the bed."

"No." Jennifer reached out and grabbed Jesse's nightshirt. "Don't go."

"But I must be hurting you."

"No." Jennifer smiled at her wife.

"Then why are you crying, darlin'?"

"Sweetheart, these are happy tears."

"Happy tears?"

KC was struggling to climb over Jesse, and she reached back to help the baby. Once free of the obstacle of her mommy's body, KC knelt on the bed next to Jennifer, placing her head on her momma's chest. Jennifer stroked the baby's head. "Didn't you hear what she called me?"

Jesse tried to remember, but her exhausted mind left everything in a fuzzy blur. "What did you say?" she asked the baby, not really expecting an answer.

"Momma." KC patted Jennifer. "Momma."

Jesse smiled at KC, tears filling her own eyes. "That's right, Sunshine. She's our momma." She pulled the baby onto her chest holding her firmly in place with one hand as she reached for Jennifer's hand with the other. It wasn't long before the family was peacefully asleep.

CHAPTER TEN

It had been a week since Jesse had galloped Jennifer into Bozeman. Doctor Fitzgerald was washing up after examining the damaged leg. Coaxed back to the house mostly out of curiosity that the schoolteacher was still alive, he was pleased with the way the leg was healing and amazed that no serious infection had redeveloped. "It looks like there's nothing more for me to do."

"Told ya tha' afore ya come up here," Bette Mae said, tucking the blankets back around Jennifer.

The doctor grumbled at the audacity of the woman. He was sure she had gained her medical knowledge by seeing to the gunshot and knife wounds of customers in establishments on the seedier side of frontier life. "I'll leave her in your care, then. I'm sure your doctor in Sweetwater will be able to see to her needs once you get back."

"Ain't got no doc in Sweetwater," Bette Mae said.

"Actually, Bette Mae sees to all the medical needs in Sweetwater," Jennifer interjected.

"But she hasn't been properly trained."

"Mos' a my patients are still alive, Doc." Bette Mae handed him his medicine bag. "Guess that's all the trainin' I needs."

Jesse entered the room, carrying KC in one arm and balancing a tray of food in the other. She gently set the baby onto the bed. "Good, you're still here. I want to thank you, Doc," Jesse offered her freed hand. "I appreciate all you did to save Jennifer." Her voice caught in her throat, and she took a moment to clear it. "And I want to apologize for the other night. Hope I didn't hurt you."

Doctor Fitzgerald reached tentatively for the outstretched hand. He still carried some bruising from when the woman had thrown him against the wall. "Guess I might have done the same in your position." He shook Jesse's hand. "You take good care of her. She'll need to be a lot stronger before you try to go back to Sweetwater."

"Thanks, Doc." Jesse nodded. "I promise she's not going anywhere until she's ready."

"Fine." He was in a much better mood than he had been just moments before. "I'll bid you goodbye."

"Goodbye, Doctor Fitzgerald." Jennifer smiled as KC gave a finger wave to the departing doctor. "And thank you."

"I'm real sorry the leg won't be much good to you." He had told Jennifer the leg was too damaged to be of much use, even recommended that she get a pair of crutches to help her get around. "But you're alive, and that's what really matters."

"Thanks again, Doc," Jesse called out as Bette Mae escorted him out of the room. Left alone with her wife and child, Jesse took the tray of food to the bed.

"Momma?" KC was lying on her belly beside Jennifer, looking at the bandaged leg propped up by several pillows. "Owie?"

"Yes, sweetie." Jennifer rubbed the baby's back. "Momma has an owie."

"You be real careful, Sunshine." Jesse set the tray on the small table that sat near the bed. "Don't touch Momma's owie."

"Otay." KC sat up and stretched out a hand toward the food tray.

"Sweetie," Jennifer said with a laugh, "you can't be hungry already. Not after that large breakfast I heard Bette Mae fed you."

KC withdrew her hand and thrust out her lower lip.

Jesse chuckled at the baby. "Here you go, Sunshine. Your Grandma Marie made this special for you." She handed the baby a cookie.

"Jesse, you'll spoil her." Jennifer shook her head but let the baby enjoy the cookie.

"Nah, she only gets one. And," she handed a second cookie to Jennifer, "this one is for you."

"Oooh." Jennifer sighed. "It's still warm."

"Yep." Jesse filled a glass with cold milk and placed it on the table within Jennifer's reach. "Best way to eat cookies."

Jennifer looked at Jesse with suspicion. "You're not having any?"

"Nope." Jesse shrugged.

"How many did you eat in the kitchen?"

"One or two." Jesse watched Jennifer's eyebrow slowly rise. "Or three. Maybe four." Seeing the doubt in her wife's eyes, she quickly added, "No more than five."

"Ha." Jennifer giggled. "Now we know where you get your appetite, sweetie," she told KC, now with cookie smeared all over her face.

"Come here." Jesse carefully lifted the baby from the bed. "Did you get any of that cookie inside of you?" KC giggled as Jesse playfully rubbed a wet cloth over her dirty face.

There was a knock at the door, and Billie poked his head inside. "Want some company?"

Jennifer smiled at their friend. "Sure."

"How you feeling?" he asked.

"Like a mountain lion used me for a scratching post," Jennifer said as she finished her cookie.

Not knowing what to say to his friend, Billie shuffled uneasily for a moment. "Doc said you're goin' ta be okay," he said, looking hopeful.

"Long as I've got Jesse and KC, I'll be fine."

"Good to hear," he said with a smile. "Um, I hate to bring this up, Jennifer, but it's about your pa."

Her mood darkened. "What about him?"

"Circuit judge will be here any day now. We need to know if you'll still be wantin' to let him go free."

Jennifer had asked the sheriff to drop all charges and release her father if he promised to leave Montana and never return. Jesse and Mary had joined Billie in arguing against Jennifer's decision, but she had insisted that she didn't want her father anywhere in Montana, even in prison. Jesse had reluctantly agreed to allow Jennifer to make the final decision.

"Has he promised to leave the territory?"

"Yes, for whatever his word is worth," Billie said doubtfully.

"Darlin'," Jesse took Jennifer's hand, "I don't think he should get away with what he's done. A man is dead, and you could have died, too."

Jennifer was adamant. "Sweetheart, I wouldn't be able to rest if I knew he was still here. Besides, he'll be in plenty of trouble that will keep him busy once he goes back East. I'll contact Andrew's father. I'm sure that he'll expect my father to do much more than apologize for his son's death. Please," she said, placing a hand on Jesse's cheek, "I don't want him here."

Jesse leaned into the caress. "All right," she conceded.

"Let him go," Jennifer told Billie. "Just be sure he gets on the stage."

"Don't worry." Billie nodded. "I'll buy his ticket and put him in his seat myself."

Sheriff Carson unlocked the cell door. "You're free to go."

"The judge set me free?" Kensington crowed. "I told you no reasonable man would keep me in jail once he heard my side of things."

"Judge had nothing to do with it." Carson tossed the ring of keys onto his desk. "Your daughter insisted that you be set free. Why, I don't know."

"'Bout time she came to her senses." Kensington stopped at the sheriff's desk. "Where can I find her?"

"It would be in your best interests to keep away from her. Just like you agreed, you're to catch the next stage out of town, head east, and don't come back."

Kensington glared at the lawman. "Where is she?"

"Stage station is at the end of town, you can't miss it. I suggest you go straight there and don't start any trouble."

Kensington turned on his heel and stomped out of the office.

"Something tells me, I ain't seen the last of that jackass." The sheriff reached for his hat. "Better warn the Bransons to be on the lookout for him."

Kensington marched to the small house where he had been directed by one of the storekeepers. He didn't bother to knock before storming into the Branson home. Stanley Branson was sitting in the parlor reading a paper. He looked up, startled, when Kensington barged into the room.

"Where is she?" Kensington shouted.

Based on his daughter's descriptions of Jennifer's father, Branson knew the identity of the intruder but decided to act as if he didn't. Carefully folding the paper, he set it on a side table and stood. "Might I ask who you are?"

"Martin Kensington. I won't ask again. Where is the bitch who is deluding my daughter?" Kensington spat.

"When in my home, sir, I will ask that you keep a civil tongue. I do not take kindly to that sort of language used in the presence of my wife."

"Never mind; I'll find the harlot myself." Kensington strode through the room to begin his search of the house.

Branson reached out to stop him. "Mr. Kensington..."

"It's all right, Poppa." Jesse descended the stairs leading from the bedroom. "He's looking for me."

"You unspeakable whore," Kensington growled. "Where is she?"

"Where you'll never touch her again," Jesse growled back.

"I should have killed you when I had the chance." Kensington started for Jesse but stopped abruptly, held in Mr. Branson's vise-like grip. "Let me go."

"Get out of my home," Branson ordered, turning him in the direction of the door.

Kensington looked at Branson with incredulity. "You're protecting that monstrous—"

"She's *my* daughter." Branson propelled Kensington toward the door. "And don't you ever forget it."

Kensington shrugged out of Branson's hold, pushing past him as he again started for Jesse. A powerful hand on his shoulder spun him around, and a fist struck his chin. He fell back against a table, knocking it over.

Branson reached down and pulled the interloper to his feet. With arms strong from many years of hard work, he tossed Kensington toward the door just as Billie rushed into the house. Kensington fell at the sheriff's feet.

Jennifer struggled to get out of bed. "I need to go down there."

"No, you don't."

"Please, Ed," Jennifer pleaded with the man who was more of a father to her than the one downstairs threatening Jesse.

Ed shook his head. "Jesse would shoot me if I let you go down there."

"I'll shoot you if you don't." Jennifer threw back the blankets. She was thankful that KC was out for a walk with her grandmothers and did not have to hear the shouting. "Please."

Ed reluctantly relented when it became apparent that Jennifer would make her way downstairs, with or without his help. He picked her up and gingerly carried her from the room.

"Sheriff, arrest that man," Kensington commanded from his position on the floor.

"Get up, you fool." Billie reached down and yanked the man to his feet. "Sorry 'bout this," he told the others. "Sheriff Carson let him go before I got there. Everyone okay?"

Stanley Branson stood beside Jesse, his hands still balled into tight fists. "Yes, but I'll thank you to remove that man from my house, before I hit him again."

Billie nodded. "Come on, Kensington. You have a stage to catch."

"I'm not leaving without my daughter."

"Yes, Father," Jennifer said as Ed carried her down the stairs. "You are leaving without me."

"Jennifer." Jesse rushed to her wife's side. "Darlin', you shouldn't be out of bed." She took Jennifer from Ed's arms.

"I had to come down, sweetheart." Jennifer rested her head against Jesse's. Turning to the enraged man she had once called Father, she angrily said, "Go home. Go home and leave me alone. I am no longer your daughter."

"You'll come with me and do as I say," Kensington insisted.

"No." Mary Kensington stepped in front of her husband. She and Marie Branson had been returning from their walk with KC when they'd heard a crash from inside the house and hurried inside. "Jennifer is her own woman now. She has a life here."

"Take care, woman. You don't know what you're saying."

"I'm saying that you're wrong. You were wrong to come here, and young Andrew lost his life because of that. I'll not have you do any more to harm our daughter or anyone else. It's time you left her alone."

"How dare you question my authority!"

A ringing slap stunned Kensington and the others in the room. Mary Kensington withdrew her hand and looked at it in wonder, then stared into her husband's face. "How dare I?" she whispered. "How dare I?" Her voice grew louder as years of pent-up anger boiled over. "I dare because I love her. Martin, go home. Go back to your sons and your precious company."

"You'll come with me." It was half a statement, half a question.

"No, I think I'll stay here. I'd like to get to know my daughter and..." she turned to look at Jennifer, "her family."

Jennifer smiled through the tears that trickled down her cheek. "I'd like that, Mother."

"You can't be serious. You must return with me."

"No." Mary turned back to her husband. "I must do nothing of the sort. One thing coming to Montana has taught me is that I don't have to comply with all of your demands. For now, I think it's more important that I stay here."

"But what will I tell our sons? What will I tell our friends?"

"To be honest," Mary gave a wry smile, "I don't give a damn."

Jennifer stared at her mother; she had never heard her use profanity ever before. Never. Not once.

"Come on." Billie shoved Kensington out of the house. "The stage is leaving soon."

"But..." Stopping on the porch, Kensington looked back. His traitorous wife was standing beside the woman who was responsible for all his troubles, the woman who held his daughter in her arms. In the face of this unexpectedly united front, his shoulders slumped. "What will I tell them?"

"You could start with what an out and out jackass you are," Billie said as he pushed the man down steps and out into the street.

Jesse sat on the front porch, KC playing at her feet, while Jennifer slept upstairs. "I want to thank you, Poppa. For yesterday."

"You're my daughter," Stanley replied. "Couldn't just sit there and let that fella talk about ya that way." He watched his granddaughter play. "About the ranch, Jesse..."

"I could have run it." Jesse's voice was barely more than a whisper.

"I know." Stanley swallowed hard. "It wasn't that. I was behind on the payments, and there wasn't anything left for me to do. Bank took it back, Jesse. Gave your ma and me one day to get out; they already had the papers signed by the new owner."

Jesse reached out and took his larger callused hand into her own. "You should have told me, Poppa, I could have helped."

"I didn't want you to know that your old man couldn't make a go of it."

"That day I came home..." She couldn't say any more; the hurt of what happened that day rushing back as if it were yesterday.

"I'm sorry, Jesse. I just didn't know what else to do. I knew how much ya wanted the ranch, but there was nothing left. We don't even own this house. Banker felt sorry for us and is letting us live here for the few dollars I earn doin' odd jobs for folks."

Jesse looked at her father. He had always been a proud man, but now she could see how much his pride had cost him. "It's okay, Poppa." Jesse smiled. "Things worked out for the best."

Stanley was surprised that his daughter showed no sign of holding the past against him. "How do ya figure?"

"If you had kept the ranch, I never would've ended up in Sweetwater. And I never would've met Jennifer."

"Ya love her? Like I love your momma?"

"Yes."

"And she loves you?"

"Yes."

"Can't say I understand." Jesse waited. "But you're my daughter. Can't turn my back on ya for who you love."

"Thank you, Poppa."

"Things have a funny way of working out sometimes, don't they?"

"Yeah." Jesse scratched her head, a thought rolling around in the back of her mind. "Poppa," she said quietly, "I can buy you a house. Or you could come to Sweetwater and live with us on our ranch. There's more than enough room for you and Mom."

"Wouldn't be right. Can't live on your charity."

Jesse stiffened. "Is that why you never answered my mail — you thought I was offering you charity?"

"It's not fittin' for a man to live off his child. Man needs to pay his own way."

"Aw, Poppa." The baby tugged on her pant leg, and Jesse bent down to lift KC into her lap. "There's more than enough work at the ranch and the Slipper to keep us both busy for years. And besides, it would be nice for KC to have a grandpa around."

"You'd want us there?"

Smiling, Jesse assured her father, "Yes. I'd *want* you there."

"What about Jennifer?"

"She'd love to have you and Mom around." Jesse chuckled at the thought of all of them living on her property. "The more the merrier."

"Ya really love her?"

"With all my heart."

"Ya got married?"

"Yes. I wanted to invite you but I didn't think..." She left the thought unfinished.

"Married folk should wear rings. You don't wear one."

Jesse looked at her unadorned hand. "Not too many places to buy one in Sweetwater."

Without a word, her father stood and disappeared into the house. "I guess that's that," Jesse said to the baby, who looked up at her questioningly.

Moments later, Stanley reappeared. "Here." He handed Jesse a small box. "Belonged to your momma's folks. Always figured we'd give 'em to our son when he married. Guess it don't make much sense lettin' 'em go to waste."

Jesse opened the box and revealed two golden wedding bands glittering in the sunlight. KC reached for the shiny objects.

"No, Sunshine." Jesse stopped the baby's hands. "Those are for your momma and me." She looked up at her father, tears flowing. "Come to the ranch, Poppa."

"Maybe," Stanley said before disappearing back inside the house.

Jesse tucked the sleeping baby under the blanket in the cradle, then slipped into bed and snuggled up to Jennifer. "How you doing, darlin'?"

"I wish I was home in our own bed." Jennifer reached out and pulled Jesse's face close to kiss her. "I love you."

"I love you, too," Jesse breathed. "I have something for you." She reached into her pocket and pulled out the small box her father had given her. She carefully opened the box, keeping the contents concealed from Jennifer. Smiling as she took her wife's left hand into her own, she slipped a gold wedding band onto the ring finger. She handed Jennifer the matching band and offered her hand to her wife.

Jennifer slid the ring onto Jesse's finger. "They're beautiful, Jesse, but aren't they too expensive?"

"Nope." Jesse brought Jennifer's banded finger to her lips and kissed it. "They belonged to my grandparents. Poppa says that folks need rings to show they're married."

Jennifer looked at the rings sparkling in the candlelight. "Your poppa is a pretty wise man."

"Glad you think so. I asked him and Mom to come live with us."

Jennifer stared. "Really?"

"Yep." Jesse nodded. "Figured KC needed some grandparents to spoil her."

Jennifer snuggled into Jesse's arms. Thinking of all the pain Jesse had suffered from thinking her parents had abandoned her, she had to ask, "You do know what you're doing, right?"

"I think so."

"I love you, Jesse Branson," Jennifer said as she clasped their banded hands together.

"I love you, Jennifer Branson."

"Sweetheart?"

"Hmmm."

"I want to go home."

Jesse shook her head. "But the doctor—"

"The doctor doesn't know how much better I will mend back in familiar surroundings, sweetheart. Please, Jesse, let's go home."

Jesse watched Jennifer's eyelids begin to droop as the exertion of the day caught up with her. "We'll go home, darlin'," Jesse murmured, removing the pillows from behind Jennifer's back so she could lie flat. "But the doctor's right, you need to be a bit stronger before we travel."

"Okay," Jennifer said sleepily. "Just don't make me wait too long."

"I won't." Jesse leaned over to kiss Jennifer, not surprised to find she was already asleep.

CHAPTER ELEVEN

Several weeks later, true to her word, when Jennifer was recovered enough to travel, Jesse took her home, along with her mother and KC.

"What do you think, KC?" Jesse asked as she climbed down from the ladder. "Think your momma will like it?"

KC looked up at Jesse. Her mommy was very happy about something and that made her want to clap her hands, so she did.

Jesse looked up at her handiwork. "Yep, I think she will, too." Jesse picked KC up. "You've been a real good girl today. I think maybe you should get a cookie; what do you think?" KC understood the word "cookie", and her head bobbed up and down in agreement.

Jesse lifted the baby up onto the cushioned seat in the buckboard, now covered in a mountain lion hide. "You sit and eat your cookie while I get the tools put away. And this time, try to get most of it into your tummy, okay?"

"Otay." KC took the treat and starting nibbling along its edge while she watched Jesse.

"Don't want you looking a mess when we pick up Momma."

After placing her tools in the back of the buckboard, Jesse laid the ladder out of the way alongside the road. She'd stop and get it on the way back to the ranch house when they returned from town.

Jennifer lifted the hair off the back of her neck in a futile attempt to cool her clammy skin. She had asked Jesse to drop her at the schoolhouse that morning so she could work on study plans for the coming school session, but now she was missing the cool shade of the ranch. Even with all the windows open, sitting inside the schoolhouse during the afternoon hours was next to unbearable. Sounds drifted in from outside on the still air — horses' hooves clomping against the hard packed street and wagon springs creaking. As she opened her desk drawer and placed her papers inside, her thoughts strayed to the events of the last few months. Had it really been such a short time since she'd come to Sweetwater to teach their children? She'd arrived in town not much more than a child herself and innocent of the difficulties that life could hold. But as often happened, events were forced upon the unsuspecting that caused one to grow up in a hurry. She thought of how much different her life was now compared to only a year before, and all because she had fallen in love the day she'd stepped off the stage in Sweetwater.

Jennifer's attention was drawn by the sound of boots crunching on the gravel path leading to the schoolhouse and a steady stream of baby gibberish. "And here she comes now."

Jennifer grabbed the cane leaning against the wall behind her desk. Limping heavily, she made her way between the rows of desks to the door. With Jesse's help and encouragement, she was working hard to regain the use of the damaged leg. Some days were better than others, but a nice long soak in a hot bath and a rubdown by Jesse helped eased her discomfort at the end of the day.

She left the stuffiness of the schoolhouse and stepped out into the relative coolness of the shade on the small porch. Smiling, she waited as her wife and daughter made their way up the path.

Jesse smiled broadly. "Afternoon, darlin'."

"Momma." KC's outstretched arms reached for the ginger-haired woman on the porch.

"Hi, sweetie." Jennifer was glad of Jesse's supportive arm around her waist as she relinquished her cane and took the baby. KC wrapped chubby arms around her momma's neck and kissed her on the cheek. Jennifer kissed her back. "I've missed you."

"What about me?" Jesse asked as she wrapped her long arms around Jennifer and pulled her close, their mouths meeting for a tender, lingering kiss.

When their lips parted, Jennifer sighed. "I've missed you, too, sweetheart."

Mindful of the balance issues arising from the still-mending injuries, Jesse traded the cane for the baby. "How's your work going? Finish it up, yet?"

"Almost." Jennifer leaned into Jesse, then gingerly shifted her weight onto her injured leg. "Come on, help me get the windows shut so we can go home."

Jesse followed her into the schoolhouse. Setting KC down on the floor, she crossed to the closest window and pulled it shut; clouds were building over the mountains to the west. "Looks like we could get thunder bumpers tonight."

"Thunder bumpers?"

"Storms we get this time of year." Jesse pulled down a window. "Usually begin to roll in just before nightfall. Lots of thunder and lightning."

"And rain?" Jennifer asked hopefully.

"If we're lucky." With all of the windows closed, Jesse glanced around for KC. "Mostly, just lots of booming."

KC peeked out from under Jennifer's desk. "Oom?"

"Yep, Sunshine." Jesse playfully approached the baby like a tiger on the prowl. "Boom, boom, *boom*," she teased.

KC giggled. "Oom, oom, *oom*," she repeated.

Jennifer wiped beads of perspiration from her forehead. "It sure would be nice to get some rain to break up this heat."

"The summer sure has been a hot one; looks like it might keep on right 'til snow starts fallin'." Jesse lifted KC from the floor. "Come on, you rascal. Looks like we better start tyin' a rope to you, you squirt around so much." When she straightened up, she saw Jennifer's disapproving look. "Only way we'll be able to keep track of her," she explained.

Jennifer tried not to smile at the image that popped into her head — Jesse walking around Sweetwater linked to KC by a long rope. She could just imagine what trouble the two of them could cause. "We'll find another way," she assured the rancher. Changing the subject before Jesse could offer any new suggestions, she asked, "Should we stop by the depot?"

The town of Sweetwater did not have a telegraph or post office. Messages and mail traveled to and from town on the stage and was held at the stage office until picked up. Jesse was hoping for word that her parents had accepted her offer to come and live on the ranch, but it seemed her father had yet to make a decision, at least not one he wanted to share with her. "Stopped by on our way here." Jesse toted the giggling KC to the front door and held it open for Jennifer. "Nothin' yet."

Jennifer stepped onto the porch, then waited as Jesse pulled the door shut, making sure it was secure before joining her. She heard the disappointment in her partner's voice. Knowing there really wasn't anything she could say to lessen it, she held out her hand, and Jesse instantly accepted it. They slowly walked down the gravel path to the footbridge spanning the creek at the bottom of the knoll where the schoolhouse sat. On the other side of the footbridge, their buckboard sat behind Boy, their patiently waiting draft horse.

Jesse helped Jennifer up into the buckboard, being careful not to jar her damaged leg, then handed KC up to her momma.

KC promptly crawled off her mother's lap and plopped down in the center of the bench seat. She liked to sit between her mothers where she could hold on to both of them while the buckboard bounced along the road. Naturally, her mothers preferred to sit side-by-side and, much to KC's dismay, Jennifer pulled her up onto her lap.

"They'll come, sweetheart." When Jesse was seated, Jennifer laid a comforting hand on her thigh. "Just give them some time."

Jesse took Jennifer's hand, brought it to her lips, and tenderly kissed the gold band that encircled Jennifer's ring finger. "I hope you're right, darlin'." She gently squeezed Jennifer's hand. "I'd hate to lose them again."

Jennifer returned the squeeze. "You won't. Bozeman isn't that far away. We can visit them as often as you like."

Jesse nodded, unwrapping the reins from the brake handle and slapping them lightly on Boy's hindquarters. The large draft horse started walking in the direction of the Silver Slipper, the women sitting quietly as he plodded along the dusty street. Used to stopping at the Slipper, the horse walked to the front of the two-story building and stopped in the shade of its wrap-around porch. Jesse hopped down from the wagon and hurried around to help Jennifer.

"Afternoon." Bette Mae stepped out of the shadows on the porch. "Why, I was jus' tellin' yer momma, it was 'bout time for yas to be stoppin' by on yer way home."

"Afternoon, Bette Mae. Sit still until Mommy can get you," Jennifer instructed KC, who was wriggling to be freed. Jennifer rolled her eyes at the child's excitement at seeing Bette Mae.

"Best take care of her first," Jesse told Jennifer, who nodded and helped KC crawl into Jesse's waiting arms. Jesse handed the baby to Bette Mae.

"Lordy, but ya is growin' like a weed. I do declare ya's bigger than ya was this mornin'." Bette Mae tickled the child's belly.

Jesse laughed. "Don't suppose it has anything to do with the treats you keep baking for her." She turned to Jennifer and carefully lifted her from the wagon, then carried her up the steps and gently set her down on the porch next to Bette Mae.

"You don't have to carry me," Jennifer protested.

"Hush, darlin'; I don't mind."

"Yes, sweetheart, I know." Jennifer leaned on her cane to steady herself, then said unhappily, "I just don't like feeling helpless."

"Oh, you're far from helpless, darlin'. Besides you'll be running up those steps in no time, and then I won't have any excuse to do it." She grinned at Jennifer. "I really like to, you know." Jesse wrapped Jennifer in a hug. "I love you," she whispered, placing a kiss on her wife's lips.

Jesse knew how difficult it was for Jennifer to do certain things, like climbing the steep stairs at the Slipper. Her wife never complained, but she did insist on doing things for herself as much as possible. She had even started riding her mare, Blaze, again, mostly for short loops around the ranch house, but she made each one a little longer than the last in hopes that she'd be able to ride to town before long.

"Com' on." Bette Mae turned to take KC inside. "Tha's not fittin' for a child to see." She smirked over her shoulder at the two women.

Breaking off the kiss, Jesse laughed. "Aw, Bette Mae, she's seen worse."

Jennifer blushed. "Jesse Marie Branson!"

"Ya best com' wit' me, angel," Bette Mae said to KC. "Looks like yer mamas are fixin' to have a spat. 'Course now," she whispered mischievously to the child, "they only fight so's they can make up."

"Come on, darlin'." Jesse scooped Jennifer into her arms. "Let's see what goodies Bette Mae has waiting for our daughter. We can make up when we get back to the ranch."

"Jesse!" Jennifer's blush deepened.

Having heard a familiar word, "goodies", KC perked up. "Cookie?" and the women were all laughing as they went inside.

Mary Kensington rose from an overstuffed chair where she had been enjoying a book from the Silver Slipper's extensive library. "I thought I heard your voices." Jesse and Jennifer both gave her a hug. "Sit, daughter." Mary pointed to a chair at the closest table. "You should be resting that leg."

"I'm fine, Mother," Jennifer assured, though she sat. "Besides, with the mothering Jesse gives me, I really don't need any more."

Mary smiled as she sat in the chair next to her daughter. "You can never have enough mothering."

"Grmm," KC told Bette Mae, pointing at her grandmother.

"Yep, angel." Bette Mae nodded. "That's yer gramma. Still havin' trouble gettin' yer little mouth around tha' big word, I see."

Jesse chuckled as she pulled a chair close to Jennifer. "You wouldn't think that was such a little mouth if you had to listen to her wail when she wakes up hungry."

Bette Mae sat KC in her grandmother's lap and then took a seat at the table. "Grmm." KC smiled at the older woman. "Cookie?"

Mary smiled nervously at the child that reminded her so much of Jennifer at the same age. "I think there may be some in the kitchen." Though she was determined to make amends to Jennifer and accept her relationship with Jesse, Mary was having trouble adjusting to her granddaughter. It wasn't so much that the baby wasn't Jennifer's by birth, but KC was her first grandchild, and she wasn't sure she was ready to be a grandmother.

"Don't you think you've had enough treats for one day?" Jennifer asked, knowing that, between Jesse and Bette Mae, her daughter never went hungry.

KC poked out a quivering lower lip. Her pout was so pitiful that all four women had a hard time keeping a straight face.

"What say we share a cookie?" Jesse reached over and gently pressed on KC's lip. "Don't want you trippin' on that when we leave," she teased. KC playfully tried to nip at Jesse's finger, but it was withdrawn too fast. "Ha, you missed," Jesse said triumphantly.

"Some day my little angel is going to catch tha' there finger, and then we'll be seein' who's doin' the wailin'." Bette Mae chuckled.

"Never," Jesse boasted.

"Right." Jennifer grinned, using her cane to steady herself as she pushed up from the chair. "Come on, speedy," she said to Jesse, "let's get her home before she can ask for something else these two would be more than happy to spoil her with."

"I do not spoil tha' little angel," Bette Mae protested. "I'm jus' tryin' to help her grow big and strong like her mommas. Ya got ta admit, she's a mite on the tiny size."

"Give her time, Bette Mae." Jesse stood. "She's not yet a year old. She's got plenty of time to grow."

"I didn't think you knew how old she was," Mary said as Jesse took the baby from her.

"We don't know for sure," Jennifer confirmed. "But we figure she couldn't have been more than eight or nine months old when we found her."

"Tha' means we should start plannin' a birthday party," Bette Mae said.

Jennifer looked at Jesse, who shrugged. "Don't see that it would hurt anything. She should have a day she can celebrate."

"But which day?" Jennifer asked.

"Guess you could pick any day you want." Mary was surprised to be feeling excited over the prospect of a birthday party for the baby. *Maybe I'm finally getting used to being a grandmother.*

"Guess we could," Jesse agreed. "Tell you what, let us give it some thought, and we'll let you know what we decide. You can plan the party then."

"Don' you worry." Bette Mae gave KC a goodbye kiss. "We'll have the biggest party this town has ever seen."

Jennifer and Jesse groaned at the same time. "Oh, boy."

The buckboard came to a halt at the front gate of the ranch, and Jesse climbed down from her seat. Looking about, curious as to why they had stopped, Jennifer noted something different about the sign. "Jesse?"

"Hmm?" Jesse was retrieving the ladder and placing it in the back of the buckboard.

"You changed the name of the ranch?"

"Thought it was needed," Jesse said as she climbed back up into the seat beside her wife.

Jennifer gazed up at the two large logs on either side of the road that marked the entrance to the property. Arching from the top of one log to the other was a third log; the side that faced incoming visitors was hewn flat. Carved into the log had been *J's Dream* but a letter had been added since Jennifer had last seen it, and now the sign proclaimed, *JJ's Dream*. She looked at Jesse and beamed. "I love it; and I love you."

"I love you, too." Jesse leaned for a kiss.

"Jesse?" Jennifer was tucking the blanket around the sleeping baby. With thunder booming and lightning crashing overhead, it had taken extra time to get KC to sleep, but she had finally given in and closed her tired eyes. "What do you think we should do about KC's birthday?"

"Don't rightly know." Jesse poured another pail of heated water into the tub she was preparing for Jennifer.

"When is your birthday?" Jennifer asked as she undressed.

"March 21st." Jesse tested the water in the tub to be sure it wasn't too hot. "Yours?"

"June 5th."

Jesse lifted the last pail of heated water from the fireplace and slowly added the water to the tub as she thought about Jennifer's birthday. Jennifer had arrived in Sweetwater around the first of June. That meant her birthday had gone uncelebrated.

Jennifer turned at the sudden silence. "Sweetheart?" Seeing Jesse's frown, she asked, "What's wrong?"

"You never said anything."

Naked from the waist up, Jennifer limped over and wrapped her arms around her lover. "We were kind of busy at the time." Her birthday had been the day after she broke Jesse out of jail to save her from a lynch mob.

"Still," Jesse sighed at Jennifer's touch, "I could have got ya a present or somethin'."

"Oh, silly." Jennifer turned Jesse in her arms and planted a kiss on the pouting lips. "You gave me the best birthday present I could ever have wished for."

"I did?" Jesse's arms enfolded Jennifer and pulled their bodies closer.

"Yes, sweetheart. You gave me you."

Thinking back on the events of that day, Jesse grinned. That was when she had first admitted to having feelings for Jennifer. "Guess I did at that."

"Yes, love." Jennifer smiled back. "You certainly did."

"Still," Jesse kissed the end of Jennifer's nose, "you could have said something."

Jennifer marveled anew at how strange it was that she felt as if she had known Jesse forever and yet there was still much they didn't know about each other.

By the look on Jennifer's face, she was a thousand miles away. "Darlin', are you okay?"

"Yes, I was just thinking." Jennifer sat on one of the chairs beside the dining table and bent over to remove her boots.

"Let me." Jesse quickly knelt at her wife's feet. "What were you thinkin'?" She carefully pulled the boot free from Jennifer's injured leg.

"How much we still don't know about each other."

"Like what?" She stood and held out a hand to help Jennifer off the chair.

"Our birthdays, for one." She leaned on Jesse as her pants and undergarments were pulled down. She lifted first one foot and then the other, so Jesse could remove the clothing.

"You know that now. As for the rest, guess we'll just find out as things come up." Jesse leaned back on her heels to enjoy the view.

Jennifer blushed as Jesse's eyes moved, unhurried, up her naked body. "Water's getting cold, sweetheart."

"I can always heat more." Jesse wiggled her eyebrows.

Jennifer reached down and pulled Jesse upright. "No, that would mean you'd have to go outside and fill those buckets at the well. I prefer to keep you right here."

"Oh, you do, do you?" Jesse laughed as she helped Jennifer step into the tub. After making sure her lover was comfortable, Jesse picked up the washrag and soap. "Now about those things you'd be wantin' to know about me. I suppose you could make up a list," she teased as she worked the soap into lather on the washcloth.

Jennifer laughed. "I wouldn't know where to start. And once I got going, I probably wouldn't know when to stop."

Knowing her wife's penchant for long shopping lists, Jesse chuckled. "Ain't that the truth."

Jennifer leaned back and closed her eyes, savoring the feel of Jesse's gentle hands moving over her body.

"Ready for your hair?" Jesse asked after several minutes.

Jennifer opened her eyes and slowly sat upright. "Yes," she said, running a hand through her tresses. "I can't seem to keep it clean, what with it being as hot as it has been. I suppose I could cut it shorter."

Jesse soaped up her hands, then carefully washed the silky hair. It took a couple of soapings to get the day's sweat out of it, but that was all right with Jesse; she loved the feel of Jennifer's locks as they slid through her fingers. "No, darlin'. I love it just the way it is."

With her hair rinsed of soap, Jennifer leaned back against the tub's smooth surface. She smiled in invitation. "Join me."

Reaching for a towel, Jesse's hand stopped in mid-air as she turned back to look at her wife. She and Jennifer had begun to bathe together soon after she had moved to the ranch. But since her accident, Jesse had refused, for fear of hurting Jennifer. "You sure?"

"Yes, sweetheart. I've missed it. I've missed you. Please, my leg is much better."

Jesse hesitated, but she had missed their shared baths, and Jennifer's leg did seem to be as mended as it was probably going to get. She grinned as she stripped off her clothes and slid into the water. Jesse sighed, leaning back to rest against Jennifer. "I've missed this, darlin'."

"Me, too." Jennifer picked up the soapy rag and washed the parts of Jesse she could reach. When her hands brushed soap over supple breasts, she felt the nipples harden at her touch. Dropping the washrag, Jennifer took the firm globes in her hands and gently squeezed. Her head bent to plant slow, tender kisses across the rancher's strong shoulders.

Jesse moaned as her body responded to Jennifer's loving touches. They had not made love since before Jennifer's kidnapping, and each longed for the feel of the other. Desperately longing to continue, she nevertheless said, "Don't think we should—"

"Hush," Jennifer whispered.

Jesse shivered as one of Jennifer's hands traced irregular circles from her breasts down her stomach and continued lower. Her head fell back against Jennifer's shoulder, and she moaned when her lover's lips claimed her.

Jennifer's tongue pressed inside to hungrily explore Jesse's waiting mouth. As they kissed, Jennifer slipped her hand between Jesse's legs, her fingers sliding smoothly in the slickness they encountered.

Jesse spread her legs invitingly and was instantly rewarded when Jennifer's fingers gently pinched her clit. While Jennifer's tongue continued its assault on Jesse's mouth, she slid her fingers down Jesse's inner lips and slipped inside.

Aching for her lover's touch, just the entry was all Jesse needed to climax. Her hands clutched the sides of the tub as her thighs clenched tight around Jennifer's hand, holding it in place. Her hips arched up, and her chest heaved as the weeks of pent-up need exploded within her. She screamed into Jennifer's kiss. Her body trembled with shivers of aftershock as she collapsed down into the tub, causing water to slosh over its sides.

Jennifer wrapped her arms around Jesse and held her as she recovered. In the throes of their passion, her leg had been wedged between Jesse's hip and the side of the tub and it was throbbing, but she didn't care. All that mattered was the love she had been able to share with her wife, something she had been aching to do for weeks.

"I love you," Jesse sighed, her body boneless in Jennifer's embrace.

"I love you." Jennifer left a trail of delicate kisses down the side of her wife's face and neck.

"Whoa, darlin'." Jesse reached up a shaky hand and gently stilled Jennifer's mouth. "Seems that's how I ended up like this in the first place. Give me some time."

Jennifer grinned. She loved making love to Jesse. "That good, huh?"

"Unh, huh." As her strength returned, she realized she had Jennifer's bad leg pinned against the side of the tub. "Oh, darlin'!" She jerked away. "I'm so sorry. Did I hurt you?" Jesse sat up and ran her hands over Jennifer's leg, searching for any fresh injuries.

"Stop." Jennifer pulled Jesse back against her. "It's fine."

"Are you sure?" Jesse couldn't believe her carelessness. "I'm so sorry."

Jennifer cupped a hand against Jesse's face, her thumb tracing Jesse's lips to quiet them. "It's okay."

"Really?"

"Really."

Jesse's tongue lashed out and pulled Jennifer's thumb inside her warm mouth. As she sucked, her eyes locked on Jennifer's.

"Oh, no." Jennifer responded, reading her lover's thoughts.

"It's only fair." Jesse grinned, releasing her wife's digit. "You've had your fun, now I should have mine." A long arm reached up and a gentle hand cupped the back of Jennifer's neck. Jesse pulled Jennifer to her and pressed their lips together. It was several moments before they parted.

"You better finish your bath and take me to bed if that's what you want."

Jesse quickly searched around the bottom of the tub for the washrag. She wasn't one to keep her wife waiting. "Yes, darlin'."

After finishing her bath, Jesse carried Jennifer to their bed and made love to her. They now lay in the tangled sheets, the scent of their recent activity hanging in the air around them. Jennifer was lying on her back with one arm tucked behind her head, her other hand playing with Jesse's hair. Her injured leg was propped up on a pillow, safely out of harm's way.

Jesse was lying half on and half off of Jennifer, with one arm draped across her wife's waist. A soft breeze blew through the open window next to their bed, washing a welcome coolness over their heated bodies.

"September first."

"What about it?" Jesse asked, not raising her head from where it rested between a pair of lovely breasts.

"For KC's birthday."

Jesse thought for a moment. "Why the first?"

"It's her first birthday. Seems right."

"Oh." Jesse lightly ran fingers up and down Jennifer's leg, raising goose bumps.

"That tickles," Jennifer said with a giggle. "So, what about it?"

"Sounds fine to me." Jesse's fingers were replaced by lips softly kissing Jennifer's stomach.

"Jesse," Jennifer purred. "You start that and we'll never get to sleep tonight."

Jesse pushed herself up on her elbow and gazed into Jennifer's sapphire eyes. "Who said anything about sleeping?" she asked seductively, as her lips claimed Jennifer.

CHAPTER TWELVE

Jennifer was still asleep when Jesse woke to the sound of KC moving about in her cradle. Knowing KC had been experimenting with trying to climb out on her own, Jesse reluctantly left the comfort of the bed and the warmth of Jennifer's body to see what their daughter was up to.

KC — wet, hungry, and ready to start a new day — was very happy to see her mommy looking into her cradle. She raised her arms in the air. "Up."

"Okay." Jesse lifted the child free of the cradle. "But you have to be real quiet; Momma is still asleep," Jesse whispered.

"Otay," KC whispered back. "Ugh," she said as her wet bottom was patted.

"Yeah, ugh," Jesse agreed, carrying KC to the dresser where they kept clean clothes and diapers. As Jesse dug in the drawer for a fresh diaper, KC peeked over her shoulder at her sleeping mother.

Jesse pulled out a small shirt and pair of britches and added them to the diaper. She carried the clothes and baby to the table in the kitchen end of the log cabin. "Since we can't change you on the bed, this will have to do," she told KC as she laid her down on the wooden surface to remove the baby's soiled diaper and nightshirt.

"Momma seep," KC whispered.

Jesse did a double-take at her daughter's first attempt at the new word, then smiled. "That's right, Sunshine, and we want her to stay that way." She never stopped being amazed by her daughter's use of new words. It seemed that once KC started talking, she was adding words to her vocabulary on an almost daily basis.

As soon as Jesse finished dressing her, KC sat up and began inching toward the edge of the table. "Nope, you keep your little behind stuck to that table until I get rid of this." Jesse deposited the dirty garments in a wash basket, then she washed her hands in a pail of water kept warming by the fire for that express purpose. Bright eyes watched Jesse's every move.

"Cookie?"

"No, not this morning. Here." Jesse grabbed a handful of soft biscuits left over from the previous evening's supper and handed one to the hungry child. "These will have to hold you until Momma cooks breakfast. We'll get you some fresh milk as soon as I milk the cow." KC took a bite as Jesse lifted her off the table and sat the baby on the floor so she could go and get dressed. "Guess you're coming with me to do chores."

She dressed quickly, not being sure how long she could count on KC's good behavior. Scooping the child up, she grabbed her boots and Stetson and left her exhausted wife to sleep in the quiet cabin.

Jesse placed KC on an upturned box outside the door to the chicken coop. "You stay right here while I check for eggs."

"Otay." The child smiled at her mother, her feet beating against the side of the box.

"Good girl." Jesse passed through the small doorway in the end of the coop and began retrieving eggs from the nests. "Oh, no," she muttered when she stepped back outside and discovered that KC no longer waited on the top of the box. Loud squawking and clucking from inside the chicken coop alerted her to the location of her missing daughter.

KC watched Jesse disappear inside the chicken coop and waited for her mother to reappear. After several minutes, she tired of sitting on the box. Slipping down to the ground, she crawled a few feet before plopping down to sit. She watched as a hen poked its head out a small opening at the side of the coop then stepped out onto a board. KC watched the hen's jerky steps as it made its way down the board and eventually reached the ground, not more than an arm's length from where she sat. As KC reached for the bird, it took one look at the baby and scurried across the yard to safety.

The baby cocked her head to one side and studied the piece of wood. She dropped back on all fours and began crawling to the end of plank. Not hesitating for a moment, she headed up the board to the chicken coop where her mommy was. Reaching the top of the board, KC poked her head inside. It was dark in the shed, and she could hardly see. Determined to find her mommy, KC crawled inside. She found herself where the chickens nested and, undeterred by the clucking hens she encountered, crawled along the shelf.

"Mornin', darlin'," Jesse greeted as she entered the cabin, ducking when she walked through the doorway so as not to bump KC, who was riding on her shoulders. KC beamed at her mother from under the Stetson she wore.

"What have you two been up to?" Jennifer asked, kissing Jesse.

"Was supposed to be the morning chores," Jesse handed a basket of eggs to Jennifer, "'til the squirt here decided to help collect eggs." Jesse reached up and carefully lifted the baby over her head. "Sure got those hens riled up when she crawled through the hen house. Probably won't see another egg for days."

"So that's what woke me up." Jennifer chuckled as she set the basket on the table, then she took KC from Jesse and plucked a chicken feather from the baby's fine hair. "So you were chasing chickens."

"Owie." KC pointed to a red mark on her arm.

"Hens got a peck or two in before I could round her up." Jesse retrieved her Stetson and hung it on a peg next to Jennifer's. "Sorry we woke you, darlin'."

"That's okay." Jennifer examined KC's arms, kissing each peck mark. "Looks like you'll live." She playfully swatted KC on the butt and then sat the baby on the cabin floor. "Next time, leave the chickens be."

"Otay." KC crawled to her toy box, and toys started flying through the air.

Jesse shook her head as she surveyed the growing disarray. "Sure glad we only have one of her," she said with a chuckle, turning back to her wife. "Something smells good."

"Thanks." Jennifer pulled a pot from the fireplace they used for cooking. "Get washed up; breakfast is just about ready."

"Come here, Sunshine," Jesse called to KC. "Time to wash up for breakfast."

KC dropped her toys and crawled to Jesse. "Up?" She pulled herself upright on Jesse's pant leg.

Jesse reached down and lifted the baby up, then stood KC on the hearth next to the wash bucket and supported her while the baby dropped her arms over the side of the bucket and started splashing in the warm water.

"No, KC," Jennifer scolded. "Wash, don't play." KC's lower lip pushed out as she did as she was told.

"Best get that lip back in place, Sunshine," Jesse whispered into the baby's ear, "otherwise you might not get to eat whatever yummy breakfast Momma has made for us." The pout instantly disappeared, replaced by a smile. "Good girl." Jesse smiled at her daughter. Using the towel Jennifer handed her, Jesse dried KC's arms and hands before placing her in the highchair.

Jennifer filled two plates with eggs, bacon, biscuits, and potatoes and set them on the table. As they ate and talked, both mothers fed KC a bowl of oatmeal, as well as food from their plates.

"I'd like to go into town again today," Jennifer said as she wiped cereal off KC's chin.

"I figured you'd want to stay here today, especially since it'll be hot again. Storm last night didn't bring more than a few drops of rain." Jesse filled a glass with milk.

"Moo?" KC asked. She liked milk as much as Jesse did.

"Here you go." Jesse held the glass for KC to drink. "Small sips," she reminded the baby.

"I'd like to finish up at the schoolhouse. I want to send my class plans over to Bannack to have Leevie Temple review them," Jennifer told Jesse. "Bannack is lucky to have such an experienced schoolteacher. I know the time she has spent talking with me has really been helpful. All her suggestions in regards to teaching so many different grade levels at the same time have really proven quite useful. I'd like to know what she thinks about my lesson plans. Oh, and I haven't had much time to talk with Ed since we returned from Bozeman. I'd like to see how he's doing," Jennifer added. "I'm really worried about how he's adjusting to the news of his sister's death."

"That had to be a shock, all right." Jesse shook her head. "And at the hands of her own husband. I'll hitch up Boy as soon as we finish here."

"Where's Jennifer?" Mary Kensington asked when Jesse and KC entered the Silver Slipper.

"At the schoolhouse. She wanted to finish up before it got too hot," Jesse told her mother-in-law.

KC held her arm out for her grandmother to see. "Owie."

Bette Mae came through the kitchen door. "Lordy, I done know'd tha' was my little angel's voice."

"Used to be me you listened for," Jesse teased.

"That was afore ya brought this little one home." Bette Mae kissed KC, then pulled Jesse down and gave her a quick peck on the forehead. "Happy?"

"Owie," KC repeated, louder.

Bette Mae winked at Jesse. Obviously, the child thought her chicken pecks deserved more attention than they were getting. "Well, now. What have we here?" Bette Mae bent to examine the arm but saw nothing more than a couple of small, red marks, about the size of a pinhead. She looked at Jesse for an explanation. Jesse obliged with a recounting of KC's morning adventure in the chicken coop.

Mary laughed. "My, that must have been a sight."

"Think them chickens will survive?" Bette Mae wiped tears of laughter from her eyes.

"Don't know." Jesse chuckled. "Most probably will, but a couple are doubtful."

"*Owie!*"

"Oh, my." Mary took KC from Jesse and sat her in her lap as she settled on a settee on the library side of the Slipper's dining room. She made a big show of checking out each and every spot, nick, and blemish on the baby's arms, placing a kiss on top of each one. "Better?" she asked the youngster solemnly.

"Otay." KC smiled at her grandmother. "Cookie?"

Dropping down next to Mary, Jesse groaned at her daughter's instant change of mood. "How did you ever raise so many, Mary? This one is more than I can keep up with."

"You're doing just fine," Mary assured her. "In fact, I think you and Jennifer are doing a fine job of raising KC. You seem to be natural mothers."

"Lordy, Jesse," Bette Mae winked at Mary, "you's doin' such a good job, I'm thinkin' ya should have two or three more." The pillow thrown at her bounced harmlessly off the door as Bette Mae disappeared into the safety of the kitchen, her squeals of laughter echoing back into the dining room.

"Don't even suggest that to Jennifer," Jesse warned Mary. "She'd have a dozen or more, if it was possible."

Turning serious, Mary asked, "You didn't want children, Jesse?"

"Never gave it much thought." KC crawled into her lap and curled up to take a nap. "Then we found KC and, well, she just kinda grew on me." Jesse absently caressed the sleepy baby.

"It's clear to see that the child loves you very much," Mary said softly. "Would you consider having more?"

Jesse thought a few moments as she watched the baby. "I don't know," she answered honestly. "But," she smiled, "if Jennifer wanted to, I couldn't say no."

"Jennifer is lucky to have you, Jesse."

"Nah." Jesse looked up from her sleeping daughter. "I'm the lucky one." She grinned. "Now if you'll excuse us, I'll go put KC down in the office."

"Of course." *I wonder what it would feel like to be loved as much as those two love each other. Heaven knows, such love is precious, and so rare.* She knew she didn't have it with her husband. She pondered exactly what she did feel for him. She had to admit that it wasn't much, not at the moment. As Jesse rose, careful not to wake KC, Mary asked, "Will you be stopping by here before you return to the ranch this evening. It seems like I've had so little time with Jennifer."

Jesse considered. She and Jennifer had fully expected Mary to live at the ranch with them, but she had chosen to stay in town. By doing so, she had limited the time Jennifer could spend with her. Knowing that Jennifer was just as anxious to find time to spend with her mother, Jesse said, "Why don't we plan to eat here tonight."

"That would be nice." Mary smiled. "Thank you."

Jesse nodded, then walked to her office, KC sleeping contentedly in her arms.

Easily balancing KC in one arm, Jesse helped Jennifer across Sweetwater's only street. That morning, Jennifer had asked that Jesse leave the buckboard at the Slipper when she and KC came to the schoolhouse. She wanted to walk to the general store and then back to the Slipper. Since the town was so small, Jesse saw no harm in letting Jennifer test her leg.

Jennifer stepped up onto the boardwalk in front of the general store, Jesse keeping close watch in case Jennifer's leg gave her problems. Jennifer smiled as Ed came out of the store's open front door, and she greeted the storekeeper warmly. "Afternoon, Ed, it's so good to see you."

"Likewise, Jennifer, how are you?" He quickly covered the few steps separating them and wrapped Jennifer up in a bear hug.

"I'm well," Jennifer said when Ed finally released her. "A little better every day, thank you."

"And little KC...my, don't you look just like your momma."

"That she does," Jesse agreed. It was remarkable, the similarities between Jennifer and her adopted daughter; both had ginger brown hair and bright sapphire blue eyes. Jesse even thought that KC had Jennifer's smile.

"Come on inside; it's cooler there. Not much, but a bit." Ed guided the women into the store. "Here you go." He lifted a chair off the peg that held it high on the wall.

"Thanks, Ed." Jennifer slumped gratefully onto the seat. She hadn't walked far, but still it felt good to get off her leg.

Jesse sat KC on the floor at Jennifer's feet. "You stay put, Sunshine." She handed KC her toy horse, then wrangled a barrel of dried beans over next to Jennifer's chair and sat down on it.

"You know, Jesse," Ed tilted an empty wooden crate onto its side and joined the women, "it'll be hell on my back to move that barrel back."

"I know." Jesse grinned. Ed was a big man; his solid muscular body toned from years of loading and unloading freight wagons, yet Jesse had always found pleasure in matching her strength against his. "I'll help you put it back," she teased.

"Good thing I like Jennifer so much," Ed responded. "Otherwise, I just might have to do something about what you call a sense of humor."

"You used that as a threat even before Jennifer came to Sweetwater," she said with a laugh.

Ed laughed along with her. "That I did."

"Be good." Jennifer slapped Jesse on the leg.

"Nothin' but, darlin'." Jesse bent over and kissed Jennifer's brow.

"So," Jennifer said as she good-naturedly pushed Jesse away, "how are you doing, Ed?"

"I'm fine," he answered, realizing that Jennifer was referring to his sister's death. "I just wish she had picked better for a husband. Shame she didn't get more out of life."

Sensing that their friend wanted to talk about it, the women remained silent.

"You would have liked Lizzie, so full of life, she was," Ed continued. "When we were kids, I don't think I ever saw her sad. But after she married that Cassidy fella, her whole life was sad." He lost himself in memories for a moment, then recollected, "Except for those few weeks they spent in Fort Benton. Funny, now that I think about it, Lizzie always smiled when she talked about that time. Don't rightly know why, considerin' that good fer nothin' spent all of his time at the gambling tables. Lost most of their money there; barely had enough left to pay to get them to Sweetwater."

Jennifer looked at Jesse, and a silent acknowledgment passed between them. It was in Fort Benton that Bette Mae had met and fallen in love with Lizzie, a love that Bette Mae had never confessed to anyone except Jesse. Now it appeared that Bette Mae might not have been alone in the feelings she'd had for the other woman.

"But she's happy now." Ed reached over and patted Jennifer's good leg. "I just know it."

Jennifer took the big hand into her own and held it. "I know it, too."

"You okay here?" Jesse asked. "I mean, Cassidy didn't leave any debts owing on the store, did he?" With Lizzie's death and her husband hanged, Ed now owned the store that he had operated for his brother-in-law — who had been busy chasing after the gold discoveries in the territory.

Ed shyly withdrew his hand. Jennifer had become the daughter he'd never had, but he was still self-conscious about some of the trappings of their deepening bond. "Store's done pretty well in the last couple of years since Cassidy left me in charge, well enough to clear the debts he had with the freight companies and put some money away in a Bozeman bank." Ed shook his head. "Always felt bad about keeping that a secret from Lizzie, but I was afraid Cassidy'd just gamble it away if he knew about it."

"You did the right thing," Jennifer assured him. "Lizzie would have agreed with you keeping it a secret."

"Guess now that she'll not be needin' it, maybe I can use it now to expand the store like I've been wantin' to." Ed looked at the crowded shelves and aisles around them. Now that he was the proprietor, he could make any necessary changes.

"That's a great idea!" Jennifer exclaimed. "What do you have planned?"

"Oh," Ed scratched his head, "thought I'd build on out back. Make a dock for the freight wagons to unload so's they don't have to pile the load out front and block the boardwalk. I could put a small room upstairs for sleepin' and enlarge the back room for holdin' the freight that's waitin' to be picked up by the ranches. Would give me room to move some of this stuff." The sweep of his hand around the room indicated the numerous crates and boxes stacked everywhere.

Jesse nodded. "Sounds like a good idea. Let me know if I can help. It's sure been a long time since anything new was built in town."

"Schoolhouse was the last," Ed supplied.

"And a lovely schoolhouse it is." Jennifer smiled. "I think it would be nice for Sweetwater to start growing."

"Don't know, darlin'," Jesse drawled. "I kinda like Sweetwater just the way it is."

"Can't say that I'd be unhappy to see a few more people around," Ed said. "And it would mean more business for the Slipper, Jesse."

"I don't know," Jesse said with a shake of her head. "Progress isn't always a good thing."

"Jesse," Jennifer injected, "if the Slipper was making more money, we could afford to do more out at the ranch, like buy that breeding bull you want." Jennifer still felt a little guilty that the money Jesse had been saving for the bull had been used to pay the doctor and other expenses during their stay in Bozeman.

Jesse was far from convinced. "Bad things happen when stuff starts to grow," she observed. A muted thud was heard at the rear of the store, and three heads immediately turned toward the sound. "What was that?" Jesse asked.

Ed frowned. "Damn. I was filling one of the bins with flour when I saw you walking across the street. Forgot I left the bag sitting atop it. Dang thing probably fell over."

"I best go see what kind of mess it made," Jesse offered as she stood. "Don't want KC wandering into it."

"Speaking of KC..." Jennifer looked around for the missing baby. "KC, where are you?" Ed helped Jennifer up while Jesse went to search for their daughter.

"KC?" Jesse called. "Where are you, Sunshine?"

The three adults converged on the sound of small hands smacking together and KC jabbering happily. "Damn." Ed stood, hands on his hips, KC smiling up at him.

Jesse frowned. "Like I said, bad things happen when stuff starts to grow."

The baby was covered from head to toe in flour, sitting atop a pile of the feathery light powder. Next to her, a keg of pickles knocked over by the falling flour bag and broken open lay on its side, its contents strewn about and the juice leaking down into cracks in the floor. KC was mixing pickle juice with the flour, then patting the mixture into small, flattened, cookie-shaped mounds she stacked around her. She picked up one of the gooey concoctions and offered it to Jesse. "Cookie?"

"Guess you'll be doin' more than puttin' that bean barrel back," Ed said dryly. He slapped Jesse on the back before doubling over in laughter.

An hour later, a very perturbed Jesse sputtered as she poured water over her head to rinse the soap from her hair. "No more cookin' lessons with Bette Mae!"

"Yes, dear," Jennifer said, trying not to laugh.

After cleaning up KC's impromptu bakery and by the time they got the baby back to the Slipper, Jesse was covered in the same white goop as her daughter. Bette Mae had taken one look at the pair and started laughing so hard she had been unable to do anything but point to the bathing room. Both Jesse and KC were stripped and put into the tub to be scrubbed clean. KC clapped her hands as though the whole affair was a funny game. Jesse did not.

Jennifer tried again to pacify her wife. "Oh, sweetheart, she was only playing." Jesse just glared at her.

KC was sitting in Jesse's lap playing with a washrag. She smiled up at her mommy with twinkling eyes but Jesse was determined to stay upset.

Turning in her mother's lap and using the side of the tub for handholds, KC pulled herself upright until she stood eyeball to eyeball with Jesse. "Mommy." KC wrapped her arms around her mommy's neck and kissed Jesse on the cheek. "Wuv."

Jesse's anger melted. She hugged the baby close. "I love you too, Sunshine." She handed the baby to Jennifer. "Let Mommy get you dressed."

As Jennifer took the baby, she grasped Jesse's hand and held it. "I love you, too."

Jesse smiled. "Wonder if Bette Mae found me any clothes." Jesse had kept clothes in her office back in the days when it wasn't unusual for her to spend a night or two in town. Since Jennifer had moved to the ranch, Jesse hadn't had the need and had removed all her personal belongings from the Slipper. A knock on the bathing room door brought her answer.

"Looky there," Bette Mae cried out cheerfully as she entered. "I do believe ya look a sight better. Ya almost scared me to death, walkin' in white as a ghost before. I swear I thought it was time ta meet my Maker, I did." Bette Mae chuckled. "Why, when I tole Billie and Ruthie wha' you done walked in lookin' like, I thought poor Ruthie would..."

Jesse didn't hear the rest, as she slipped under the surface of the bath water.

Jesse joined Jennifer and her mother at a table in the Slipper's dining room. She wore the clothes that Bette Mae had managed to find — a pair of denim jeans a size too big and a well-worn denim shirt a size too small. At least she had been able to put her own boots back on.

"Evening, Jesse. Heard you had quite the afternoon," Mary said as Ruthie set plates of food on the table.

"Bet the whole valley has heard by now," Jesse grumbled as she scooped up a fork full of the whipped potatoes.

"Oh, I doubt everyone knows." Jennifer handed a bite of cooked carrot to KC, who hungrily shoved it into her mouth. "I'm sure only the people in town have heard. It'll take a few days to reach all of the ranches."

"Not to mention the mining camps," Bette Mae added as she set a pitcher of cold milk on their table before hurrying back to the kitchen.

"Funny." Jesse jammed her elbow on the table and plopped her chin into her cupped hand. "It'll probably be weeks before anything happens to give folks something else to talk about," she said. She looked at KC, happily munching on a biscuit covered with a small amount of butter and honey. It wasn't long before the baby had butter and honey smeared all over her face with biscuit crumbs sticking to the mess. Jesse brightened. "Then again, with you and KC around, you just never know what might happen."

"Bad, Jesse."

"Now, darlin'," Jesse sat up straight, "you have to admit since you hit town, it has been plenty excitin' around here."

"Ain't tha' the truth," Bette Mae chirped in as she walked by carrying a pot of coffee.

"That's not fair," Jennifer protested.

"It's okay, darlin'. I wouldn't have it any other way."

"Good thing."

Mary had watched the playful exchange in silence, but now observed, "A lot *has* happened to you, Jennifer."

"Yes, Mother, it has," Jennifer said suspiciously.

"And yet, you are happy, aren't you?"

"I am very happy." Jennifer smiled at Jesse who was intent on their conversation.

"I'm happy for you." Mary reached over and took Jennifer's hand into her own. "I truly am."

"Thank you, Mother."

"I just hope things will be a little less exciting in the future," Mary added wryly.

Jesse raised a glass of milk and nodded. "Hear, hear."

"Mooooooooooo." KC loudly let her feelings be known.

The women finished their meal and moved from the dining room to Jesse's office, where they could enjoy a quiet conversation away from the Slipper's other diners. Jesse and Jennifer sat on the couch, Jesse's arm draped over Jennifer's shoulders. Mary was in the armchair with KC sleeping in her lap.

In the peaceful setting, Jennifer decided to broach an old topic. "Mother, why won't you come live at the ranch? We'd have more time together." It had hurt her when her mother had decided to stay in town, although it was true that the one-room log cabin that served as the ranch house wasn't much bigger than the office in which they currently sat.

"It wouldn't be right, all of us living in that small cabin."

"I don't understand—"

Mary's face reddened. "You and Jesse would have no privacy, dear." Jennifer looked at her quizzically.

"I think she means that she'd be uncomfortable with us..." Jesse began. "Well, you know..."

Jennifer looked from Jesse to her mother and back, and suddenly she understood. "Oh." She blushed. "I guess that would be a problem."

The women fell silent, thankful that no one had had to actually speak the words.

"You know," Jesse said, thinking out loud, "we've got that old storage shed that isn't used for anythin'. Fact is, I think the man that owned the ranch used it for livin' in before he built the ranch house. We could clean it up and make it livable. It would give you your own place. That is, if you'd like."

"That's a wonderful idea, Jesse," Jennifer said, excited at the prospect of having her mother closer. "It wouldn't take much to fix it up. A good sweeping out, some curtains and such."

"Needs a new roof," Jesse added.

Mary wavered. "I don't know. Seems like a lot of extra work for you."

"Nah," Jesse told her. "Couple of days and it'll be all shiny and new. It's just the one room, though, not room for much more than a bed and table. 'Course we'd expect you to take your meals with us."

"Please, Mother. I really would like to have you at the ranch. So would KC."

"What about you, Jesse?" Mary asked.

Jesse took a moment to consider how she felt about it. She enjoyed having the ranch as a place for just her family, and it would be different having someone else living there, but she had asked her folks to come live with them and Jennifer had voiced no objections. *Mary is family now, isn't she?* She looked at Jennifer, who was watching her expectantly. "The ranch is for my family, and you're family. Of course I'd like you to come and stay. For as long as you'd like," she added as Jennifer released a sigh of relief.

"Thank you, Jesse. But I'll accept only if you let me help fix it up."

"Agreed," Jennifer said before anyone could change their mind. "Sweetheart, why don't we stay upstairs tonight, then Mother can ride out with us to the ranch tomorrow. We can fix up a cot for her in the house until her cabin is ready."

Jesse nodded. "I'll ask Bette Mae which room we can use tonight. Be right back." She rose from the couch.

"Better bring some milk for KC, she'll be hungry before too long," Jennifer called after Jesse as she left the office.

"I don't have to stay at the ranch, dear," Mary said after Jesse had left the room. "I can stay here until the cabin is ready."

"No, Mother. It will only take a few days to get the cabin ready, and I'm tired of not seeing you except for a few minutes at a time."

"If you're sure."

"I am. Before we leave town tomorrow, we'll go by Ed's and get everything we need to fix the place up proper for you.

"Momma?" KC whimpered as she woke.

"I better go find, Jesse." Jennifer stood. "This one will be crying for her mommy and her moo before long." She took the half-asleep baby from her mother. "We'll see you in the morning."

"I should get to bed as well. Sounds like the next couple of days will be quite busy." Mary stood and kissed Jennifer's cheek. As she walked with Jennifer to the office door, she added, "Say goodnight to Jesse for me."

"I will. Goodnight, Mother."

Jesse loaded Mary's few belongings into the back of the buckboard while her mother-in-law was still inside saying her good-byes to Bette Mae and the other women who worked at the Silver Slipper.

Jennifer, holding KC, stood on the porch enjoying what coolness there was in the morning shadows. There had been another rainless thunder bumper the night before and the day was well on its way to being another scorcher.

A horse and rider passed on the road, and Jennifer watched as the rider dismounted in front of the general store. The man wore buckskin pants and vest without any shirt, his dark skin exposed to the sun's harsh rays. Long black hair, decorated with eagle feathers and beads, hung in two braids down his back. Instead of boots, his feet were wrapped in a covering that looked more like a pair of slippers than shoes. "Sweetheart," Jennifer called softly to Jesse, "isn't that an Indian?" She had read many stories about the native people, but this was the first time she had actually seen one.

Jesse turned to look down the street to where the man was pulling a bundle of furs off the back of his horse. "Yep."

Ed came out of the store, walked to the edge of the boardwalk, and began making hand gestures at the man. The Indian responded with gestures of his own. After a few minutes, Ed accepted the bundle of furs, taking them inside his store. He reappeared with some smaller sacks and what appeared to be a sack of flour, and he handed them to the man. The Indian tied the sacks together, then threw them over the neck of his horse. Before remounting, he stepped to the edge of the boardwalk and clasped arms with the storekeeper. Moments later, he was riding back toward the Slipper.

As he rode past the boarding house, the rider glanced in Jesse's direction. Jennifer was surprised to see her wife nod in acknowledgement before he disappeared around the side of the Slipper and out of town.

"Oh my, is it safe?" Mary gasped, having caught a glimpse of the passing native.

"Yep." Jesse climbed the porch steps to help Jennifer descend. "He's a friend."

Jennifer caught the undertone in her voice and looked at Jesse quizzically. "But?"

"We'll talk later," Jesse told her. "Come on, let's get to Ed's and get those purchases taken care of. I want to get back to the ranch before noon; the horses need tending to." She took Jennifer's arm and guided her to the steps.

Confident that Jesse would tell her about the man at a later time, Jennifer let the matter drop. "Come on, Mother," she called back to Mary who was discussing the rider with Bette Mae.

"Ya go on, now," Bette Mae assured the woman. "Jesse knows what she's doin'. She'll take right good care of ya. There's nothin' ta be concerned over."

Unconvinced, Mary reluctantly joined Jesse and Jennifer at the buckboard.

As they entered the store, Ed immediately directed the women to the front end of the long counter where he normally conducted business. A space approximately three feet square had been fenced off with a length of chicken wire; every few inches, the wire was tacked to the wood floor. Inside the enclosure, a blanket had been spread out and a few toys were scattered atop the blanket.

"And just what is that supposed to be?" Jesse asked.

"That," Ed said proudly, "is a holding pen for that there young 'un of yours."

Jesse considered the unlikely prospect of the flimsy wire holding KC for very long, "Let's give it a try." She dropped KC inside the wire fence and set her down on the blanket.

KC looked suspiciously at her surroundings. "Up," she demanded.

"No, sweetie," Jennifer told the baby. "You stay there and be good while Momma shops." KC pouted, her lip jutting out.

Jesse reached down and ruffled KC's silky hair. "We won't be long, Sunshine, then we'll go home and feed Dusty and Blaze."

"Otay." KC picked up one of the nearby toys and chewed on it.

With the baby settled and, hopefully, contained, Jennifer looked around the store, deciding on the best approach for finding the items on the list she had written out during breakfast. With a plan of action decided on, she set off.

Ed returned to his stool behind the counter and watched as Jennifer went through the store's inventory with the precision of a military quartermaster. To his amusement, every time she filled Jesse's arms with items, she would send the rancher back to the counter so he could make a record of them in his ledger. Once they were recorded, Jesse would rejoin Jennifer, and she would resume her shopping. Mary chose to sit quietly next to KC's holding pen and watch her daughter foraging.

"Anythin' else, darlin'?" Jesse asked as she returned from placing the last of the purchases into the back of the buckboard and making sure the load was secure.

"Let's see." Jennifer reviewed her list. "No," she said crumpling the paper and tossing it into a small basket Ed kept behind the counter for rubbish. "That's all of it. Guess you can go ahead and pay."

"Thanks." Jesse smirked. "Glad I'm good for something."

"Me, too." Jennifer gave Jesse a pat on the rear end, her hand lingering for a moment.

"Ooo," Jesse purred. "Someone woke up in a happy mood this morning."

"Sweetheart, I always wake up happy when I wake up next to you."

"If you two lovebirds are done," Ed chuckled, "I do have other customers waitin'."

Jesse looked around the store, finding it empty except for her family. "Where? In Bozeman?"

"Don't be smart," Ed teased. "With what you got today, plus," he paused to clear his throat and then loudly announced, "one bag of flour and one gallon of pickles..."

Jesse glared. "Just add it to the bill."

Ed grinned at Mary. "Sure you're ready to be around this grouchy one all day?"

Jesse scowled at Ed, but there was a twinkle in her eyes. "Keep your opinions to yourself."

He made a notation in his ledger, then leaned across the counter and whispered loudly enough for everyone to hear, "Let's just see how long it is before you're making excuses to come to town to get away from all the womenfolk you have out at the ranch now."

Jesse leaned on the counter and whispered just as loudly, "I'm *one* of those womenfolk."

"Yeah," Ed whispered back, "but you don't count."

"You're probably right about that." Jesse laughed and slapped him on the shoulder. "Come on, ladies." She bowed to Jennifer and Mary and gestured toward the door.

"Oh my, how gallant," Mary gushed.

"My knight in shining armor," Jennifer said as she passed Jesse on her way out. "Don't forget the baby."

"I don't know, Ed," Jesse said, collecting KC from the holding pen. "I think I may be in way over my head."

"You're outnumbered, that's for sure." Ed chuckled. "But I think you'll do just fine, Jesse. You know where to find me if you need a break."

"Thanks. I think."

"Mommy?" KC asked as Jesse walked to the door.

"Yes, Sunshine." KC pointed at the toys she had left behind. "Don't you think you have enough of those at home?" Jesse asked.

"No."

"Yep, Jesse." Ed walked over and handed KC a small, brightly painted bird. "You are definitely outnumbered."

"Don't suppose this is on the house?" Jesse asked.

KC grabbed the bird, imitating the sounds she heard every morning at home. "Cheep, cheep."

Ed sniggered and without another word, Jesse went outside to join Jennifer and Mary.

"Ready, darlin'?" Jesse asked, settling on the seat next to Jennifer.

"Yes, sweetheart." Jennifer slipped her arm around Jesse's. "Let's go home."

Jesse released the brake and with a slap of the reins, Boy started down the street in the direction of the Silver Slipper and the ranch beyond.

Mayor Miles Perkins strode into the general store as if he were the owner. "Ed, I need to place an order," he informed the storekeeper who was engaged with another customer.

"Be with you in a minute, Miles." Ed didn't like the arrogant mayor who thought his business should take priority over anything and anyone else, an attitude that some in Sweetwater said had gotten more forceful in the last few months. But he was a good customer and paid his bills on time. "That should take care of your order, Ruthie. Tell Bette Mae that I'll bring it over as soon as I'm done unpacking this morning's freight delivery."

"Thank you, Mr. Granger."

"Are you done now?" Mayor Perkins asked her impatiently, perturbed at having to wait.

"I'll thank you not to use that tone with Miss Ruth," Billie said as he stepped in from the boardwalk. He had seen Ruthie walk past the jail on her way to the general store and had planned to wait for her outside, but hearing Mayor Perkins' tone he decided to go inside and speak up for the shy girl he was courting.

"I have important business," Mayor Perkins blustered.

"You can wait your turn like everyone else," Ed told the mayor. "Besides, what can be so important? Your boys eat through the pantry again?" It was well known that the mayor's sons could put away more food than half the ranch hands in the valley. It was a wonder the man could afford the cost of feeding them.

"No," Perkins replied indignantly. "I have received a charter from the territorial governor to establish a bank in Sweetwater. I need to place an order for building materials."

"A bank?" It wasn't easy to be granted a bank charter, especially for a small town like Sweetwater. Billie moved over to stand next to Ruthie by the counter. "How'd you get a charter for a bank?"

"Doesn't matter." The mayor slapped a piece of paper on the counter. "This is a list of the materials that I will need. My architect drew it up, so follow it exactly when you send in the order," the mayor stated pompously.

"Ark-e-tek, huh," Ed repeated as he picked up the sheet. "Let's see...lumber shouldn't be a problem, but you'll probably have to wait a few weeks since I sent in a large order a few days ago. Bricks and sandstone blocks?" He read the next items. "Goin' ta be a mighty fancy building, Miles. You sure Sweetwater needs somethin' like that?"

"We need a bank," Perkins stated flatly.

"Never said we didn't." Ed was just as aware as the mayor that it was a nuisance to have to travel to Bozeman to the closest bank, especially during the winter months. "Just wonder if we need such a fancy one."

Ignoring the storekeeper's implied criticism, Mayor Perkins asked, "Can you get those supplies or not?"

"Yep." Ed pulled a form from under the counter. "Will take several weeks for the bricks. Might be several months on the sandstone."

"I need it sooner than that," Perkins insisted.

"I can put a rush on it," Ed offered, "but it probably won't make much difference. Don't even know if my suppliers in Bozeman can handle an order this big. And they're goin' ta want a deposit."

"Send the order, Ed. Let me know if they can handle it. If they can't, I'll send to Denver. Already had to order the safe through there; it's coming from a company in New York City. Best safe makers in the country," Perkins boasted. "If they need a deposit, I'll take care of it." He turned and marched out of the store.

"Damn." Billie blew out a breath. "Wonder how he got the governor to give him a charter?"

"I wonder where he's getting the money." Ed started transferring the information on the mayor's paper to the order form. "This stuff ain't cheap."

"Good question." The sheriff glanced at the list of materials. "Maybe I should do a little checking into our mayor's activities. Seems to me, I heard he took a trip to Denver not too long ago."

"Yep. While we was in Bozeman with Jesse and Jennifer."

"I'll stop and see if Thaddeus knows anything." Turning to the young woman who was standing quietly beside him, Billie said, "Can I walk you back to the Slipper, Ruth?"

She smiled shyly. "I'd like that."

"Shall we?" Billie held out his arm, and Ruth timidly took it.

As the couple left the store, Ed smiled to himself. "Almost as cute as Jesse and Jennifer."

After walking Ruth back to the Slipper, the sheriff stopped at the *Gazette*, the valley's only newspaper, and spoke with the owner and editor.

"I can't help you, Billie," Thaddeus said, shaking his head. "I heard Miles had gone to Denver, but if he told anyone why, I haven't heard about it. Why are you asking?"

"He was in Ed's earlier, ordering building materials for a bank. Seems he got a charter from the territorial governor."

Thaddeus was surprised at the news. "For here in Sweetwater?"

"Yep. Wonderin' how he was able to do that, is all."

"You think his trip to Denver has something to do with it?"

"Could be." Billie took off his hat and scratched his head. "Don't see that he would have that kind of influence on his own, not to mention the money it would take."

"Been rumors of some Eastern financiers taking an interest in the valley. Seems one or two of the mines are starting to show some good color. Miles would be the man they'd talk to if they were thinking of doing anything around here."

"Guess it makes sense that the mayor would be the one they'd talk to first."

"I've been planning to take a ride out to some of the larger mining camps in a day or so to see if there's anything happening that would interest the *Gazette*. Let me do some checking, Billie. If anyone knows anything, I'm sure I'll hear about it."

CHAPTER THIRTEEN

Jennifer rounded the corner of the small outbuilding that was soon to become the living quarters for her mother. Perched on a ladder against the back wall, Jesse was nailing down the last row of shingles that would complete the roof repair.

"Sweetheart." Jennifer held her hand up to shield her eyes against the bright sun as she looked up. "Mother has made tea. And there's cold well water. Why don't you come in and rest for a while? You've been at it since breakfast."

"I only have about a dozen shingles left, and I'd sure like to get it done and get in out of this darn heat." Her hammer pounded rhythmically, punctuating her words. "Give me a few more minutes and I'll be finished," she said without stopping.

"All right." Jennifer gave Jesse's leg an affectionate pat before walking back around to the front of the small building.

"Isn't she coming?" Mary asked when Jennifer entered the almost completed home.

"She'll be here in a minute. She wants to finish." Jennifer sat on the edge of the bed.

KC, who had been playing on the floor with her toy horse, quickly crawled to Jennifer and pulled herself upright on her momma's leg. "Up." Jennifer lifted the baby into her lap.

"Can't say I'll miss the noise." Mary handed Jennifer a cup of tea.

"Mommy." KC pointed to the roof, then held her hands over her ears.

"Yes, sweetie, Mommy is making a lot of noise, but she's almost done." As she listened to the sound of Jesse's hammering, Jennifer glanced around her mother's new living quarters.

A single room of no more than ten by twelve feet, there was only one entry, a door set slightly off center in the front wall. Each of the walls held a window, which made the interior surprising bright, especially after the window glass had received a good scrubbing. Standing in the corner was a wood stove that would be used for both heating and cooking. Several rugs covered the rough plank floor, placed in an effort to help control dust and make the room more comfortable.

The day before, after Jesse had emptied the cabin of its meager furnishings, Jennifer and Mary had set to work cleaning the years of cobwebs and dirt. As they had worked on fixing up the inside, Jesse worked on the outside of the cabin, re-hanging the door and replacing missing chinking between the logs to keep out the nastier weather. She repaired a broken window and constructed a new frame for it, the old one having rotted through. And the small porch had needed some attention.

That morning while Jesse worked to repair the leaky roof, Jennifer and her mother had decorated the interior. New curtains hung in the windows. The bedsprings had been thoroughly cleaned and now held a new mattress and bed coverings. The bed occupied one end of the room, and a table and chair sat in the front corner at the other end, the arrangement offering anyone sitting there a view out two windows. A few dishes and some food staples had been neatly stacked on a shelf near the stove. Although Mary would typically take her meals with them, Jennifer wanted her to have the items for any time she might want to stay in her own cabin.

As she took note of the sparse furnishings, Jennifer wondered if her mother, who had been surrounded by much more luxury back East, would be happy in the small building.

"Mother?"

Mary was sitting at the table, enjoying the view of the ranch yard and forest beyond. "Yes, dear."

"Are you going to be happy here? I mean, this isn't exactly how you're used to living."

Mary turned and looked at her daughter. KC had crawled off Jennifer's lap and was happily rolling around on the soft bed, giggling as she entertained herself. Mary rose from the chair and crossed the room to sit next to her apparently apprehensive daughter. She took Jennifer's hands into her own and rubbed them lovingly. "I'll be very happy, dear."

"Are you sure?"

"Yes, I'm very sure. I can sit and listen to birds singing in the trees instead of freight wagons rumbling under my window." Mary referred to the daily activity on the stage road through Sweetwater. "This room may not be as fancy as my sitting room back home, but it provides me an opportunity I don't have there. I'm able to spend time with you and Jesse and your beautiful baby. I couldn't ask for anything better."

"But—"

"I'm happy, Jennifer," Mary interrupted. "I really am. This is the first time, in a very long time, that I'm doing exactly what I want to do."

"I'm glad." Jennifer leaned over and kissed her mother's cheek. "I'm really glad you're here."

"Where's that water you mentioned?" Jesse asked, entering the cabin. She pulled a kerchief from her back pocket, lifted her hat, and wiped the sweat from her brow and neck.

"Mommy!" KC cried out at the sight of Jesse. She started crawling toward the edge of the bed.

"Whoa there, Sunshine." Jesse snatched the baby off the bed before she could fall over the side. "That's a mite far for you to bounce."

"Finished?" Mary asked as she went to the table to pour a glass of water for Jesse.

"Yep." Jesse gratefully accepted the cold drink and took a long swallow. "Better than new, if I do say so myself."

KC grimaced at her mother, her tiny hands covering her ears. "Owie."

"Sorry, Sunshine." Jesse kissed the tip of the baby's nose. "But we couldn't let your grandma be rained on, now could we?"

KC reached for Jesse's glass.

Jesse allowed KC a drink. "Mo?" KC asked.

"Nope." Jesse emptied the glass and then placed it back on the table. "Sure looks nice in here," she said. "You wouldn't know it was the same room we had to kick our way into yesterday."

Jesse had carried out box after box of bits and pieces before they could start cleaning and converting the small storage building. Most of the discards were piled in the yard, waiting to be burned. They discovered that what hadn't been eaten by bugs and mice was too rotten or too rusty to be of any use.

"It was a lot of work, but it does look nice, doesn't it?" Jennifer said with pride.

"Yep." Jesse shifted KC in her arms, which were sore after all the heavy work she had done. She was glad the roof repair was finally finished and was looking forward to a nice, long soak in the tub after dinner. But there were still a few chores to finish before she could call it a day. "I think I'll leave you ladies and go check on the horses. You want to come, Sunshine? I can use your help milkin' that cow you like so much."

Jennifer was concerned about Jesse working any longer in the hot afternoon. "Will you be long, sweetheart?"

"Nope. There's another storm brewin' over the mountains. Looks like this one could have some rain in it. I'll just make sure the horses are bedded down and everythin' is put away so it won't get wet if we do get rain." KC reached for Jesse's Stetson as they disappeared out the door.

Jennifer looked out of the window that faced west. Dark clouds were building over the mountains. "Does look like a nasty one," she said. "I'd better get back to the house and start supper."

After the evening meal, the three women sat around the table, talking and watching the storm outside. KC sat in Jesse's lap, alternating between playing peek-a-boo with her grandmother and covering her ears whenever thunder boomed. Outside, a bolt of lightning flashed, followed a few moments later by a long clap of thunder rumbling across the dark sky. A gust of wind hit the side of the ranch house, shaking the window glass.

Jennifer flinched as another lightning strike illuminated the yard. "It looks pretty bad out there."

"Goin' to get worse before it gets better." Jesse wasn't very happy that she had had to postpone her bath, but she knew she might have to go out during the storm if something happened. "Good thing I put the horses in the barn tonight." It was her practice to let the horses stay out in the open corral on hot nights.

"Think we'll get much rain?" Jennifer asked, just as the heavens opened and rain sluiced down. The drops were so big that they sounded like stones being hurled at the windows. "Guess that answers my question."

KC stopped her game and looked at the window. She had never seen rain before. Using Jesse's shirt, the baby pulled herself up to get closer to the window and pressed her nose against the glass. Another bolt of lightning zigged through the sky, the bright flash startling KC, who whimpered and fell back into Jesse's lap.

"Hey, I think you'd better stay away from that window, Sunshine," Jesse said to comfort the baby. "Don't want your pretty hair to get frizzled."

Jennifer reached over and gently rubbed KC's back. "Sweetie, are you okay?"

"Owie."

"I know." Jennifer looked at Jesse. "Think we can get her to go to sleep?"

Jesse looked outside as another bolt of lightning lit up the sky, the strikes moving closer to their side of the valley.

"Maybe I should get back to my cabin before it gets any worse," Mary said.

"No." Jesse handed the baby to Jennifer. "I'll get her some milk. Try rockin' her," she suggested, then turned back to Mary. "This will be over in another hour. It's best you stay put until then."

Not really wanting to go out into the storm, Mary breathed a sigh of relief. "All right."

Jennifer carried the distressed baby to the rocking chair Jesse had made. As she rocked, she hummed softly. KC quieted, but her eyes remained on the window and the storm.

"You really think this will be over soon?" Another burst of lightning lit up the yard, and Mary could see the closest trees were nearly doubled over by the wind.

"Yep." Jesse seemed unconcerned about the storm as she filled a baby bottle with milk. "It'll blow like crazy, rain like there ain't goin' ta be a tomorrow, then it'll just stop. Clouds will move on east and the stars will come out. Tomorrow you'll wonder if you didn't dream the whole thing."

Mary instinctively pulled away from the window as drops from another cloudburst beat against the glass. "I doubt that."

"At least, it should be cooler tomorrow," Jennifer said.

"Don't count on it, darlin'." Jesse handed her the bottle. "Soon as that sun peeks over those mountains, it'll be just as hot as today, maybe hotter."

"Really?" Mary's face showed her surprise. "All this rain won't have any effect on the heat."

"Nope." Jesse shook her head. "Not only won't it have any effect, but you'll be raising dust clouds when you walk across the yard."

"Come on, Jesse," Jennifer protested. "All that water must have some effect."

"Wait and see," Jesse told the doubting women as she again sat at the table with Mary. "You'd think this valley was at the bottom of a lake the way water runs off it. All I can say is it's a good thing we have as many rivers in the valley as we do. Otherwise, the land wouldn't be much good for growing anything but rocks."

"Guess we'll see," Jennifer murmured as she took another look at the storm raging outside.

A little over an hour later, Jennifer was putting KC to bed as Jesse walked Mary back to her cabin. Jesse's repairs on the roof had held, and the cabin appeared to be in good order. She bade Mary goodnight.

"Don't forget, you have any trouble, pull on that string. Any trouble at all, even if you just want someone to talk to." Jennifer was concerned about her mother being alone in the cabin, so the day before, Jesse had strung a cord from Mary's cabin to the ranch house. A cowbell tied to its further end would serve as a distress signal.

"Thank you, Jesse. I'm sure I'll be fine. I promise that I'll pull on the string if I need anything. Now go back. I'm sure Jennifer is starting to worry."

Before returning to the ranch house, Jesse went to the barn and checked on the horses. Satisfied they were okay and the barn had survived the storm without damage, she walked back across the yard. Overhead, the moon was peeking out from behind one of the few remaining clouds, and thousands of stars twinkled in the black sky. Jesse stopped for a moment to enjoy the night. As she stood looking upward, she heard footfalls approaching.

"Beautiful, isn't it." Jennifer wrapped her arms around Jesse and pressed her body against the woman she loved.

"You certainly are." Jesse claimed Jennifer's lips.

Jennifer sighed as their mouths parted. "I was talking about the stars."

"I know." Jesse leaned forward until their foreheads touched. "But I do believe you are the most beautiful sight my eyes have ever been blessed with."

"Aw, Jesse." Jennifer's eyes filled with tears. "You are so romantic."

"I love you," Jesse whispered. "More than anything else on this earth." A tear trickled down Jennifer's cheek, and Jesse tenderly wiped it away with her thumb.

"Don't ever leave me, Jesse. I don't think I could live without you."

Jesse pulled Jennifer closer. "Ain't goin' nowhere, darlin'."

Jennifer twisted in Jesse's arms and laid her head on the strong shoulder. The world around them faded until there was nothing but the two of them happily enveloped in each other's love.

"How about that bath?" Jennifer asked after some time. "The water is hot."

"Oooo, I thought you'd never ask." Jesse grabbed Jennifer's hand and led her back to their cabin.

Jennifer sat on the bed waiting for her wife to finish drying off after their bath. "Jesse?"

"Hmm."

"I think I owe you something for stringing the alarm bell to Mother's cabin."

"Oh." Jesse tossed the towel she had been using over the back of a chair. "Just what were you thinkin' would be fittin', darlin'?"

"A reward, maybe," Jennifer teased, scooting back on the bed and lying down. She held out a hand and when Jesse took it, she pulled her lover on to the bed. Jesse stretched out on top of Jennifer, pressing their naked bodies together.

Jennifer's hands roamed over Jesse's back before pulling her even closer. Slowly she lifted her stronger leg, guiding it between Jesse's. When Jesse opened for her, Jennifer thrust her thigh upward and felt Jesse's warm wetness spread over her cool skin. Jesse moaned, slowly rubbing against Jennifer's thigh. She locked her arms on either side of Jennifer, giving her the necessary support to rock harder against her lover's thigh.

Jennifer slid her hands around to Jesse's chest, cupping her breasts and squeezing the firm mounds. She lifted her head to suck hard nipples into her mouth, her teeth raking across the sensitive skin. Jesse responded to the overwhelming sensations, throwing her head back and forcing her breasts against Jennifer's caressing hands. Jennifer continued kneading Jesse's breasts with one hand as she slowly slid the other down Jesse's stomach and between their bodies. Her fingers slipped into Jesse's wetness, quickly finding the hard clit and firmly pressing against it. Jesse's body jerked, her nipples unwillingly pulled from Jennifer's sucking mouth. Jennifer reached up and pulled Jesse down to her, capturing Jesse's lips and crushing their mouths together.

As her urgency for release built, Jesse pressed harder against Jennifer's hand, spasms intensifying at her center and expanding outward. Jennifer slipped inside, moving her fingers rapidly in the circular motion Jesse liked. Jesse's back arched, her body going rigid as vaginal walls clenched around Jennifer's fingers. "Oh, yesssssss!" she cried, as wave after orgasmic wave crashed through her. Moments later as the tension abated, Jesse collapsed onto the bed beside her lover. Jennifer rolled onto her side to gently rub Jesse's back as she regained her breath. "I liked my reward," Jesse gasped.

Jennifer tenderly traced irregular patterns on Jesse's heated, sensitive skin. "I thought you would."

Jesse adjusted her position so she was facing Jennifer. "I love you, Jennifer Branson."

"I love you, Jesse Branson." She bent forward, kissing her wife.

"Now, darlin'," she tenderly pushed Jennifer onto her back, "I'm going to show you just how much."

She kissed Jennifer, starting with her mouth and then leaving a wet trail of kisses down her neck, around her breasts, and down her stomach to the patch of curly hair at the apex of her legs. She inhaled deeply, breathing in the scent of her lover. Jennifer's hands clutched at the bed sheets as Jesse set her skin on fire, her breathing becoming unsteady panting.

Jesse slid between Jennifer's legs, lifting them onto her shoulders. She tenderly kissed up and down the inside of first one thigh and then the other, moving closer to the center of Jennifer's passion with each pass.

"Please." Jennifer whimpered. Jesse was driving her mad.

Jesse slid her hands between Jennifer's thighs and gently spread her legs wider, opening her lover up to her. For a moment, she simply gazed at the beauty before her, then, slowly, she examined Jennifer with her lips and tongue, the tip of her tongue barely touching the sensitive clit that pulsed beneath it.

Jennifer moaned, wordlessly asking for more contact. Jesse adjusted to press her tongue firmly against the nether lips it explored, enjoying the sweet, tangy juices.

"Inside," Jennifer begged.

Jesse did as she was asked, driving her tongue inside her wife. She pulled out and thrust in again, at the same time, pinching Jennifer's clit between her fingers.

Jennifer ground her heels into the mattress as her body bucked upward, the motion forcing Jesse's tongue deeper inside her. "Jesseeeeeeeeeeeeee."

CHAPTER FOURTEEN

KC tucked her head against Jennifer's shoulder and watched woefully as Jesse mounted her golden mare, Dusty, and prepared to ride to Sweetwater.

"I won't be long, darlin'. Just want to check on Bette Mae and make sure the Slipper survived in one piece."

Hearing the familiar name of her baking buddy, KC brightened. "Cookie?"

Jesse smiled at the baby. "I'll see what she's got in the oven." The rancher shifted in the saddle and leaned down to give Jennifer a kiss. "I'll be back before nightfall. Stick close to the house. Please."

"Is something wrong, Jesse?" Jennifer asked again. Since they'd awakened that morning, Jesse had seemed preoccupied, but she refused to share her concerns.

"Stick close. Promise?" Jesse looked into Jennifer's eyes.

"Yes, I promise. I just wish you'd tell me what's bothering you."

"Not sure." Jesse straightened in the saddle. "Just a feeling I've got." She urged Dusty forward.

"Be safe, sweetheart," Jennifer called. With a wave of her hand, the rancher rode toward the gate.

"Come on, sweetie," Jennifer said to the unhappy child watching her mommy disappear over the hillock. "Let's go see if your grandma is up yet."

Mary's cabin was about twenty yards away from the ranch house and separated from the barn and outbuildings by the garden. As Jennifer passed it, she smiled at the neat rows of vegetables and flowers enclosed by a new picket fence. After she'd moved to the ranch, she and Jesse had spent several days pulling weeds and tilling the ground so it could be useful again. It was a good feeling, knowing that their hard work had turned the neglected, weed-infested patch of ground into something so beautiful.

Through the open door of her cabin, Mary saw Jennifer approaching. "Come in, dear," she called out.

KC perked up when she heard her grandmother's voice. "Grrma."

"Everything okay, Mother?" Jennifer asked as she entered the cabin.

Mary was sitting at the table, sipping a cup of tea. "Yes. I'm fine. Water's hot if you'd like some tea." Mary pushed her cup toward the center of the table, and KC was placed in her waiting arms. "How are you this morning?" she asked, kissing the baby's cheek. When KC pouted, Mary shot her daughter a questioning look.

"Jesse went to town. KC wanted to go too," Jennifer explained. "We were expecting you for breakfast." She sat on the bed, the cabin being too small for a second chair.

"Oh? I just woke up a short time ago."

"Did you sleep all right?"

Mary chuckled. "I can't remember ever sleeping as well as I did last night. That is, once I got used to the quiet."

"It is quiet here, isn't it?" Jennifer thought back to the town she had grown up in. There was a constant stream of horse-drawn carts and buggies traveling the cobblestone streets. And the business district around the train depot was never tranquil, the noise from the saloons and freight wagon yards carrying far on the still evening air. Many a night, she had lain awake, unable to block out the noise.

"Do you ever miss it, dear?"

"You mean being back East?"

"Yes. Do you ever miss home?"

Jennifer was silent for a moment. "This is home for me, Mother. Wherever Jesse is, that will always be my home." She watched as KC slipped from her grandmother's lap, dropping to the floor to crawl toward her. "But do I miss where I grew up? No, Mother, I don't."

"Was it really that bad?" Mary pulled her teacup close and took a sip.

"It was never right for me." Jennifer reached down and helped KC up. The baby curled up in her lap and yawned. "I felt trapped there, Mother. All I ever wanted was to travel and make my own way in life. But, Father..."

Mary nodded somberly. "He believes in his ways."

"His ways are wrong." Jennifer's longstanding frustrations poured out. "How often did you hear him complain about needing someone he could trust in the shipping office? Or wish for someone to handle the correspondence from his suppliers and customers so he would be free to see to the ships and their cargo? I could have done that, Mother. I could have contributed to the company. But he only saw me as a means to make a business deal."

Mary understood the resentment Jennifer had over being left out of the family business. After all, it had been her own arranged marriage to Jennifer's father that had provided the funding to keep the business afloat.

"What about your brothers, dear? They love you."

Jennifer laughed, a touch of bitterness belying the mirth. "My brothers barely acknowledged me, Mother. I have no memory of any of them playing a game with me or reading to me. Or even talking to me, except to order me about." Jennifer shook her head. "No, Mother, there is nothing in the East that I miss. Or wish to return to," she said before her mother could suggest a visit.

"I'm sorry, Jennifer." Mary returned her empty teacup to the table. "I knew what your father expected of a daughter; my father had expected the same of me. I did try to talk to him after you were born. I didn't want my daughter forced into a loveless marriage as I had been. But your father is a very stubborn man."

Jennifer was surprised to hear that her mother had protested her father's actions. She could not remember a single time her mother had even questioned her father during her years growing up. She was getting to know a completely different side of her mother. "You talked to him?"

"Yes. But it was no use." Mary stared into her empty cup. "Unfortunately, the more successful your father was determined to make the business, the more he seemed to lose touch with what was really important. When your brothers were young, your father would take us on walks about town every Sunday morning. I loved those times," she said softly. Looking unseeing out the cabin's window, Mary watched the memories replay in her mind's eye. "He smiled a lot back then. I think he was actually happy. But, by the time you were born, the business was everything to him. I hoped he would not repeat my father's actions." She sighed and sat in silence for several minutes. "I was so scared when you left, Jennifer," she said, turning to face her daughter. "But I was also glad. And I prayed you had somehow found a path to your happiness." She smiled, knowing Jennifer had found that and more. "I just wish you had sent word telling me that you were all right."

"I'm sorry, Mother."

"I now understand your reasons." Mary rose to prepare herself another cup of tea. "Tea, dear?"

Jennifer shook her head. "Who told Father where to find me?" The question had troubled her since her father told her of receiving a telegram from Bannack.

"I'm not sure." Mary returned to her chair with a fresh cup of tea. "He received a telegram one day and announced he would be leaving immediately. He wouldn't tell me who had sent the telegram, but I did see it for a brief moment. I think the name at the bottom was...Thomas." She considered the sound of the word and decided it wasn't quite right. "Or something like that."

Jennifer thought the name sounded familiar. "I knew it," she cried. KC fussed in her arms at the abrupt sound. "Sorry, sweetie." She rubbed the baby's back until she settled. "The dress shop in Bannack...*Thompson's* Dress Shop. I knew that man made me uneasy; now I know why."

"Of course." Mary nodded. "Marcus Thompson. He did some work for your father before he and his wife left for the West."

"I'll have to remember to pay him a visit next time I'm in Bannack," Jennifer vowed. "I'm real sure Jesse will want to stop by and say howdy."

Mary grinned. "Bet he won't send any more telegrams after Jesse is finished with him."

"No, I'm sure he won't. Speaking of that dressmaker, I haven't had a chance to try on the dresses she made me. And considering the poor job she did fitting my wedding dress, maybe it wouldn't be a bad idea. Want to help?"

"Of course."

"Good." Jennifer stood, careful not to wake KC. "Let's go put her to bed. Maybe when she wakes up, we can take a walk down by the river."

"That would be nice."

Jesse was on the porch of the Slipper, sweeping up broken glass. She had been happy to learn that the building had weathered the storm with only a smashed window, a broken branch having blown into it. "Anything else you need me to do, Bette Mae?"

"Nope." Bette Mae righted another toppled chair. "Broken glass from that window was all we found this mornin'. Ruthie and Nancy checked all the rooms upstairs. I gave yer office a quick peek; couldn' find anythin' amiss."

"All right. I'll go see if Ed has the glass for a new window or if we have to order it from Bozeman. Either way, I'll come back and cover that hole."

"Ya can pick me up sum salt whilst ye're there," Bette Mae called as Jesse walked down the steps.

Jesse stepped from the shade of the porch into the harsh sunlight. It was hard to believe that a rainstorm had been raging less than ten hours before. As she walked toward the general store, she spotted Miles Perkins standing in front of the empty space on the far side of the store. His arms swung wildly about as he talked to a man she didn't recognize.

Ed was standing on the boardwalk in front of his store, also watching the mayor. "Have you heard what Miles is planning?"

"Nope." Jesse gratefully stepped into the shade alongside Ed.

"He's building a bank."

"Really?"

"Yep. He was in here a couple days ago ordering the material for the building. Goin' ta use sandstone blocks, make it real impressive. Even has a safe coming all the way from New York City." Though his words were full of awe, his voice indicated somewhat less enthusiasm about the mayor's plans.

"I guess a bank is one thing Sweetwater can use." Jesse took off her Stetson and wiped her sweaty brow with her sleeve. "Can't believe how hot it is after all that rain last night."

"Funny, isn't it?" Ed agreed. "What brings you to town, Jesse?" The storekeeper was glad for something to occupy his time other than the mayor's activities. "Tired of being surrounded by women already?" Ed chuckled.

"No." Jesse smirked at her friend as she returned the Stetson to her head. "Came in to check on the Slipper. Need some glass cut; you have any in stock?"

"Think so." Ed turned toward the door. "Let's go see."

Jesse followed him into the store and through to a back room he used for sleeping. A small cot, looking too small to hold the big man, was shoved out of the way of the many boxes and crates stacked in the room. Ed moved a couple of the boxes and looked behind them.

"Thought I had one piece left," he said as he gingerly lifted the glass free. "Hope this is big enough for you."

"Looks to be," Jesse said. "I'll be sure as soon as we can set it down and measure it."

It didn't take long for Ed to find a safe spot to lay the glass down so it could be measured and cut to size. He offered to wrap it in paper for Jesse but she declined.

"I'm taking it right back and sticking it in place. No use to waste the paper."

"Anything else for you today, Jesse?" Ed asked as he carefully disposed of the left over slivers of glass.

"Bag of salt."

Ed walked a few paces down the counter and pulled the requested item off one of the shelves lining the wall behind it. "How's the work comin' out at the ranch?"

"Finished." Jesse accepted the salt from the storekeeper. "Looks real nice, too."

"Jennifer's momma sure seems like a real nice lady." Ed opened his ledger and made a notation of the purchases.

"She is."

"Too bad the father is such a bad character." Ed completed his calculations. "You still have money coming, Jesse. I'll just put this against it."

"Thanks, Ed." Jesse readjusted the piece of glass under her arm. She wanted a firm grip on it before she left the store. "You order the lumber for your add-on, yet?"

"Yep. Sent the order to Bozeman last week. Miles wasn't too happy to hear he'd have to wait 'til mine was filled. Seems he was hoping that there fella could start building right away."

"Who is he, anyway?"

"Miles called him a... What was it now? Oh yeah. Ark-e-tek. Came all the way from Denver."

Jesse rolled the word around on her tongue. "Ark-e-tek. Wonder what that fancy name means."

"Somebody who makes fancy buildings, I reckon," Ed muttered as he replaced the ledger.

"I reckon."

"Glad I caught you, Jesse."

"Something wrong, Billie?" Jesse was putting away her tools after installing the new window glass.

"Wanted to tell ya that I talked to a couple of the Rocking B boys this mornin'." Conrad Billingsley's Rocking B ranch was the oldest and biggest ranch in the valley. "They said that lots more rain fell in the mountains last night. And they expect the rivers to start rising sometime today. Thought you'd want to keep a lookout for high water, seeing's how the river is so near your place."

Jesse's heart dropped into her boots, and she gasped as if someone had slammed a fist into her stomach.

Billie was troubled by the look of panic spreading across her face. "Hey, you okay?"

"I've got to get back to the ranch!" Jesse dashed off the porch. Moments later, she and Dusty were galloping out of town.

"Wha' bit her in the butt?" Bette Mae asked the sheriff at Jesse's sudden departure.

"Don't know." Billie looked after his friend. "Think maybe I'll ride out to the ranch, just to be sure everything's all right."

After spending the morning trying on dresses, Jennifer finally pulled the last, a pale yellow dress with a flowery pattern, from the box. "This is the last of them." She stepped into the dress and pulled it up her slender body.

"I don't know, dear." Mary scrutinized the fit of the dress. "I'm not sure that this one is any better than the others."

"My measurements couldn't have changed that much." Jennifer looked at her reflection in the full-length mirror that stood in the corner of the cabin. The dress bagged around her waist and was at least half a foot too short. "And I certainly didn't grow since we were in Bannack."

"My," Mary said as she examined the length of the sleeves. "Her talent as a dressmaker is somewhat lacking. This work would never have been accepted back home."

"Maybe that's why she moved to the West." Disgusted, Jennifer removed the dress and tossed it beside the others on the bed. She retrieved her denim pants and pulled them on. She was buttoning up her shirt when the door burst open.

"Jennifer!" Jesse shouted.

KC, playing on the floor, jumped as Jesse charged into the room. The noisy appearance of her mother scared the baby, and she howled.

"Jesse, what's wrong?" Jennifer was so surprised at Jesse's sudden entrance, she nearly fell before she managed to steady herself with her cane.

"You're here." Jesse bent to pick up the sobbing baby.

"Where else would we be?"

"You didn't go down to the river today, did you?" Jesse was rubbing the baby's back, attempting to calm her.

"We were going to," Jennifer admitted, "but then I remembered my promise to you that we would stay near the house."

Jesse dropped into the rocking chair, her arms encircling KC. "It's okay, Sunshine," she soothed. "Mommy didn't mean to scare you."

"She's not the only one you scared," Jennifer scolded. "Mind telling us just what that was about."

Jesse shrugged sheepishly. "I just had a feeling something bad was going to happen today. Then when Billie told me that the river was rising...I know how much you like to walk down to the river in the afternoon. And I just...I guess I just figured that if somethin' was bound to happen, that would be it."

"Sweetheart, what are you talking about?" Jennifer walked over and caressed Jesse's cheek. "Take a deep breath and tell me what happened."

Jesse did as she was told, and started again. "Billie said that there had been a lot more rain in the hills last night than what we got here in the valley. And he said that the rivers were probably going to be rising, causing some flooding. I thought that if you went down to the river like you like to do..." The words rushed out in a torrent of their own.

"You thought we might get trapped by high water," Jennifer said softly. Jesse nodded. "Oh, sweetheart." Jennifer lifted the baby from Jesse's lap and took her place. "I promised to stay here, and I would never break a promise I made to you."

"I..." Tears streamed from Jesse's eyes. "I was so scared, darlin'. I thought that was what my bad feeling was about. I had to know."

Jennifer kissed Jesse's wet cheeks. "I understand. I would have done the same thing under the circumstances." She pulled Jesse's arms around herself and KC.

"Mommy?" KC reached for Jesse, a sad look on her miniature face.

"It's all right, sweetie." Jennifer kissed the top of KC's head. "Mommy is okay. She was just worried about us, like any good mommy would be."

Jesse remained silent as the adrenaline rush ebbed, leaving her feeling exhausted. "Guess I kinda overreacted." She smiled weakly.

"No." Jennifer kissed her forehead. "You just love us."

"I must say," Mary finally got over the shock of the rancher's abrupt entrance, "it is extremely exciting around you two."

Jennifer looked at her mother, then at Jesse. Both women broke into giggles.

After several minutes, Jesse realized that there were dresses and undergarments strewn about the room. "What have you two been up to?"

Jennifer shifted to rise from Jesse's lap but strong arms held her tight. "I decided I should try on the dresses we bought in Bannack. Good thing I did."

"Don't you like them?" She had spent a lot of money to have the dresses made and shipped to Sweetwater. If there was a problem, she wanted to know.

"Not a single one fits. They're worse than the wedding dress."

"Guess I'll be sending a letter to Mrs. Thompson."

"There's something else you need to know about the Thompsons," Jennifer said hesitantly. "Mr. Thompson is the one who told my father where to find me."

Jesse said nothing, but her jaw muscles tensed and the veins in her neck stood out. That man was behind all the pain Jennifer has suffered. Mr. Thompson would be receiving more than a letter.

Jennifer watched her lover's face change various shades of color as the anger built inside her. "Sweetheart, would you please breathe before you pass out?" She guessed that if she and KC weren't occupying Jesse's lap, her protector would have already been on her way to Bannack. "He's not worth it, Jesse. Let it go."

"He hurt you."

"I know, sweetheart." Jennifer gently kissed her agitated wife. "But I'm all right now. If you go after him, I'll just be hurt all over again."

Jesse stared into Jennifer's eyes. She loved this woman so much, she never wanted to do anything to hurt her. "All right. I'll let it be."

Jennifer smiled. "Good girl."

"For now."

Down by the river, the pine tree that Jesse, Jennifer, and KC liked to sit under when they took their afternoon walks was undercut by a current swollen with the recent rain. Slowly tilting, until it could no longer hold itself upright, the tree crashed into the rushing water and was hurtled downstream. The riverbank vanished under the churning flow until nothing was left of their favorite picnic spot.

When Billie rode into the ranch yard, he found Dusty standing in front of the cabin, her reins hanging loose in the dirt and the door standing wide open. He dismounted cautiously, pulling his pistol as he stepped onto the porch. "Jesse, everything all right?" he called into the cabin, the gun ready for use.

The women had heard Billie's horse enter the yard. Looking out a window, they had seen it was him and gave little thought to his unexpected arrival. "Everything's okay," Jesse called back as she finished changing KC's britches. "Come on inside."

"Billie?" Jennifer peeked out the door. "Goodness, put away that gun before you hurt somebody."

Jesse patted KC on her padded rear end. "There you are, Sunshine. All nice and dry again."

"Dow." KC raised her arms, asking for help getting off the bed.

Jesse took hold of the baby's arms and dropped her safely onto the floor. KC crawled immediately for her toy box. "Come on in," Jesse repeated as she dropped the soiled diaper in the wash basket. Billie still stood outside the door, mouth agape. "What's wrong, you never seen a diaper changed before?"

"Damn, Jesse," Billie said as he holstered the pistol and stepped inside. "The way you lit out of town, I thought maybe Jennifer or KC was in trouble."

"What?" Jesse looked confused until she remembered the abrupt manner in which she had left Sweetwater. "Oh. Sorry 'bout that."

Mary chuckled as she cut vegetables for the stew Jennifer was preparing for supper. "Never a dull moment with you two, is there?"

"Hush, Mother." Jennifer playfully swatted at her with a towel. "Staying for supper, Billie?"

Billie stared at the happy family scene before him. "I guess. But only if you tell me what happened."

"Go on and sit down, Billie." Jesse laughed as she filled two cups with fresh brewed coffee from the pot. She joined the sheriff at the table and began to tell him why she had ridden out of town like someone had lit her on fire.

"So none of the dresses fit?" Billie asked as he finished off his second piece of apple pie.

"Not a single one. I'll have to ask Ruthie if she'll mind fixing them." Jennifer poured coffee into Jesse's empty cup. "I probably should have just had her sew them in the first place."

"Thanks, darlin'. You know," Jesse sipped from her cup, "that might not be such a bad idea."

"What?" Jennifer asked, feeding a small bite of pie to KC.

KC held onto the fork as if more pie would magically appear on it. "Mo'."

"Having Ruthie sew your dresses."

"You lost me, sweetheart." Jennifer gently pulled the fork from KC's grasp.

"Much as I hate to admit it, Sweetwater is beginning to grow. Ed's going to add on to the store, and Mayor Perkins is opening a bank."

"He is?" Jennifer interrupted.

Jesse hadn't had time to share her earlier conversation with Ed. "Yes. Somehow he got a charter from the governor. But as I was saying, there'll be more folks in town. Women aren't going to be willing to travel to Bozeman or wait for the freight wagons every time they need a new dress or their young 'uns need clothes."

"What are you suggesting?" Billie took a gulp of coffee.

"Opening a dress shop."

Billie choked on his coffee. "You plannin' to take up sewing, Jesse?"

"No." She scowled at the sheriff. "I was thinkin' that Ruthie might be interested."

"That's a wonderful idea, sweetheart," Jennifer agreed enthusiastically.

"That's a nice thought, Jesse, but Ruth can't afford anythin' like that."

"Wasn't expectin' her to pay for it, Billie. We'd set up the shop," Jesse told her friend. "All she'd have to do is the sewing."

"I don't know." Billie knew how shy Ruthie was, but it would be nice to see her doing something she truly enjoyed rather than just working in the kitchen at the Slipper. "Guess it wouldn' hurt none to ask her."

"She could use your office at the Slipper," Jennifer said. "You're barely there anymore."

After convincing Jesse to let her help with the Slipper's bookwork, Jennifer had moved most of the ledgers and other records to the ranch house so she could do the books at home. The office was only used now for Jesse to catch up on reading the Sweetwater *Gazette* while Jennifer was busy elsewhere in town.

"It's kinda dark in there for sewing, don't you think?" Mary asked, having seen the windowless room.

"Guess we could put in some windows." Jesse hadn't really thought about converting her office into a dress shop but it did make sense to use the idle space. "Be obliged if you didn't mention this to Ruthie, Billie. I want to give it some more thought. We'll talk to Ruthie and Bette Mae next time we're in town."

"Sure, Jesse."

"Mommy?"

KC looked sleepy, and Jesse lifted the baby from the highchair. "Guess it is past your bedtime, Sunshine."

"Time for me to be gettin' back to town." Billie stood. "Thanks for supper, Jennifer."

"You're welcome any time." Jennifer handed the sheriff his hat. "Come by more often."

"Goodnight, Miss Mary," Billie nodded to Jennifer's mother. "'Night, Jesse."

"I'll walk you out." Jesse kissed the top of KC's head before passing the tired baby to Jennifer. "I need to check on the horses."

"I'll come, too." Mary gave Jennifer and KC goodnight kisses. "If you'll be so kind as to walk me to the cabin, Jesse."

"Glad to." Jesse held the door open. "Be right back, darlin'." By the time Jesse returned to the house, KC was fast asleep in her crib and Jennifer was soaking in the tub.

"Better hurry before the water gets cold, sweetheart," Jennifer purred as clothes began to fly.

CHAPTER FIFTEEN

Bette Mae had just set Ed's breakfast in front of him when the door to the Slipper opened and a nattily dressed man entered the dining room.

"I'm looking for the proprietor," the man announced pretentiously.

"Jesse ain't here," Bette Mae said, filling Ed's cup with hot coffee. "Somethin' I can help ya with?"

"I sincerely doubt it. When can I expect him to arrive?"

Bette Mae looked the man up and down. He wasn't very tall, just coming up to her chin and she wasn't a tall woman. He had dark hair with a handlebar mustache to match. His eyes narrowed to slits as he bristled at her assessment. "*He* is a *she*," Bette Mae said slowly. "And when Jesse comes to town is her business. Now, you interested in havin' breakfast or ya just goin' ta stand there wastin' my time."

The man shuddered at the thought, ignoring what the woman had said about Jesse. "Eat *here*; I think not."

"Then I s'gest ya turn around and walk yer uppity arse back outside. Ya's scarin' my customers."

The man looked around the dining room at the several tables that were occupied with folks eating their morning meal, many of them sniggering at the comment. He took a deep breath, holding it for a moment before releasing it. Then he turned and left the Slipper.

"Looks like Mayor Perkins done got him sum competition for town's mos' pompous ass," Bette Mae observed as she made her way back to the kitchen.

After spending several days at the ranch, Jesse and Jennifer decided a trip to town was in order; Mary asked to accompany them. Their first stop was at the Slipper to check in with Bette Mae, who told them of the strange visitor.

"Who was he?" Jesse asked.

"Didn' say," Bette Mae told the women. "Jus' said he wanted ta talk to the *proprietor*. Said it like he thought he was real important, he did."

"I guess we'll just have to wait until he comes back when I'm here. Or Jennifer."

Bette Mae didn't care if the dandy ever returned. "Plan ta do sum work in the office?" she asked.

"Nope."

"Got shoppin' ta do?"

"Nope."

"Jennifer workin' at the schoolhouse?"

"Nope."

"Then what did ya come all the way inta town for?"

"We were kinda hopin' to talk with you."

"And Ruthie," Jennifer added.

"Oh lordy," Bette Mae exclaimed. "What trouble ya got yerselves inta now?"

Jesse laughed. "No trouble, Bette Mae. Just find Ruthie and come into the office."

"Alrighty. But I do not trust you, Jesse Marie."

"Ooh." Jennifer waggled a finger in Jesse's face. "You're in trouble now."

"Ha, ha." Jesse brushed the finger aside. "Mary, you're welcome to come into the office, too."

"Thank you, Jesse, but I think I'll look through the books."

"It shouldn't take long, Mother."

"You take all the time you want. I'll be fine. Would you like me to watch KC for you?"

Jesse hesitated. Since Jennifer's kidnapping, KC had fussed whenever she was out of sight of her mothers. "Sunshine, do you want to stay with Grandma while Momma and I go in there?" Jesse pointed to her office door.

"No." KC vigorously shook her head.

"Sorry, Mary."

"It's okay, Jesse." Mary patted the rancher's arm. "She needs to feel she's safe."

Mayor Perkins entered the Slipper, followed close behind by another man. "Ah, Jesse, there you are. I thought that was your wagon outside."

"Miles," Jesse acknowledged with a nod.

"Jesse, I'd like to introduce Mr. Tobias Harrington." The mayor motioned the other man forward.

Bette Mae came out of the kitchen door with Ruthie in tow. "Tha's him, Jesse."

Harrington looked at Jesse, perplexed. When Mayor Perkins had told him the Silver Slipper's owner was a Jesse Branson, he had assumed the owner was a man. "*You* are the proprietor of this establishment?" He realized that he might have known that had he taken the time to listen to what the cook was telling him a few days before.

"If you mean, do we own the Slipper, the answer is yes, we own her," Jesse said, including Jennifer.

"I wasn't expecting a woman."

"Well, you got one. You have a problem with that?" Jesse's demeanor dared the man to answer in the affirmative.

Hesitating, Harrington decided the safest course was to ignore the intimidating woman's question. "I have a proposition for you," he stated. "I expect you have somewhere private we can talk."

"We have an office," Jesse responded. "If'n we were wanting to talk to you *privately.*"

"Very good." Harrington gestured for the mayor to lead the way. "Shall we?"

"Yes, yes, very good." Mayor Perkins pointed to the office door. "This way."

"Bring us some coffee," Harrington ordered presumptuously. Before Bette Mae could respond, Jesse stepped in front of the men, blocking their path.

Sensing Jesse was ready to throw them out of the Slipper by the seats of their pants, or worse, Jennifer spoke before her wife had a chance. "Mr. Harrington, we are not accustomed to our staff being treated so rudely. Perhaps, if you wish to have some coffee, it would be better for you to ask for a cup."

"I don't have all day, Perkins."

Harrington tried to brush Jesse aside, but she refused to move, and there was no way the small man was going to be able to force her. "Jesse, please," the mayor pleaded. "Just a few minutes of your time."

It was clear that Jesse had no inclination to listen to what the arrogant interloper had to say, but Jennifer was curious. "Perhaps we could give them five minutes, sweetheart," she said to her truculent wife.

"We have other business to attend to today, so this better not be a waste of our time." Jesse glared at the men. "Forget about the coffee, Bette Mae," she said. "They won't be here long enough to drink it."

"Tha' suits me jus' fine."

"Perkins, you have five minutes." Jesse led the way to the office, holding the door open for Jennifer.

"My business is with you," Harrington stated.

Jesse had had all she was going to take off this narcissistic jackass. "Look, mister, I don't know who you are or what you want, but you want to talk business about the Slipper, then you talk to me *and* Jennifer. Or you can turn around and leave right now."

"And don' let the door hit ya in the arse on the way out," Bette Mae muttered on her way back into the kitchen.

"Come on, Tobias." Mayor Perkins pulled Harrington toward the office. "I told you they were partners."

If Harrington hadn't been under orders from his employers to quickly complete the offer on the Slipper, he would have turned on his heel and left rather than continue dealing with this unreasonable woman. He reluctantly followed the mayor.

Once the office door was shut and Jennifer, holding KC, was seated comfortably in the chair behind the desk, Jesse barked, "What the hell do you want?"

"Miss Branson," Harrington began.

"Mrs.," Jesse corrected.

"If you are married," Harrington stammered, "I should be talking with your husband."

Mayor Perkins looked like he had swallowed something bad for breakfast and was seeking the quickest way to be rid of it. "I explained all of this to you, Tobias. Jesse and Jennifer are married. To each other."

Harrington looked at the women, then at the mayor. "How is that possible?"

"Doesn't matter," Jesse said. "It is. We are. Deal with it."

"Mr. Harrington," Jennifer smiled pleasantly, "did you wish to discuss something with us or not?"

"Go on," Mayor Perkins urged.

Confused and frustrated at the seeming lack of options, Harrington nodded curtly. "I represent a group of investors in the East. They have plans for the town of Sweetwater, and they wish to purchase your establishment."

"No," Jesse and Jennifer said at the same time.

"Excuse me."

"The Silver Slipper is not for sale," Jennifer explained.

"I am authorized to make you a generous offer."

"As my wife said," Jesse walked to the office door and opened it, "the Slipper is not for sale. Not at any price, not at any time, and especially not to you. Good day, gentlemen." She waited for the visitors to leave.

"You are making a big mistake," Harrington protested. Things were not going at all as he expected.

"*Get out!*" Jesse ordered.

After Harrington and the mayor left, Jennifer patiently waited as Jesse stormed about the office until the steam she had built up over Harrington's pompous attitude finally abated.

"Ugh," KC muttered as she watched her mommy.

"Yes, sweetie." Jennifer chuckled at her daughter's innocent insightfulness. "Ugh."

Tobias Harrington paced around Mayor Perkins' office. "This is going to cost my employers money they weren't expecting to spend."

"I told you she was a difficult woman. Can't your employers just build another boarding house?"

"Of course they'll build another one," Harrington snapped. "It would have saved time and money if that woman had accepted the offer. I'll just have to go back and talk to her, make her understand that there are changes coming to this town. Important changes."

The mayor shook his head. "You won't change her mind. She runs the Slipper like those women are her family."

"All whores, from what I hear." Harrington stopped pacing and looked out the office window to the building at the far end of town. "Decent people shouldn't have to do business with whores. And what about the relationship between those Branson women?" He turned to face the mayor. "Indecent, if you ask me. How could you allow something like that to take place?"

The mayor stayed silent rather than tell his new business partner that he had not only allowed it, but had also performed the wedding ceremony.

"Downright indecent," Harrington repeated. "It appears I have no choice but to return to Boston and inform my employers of this unfortunate development. What time does the next stage leave for Denver?"

In the adjoining office, Thaddeus Newby was thankful for the thin wall between his office and the mayor's. From his desk drawer, he pulled out a clean piece of paper and began to quickly jot down a message to a newspaper friend in Denver who might be able to uncover the reason for the mayor's recent trip to the city. Thaddeus sealed the note in an envelope and addressed it, then stood and picked up his hat from the corner of the desk. He hurried from his office; the stage was due soon, and he wanted to be sure his letter was in the mail pouch when the coach left town.

When Jennifer asked Bette Mae and Ruthie to come into the office, Jesse was slumped in the armchair, still simmering over Harrington. KC was crawling around Jesse's chair and climbing under and over her mother's long legs. Bette Mae sat in the desk chair while Jennifer sat with Ruthie on the couch and explained their idea for a dress shop.

"Lordy," Bette Mae exclaimed. "Tha's a right fine idea."

"I don't know, Miss Jennifer." Ruthie looked down at the floor. "I don't think I could."

Ruthie wasn't much older than Jennifer but had seen a much different side of life growing up. Shortly after her fifteenth birthday, she had been forced into a life of prostitution when her mother died and her father abandoned her. Her face bore the scars from a knife wielded by a customer that had wanted more than Ruthie was willing to give.

Jennifer tenderly laid a hand on the girl's knee. "I know you're self-conscious about your scars." Jennifer stopped Ruthie's hand from instinctively covering her face. "But you are a very pretty girl and a very talented seamstress. And I know that you'd rather make dresses than work in the kitchen; you've told me that yourself. But Jesse and I don't want you to take this on unless you want to."

Ruthie considered. It was true; she did like sewing a lot better than working in the Slipper's kitchen and serving folks their meals. But she felt uncomfortable whenever people stared at the scars the bastard had left on her, and she could only imagine the questions she might face from ladies having dresses fitted.

"Can't hardly see them scars anymore, Ruthie," Bette Mae said softly.

She had been so frightened when she'd heard Ruthie crying for help that night. She hurried to the girl's room to find the man straddling Ruthie on the bed, his arm raised to drive the bloodied knife into the girl's chest. Without hesitation, Bette Mae had pointed and fired the six-shooter she'd grabbed when she'd heard the first terrified scream.

"If you decide you can't do it," Jesse said reassuringly, "you just say so."

Ruthie felt she owed Jesse a debt. Refusing to be with any other men after that night, she'd been sure that the owner would tell her to leave. But a few days later Jesse arrived in Sweetwater, having won the Slipper in a poker game. She not only kept Ruthie on, but had also paid for her to go to Bozeman and see the doctor. "Miss Jesse, I'd like to try."

Jesse smiled. "Good."

"So, where's ya plannin' ta build this dress shop?" Bette asked.

"Actually," Jennifer told her, "we thought we'd do it here."

"Here?"

"In this room."

Bette Mae looked around the office. The few furnishings consisted of the couch, a small table beside it, the desk in the center of the room, the small armchair Jesse was slouched in, a liquor cabinet that was unused, and a set of shelves behind the desk. It wouldn't take much to convert the room into a seamstress shop for Ruthie. Only one problem she could see, the room was windowless.

"Mighty dark in here, don' ya think?"

"Figured I'd use Harrington's head and knock a hole or two in the walls," Jesse grunted, her lips twitching as she tried not to smile.

"Bet ya'd like that." Bette Mae wasn't certain that Jesse was only kidding.

KC climbed as far up Jesse's leg as she could before asking for help. "Up."

Jesse pulled the baby the rest of the way to her lap. "Getting tired, Sunshine?" KC yawned. "Unless there's anything more to discuss," Jesse placed a supporting hand on KC's back as the sleepy baby snuggled against her chest, "Jennifer and I will make arrangements with Ed to order the windows."

"We'll see if he has any catalogs, Ruthie," Jennifer said. "So you can start ordering dress material and other supplies."

Ruthie blanched. "Don't worry, Ruthie," Jennifer quickly added when she saw the girl's reaction to the thought of having such responsibility. "Jesse and I will help you."

"Come on, Ruthie." Bette Mae stood. "Let's go git my little angel some milk so's she can take a nap. Ya can worry 'bout bein' a high and mighty seamstress after ya git them taters peeled."

After Bette Mae and Ruthie left, Jesse carried KC over and joined Jennifer on the couch.

"Some morning, huh?" Jennifer asked as KC switched laps. She leaned against Jesse and felt the warmth of her wife's arm drape over her shoulders.

"I'll say."

"Sweetheart, why do you think Harrington's investors are interested in Sweetwater?"

"Pompous ass," Jesse muttered, before she answered. "Probably has something to do with the mines."

"How's that?"

"Takes a lot of money to get the ore out of the ground," Jesse explained. "Investors back East have that kind of money."

"But the mines are all in the mountains. What would they be doing in Sweetwater?"

Jesse leaned back, pulling Jennifer with her. "When a mine hits pay dirt, Eastern investors send their errand boys to sniff around like buzzards on a carcass."

"You mean like Harrington?"

"Yep. They offer the claim owner a fraction of the mine's anticipated value."

"Why would they accept so little?"

"Like I said, it takes lots of money to turn a pile of rocks into a gold brick. Men who stake the original claims and do the work to find the ore don't have that kind of money. So when a vein is struck, they sell out. They get a lot more than they ever dreamed of, and the investors get the future profits."

"But that doesn't explain why they'd be interested in the Slipper."

"To make the mine pay, they have to bring in machinery, stamp mills, processors, stuff like that. To get that equipment to the mines, they have to build roads. They'll bring in mining engineers, assayers, and workers to build the roads and take care of the ore wagons and mining equipment. Those men will need somewhere to stay until lodging can be built closer to the mine. Then the investors will want to come and see what their money is being spent on, and they'll need a place to stay."

"They can stay at the Slipper even if we own it, can't they?"

"Yes, but investors like to own what they use. That way they keep more of the profits. That's probably also why Perkins got the bank charter. My guess is that Harrington's investors will also own the bank. All those workers will need to get paid, and it wouldn't be too safe bringing the payroll in from Bozeman every month."

"Can't they just build their own rooming house?"

"Probably will, since we turned down their offer. Just would have been cheaper for them to buy the Slipper."

Jennifer considered all that Jesse had just told her. "Sweetwater is really going to grow, isn't it?"

"'Fraid so." Jesse sighed.

Bette Mae came into the office carrying a tray with a pitcher of milk and glasses. It also held a plate of sandwiches and another of cookies, straight out of the oven.

"Thought ya might be hungry." Bette Mae set the tray down on the desk. She filled a baby bottle with milk and brought it to KC. "There ya go, angel."

KC hungrily grabbed at the bottle. Lying back in Jennifer's arms, she started sucking down the contents.

"Tha's a right nice thing ya is doin' for Ruthie," Bette Mae said.

"Thanks." Jennifer watched KC, making sure she didn't drink too fast. "Would you ask Mother to join us?"

"She said ta tell ya she'd be back in a bit."

"Oh. Do you know where she went?"

"Headed down ta Ed's," Bette Mae said as she left the room.

Jennifer looked puzzled. "She didn't say anything about needing anything from the store."

"Maybe she just wanted to stretch her legs," Jesse offered.

"Maybe."

Mary took the envelope out of her bag and turned it over in her hands. She debated anew whether or not she should send the letter or leave well enough alone. She was saddened by Jennifer's memories of a childhood devoid of any affection from her brothers. Maybe it wasn't too late to right the wrong she had allowed her husband to commit by impressing his views of women onto their sons. *Yes, I have to try.* She approached the counter. "Could you please post this letter for me, Ed?"

"Why sure," he replied.

"When is the next stage?"

"Let's see." Ed pulled a pocket watch from his shirt pocket and took a look at the time. "Should be coming in about two hours. That is, if it's on time. Most days it runs late. I was fixin' to walk over in another few minutes."

"I hate to be a bother," Mary said, but having Ed post the letter made sense. If Jennifer saw her going into the small adobe stage station, she would most definitely have questions.

"No bother at all," he replied. "I have a few letters to post myself; got some orders to send to my suppliers in Bozeman, too. I can toss yours on the pile."

"Thank you. I really appreciate it." Mary returned to the Slipper, arriving just as Jennifer came out of the office.

"Mother, we were just going to go search for you. We're ready to leave."

"I'll just say goodbye to Bette Mae." Mary hurried into the kitchen before Jennifer could ask about the purpose of her walk.

"Your own shop?" Billie was sitting with Ruthie in the dining room of the Slipper. True to his word, he didn't mention he already knew of the plan Ruthie had just told him about. "Jesse is supplying everythin'?"

"And Miss Jennifer," Ruthie reminded.

"I can't believe it. That's a mighty fine thing for them to do."

"I don't know if I can do it, Billie," Ruthie said uneasily.

"Why not, honey?" Billie smiled nervously, the use of the endearment still sounding strange to them both. "It's what we've talked about doin', if we ever had the money."

"I know, but," Ruthie touched the scars on her otherwise pretty face, "you know I don't like people looking at these."

Billie smiled and pulled her hand away from her face. "Bette Mae is right, Ruth. They've faded to where you barely notice them. Besides, I think you're the most beautiful woman in the entire valley."

"Miss Jesse and Miss Jennifer are the most beautiful."

"Not to me, honey." Billie captured her hand and held it. "I think you should give it a try, Ruth. Jesse said you could pull out at any time, right? What do you have to lose?"

"I guess it can't hurt to try."

"That's my girl." Billie smiled proudly. "Now, would you allow me the honor of buying you dinner?"

Back at the ranch, the women spent a few hours weeding and tending the rows of vegetables while KC plucked flowers and played in the dirt. It wasn't long before the baby was covered from head to toe in grime. Mary returned to her cabin to rest before supper while Jesse and Jennifer gave the baby a bath.

"More coffee, Jesse?" Jennifer filled her own cup as she watched KC splashing happily in the tub.

"No thanks, darlin'. Think I'll go check on the horses. Might as well take the buckets with me; I can refill them on the way." She picked up the water buckets they would heat for their own bath later in the evening.

The baby reached for Jesse when she saw her take her Stetson down from the peg beside the door.

"Sorry, Sunshine." Jesse knelt down beside the tub. "Can't carry you and the buckets. You stay here and keep an eye on your momma for me. Besides, we just got you clean."

KC frowned, water dripping off her nose. "Otay."

Jesse stood and drew Jennifer to her until their lips met. "I'll be back before you get the squirt dressed," Jesse breathed into Jennifer's mouth.

Jennifer felt her body reacting. "Maybe she'll go to sleep early tonight."

"Let's hope so."

A knock on the cabin door interrupted the moment of closeness. Jennifer knew her mother would have called out after knocking. "Who could that be?"

"Don't know." Jesse was concerned that she hadn't heard anyone approach the cabin. Whoever was at the door could be trouble. "Stay here with KC," she told Jennifer, quickly crossing to the cabinet that held her weapons. She pulled a rifle from the rack and checked to make sure it was loaded, then she walked to the door. "Who is it?" she asked cautiously.

"A friend, Buffalo Heart."

Recognizing the voice, Jesse quickly pulled the door open. "Walk? Damn, you gave me a scare."

Jennifer, with KC secure in her arms, saw the Indian they had seen in town several days before. Jesse had told her the man was known to his people as Walks on the Wind and he was an old friend; she'd met him during the time she had wandered the West before winning the Slipper in a card game in Denver.

The native smiled and stretched out an arm, which Jesse immediately clasped. "You must be getting old, Buffalo Heart. Even a young boy would have heard me from the time I put my horse in your corral."

"Come in, old friend." Jesse pulled the man into the cabin. As she returned the rifle to the gun cabinet, she continued, "I figured you would be stopping by after we saw you in town."

KC shivered. "Sorry, sweetie." Distracted by the new arrival, Jennifer had forgotten the baby in her arms was naked. "Come on, let's get you dressed." She started across the room, but Jesse stopped her.

"You have a family, Buffalo Heart."

"Yes." Jesse smiled proudly. "This is my wife, Jennifer. And this," she took the baby from Jennifer, "this is our daughter, KC. Darlin', this is my friend, Walks on the Wind."

Jennifer smiled. Though she was nervous about the stranger, she trusted Jesse. "It's nice to meet you."

Walks on the Wind looked at Jennifer, then at the baby. The resemblance was startling. "I knew you were of two spirits, Buffalo Heart, but I didn't know you could make a baby."

Jesse laughed as she handed KC back to Jennifer so she could dress the baby. "I can't. Here, sit." She gestured Walk to a chair. "We found her after her folks were killed. When we couldn't find any other family, we decided to raise her ourselves."

Once dressed, the baby asked to be put on the floor, and Jennifer complied. Without hesitation, KC crawled to Walks on the Wind and pulled herself upright on his leg. "Up," she demanded.

The warrior cheerfully lifted KC into his lap. Jennifer's fears for the baby's safety quickly evaporated as she watched KC engage the man in a conversation of gibberish.

"Looks like KC has taken a likin' to ya." Jesse laughed as her daughter pointed and gestured. After a few minutes she reclaimed her daughter. "She'll talk your ears off if you let her. Go on and play with your toys for a while," she told KC as she sat her near the toy box. Returning to her friend, she said, "We were just gettin' ready to fix supper. You'll join us?"

"I'd like that."

Mary tapped on the cabin door. "Hello?"

"Come in, Mother."

Mary gasped as she entered the cabin and spied the Indian. "Oh, my."

"It's all right, Mother." Jennifer took her mother's hand to reassure her. "This is Walks on the Wind, a friend of Jesse's. He's having supper with us."

Walks on the Wind stood and held out a hand to Mary.

The women and their guest were finishing up their evening meal. KC was sitting in Mary's lap fighting sleep.

"I must say, Walk," Mary said, addressing him as he had requested, "your English is..."

"Pretty good for an Injun?" Walk finished for her.

Mary was embarrassed. "Well, yes...I mean, no."

"It's all right, Mrs. Kensington." Walk smiled to ease her discomfiture. "My mother married an English fur trapper; he taught me the language. And I spent a couple of years at a missionary school."

"I see." Mary was discovering that she liked the genial man. "So you are part white?"

"No. The trapper was my mother's second husband. My father was killed by soldiers when I was a child."

"Oh. I am sorry."

Awkwardness pervaded the room and Jennifer changed the subject. "The other day in town, you didn't speak with Ed. You..." She moved her hands, trying to imitate the gestures she had seen Walk and Ed use.

"Sign language," Walk said.

"Why didn't you just speak to him?"

"Sometimes, it is best not to speak your language."

"I don't understand."

"Unfortunately, darlin', there are many folks who have nothing good to say about the Indians. By not letting everyone know he understands English, Walk can hear things that might come in handy. You'd be surprised what folks will say in front of Indians because they think they're too dumb to understand."

"That's so sad."

"What kind of things, Jesse?" Mary asked.

"If a new Army outpost is coming or where new settlements are growing, for example," Jesse explained.

"Or plans to attack our villages," Walk added bitterly.

"Hopefully, some day that won't be the case," Jesse told her friend.

"There is always hope, Buffalo Heart," Walk agreed, but both women knew that most likely the frontier's future would not hold fairness for its native peoples.

"Why do you call Jesse Buffalo Heart?"

"She's never told you of her first buffalo hunt?"

"No."

"And I don't think now is the time to talk about it," Jesse warned Walks on the Wind. "Come on, darlin', help me clear the table."

Jennifer refused to budge from her chair. "No, I want to hear this. Please."

Ignoring the pointed looks he was receiving from Jesse, Walks on the Wind recounted the story.

"Buffalo Heart joined my village on a buffalo hunt when she was not much older than some of the young boys we allow to take part in their first hunt. And, like the boys, she wanted to prove she was as good, or better, than the seasoned hunters. So she was determined to kill the largest bull in the herd. She tracked that bull for three days before she got close enough to shoot it and brought it down with one shot to the heart. Some of the young warriors were jealous and told her she had to rip the heart from the animal and eat it raw to prove her worth as a hunter. Buffalo Heart met their challenge."

KC yawned, and Jesse took her from Mary to rock her to sleep. The baby curled up in her arms and promptly went to sleep. Seeing that the baby didn't need further rocking, she carried KC to her cradle and put her to bed.

"The medicine woman gave her the name that night in a ceremony thanking our gods for a good hunt," Walks on the Wind concluded.

"Most disgusting thing I've ever eaten." Jesse shivered at the memory.

Jennifer held up her hands. "I don't want to hear any more details."

"I agree." Mary looked as if her supper was trying to make a reappearance. Jesse and Walks on the Wind began to laugh.

"So what brings you to Sweetwater," Jesse asked. "It's a bit out of your way, isn't it?"

"I came to ask you to join us on our hunt this season." He turned to Jennifer. "Every summer, our hunters leave our homeland in the west and travel over the mountains to track the buffalo herds east of the Rocky Mountains. Hunting the buffalo provides the meat our people need to survive the winter."

"Sorry, Walk." Jesse returned to the table. "I have my own family now. Can't take a chance on something happening to me."

Though she appreciated that Jesse was putting her family's well being first, Jennifer was disappointed that Jesse declined the invitation. She would have loved the opportunity to see the large animals she had read about.

Hoping Buffalo Heart would change her mind and join the hunt, Walks on the Wind was telling Jesse, "We are traveling on the southern trail."

Later that night, blankets were spread on the cabin floor in front of the kitchen fireplace to provide Walks on the Wind a comfortable spot to sleep. When Jesse awoke the next morning, her friend was gone.

CHAPTER SIXTEEN

Martin Kensington stood in his parlor, his three sons in various postures around him. He had just informed them of his plans to return to Montana and, with their help, force their sister to return home. His wife would also be brought back to his house to resume her proper duties. Once he had the women where they belonged, he would make new arrangements for Jennifer's marriage. "We're leaving tomorrow."

"Father, I don't think that is wise," his eldest son said.

"And why not, Thomas?" Kensington bellowed. "Am I to leave my wife and daughter in the hands of a perversion, an outlaw?"

His son continued as calmly as possible, "That is not what I'm suggesting. I just think that there are better ways to handle this."

"Such as?"

"I don't know." He saw the look of contempt flash across his father's face and quickly suggested, "Give me time to make inquiries into the matter."

"No. They belong here. I will not allow them to defy me one more day."

"But, Father," William, his youngest son, injected, "did you not say that you were allowed to leave Montana Territory only because you swore you would never return?"

"Do you expect me to honor such an oath?"

"It is legally binding," Thomas asserted.

"There is nothing about that godforsaken land that is legal. If there had been any law, that bitch would have been sent to prison for causing Barrish's death, and your sister and mother would be here, as they should be."

"I don't think that is necessarily the case," Thomas countered.

"Besides," Howard added, "sounds to me like Jennifer is pretty happy where she is. Why should we interfere?"

Martin's head whipped around to look at his second son. Thomas and William exchanged fearful glances. "How...do...you...know...that?" Kensington demanded, his words deliberate and his anger barely contained.

Howard looked embarrassed, as if he'd been caught doing something wrong. "Damn."

"Answer me."

"We received a letter from Mother," Thomas admitted.

"You what?" Kensington boiled at the disclosure. "And you chose to keep this from me."

"She asked us to."

"Since when do you let a woman tell you what to do!" Kensington raged.

Howard said in a shaky voice, "Calm down, Father." His father's large hand struck him across the face, knocking him backward.

"Father, stop." Thomas grabbed his father's arm while William knelt to check on Howard.

Thomas Kensington had not inherited his father's temper, but he had inherited his size, and, after years of loading and unloading cargo from the family's ships, he was more than a match for the larger man. He easily resisted Martin's attempts to break his hold.

"Let me go!" Kensington screamed.

"I will, as soon as you calm down." Thomas tightened his grip. "How is he?" he asked his younger brother.

"Dazed, but he should be all right," William reported. "He's got a pretty nasty gash on the back of his head. He must have hit it on something when he fell."

"Think you can get him to the doctor by yourself?"

"Yes." William helped his brother stand on wobbly legs. "You going to be all right?" he asked, concerned about leaving his eldest brother alone with their father.

"Yes, get him out of here."

"We'll be back as soon as we can."

William half-carried his brother to the door. Martin watched dispassionately as his two youngest sons left the house. "I want to see the letter," he demanded.

"No." Thomas released his grip.

"Give me the letter."

"I burned it," Thomas lied as he carefully sat on one of the delicate chairs with which his mother had furnished the room.

"Something else she asked you to do, I suppose."

"Sit down and we'll talk."

Not caring how his large stature strained the fragile frame, Martin dropped into a matching chair. "With or without your help, I'm going back to Montana."

Thomas remained silent. He was years older than his sister and had almost nothing to do with the girl as she grew. It wasn't really intentional. At the age of twelve, he was already working in the family business when Jennifer was born and had little time to spare for the new arrival. He smiled as he thought of the little girl who always seemed to have a thousand questions. She had been so full of spirit. He now realized that over the years that spirit had gradually disappeared under their father's discipline.

Thomas had been upset by his mother's letter, as had his brothers. It had been disturbing to read of their sister's memory of them, and, looking back, they knew that they had allowed their father's opinion of women to shape the attitudes they had shown their mother and sister. The brothers had discussed whether there was any way to make up to Jennifer for such a lonely and unhappy childhood.

He studied the look of determination on his father's face and knew that nothing he could say would change his plans. In his mind, he reread his mother's letter describing his sister's new life in Montana. He was still trying to understand the concept of his sister marrying another woman, but from what his mother had written, Jennifer was happy and that was all that mattered to him. His mother had gone on to recount the events of his father's trip to Montana. Thomas compared the details in the letter to the version his father had told upon his forced return. It seemed his father had left out quite a few facts, especially his role in the tragic events that cost Andrew Barrish his life and had almost cost Jennifer hers. He wondered what the consequences might be if his father carried out his current threat to go back to Montana.

As he watched his father seethe, Thomas determined not to allow him to destroy the happiness Jennifer appeared to have found. "I will accompany you to Montana, but only I will accompany you and only under the following conditions."

Kensington glared at his eldest son. "If I refuse?"

"I will send word to the territory authorities, alerting them to your intentions."

"You wouldn't dare."

Thomas stared at the man who had come to control his family through the use of intimidation. No wonder his sister had chosen to run away. He marveled that he himself had never taken the same option. "Yes, Father, I would," he promised. When his father didn't reply, Thomas stated his terms. "Condition one, you will not seek Jennifer's return. Condition two, you will allow Mother to make her own decision as to whether she returns to live with us or stays with Jennifer."

"Then what's the point in going?" Kensington ground out through gritted teeth.

Exactly. "The point is for me to talk to them and ascertain if they are well and what their wishes are. And for me to *ask* Mother to return," Thomas said. He missed his mother and wanted her to be a part of his life again, especially now that he was preparing to ask a wonderful young lady to be his wife.

"Not your sister?"

"Jennifer has a new life, Father. She is married and has a child. There is nothing for her here."

"Living with a whore and a bastard." Kensington snorted. "Some life."

Thomas' jaw clenched. "Do you agree to my conditions, or not?"

"When I get your mother and sister back here where they belong, I will make sure they understand the consequences of defying me. Train leaves tomorrow," Kensington said as he rose from the chair. "Whether you go or not is your choice." He stormed from the room.

"For Jennifer's sake, I hope the love she shares with her Jesse is as strong as Mother claims," Thomas muttered. He made a silent vow that he would not let his father hurt Jennifer ever again. And if his mother chose to return, things would be different for her also.

The heavyset bald man puffed on a cigar, then jabbed it at Harrington. "What do you mean, married to another woman?"

"Just what I said," Tobias Harrington insisted. "Two women, married to each other. All nice and legal, according to Mayor Perkins."

A tall, thin man shook his head. "Scandalous."

"They refused our offer?" another asked.

"Never heard the offer," Harrington corrected. He was standing at the head of a large circular table, around which sat a dozen men who formed the investment group that employed him. He had returned to their Boston offices to report on the developments in Sweetwater. "They turned me down before I could give them any details."

"This mayor..." A man with curly red hair and bushy sideburns spoke. "Did he not promise he could make things happen for us in this town? What's the name of it?" He reviewed several pages of notes spread out before him on the table. "Sweetwater?"

"Yes, but—"

"Yet," the red haired man continued without letting Harrington finish, "the first thing we ask of him fails to happen."

"I don't understand," the bald man interrupted. "How can such a marriage be legal?"

"Will you shut up!" the red haired man shouted. "I don't give a tinker's damn if the women are married to each other. I do care that we are now required to build a hotel, something we hadn't budgeted for. And," he directed his barb at Harrington, "I wonder if the men we entrusted this project to are worth the money we're paying them."

Harrington felt the ground slipping out from under him, and he struggled to regain solid footing. "Mayor Perkins is very influential in Sweetwater."

"Doesn't appear to be."

Harrington searched the faces around the table, uncertain which of the men had spoken.

"Can we trust him?" a man sweating heavily asked. "And do we even need him?"

"We do need Perkins for the bank charter," Harrington answered. "Has to be a resident of the territory."

"Hell, we can get any idiot to front for us on the charter," the red-haired man argued. "Perkins is supposed to be able to get things done and do it without costing us money."

"Perkins not withstanding," everyone at the table quieted as the elderly man spoke, "is there any chance of getting these women to change their minds?"

"I don't believe so, sir."

"Then there is no sense in us continuing this discussion." The others nodded; the elderly gentleman was the president and founder of their investment company. "Harrington, I want you to return to Sweetwater and oversee our operations there. You are to make arrangements for the building of a hotel at as little expense as possible. Do you understand?"

"With all due respect, sir," Harrington objected, "it was my assignment to secure an ally in Sweetwater. That I have done. I do not see any reason for me to have to return there."

"You are correct, Mr. Harrington," the company president replied, "to a degree. It was also your assignment to provide us with a good starting position. Which, it is quite evident, you have not done. Why was the offer for the boarding house handled so inefficiently? You said that the owners never actually heard our offer, yet they turned you down. What happened?"

Harrington couldn't believe he was being held accountable for those unnatural women refusing to sell, but he wasn't about to tell these men why his attempt at making the offer had been so abruptly rebuked. He didn't believe his own demeanor in the Slipper had played any part in the rejection. "Mayor Perkins believed that—"

"Mayor Perkins is a fool." The president slammed a fist on the table. "And you should have made a better choice for our advocate. Now we are stuck with this man who seems to be incapable of following instructions. I have just today received the list of building materials he ordered for the bank building."

Oh, no. I knew I shouldn't have left that up to him. Harrington cleared his throat nervously, but didn't get the chance to defend himself.

"Did you know he has engaged the services of a Denver architect to design the building?"

Harrington vaguely remembered Perkins mentioning something about that, but the man rambled on so that he tended to tune him out. Maybe he should have paid closer attention. "No, sir."

"Did you know he is planning to use brick and sandstone blocks in its construction?"

He definitely should have paid closer attention to the mayor's ramblings. "No, sir."

"Did you know he has ordered the most expensive safe available from New York City?"

"No, sir." He would strangle that overly talkative rotund mayor when he got back to Sweetwater.

"It is apparent to me, Mr. Harrington, that you have not performed your duties in a satisfactory manner. Therefore, I want you on the next train back to Montana Territory. And you will not return until you have successfully completed this undertaking. Do I make myself clear?"

"Yes, sir."

"And keep an eye on Mayor Perkins. I do not want him causing us any more problems. Or more importantly, costing us any more money."

"But, sir—"

"You are dismissed."

Harrington nodded and quickly backed away from the table. *Those Branson women are the cause of this. If only they had accepted the offer for their boarding house. One way or another, I will most definitely make them pay.*

CHAPTER SEVENTEEN

It was dark in the mine tunnel; dark, damp, dirty, and smelly. But he wouldn't have to put up with the conditions much longer. The Songbird mine would soon be someone else's problem, and he'd be heading back to St. Louis, to his wife and children, with a bag full of money. He whistled tunelessly as he worked to clean up the shaft, doing his best in the dim light his lantern provided. There was no reason to leave anything lying about now that the assayer had come and gone. All he had left to do was sign the papers and get his money, which he would do the next day. Yes, soon he would be living on Easy Street and those big shots from back East could deal with this mountain of rock.

The stagecoach left Denver at sunrise with three passengers. Just before nightfall, the horse team was reined to a stop at an overnight depot. The men inside the coach were relieved that the first day of their journey was over.

At the best of times, traveling by stagecoach was never pleasant. If the roads were wet, mud would be thrown everywhere, caking into globs of sticky goo. If the roads were dry, dust would coat the horses, coach, baggage, and passengers without prejudice. Either way, the coach's canvas window covers were almost always tied down to protect the passengers as much as possible. The curtains did help keep the mud and dust out, but they also kept the heat and stale air in, making for steam-bath conditions inside the coach.

Stage roads were seldom more than ruts, pocked with potholes and strewn with rocks, causing the stage to lurch violently as it rolled over the obstacles. On the rare occasion that the stage traveled along a relatively smooth stretch of road, the coach would still sway robustly. No matter the road conditions, the passengers inside were continually thrown against one another and the sides of the coach. Any attempts at carrying on a conversation while the stagecoach was in motion were quickly abandoned when passengers found all their energy was required just to maintain their seats. Thus it was that the three passengers had spent an entire day together with no more than a nod of the head between them.

The one-story way station made of roughly hewn logs was separated into three sections. A dining area in the front half of the building was separated from the cooking area at its side by a partial wall. The sleeping area for the stage driver and passengers took up the rear half of the station. In the middle of the dining room sat a serviceable table that was nothing more than a wide plank resting on two blocks of wood. Benches on either side of the table were similar in design, only not as wide and not as high.

As the three passengers carried their luggage into the building, the stationmaster's wife was placing bowls of food on the table. "Put your bags back there." She pointed to a doorway leading into the back room. "Best come eat while it's hot."

All three men groaned as they surveyed the sleeping quarters. A dozen cots were spaced unevenly about the room, some looking as if their days of usefulness had passed years before. The cots were outfitted with linens, pillows, and blankets, all of which were dirty, stained, and full of holes and, unquestionably, bed bugs. Quickly claiming the cots that seemed to pose the least danger, the men set down their luggage and returned to the other room.

"Privy is out back," the woman said as the men took seats at the table. "Best be careful where you step; rattlers get pretty active this time of day." She set a pot of coffee in the center of the table. "If'n you be wantin' a bath, you'll have to use the trough by the barn. Just don't get it too muddy. Horses don't take kindly to that." Her duty done, she disappeared into the cooking area.

The men looked dubiously at the meal provided for them. It was hard to deduce what many of the serving dishes held, but they were hungry after the long day and filled their plates.

As he reached for the coffeepot, Harrington glanced at the men sitting on the opposite side of the table. One was obviously older than the other and, judging by their resemblance, he presumed them to be father and son. "Coffee?" Harrington offered, and he filled their cups when they nodded. "I'm Tobias Harrington."

"Kensington," the older of the two responded. "Martin Kensington, and this is my son, Thomas."

"Kensington?" Harrington took a bite of the stew, frowning when he couldn't readily identify the animal the meat had come from. "Seems I've heard that name before. On the Coast, perhaps."

"Kensington Shipping Line," Martin said proudly.

"Ah, yes." Harrington nodded. "Mighty fine company you have, sir. It is well known as one of the best." *Maybe this trip won't be so bad after all.*

"Thank you." Martin reached for more biscuits, thinking that they were safer to eat than the meat Harrington was having so much trouble chewing. "However, I prefer to think of it as being the best."

"Yes, of course." Harrington gave up on chewing the meat and quickly swallowed to get rid of it. "You built it on your own?"

"Took it over from my father and his father before him, as my sons will one day take over from me."

"A business to pass on to your sons is a wonderful legacy." Harrington decided to give the bowl of roasted potatoes a try.

"Yes," Martin agreed.

"What brings you west, Mr. Kensington?" Harrington used a knife to cut through the undercooked vegetable. "There aren't any seaports in the territory that I know of," he added lightly, so his dinner companions wouldn't think he was prying.

"No." Kensington struggled with a potato of his own. "Personal business. I've come to escort my wife and daughter back home."

"Visiting relatives, are they?"

"Excuse me, Mr. Harrington," Thomas interrupted, "but I do believe our family business need not be discussed with strangers." He did not want to listen to any more of his father's ravings about Jennifer and her wife, which was all he had heard on the long train journey to Denver.

"Thomas, Mr. Harrington meant no harm."

"It is a private matter, Father."

Martin fumed at his son's impertinence but rather than create a scene in front of the other traveler, he chose to drop the matter. "I'm sorry, Mr. Harrington." Martin smiled uneasily. "It has been a long trip, and my son is tired."

"No offense taken." Harrington saw no reason to alienate the man when he saw potential for a future business relationship with Kensington's company. "I think I'll stretch my legs before turning in." He smiled pleasantly as he stood.

The stationmaster and coach driver entered, their work rubbing down and feeding the horses completed.

"Best git ya some sleep," the driver told Harrington as he headed for the front door. "We'll be leaving at dawn. You'll git called fer breakfast a hour b'fore."

"Just a short walk to stretch my legs," Harrington replied.

"Keep a watch out fer snakes."

"I don't know, Miss Jennifer." Ruthie was looking through the pages of a catalog, each page filled with descriptions of different kinds of cloth and their advantages for different types of clothing. "It's hard to know what to order when you can't see it." The catalog lacked pictures.

"I agree." Jennifer was looking through a second catalog. "And all the descriptions are so general. Like this one." She pointed to a spot on one page. "Yellow flowers on pale background. How are you supposed to know what that is?"

"This one jus' says gingham." Bette Mae pointed at another part of the page. "Doesn't even say what color."

"And the notions are even worse," Mary added.

"Notions?" Jesse asked without looking up from the paper she was sketching on.

"Thread, ribbons, buttons, etcetera," Jennifer explained. "Here it says the thread comes in red, blue, green, black. That's it, no shades of red, just red."

"So?" Jesse asked absently as she continued to draw.

"What if you're sewing a rose dress?" Jennifer asked. "What color thread will you use so it blends in and doesn't show?"

Jesse lifted her arm and examined the sleeve of her cotton work shirt, cocking her head to the side. The thread didn't blend in. In fact, it was quite easy to see. "Does it matter?"

Jennifer chuckled. "Yes, you old cowhand. For a lady's dress, it most certainly matters."

"Oh." Jesse went back to her diagram.

The women were in the office at the Slipper. Jennifer and Ruthie were sitting on the couch with the catalogs Ed had from the Bozeman suppliers spread out on their laps. Mary was sitting on a chair brought in from the dining room, and Bette Mae had pulled the armchair next to the couch. Mary and Bette Mae were leaning forward to see the books held by Ruthie and Jennifer. Jesse sat at her desk with KC perched next to her, the baby watching Jesse intently.

Jesse was evaluating her sketch of the interior of the office, with an eye to the best way to remodel it into a dress shop. "How 'bout we put that window in this wall?" She pointed to a spot on the drawing.

"Otay," KC agreed.

Jesse drew in a window. "Now, where should we put the next one?"

"Jesse?"

"Hm?" Jesse drew another window on the outside wall.

"I think we should make a trip to Bozeman," Jennifer said.

"Oh," Jesse responded absently as she reviewed her drawing. She wasn't sure how many windows it would take to brighten the dark room or the best place to locate them. The office had two outside walls, but she had the covered porch on the other side of those walls to take into consideration.

"We can't possibly know what to order by looking at these catalogs. I think we should take Ruthie and go visit the suppliers ourselves. That way we can see what the material actually looks like."

"Oh, Miss Jennifer, I couldn't," Ruthie protested.

"Hush, child," Bette Mae shushed. "Ain't nothin' ta go ta Bozeman. B'sides, ye're gonna have ta learn ta do some of this by yerself. Jennifer ain't gonna always have time, 'specially when school starts again."

"Bette Mae is right, Ruthie." Jennifer smiled reassuringly. "Once school starts, I won't have time to do as much with the shop. And we know Jesse isn't going to be of much help."

"Hey." The rancher pouted playfully. "I can help. I know what I like to see on my wife and," she grinned mischievously, "what I like to see off."

"Jesse!" Jennifer's cheeks colored as the other women giggled. "You are so bad."

"Well, Sunshine," Jesse winked at Jennifer, "guess Momma is goin' ta have ta spank me when we get home."

"Jesse Marie Branson!" Jennifer cried.

"Uh, oh," Bette Mae whispered to Mary. "Seems these two are fixin' ta have a spat. Care ta join me for a cool drink in the other room?"

"I think that would be a wise course of action." Mary stood. "Come on, Ruthie." She waited for the younger woman to join them.

"Mommy." KC pouted, upset Jesse was no longer focused on the drawing and her.

"Just a minute, Sunshine," Jesse said as she saw the look on Jennifer's face. "I'm thinking I might have just stuck my boots in a cow pie." Picking up KC, she walked to the couch and sat beside her steaming wife.

"My mother was in the room, Jesse," Jennifer said quietly.

"I know." Jesse draped an arm around her wife's shoulders and pulled her close. She was relieved when Jennifer didn't resist. "I'm sorry, darlin'. Guess I jus' wasn't thinkin'."

Jennifer remained silent but leaned into Jesse's embrace. "So," she purred after several long and awkward minutes, "just what sort of clothes do you like to see off of me."

Jesse was relieved Jennifer wasn't going to stay angry at her. She hooked a finger under Jennifer's chin and tenderly tilted her face upward. "Just about anything you have on, I like to see come off. I love you," she sighed as she softly pressed her lips against Jennifer's.

"Mommy."

When Jesse had plucked KC off the desk, KC had done the same with the drawing. She poked a finger at the paper. "Do you really think we need to go to Bozeman?" Jesse asked, taking the paper from the baby.

"Sweetheart..." Jennifer lifted her head off Jesse's shoulder so she could look into the eyes she so loved. She leaned close to kiss sweet lips. "I know why you don't want to go," she whispered, "but I think you'll feel better if you talk to him."

"Maybe you're right. But what will I say to him?"

"Don't worry." Jennifer patted a muscled thigh. "You'll figure something out."

CHAPTER EIGHTEEN

Thaddeus returned from visiting the surrounding mining camps and found a letter waiting for him. After reading it, he immediately took the letter to the sheriff's office.

"Are you sure about this?" Billie asked the editor of the *Gazette*.

"Yes. Got it from a newspaperman in Denver. He has a friend back East, and they checked the details twice before sending that to me."

Billie reread the letter. "Damn." He shook his head. "I can't believe he'd do this without telling anyone. Folks should have had some say in this."

"I agree." Thaddeus took the letter from Billie and tucked it securely into his jacket pocket. "I'm sure they'll have plenty to say when the next edition of the *Gazette* comes out."

"You printing all of it?"

"Yes. I'll give Miles a chance to tell his side of it, but like you said, folks have a right to know."

"How many mines we talking about?"

"One, for sure. Possibly a couple more."

Billie knew the mountains around Sweetwater were dotted with hundreds of claims — anywhere from small placer mines worked by one or two men to larger operations requiring several men and heavy equipment to extract the ore from the ground. "I wonder which ones."

"Word in the camps is that the Songbird hit a vein," Thaddeus replied.

"Hell, that's at the top of a mountain." Billie was aware of the general location of the Songbird claim but didn't know much about the miner who worked it. He was a loner and talked very little on his few visits to town.

"The road that'll be needed to get equipment up to it will cost thousands. Add that to what the bank and hotel are costing..."

Billie whistled. "That's a lot of money. If it is the Songbird, there must have been a pretty good assay. There would have to be a mighty high percentage of ore in the rock for the backers to think that the potential earnings would be worth the investment."

"Yep, and Miles stands to share in the profit."

"Think I'll ride out and talk to Jesse."

Thaddeus pulled a second envelope from his pocket. "If you're going that way, will you give this to Jennifer? Got mixed in with mine."

Jesse was mucking out the horse stalls in the barn. Knowing better than to leave her inquisitive daughter free to wander, she had KC safely corralled in the carry sack on her back.

"Mommy." KC pointed over Jesse's shoulder to a pile of manure that had been missed in Boy's stall.

"Thanks, Sunshine," Jesse muttered as she re-entered the stall she thought she had finished cleaning.

"Jesse, I think you should take this more seriously," Billie said from his cozy perch on a hay bale.

Jesse emptied the pitchfork into the wheelbarrow. "I can't stop them from building a hotel. Besides, if they're planning to do all the stuff you say, there'll be plenty of new folks coming to town and plenty of business for both their hotel and the Slipper."

Jennifer entered the barn to take charge of KC. "Hello, Billie. What brings you out here?"

"Came to warn us that a hotel is being built in Sweetwater." Jesse started on Dusty's stall.

"Sweetheart, give KC to me. Harrington's investors?" she asked.

"Yes." Jesse came out of the stall and turned to let Jennifer remove the sack and baby from her back. "Seems they may be buying one of the mines and expanding the operations." Freed of KC's weight, she stretched the muscles in her back. "Miles is working for them. That's how he got the charter for the bank."

"When we refused to sell the Slipper, we figured that they'd build their own hotel." Jennifer pulled a few stalks of hay from KC's hair and looked at her dirt-stained face and arms. "How you manage to get so dirty, I'll never know." She had a suspicion, though. She looked at her wife and, sure enough, Jesse was just as dirty as KC. "Guess you do take after her in that way."

Billie presented his argument again for Jennifer. "A new hotel is goin' to take business away from the Slipper."

"Seems like more people coming to town will only help the Slipper's business." Jennifer unknowingly echoed Jesse's earlier comments as she dunked a handkerchief in a bucket of water. Wringing the cloth of excess water, she used it to clean some of the dirt from KC's face.

"Phttttt." KC stuck out her tongue, shaking her head from side to side to avoid the wet cloth, not at all happy at having her face washed.

"All right." Jennifer gave up. "You'll just have to wait and take a bath with Mommy."

"Otay." KC grinned. "Dow."

"No, you can leave some of the dirt on the barn floor today." Jennifer kept a firm grip on the baby. "You and Mommy are wearing more than enough already." KC's lower lip slowly pushed out into a pout.

"What about the Slipper?" Billie asked.

Jesse stopped her work and leaned on the pitchfork. "Billie, ain't nothin' we can do, one way or the other. We'll just have to see what happens when their hotel opens. Hopefully, it won't hurt the Slipper, but if it does, we still have the ranch."

Jennifer said nothing, but she knew Jesse was aware that without the Slipper's income, they would be unable to afford the ranch. If they again ever set aside enough money to get the breeding bull Jesse wanted, then maybe the ranch would begin to pay. She had already decided to give Jesse her stipend for the coming school year to help replace the funds spent for doctor bills.

Billie stood up and brushed off his pants. "Guess ye're right, Jesse. We'll just have to wait and see. Mayor Perkins will have a lot of explaining to do as soon as Thaddeus gets the *Gazette* out this week. Maybe then we'll know more about just what those investors have up their sleeves."

"Staying for supper, Billie?"

"Thanks, Jennifer, but I'm meeting Ruth."

"When you goin' to ask her to marry you?" Jesse asked as she came out of Dusty's stall with the last pitchfork load of manure.

"Damn, Jesse." Billie reddened. "Ain't talked to her about that yet."

Jesse leaned the pitchfork against the wall and bent to lift the handles of the wheelbarrow. "How long ya need? You know ya love her." She pushed the wheelbarrow out of the barn to dump its contents.

Jennifer patted Billie's arm. "You take your time, Billie."

"Thanks, Jennifer."

"Just don't take too long." Jesse teased, returning with an empty wheelbarrow.

"I'll see you two later." Billie shook his head at the good intentions of his friends. "Oh, wait a minute. I almost forgot, Thaddeus asked me to give this to you." He pulled the envelope from his pocket and handed it to Jennifer. "Here."

"What is it?"

"Letter came for you."

"Oh?" Quizzical, Jennifer read the return address.

"I'd best be gettin' back."

Jennifer and Jesse followed him outside, tucking the letter into her pocket. Seeing the worried look on her wife's face, Jesse waited until Billie rode off and then asked, "What is it, darlin'?"

"A letter from Andrew's father."

"Aren't you goin' to read it?"

Apprehensive about what it might contain, Jennifer didn't want to open the letter. Though she had truly played no part in the young man's death, she continued to feel responsible. While still recovering from her own nearly fatal wounds, she had written a long letter to his family.

Could Mr. Barrish be writing to place blame on me? "I'll read it while you and KC have your bath. Speaking of which, I better go start heating the water."

"Darlin'?" Jesse walked at Jennifer's side. "Are you okay?"

"I'm just afraid of what he might have to say. I'd rather read it later."

Jesse wanted to wrap Jennifer in her arms, but considering the chore she had just completed, she opted to kiss her on the forehead. "Why don't you take KC inside, I'll just finish up here; won't take long."

> *Dear Miss Kensington,*
>
> *I write this letter for two reasons. First, and foremost, I wish to thank you for the kind words you wrote regarding our son, Andrew. It was with strong reluctance that I agreed he should accompany your father. As you may know, Andrew was our only son, and we should have considered that harm might come to him in such a wild and dangerous country. However, circumstances clouded our judgment and, for that, I will always blame myself.*
>
> *I was outraged to hear of your father's demands that Andrew assist in his efforts to forcibly remove you from your home and further, that he participate in the unspeakable treatment of you during that terrible ordeal.*
>
> *It is thereby that I come to the second reason for this letter. It has come to my attention that your father has recently booked rail passage to Denver. I can conclude no other purpose for doing so than that he intends to, again, attempt to force your return to the East. I sincerely hope that this warning reaches you in time to prepare you for his arrival.*
>
> *I wish for you to know your description of our son's honorable conduct from his arrival in Sweetwater to the event that eventually led to his death has done much to ease the pain of his loss. I shall be forever grateful to you for giving that to us.*
>
> *Yours,*
>
> *Mr. Benjamin Barrish*

Jennifer sat on a chair next to the tub reading the letter to Jesse as she washed the day's grime from her body. KC was enjoying their shared bath and splashing noisily between her mother's legs.

"Bastard!" Jesse exclaimed. "Sorry, darlin'."

"I completely agree with you. I cannot believe he would dare return." Jennifer silently refolded the letter and returned it to its envelope, uncertainty and fear rising within her. "What are we going to do?"

Jesse reached out, resting a comforting hand on Jennifer's knee. "Don't worry, darlin'." She looked into worried eyes. "I'll never let him hurt you again."

The sun had dropped from the sky, and the moon was rising in its place. After finishing their meal in the Slipper's dining room, Billie escorted Ruthie outside to the porch where they sat in the shadows.

"Ruth, have you ever thought about..."

"About what, Billie?"

Billie took her hand and squeezed gently, thinking back to the night he had first noticed the shy girl. It was the night he had been shot while attempting to control a lynch mob determined to hang Jesse. He remembered how afraid he was when several weeks later he finally mustered the courage to ask Ruth if he could court her. And how proud he was when she agreed. "Do you remember that buggy ride?"

Confused a little by the change in subject, Ruthie hesitated. Then she smiled. "Yes, Billie." She giggled. "I remember."

Billie chuckled. "Made quite a fool of myself that day."

"No, you didn't. I thought you looked cute."

"I looked like a drowned rat."

"A very cute drowned rat." When Billie rose from his chair and moved in front of her, kneeling down on one knee. Ruthie's heart began to race.

"Ruth," Billie took both of her hands into his, "that day at the lake, I fell in love with you. And each day since, my love has grown. I've tried to come up with a romantic way to say this, but I think I just have to get it out." He took a deep breath, slowly releasing it. "Ruth, I love you. And I would be the proudest man in the territory if you would do me the honor of becoming my wife."

Tears rolled down her cheeks. "Yes," she whispered. "I would be honored to marry you, Billie."

Cupping his hands around his beloved's face, he gently brought their lips together and tenderly kissed her for the first time.

Jennifer and Jesse were talking over their options with Mary. Jesse was standing by the fireplace while Jennifer and her mother sat at the table. KC had been put to bed many hours before.

"I'm not running from him, Jesse."

"I'm not saying to run, darlin'." Jesse picked up the coffeepot to refill her cup, then set it back down without doing so. She'd had so many cups in the last few hours she'd lost count, and the thought of drinking any more was suddenly very unappealing. "Just suggesting gettin' out of Sweetwater long enough for Billie to handle things."

Mary was just as upset as the others over her husband's plan to return to Montana. "I think Jesse is right. Who knows what he has planned, Jennifer? You can't give him the opportunity to cause you or Jesse any more pain."

"This is our home," Jennifer whispered. "Why do we have to leave? He's the one in the wrong."

Jesse sat next to Jennifer and spoke quietly. "The ranch won't mean anything to me, darlin', if something happens to you. It's best we let Billie take care of your father. When he tells us it's safe, we'll come home." Taking Jennifer's hands into her own, she pleaded, "Please, darlin'. I would die if anything happened to you or KC."

Jennifer looked at the crib where their daughter was peacefully sleeping. Jesse was right. If anything happened to any of them...Jennifer leaned into Jesse, "Where will we go?"

"You wanted to see the buffalo."

"Walks on the Wind?"

Jesse nodded. "There's no way your father can find us there. But we can't take the wagon on the trail; it would mean you'd have to ride Blaze."

"Okay." Jennifer agreed even though she wasn't sure her leg would be able to handle the stress of a long ride. But she was determined to do whatever she had to, to save her family from her father.

"I think you two should get some sleep." Mary stood, yawning. "I know I can sure use some."

"I'll walk you," Jesse offered.

"No. You stay here with Jennifer." Mary bent to kiss each of them on the cheek. "When I get to the cabin, I'll pull the bell cord to let you know I got there."

"We don't know when your father left, so it's best we leave as soon as possible. We'll go to town in the morning and talk to Billie," Jesse said. "And get supplies. Mary, it'll be safer for you to stay at the Slipper while we're gone."

"I have no interest in waiting for him to arrive. I'm coming with you."

Jennifer was surprised at the forceful manner in which her mother stated her intention. "Mother, are you sure?"

"Yes. I'll see about a horse at the livery tomorrow. Besides, I think I'd like to see those buffalo Walks on the Wind talked about."

"Are you sure he's coming here?" Billie asked.

"Yes." Jennifer watched KC playing on the floor at her feet. "Can you have him arrested?"

"Considering that part of the deal was for him to leave the territory..." Billie searched in his desk drawer for the paper provided by the Bozeman sheriff detailing Kensington's agreement to leave the territory under threat of immediate arrest should he ever return. "I'll wire all the sheriffs between here and Denver to arrest him on sight and take him to the territorial prison at Deer Lodge."

"Good." Jesse blew out a breath. "Send word to us when he's locked up."

"It's a good idea for you to stay at the ranch until this is taken care of. Ah," Billie pulled some papers out of the drawer, "got it."

"We're not staying at the ranch." Jesse was standing behind Jennifer, her hands resting on her wife's shoulders gently massaging the tense muscles.

"You're not?"

"No. We're going where he won't be able to find us. I don't want to take the chance of him trying anything with Jennifer again."

Billie was concerned about the women running into trouble and there being no one to help them. "You sure ya need to leave?"

"I think it's best."

"Where ya plan on going?"

"East of the mountains. Jennifer wants to see the buffalo herds and Walks on the Wind is there with a hunting party."

Billie had met the Indian a few times at Jesse's ranch and liked the quiet man. "So, you're planning on meeting up with him?"

"Yes, you can send word there. It'll be safer."

"You're probably right." Billie made a notation on the paper. "I'll get the telegrams sent. You going to the Slipper?"

"No, Ed's. We need supplies for the trip."

"Mary staying in town?"

Bored with being on the floor, KC tugged on Jennifer's pant leg. "Momma, up."

"She's going with us." Jennifer lifted the baby into her lap and hugged her. Her voice charged with emotion, she said, "I don't want him to find us, Billie."

"He won't, Jennifer," the sheriff promised. "Just be careful. The less folks you tell about your plans, the better."

"No one will know except you, Ed, and Bette Mae," Jesse assured him.

"When you plan on leavin'?"

"First thing in the morning." Jesse helped Jennifer up from the chair. KC reached for Jesse, and she took her from Jennifer's arms.

"All right." Billie rose to walk the women to the door. "You stay put with Walk and his folk until you hear from me. And don't fret about the ranch, I'll check in on it."

Jesse clasped her friend's shoulder. "Thanks, Billie."

"Be safe, both of you."

"Goodbye, KC." Billie rubbed KC's head. "You take care of your mothers for me."

"Otay." KC held up her hand, fingers waggling up and down.

"I can't believe it," the storekeeper said after Jennifer told him about the letter she'd received.

"You can't tell anyone, Ed."

"I won't." Ed pulled Jennifer into a hug. "You don't worry 'bout anything; Billie and I will take care of your daddy."

Jennifer burst out, "I thought this was over."

"Darlin'?" Jesse was worried about Jennifer. It was a good thing they were leaving Sweetwater because if they'd stayed and she saw Kensington, she'd take care of him herself. And she'd make sure he could never hurt Jennifer again.

"I'm all right." Jennifer withdrew from Ed's embrace and dried her tears on her sleeve. "Let's get what we need. I want to get out of here as soon as possible."

As KC watched from her holding pen, her mothers and Ed quickly filled the back of the buckboard with the necessary supplies. It wasn't long before Boy was pulling the wagon toward the Silver Slipper.

Mary was waiting on the porch at the Slipper. A dark brown horse was tied to the hitching post next to the stairs, evidence that her trip to the livery had yielded a mount. The women hurried inside to find Bette Mae.

"Lordy, but tha' man must be thicker than a tree stump," Bette Mae said when she heard about the letter. "Don' ya be worryin' 'bout me. Ya go on and git," she told them. "The Slipper'll be jus' fine. And I'll help Billie keep an eye on the ranch for ya."

"No one can know that we're not there, Bette Mae," Jesse said.

"No one will." Bette Mae wrapped her arms around the rancher and hugged her tight. After a few moments, she released Jesse and hugged Jennifer. "Now, git."

Jesse and Jennifer stayed just long enough for KC to give Bette Mae a hug and kiss, then they returned to the buckboard. "We can tie him on back," Jesse told Mary, gesturing at the horse.

"That's okay." Mary pulled herself into the saddle. "I think I'd better ride. It'll give me a chance to get used to it again."

Jesse helped Jennifer climb into the wagon, being mindful of her damaged leg. She was concerned about the leg and the long ride ahead of them, but if it gave Jennifer trouble it would be easy enough to hole up somewhere in the mountains. And there was one added advantage to doing that: Kensington would have no hope of finding them.

Jesse settled beside Jennifer and slapped the reins against Boy's hindquarters, and the women were quickly on their way out of town.

In the office of the *Gazette*, a controversy was taking place. "Damn it, Miles." Thaddeus sat back in his chair as the mayor paced around his office, the mid-day sun streaking through the windows. "Those weren't decisions you had the right to make."

"I had every right." Miles Perkins was not amused at having been summoned to the newspaper editor's office to answer questions. "As mayor, I speak for the town."

"The position of mayor is an honorary one, Miles. You have no authority except for presiding at weddings and funerals. Heck, we don't even have a town council. You know it's always been the custom for the citizenry to vote on this kind of stuff."

"What's to vote on, Thaddeus? They're giving us a bank, building a hotel, improving the road, and hiring workers — all good things for Sweetwater."

"But at what price? You guaranteed them water rights on stretches of the river that belong to the ranchers. You promised to let them cut timber on land that doesn't belong to you. You told them Jesse and Jennifer would sell the Slipper."

"The owners of those properties will be compensated. And Jesse would have been paid substantially more than that old building is worth if she'd only listened to the offer instead of throwing us out of her office."

"That's not the point. They should have been asked before you promised."

"There wasn't time," Perkins protested.

"Especially since you would have had to settle for a lower percentage if you said you had to ask first."

Perkins turned white. "You know about that?"

"Yes, and soon everyone else in the valley will too. Here's the next edition of the *Gazette*. Care to make a comment, Mayor Perkins?" Thaddeus tossed a newspaper at the mayor. In bold print, the headline screamed:

MAYOR PERKINS SIGNS CONTRACT
WITH MINING COMPANY
GIVES AWAY VALLEY'S WATER AND TIMBER RIGHTS

CHAPTER NINETEEN

"Sweetheart, should I pack our heavy coats?" Jennifer asked as she laid out the clothing they would take.

"No." Jesse was filling a pack with foodstuffs. "It's too hot for those. Our jackets should be fine."

"Won't it be cold in the mountains at night?"

"As hot as it's been, it'll only get cold for a few hours. Our blankets should be warm enough." Jesse carried the pack to the door and set it on the floor with the other items they were taking. "Besides, coats will be bulky, and we don't want to overload Boy." With KC's needs and Mary accompanying them, she had decided to take Boy along as a packhorse.

"All right." Mary lifted a saddlebag from the table to test its weight. Satisfied she could handle it, she set the bag down with a laugh. "That's it for me. One benefit to having so few things."

Jesse went to check on Jennifer's progress. "If we want to leave at dawn, we better get to bed soon. I think we need to start supper."

Jennifer nodded. "Why don't you finish here, and I'll make us something quick."

"I can help," Mary said as she cleared the table.

KC crawled to where Jesse was placing their folded clothes into a pack. The baby pulled herself up on Jesse's leg. "Mommy?"

Jesse stopped her work and lifted the baby into her arms. "What's up, Sunshine?"

"Go?" KC pointed to the clothing spread on the bed.

"Yep." Jesse kissed the baby's cheek. "You, Momma, Grandma, and me — we're all going on a trip to see buffalo." KC smiled. "Why don't you sit right here while I finish packing." Jesse set the baby down in a clear spot on the bed. By the time she finished packing their clothes and adding them to the pile by the door, Jennifer and Mary had supper ready. Jesse washed her hands and joined her family at the table. "Smells good, darlin'."

"Thanks." Jennifer blew on a spoonful of stew broth to cool it before feeding it to KC.

"Jesse," Mary filled a glass with milk and set it by Jesse's plate, "how does one find the buffalo herds?"

"That's pretty easy." Jesse settled into her place. "The herds are so big that once you get within fifty miles of them, you'll see the dust cloud they kick up when they're on the move. The closer you get, you'll start to hear them grunting and the bulls buttin' heads. If the herd happens to be running, you'll feel the ground shake. It's really a remarkable sight."

Mary tried to visualize a herd of animals so large they could make the ground shake from so far away. "Hard to imagine that."

"In a few days, you won't have to," Jesse said with a smile.

"Walks on the Wind said they were taking the southern trail. Is that how we'll go?" Jennifer asked.

"No." Jesse took over feeding KC so Jennifer could eat. "That trail is further south than the one we took over the mountains to Bannack. We'll head due east from here and take an old trail that's seldom used anymore. It's a bit rougher, but it'll get us there quicker. Chances of meeting anyone on it are next to nothin', and we won't have to risk someone seeing us riding south through the valley."

Still apprehensive about her ability to ride any distance with her damaged leg, Jennifer asked, "How long of a ride do you think it is, sweetheart?"

"Four, maybe five days if the trail over the pass is in good shape. Another day or two, if not." Knowing why Jennifer was concerned, she added, "We can stop anytime, darlin'. We don't have to get to the hunting camp. Anywhere along the trail, we can hole up and wait for Billie to find us. You just say you can't go any further and we'll stop."

Jennifer smiled. "That makes me feel better."

"Any time, darlin'," Jesse repeated, "you say stop and we will." Jesse sniffed the air a few times. "Darlin', are you trying to burn somethin'?"

"Darn." Jennifer jumped to her feet and grabbed a towel to pull a pan away from the coals in the fireplace. She carefully sliced the contents and served a piece of the slightly overcooked cake onto four plates. In the center of one piece, she pushed a small candle, then carried the plates to the table.

"What's this?" Jesse asked.

"It'll be KC's birthday in a few days. Under the circumstances I figured we'd celebrate it a little early."

Mary remembered them talking about the baby's first birthday, but couldn't remember any date having been decided on. "It is?"

"Yes." Jennifer set the piece with the candle in front of KC. "Not yet, sweetie," she told KC when the baby reached for the plate. "We need to light the candle."

"Guess I kinda forgot all about it," Jesse admitted ruefully.

"Actually, I did, too." Jennifer took her seat. "But today when we were in the general store, I happened to see the calendar Ed has on the wall. Sorry, Mother, I meant to tell you, but somehow, with everything going on, I forgot."

Mary reached over and patted Jennifer's hand. "I'm just glad I'm here to celebrate with you."

"Me, too."

"Bette Mae is sure goin' ta be mad when she finds out," Jesse said.

"Oh." Jennifer laughed uneasily. She knew the older woman would be hurt that she'd missed the occasion. "I guess we'll be drawing straws to see who has to tell her."

"Nah." Jesse winked at Jennifer. "We'll let Mary do it."

"Momma."

"Oops, seems the birthday girl wants her cake." Jennifer reached back and snatched the box of matches off the fireplace. "Do you want to blow out your candle, KC?" KC cocked her head and looked at Jennifer.

Mary laughed at the baby's expression. "I guess she doesn't know what that means."

"Here, KC." Jesse leaned close to the baby. "Do this." She took a deep breath, puffed out her cheeks, and blew. The released air tickled the baby's face. KC giggled. "Come on." Jesse tried again. "Do this." She repeated her attempt to teach the baby.

KC looked intently at Jesse, puckered her lips, took a deep breath, puffed out her cheeks, and...

The women waited. And waited. And waited. Jesse reached out and gently poked a finger in a bloated cheek, releasing the confined air before the baby turned blue from holding her breath.

Figuring she had done what her mommy asked, KC pointed to the cake. Mary chuckled.

"Guess that's going to take a little practice," said Jesse.

"Here, sweetie." Jennifer pulled the candle out and pushed the plate close enough for KC to help herself. With the cake within her reach, KC dug in with both hands.

The men had endured several rough days of stage travel. Harrington had made no further attempts to question the elder Kensington about his reasons for traveling west, deciding to wait until he could have a private conversation with the businessman. So far Kensington's son had kept close by his father's side, but Harrington was patient. His patience finally paid off one night when he took his after-supper walk. Martin Kensington stood next to the cascading waters of a small creek.

"Mr. Kensington," Harrington said as he approached.

"Mr. Harrington."

"Seems our trip is almost complete." Harrington sat on log stretched part way over the creek.

"And none too soon for me."

"Yes." Harrington adjusted his position to move off a sharp piece of bark poking him in the backside. "I, too, will be glad for this trip to end. Although I am not anxious to face what awaits me."

"What does bring you, obviously a man of some refinement, to this godforsaken country?" Kensington sat on the log an arm's length from Harrington.

"My employers have sent me to oversee their investments. They have been forced to unnecessarily expend funds because the proprietor of a rundown, worthless boarding house in the town of Sweetwater—"

"Jesse Branson," Kensington spat out.

Harrington looked surprised. "You know her?"

"She is the very reason I have come west." Kensington proceeded to tell Harrington of his earlier trip to Sweetwater, its purpose, and its unfortunate outcome. He conveniently left out his part in the sordid affair.

"But the law, Mr. Kensington, did they do nothing?"

"Law, ha." Kensington stood and began to pace, his agitation growing with each step. "The sheriff in Sweetwater is her best friend. There is no law, not for decent people like you and me."

"I can't believe this. I have been guaranteed that Sweetwater is a law-abiding town."

"By whom?"

"Mayor Perkins."

"That son-of-a-bitch. Why, he's the bastard that officiated at my daughter's so-called marriage to that travesty of a woman."

Harrington leapt off the log in shock. "He *what!*"

"It seems he left that little fact out of his resumé." Kensington laughed humorlessly.

"I must wire my employers about this immediately. They will not be pleased to hear that the law in Sweetwater cannot be trusted. They will want to take the appropriate action."

Kensington became very interested in what Harrington was saying. "What can they do?"

"They can have the territorial governor assign a U.S. Marshal to look into these matters."

Kensington studied the man he had, until now, taken little notice of. "Your employers seem to have friends in high places, Mr. Harrington."

"It is in their best interest to ensure their money is not wasted."

"Maybe, Mr. Harrington, we can help each other."

"How so?"

"You want the Silver Slipper."

"Admittedly."

"I want that Branson harpy out of my daughter's life." Harrington listened, saying nothing as Kensington continued. "If you were able to have her arrested and put in prison, ownership of the Slipper would revert to my daughter. Once that happened, I would have Jennifer sign all rights over to you."

Harrington considered the proposition. If he could deliver the Slipper to his employers he would regain their trust and, quite possibly, be able to return east. On the other hand, if he could put Jesse Branson behind bars, Kensington might just be grateful enough to offer him a position with his company. Either way, he couldn't lose. "And what would you have her arrested for?"

"I have it on good authority that the child being referred to as my granddaughter was orphaned when its parents were murdered."

"That seems to be common knowledge in Sweetwater."

"Do you know the entire story?" Kensington asked. When Harrington shook his head, he continued. "The story told is that the child was discovered by my daughter and Branson when they traveled to Bannack. When they arrived there with the child, they reported to the sheriff that outlaws had killed the parents during a robbery attempt."

"And?"

"I have an acquaintance in Bannack who confided to me that when Sheriff Logan went to investigate their story, instead of outlaws, he found evidence that Branson had actually been the killer."

"Why wasn't she arrested?"

"She managed to get Logan hanged before he could do anything about it."

"How'd she do that?"

"She talked her friend, Sheriff Monroe, into sending a telegram to the territorial governor reporting Logan to be the leader of a gang of outlaws. Vigilantes heard that and took the law into their own hands."

"If what you say is true..."

"It's true enough." Kensington figured if it would get Jesse hanged, it didn't hurt to stretch the facts a little. "I suggest you have that U.S. Marshal check into it."

"Mr. Kensington, if what you have just told me proves to be true and you do, in fact, deliver the Silver Slipper to me. I will make sure that you are rewarded with a percentage of the Montana mining investments of my employers."

"You take care of Branson," Kensington held out his hand, "I'll take care of Jennifer."

"You have yourself a deal." Harrington put out his own hand, and the men smiled as their deal was sealed.

"Father?" Thomas, who had been looking for his father, saw the two men shaking hands. "What's going on here?"

"Nothing that concerns you, son." Kensington nodded to Harrington before turning back to the stage depot.

"Good evening," Harrington said to Thomas as he followed.

The younger Kensington stood looking after them. *What the hell are they up to?*

CHAPTER TWENTY

The sun's rays were just starting to peek over the mountains in the east, the sky unsurprisingly cloudless after another night of light rain. Jesse, with KC snug in the carry sack on her back, mounted Dusty. Moments before, she had assisted Jennifer onto Blaze while Mary mounted her hired horse.

Jesse made a last visual inspection of the ranch buildings. Satisfied nothing looked amiss, she knew it was time to leave. She tapped her heels against Dusty's sides, and the large palomino started walking, Jennifer and Mary urging their horses to follow. Boy had no choice but to follow since his lead was wrapped around Jesse's saddle horn.

She led the group due east from the ranch. Within an hour, they'd left the rolling hills of the valley floor behind them and entered the pine forest at the foot of the mountain range. At first, with no trail to follow, Jesse guided Dusty through the trees and underbrush picking the best path as they rode. As their horses kept pace, Jennifer and Mary looked in awe at the forest through which they were riding.

Ponderosa pines stood hundreds of feet high, with trunks several feet in diameter. The reddish brown bark shone bright wherever the sun's rays penetrated the dense, leafy canopy. The recent rains had encouraged wildflowers to bloom, and the forest floor was carpeted in a palette of yellows, blues, and reds. High above their heads, squirrels chattered from the safety of the branches, and unseen birds sang their morning songs and chirped at the travelers. Occasionally, startled by the intrusion of the riders, a deer or elk would bound through the trees.

It was late morning when Jesse pulled Dusty to a halt next to a small creek. "Let's take a break," she said as she swung her leg over the mare's back. "How ya doin', darlin'?" she asked as she helped Jennifer to the ground.

"So far, so good." Jennifer gingerly put weight on her damaged leg; it was sore but seemed all right. She pulled her cane from its storage in the rifle scabbard on her saddle.

"This is beautiful," Mary said, walking to the edge of the creek where the forest yielded to a small clearing covered in pine needles and moss.

Small boulders lay jumbled in the creek, tumbling its water over and around them. More boulders were scattered about the clearing, providing handy places to sit and rest. A large pine tree, probably blown down the previous winter, lay on its side stretching from the clearing across the creek and beyond into the forest on the opposite bank. The water flowed under the fallen tree.

"Water's a little dirty," Jesse commented as she and Jennifer joined Mary.

"Is that bad?" Jennifer asked as she sat on one of the larger boulders.

"May mean trouble up higher." Jesse slipped her arms free of the carry sack and gently set it next to Jennifer. She helped KC out of it. "Let's check your britches, Sunshine."

KC, released from the carry sack's confinement, started scooting for the rock's edge.

"Hold on there, squirt." Jesse grabbed KC before she could get too far. "You stay right here with Momma while I get you a fresh diaper."

"Pfttt." KC expressed her disappointment.

Jennifer lifted the pouting baby into her lap. "Sweetie, I know you want to play but you need to stay with Mommy or me or your grandma, okay?" KC continued to pout, and Jennifer kissed the baby's forehead. "I don't want you to get hurt. You be a good girl and I promise, Mommy and I will let you play when we stop for the night."

"That's right, Sunshine." Jesse returned with the saddlebag Jennifer had filled with the baby's diapers and clothing. "You be a good girl and I'll take ya in the creek after supper."

Mary had been exploring the clearing and spotted what looked like a path coming out of the trees on the opposite side of the creek and then turning to follow the creek eastward. "Is that the trail, Jesse?"

Jesse didn't look up from changing KC's soiled diaper. "Yep, it's an old Indian trail. This end isn't used much any more. It'll take us all the way up to the pass and down the other side."

Jennifer could just make out the overgrown path from where she sat. "Why has it fallen into disuse?"

"It's not safe for them now, not with so many white men in the valley. They still use it from the other side to reach their hunting grounds near the summit."

"Will we run into Indians?" Mary asked, suddenly concerned for their safety.

"Maybe." Jesse finished with the baby and sat her up. "There ya go, Sunshine. All ready until we stop again." Returning her attention to Mary, she answered, "Might be a hunting party around, but I don't expect we'll have any trouble with them. Most are pretty friendly unless you give 'em a reason not to be."

Mary regretted her apprehension. She knew her fear was wrong, especially after the pleasant evening she had enjoyed with Walks on the Wind. Remembering how affable the man had been, she wondered why the Indians were generally referred to as savages, or worse. Back home, she had read many gruesome newspaper accounts of violent Indian attacks against settlers, but Walks on the Wind had said his father had been attacked and killed by white men. She had talked to Jesse about that and had been surprised by her daughter-in-law's response.

"Been bad things done by folks on both sides," Jesse had told her. "I've learned it's best not ta judge a fella by what his kinfolk have or haven't done. Way I figure it, there's good and bad in every group of people, so I try to take each person for who they are, not what they are."

It was good advice, and it made Mary aware that she was going to have to work a lot harder to overcome her own preconceptions concerning the native people.

Jesse carried the saddlebag back to Blaze and tied it in place. She retraced her steps to KC, who raised her arms as Jesse approached. Jesse bent down and lifted the baby.

"Here, let me help," Jennifer stood and took their daughter, allowing Jesse to slip her arms into the straps of the carry sack. Then she made sure the baby was comfortable in the sack's pocket. "All set."

Jesse turned to face Jennifer, pulling her wife into a hug. "I love you."

Jennifer melted into Jesse's embrace and sighed. She wasn't sure what had prompted Jesse's declaration, but she was glad of it. "I love you, too."

KC, not wanting to be left out, wrapped her arms around Jesse's neck and squeezed hard. "Wuv."

"Ack." Jesse laughed, choking a little. "Not so tight, Sunshine."

Jennifer reached up and gently loosened the baby's grip. "You're getting strong, KC. She is, isn't she, Jesse?"

"Yep. She's not the little tyke we found any more."

"No, she's not." Jennifer looked at the baby riding on Jesse's back. No longer the tiny infant discovered buried under the remains of a burned-out wagon, KC was growing into a healthy, robust child. "She's getting so big," Jennifer said sadly as she remembered the infant.

Chuckling, Jesse tightened her hold on her tearful wife. "Darlin', she's still a baby. Don't go marryin' her off just yet."

Jennifer sighed deeply. "I'm being silly." She sheepishly grinned at her wife.

"Nah." Jesse leaned to kiss her forehead. "You're just bein' a momma."

"I am, aren't I?" Jennifer's smile widened. It was amazing: right there in that little forest clearing, she had everything she had ever dreamed of — a spouse she loved and who loved her in return and a beautiful child. She was blessed. Then she remembered the threat looming over that blessing, and her thoughts darkened. "Let's get going." She pulled out of Jesse's embrace. "We've rested long enough."

Jesse guessed at the cause of Jennifer's sudden mood change and agreed it was time to get moving. "Ready, Mary?" she called to her mother-in-law.

"Yes, I'm coming."

Jesse guided the horses through the shallow water of the creek and onto the trail. It showed evidence of having once been a heavily used path, wide enough for two people to walk side-by-side along its surface of hard-packed dirt covered by leaves and pine needles. The trail paralleled the creek as it wound its way east through the forest to the mouth of a canyon. After a mile or two, the trail began a gradual ascent with the path narrowing and becoming rocky and irregular, making travel more difficult for the horses and riders. The trail started to distance itself from the creek and, though it was soon lost from sight, the riders continued to hear the water tumbling and cascading down the canyon to the valley now far below them.

The further into the canyon Jesse led the group, the closer the canyon's steep stone cliffs closed in on them.

The trail eventually found its way back alongside the creek, and the horses were making their way across a sandy stretch enclosed by a rock ledge on the one side and the creek running along the other. It was a welcome break for the horses that had spent the better part of the last miles picking their way along the rough, stone-littered path.

Being so close to the water did little to relieve the heat building in the canyon. As the sun beat down, its warmth was absorbed by the rock and radiated back out, baking everything between the canyon walls.

Sweat rolling off her back where KC sat, Jesse looked for a camping spot. They would stop as soon as she could find an appropriate site.

Riding at the front of the group, Jesse could not see Jennifer's strained features. Her leg had begun to throb and ache, and no matter how many times the schoolteacher adjusted her position in the saddle, she could not ease the pain. She knew she only had to ask Jesse to stop and her wife would do so immediately, but she refused to say anything. She would wait to rest her leg. First she wanted to get her family as far away from her father as she could. And she was more than willing to endure any pain to do so. Jennifer looked up at the sky and saw that the sun was past the midday point. She was sure Jesse would be calling an end to the day's travel sometime soon.

The horses crested a rise and the rocky, uneven trail leveled and smoothed. A small clearing opened before them. Jesse looked around. The creek was close, the ground was relatively level, there were plenty of trees for shade and a good supply of firewood lying about. "We're camping here," she announced and wasn't surprised when she heard no objections.

Jesse swung herself down from Dusty and turned to help Jennifer, who was struggling to dismount. She grasped her wife around the waist and carefully set her on the ground. When Jennifer maintained her hold on the saddle and made no attempt to remove herself from Jesse's steadying hands, the rancher knew something was wrong. She scooped Jennifer up into her arms and carried her to a nearby tree, setting her wife down softly on the bed of pine needles at its base. "How bad is it?"

"It's not too bad," Jennifer lied. "I just need to rest it for a while."

"You should have said something," Jesse scolded as she slipped KC and her carry sack off her back.

Mary joined them and handed Jennifer a canteen. "Here's some water." She knelt beside her daughter, extremely concerned about the paleness of her skin. "You don't look well." When she caressed Jennifer's cheek, the skin was damp and clammy.

"I'm okay." Jennifer tried to smile, but the pain was too great. "I just need to rest."

"Stay with her, Mary. I have to take care of the horses."

"Momma?" KC crawled to where Jennifer sat and climbed onto her good leg. "Yum."

"Are you hungry, sweetie?" Jennifer reached to lift the baby into her lap but stopped immediately when the action caused a stab of pain in her leg.

"You sit still." Mary sat KC next to Jennifer. "I'll get you both something to eat."

Jesse had pulled the saddles and packs off the horses and was standing near the creek, letting the animals enjoy a long drink. Mary knelt by the packs and began to open the ones holding the cooking utensils and food. Each of them, feeling guilty for not paying closer attention to Jennifer's discomfort during the day's ride, kept a remorseful eye on the injured woman.

Happy to be out of her carry sack and unaware of her momma's suffering, KC pulled herself upright to stand leaning against Jennifer's shoulder, pointing and jabbering about the surrounding sights. Jennifer tried to pay attention to KC's gibberish, but she found it hard as she watched Jesse and her mother prepare the campsite. She was exasperated and angry at not being able to help.

Jesse let Dusty and Blaze loose, knowing they would not wander far, but Boy and Mary's hired horse were picketed next to the creek with a good supply of grass within reach. Next, she set to work getting the campsite set up. Water for cooking was brought from the creek, a fire was started, and bedrolls were laid out. She made sure Mary had everything she needed to prepare their supper, even offering to help cook, but Mary insisted she could manage on her own. With no chores left to put off facing Jennifer any longer, the embarrassed woman walked to where Jennifer waited.

"I got your bed ready, darlin'." Jesse knelt beside Jennifer. "It'll be more comfortable than sitting here on the ground. I'm so sorry, Jennifer," Jesse blurted, cupping her wife's cheek in her hand. "I should have been payin' closer attention. I should have stopped hours ago."

Jennifer's eyes filled with tears at the mortified look on her lover's face. "You have nothing to be sorry for, sweetheart. I should have said something but," she leaned into Jesse's touch, "I wanted to get as far away from Sweetwater as we could. I'm so sorry."

Jesse shifted positions so she could sit behind Jennifer and lovingly wrapped her arms around her wife, relieved when Jennifer leaned back into her embrace.

"Come on, KC. Let's get your pants changed, and then you can help me make supper," Mary told the baby, knowing the couple needed some time alone.

Jennifer awoke to the sound of water splashing and KC giggling.

"Hush, Sunshine," Jesse whispered. "We don't want to wake Momma."

"Otay," KC whispered back. But, as babies will do, she continued making noise as she played.

Jennifer opened her eyes to discover the sun was well up in the sky. "Guess yesterday took more out of me than I thought," she said, not thinking anyone would hear.

"It sure seemed to." Mary was sitting close by. She had been watching Jesse and KC play as Jennifer slept.

Jennifer grimaced as she stretched to work out the soreness that sleeping on the ground had caused.

The night before, Jesse, unable to provide a hot bath for her wife, had soaked towels in hot water and wrapped them around the aching leg. Just before they went to bed, she had lovingly massaged Jennifer's tired body, lavishing special attention on her leg. By the time sleep claimed Jennifer the pain had lessened considerably. Unfortunately, stretching the muscles reawakened the raw nerves.

"I'd ask how your leg was, but seeing the look on your face, I think I have a pretty good idea." Mary frowned. She was still feeling guilty for not noticing Jennifer's distress the day before. "Are you hungry?"

"A little." Jennifer smiled to ease her mother's guilt. "And the leg isn't as bad as I expected. It really isn't much worse than on a normal morning."

Mary knew better than to question Jennifer further. She had come to appreciate that Jennifer lived with a great deal of pain and discomfort and respected how her daughter never allowed herself to complain. For her daughter, the limitations of the injured leg were just a fact of her life now and didn't need to be discussed. It had taken Mary some time to understand that Jennifer found it easier not to talk about the leg because that kept away the awful memories of the cougar's attack and Andrew Barrish's death.

As more laughter floated across the campsite, Jennifer propped herself up on her elbows so she could see what KC was doing that sounded like so much fun. Jesse was sitting in a small, shallow pool with KC sitting on her legs, and the two were splashing each other unmercifully. Several large stones encircled the pool of calm water, separating it from the creek rushing beside it.

Jennifer didn't recall seeing the pool the night before, so she assumed Jesse must have created it that morning. She chuckled, watching her wife and daughter play.

"Jesse sure has a way with the child," Mary observed as she followed Jennifer's gaze toward the creek.

"Yes, she does." Jennifer, now fully awake, realized how warm the day was and how hot she was under the blankets covering her lower body. She threw the blankets aside. "And KC simply adores her."

"Seems she adores both of you."

The movement of the blankets attracted KC's attention. "Momma."

"Good morning, sweetie," Jennifer called to the baby. "You're not getting Mommy too wet, are you?" She laughed when KC punched her little fists into the pool, causing water to fly everywhere.

Jesse held up her hands to protect herself against KC's assault. "Afternoon, darlin'."

"Afternoon?"

"Yes, dear. Jesse didn't want to wake you; she said you needed to rest. She does look after you, doesn't she?"

That was one of the things Jennifer loved most about Jesse — she was always there for her. Even when Jennifer herself didn't think she needed it, her wife would surprise her with a thoughtful word or action and her heart would melt all over again. Like now, when she looked to the pool and saw the center of her life playing with their baby as if they didn't have a care in the world.

"Yes, Mother." Jennifer sighed contentedly. "She does."

Jesse stood up, lifting KC from the water along with her. The baby was not happy to be removed from the pool, but Jesse whispered something in her ear and KC giggled. Jesse sloshed to the edge of the pool, then up the bank to the campsite.

Jennifer suddenly became aware that Jesse was as naked as KC. "Jesse!"

"How ya doin'?" Jesse settled on the bedroll next to Jennifer, the sun's warmth making quick work of drying the water droplets from her tanned skin. KC climbed from Jesse's lap onto Jennifer's.

"You're naked," Jennifer whispered.

Cocking her head to the side, Jesse scratched behind her ear, bewildered at Jennifer's comment. "Usually am when I take a bath."

"But Jesse," Jennifer wrapped her discarded blanket around the naked body, "someone could see you."

"Darlin," Jesse laughed, "ain't nobody around here for miles. How's the leg?" she asked, her tone turning serious.

Remembering how hurt Jesse had been the day before when she'd kept her pain to herself, Jennifer decided to tell Jesse the truth. "It hurts. I don't think I can ride very far today."

Jesse bent to kiss Jennifer. "Well, that works out just fine, then. We're staying here, aren't we, Sunshine?"

"Yep," KC said proudly.

Jennifer laughed at the baby's imitation of Jesse. "How long have you been working on getting her to say that?"

"A while." Jesse smirked. "Thought since she looks like you, she should sound like me."

"Oh, you did?" Jennifer shook her head, amused. "I'm not sure I'm ready for that."

"Too late. Come on, KC." Jesse reached out to steady the baby. "Get off your momma so she can get up."

"Otay." KC swung her feet over Jennifer's side, then slipped off to sit next to Jesse on the bedroll.

Placing a hand on Jesse's arm, Jennifer said, "Sweetheart, maybe we shouldn't stay here today. Father could already be in Sweetwater."

Jesse was more concerned about Jennifer's leg than about where her father-in-law was. "We don't know that he's even arrived in the territory yet. And even if he has, he can't find us here. Very few people know about this trail, and the ones that do won't be tellin' him anything. Besides," she delicately ran her hand the length of Jennifer's leg, "you need to rest."

Jennifer wasn't convinced that her determined father wouldn't be able to find them. "But—"

"No," Jesse said softly. "We stay here today. Tomorrow, too, if we have to."

"All right," Jennifer agreed. There really was no point in arguing; Jesse was right — her leg needed the rest.

"Miles, what in the hell were you thinking?" Conrad Billingsley demanded.

The citizens of Sweetwater crowded into the dining room of the Silver Slipper, it being the largest room in town for such a gathering. The day before, the *Gazette* had broken the story of the mayor's association with the Eastern investment group and of the guarantees he had provided them. It wasn't long before a town meeting was called.

The embattled mayor tried to worm his way out of the fact he had promised rights to valley resources he did not own or control. "It's good for Sweetwater."

"I'm not giving up my water rights so some group of dandies back East can dig up a mountain." Conrad Billingsley had built his Rocking B ranch into the largest in the valley and, with it, controlled more than half the valley's water.

"They will compensate you, Conrad," Perkins told the angry man. "Rather handsomely, I might add."

"You fool." Billingsley reached for the mayor's neck. "I can't water my herds on their greenbacks."

"Back off, Conrad." Billie stepped between the two men before any harm could come to the mayor. "Sit down," Billie commanded the rancher. "We need to talk about this, but I'm not going to let anyone get hurt."

Billingsley stood his ground. "He promised them my water rights."

"And mine," added Marcus Butler, owner of another of the valley's larger ranches. "I don't care how much money this Harrington and his investment group plan to pay, I'm not selling those rights."

"*Sit.*" Billie was tired of everyone trying to outshout the others. "So we can discuss what we can do."

"Hang the bastard," someone yelled. Many in the crowd quickly voiced their agreement. Perkins paled, instinctively reaching for his throat as if a noose was tightening around it.

"No one's going to be hanged," Billie told the angry people. "I know what Miles did was wrong, and he'll pay. As for selling your rights, you don't have to accept their offers."

"Billie's right." Thaddeus Newby moved from where he had been watching the proceedings to stand next to the sheriff. "You can tell Harrington and his group you refuse, just like Jesse and Jennifer did."

"What about Jesse?" Billingsley asked the newspaperman.

"Tha' Harrington waltzed in here and said he was ta buy the Slipper," Bette Mae told the room. "Miles done told him they'd be happy to sell."

"I did not," Perkins protested. "I simply said that Jesse and Jennifer were too busy to bother with this place." His arm swept around the room. "And that they'd probably be real glad to have someone offer to take it off their hands."

"What 'bout me and the girls?" Bette Mae glared at the mayor. "What was we supposed ta do?"

"I'm sure you could find jobs in Bozeman or Bannack or one of the mining camps," the mayor hedged. "After all, your services aren't exactly dependent on Sweetwater."

"Why ya little..." Bette Mae stormed toward the arrogant mayor, several of the women who worked for the Slipper following close behind.

"Stop." Billie moved to block the angry women. "Killing him won't solve anything, Bette Mae." Even though after hearing the mayor's offensive remarks, he could have killed the man himself for insulting the Slipper's employees, who happened to include his fiancée.

"Miles Perkins." Loud and clear, a voice from the middle of the room cut through the confusion of angry shouts. "I knew you were a horse's ass when I married you, but I will not sit here and listen to you say such terrible things."

"Why now, I think Mayor Perkins simply spoke the truth. The Silver Slipper is nothing but a whorehouse, and it's scandalous that decent folks are expected to allow such an establishment in their town."

Everyone in the room turned to look at the man who had spoken. Billie recognized Martin Kensington, standing just inside the Slipper's front door. At his side stood a younger man who appeared to be another Kensington, and Tobias Harrington. Few in the room would have seen any of the trio before.

"Kensington, what the hell are you doing back here?" Ed Granger roared. Seeing the Easterner brought back the memory of fear on Jennifer's face when she had told him of her father's intentions to return to Sweetwater.

"Mr. Kensington has a right to be here," Harrington confidently told Ed.

"Like hell he does." Bette Mae directed her anger away from the mayor and toward the man who had caused Jesse and Jennifer so much pain.

"Who the hell is that?" Billingsley and Butler both demanded at the same time.

Mayor Perkins, anxious to focus the gathering's attention on someone else, literally ran to greet his benefactor, an action his dismayed wife could not recall ever seeing before. "Mr. Harrington, it's so good to see you again."

"That's Harrington?" Billingsley started for the small man at the door.

All at once, everyone in the room was shouting. Their rage was directed at Harrington, Kensington, and Perkins, individually or together, depending on their situation. Chairs were overturned and tables knocked aside as folks attempted to get to the men standing near the front door.

"Dammit!" Billie yelled over the growing bedlam. "Everyone calm down."

Seeing a hostile crowd surging toward them, a bewildered Thomas Kensington pulled his father and Harrington back out the door. Mayor Perkins squeezed through the opening seconds before Thomas yanked the door shut for the slight protection it might provide. "Run!"

"Where?" Harrington asked.

"This way." Perkins took off down the stairs. "My office."

Harrington and Kensington followed as Thomas struggled to hold the door against the frantic but uncoordinated efforts to open it from inside the Slipper. As he felt the door being pulled from his grasp, Thomas released his grip and took off at a run after the others.

Inside the Slipper, chaos reigned. Shouting, pushing, arguing, everyone seemed to have a different idea as to what should be done with Kensington, Harrington, and Perkins. And they were voicing their opinions quite loudly as they struggled to crowd through the door.

Thaddeus looked at Billie, shrugging. "Another orderly meeting of Sweetwater's finest." His tone was mocking as he remembered a night not too long ago when he and Billie had faced down another mob.

"Seems there's only one way to get their attention." Billie pulled the pistol from the holster he wore around his waist.

"Jesse won't like another hole in her ceiling," Thaddeus observed.

"Doubt if she'd like them tearing the Slipper apart." Billie pointed the gun toward the ceiling and pulled the trigger. Everyone froze. "Please," Billie glared at the crowd, "sit down." Folks grumbled but followed the sheriff's order.

Conrad Billingsley, still standing next to the door, which he had given up trying to open when the gun was fired, asked Billie, "What do you plan to do about Miles?"

"And Kensington?" Bette Mae added.

"You're letting them get away!" someone shouted.

"No one is getting away." Billie's gun remained in his hand, ready if needed. "Miles won't go any further than his office, and I'm sure the others are with him."

"So what are you going to do?" Billingsley repeated.

"I'll go over there and talk to them. Before you say anything, Bette Mae, I'm arresting Kensington for violating his release agreement."

"You can tell that Harrington, I'm not selling my water rights, no matter how much he offers to pay," Billingsley said. Others in the room echoed his sentiment.

Billie nodded. "I'll tell him. Now I want you all to go back to your own business."

"This is our business," Butler shouted angrily from where he stood beside Billingsley.

"I know that," Billie shouted back, just as angry. "Let me handle this. Anyone that wants to can come by my office and file a complaint against Mayor Perkins. I'll tell Harrington the dealings he had with the mayor are invalid, and he'll have to approach each of you individually so you can make your own deals with him. If you have a mind to."

"All right, Billie," Billingsley told the sheriff. "We'll let you handle it for now. But if that man sets one foot on my property, I'll blow his head off."

"You talkin' Harrington or Perkins?" Butler asked.

"Both."

After the townsfolk cleared out of the Slipper, Billie took a moment to talk to Ruthie. The young woman was worried about the sheriff facing the mayor and other men alone.

"Why don't you take Mr. Granger and Mr. Newby with you?"

"I'll be fine, honey," Billie assured his fiancée. "Thaddeus is coming with me. He'll be wantin' to write up Kensington's arrest for the *Gazette*."

Ruthie wasn't at all appeased. "You be careful. I don't trust Miss Jennifer's father. And that other man he brought with him looks just as mean."

"I'll be careful."

"Billie, ya ain't plannin' ta keep tha' sorry excuse for a papa in yer jail, are ya?" Bette Mae walked up to the couple. "'Cause I'm thinkin' he ain't goin' ta be too safe there. 'Specially since I do all the cookin' for yer prisoners." She grinned wickedly.

"Hope that's not a threat."

"Yes, sir. Tha's 'xactly what tha' is."

Billie knew Bette Mae disliked Jennifer's father. Disliked probably wasn't a strong enough word to describe her feelings, yet she wasn't about to poison the man. At least he didn't think so. However, she just might be willing to make him a little sick. "You promise not to poison him, and I'll take him to Deer Lodge in the morning."

"Make sure ya git the nastiest horse the livery has to drag his sorry butt there," Bette Mae huffed as she straightened up the mess left behind by Sweetwater's citizenry.

"I've got to go," Billie told Ruthie as Bette Mae walked away. "I won't be able to see you tonight. I'll have to stay at the jail."

Ruthie smiled demurely. "I love you."

"I love you, too." Billie pecked Ruthie on the cheek.

Ruthie's face tinted with a blush. "Be careful."

"I will." Billie walked to the door. "Coming, Thaddeus?"

"Right behind you." The newspaper editor smiled. He had watched the exchange between the couple and knew a story when he saw one. Billie would be answering some questions of his own before the day was done.

From the Slipper, Billie and Thaddeus went straight to the sheriff's office. The sheriff took a shotgun out of the rack behind his desk and loaded it, putting extra shells in his pocket. He marched out of his office and crossed the few feet to the office next door, the newspaper editor on his heels.

Mayor Perkins sat at his desk while Harrington paced nervously about the room. Martin Kensington and his son sat in chairs opposite the desk, watching the distraught man.

"Perkins..." Harrington stopped momentarily to look out the window at the Slipper. Seeing no activity outside the building, he turned back to the others. "Your mess just keeps getting bigger."

"But I—"

"Shut up." Harrington was pacing again. "I have to think. Mr. Kensington, you've dealt with these people. What do you think they'll do next?"

Thomas couldn't understand the angry reactions his father's appearance had provoked from some of the people in the Slipper. Not to mention, the very vocal hostility directed at Tobias Harrington. "Father, what in the hell have you gotten us mixed up in?"

"Be quiet," Kensington hissed. "You wanted to come along. Don't start questioning me."

"I agreed we'd talk to Jennifer, nothing more."

"Look," Harrington slammed a fist down on the mayor's desk, "right now, I don't give a damn about your family problems. I have a job to do, a job that just got much more complicated thanks to you, Perkins. Nonetheless, I have every intention of doing as my employers have directed. Now," he demanded, "I need to know what the townspeople are likely to do and how I can—"

The door burst open, and the men were shocked to find themselves looking down the barrel of a loaded shotgun held in the sheriff's rock-solid hands.

"Nobody move." Billie stared at each of the four men, making sure they knew he was serious. "Martin Kensington, you are in violation of your agreement to never return to Montana Territory. By order of the Bozeman court, I'm placing you under arrest."

Kensington stood. "Just a minute..."

"I said, don't move," Billie ordered.

Thomas could see that the sheriff was in no mood for a confrontation. "Father, sit down. Please."

Kensington shook off his son's restraining hand. "I will not have this incompetent lawman arrest me again."

"Kensington, you take one more step, and I'll blow a hole clean through you." Billie calmly aimed the shotgun barrel at the man's chest. "And," he smiled viciously, "I'll take great pleasure in pulling the trigger."

"Just a minute, Sheriff," Harrington protested. "You have no authority to arrest Mr. Kensington."

"You have enough trouble of your own, Mr. Harrington, without taking this on. By the way, any agreements you've made with Mayor Perkins are being declared invalid until the circuit judge gets to town. Until then, you talk directly with the property owners. If they want to deal, okay; if not, you get nothing." He looked at the younger version of Kensington sitting beside the man. "You related?"

"His son."

Billie wasn't surprised at the man's identity, considering he looked so much like his father. "Jennifer's brother?"

"Yes."

"You here to make trouble?"

"No. I just want to talk to her and my mother."

"Guess that's up to them."

"Will you ask them if they will see me?"

"Right now, I need to get your father to the jail and locked in a cell for the night. I'll be taking him to Deer Lodge first thing in the morning." Relying on his instincts, Billie felt he could trust the younger Kensington. "Once I get back, I'll talk to Jesse and Jennifer."

"Fair enough," Thomas agreed knowing he couldn't do otherwise.

"Let's go, Kensington." Billie motioned for the man to accompany him.

"Don't worry, Martin," Harrington told his secret partner. "The marshal should be here any day."

"Marshal?" Thaddeus Newby had been quietly taking notes as he stood off to the side of the room.

"Yes." Harrington puffed up. "My employers have arranged for a U.S. Marshal to be assigned to bring law to Sweetwater."

"We have already have law here." Thaddeus pointed at Billie with the end of his pencil.

"Honest law," Harrington sneered. "Not someone who turns a blind eye to the unlawful acts of certain individuals." Billie's comments about shooting Kensington had convinced him that the man had been telling the truth about the sheriff's willingness to turn aside the law in order to protect the Branson women.

"What are you talking about?" Thaddeus asked.

"I think the sheriff knows the answer to that," Harrington challenged.

Billie had no idea what Harrington was talking about and really didn't care. "I don't have time for your games. Come on, Kensington." Billie led the man from the room, Thomas following at a safe distance.

"Care to explain your comments?" Thaddeus asked again after Billie left with his prisoner.

"No," Harrington replied smugly as he sat on the edge of the mayor's desk. "I think it will become apparent when the marshal arrives."

"And when will that be?"

"Any day now."

CHAPTER TWENTY-ONE

Jennifer woke up giggling with Jesse nipping and nuzzling her ear. It was still dark, and she was glad for the warmth of both their bedroll and Jesse's body wrapped protectively around her. She batted at Jesse playfully. "Stop that."

Jesse continued to suck on the silky earlobe. "If your mother wasn't sleeping on the other side of the fire, I'd be doing much more than this." Her warm breath puffed softly across Jennifer's skin, awakening other areas of her body.

Jennifer turned her head and captured Jesse's busy lips with her own. She moaned quietly when her wife's tongue traced around her lips before teasing them open. After several long moments of shared exploration, the women pulled apart.

"We can't," Jennifer whispered as she twisted her body to face Jesse.

"I know, but this is good, too." She smiled as she pulled Jennifer close. "How do you feel this morning?" she asked, hoping the day of rest had helped the painful leg recover.

Jennifer stretched her leg, testing it for soreness. "Actually," she reported happily, "it feels pretty good."

"Think you can ride?" Jesse kept her voice low since Mary and KC were still asleep, and there was no reason to wake them if they weren't going to break camp.

Jennifer was unsure how to answer. "How far would we be riding?"

"Summit is 'bout half a day's ride," Jesse told her, thinking that if they could make the summit it would be enough riding for the day. "But it's rough trail the last few miles, and the canyon really narrows at the top. We'll have a drop off to one side and a steep cliff on the other. There'll be nowhere to stop once we start up."

"I think I'm ready." The worried look on her face said otherwise.

"You need to be sure, darlin'. We can stay here for as long as you want."

Jennifer considered their options. They could remain in the camp; it was a nice spot and probably far enough away from Sweetwater to keep them safe. On the other hand, she wasn't sure to what lengths her father would go to find her. Even if Billie arrested him, she was convinced that her father would never have returned to Montana without a plan to circumvent his agreement with the territorial authorities. And if he somehow found the trail they had taken out of the valley, they were less than a day's ride from the ranch. No, it would be better to keep going. The more distance they could put between themselves and her father, the better it would be. "I can make it," she said, her determined tone more to convince herself than Jesse.

"If you're sure." Jesse looked into Jennifer's eyes in order to catch any doubt that might flash through them.

"I'm sure, sweetheart." Jennifer nodded, her jaw firmly set to the day's task. "When should we leave?"

Jesse wasn't sure Jennifer was telling her everything, but she was just as anxious to reach the summit and put the worst part of their journey behind them. "As soon as we can. We'll want to get to the top before the afternoon heat sets in."

"All right." Jennifer tried to push herself upright, but she was still securely wrapped in strong arms.

"I love you." Jesse tenderly kissed her wife's lips. "What say I see about catching us some fish for breakfast while you get the sleepy heads up." She pulled away just as Jennifer tried to tighten the embrace.

"That wasn't nice," Jennifer pouted as Jesse sprang to her feet, leaving her alone in their bedroll.

The citizens of Sweetwater watched as freight wagon after freight wagon rumbled along the stage road and pulled into the open field next to the general store. As several men climbed down from their perches atop the heavy wagons to start unloading, Mayor Perkins and Tobias Harrington rushed out of the mayor's office to greet the men. One of the workers broke away from the rest.

"Mr. Harrington?"

"You're late," Harrington grumbled as he hurried past the man's outstretched hand to inspect the materials being unloaded. "Be careful, there," he shouted at a couple of men struggling with the weight of a large, bulky crate. "Anything broken will be deducted from your wages."

"Mr. Harrington. My name is Frank Wilson. I'm the foreman sent to—"

"I know who you are and why you're here." Harrington kept his eyes on the workers. "What I don't know is why you are late."

Frank Wilson had not been happy to hear he would be working with Tobias Harrington in Sweetwater. The diminutive man was known for doing whatever was necessary to complete his assignments. He also had a well-earned reputation for being rude, arrogant, and uncooperative. But when orders arrived to pick up building supplies in Bozeman, hire a work crew, and proceed to Sweetwater to build a bank and hotel, Wilson complied without comment. He only hoped Harrington would make himself scarce once he saw that the foreman was more than capable to carry out his tasks without help. Until then, he would have to try to get along with the supercilious Harrington.

"We came as quick as we could. The loads were heavier than we expected; it's been tough on the horses."

Harrington grunted. "You have the invoices, I assume." Wilson handed over an envelope. "Let's hope you didn't leave anything behind." Harrington ripped open the envelope and began to scan the papers inside. "How soon can you start building?"

"Soon as we get unpacked and I get the men rooms at the boarding house."

"Don't be a fool. You know there are tents and cots in the wagons. Who did you think they were meant for? You can set the tents up there." Harrington pointed to the opposite side of the town's only street. "You and the men will be staying in them. I've hired a cook to prepare your meals. One of the tents will need to be set up near the creek for him."

"What?" Wilson had been told to house the work crew wherever he saw fit. And sleeping outside in a tent was not what he had in mind. Especially since he'd heard the Slipper offered clean rooms and good meals.

"Silver Slipper is off limits to employees of the company." Harrington shoved the papers back inside the envelope. "I suggest you get the hotel built quickly if you don't like the arrangements," he told Wilson as he walked past, returning to the mayor's office, which he now considered his own.

"Hey, wait a minute," Wilson called after Harrington, who never broke stride.

"Perkins will answer any other questions you may have."

Wilson looked at the mayor, who smiled tensely.

"Mr. Wilson, I have the building plans for you." Perkins handed the disgruntled foreman several rolled-up drawings. "The hotel is to be built on that lot." He pointed to the empty space next to the stage station. "And the bank is to be built here." He pointed to where the men were unloading the wagons next to the general store. "You might want to stack your materials elsewhere," he suggested nervously.

"Damn." Wilson took the drawings, mumbling, "This is starting off great. You men," he called to the workers. "Stop unloading. We need to move the wagons further back." *Ah yes*, he thought as he listened to the men grumble, *starting off very nicely indeed.*

"If you have any questions or require anything, you can find my office there." Mayor Perkins pointed to the building on the other side of the general store. "Nice to meet you," he said, scurrying away before the man could pose any questions.

Sheriff Billie Monroe looked up as the door to his office opened and a form stepped through, blocking out the late morning sunlight. He had planned to leave for Deer Lodge at first light but trouble with a couple of drunks at the Oxbow Saloon had delayed his departure.

"I'm looking for the sheriff," said a man wearing a badge over his left breast.

"I'm Sheriff Monroe." Billie figured that the mysterious marshal had finally arrived. "How can I help you?"

The man stepped further into the small office and shut the door behind him. He was about the same height as Billie but was thinner and older. He wore a faded blue cotton shirt tucked into a pair of denim pants. His worn leather coat and boots were thickly covered in trail dust. A black Stetson was pulled down tight over his eyes so a thick salt and pepper mustache was about all of his face the sheriff could make out.

"I'm United States Marshal Bret Morgan." The lawman pulled a wrinkled paper from his pocket. "I have an arrest warrant for one Jesse Branson."

Taken aback by the man's announcement, Billie leapt out of his chair. "What the hell are you talking about?"

Kensington laughed from his cell. "I told you things would be changing around here."

"Shut up, Kensington!" Billie shouted.

"Would that be Martin Kensington?" the marshal asked.

"What if it is?"

"Yes, Marshal," Kensington called from his cell. "I'm Martin Kensington."

The marshal reached back into his pocket and pulled out a second wrinkled paper. "I have a release order for Mr. Kensington."

"From who?" the sheriff asked in dismay.

"Territorial governor." Morgan tossed both papers onto Billie's desk. "All charges against Mr. Kensington have been suspended, pending investigation into the charges against Branson."

"I don't believe this." Billie collapsed back into his chair. He picked up the papers and read them very carefully. "You can't be serious," he told Morgan as he read. "There's no truth to these charges against Jesse."

"That's for a judge to decide. Where can I find her?"

Thaddeus had been watching the activity around the freight wagons when he'd seen the marshal ride into town. Following the story, he entered the jail where he took in the tension with a practiced newspaperman's eye. "What's up, Billie?"

"See for yourself." Billie handed the papers to the newspaperman and then opened his desk drawer to retrieve the keys to the cell.

"Now, Sheriff," Kensington said as Billie unlocked his cell, "you can take me and the marshal to my daughter."

At that moment, Billie was very glad Jesse had had the forethought to leave the valley with Jennifer and KC. "Sure. We can ride out to their ranch."

Thaddeus looked up in surprise. "Billie, are you crazy?"

"Marshal has a warrant," Billie told him. "I have to cooperate."

"Jesse didn't do this. You'll be giving her over to the hangman."

"Why don't you ride with us, Thaddeus?" Billie could use help in making the marshal's job as hard as possible, something he knew Thaddeus would be glad to do once he realized Billie wasn't riding out to arrest Jesse.

"That's a good idea," Kensington said. "I'm sure you'll find plenty of news to write about in the *Gazette.*

"Dammit, Kensington," Billie grabbed his hat from a peg on the office wall, "don't you ever get tired of making a fool out of yourself?"

"Father?" Thomas had entered the sheriff's office expecting to find his father behind bars. "What's happening?"

"We're riding out to find your sister."

"You can't do that."

"Sheriff, I'd like to get this taken care of as quickly as possible," the marshal said, tired of all the talk. Especially since he couldn't figure out how half of it was possibly related to his business.

Billie nodded. "Let's go."

The trail narrowed, becoming increasingly rocky and treacherous. Recent rains had loosened the ground further up the canyon walls, causing slides that covered many stretches of trail with mud and jagged stones. A few of the slides had been big enough to wash out small sections of trail. The women let the horses pick their own path around the obstacles as they slowly made their way toward the summit.

Jesse knew they were rapidly approaching the point where turning around would be impossible; she had to stop and ask Jennifer how she was doing. Choosing a spot where the trail widened as it re-entered the cover of trees for a short stretch, Jesse pulled Dusty to a stop. "Jennifer," she turned in the saddle as her wife rode up beside her, "if we have to turn around, this is the last chance to do it."

Jennifer knew what Jesse was asking. She took her booted foot out of the stirrup and tested the leg. It was sore, and she had begun to feel a little pain about an hour before, but it didn't feel unbearable. "How far to the top?" she asked as she reached behind Jesse to give KC a drink from her canteen.

"Two miles." Jesse drank from her own canteen. "Three, at the most."

"Mother, how are you doing?"

"I'm fine." Mary had dismounted to stretch her own legs. "I can make another few miles."

"It's going to be rough," Jesse told both women. "Rougher than what we've already seen."

Mary considered this information. The past few hours she had spent holding on to the saddle horn with a death grip, hoping that her rented horse wouldn't suffer a misstep that would send both of them plunging down the steep slope to the creek several hundred feet below. If the miles ahead were worse... Of course, once they reached the summit, the frightening trail would be behind them. "I can go on." Mary remounted.

Jennifer reached for Jesse's hand and brought it to her lips, placing a tender kiss on the soft skin. "I'm okay, sweetheart."

"All right. Let's check KC's britches and get moving. If we don't run into trouble, we should make the summit in a couple of hours."

They wasted no time in seeing to the baby's needs and getting back on the trail. Half of the remaining distance to the summit had been covered when Dusty rounded a granite outcropping and came to a stop. Unable to go any further, the draft horse trailing Dusty came to a stop before clearing the outcropping. The trail ahead was gone.

"What's wrong?" Jennifer called out to Jesse when Boy blocked her way.

"Wash out," Jesse called back over her shoulder. Carefully, she stood in the stirrups to get a better look at how much of the trail had been destroyed. "Damn," she muttered, frustrated that she couldn't see an end to the damaged section. There was no way to turn the horses around and go back, and it was too dangerous to try to back them down the trail. She would have to find a way across. "Stay there," Jesse told Jennifer. "I'm coming back to you."

To her left, the slope of the mountain was almost perpendicular and offered no place to safely dismount. To her right, the drop was so steep she could see straight down to the bottom of the narrow canyon. "Easy, girl." She settled Dusty, the horse as uneasy as she was with their predicament. With the baby on her back, she didn't need the mare getting nervous just now. Jesse turned her head to look into the baby's eyes. "Sunshine, I need you to sit very still."

Jesse edged Dusty as close to the left as possible, then carefully swung her leg over the saddle. She made sure her foot was on solid ground before putting all her weight on her leg. Cautiously, she worked her way alongside Dusty, then Boy, breathing a sigh of relief when she reached the open trail behind the horses.

Jennifer saw the trepidation on Jesse's face. "Sweetheart?"

Jesse was glad to see that the section of trail where Jennifer and Mary waited was actually wider than she'd thought. It would provide a spot for them to wait without worrying about being right next to the steep drop off. It wasn't a lot but it would have to do.

"Mudslide took the trail out." Jesse helped Jennifer and then Mary carefully dismount.

"What are we going to do?"

"You're staying here. I'm going to lead Dusty across and set a trail."

"No." Jennifer shook her head violently. "We can go back."

"Darlin'," Jesse cupped her hands around Jennifer's face and looked directly into her eyes, "we can't. Not without leaving the horses."

"Jesse, please."

"Listen, Dusty is the most sure-footed horse I know. We'll go slow and find a way across, then I'll come back for you."

"No, Jesse." Jennifer was on the verge of tears. "I can't lose you," she whispered, desperately afraid of Jesse losing her footing and falling down the steep slope to her death.

"I'm not going anywhere." Jesse wiped the tears away with her thumbs. "I promise, darlin'. I'll be back."

Mary wrapped her arms around her distressed daughter. "Jesse, are you sure that's the only way?"

"The trail is too narrow for the horses to turn around. This slide can't be that long; we're almost to the summit. I'll be back before you know it."

"Be careful," Jennifer pleaded.

Jesse pulled Jennifer close and kissed her. Her voice full of emotion, she reassured the woman she loved more than anything. "I love you, Jennifer. You are my life. I won't do anything to lose you now." She slipped the pack off her back and passed KC to Jennifer. "I love you." She kissed the baby's forehead. "You be a good girl."

"Wuv." KC threw her arms around Jesse and held tight.

"I love you, Jesse." Jennifer gently pulled the baby off Jesse. "Come back to us."

"I will, I promise." Jesse turned to work her way back to Dusty. "I'm going to untie Boy's lead. Make sure you take hold of it so he doesn't try to follow us."

Jesse eased her way back alongside Dusty, pausing to untie the rope wrapped around the saddle horn. She waited for Jennifer to pull it back out of the way before she moved to stand in front of her mare, surveying the potential paths through the debris field. It didn't look good; rocks, tree branches, and dried mud covered the mountainside in front of her. Jesse was scared. One wrong move and she'd be sliding down to the canyon bottom before she could stop herself. "Guess there's only one way to do this," she muttered as she led Dusty off the relative safety of the trail remnant holding the reins loosely in her hand, not wanting to be pulled over the side if Dusty lost her footing. She thought of Jennifer and KC waiting for her and with a determination only love can produce, she started to pick her way across the rubble.

After working almost thirty feet across the washout, Jesse found herself standing on a solid ledge buried under the debris; she was grateful for its sturdy support on the otherwise tenuous slope. Just at the far end of the ledge, a boulder blocked her progress. She thought she might be able to climb over it but there was no way for Dusty to follow. Inching forward, Jesse studied the situation. She noticed a small branch wedged under the rock that was apparently holding the rock in place. If she could remove the branch, the boulder would fall down into canyon and out of the way. But there was no telling how much more of the hillside would go with the rock.

Calculating that the ledge she and Dusty occupied was relatively secure, Jesse decided to try to remove the branch and hope for the best. She really didn't have any option. She could go back to where Jennifer and Mary waited, but Dusty could not.

Warily, she climbed upslope of Dusty so she could pull the rope coil from her saddle, then she returned to the more stable footing on the rock slab. Opening a loop in the rope, she expertly flipped it over the end of the branch.

"Please let this work," Jesse prayed, bracing her boots and tugging on the rope as hard as she could. At first the branch resisted her efforts. Then, ever so slowly, it began to pull out of the partially dried mud. The branch had only been partly freed when the boulder started to budge. Sensing the movement, Jesse released her hold on the rope so she wouldn't be pulled over the side if the branch got carried down slope with the rockslide. Jesse froze as seconds later the boulder rolled free, bouncing and crashing all the way to the bottom of the canyon. Breathlessly, she waited to see how much of the debris would follow in its wake. She let out a long sigh when the ground beneath her feet held firm.

"Hope we don't have to do anything like that again, Dusty."

Looking beyond where the boulder had rested, Jesse spied the end of the washout less than fifty feet ahead and just before the trail passed over another sturdy ledge before curving back out of sight behind a rocky crag. Though the distance wasn't far, it seemed to take forever for her and Dusty to be standing back on solid ground.

Jesse continued around the crag and was thankful to see the canyon slope start to fall away at a more gradual grade and the trail start to widen. She led the horse to the shade of a large pine tree.

"Ain't much, but it's better than waitin' out in the sun." The rancher patted the mare's neck. Pulling the canteen free, Jesse removed her hat and filled it with the water. Dusty wasted no time in drinking. "Sorry, girl," Jesse put the wet hat back on, "that's all the water we have for now. If I remember right, there's a creek not too far up the trail, but don't go off on your own just yet." She rubbed Dusty's nose. "There's no telling if this is the only washout, and I don't want you gettin' into any trouble." Jesse turned to retrace her steps back to her family.

CHAPTER TWENTY-TWO

The sheriff led the men into the ranch yard and made a show of calling out for Jesse and Jennifer. When no response came, Kensington kicked in the door to the ranch house, searching for his daughter. The marshal rode to the barn to check there and Thomas went to investigate the smaller cabin.

"Where are they?" Thaddeus whispered to Billie so the other men wouldn't hear.

"Gone."

"Where are they?" Kensington demanded as he stormed out of the empty ranch house. Billie shrugged.

"Sheriff, do you know where they are?" the marshal asked, returning from the empty barn.

"Nope. Figured they'd be here since they weren't in town."

"You know where they are." Kensington tried to pull Billie from his horse.

Thomas pushed his father away from the lawman. "Stop it, Father. How would he know where they are? They could just be out for a ride."

Kensington brushed his son's hands away. "They must have known I was coming."

"How?" Thomas countered. "You didn't send word telling them, did you?"

"No. But you could have," Kensington accused.

"I wish I had." Thomas mounted his horse. Disgusted by his father's behavior, he hoped Jennifer had had prior warning and was somewhere very far away.

"Guess I'll just have a look around." The marshal looked at the sheriff, trying to gauge his reaction. He had a gut feeling the lawman knew more than he was saying, and considering he had been sent to Sweetwater because the sheriff was accused of collaborating with Jesse, he was determined not to trust the man. "Maybe I can pick up some tracks."

"Suit yourself." Billie shrugged, confident in the fact that Jesse was one of the best trackers in the territory and was just as skilled at hiding tracks. He was sure she had left nothing behind to give away their movements. "Think I'll swing by the river on the way back to town."

"Where they like to picnic?" Thaddeus asked, picking up on Billie's attempt to keep the marshal chasing his tail for a while.

"Yeah, by that big pine tree."

The marshal watched Billie and Thaddeus ride away, Thomas and his father close behind. He looked around at the empty ranch yard and scowled. There were a hundred different ways his fugitive could have ridden away from the ranch, and most would take her to extremely remote parts of the territory. The younger Kensington was right, if they hadn't had prior warning they were probably just out for an afternoon's ride or picnic. They were sure to show up sooner or later. Maybe he'd do well to follow the sheriff. Morgan kicked his horse into a trot and rode after the others.

Jennifer waited, her heart in her throat, as Jesse carefully made her way back across the washout. She had refused to wait with Mary but instead stood at the edge of the slide, watching every move Jesse made. She had almost screamed when Jesse loosened the boulder, sending it to the bottom of the canyon. But she hadn't, afraid it would startle her wife and cause her to lose her footing and fall. Now Jesse was returning to her, and she could breathe again.

Jesse wrapped her arms around her wife and hugged her tight.

"You okay?" Jennifer asked from the safety of Jesse's arms.

"Yep." Jesse tightened her hold. "I am now." Jesse released Jennifer, then helped her back around the outcropping to Mary and KC.

Mary rushed to hug Jesse, KC in her arms. "You're back."

"Mommy."

"Hi, Sunshine." Jesse laughed as the baby leapt into her arms. "Have you been good?"

"Yep." KC giggled.

"What now, Jesse?"

"Now I take the horses across. Then I come back for you."

"Can't we go at the same time?"

"No." Jesse picked up a canteen and took a long drink. The heat was building between the canyon walls, and she was starting to suffer from its intensity after her two treacherous trips across the washout. "It's not safe, too much could go wrong." She pulled the other canteens from the saddles. Even though she had emptied the canteen Dusty carried, she would leave these with Jennifer and Mary.

"But sweetheart," Jennifer could see that Jesse appeared drained, "that means you have to cross three more times."

"It's okay." Jesse smiled in reassurance. "I know the way now, won't take nearly as long this time. Besides, the horses will beat down a path and make it that much easier when I come back for you."

"I don't know, Jesse." Jennifer wanted to be able to get everyone across and be done with it.

"Trust me, darlin'. I'll be back before you know it."

Jesse would have preferred to lead the horse most unfamiliar to her but with no room to rearrange their order, she was forced to take them across in the order they now stood. She tied Blaze to Boy's saddle horn and Mary's horse to Blaze, making sure the leads were loose enough that if one horse lost its footing, it would not pull the others over with it.

With quick kisses planted on Jennifer's cheek and KC's forehead, Jesse started back across the washout. It was getting hotter, and it didn't help that the section of trail was in the open and provided no protection from the midday sun. As she again picked her way along her chosen path, Jesse could feel the sweat rolling down her back, legs, and arms. Having Dusty's hoof prints to follow was a big help, and with no large boulders to have to move, it didn't take nearly as long before she reached safety at the far side of the washout.

She led the horses to where Dusty waited. After securing Boy and Cinnamon, Mary's horse from the livery, to the pine so they wouldn't wander, Jesse slumped against the tree trunk. Sweating profusely from the heat in the canyon had sucked moisture from her body, and she desperately needed water. She thought about taking Dusty and trying to find a creek but knowing that would take her away from her family, she quickly discarded the idea. Figuring there'd be plenty of time to get water after she retrieved Jennifer, KC, and Mary, she started back.

Jennifer met Jesse with a canteen, which was quickly drained. "Glad this is the last trip," Jesse said as she picked up KC's pack and prepared to put the baby into it.

Jennifer reached for the sack. "Why don't you let me carry her?"

"No, darlin'." Jesse kept the sack out of Jennifer's grasp. "Your leg will have strain enough just walking across; I'll take KC."

Jennifer knew Jesse was right. Trying to make her way across the narrow, uneven path would be all she could handle. If she was honest with herself, she wasn't really sure she could do even that.

"Here ya go, Sunshine." Jesse slipped the baby into the carry sack. "You need to sit real still for Mommy."

"Otay."

"You've been a real good girl today, Sunshine." Jesse twisted her head around to look at KC. "There's a nice lake not too far away, and when we get there, we'll go swimming. Does that sound good?"

"Yep." The baby smiled back, then hunched down in the pack to do as her mommy asked.

"Good girl." Jesse smiled at the waiting baby. "Mary?"

"I'm ready." Mary wasn't so sure, but she'd made it this far. What was another hundred feet? She had the canteens tied around her waist. Most were empty, so they didn't add much weight to her small frame.

"Darlin'?"

"Yes, I'm ready, sweetheart."

Jesse adjusted the pack on her aching back. "I'll go first, then Jennifer, then Mary. Follow the path the horses left. If you have any trouble, call out. It's better to rest than try to force your way across." She looked at the women to make sure they understood. Both nodded. "Let's get out of here." Jesse led the women out of their temporary sanctuary.

Leaning heavily on her cane, Jennifer had labored halfway across the washout when she realized she could go no further. Picking her way through the loose, uneven debris had taken its toll on her stamina and the limited strength of her damaged leg. And to make matters worse, her bad leg was on the downhill side, raising serious concerns about the leg collapsing under her and causing her to tumble down the mountainside.

"Jesse," Jennifer called to the rancher several feet ahead of her.

Hearing the anguish in her wife's voice, Jesse froze. "What?"

"I can't go any further."

"Don't move," Jesse shouted back as she continued across the mudslide. With KC on her back, she couldn't help Jennifer without endangering all three of them. "I'll be right back."

Unable to continue, Jennifer could do nothing but watch Jesse move steadily away from her.

Reaching the spot she had left the horses, Jesse set the carry sack in the shade with KC still inside. "KC," she told the baby, "I want you to sit right here with Dusty and Blaze. Don't move. I have to go get Momma." Jesse wasn't sure the baby understood but leaving her in the carry sack would limit her ability to go anywhere and the horses would look after her. "Sit right here."

The baby looked up at Jesse. "Otay."

"Good girl." Jesse bent to kiss the baby and had to put a hand on the tree to keep herself from keeling over. She was exhausted. Taking her time, she stood and waited for the dizziness to pass. *Come on, you only have one more trip to make. You can do this.* She couldn't take time to rest; she had to get back to Jennifer and Mary.

Jennifer was getting concerned when Jesse didn't reappear around the outcropping at the far end of the washout. She was about to call to her when the rancher edged around the crag and started back through the rock field. The closer Jesse got, the more Jennifer could see how worn out she was. "Tomorrow, we're resting in camp for *you*," Jennifer said softly.

Too concerned with where she was placing her own feet, Mary had not realized Jennifer was having problems until she'd called to Jesse. At first, she had been happy to wait and rest, but now she was anxious to be off the unstable slope and away from the sheer drop-off where she was standing. "What's that?" Mary asked from where she waited a few feet behind Jennifer.

"Nothing, Mother." Jennifer's eyes never left her wife. "Jesse is on her way back." By the time Jesse reached her stranded wife, she was breathing hard, and her clothes were soaked through with sweat. "Are you okay?" Jennifer asked as soon as Jesse stood in front of her. She was much more concerned over the rancher's condition than her own.

"Fine." Jesse smiled, but her tone said otherwise.

"You need to rest."

"Let's get you over there so we can all rest." Jesse cautiously shuffled her feet until her back was to Jennifer, then she bent down, bracing her hands on her knees. "Climb on."

"Jesse!" Jennifer screamed, thinking her wife had lost her mind. "You can't carry me."

Slowly, Jesse pushed herself upright, then shuffled back around to face Jennifer. She took a deep breath before speaking. "Darlin', you can't walk. Can you think of any other way to get you across?"

Jennifer couldn't imagine Jesse carrying her in her present state of exhaustion. "You can't carry me."

"Then what?" Jesse asked, frustrated with Jennifer's stubbornness and too tired to deal with it. Before her wife could respond, she quietly added, "KC is all alone over there, darlin'. No tellin' how long before she decides to try and find us. Please, climb on my back so we can get this over with," Jesse urged.

Mary said a silent prayer as she listened to their conversation, knowing the fatigued woman would get her daughter to safety even if it cost her her own life. Mary hoped it wouldn't come to that.

Jennifer grew angry. It was times like this that she hated her father. If it hadn't been for him, she would not be in this situation. She and Jesse would never have been forced to leave their home. She would not have been attacked by the mountain lion. She would not be dependent on an exhausted woman to carry her to the top of a mountain. *Damn you, Martin Kensington. If I ever see you again, I'll make sure you never, ever do this to us again.*

Jennifer nodded, and Jesse turned to present her back to her wife. Jennifer climbed on and waited breathlessly while Jesse got her balance and straightened. Her steps were shaky, and she had to stop often to regain her breath, but Jesse carried Jennifer across the washout, setting her safely down next to KC before collapsing to her knees.

"Jesse?" Jennifer cried.

"Water," Jesse asked, her throat so dry the words hardly made a sound.

"Here." Mary handed Jesse the last canteen that carried any of the precious liquid. Jesse gulped the water down, sucking in the last drop.

"We're camping here," Jennifer announced, even though they were only on a wide spot in the trail with the horses tied to a tree standing within inches of the path.

"No," Jesse said, her energy returning as she resolved to get her family to the security of the summit. "The top of the pass isn't far from here."

Jennifer was just as determined that they would go no further. They could get to the summit tomorrow, or the next day, for all she cared. "Jesse, you need to rest."

"Darlin', we need water." Jesse pushed herself upright. "If we don't run into any more problems, we'll be there in less than an hour. Then we'll rest. For as long as you say," she added, when she saw Jennifer was about to protest.

Jennifer glowered; she'd been outmaneuvered. "Just remember, you promised."

"I'll remember."

"You get the horses, I'll carry KC."

"Deal."

As the women prepared to remount their horses, a loud rumble came from the trail behind them. They rushed to the edge of the crag just in time to see the ledge in the middle of the washout pull away from the hillside and tumble to the bottom of the cliff, taking a good portion of the debris field with it. Left in the wake was a gapping cavity that would be impossible to cross.

Jennifer began to tremble when she looked at the spot where she had been standing just a few moments before and watched the remnants disappear from sight.

"Let's go, darlin'. No point standing here and looking at it." Jesse wrapped her arms around her wife, gently turned her around and led her back to the waiting horses.

"Martin Kensington," Mary murmured as she looked at the now impassable mountainside, "I will never forgive you for this."

KC sat on Jesse's stomach, splashing and laughing as the rancher lay in the cool waters of a mountain lake with hardly any part of her body visible except her face. Jesse had been underwater since the women finished setting up camp.

Jennifer sat nearby on a smooth rock, her bare legs dangling in the water. "You planning on staying in there all evening?" she inquired of her submerged mate, who continually refused to leave the lake to eat the meal Mary was keeping warm.

"Yep," KC answered.

Jennifer could see the ripples in the water created by Jesse's silent laughter. "I give up." She lay back on the rock to enjoy the setting sun. They were together and they were safe. Supper would wait.

CHAPTER TWENTY-THREE

Jennifer sat on the same flat rock she had used the night before to watch Jesse and KC playing in the lake. From her perch, she could see for hundreds of miles in every direction. It was a panorama she had never in her life envisioned, and she was enjoying every second of it as she watched the sun rise in the east, painting the sky in pinks, reds, and oranges. It was a glorious morning. Especially when she considered that less than twenty-four hours earlier she had been trapped on the side of a cliff, unsure whether she or her family would survive. Not to mention just how close they had come to being swept down the mountain when the trail completely collapsed.

Jennifer surveyed their campsite, which was situated in an alpine meadow that gently sloped down to the crystal clear waters of the lake. The meadow was quite large, keeping the trees of the surrounding forest at some distance from the camp. Their supply packs were stacked about fifty feet from the shoreline, and a campfire had been built between them and the water. The fire glowed softly, surrounded by dark forms still tucked in their bedrolls. The horses were contentedly munching on an early breakfast of ankle-deep, dew-covered sweetgrass and tender wildflowers.

Jennifer heard a sound. Instantly alert, she scanned the area for the source. Across the meadow, an elk cow and her calf cautiously emerged from the shelter of the forest. At the same time, far off in the distance, Jennifer heard the call of a coyote greeting the dawn. The mother elk lifted her head and listened, taking a few sniffs of the air while her calf pranced nervously at her side. Deciding the coyote posed no immediate threat, the elk put her head down to graze. The gangly calf edged close to the cow and nosed underneath her belly for the tit and warm milk it knew would be there.

Watching the elk, Jennifer was reminded of her own wife and child sleeping a few feet away, and she adjusted her position on the rock to observe her family. Jesse lay on her back with KC sprawled on top her. The baby's head was nestled between the rancher's breasts, and a long arm was draped protectively over the child's back. Jennifer felt the sting of tears as she surveyed the peaceful sight. This was the life she had always dreamed of, and she now wanted more than anything to protect it from any and all threats, including, and especially, her father.

Billie arrived at the Slipper to have breakfast with Ruthie, and he was telling her and Bette Mae about the marshal's arrest warrant for Jesse.

Ruthie looked at him in disbelief, "They can't arrest Miss Jesse. What they are saying is not true."

"What ya plannin' ta do about this, Billie?" Bette Mae asked when the lawman remained silent.

"Nothin' much I can do." Billie shook his head. "Warrant is legal. If the marshal finds Jesse, he will arrest her."

Bette Mae slumped in her chair, looking expectantly at their friend. "Must be somethin' ya can do."

"Been doin' what I can," Billie said in a low voice.

"It's bad enough that Miss Jennifer's father has come back." Ruthie was close to tears thinking of the women who had been so kind to her. "But to be accused of this... Poor Miss Jesse. And what will Miss Jennifer do?"

Billie, unthinking, gently took his fiancée's hand into his own. "I'd like to know who made up such a story and how they got the governor to believe it."

"I'll bet tha' sorry excuse for a papa has somethin' ta do with all this," Bette Mae said as she thoughtfully considered the intimate gesture. "Somethin' the two of ya wants ta be tellin' me?" she asked in a lighter mood and smiling at the pair.

"Oh." Ruthie's cheeks turned a deep rose as Billie quickly withdrew his hand.

"Been kinda wondering that myself," said Thaddeus Newby, who had entered the Slipper in search of breakfast.

Billie, his skin also a slightly deeper shade than normal, looked at Ruthie. "Guess we were plannin' on breakin' the news sometime, weren't we, honey?"

Ruthie smiled bashfully. "Go ahead, Billie."

"We did kinda want to wait until Jesse and Jennifer were here, but..." Billie reached out and re-took Ruthie's hands. "Ruth has agreed to be my wife."

"Lordy," Bette Mae chuckled, "it's abou' time ya asked her. Little Ruthie, a married woman. Ain't that grand." She smiled broadly at the blushing soon-to-be-bride.

"Congratulations, Billie." Thaddeus thumped the sheriff on the back. "And to you, Ruthie. When do you plan on tying the knot?"

Ruthie immediately spoke up. "Not until Miss Jesse and Miss Jennifer come back."

"Maybe by then you'll get use to not using the 'Miss' with their name, like they keep askin'," Billie teased.

"Come back from where?" The voice came from the steps leading up to the boarding rooms.

"Damn," Billie muttered.

Marshal Morgan completed his descent of the stairway and sauntered across the dining room to the table.

"Come on, Ruthie." Bette Mae abruptly stood. "We have work ta do in the kitchen. Jesse don' pay us to sit around all mornin'."

"Yes, ma'am." Ruthie sprang to her feet, petrified she had given away Jesse and Jennifer's secret.

"I ask again, Sheriff," the marshal repeated, "come back from where?"

"From wherever they've gone off to." Billie calmly poured himself a cup of coffee from the pot on the table. "Care for a cup, Marshal?" he asked casually.

Morgan studied Billie as he took a seat and accepted a cup of the hot coffee. Until he could prove the man was keeping information from him, he would have to believe what he was told.

Bette Mae came out of the kitchen carrying two plates heaped high with eggs, ham, and potatoes. "Here's yer breakfast, Billie." She slid one in front of the sheriff and the other in front of the newspaperman. "And yers, Thaddeus." Turning to the unwelcome third man at the table, she asked scornfully, "Ya be wantin' anythin', Marshal?"

"Bring him a plate, Bette Mae," Billie answered with a wry smile. "Just 'cause he has a job to do, don't mean we can't be hospitable."

"If tha's wha' ya be wantin', Billie," Bette Mae said without acknowledging the marshal. "Though I don' rightly know why we have to put 'im up and feed 'im when he wants ta arrest Jesse," she mumbled as she disappeared back through the kitchen door. Moments later she returned with a plate, not half as full as the others.

Marshal Morgan ate in silence while Billie and Thaddeus, not wanting to inadvertently say anything of interest in front of the marshal, discussed an engagement announcement to be published in the *Gazette*.

When all three plates were empty, Billie asked, "What are your plans today, Marshal?" He hoped he could spend another day leading the man on a fruitless search for the missing women.

"Think I'll talk to folks around town." The marshal pushed his chair away from the table and stood. "Maybe someone heard or saw something last time Branson was in town."

"I'll come along." Billie downed the last of his coffee. "If you don't mind."

"Actually, Sheriff," Morgan said as he walked to the door, "I think it's best I do this alone."

"Suit yourself." Billie reached for the coffeepot to refill his empty cup. "Let me know if you need my help." He smirked when the marshal's only response was a grunt as he walked out of the building.

"Aren't you afraid he might talk to the wrong person?" Thaddeus asked.

"Nah." Billie leaned back in the chair. "Nobody knows nothin'. Jesse and Jennifer kept their plans to themselves." Billie figured the white lie was better than telling any more to the newspaper editor and having him accidentally say something that could get back to the marshal. It was bad enough that Ruthie had made the slip earlier. Luckily that one was easy to cover, but there was no guarantee the next would be. No, it was better to keep the information of the women's whereabouts as secret as possible. He would make a point of telling that to the others that knew — Bette Mae, Ruthie, and Ed — when he could talk to them privately.

"Guess I'll take a walk and see what Perkins and Harrington are up to this morning," Thaddeus said. "Heard that they might be riding up to the Songbird mine today to take a look around."

"Say, Thaddeus, you've been up to the mining camps. What's the hearsay on the Songbird?"

"What do you mean, Billie?"

The sheriff usually knew when miners struck a good vein or found a few nuggets; they would usually come to town and drink up any money they received for their find. And when miners drank, they talked. It was rare for a miner to keep a rich strike a secret. Billie scratched his jaw. "Seems to me that the fella who was workin' it never had much more than two coins to rub together when he came to town for supplies. Fact is, he always had a balance owing at Ed's. Kinda surprisin' to hear that the Songbird is worth the effort Harrington and his investors are goin' to."

"It might be worth looking into. I'll ask around and see what I can find out."

"Let me know."

"Will do."

"Keep an eye out for the marshal, too."

Ed Granger was sweeping off the boardwalk in front of the general store. As he swept, he heard the sound of quarreling coming from the formerly unoccupied field next to his store. He walked to the end of the boardwalk to see what was causing the ruckus.

Freight wagons were lined up at the back of the field with piles of lumber and other supplies stacked next to them. Several men were milling about; most looked unhappy, and many were grumbling among themselves. Near the road, two men stood toe-to-toe, one towering over the other, and both trying to out-shout the other.

"I'm telling you, Perkins," Frank Wilson shoved a finger into the mayor's chest with some force, "I can't ask these men to work without feeding them first." If it hadn't been for the mayor's solid girth, the foreman would have had no trouble pushing the shorter man backward.

"The cook hasn't arrived." Mayor Perkins held his ground against the foreman, who stood more than a foot taller than he did. "He should be here soon. As soon as he comes, the men will be fed."

"Are you an idiot?" Wilson shouted. It was only his second day in Sweetwater, and already he was wishing he was anywhere else. "These men have to eat. And I'm not going to eat any more of that slop they serve at the Oxbow," he shouted, referring to the saloon next to the stage station where Tobias Harrington had insisted they eat the night before.

The Oxbow's clientele was made up of cowboys and miners who came to town for a night of drinking and gambling, and they normally weren't too particular about the food that might accompany their liquor.

"There's nothing I can do," the mayor shouted right back, although he wasn't really sure why he and not Harrington was handling this situation.

"There's something I can do," Wilson said stubbornly. "I'm taking them to the Silver Slipper for breakfast." The foreman's words were greeted with cheers from the hungry men, who immediately started moving in the direction of the building at the opposite end of town.

"That's not allowed," Perkins sputtered as the men charged past him.

"If Harrington doesn't like it, he can get his ass out here and start cooking." Wilson joined the workers, leaving the hapless mayor standing alone in the street.

"Morning, Miles." Ed smirked from his vantage point on the boardwalk. "Trouble?"

"Ah, no." Mayor Perkins looked at the departing men. "Just a misunderstanding. Nothing for you to concern yourself with."

The storekeeper chuckled. "If you say so."

Muttering under his breath, the stout Perkins stepped up onto the boardwalk. He wasn't sure how he would explain the morning's events to his business partner, but he was sure that no matter how he spun the story, Harrington would blame him.

"Bet Harrington will be real pleased to see the Slipper's bill for feeding that group," Ed called after the mayor as he hurried along the boardwalk to his office. "I know Jesse will be more than happy to collect on it." Ed laughed at the retreating figure. As he returned to his morning chores, he noticed a man coming out of the stage station and looking his way before striding directly across the street toward him. As the man neared, Ed saw the badge he wore on the front of his shirt. He waited as the marshal stepped from the dusty street onto the wooden boardwalk.

"I'm Marshal Morgan. I'm looking for Jesse Branson. Understand you're a good friend."

"That I am."

"Do you know where she is?"

"At their ranch, I s'pose."

"She's not there."

"She ain't here, either." Ed turned to go into his store.

"Damn friendly town," the marshal grumbled.

Since leaving the Slipper he had talked to a dozen people, all denied any knowledge of Jesse Branson's whereabouts. He decided he might have better luck with the ranchers in the valley and stepped off the shaded boardwalk to retrieve his horse from the livery.

Martin and Thomas Kensington were just finishing their breakfast when the door to the Slipper's dining room opened and several obviously hungry men rushed in, grabbing every available chair. Two men promptly sat in the empty chairs at the table occupied by the father and son.

"What the hell is the meaning of this?" Kensington bellowed as one of the men helped himself to the coffee remaining in the pot.

"I'm sorry, sir," Frank Wilson apologized. "But my men haven't had a decent meal since we left Bozeman."

"I don't give a damn."

"Father," Thomas interrupted, "we were finished. Let's just go."

Martin pushed back from the table and stood. "Is there no civility in this godforsaken country?"

"For a man tha's mighty lackin' in manners, I wouldn' be so uppity," Bette Mae said as she cleared the table of the dirty dishes in preparation of serving the new diners.

"When my daughter takes over ownership of this establishment..." Kensington began a threat that had been heard several times since he and Thomas took rooms at the Slipper the day before.

Bette Mae had only agreed to let the two men stay at the Slipper because they were Jennifer's kin, but she was regretting the decision more and more. "Jennifer already owns the Slipper, and I'm still here," Bette Mae countered. "So if'n ye're done with yer meal..."

"We're leaving, Bette Mae." Thomas smiled apologetically. "Thank you."

"Ye're welcome, Thomas." She was beginning to like Jennifer's brother.

"Let's go, Thomas," Kensington growled. He would see the innkeeper run out of town if it was the last thing he did in Sweetwater. "I've got things to do."

"What things?" Thomas asked as he followed his father to the door.

The night before, Jesse hadn't given any argument when Jennifer finally told her to leave the cool waters of the lake and go to bed. And the fact the rancher was still sound asleep was evidence of how exhausted she had been after the harrowing experience of the previous day.

Jesse groaned as she forced her eyes open. She was lying on her side with one arm folded under her; it tingled from lack of blood. She flopped over onto her back to free the arm. Everything hurt, and she decided she would just lie there until the others woke up. It took her brain, still muddled with sleep, a few minutes to realize she was alone on the bedroll. Glancing skyward, she was surprised to see that the sun had already reached the midway point in its day's journey. She grudgingly pushed her sore body up into a sitting position and looked around the empty camp.

The fire, not needed during the hot day, had been allowed to burn down but was banked to keep a small flame burning under a pot. Jesse's stomach growled as her nose picked up the scent of one of the cooking spices Jennifer liked to use.

Jesse wondered where her family had gone. Lifting a hand to shield her eyes from the harsh sunlight, she spotted the missing women at the far side of the small lake, leisurely exploring the shoreline. Jesse smiled as she watched Jennifer, always the teacher, pointing out interesting things to KC.

Sensing she was being watched, Jennifer looked across the water and saw Jesse sitting up. "Mommy's awake," she told KC as she waved.

KC bounced in Jennifer's arms, excitingly calling, "Mommy, Mommy."

Jennifer quickened her steps to return to camp.

Jesse stood with the intention of walking to meet Jennifer and KC, but her body had other ideas. She took a few tentative steps before being forced to stop by legs stiff from the previous day's exertions. Her back ached, and it was difficult to find a position that didn't add to its pain. She was also a little lightheaded from having slept so long and so deeply. She looked for a place to sit. A short section of a fallen tree had been rolled into camp the previous night to use as a bench, and she dropped down on it to wait for Jennifer and Mary.

Jennifer hurried into the camp. "Sweetheart?" She bent over so she could look directly into her wife's eyes. "Are you all right?"

"Little sore, darlin'." Jesse smiled in a futile attempt to allay Jennifer's concern.

KC reached for Jesse. "Mommy."

"Hi, Sunshine." Jesse opened her arms, and Jennifer handed the baby to her. When she tightened her arms in a hug around the child, she grimaced in pain, her back protesting loudly.

"Jesse?" Jennifer saw the expression. "Sweetheart, maybe you should lie back down." She took the baby back. "Hush, sweetie," Jennifer told KC when she fussed at being removed from Jesse's lap. "Mommy can't hold you right now. Come on, you can sit next to Mommy over here." She carried KC to the bedroll and sat her down. "Stay here while I help Mommy."

Jesse didn't complain when Jennifer helped her up off the log; she was happy to have the assistance. She leaned on her wife as they slowly made their way to where KC was waiting, groaning as she lowered her tender body back to the ground.

"What can I do to help?" Jennifer asked as Jesse eased herself onto the bedroll.

"Not sure."

KC crawled to Jesse's side and laid her head on her mother's stomach, her eyes looking up sadly.

Jesse smiled at the baby, ruffling her fine hair. "A rubdown might be nice," she told Jennifer.

"Let me get a pot of water heating so I can wrap you in hot towels afterward." Jennifer had found the hot wraps Jesse used on her leg to be extremely effective in relieving the pain and soreness she experienced at the end of a day. "Then we'll get started." She used her cane to push herself upright and started for the lake, picking up a bucket on her way.

"Is there anything I can do?" Mary asked, smiling uneasily at her daughter-in-law. She was aware that without Jesse's extraordinary efforts the day before, they probably would not have made it safely off the cliff, and she felt awkward that the woman was suffering today while she was unscathed.

"No. I'll be all right, Mary. Just need a little rest."

"Which you'll have plenty of," Jennifer said as she added wood to the campfire, stoking the flames before she put the large pot of water on a rock in the center of the fire. "I don't see any reason for us to leave here for a couple of days."

"Darlin', we can't stay here."

"Yes, we can. No one would be fool enough to follow us across that slide. Besides," Jennifer limped back to Jesse, "you said we would stay here as long as I wanted. So we'll stay. Now take off your clothes and turn over."

Jesse unbuttoned her shirt. "Guess I did, didn't I?"

"Yes." Jennifer grinned, enjoying the view of Jesse undressing.

Jesse sensed her wife's eyes on her, and her skin colored with a light blush.

"Roll over," Jennifer instructed, her eyes twinkling as they dropped down the length of Jesse's muscular, lithe body, pausing momentarily on her gorgeous breasts and again at the tantalizing apex of her legs.

"Now that's not nice, darlin'." Jesse blushed deepened as she followed Jennifer's gaze, embarrassed by her wife's candid display of desire. "What will your mother think?" she whispered, even though Jennifer's mother was standing only a couple of feet away, her back conveniently turned to the women.

"She'll think that her daughter has married a very beautiful woman," came a voice filled with mirth.

Both Jesse and Jennifer looked as if Mary had just spouted a second head. They never would have expected the demure woman to make such a comment.

"I think I'll take a walk." Mary chuckled as she left the two slack-jawed women alone.

"Wow," Jesse murmured after a few moments.

"Yeah." Jennifer looked after her mother. "Wow."

Ed Granger went out to greet the driver of a heavily laden freight wagon that had just pulled to a stop in front of the general store.

"Afternoon," Ed said as the driver climbed down from the bench seat.

"Afternoon, Ed. Sorry I'm late, but I had some trouble on the road."

"Nothin' serious, I hope," the storekeeper asked, looking over the load.

"Nah, just some boys thinkin' their loads was more important than mine. Found it best to pull over and let them go by 'fore they caused some real problems."

The freight road over the mountains was narrow, with few places for the big freight wagons to pass one another on the twisting path. It wasn't unknown for a wagon to get too close to the edge and roll over the side, destroying the wagon, its contents, and, many times, the driver.

"Let me guess." Ed looked to the end of the boardwalk and the men working in the field there.

The driver followed his gaze. "Yep. Them boys was sure in a hurry ta git here."

"Kinda wondered how they got their supplies 'fore me, considerin' how I sent their orders in a couple days after mine."

The driver stomped his boots on the boardwalk, trying to shake some of the dust clinging to them. "Ya don't know the half of it. Sum fellow was bullying the stores in Bozeman to fill their orders first; got real nasty when the storekeepers refused. What's going on in Sweetwater that's so important?"

"Harrington," Ed muttered, not really answering the man's question. "Come on inside." Ed slapped the driver on the shoulder, regretting it when a cloud of dust rose off the man's shirt. "I was just goin' to pour me a glass of cold cider. Bet you could use one yourself."

"Sure could, Ed. Thanks."

"Way things are going," the livery hand was telling Thaddeus Newby, "we gonna need to buy some more horses."

"Why's that?" the newspaperman asked as he saddled his horse. Thaddeus was in the livery to get the horse he boarded there. After hearing the sheriff's questions about the Songbird, he figured it would be worth another ride out to the mining camps to ask some of the miners their thoughts on the recently purchased mine.

"With so many folks askin' to rent our horses, ain't got 'nough to go around."

For the first time, Thaddeus noticed that most of the stalls were empty. "Who's been renting them?" As the editor of the valley's newspaper, he was also alert to possible story sources.

"First, Miss Jennifer's ma came in and asked for one. Then that Harrington fella got one to use whilst he's in town, and Wilson, his foreman, came by yesterday and hired a couple more. Jus' this morning, that Kensington fellow came by and got two more. Don't leave any but the old mare, and she's no good for ridin' anymore."

"Sounds to me like business is pretty good," Thaddeus said as he wondered where Kensington would be going that he needed a horse. There was only one place he could think of, and he hoped he was wrong. He walked his horse out of the livery, mounted, and rode straight for the sheriff's office.

"Billie, you in there?" Thaddeus called as he approached the jail.

The sheriff stepped out of the building and crossed the wide boardwalk to stand at its edge. "What's up, Thaddeus?"

"Thought you might want to take a ride out to Jesse's."

"What for?"

"I was just over at the livery. Kensington rented a couple of horses this morning. Can't think of anyplace else he'd be riding to."

"Damn." Billie's gut clenched. "He better not be up to anything."

Thaddeus didn't like the idea of Kensington being out at Jesse and Jennifer's any better than the sheriff did. "Chances are, he is."

"I'll leave now," Billie said as he reached back inside the door for his hat, then pulled the door closed. "You headed that way?"

"No. I'm going out to the camps. Be back in a couple of days."

"Be careful," Billie said as he stepped off the boardwalk to retrieve his own horse from the livery.

"You, too." Thaddeus urged his horse into a trot and was soon leaving a cloud of dust behind as he rode out of town.

"Father, what are we doing here?" Thomas asked as they rode under the arch marking the ranch property.

"Don't you want to see if your sister is home?"

"I can see that she isn't here." He had already noted the lack of smoke from the chimneys or any evidence of people moving about the ranch yard. "We shouldn't be here, especially since Jennifer isn't here."

"That's exactly why we should be here." Kensington rode up to the ranch house, its door hanging haphazardly from being kicked in during their earlier visit. He dismounted and tossed the reins over the hitching rail, disappearing inside the house before Thomas could dismount.

Martin Kensington had gone to the ranch hoping to find out more about the property the women owned. After his attempts to gain access to Jesse's office were blocked by an extremely watchful Bette Mae, he had remembered Jennifer's comment that she helped with the Slipper's bookkeeping and wondered if the information he sought might not be at the currently unoccupied ranch.

Kensington stood in the center of the log building that his daughter called home, surveying the room's simple furnishings. He was looking for a desk or other likely space where ledgers and business records might be kept. His eyes abruptly stopped when they fell on the room's sole bed. "Jezebel," he growled at the perceived symbol of the aberrant power that Branson seemingly held over his daughter.

"Father?" Thomas entered the plain but cozy cabin. "What are you doing?" he asked when he saw the coverings being pulled off the bed and thrown into the fireplace used for warming the sleeping area of the room.

"It's unnatural," Kensington didn't hesitate in his frenzied activity, "for them to be sleeping in the same bed."

"Stop it." Thomas ran to his father and tried to remove the bedding from his grasp.

Kensington yanked away and, catching Thomas unbalanced, pushed him aside. "I will not have my daughter doing such things." He tossed the bulky blankets at the stone-lined opening. Grabbing a lantern off the mantle, Kensington threw it against the back of the fireplace. The lantern exploded, spilling its contents.

"Father," Thomas screamed, "you can't do this!"

"Shut up." Kensington's rampage continued as he crossed to the chest of drawers, yanking each drawer free. Clothes flew everywhere as he hurled the drawers around the cabin. He spotted Jesse's bookcase and ripped it from the log wall, the books tumbling off the carefully constructed shelves. Then he stormed to the kitchen area, frantically demolishing the neatly stacked cups and dishes. The shelves were pulled from the log walls and the table and chairs tossed outside through the windows.

"Please, Father," Thomas begged, though he knew his pleas were falling on deaf ears. He couldn't believe what he was witnessing; his father was destroying everything. He made several attempts to stop the destruction, but the older man's rage seemed to give him strength, and he easily eluded the efforts.

The fuel from the broken lantern slowly dripped down the rock surface at the back of the fireplace, pooling in the coals remaining from the fire Jesse had tended during the last night she and Jennifer had spent in the cabin. Buried deep in the ashes, a small piece of wood still smoldered. When the flammable liquid reached this source of heat, it burst into flame, igniting the linens that lay within the fire's reach. Licking its way along the layers of blankets and sheets that stretched from the fireplace to the bed, the blaze began to spread onto the wood floor. The tongues of flame discovered the clothing scattered in their path and fed hungrily on this additional source of fuel. It didn't take long for the inferno to spread to the furniture and then up the log walls.

Thomas, concentrating on his raging father, wasn't aware of the fire until he smelled the smoke. When he turned to look, he saw the entire sleeping end of the cabin in flames. He knew there was no way to save the log structure. "Fire!" he shouted. "We have to get out!"

At first, Kensington did not heed his son's warning. Only when the thickening smoke made breathing difficult and he coughed on the caustic fumes did he take notice of the flames engulfing the other end of the building. He laughed.

"Father." Thomas pulled at his father, who was gleefully watching the flames spread. "We have to get out."

"Yes," Kensington cackled. "Yes, let's go outside and watch it burn."

Thomas pulled his father outside to the safety of the open yard. Seeing a bucket next to the water pump, he ran to fill it. Pumping furiously, Thomas watched as flames broke through the roof and black smoke billowed into the blue of the sky. With the bucket full, he ran back to the porch and threw the water fruitlessly on the flames.

"Don't waste your time," Kensington crowed. "Let it burn."

Knowing it was futile to attempt to put out the fire by himself, Thomas dropped the bucket and watched as his sister's home was consumed. Shaken, he asked, "How could you?"

"How could I?" Kensington barked. "How could I? Your sister defies me. She runs away to live here, away from her family responsibilities and in an unnatural relationship, and you ask 'how could I'? If you were anything of the man I raised you to be, you would have done this and saved me the trouble. How dare you ask how could I?"

Thomas stared at the man before him, a man he realized he truly didn't know. "You're right, Father," he said. "I'm not the man you raised me to be. And because of that, I could never have done this. Not to Jennifer, not to anyone." He went to the horses that had pulled free of the hitching rail as the fire grew and were standing nervously next to the corral fence. He walked them inside the corral and closed the gate, then he returned and picked up the discarded bucket. Filling it at the pump, he began to wet down the other buildings to keep any stray spark from igniting them.

"What are you doing?" Kensington asked as Thomas made another trip to the water pump.

"Making sure you don't destroy anything else."

Kensington tried to wrest the bucket from his son. "Let the damn place burn."

"No." Thomas pushed his father away. "Go back to Sweetwater and your friend Harrington. Better yet, go home. You've done enough here." He returned to his undertaking.

"Come back here!" Kensington yelled after his son. When Thomas continued to douse the buildings with water, Kensington shrugged. "Good riddance. You were never much good as a son, anyway," he muttered as he turned back to the burning structure, the roof collapsing as he watched.

CHAPTER TWENTY-FOUR

Ed finished explaining the recent events in Sweetwater to the freight wagon driver. He had left out the part about the marshal and Jesse, figuring the man didn't need to know. "Guess that's it."

"Sounds like Sweetwater done got itself a wagon-load of trouble. Been my experience that folks make a big fuss whenever they think they've hit pay dirt. Build everything up, then leave it all to rot when the ore doesn't produce or runs out. Seems to me, they'd do better to leave things alone. Be a lot less broken lives, if ya ask me," the freight driver said, finishing off his glass of cider. "I best be getting the wagon unloaded so I can head back. Thanks for the cider."

"You're not staying in town tonight?"

"Can't. Lettin' them other wagons go by put me behind schedule. Got to git back to Bozeman; got me a load waitin' ta go ta Virginia City."

"I'll give you a hand, then."

The wagon driver grinned at the large man, who could lift three times the weight he could. "Much obliged. Work goes a lot faster when you help."

The two men worked non-stop to unload the wagon. By the time they finished, Ed was glad he'd decided to make some changes to the general store. One thing was for sure, the dock he was planning for the rear of the building would make the unloading of freight much easier. With the wagon's load spread out on the boardwalk, Ed saw that it contained the items Jesse had ordered for the redesign of her office at the Slipper. He hoped she was safe.

"Feeling any better?" Jennifer asked as she sat beside Jesse, who was resting on the flat rock by the lake.

Jesse laid her arm around Jennifer's shoulders and pulled her close. "Much. KC asleep?"

"Yes." Jennifer melted against Jesse. "Mother is napping with her." She had finished Jesse's massage a short time earlier and, after a lunch of trout and biscuits, the baby had been put down for a nap. The women sat silently, content just to be with each other. Jennifer finally broke the silence. "It's beautiful here."

"It is."

"I saw an elk this morning in the meadow, sweetheart." She smiled at the memory. "Oh?"

"Yes. She was so beautiful, and she had a baby with her." Jennifer looked down at her hands. "It made me think of you and KC."

Jesse hooked a finger under Jennifer's chin, and she gently tilted her wife's face and leaned over to capture her lips. At first, the kiss was tender as Jesse softly explored Jennifer's welcoming lips, but after a few moments the kiss deepened. The women's tongues danced and twisted around one another as they expressed their desire. Needing to breathe, the women ended the kiss by clinging together. Jesse laid back, pulling Jennifer with her.

"No, sweetheart." Jennifer pushed a hand against Jesse's chest to stop her. "We can't do this with Mother so close."

Jesse smiled at her wife. "She's asleep." Jennifer glanced over her shoulder at the campsite. "I love you," Jesse whispered. Placing a hand against Jennifer's cheek, she guided the lips she loved close. As they renewed their kiss, she rolled Jennifer over onto the smooth surface of the rock, her nimble fingers opening the buttons of her wife's shirt.

Jennifer arched into Jesse's touch as gentle hands cupped her breasts, squeezing lightly. Feeling aroused nipples pressing against her palms, Jesse pinched them while her lips covered the breasts with feathery light kisses. Jennifer moaned, burying her hands in Jesse's long hair, urging her to continue.

Jesse complied, planting soft kisses around the outside of the mounds of soft tissue. Slowly her lips trailed down to Jennifer's taut stomach, the skin twitching beneath her kisses. With her lips exploring her wife's body, Jesse unbuttoned Jennifer's pants and pushed them down below her knees. Loving hands glided back up the inside of damp thighs, teasingly stopping just below the spot where Jennifer needed them most. Jennifer gasped as she spread her legs, opening herself to her lover.

As her lips neared the thatch of silky hair, Jesse detected the sweet, musky bouquet of Jennifer's arousal. Her lips retraced their path back to Jennifer's firm breasts, then broke new trail up a smooth neck, along her jawline and, finally, back to waiting lips. She slipped her hand between her lover's legs, stroking the clit, her fingers sliding easily through a silky wetness along drenched nether lips to ring the opening into her lover. Jennifer's clenched fingers digging into the skin of her back reinforced her desire. Wasting no time, Jesse plunged three fingers inside, curving them forward to press against an extremely sensitive spot she had discovered quite accidentally during an evening of lovemaking. She felt muscular walls tightened around her fingers as her lover climaxed.

Jennifer's heels braced against the rock's hard surface. Her hips thrusting hard against the fingers inside her, she moaned her lover's name.

Feeling her wife's thighs clamp together, trapping her hand, and hearing Jennifer cry her name were all Jesse needed to join her lover in a shared ecstasy. Her back arched, and her body stiffened as orgasmic waves washed through her. Their energy spent, the Bransons collapsed, their bodies pressed together.

Jennifer recovered first. She lay under Jesse, kissing and caressing her face. "Jesse Marie Branson, I love you so much."

"Mmmmmm," was all Jesse could manage.

Billie saw the black smoke before he reached the gate to the ranch, his horse already at full gallop. As he rode over the rise just before the road dropped down to the ranch yard, the sheriff caught sight of the burned-out shell of the house. He pulled his horse to a stop several feet from the smoldering remains, not bothering to dismount. The cabin had been completely consumed, along with everything inside. He wondered if Jesse had had the foresight to take the Slipper's business records into town so Bette Mae could safeguard them.

"Damn, Jesse," the sheriff whispered. "I'm so sorry." There was little doubt as to what had happened. As he had raced toward the ranch, Billie had passed Kensington riding away from it. Noting a horse owned by the livery inside the corral, he pulled his pistol. Looking around and not seeing the rider, he called out, "Who's here?"

"It's me, Sheriff." Thomas came out from behind the smaller cabin "Find a shovel and come help me," he said before disappearing again.

Billie dismounted and hurried into the barn to find a shovel, then he rushed to find Thomas. Rounding the corner of the hut, he saw Jennifer's brother trying to contain flames climbing up its side. Using the shovel, Billie threw dirt on the blaze while Thomas doused it with buckets of water. It didn't take long for the men, working together, to put out the fire that had started when a spark had drifted across the yard.

"Glad you came along, Sheriff." Thomas wiped his brow with a sooty sleeve, leaving a streak of black across his sweaty skin. "Wasn't sure I could stop it by myself."

"How'd this happen?"

"It was an accident. I'm not excusing what he did," Thomas quickly added when he saw the look of disbelief on the sheriff's face. He went on to explain the events after his father had entered the cabin. "My father is to blame, but I don't believe he came here with any intention of burning it down."

"Doesn't much matter whether he intended to or not." Billie handed the other man his bandanna and pointed at his smeared forehead. "He's the cause, and no matter what the governor says, I'm going to arrest him as soon as I get back to town."

Tobias Harrington was sitting at the mayor's desk going over the purchase papers for the Songbird mine. Mayor Perkins, sitting in one of the chairs on the opposite side of the desk, struggled to read the papers upside down. Both men looked up when the office door burst open.

Martin Kensington strode in covered in soot and ashes and reeking of smoke, none of which he seemed to notice. "Afternoon, gentlemen," he said cheerfully as he dropped into the chair beside the mayor.

"Kensington?" Harrington looked suspiciously at the man. "What have you been up to?"

"Taking care of some business." Kensington leaned back in the chair. "Went out to my daughter's ranch to have a look around. Unfortunately, there was a small accident while I was there."

"Anybody hurt?" Harrington asked, although he really didn't care.

"No." Kensington brushed some ash off his pant leg. "What they referred to as a house caught on fire."

Mayor Perkins gasped. "You burned down Jesse's house!"

"I did not burn it down. It just happened to catch fire while I was there."

"Don't suppose you had anything to do with that?" Harrington was beginning to believe that Kensington might not be the answer to his problems as he had once believed. In fact, the businessman was beginning to be more trouble for him than the mayor. Maybe he should have just left him in the sheriff's custody.

"Oh, my god." The mayor drooped in his chair. "We can't have these things happening," he said to Harrington.

"What do I care if their house burns down?" Harrington told the mayor. "It's not like they'll be needing it."

"What are you talking about?"

Kensington smiled smugly. "When the marshal finds Jesse, she'll be going to prison, if she's lucky. And Jennifer will be going back East with me, where she should be," he informed the mayor. "Neither one of them will be coming back to Sweetwater. And I'll have Jennifer sign over her interest in the boarding house to Harrington." *I'll have the Slipper signed over, if I decide not to keep it for myself.*

Harrington wasn't happy with their secret plans being so openly discussed in front of the gossipy mayor, and he interrupted before Kensington could reveal anything more. "I have to ride up to the Songbird with Wilson this afternoon, and I have a lot to go over with Perkins before I leave. Is there something you wanted, Kensington?"

"Don't take that tone with me. I just wanted to know if the marshal has come up with anything yet."

"Haven't seen him," Harrington said dismissively, his attention returning to the papers in front of him. "I suggest you find the marshal and ask him yourself."

Kensington stood. He really didn't like the small man's attitude. Harrington needed to be put in his place, and he knew just how to do that. "Don't let me keep you from your work." He stomped out of the room.

"Fool," Harrington muttered under his breath.

Mayor Perkins was beginning to regret the events he had helped set in motion in Sweetwater. What he had thought to be an opportunity for the small town was rapidly turning into anything but. "What did he mean he would have Jennifer sign over the Slipper to you?"

"Doesn't concern you." Harrington neatly stacked the papers in the top drawer of the desk. "I have to meet Wilson," he said as he pushed himself up from the desk.

Marshal Morgan returned to Sweetwater after a long day of riding. He had visited many of the ranches in the valley, only to be met with the same response at all of them; no one knew the whereabouts of Jesse Branson. As he rode up to the livery, he silently considered his options. It was apparent that the people of Sweetwater weren't going to help him find the fugitive. Maybe he should head back to the woman's ranch in the morning and see if he could pick up any tracks.

"Surprised to see you back in town, Marshal," the livery hand said as the tired man walked his horse inside the barn.

"Why's that?" Morgan didn't recall seeing the boy before. There had always been an older man at the livery when he'd been there.

The boy took the reins of the marshal's horse. "Thought ya was goin' after Jesse."

"Haven't found her yet." Morgan followed the boy to the stall where he was pulling the saddle off his horse's back. "No one in the valley seems to know where she is."

"She ain't in the valley."

"You know where she is?"

"Yeah. They went over to the other side of the mountains." The boy picked up a pair of brushes and went to work on the horse's coat.

Morgan was annoyed. He had been looking for the woman all over the valley, now he was hearing that she'd left Sweetwater and quite possibly people in town knew about it. "How do you know?"

"Miss Jennifer's ma came in a few days back and got a horse. Said they was going to meet up with a friend to see the buffalo herds."

"What friend?"

"Don't know. Some Injun, I think."

"Why didn't you say anything before?"

"Nobody asked me. 'Sides, this is the first time I seen ya. Been gone the last couple of days visiting my brother in Garnet."

"Brush him down and feed him, then get his saddle back on. I'll be leaving as soon as I talk to a few people." The marshal turned and left the boy to his task. As he walked out of the livery, he saw the sheriff and Thomas ride up to the Slipper and quickly go inside. He had intended to talk to Tobias Harrington about what he had just learned but seeing the sheriff, he changed directions.

"He burned their house down!" Bette Mae cried as she listened to Billie and Thomas. They had just returned from Jesse and Jennifer's ranch and figured they'd start their search for Kensington at the Slipper.

"Not intentionally," Thomas said. "But yes."

Tears flooded Bette Mae's eyes and flowed down her cheeks. "Tha' house meant everythin' to them two. They worked on it together ta make it their home. Why'd ya let 'im do it?"

"I didn't let him, Bette Mae," Thomas protested. "It happened too fast; I couldn't stop it." Thomas felt sick over the loss of his sister's home. "What could I do?"

Bette Mae looked at the dejected young man. He was nothing like his father, and she was sure he'd had no hand in the burning of the cabin, other than having the misfortune to be there as a witness to his father's rampage. "I'd be obliged if ya was ta go upstairs and pack yer papa's things up. He ain't welcome in the Slipper no more."

Thomas didn't have the energy to argue, not that he saw any reason to. His father had gone too far in his attempt to destroy Jesse and Jennifer's life together. He could face the consequences of his behavior, starting with finding himself somewhere else to stay if he chose to remain in Sweetwater.

"He ain't gonna need his things, Bette Mae," Billie injected.

At that moment, Kensington, still fuming over Harrington's treatment of him, entered the Slipper. "Thomas," he said as soon as he spotted his son among the people standing together, "I'm glad you're here. I need to send a telegram; you can leave immediately."

"Martin Kensington." Billie officially addressed the man, still covered in ash and soot. "I'm placing you under arrest."

"What the hell for?"

"Trespassing, for starters. Destruction of property," Billie glared at the man, "and arson."

Kensington laughed at the lawman. "You can't arrest me. Aren't you forgetting about the governor's order?"

"That order applies to past crimes," Billie rested a hand on his gun, ready to use it if that was what it would take to put the man in a jail cell, "not laws you broke today."

Thomas, in an attempt to pacify his father and avoid any further trouble, said, "I told the sheriff you had no intention of setting fire to the house, that it was an accident. I'm sure the judge will understand that when you talk to him."

"I don't need you to defend me."

"You're gonna need somebody," Billie said as he approached the angry Kensington. "Now don't give me any trouble. You are under arrest."

Marshal Morgan shoved the door open and entered the Slipper in time to hear Billie's last words. "Hold on there, Sheriff."

"This ain't your business, Marshal," Billie said. "Kensington set fire to Jesse's ranch house."

"Speaking of the elusive Miss Branson, did you know she made plans to leave the valley days ago?"

"She what?" Kensington spun around to face the marshal. "Is Jennifer with her?"

"And your wife, apparently."

"Who told you that?" Billie asked. He knew he was in trouble and was trying not to get in any deeper. He wouldn't be of any use to Jesse and Jennifer in a jail cell.

"Livery hand."

"What are we waiting for?" Kensington moved to the door. "Let's get going, Marshal."

The marshal ignored Kensington as he stared at Billie, waiting for a reply. "I need to know, Sheriff."

Kensington would not be ignored. "We're wasting time, Marshal."

"No," Billie lied. The marshal was wrong. The warrant was wrong. Harrington was wrong. He was sure Kensington was behind all of it. He would protect Jesse, no matter the cost. The mayor could take his badge, he didn't care. "I didn't know. You have any more information 'bout where she might have gone?"

Marshal Morgan knew the sheriff was lying, but he didn't have the time to deal with it just yet. It would wait until he had Jesse Branson behind bars.

"Boy said Mrs. Kensington mentioned meeting a friend somewhere near the buffalo. An Indian."

"Walk."

"Excuse me?"

"Walks on the Wind," the sheriff explained. "He's a friend of Jesse's. His tribe hunts buffalo every year 'bout this time."

"You know where to find them?"

Billie knew he had no choice but to guide the marshal to the buffalo hunting grounds. "Yes. I'll be ready to ride in half an hour."

"I'll meet you at your office. I need to talk to Mr. Harrington before we leave."

"I'll be right behind you, Marshal," Kensington said as he followed the lawman outside. He had returned his horse to the livery and needed to reclaim it.

Billie shook his head in disgust. "You coming?" he asked Thomas, hoping he'd agree to accompany them. He could use an ally on the trip.

"What about my father?"

"I'll deal with him later. I can't leave town with a prisoner in the jail, and I can't do Jesse and Jennifer any good sittin' here."

"I'll get my things."

"Where's Ruth?" Billie asked Bette Mae when the two of them were left alone.

"In there." Bette Mae pointed to the kitchen door. "You bring my girls home," she told the sheriff. "All of 'em."

"I will," he promised.

CHAPTER TWENTY-FIVE

They rested two days by the mountain lake before Jennifer finally allowed that Jesse was fit to continue their journey. They packed the horses, cleaned their campsite, and headed down the eastern slope of the pass. The women also agreed that, due to Jennifer's limitations and Jesse's exhausting experience, they would travel shorter days and by mid-afternoon would begin to look for a suitable site to camp and call a halt to the day's travels. The trail wasn't as rocky or steep as it wound its way east through the pine forest. With the easier descent, they made good time, even though they were traveling fewer hours. It was the morning of the third day since they'd left their camp at the mountain summit.

Jennifer tilted her head to better listen to an unfamiliar roar sounding through the trees that surrounded them. "Sweetheart? What is that?"

"Waterfall," Jesse said as she guided Dusty along the trail. She'd been hearing the distinctive sound for quite some time.

"It must be big. Will we see it?" Jennifer loved the plummeting cascades of water that they'd found on the creeks and rivers they passed. When they traveled alongside the waterways, hardly a mile went by that they didn't get to enjoy water tumbling over some rocky ledge or obstacle.

As they continued through the trees, the roar grew louder. Looking down the trail, they could see a misty cloud billowing around the trees and knew they were getting close to the falls. They rode into a small clearing and found themselves literally at the base of the falls, the thick forest concealing the watery splendor until the very last moment.

The women looked up in awe as water plummeted down a half dozen stone precipices to plunge into a deep pool carved out by the pounding water. The top of the falls was over one hundred feet above them, and the spray caused by the tumbling water reached almost as far outward. The droplets falling on them were as drenching as a light rain.

The churning water made talking impossible, and Jesse pointed to a spot across the creek that was somewhat protected from the spray but still afforded a view of the falls. When Jennifer nodded, the rancher led the horses into the creek to cross. Given the torrent of water cascading over the falls, the creek was surprisingly not more than a few inches deep, as the water spread out over a large area before eventually finding its way back into a narrow channel hundreds of feet downstream. Once they were protected from the spray, the women sat on their horses to enjoy the natural spectacle.

"Uck," KC said as she wiped water droplets off her forehead.

"Yep, Sunshine." Jesse chuckled. "It's a little on the wet side."

"But it's so beautiful," Mary said. She had never seen such displays of nature before coming to Montana. The falls she was used to seeing were mostly narrow chutes of water falling a few feet. Nothing like what she was looking at now.

"Yes, it is beautiful," Jennifer agreed. "Can we stay here for the night?"

Jesse smiled regretfully at her wife. "Better not." With the falling water drowning out all other sounds, she was concerned she'd be unable to hear any danger that might threaten the group. And KC was right about it being damp so close to the falls. "We don't have much further to go before we reach the valley. We should be able to spot the buffalo herds before nightfall. I'll feel safer when we find Walk and his people."

"You're right." Jennifer reached out and patted Jesse's arm. "Maybe we can come back when all this is over."

Jesse lifted Jennifer's hand to her lips, kissing it lovingly. "I promise."

The women left the roar of the waterfall behind them and continued east. Shortly after they stopped to change KC's britches and grab a quick snack, the trail left the cover of the forest for the last time and gradually became indistinguishable from the valley floor before disappearing altogether.

Jennifer scanned the ground around them. "What happened to the trail?"

"Don't need it anymore." Jesse stood in her stirrups, studying the horizon. "The trail is only used to get over the pass. In the valley, you just go wherever you need to."

"And where do we need to go?"

"There." Jesse pointed southeast. "See that cloud of dust?"

Far in the distance, Jennifer could make out a hazy cloud at the bottom of a bluff. "I think so."

"That's where the buffalo are." Jesse settled back in the saddle. "That's where we go."

"Is that where Walk will be?" Mary asked as she looked to the horizon for Jesse's dust cloud.

"Somewhere close by."

"Will we find him by nightfall?" Jennifer pulled her canteen free and offered KC a drink.

"Only one way to find out." Jesse waited for KC to finish drinking before she urged Dusty forward. She had an unexplainable feeling that something was wrong, and she wanted to get to the safety of her friend's camp as soon as possible.

Dusty started across the valley at an easy trot with the other horses following. Around midday, the women stopped at a small grove of trees along a creek for a short rest. While Jesse saw to the baby, Jennifer carried their canteens to the creek to refill them. She kept looking up at the sky and shaking her head. After the third time she saw her wife look skyward, Jesse asked, "What's wrong, darlin'?"

"I'd swear I hear thunder, but there isn't a cloud in the sky." Jennifer carried the canteens back to the others.

"It's the buffalo." Jesse put KC back into the carry sack and swung it up on her back. "The herd must be moving."

"What are you taking about, sweetheart? How can a group of animals rumble like thunder?"

"I'll show you." Jesse helped Jennifer remount Blaze, then pulled herself aboard Dusty. "Come on." She led away from the grove of trees to the top of a small bluff not too far away. From there the women could look down into a wide valley at a dark mass moving in their direction.

As they watched the flow come closer, the horses began to fidget, and the women dismounted to calm them. They could feel the ground beneath their boots tremble, and small rocks dislodged from the bluff's edge and fell to the valley floor some distance below.

Jennifer could not believe the number of buffalo in the valley; the herd had to number over a hundred thousand strong. She had read many descriptions of the shaggy-haired, short-legged animals, but she realized now that the authors of those descriptions had not done justice to their subject.

Gradually the herd slowed, and the women could follow the movement of distinct animals as they grazed on the grasslands. Mixed in with the larger animals were several smaller ones, their coats a much lighter shade of brown.

"Why do some of them have lighter-colored coats?" Jennifer asked.

"Those are the babies." Jesse kept her eyes focused on several men on horseback following the herd at a safe distance. They were too far away to make out individual features, but she hoped one of them was Walks on the Wind.

"Isn't that an unusual color?" Mary commented on the orange-tinged coats of the younger animals. "It sure stands out."

"You wouldn't think so if you were a wolf or coyote. They can't distinguish the color from the grass and shrubs. Makes it safer for the babies," the rancher informed her mother-in-law, her eyes still on the outriders as one broke off from the others and headed their way. Jesse smiled as she recognized the approaching rider. "It's Walk," she told the others as she turned away from the bluff's edge to greet her old friend. Jennifer and Mary turned also.

Walks on the Wind raced his horse up the bluff's moderate slope, leaping to the ground when he reached the women. "Jesse, Jennifer, I wasn't expecting you."

Jesse grasped Walk's outstretched arm. "Changed our minds."

"You are always welcome in my camp."

KC peeked over Jesse's shoulder. She remembered the man who had played with her when he visited their home not so long ago. She smiled and let out a string of gibberish in greeting.

"You, too, KC." Walk playfully tapped the baby on the nose. "We have some young ones in camp about her age."

Jesse groaned. "Not sure I've got the stamina for more than one of her."

"They keep each other busy and leave the elders free to rest during the day."

"Funny," Jesse growled.

"Serves you right." Jennifer elbowed Jesse in the ribs. "You know you love chasing KC around all day. It's hard to tell which of you enjoys it more." She turned to Walk. "Is your camp near?"

"Not far." He looked to the bottom of the bluff where one of the other riders was calling to him. He responded in his native tongue, and the man rode away. "I told him Buffalo Heart has come to join our hunt. He's going back to let the others know."

Jesse became serious. The Indians were her friends, and she didn't want them to suffer because of her trouble with Kensington. "Walk, there's a reason we're here, and I think you need to know it before you invite us into your camp. It could mean trouble."

"You are our friend, Buffalo Heart. Your trouble is ours."

"I appreciate that, but I'd feel better if you knew what was going on."

Walk had reasoned that unexpected appearance of his friends was the result of a problem. "You can tell me as we ride."

"It should be over there." Billie pointed to a bluff a couple of hours ride across the valley. "Walks on the Wind usually camps around there during the hunt."

"How do you know?" Kensington asked.

"Joined Jesse on a hunt last year." Billie frowned, remembering the good times he'd had in the Indian camp. He knew this wasn't going to be another.

"Let's go." Marshal Morgan urged his horse forward. "I want to get there before nightfall."

Billie had led the party from Sweetwater to the lush valley country where the buffalo herds gathered in the late summer. At the marshal's insistence, they had ridden non-stop, both day and night, only stopping every few hours just long enough to rest the horses. What the sheriff had hoped would be a ten-day trip had been accomplished in less than half that time. There was nothing to do now but hope Jesse and Jennifer had decided to stay somewhere in the mountains, safely tucked away where their pursuers couldn't find them.

"Where's Billie?" Thaddeus Newby asked Bette Mae. He had arrived back in Sweetwater after spending several days riding between mining camps. He wanted to talk with the sheriff and, finding his office vacant, had walked to the Slipper on the chance that Billie would be there with his fiancée.

"On his way to arrest Jesse."

"What!"

"Marshal found out tha' they'd gone over the mountains to get away from Kensington. Billie couldn' do nothin' but go with him. Took Kensington and Thomas with 'em."

"Damn." Thaddeus plopped down in an unoccupied chair.

"Tha' ain't the half of it." Bette Mae joined him at the table. "Kensington set fire to the ranch house. Burned it to the ground."

Thaddeus' shoulders slumped. Obviously, his warning to the sheriff about possible trouble at the ranch hadn't been in time. "What can happen next?"

"They can hang Jesse."

"Jesse's not going to hang. No judge in the territory will believe the charges they've made against her."

"But Jennifer's papa..." Bette Mae wiped at the few stray tears rolling down her cheeks, the strain of worrying about her friends becoming too much to hold back. "Why won' he leave 'em be? Ya know what it'll do ta Jennifer if anything happens ta Jesse."

"I know."

"He's twisted inside, Thaddeus. Bent and twisted like the vines in the forest. He don' know wha's right anymore, jus' knows what he wants. And he wants Jesse dead."

"That won't happen." He hoped that was true, but he wasn't foolish enough to believe that Kensington wouldn't do everything in his power to make it happen.

A warning call echoed through the Indian camp when the approaching riders were spotted.

Jennifer had just finished feeding KC and she carried the baby to where Jesse had paused in the process of spreading out their bedrolls.

"Sweetheart, isn't that Billie's horse?"

Jesse frowned. It was Billie, and he wasn't alone. Jesse knew that could only mean one thing. At Jennifer's gasp, she said, "What is it, darlin'?"

"It's Father."

Mary rushed to her daughter's side. "Are you sure?" she asked, the men still too far for her to see them clearly.

"Yes. And Thomas is with him."

Jesse closed the distance between them to wrap her arms around her wife. "Thomas?"

"My brother."

"I wonder who the fourth man is," Jesse muttered.

Walks on the Wind joined the women. "Is this your trouble?"

"Seems to be," Jesse told him.

"I can have them chased away."

"No." Jesse shook her head. "We best face this and get it done with."

The men rode into the Indian camp. Billie tried to reach the women first, but the others were right behind him.

"It's about time we found you." Martin Kensington was off his horse and storming toward Jennifer. "Take your hands off my daughter!" he screamed.

Jesse pushed Jennifer behind her and faced the angry man. "Back off, Kensington."

Recognizing the large man who had hurt her mothers before, KC frantically wrapped her arms around Jennifer's neck and began to cry.

Thomas ran after his father, grabbing him by the arms and pulling him away from his sister's wife. "Father, stop."

Marshal Morgan dismounted and reached into his saddlebags for his set of handcuffs. Carrying them toward the fugitive, he said, "Jesse Branson, you're under arrest."

"What the hell are you talking about?" Jesse asked.

Though she knew her husband was intractable, Mary cried out, "Martin, why are you doing this?"

Jennifer, refusing to remain behind her protective wife, forced her way to stand beside Jesse. "What does he mean you're under arrest?"

KC heard the fear in her momma's voice. As she felt the arms holding her start to tremble, her cries turned into wails.

Billie yanked the marshal around to keep him from Jesse. "Back off."

"Get out of my way," Kensington ordered, as he tried to break loose from his son's grasp.

Walks on the Wind stepped in front of Jesse and Jennifer. "Enough." He held his arms up, palms facing the lawmen and the Kensingtons. "You have entered our camp uninvited," he said. "If you wish to remain, you must obey our customs."

Several of the other men in the camp stood behind the women, ready to protect them if Walk gave the signal. "Buffalo Heart is a friend of this camp, and she must be treated as if she were one of us."

"We're not looking for any trouble," Marshal Morgan said to Walks. "But I aim to carry out my duties and arrest her."

"Your law does not belong in our camp."

"Like hell!" Kensington protested.

"Shut up," Marshal Morgan hissed. "I have a job to do, and I won't have you making it any more difficult than it has been already." He faced Walk. "We won't be staying any longer than it takes to handcuff my prisoner and get her on a horse. I suggest you don't try to prevent it."

"Billie?" Jesse asked from behind Walk. "What's going on?" Her friend's troubled eyes told her that the news wasn't good.

"This is Marshal Morgan. He has a warrant for your arrest."

"For what?" Jennifer asked as she felt Jesse's shaking arms encircle her.

"For the murders of Kenneth and Catherine Williams," the marshal answered, "and the kidnapping of their infant daughter."

Jesse's knees went weak, and if it hadn't been for her arms wrapped around Jennifer, she would have fallen to the ground.

Jennifer felt like a fist had slammed into her stomach. This couldn't be happening again. "Father, what have you done?"

"Just told the governor what I heard from the good people of Bannack," Kensington boasted. "Maybe now you'll understand what this conniving bitch is really like."

"Have you gone mad?" Jennifer screamed. "I was with her when we found KC. She didn't kill the Williamses; Sheriff Logan's men did."

"Not the way I heard it."

"Martin, please don't do this," Mary pleaded. "I know Jesse; she's a good woman. And Jennifer loves her very much."

Kensington grunted. "She can't love another woman. It's not natural."

"Please, Martin."

"I see the she-devil has corrupted you, too. I'll fix that as soon as we get back home."

"Thomas, are you here to help him?" Mary asked.

"No, Mother. I came to try to keep him from causing you and Jennifer any trouble. Unfortunately, I haven't done a very good job."

"Sweetheart?" Jennifer felt Jesse's silent sobs. "Oh, Jesse..."

"I can't lose you," Jesse whispered.

"I'm not going anywhere, sweetheart." Jennifer adjusted her position so she could hold Jesse and the baby. "You didn't kill anyone, and we'll prove that in every court in the territory if we have to."

"Don't leave me."

"Never, my love." Jennifer kissed Jesse's cheek, tasting her tears. "Never."

"All right, enough of this," Kensington snapped. "Thomas, get your mother and sister on their horses. You can leave the brat here for the savages to take care of."

"No," Thomas told his father.

"What did you say?"

"I said no. I will not help you force them to do something they don't want to do. What you've already done to them is bad enough."

"Get the horses."

"No."

"Marshal, I want my wife and daughter taken into protective custody."

"No."

Kensington glared at the marshal. "You were sent here by the governor—"

"Mr. Kensington, I am well aware of the duties I was assigned by the governor. And they do not include anything to do with your wife or daughter."

"If I have to do this myself, I will." Kensington set off to find two horses for Mary and Jennifer to ride.

Walk signaled to a couple of the men standing nearby, and they left to make sure Kensington wasn't successful in his search.

"I need to handcuff you," Marshal Morgan told Jesse, still standing behind Walk. "I don't want any trouble."

Walk and the other men of the camp readied their weapons. "No," Jesse called out. "I don't want a fight," she told Walk when he turned to question her. "I don't want anyone to get hurt." She knew the consequences the Indians would most probably face if they killed the marshal or the Kensingtons. "I'll go with you, Marshal." She kissed Jennifer and KC, then tried to extricate herself from her wife's grasp.

"Don't, Jesse," Jennifer pleaded. "You didn't do anything. Walk will help us."

"Please, darlin'. I don't want anyone to get hurt. Let me go with the marshal; we can sort this out with the judge."

Jennifer refused to let Jesse go. "I love you."

"Be a good girl, KC." Jesse kissed the baby. "I love you." Jesse hugged Jennifer one last time before gently pushing her wife away. She stepped past Walk and stood in front of the marshal, her hands held out before her.

Morgan clamped the handcuffs on her wrists. "Where's your horse?"

Jesse whistled, and Dusty trotted over from where she had been standing nearby. She still wore her saddle; they had not been in the Indian camp long enough to unsaddle the horses.

"Get on up," the marshal commanded. Once Jesse was settled in the saddle, he pulled some pigging rope from his vest pocket and tied her legs to her stirrups.

Jennifer retrieved Blaze and Boy. Her face stained by tears, KC huddled in the carry sack on her momma's back. She reached for Jesse and couldn't understand why her mommy didn't lift her into her arms.

"Marshal Morgan."

"Yes, Miss Kensington?"

"Mrs. Branson," she corrected. "Where are you taking my wife?"

"Bannack, Mrs. Branson." The marshal acknowledged the unusual relationship. "She'll stand trial there."

"Then I will be accompanying you there."

Mary led her horse up beside Jennifer. "As will I."

"I suggest you and your mother return to Sweetwater," the marshal said.

"You don't know these two." Billie smiled at Jennifer as he helped her mount Blaze. "Where one goes, the other is right behind."

The marshal lowered his voice to speak to Billie discreetly. "Sheriff, with what is likely to happen in Bannack, I think you should take them home."

"Jesse didn't kidnap that baby, Marshal. And she sure as hell didn't kill anyone." Billie pulled himself back onto the saddle of his horse. "We're all going to Bannack."

"Do what you want, but keep back and don't get near my prisoner." The marshal remounted his horse. "I have orders to deliver her to the judge in Bannack, and I'll do whatever it takes to get her there." Everyone understood his unvoiced threat. "Let's go, Branson."

Marshal Morgan escorted his prisoner southward. With her bound hands, Jesse hung on to Dusty's saddle horn; the reins were controlled by the marshal who was taking no chance of having her ride off. Not that she would, with Jennifer and KC following behind them.

Sitting in the carry sack, a whimpering KC rested against her momma's back. Jennifer shared the baby's pain and hoped the marshal would let Jesse hold their daughter when they camped for the night. If they camped for the night.

The riders reached the end of the valley and started over a low pass that would take them into the adjoining valley. Determined to reach Bannack as quickly as possible, the marshal refused all requests to stop. "Y'all can do whatever you want, but I plan to travel straight through the night."

Jesse's bound wrists and legs were tingling from a lack of circulation. "Marshal," she addressed the single-minded man who rode beside her. "I need a break."

"You'll have plenty of time to rest in Bannack."

"I've lost feeling in my legs," Jesse explained. "Just let me walk around a bit. And Jennifer needs to rest." Jesse was concerned about her wife after the long day in the saddle.

"She can stop whenever she wants." The marshal kept riding.

"Mommy," KC cried when she heard Jesse's voice.

The despair in the small voice tore at the hearts of the others, even the marshal, but having a job to do, he tried to ignore the baby's cries.

Jesse couldn't take it any longer. If she was sore and tired, then Jennifer must really be suffering, not to mention how their little daughter was feeling. "Dusty, stop," she instructed the golden mare, who immediately obeyed.

"What the hell?" Morgan yelped as his arm was yanked backward by his grip on Dusty's reins, the sudden stop almost unseating him. He pulled on the leather to get the mare to move. "Come on, you dumb—"

"She ain't goin' nowhere." Billie rode up beside the marshal. "Seems like a good spot to camp for the night."

"I'm taking my prisoner to Bannack. Tonight." The marshal kept pulling on the reins but failed in his efforts to get Dusty to move. "Damn it." He glared at Jesse. "Make her move."

"No." Jesse stared down the marshal. "If you haven't noticed, Marshal, my wife suffered a severe injury not very long ago, and she needs to rest. You can yank on Dusty's reins all night, but she won't move until I tell her to. So," Jesse smiled at the man, but her eyes held no humor, "I suggest you agree to stop for a few hours."

The marshal knew he had no real choice. He was outnumbered five to one, and he again wondered why the elder Kensington had not accompanied the group when they left the Indian camp. The man was more trouble than he was worth, but at least he would have helped even the odds. "All right," the marshal reluctantly allowed. "But we're leaving at dawn. I want to be in Bannack tomorrow."

Billie slipped off his horse and helped Jennifer dismount. Her leg throbbed, and she was grateful for his help. She just wished it were Jesse's arms around her instead rather than the sheriff's.

"Why don't you take KC over there," Billie indicated a grassy spot not too far from where they were standing, "and I'll see about getting the marshal to let Jesse sit with you."

"Thanks, Billie." Jennifer grimaced as she pulled her cane free of the scabbard. She couldn't wait to stretch out her aching leg. But what it really needed, she knew she wasn't going to get this night — a rubdown from Jesse's gentle hands. "But I need to get some stuff out of the packs. KC needs fresh britches, and she's hungry."

"Go sit down." Thomas stepped up beside his sister. "I'll take care of that for you."

Jennifer looked up at her brother. She had been shocked to see Thomas riding toward the Indian camp, thinking that he had come to assist their father in his quest. She had been even more surprised when he had done just the opposite. "Thank you, Thomas." She leaned heavily on her cane. "I'm not sure I could manage by myself."

"Go on." Thomas smiled sadly. He had known of his sister's injury but had been unaware until just that moment how much she suffered because of it. "Mother, why don't you go with her?" he said as Mary joined them.

Billie went over to the marshal who had dismounted and was untying Jesse's legs. "Have a favor to ask, Marshal." He stood a few feet away, not wanting the other lawman to think he was a threat. "The baby's been crying for Jesse," he needlessly told the marshal, who had been listening to the child's sobs along with the others. "It would do her a world of good if Jesse could hold her, just 'til she falls asleep."

"That child is not my problem, Sheriff." The marshal finished freeing Jesse's legs and motioned her to dismount. "Prisoner will be tied up until we leave in the morning."

"Suit yourself, Marshal." Billie winked at Jesse, who was stomping her feet to get the blood moving again. "But if I know little KC, she'll be wailing all night if you keep them separated. Jesse will promise not to cause any trouble if you let her be with her family, won't ya?"

"Yes." Jesse nodded sincerely. She would do anything to be allowed a few moments with her family. "There won't be any trouble."

The marshal looked over at KC, who was reaching for Jesse even as Jennifer tried to change her. *If it would get the kid to stop her relentless crying...* "You'll be shackled," he told Jesse, and she nodded. He pulled a set of leg shackles from his saddlebag. "All right."

Jennifer watched hopefully as the marshal led Jesse in her direction. KC, seeing her mother approach, began to crawl toward her. Jennifer stopped the baby. "Stay here, sweetie."

Jesse was led to a small tree close to where Thomas had set out the women's bedrolls. "Don't move," the marshal commanded before kneeling down to attach one of the shackles around his prisoner's booted ankle. He secured the other shackle around the tree, then stood up.

"What about these?" Jesse held up her wrists to display the handcuffs.

"They stay on," the marshal said as he walked away.

"Thank you," Jennifer called after the marshal, who did not respond. With KC, she rushed to Jesse and wrapped her arms around her wife.

Jesse choked back tears. It felt so good to feel Jennifer pressed against her. "How ya doin', darlin'?"

"I'm fine," Jennifer sighed, and she was, now that Jesse was in her arms.

"Mommy." KC grabbed for Jesse but, with her hands restrained and her arms wrapped in Jennifer's, the rancher couldn't hold the baby.

"Let's sit down," Jesse suggested.

"Wait a minute." Jennifer released her wife and handed the baby to Jesse, who happily accepted the child. "Let me pull our blankets over here."

KC, overjoyed to be in her mommy's arms, didn't care that the woman's hold on her was awkward. "Mommy." She wrapped her arms around Jesse's neck. "Wuv."

"I love you, too, Sunshine." Jesse cried with the baby.

With Mary's help, the bedrolls and blankets were quickly moved closer to the tree that tethered Jesse, then Jennifer helped her wife sit as KC continued to cling to her mother.

"I want to hold you," Jesse whispered as Jennifer snuggled next to her. She scooted back so she could lean against the tree trunk and spread her legs. "Sit here a minute, Sunshine," she said, placing the baby on the blanket next to her. When Jesse lifted her arms up and out of the way, Jennifer slipped between her legs. KC crawled into Jennifer's lap and Jesse dropped her handcuffed arms over Jennifer's head to wrap them around her family. "I love you." Jesse kissed the top of Jennifer's head.

Jennifer relaxed against Jesse and closed her eyes, safe once again in her lover's arms. "I love you," she sighed.

Marshal Morgan watched the exchange as he pulled the saddle off his horse, the first seeds of doubt creeping into his mind.

Billie and Thomas collected firewood and built a campfire. They unburdened Boy of his packs and unsaddled the other horses before brushing and picketing them for the night. As they worked, Mary prepared a hot meal. After eating, the group settled into their bedrolls for the remainder of the night.

Jesse lay on her back with KC sprawled on top of her. Jennifer snuggled beside them, an arm and leg draped over her wife's body under the blankets. Unable to sleep, Jesse watched the moon rise from behind the mountains to the east. The camp was quiet with everyone asleep. Even the marshal, having decided his prisoner wasn't going to try to escape, had nodded off. Jesse clumsily adjusted her arms, not used to having her hands bound.

"You should be sleeping," Jennifer whispered as Jesse fidgeted.

Jesse gave up trying to find a comfortable position. "So should you."

"Can't." Jennifer nestled closer and began to massage the manacled wrists.

"That feels good." The handcuffs were tight, and the rough surface of the metal was scraping Jesse's skin raw. "How are you doing?" she asked, keeping her voice low so as not to wake the others.

"Wishing we were home in our own bed."

"Me, too."

"Jesse?" Jennifer looked into her wife's eyes, the moon's reflection shining brightly in them. "Why is this happening?"

Jesse didn't answer right away. She knew as well as Jennifer did what, and who, was behind their present predicament. She also knew that wasn't what her wife was really asking. Why did their relationship seem to be such a threat to others?

Even in Sweetwater, surrounded by friends who supported their love, they faced intolerance. People who would whisper as they walked by or stop talking whenever they entered a room. Some disliked them because they were women owning and operating businesses. Some because they were strong and stood up for themselves. But some disliked them simply because of the love they held for each other. Why couldn't people like Jennifer's father just accept them for who they were?

Jesse wondered if there would ever come a day that they would not have to defend themselves against other folk's unreasonable beliefs. "I don't know, darlin'," she finally said. "I don't know why some folks are so against us loving each other. Seems they won't be happy 'til they destroy what we have."

"They can take away everything, sweetheart, but I'll never stop loving you," Jennifer vowed, She tightened her hold on her wife. "No matter what, I'll love you forever. Even after we leave this life, you will always hold my heart."

Tears filled Jesse's eyes as her aching soul basked in the balm of her wife's words. "You are my life, darlin'. Nothing will ever change that."

CHAPTER TWENTY-SIX

"Any news?" Ed asked Thaddeus when the newspaperman returned from meeting the stagecoach.

It had been several days since the marshal had left town in search of Jesse and Jennifer. Thaddeus met every stage in hopes that a message would come, telling them what was going on. He shook his head. "Nothing."

"Been thinkin' I might close up the store for a few days and go lookin' for them. Been putting it off hopin' Billie would send word, but maybe I should just do it."

Thaddeus stepped onto the boardwalk beside the large man. "Might give it a few more days. By now they could be anywhere, and you'd just be riding around in circles. I'd ride out to look myself but there's too much happening here." There had been recent upsurge of activity in town that he was obligated to report on for the *Gazette*.

Ed looked at the lot beside his store where men were hammering a new building into existence. Similar activity was taking place across the street next to the stage station. "I'll wait two more days," he decided, "then I'm leavin'."

"Can you afford to close the store?" Thaddeus asked. The mercantile was the only store in the valley where folks could buy their necessities.

"No," Ed answered honestly. "Guess I'll talk to Bette Mae 'bout a couple of the girls keeping an eye on it for me. Shouldn't be a problem. But if I have to, I'll lock it up." He looked at Thaddeus. "Right now, I'm more concerned about Jennifer and Jesse than I am about the store."

Bette Mae listened to the storekeeper's plans to find Jesse and Jennifer. "Ruthie and Nancy can take care of the store for you for a few days."

"Thanks, Bette Mae." Ed was relieved that he wouldn't have to lock the doors. Not that he minded losing the income, but he didn't want to cause any hardship for his customers.

"But I'm comin' wit' ya."

Ed knew it would be useless to argue.

"Bette Mae," Ruthie had been listening to the conversation and boldly approached the pair, "I'd like to go with you. I'm worried 'bout Billie."

"It'll be a long ride, Ruthie," Bette Mae gently told the girl she knew had spent very little time on the back of a horse.

"I don't care," Ruthie said, determined that she be allowed to accompany Bette Mae and Ed when they left town. "I want to go."

Bette Mae studied the young woman who had recently become engaged to the sheriff. She seemed like a completely different person from the one Bette Mae knew. The old Ruthie would never have made her request, no matter how much she wanted to. She wondered how much of the girl's maturity was due to the confidence given her by Jesse and Jennifer and how much was due to the sheriff's love. She decided it really didn't matter.

"All right, Ruthie." Bette Mae smiled. "Nancy can take care of things here."

Nancy tended bar in the Slipper's saloon, and the men in town had quickly learned not to cross the tall redhead who kept a double barreled shotgun under the bar, loaded and ready to use.

"We'll be ready, Ed. Ya jus' say the word."

Frank Wilson picked his way up the narrow, rocky trail snaking to the top of a mountain outside of Sweetwater. Nearing its end, the trail leveled and approached a slope devoid of most vegetation due to numerous snow slides that every winter raced down the incline carrying everything in their path down with them. At the edge of this gradient, cut into the hillside, was an opening just large enough for a man to pass through. Stretching behind that breach, Wilson knew there was a tunnel carved into the mountain for approximately two hundred feet. He was looking at the entrance to the Songbird mine.

When he had visited the site a few days earlier with Harrington, Wilson had been bothered by something but had been unable to pinpoint the reason for his uneasiness. He just knew that something didn't seem right in the mine. The sensation had continued to nag at him, and he had come back to the mine alone to see if he could identify what was causing his sleepless nights.

"Howdy, Mr. Wilson," greeted the ex-cowboy hired to guard the mine. "Wasn't expecting anyone today."

"Spur of the moment trip," Wilson told the guard. "Just need to check out a couple of things."

"Need my help?"

"No." Wilson didn't want anything, or anyone, to disturb his thoughts while he was in the mine. "I can handle this myself."

"Fine with me. I don't much like going in under that much rock, and pretty much in the dark, to boot. But give a holler if you change your mind."

"Thanks."

Lighting the lantern kept at the tunnel's entrance, Wilson left the brightness of the day and walked into the dark mine tunnel. Cautiously, he stepped a few feet into the chasm and stopped to study his surroundings. Near the entrance, the tunnel's walls were heavily braced to keep the enormous weight of the mountain from collapsing them, but as he raised the lantern shoulder high and scanned down the length of the tunnel, he noticed that the braces became further apart until they disappeared altogether.

"Not too smart to work in an un-reinforced shaft," Wilson declared, thinking the mine's original owner had probably been unwilling to continue the arduous work of cutting and installing the fortifications, preferring instead to use his energy and resources to dig out the valuable ore. He slowly moved deeper into the tunnel, closely examining the walls as he passed. When he reached the end, he studied the rock face that had caught his eye days before.

He held the lantern as close to the rock wall as he could and ran his finger along what appeared to be a vein of ore running several feet across the stone face. He scraped at the vein with his fingernail and then pulled out his pocketknife and scraped some more. He frowned when tiny bits of the shiny material flaked off and fell to the ground at his feet. Kneeling, he picked up some of the flakes and rubbed them between his fingers.

Wilson hurried back down the length of the tunnel to reappear into the midday sunlight. "Damn," he muttered, "I wonder if that fool knows about this."

"You say something, Mr. Wilson?" The guard was sitting in the shade of a tree near the mouth of the mine.

"No, nothing." Wilson blew out the flame and returned the lantern to its hook, ready for the next person to use. Wilson nodded at the guard before turning to retrace his way down the mountain. He was grateful for the time the descent would take. He had to figure out what to do about the discovery he had just made.

"You can't keep me here!" Martin Kensington yelled for the umpteenth time.

"You're free to leave at any time," Walks on the Wind, sitting casually by a fire, told the irrational man. It wasn't the first time Walk had made the offer.

A man sitting near Walk said something in their native language, and Walk nodded. "Brave Bear asks that you quit yelling; it is making his head hurt," he informed Kensington.

"Give me my damn horse!" Kensington screamed, ignoring the request for a more moderated tone.

"Mr. Kensington..." Walk took a deep breath. Their exchange had been going on since Jesse was taken away from their camp the night before. "As I have told you, the horse is no longer here, and we cannot give you one of our horses as they are needed to get the buffalo meat back to our village."

Kensington was beyond furious. Not only had the man remained calm in the face of his own anger, but he also spoke English better than most white men in the frontier territory. And he knew the Indian was speaking the truth about his horse. When he had ridden into the Indian camp the day before, he had failed to secure his horse, and it had wandered off during the confrontation between the marshal and Jesse. At least that's what he had been told when he couldn't locate the animal. But there were several Indian ponies in the camp, and he saw no reason for the continual refusal to give him one of them.

"Look," Kensington started.

"No." Walk had finally had enough. By now Jesse and Jennifer must be close to Bannack, and he no longer needed to detain Kensington to keep him from causing them any problems on the trip. "We will not give you a horse. Bannack is south, over that small range of hills." He pointed out the proper direction in case the Easterner didn't know. "You can walk there in three or four days. You may even get lucky and find your horse on the way. Mr. Kensington, I am asking you to leave our camp." The last words were spoken in a hard voice that warned the man not to refuse.

Kensington stared at the native who dared to talk to him in such a manner. His features hardened, and he took a step in Walk's direction. Before he could take another, he was surrounded by the other warriors of the camp. Words were exchanged between Walk and the men, then Kensington was roughly forced away from the fire.

"Mr. Kensington," Walk called to the man fighting his escort, "I can no longer protect you." He gestured at the angry warriors who considered Jesse a trusted friend. If the man hadn't been Jennifer's father, he would not have protected him for this long. "Please do not attempt to return to our camp." Walk spoke in his native language, and Kensington was shoved away from the camp. "If you do, you will not receive a pleasant welcome."

With no other option, Kensington began to walk toward the south end of the valley. He took a moment to cast a final glare over his shoulder at the Indian camp and its occupants.

Walk smirked as he watched Kensington march away. He would give the belligerent man a head start, and then he would ride for Bannack himself, making sure to stay out of the man's line of sight. And, he laughed to himself, he'd take Kensington's horse with him.

Jennifer, with KC on her back, rode beside Jesse. The baby had wanted to ride on Jesse's back but had settled in on Jennifer's as long as she could see her mommy.

"How's your leg?" Jesse asked. They had been riding since dawn, and except for a few short stops to see to KC's needs, Jennifer had been in the saddle the entire time.

"I won't lie to you." Jennifer had learned that lesson the hard way and wasn't about to forget how much Jesse had blamed herself for the resultant suffering. "I will be more than glad to get off Blaze, for good. But I would stay up here forever if it meant keeping you out of jail."

"Don't think that's goin' to happen, darlin'," Jesse said sadly. "We should be in Bannack before nightfall." She figured there'd be no excuse for her wife not to rest once she, herself, was locked in a jail cell.

"That's enough talk," Marshal Morgan called over his shoulder. That morning as he was attaching the shackles to both of Jesse's legs, the chain hanging under Dusty's belly, he had relented and allowed that the two could ride side by side, but only if they didn't talk. He had permitted it for no other reason than to save his ears from another day of the baby's unhappy wails.

Jennifer mouthed the words *I love you* to her wife as they obeyed the marshal's warning. Neither wanted to do anything that would cause the lawman to reinstate his restrictions.

Thomas was riding beside his mother. Not knowing what to say to the woman who raised him, he hadn't spoken a word since they broke camp that morning.

Mary decided it was time to break the forced silence. "Thomas, why are you here?"

Listening from where they rode several feet ahead, Jesse and Jennifer were both interested in his answer.

Thomas took a deep breath. "Father insisted on returning here for Jennifer. And you. We tried to talk him out of it but he wouldn't listen. He said he was going to come back, no matter what. I agreed to accompany him only on the condition that he would let Jennifer make up her own mind about where and how she wants to spend her life, and I came because I wanted to ask you to come home."

"You mean you came to order me back home," Mary suggested skeptically to the son that had always copied his father's every attitude.

"No." He shook his head. "I've asked a wonderful young lady to marry me, and she's agreed." He smiled as he thought of his fiancée waiting for him to return. "I want you to come home for the wedding and," he emphasized, "to be part of our family."

Mary looked at her son thoughtfully. Before she had come to Montana, she had been unaware Thomas was courting someone and wondered why he had felt it necessary to keep it secret.

"I never would have come here," Thomas continued, "if I'd known what Father was capable of. Never." He looked at Jennifer and Jesse, who were looking back at him. "I'm so sorry."

Wondering why her eldest son seemed so upset, Mary gently asked, "Thomas, what has your father done?"

"You don't know?" Thomas looked at Billie. He was sure the sheriff would have found the time to tell Jesse and Jennifer about their home.

Billie hadn't said anything to the women, wanting to save them from any more heartbreak. "Thought it best to wait until all this was over."

"Know what?" Jesse brought Dusty to an abrupt stop, and Jennifer pulled Blaze up next to her.

"What's going on?" the marshal asked when he found himself moving forward alone.

"Know what?" Jesse repeated, her voice more demanding.

"I'm so sorry, Jennifer," Thomas tearfully told his sister. "I should have stopped him, but I didn't."

"What the hell did he do!" Jesse shouted.

Billie spoke up when it became apparent that Thomas was unable to answer. "He burned down the ranch."

"What!" Jennifer shrieked.

"I'm sorry," Billie said.

"All of it?" Jesse asked, stunned by the news.

"No, just the cabin. Thomas saved the rest of the buildings." The sheriff hoped that news would speak well for the distraught man.

"How?" Jesse asked.

"Why?" Jennifer asked at the same time.

"It was an accident." Thomas finally found his voice. "He didn't go there to do it, it just happened."

"Why was he there, Thomas?" Jennifer demanded.

"I don't know. He never told me."

Jennifer couldn't believe her father had managed to destroy the one thing that meant so much to Jesse while the entire town was supposed to be watching him. "Why wasn't he in jail, Billie?"

"He was," Billie explained. "I arrested him as soon as he set foot in Sweetwater. The next day, the marshal here arrived with a warrant for Jesse and a writ from the governor releasing your father. I had to let him out."

Jennifer glared at the hapless marshal who could only sit on his horse and listen to the conversation unfold around him. "You let my father out of jail," she accused. "After everything he did to us, you let him out of jail."

KC began to whimper. Jesse softened her voice and smiled at the baby. "It's okay, Sunshine." She turned to the marshal. "Kensington was ordered out of Montana, never to return," she said. "Why in hell would the governor rescind that order?"

"Tobias Harrington," the marshal said succinctly.

Jennifer was dumbfounded that the condescending little man was involved. "What does he have to do with any of this?"

"He provided the information to the governor about your crimes," Morgan told Jesse. "And about your father being wrongly accused," he said to Jennifer.

"Oh, my god." Jennifer would have laughed if the situation hadn't been so serious. "And the governor believed him?"

"Harrington is an old acquaintance of the governor's. He had no reason to disbelieve him."

Jennifer could not believe what she was hearing. "Did the governor think we made the whole thing up? How my father beat Jesse senseless and kidnapped me? How Andrew was killed because of my father? And what about this?" She slapped her damaged leg, uncaring about the pain the action caused. "Did I make this up, too? My father is responsible for all of that and much more." She glared at the marshal. "Not to mention KC. Tell me, Marshal, did anyone even bother asking the people in Bannack what happened? That we reported finding the Williamses murdered? That Jesse and I buried them? How we searched for any relatives of the baby? Well, Marshal, did you?"

"You can ask them yourself, during the trial." Morgan was uncomfortable with the accusations thrown in his direction. Not to mention that he was beginning to have some serious doubts as to the validity of the information he had been given. "It's time to get moving."

Jesse sat quietly, her mind reviewing everything she had just heard. Things were starting to make sense. "Come on." Jesse kneed Dusty into motion.

Jennifer reached out to stop the rancher. "Jesse, what are you saying?"

"The sooner we get to Bannack, the sooner we can prove I didn't do anything and I can get rid of these." She shook the handcuffs. "And then I can find your father and finish this once and for all." She shrugged off Jennifer's hand. "Let's get going."

"I hope that wasn't a threat," the marshal said as his horse fell in step beside Dusty.

"Nope," Jesse said. "That, Marshal, was a statement of fact. Something you seem to be pretty much lacking for."

When Frank Wilson returned to town, he rode directly to the stage station. He had made a decision and wanted to carry through with it before anyone could change his mind. "Need to send a telegram," the foreman told the stationmaster inside the old adobe building.

"Write it up." The stationmaster pointed to a small desk with a supply of paper, a pen, and bottle of ink. "It'll go out on t'morrow's stage."

"Any way to get something out sooner?"

"Messenger, but don't know if anyone is available to carry it."

"I'll pay extra."

The stationmaster considered the offer. "Seems I saw Pete ridin' up to the Oxbow a while back. Let me see if he's interested." The man hurried out to find the cowhand who often carried messages between Sweetwater and the nearest telegraph office. It wasn't long before he returned with the cowboy.

Wilson handed Pete a sealed envelope and a five-dollar bill. "I'll give you another when you return with an answer."

That was more than the cowpuncher made in a couple of months. "Yes, sir."

"It's important. Don't lose it. And don't let anyone read it before you give it to the telegraph operator. Make sure you wait for an answer, then bring it directly to me. Understand?"

"Yes, sir." Hearing no further instructions, Pete ran out of the station, mounted his horse, and galloped out of town.

From the mayor's office, Tobias Harrington had watched the foreman enter the stage station and was watching when the cowboy charged out of town. He wondered what Wilson was up to and decided to ask him. He crossed the street to meet the foreman as he came out of the stage station.

"Afternoon, Wilson." Harrington smiled pleasantly, yet his eyes were guarded.

Wilson wasn't surprised to see Harrington and was glad his message was already on its way out of town. "Afternoon."

"I noticed you rode out of town earlier. Did you go up to the Songbird?"

"Yes." Wilson started walking toward the construction site of the new hotel.

"Any particular reason?"

"Just wanted to double check something."

"It pays to be cautious," Harrington said, not liking his foreman's lack of forthrightness. "But I do expect to be informed of such things."

Wilson didn't know if Harrington was aware of the mine's true status and was simply trying to find out what he knew, or if his boss was unaware and just being his normal obtrusive self. Either way, he didn't trust the overseer and was not about to share his recent discovery with him.

"Look, Harrington, I've got two buildings to put up and a road to construct. I don't have time to play games with you. I went up to the mine to check out some things. That's my job. If you don't like it, have me replaced. Until then, leave me the hell alone." Wilson stomped off.

It had been several hours since Martin Kensington had been banished from the Indian camp. His feet, not used to walking long distances, were sore and blistered. He was following the trail of hoofprints left by the group of riders and still had some distance to go before reaching the small string of hills that split one valley from the next. It hadn't been until he was some distance from the Indian camp that he realized he had no supplies: no weapon, no food, no sleeping gear, no water. Luckily, he had crossed a few small creeks and had drunk from those. Now as the end of the day neared, Kensington was hungry, cold, and scared.

For all his arrogance, Martin Kensington was only comfortable in the confines of a large, noisy city. He didn't like this wide-open quiet country where one could travel all day and not encounter so much as another person. And now he found himself completely alone. He could have yelled as loudly as he wanted, and there was probably no one for miles to hear him.

Kensington knew he needed to find somewhere safe to spend the night because it would be foolhardy for him to attempt to continue walking in the dark. He looked around and saw nowhere that looked promising. He would have to sit in the open, without a fire or weapon, and hope nothing threatened him during the night. His thoughts swept back to the day his daughter had been attacked by the cougar, the cat's claws ripping a gash the length of her leg, exposing the bone usually deep beneath protective tissue and muscle. He shook his head to clear the terrifying memory from his mind. He definitely was not looking forward to the long, dark hours ahead.

Atop a ridge a few hundred feet behind Kensington and hidden by the tall grass, two dark eyes kept watch on the Easterner's movements.

CHAPTER TWENTY-SEVEN

Crossing Grasshopper Creek, the group of riders could hear the sounds of the active mining camp in the distance. Even though it was almost dark, there were men still panning the gravel creek bed hoping to find an elusive gold nugget. Passing through the shantytown of Yankee Flats, the marshal led the group into the town of Bannack. They rode by the residences at the beginning of town and continued on to the commercial buildings that lined the main street. Most of the buildings were made from rough-hewn logs or wood planks with only a few adobe structures and tents scattered among them. The group attracted attention from everyone they passed.

Jesse was embarrassed to be led into town in handcuffs and leg shackles, but she held her head high. Jennifer inched Blaze up beside Dusty so she could proudly ride into Bannack beside her wife.

Marshal Morgan pulled his horse to a stop as a couple of miners staggered out of one of the numerous saloons that dotted Bannack's main street. "Where can I find the sheriff?" he asked.

One unsteady man lifted his head and attempted to focus bloodshot eyes on the rider. "Ain't got one."

The marshal tried again. "Where's the town's law then?"

"Ain't got one," the miners echoed. He looked quizzically at the marshal. "Are ya deef?"

"You got a jail?"

"Yep," the men said together as they stumbled away down the boardwalk.

Billie smirked at the drunks failing to provide any usable information.

Even though they knew the location of the town's jail, Jesse and Jennifer weren't in much of a mood to be helpful and sat patiently waiting for the marshal to decide on his next move. Morgan rubbed his chin, then led the group down the street to some other bystanders.

A young boy ran up to the riders. "What's she done, Marshal? She kilt sumbody?"

Jesse tensed at the boy's words.

"You live in town?" the marshal asked.

The boy pointed down the street. "Live down there with my pa. Why?"

"Is there a lawman in town?"

"Nope."

"Who takes care of that kind of thing?"

"Judge at the courthouse." The boy pointed to a two-story brick building about halfway down the street. The marshal nudged his horse toward the courthouse.

Jesse didn't remember seeing the large brick structure before and concluded it must have been constructed recently.

"Ain't nobody there this late in the day," the boy said as he skipped alongside the horses. "Judge'll be at the Goodrich having supper. Want me ta show ya?"

The marshal nodded, and the boy ran ahead to the two-story wooden structure a few doors past the courthouse.

Jesse was familiar with the Goodrich Hotel, she and Jennifer having stayed there during their first visit to Bannack.

"Sheriff, can I trust you to guard the prisoner while I go in to talk with the judge?"

"I'm not going anywhere," Jesse answered, forestalling Billie. "Just be quick about it. I don't want Jennifer to have to stay in the saddle any longer than necessary."

The marshal looked at Jesse. Despite all the trouble she was in, her first thoughts were always for the woman she referred to as her wife and the child she was accused of kidnapping. Maybe the governor had acted on bad information.

"I'll be as quick as I can. Perhaps, Mrs. Branson," the marshal said to Jennifer as he dismounted, "it would be best if you went inside and obtained a room for yourself and the child."

Jennifer glared at the marshal, still infuriated that the lawman was indirectly responsible for letting her father out of jail. "I'll stay with Jesse until she's settled."

"Momma," KC whimpered from the carry sack.

Jesse's arms ached to hold her baby. "Darlin', why don't you go on and get a room? You'll be needing someplace to stay."

"KC won't sleep in those noisy rooms," Jennifer said quietly. "And neither will I."

"Jennifer, Jesse, is that you?" Leevie Temple hurried down the boardwalk toward them. "It's so good to see you," the woman happily greeted them before spying Jesse's restraints. Her smile turned to concern. "What's wrong?"

"Jesse's been arrested, Leevie."

"What on earth for?"

"For kidnapping KC and killing her parents." Jennifer choked out the awful words.

"What?"

"That's what they're sayin', Leevie. Darlin', please go in and get a room," Jesse repeated.

"Nonsense," Leevie said. "You'll stay with me."

Happy at the prospect of staying with her friend instead of at the hotel, Jennifer instantly accepted. "Thank you."

Another man accompanied Marshal Morgan out of the Goodrich Hotel. "These *all* your prisoners?" he asked, not having expected the large group of people waiting for the marshal.

The marshal retrieved his horse's reins. "No, Judge." He was too tired to explain Jesse and Jennifer's relationship. "This one is the prisoner, Jesse Branson. The rest are her kinfolk."

"All right," the judge said. "Let's get her locked up."

The marshal followed the judge, leading his horse and Dusty. Jennifer and the others followed, with Leevie bringing up the rear.

The judge led the group across the street and down the alley alongside of Carpenter's general store to the jail buildings located there. Morgan stepped next to Dusty to remove the shackles around Jesse's ankles so she could get down. Billie slipped from his horse and helped Jennifer to the ground, keeping a steadying hold on her while she tested her leg. Already off his horse, Thomas helped his mother.

Several townsfolk had stopped their evening activities to watch the procession pass, then fell into step behind it, rapidly filling the alley between the store and the jails. Someone asked Leevie what Jesse was charged with, and she passed on the information she'd been told just moments before. Word spread quickly through town and what had been a small crowd soon grew into a large throng. Some in the gathering remembered Jesse and Jennifer from their previous stay in Bannack and their attempts to find KC's family. Those jeered the marshal for arresting the woman on what they knew to be bogus charges.

Bannack had two jails. One was mainly used for miners who were too drunk to be on the streets until they sobered up, while the other, a more sturdily constructed building, was used to detain prisoners accused of serious crimes. After lighting a lantern that was hanging on the side of the sturdier building, the judge unlocked the door and ushered the marshal and prisoner inside. Before he could shut the door, Jennifer forced her way in. The noise of the crowd dimmed behind the jail's thick door.

Wide eyed, Jesse and Jennifer looked around the small, dismal room. The jail had been assembled by stacking squared logs atop one another and was separated into three parts. Half of the building consisted of a room where a guard could sit to keep watch on the prisoners; the other half consisted of two cells, each about six feet square. These cells were separated from the rest of the room, and each other, by solid log walls and were entered through a small door. A heavy ring was anchored into the flooring of the cells, and prisoners were chained to the ring to prevent them from escaping through the sod roof. The cells had no windows, and when the cell door was closed, a prisoner would be confined in the dank cell, engulfed in total darkness.

"I must say, Marshal..." The judge hung the lantern on a peg, struck a match, and lit another lantern, adding more light to the dark room. "I'm a bit surprised myself at the charges against Miss Branson." He had heard of Jesse's role in bringing the former Bannack sheriff to justice for being the leader of a band of thieves and murderers. "I certainly hope you have evidence to back up your warrant."

"I have a list of witnesses who live in Bannack and are willing to testify against her."

"Really?" The judge was astounded to hear that anyone in Bannack would be willing to swear in court that someone besides Sheriff Logan had been responsible for the murders of the baby's parents. Especially since the encompassing reign of terror had ended with the sheriff's death. "I'll be interested in seeing that list, Marshal. I take it you'll be staying here with the prisoner? We haven't found anyone to take the job of jailer or sheriff since the vigilantes hanged Logan."

Morgan accepted the ring of keys the judge held out. "Yes, I'll be staying with her."

"And the sheriff?" the judge asked, wondering why the other lawman had been left outside.

"No, just me," Morgan said as he unlocked one of the cells. "Inside, Branson."

"May we have a few moments together?" Jennifer asked softly. The thought of Jesse being incarcerated in the tiny cell was tearing at her heart.

"You can see her in the morning."

"Don't see the harm in giving them some time," the judge told the marshal. He remembered seeing the pair walking around Bannack only months earlier. They had introduced themselves as sisters, but something about their behavior led him to believe there was much more to their relationship than sisterhood. Seemed he'd been right.

Reluctantly, the marshal gestured for Jennifer and KC to join Jesse inside the cell. A knock at the door drew everyone's attention. The judge opened the door and found Billie standing outside holding a sack.

"They'll be needin' this for KC," the sheriff said as he handed the sack to the judge. "Tell Jennifer we'll wait for her out here. Sent the town folk away so's the marshal don' have to worry 'bout them."

"Thank you, Sheriff." The judge looked over Billie's shoulder. Sure enough, except for Leevie and those that had ridden into town with the prisoner and marshal, the alley was clear. He accepted the sack and closed and secured the door before carrying the sack to the cell. "This is for you." He smiled as he handed it to Jennifer. "Marshal, remove these shackles," he ordered.

"But—"

"I don't think Miss Branson has any plans to leave town without her family," the judge said. Jesse nodded in agreement. "Remove those shackles and bring one of those lanterns in here. We don't want the dark to scare the baby."

"Thank you," Jesse said.

"You're taking a big chance," the marshal mumbled as he knelt to unshackle Jesse's legs.

"I don't believe in treating prisoners like animals unless they've been found guilty. Until then, we can treat her decent. Take off the handcuffs, too."

When the marshal backed out of the small cell, he left the door open so he could keep an eye on the women.

"Pull the door shut, Marshal." The judge sat in the room's only chair. "Give them some privacy."

The marshal pulled the cell door shut and leaned against the wall beside it. "You're mighty trusting of your prisoners."

"Only when I question the legitimacy of the reason they are being brought before me. Now if you don't mind, I'd like to take a look at that list of so-called witnesses you have."

There was only one customer in Finney's saloon. At a table in the back corner of the rectangular building, a man sat nursing a bottle of whiskey. He had watched the women riding into town earlier and had instantly recognized them, and his thoughts flashed back to a day not long before when he had been sharing a drink with a friend and another man at a table near the front of the bar. They had watched as the same two women rode out of town. Moments later they had been joined by Sheriff Logan, who ordered them to go after the women. Now the two were back in town, and word was that one had been charged with a murder that he had helped commit. He reconsidered the wisdom of remaining in Bannack after Logan's death, knowing it was only a matter of time before the vigilantes would connect him to Logan's gang. Maybe it was time to leave town for good.

The bartender took a dirty rag and wiped down the long bar that stretched along one entire side of the saloon. As he worked, he kept watch on the other man out of the corner of his eye. The barkeep knew the vigilantes were convinced he had taken part in Logan's illegal activities and were seeking a reason to put a noose around his neck. As he wiped, he tried to figure out the best way to pass on the information he had without ending up at a necktie party in his honor. Maybe the woman's impending trial would give him the opportunity to slip out of that noose.

"Mommy!" KC repeated her pitiful cry as the cell's door closed. She was tired, hungry, and wet. And she wanted her mommy to hold her.

Free of restraints, Jesse lifted the baby out of the carry sack. "Here, darlin'," she told her exhausted wife, "sit down."

"Hold me," Jennifer whispered as she pressed her body against Jesse's. It was the first time the women had been alone all day, and she ached for her wife's touch.

Jesse eagerly complied, but it was tricky trying to hold the fussing baby and Jennifer. Releasing her arms from around her wife, Jesse sat on the dirty blankets that covered the cot and pulled Jennifer down beside her. They clung together for several minutes until KC whimpered.

"She needs changing."

"I know, but let her eat first." Jennifer lifted the sack onto the cot. Opening it, she pulled out some leftover biscuits from a meal earlier in the day. KC hungrily grabbed at the small pieces Jennifer broke off for her. Jennifer leaned against Jesse. "It's been a rough day for her."

"Been rough for all of us." Jesse sighed as she rested her head against Jennifer's. "What about you?"

"I'm okay. But when this is all over, you, dear wife, are giving me a rubdown that will last a month." She smiled, but her weary heart wasn't behind it.

Jesse grinned, trying to cheer her. "Sounds like a mighty fine idea." She reached out to wipe a crumb off the baby's cheek.

"Oh, sweetheart," Jennifer cried when she saw the damage the handcuffs had done to Jesse's wrists. "We need to take care of that." She pulled a clean diaper from the sack and tore it into thin strips. Wetting a cloth with water from the canteen Billie had thoughtfully placed in the sack, she cleaned Jesse's wounds as best she could. "Maybe I should ask to have a doctor look at these," she said as she tenderly wrapped the makeshift bandages around the abrasions.

"Don't think the marshal will go for that."

Recognizing the bandaging for what it was, KC bent forward and kissed Jesse's wrists. "Owie." Jesse gently rubbed the baby's smooth cheek.

"Wasn't planning on asking *him*," Jennifer said. "I'm sure the judge will agree."

"Guess it wouldn't hurt to ask." Jesse didn't want to admit how much her wrists were hurting, so she left it at that. She noticed that KC was starting to doze now that her stomach was full. "Let me change KC." She pulled the dirty blankets back, exposing the not much cleaner straw mattress below. "Hand me a clean towel," she told Jennifer. "I need something to lay her on."

Jennifer scooted to the end of the cot to give Jesse room to work on the baby. She handed her wife the requested towel and then pulled a clean diaper and nightshirt out of the sack. "I wish I could stay with you tonight," Jennifer murmured as she watched Jesse changing KC's clothing.

"No you don't," Jesse countered. The thought of spending the night in the, dirty, dark cell wasn't very pleasing to her. And there was no way she would allow Jennifer to experience it, even if the marshal would agree. "I think you should take KC and go." Jesse lifted the sleepy baby off the cot and cradled her in her arms.

Jennifer scooted back and snuggled against Jesse. "I want to stay until they make me go."

"I know, darlin'." She draped an arm around Jennifer and pulled her close. "But Billie and your mother are waiting outside. And I'd feel better if I knew you were off that leg for the night."

"I love you." Jennifer tilted her head invitingly.

Jesse kissed her. Pulling Jennifer tight against her, she deepened the kiss. Pounding on the cell door broke the women apart and startled KC awake.

The marshal pulled the cell door open. "You've had your time for tonight."

"I'll be back first thing in the morning," Jennifer assured Jesse as she was handed the baby, now cranky from being awakened. "I love you."

"I love you, too."

The marshal pulled the door shut as soon as Jennifer cleared the wood frame.

"I want a doctor to take a look at Jesse's wrists."

"I'll see what I can do," Morgan said, but his tone indicated he really didn't care.

Hearing the marshal's less than wholehearted response, the judge said, "I'll have a doctor check her out in the morning."

Jennifer wanted to get the grounds rules settled while the reasonable judge was there to overrule the uncooperative marshal. "Will I be allowed to visit her during the day?"

"No reason you shouldn't," the judge told her. "Is there, Marshal?"

"None you'd agree with." Opening the jail door, the marshal waited for Jennifer to leave.

"Thank you." Jennifer smiled at the judge. "Good night, Marshal," she said.

"Good night, Mrs. Branson." The marshal saw her outside, then slammed the door shut.

"*Mrs.* Branson?"

"Seems the two of them are married."

"Seems they are." The judge smiled to himself, pleased to know that his earlier feelings about the relationship had been correct. "Goodnight, Marshal." He moved to the door. "I expect you to cooperate in allowing Mrs. Branson and the child to visit the prisoner," he said as he unbolted the door and stepped outside.

Mary rushed to Jennifer's side as she limped out of the jail. "How is she?"

"As good as anyone would be who has been locked up for something they didn't do." Jennifer was too tired to keep the anger and frustration from her voice. She just wanted to be able to take Jesse and KC and go home where they belonged. A home, she suddenly realized, that no longer existed.

"I'm sorry," Mary softly said.

"No, Mother." Jennifer shook her head. "I'm sorry. I shouldn't be taking this out on you."

"We're all tired." Mary kissed Jennifer's cheek. "I think it best we all try to get some sleep and then see what we can do in the morning."

"You're probably right." Jennifer definitely needed to get off her leg and try to get a good night's sleep. She wasn't at all sure that was possible under the circumstances. "Did you get rooms at the Goodrich Hotel?" she asked, adding, "Where's Billie?"

"Thomas is on his way to the hotel now. The sheriff has taken the horses to be stabled and then was going to send a telegram to Sweetwater."

"Thank goodness. I completely forgot about Bette Mae. She must be worried sick."

"I think we should get you and KC to bed." Leevie stepped forward and offered to take the child.

Jennifer thankfully passed the sleeping baby to her friend. "Mother," she said in answer to the questioning look, "this is my friend, Leevie Temple. She is the schoolteacher here, and she was very kind to Jesse and me when we last visited Bannack."

"It's a pleasure, Miss Temple," Mary said uncertainly. She wasn't too sure she liked the idea of Jennifer staying somewhere besides the hotel where she could help care for her daughter and granddaughter.

"I'm pleased to meet you," Leevie said more enthusiastically. "I'm sure we'll have plenty of time to get better acquainted in the coming days, but now I really think Jennifer needs to get some sleep. Jesse is going to be needing you tomorrow," she told her exhausted friend.

Thomas reappeared around the corner of Carpenter's store. "Mother, I have rooms for us and the sheriff. Are you all right?" he asked his sister.

"Yes. Please take Mother to the hotel."

Thomas leaned down and picked up his mother's saddlebag and the travel bag that contained his clothes. "What should we do tomorrow?"

"I can't think about that now." Jennifer yawned. "We'll meet in the morning after I see Jesse and discuss things."

The group walked alongside Carpenter's store and said their goodbyes when they reached the boardwalk. Thomas and Mary crossed the street to the Goodrich Hotel while Jennifer accompanied Leevie down the wooden sidewalk to the log cabin she called home at the other end of town.

"You sure that will reach Sweetwater tomorrow?" Billie asked the telegraph operator. He had left the horses at the livery and walked to the telegraph office located in the courthouse at the front of the main floor.

"Yes." The operator finished the transmission. "I marked it urgent so they'll send it by messenger to Sweetwater."

"Fair enough." Billie wanted the telegram to reach town as quickly as possible; he didn't want Ruth to be worrying about him. "How much do I owe you?"

"Let's see." The operator counted the words Billie had sent. "That'll be a dollar, Sheriff."

Billie handed the man a few coins and headed outside. He was ready to fall into bed and hoped there would be a room waiting for him when he got to the hotel.

Sitting on top of a hill above the north side of town, Walks on the Wind had seen the riders approach Bannack. He had tracked their progress as they rode into town, eventually ending up in front of two small structures behind the larger buildings lining the main street. He observed Jesse as she was taken inside one of the buildings, and he saw Jennifer when she came out of the building some time later. He watched Jennifer and the other woman walk along the boardwalk and enter a small cabin. He continued to watch the cabin until the lights inside went dark. Only then did the man who had ridden hard most of the day to reach Bannack lie down in the grass and close his eyes.

For a long time after Jennifer left, Jesse sat in the cell staring at the emptiness, the lantern slowly burning down as its finite supply of fuel was consumed. As she sat in the fading light, the walls seem to close in on her, and she wondered if she would survive the night in the depressing surroundings. A vision of Jennifer formed before her eyes, and Jesse had her answer. There was too much of her life outside the log walls to give up now. Closing her tired eyes, Jesse laid back on the cot. "Sleep well my darlin'. I love you."

CHAPTER TWENTY-EIGHT

Jennifer was relieved not to have to stay in one of the hotels in town, where noise from the many saloons would have kept her and KC awake. As it turned out, worrying about Jesse kept both of them awake most of the night anyway. The baby slept fitfully, crying out periodically for her mommy, and Jennifer spent the night tossing and turning as she worried about Jesse locked in the dismal jail cell. Since she obviously wasn't going to get any rest, Jennifer decided there was no point in remaining in the bed that she was sharing with KC. She rolled away from the baby to slip off the bed without disturbing her, but KC woke with the movement and cried out for her. "It's okay, sweetie." Jennifer pulled the baby close to her.

"Mommy," KC whimpered.

"I know." Jennifer scooted back against the headboard, pulling KC into her lap. "I miss Mommy, too, but we'll go see her after breakfast."

"Otay." KC snuggled despondently against Jennifer's chest.

Jennifer wrapped her arms around the baby and began to rock slowly. She stared unseeing out the window as the approaching sunrise began to lighten the darkness outside. By the time Jennifer and KC arrived the night before at the home of Bannack's schoolteacher, she had been too tired to do much more than fall into bed with her daughter. With the coming morning, she would welcome the chance to talk with her friend and thank her properly for taking them in.

Having just one bed, Leevie had insisted Jennifer and KC sleep in it while she slept on the floor. A rope was strung across the center of the room and a blanket hung over it, providing privacy to both women. The sound of someone quietly moving about in the other half of the cabin told Jennifer that Leevie was already up.

Keeping a firm hold on KC, Jennifer swung her legs over the side of the bed. Her cane was leaning against the wall next to the headboard, and she grabbed it before attempting to stand. He leg was tired and sore, and she knew she would have to rest it as much as she could during the day. She hoped she'd be able rest the leg *and* do whatever was needed to get her wife out of jail. Straightening her nightshirt, she took the few steps to the improvised curtain and pulled it back a few inches to peer around its edge.

Leevie caught the blanket's movement out of the corner of her eye. "Good morning. I was hoping you were sleeping, but I figured you probably weren't." During the night, she had heard the baby's cries and Jennifer's restlessness.

"No." Jennifer slipped past the improvised curtain to join her friend. "I'm afraid neither of us slept much."

"Sit," Leevie ordered when she saw how much her friend was depending on her cane. She immediately pulled a chair away from a small table tucked into the corner of the cabin and gestured Jennifer into it. "I've just put some water on to heat. We'll have coffee soon, and I can whip up some eggs and bacon. Even have some oatmeal I'll cook up for KC."

"Don't go to any bother, Leevie." Jennifer eased herself down onto the chair and stretched her leg out in front of her. "We're supposed to meet the others at the hotel for breakfast."

"I suspect that will be some time from now. And I doubt if you ate much yesterday," she said, placing various foodstuffs on her wood stove in preparation for cooking. "So indulge me and let me cook for you."

"Yum," KC answered for her mother.

In the growing morning light, Jennifer looked around the compact log cabin Leevie called home. It measured fifteen by twenty feet and had been built by notching the end of logs so they would sit on top of one another without need of fasteners. Mud chinking was stuffed into the spaces between the logs to keep out the wind and rain. The cabin was dark inside and the small windows at each end did little to light the interior, which explained why Leevie usually did her schoolwork on the front porch.

At one end of the cabin, a wood stove served both heating and cooking duties. A cupboard near the stove held dishes and food staples, and a bed and dresser occupied the sleeping end of the cabin. The small table and chairs where Jennifer sat completed the furnishings.

"I've got some fresh milk. Bought it yesterday, so best we drink it before it spoils. Store has some of that new condensed milk in tins. It's supposed to last longer, but I don't much like the taste of it." Leevie lifted the lid off a wooden container and ladled milk into a glass. "I'm sorry, I don't have any bottles."

Jennifer accepted the glass and held it for KC to drink. "Jesse's been teaching her how to drink from a glass."

Hearing her mother's name, KC stopped drinking and looked hopefully around the room. "Mommy?"

"No, sweetie. Mommy's not here," Jennifer said, encouraging KC to finish the milk.

"Care to tell me what's going on?" Leevie asked, not beating around the bush.

Jennifer set the empty glass on the table and wrapped her arms around the baby snuggling against her. With everything that had happened over the past few days, she really hadn't had much of a chance to get it all straightened out in her own mind. "I don't really know where to start, so much has happened."

Leevie cracked open several eggs and dropped them into a frying pan. "Start at the beginning. We'll take it from there."

"I wrote you about what happened when Jesse and I returned to Sweetwater after our trip here."

"I was so upset to hear how seriously you had been hurt." Leevie eyes conveyed the pain she felt for the other woman. "I must say I'm surprised to see you walking after what you wrote in your letters."

Jennifer absently rubbed the injured limb. "It's been hard but with Jesse's help, it has gotten much better."

"Mommy." KC sat up and looked around the cabin again.

"Guess I'm going to have to stop using her name," Jennifer said sadly as the baby, disappointed at again not finding Jesse, nestled back against her.

Leevie nodded in silent agreement to avoid using the name. "I can't see how your injury can have anything to do with what's happening now, but I'm going to guess that it has something to do with your father."

"You'd be right."

"I thought he was banished from the territory."

"So did we. He decided to return and finish what he had started on his first trip. On his way here he met a man that works for a company back East that is developing a mine near Sweetwater. Somehow, and I'm still not sure how, he got Mr. Harrington to contact the territorial governor and rescind the arrest warrant that was to be executed in the event that Father ever returned to Montana. At the same time, my father convinced this Mr. Harrington, who in turn convinced the governor, that Jesse had murdered the Williamses and kidnapped KC."

Leevie was standing by the stove looking at Jennifer, her mouth hanging open. "How in the hell..."

Jennifer sniggered at the expression on her friend's face. "My feelings exactly." KC asked for more and, holding the empty glass up, Jennifer asked, "May we?"

"Of course." Leevie refilled the glass and handed it back.

"I received a letter from Andrew's father." Seeing the questioning look on the other woman's face, she explained, "The young man my father arranged to be my fiancé."

"Oh, yes."

"Mr. Barrish warned me that Father was planning to return to Montana. Jesse and I decided not to give him the chance to cause us any new problems. We left the ranch, planning to meet a friend near the buffalo herds and wait for word from Sweetwater telling us when it was safe to return." She wiped a few drops of milk off KC's chin with her finger. "Feel better, sweetie?" In answer, KC snuggled back against her. "We no more than rode into Walk's camp when my father, Thomas, Billie, and the marshal rode up."

"Who?"

"I told you it was complicated. Thomas is my oldest brother; Billie Monroe is our friend and Sweetwater's sheriff; and Marshal Morgan is the one who was sent by the governor to free my father and arrest Jesse."

Leevie set two plates of scrambled eggs, bacon, and biscuits on the table. She returned to the stove for a bowl of cooked cereal and the coffeepot. She took two cups from the adjacent cupboard and added silverware and napkins before sitting down to join Jennifer.

KC perked up when she saw the food within her reach. "Hold on there, sweetie." Jennifer laughed as she stopped small hands grabbing at the food. "Let me feed you this cereal, or we'll spend the morning scrubbing you clean." KC pouted but waited to be fed.

"You said Walk's camp?"

"Walks on the Wind. He is an Indian and an old friend of Je..." Jennifer stopped herself. "An old friend," she said as Leevie nodded understanding. "He travels to find the buffalo herds every summer to hunt for his people."

"And your brother?"

"Yes." Alternating between feeding herself and feeding KC, Jennifer swallowed a bite before continuing. "I was shocked to see him. As it turns out, he came along to try to keep my father from doing anything. Unfortunately, he hasn't been very successful."

"You mean because of the governor?"

"That and..." Jennifer paused and took a deep breath; she had yet to accept the reality of what she was about to say. "Father burned down our home."

"What!"

Jennifer could only nod; the pain of repeating the heartbreaking news was too much.

"Oh, Jennifer." Leevie reached out and squeezed her friend's hand. "I'm so sorry."

The women ate in silence for several minutes. "Does the marshal really believe she killed Mr. and Mrs. Williams?" Leevie finally asked, careful to omit Jesse's name from her question.

"I don't know." Jennifer wiped the baby's face and hands with a cloth. "I can't imagine why anyone would believe that, especially after we tried so hard to find any family KC might have. Morgan told the judge that he has a list of people here in Bannack that are willing to testify against...her."

"Hogwash," Leevie exclaimed as she collected the dirty dishes.

KC giggled at the funny phase. "You think that's funny, do you?" Jennifer tickled the baby, glad to see her smiling. "Leevie, I want to thank you for letting us stay here. I know it's a hardship on you."

"Nonsense," the woman replied. "Having friends about is never a hardship. Now let's get dressed and get on with the business of getting you-know-who out of jail."

Martin Kensington woke abruptly; something had roused him out of a deep sleep. He quickly sat up when he heard the noise again, a deep, menacing growl rumbling from somewhere in the grass not far from where he had been sleeping. As he listened, the growl changed to a series of high-pitched yips, then stopped altogether. After several minutes of silence, he decided whatever it was must be gone and he was again safe. At least, as safe as he could be alone in the middle of the wilderness.

He rubbed his eyes and stretched his sore back and legs. He wasn't use to sleeping directly on the cold, hard ground. Reaching for his shoes, he started to put them on but had to give up the attempt when he discovered his blistered feet had swollen overnight. He looked to the south and estimated that he had another full day of walking just to reach the hills that he needed to cross. "When I get my hands on that bitch..." Kensington mumbled as he crammed his bloated feet into the leather shoes. "She'll wish she'd never crossed me." Tentatively, he started on the day's forced march, his empty stomach grumbling loudly.

Two dark eyes followed him. When the man had moved far enough downwind, the watcher crept out from the cover of the tall grass to check on his recent kill. The wolf had been stalking the man, but he had stopped it before it could reach their common prey.

Walks on the Wind walked down into the town. He dropped into a small gully, following it until it crossed the road that curved around Cemetery Hill and entered town through Hangman's Gulch, so named because it was where the vigilantes had built a gallows and served justice on the town's former sheriff. The streets were starting to fill with miners and businessmen on their way to work. A few looked curiously at the Indian as he strode past the stonemason's shop and livery, but considering the town was named after the local Indian tribe, most folks paid him little mind; they were used to seeing Indians in town. Walk hunkered down in the morning shadows at the corner of a building to wait.

"Any sign of her?" Mary asked Thomas again. They had left their rooms on the second floor of the hotel and were waiting in the lobby for Jennifer. Thomas was frequently going outside to look for his sister, then returning to report to his mother.

"No," he said as he moved to stand at the window by the front door. "But Billie is coming back from checking on the horses."

As the lawman rounded the corner from the livery onto the main street, Billie saw a familiar figure across the street partially hidden in a narrow passageway between two buildings. Without pausing, the sheriff exchanged a silent acknowledgment with the Indian before continuing to the Goodrich Hotel.

"Sheriff, did you see Jennifer?" Mary asked as soon as Billie entered the lobby.

"No. Why don't you go in and get breakfast? She probably stopped by the jail before coming here. I'll go check."

"But we were to have breakfast together," Thomas said, worried about how his sister had passed the night.

"Wouldn't surprise me to find out she's already eaten. Go on. No sense in you walkin' a hole in that fancy rug."

"You're going to have to bring her out of that cell, Marshal." The doctor had been summoned to tend to the prisoner's injuries and was standing in the street just outside the threshold of the jailhouse. "I can't treat what I can't see."

The marshal wasn't at all happy to have had the doctor knock on the door, believing there was no reason for his prisoner to leave her cell until the trial started. "I'll have to handcuff her."

"Come now, Marshal. I was led to understand her wrists are where her injuries are. I won't be able to do anything if you have her in handcuffs. Now bring her out here in the sun where I can get a good look."

On his way to make sure the doctor was being allowed to treat the prisoner, the judge walked out from alongside Carpenter's Mercantile in time to hear the doctor's request. "Is there a problem?"

The doctor turned. "Marshal expects me to examine the prisoner in the cell. Either she gets brought out in the sun or I'll go back to my office. I don't have time for this."

The judge was also becoming frustrated with the lawman. "Marshal, bring the prisoner out. She's not going to try and escape; I have her word on that."

Jesse had been standing on the other side of the heavy wooden cell door since before dawn. She knew the door would have to be opened at some point, and she couldn't wait. She felt as if she were smothering in the close quarters. When she heard the chain securing the door start to rattle, she thought she would faint with relief.

"Back off, Branson," the marshal said as he spied Jesse standing so near the opening door. She quickly backed up until she bumped into a log wall. "Doctor wants you outside. Don't do anything to make me shoot you." He pulled the door wide open and motioned her forward.

Jesse followed the marshal's directions and moved to the outside door. Stepping through the doorway, she lifted her arm to shade her sensitive eyes against the morning sunlight.

"Over here, please," the doctor directed. In a shaft of sunlight shining between two buildings, a pair of chairs had been set facing one another. The doctor sat in one chair and indicated Jesse was to sit in the other. "Let's see what we have," he said as she took a seat. He took Jesse's hands into his own, unwrapped the bandages Jennifer had applied the night before, and slowly rotated the wrists. "Nasty business, handcuffs," he said as he examined the torn, raw skin. Reaching into his bag for some ointment and fresh bandages, he reprimanded the marshal. "You should file the inside of those things smooth before you put them on another prisoner."

The salve was cool on her abraded skin as Jesse held her arms steady while the doctor wrapped clean bandages around her wrists.

"Mommy," KC cried when she spied her mother sitting in the sunlight.

Jesse tensed as she caught the motion of the marshal pulling a pistol free of his holster. "Don't shoot!"

Leevie was leading Jennifer up a back alley from her cabin to the jail buildings. As soon as the schoolteacher heard Jesse's scream, she yanked Jennifer and the baby behind one of the privies that lined the alley. It wouldn't be much of a shield if the marshal fired, but it was all they had. The women huddled behind the privy, protecting KC as much as they could.

"Put that gun away, you fool," the judge ordered. "Or do you plan to shoot one of my witnesses? It's all right, Mrs. Branson," he called. "The marshal has put his weapon away."

Jennifer peeked around the corner of the small building. Seeing Jesse looking anxious, she limped to her wife's side. "Sweetheart, are you okay?" She was instantly engulfed in Jesse's arms.

"I'm fine, darlin'." Jesse thought she was going to cry, holding Jennifer felt so good.

"Mommy," KC called excitedly, reaching out her arms.

"She'll be fine," the doctor told both women, seeing he was no longer needed. "I'll come back later and change the bandages."

Jesse's arms were tightly wrapped around her family. "Thank you, Doctor."

"My pleasure." The doctor smiled. "Marshal," he turned to the lawman, "I don't want to see those handcuffs anywhere near her wrists again."

"She's a prisoner."

"It's my personal belief, Marshal," the doctor closed his bag, "that she won't be for long. Damn fool charges you've made against her," he muttered as he walked away. He had treated enough of the victims of the outlaw gang to know the marshal's prisoner had nothing to do with those crimes.

"Mrs. Branson." The judge approached the two women but addressed Jennifer. "I'm happy to see you this morning."

Jesse released her hold on Jennifer and gently pushed her into the chair she had recently occupied. KC was demanding to be held by Jesse, and her mother happily obliged. She stood behind Jennifer, a hand tenderly resting on her wife's shoulder. Unthinking, Jennifer reached up and entwined her fingers with Jesse's.

Though he noticed the intimacy, the judge made no mention of it as he sat in the other chair. "Mrs. Branson, I have decided to release you into the custody of your wife."

"Now just a minute," the marshal said. "You can't do that."

"Marshal, must I remind you that I represent the law in this town? I can do whatever I wish to do."

"But there have been charges brought against her."

"I am aware of the situation." The judge glared at the marshal. "I said I was releasing her into the custody of Mrs. Branson; I did not say I had dropped the charges. Now..." He returned his attention to the two women and grinned when he noticed that KC had climbed high up on Jesse's chest and was wrapped tightly around the woman's face and neck. Jesse was incapable of doing much about it, since one hand was supporting the baby while the other was held firmly in the grasp of her wife. "I'm sending out subpoenas this morning to everyone on the marshal's list of witnesses," the judge announced. "I've informed them that they are to be in my courtroom at one o'clock this afternoon. I see no reason not to start your trial immediately, do you?" he asked Jesse.

"No, sir," the accused mumbled around the tiny hand that was covering her mouth.

Hearing Jesse's muffled voice, Jennifer looked up and saw the stranglehold their daughter had on her wife.

"Oh, sweetheart," Jennifer laughed. She was joined by the judge and Leevie, who had also been quietly watching the rancher's dilemma. Jennifer relinquished Jesse's hand, allowing her to get control of KC and maneuver the squirming child to a more comfortable position in the crook of her arm.

Jesse laughed with the others. "Dang, she's getting strong."

Only the marshal found no humor in the incident and maintained a stern look. Still, behind the unyielding mask, he wondered why a child that had supposedly been kidnapped and was being ill-treated would behave so affectionately toward the woman.

"As I was saying," the judge chuckled, "I see no reason not to start the proceedings today. I am releasing you to your wife's custody, should you wish to obtain witnesses of your own. I expect to see all *three* of you in my courtroom at the appointed time."

"We'll be there."

Tears in her eyes, Jennifer leaned forward and clasped the man's hands. "Thank you."

"This jail was never meant to hold ladies."

"Will she have to stay there again tonight?" Jennifer asked hopefully.

"Let me think on it." The judge stood. "I'll let you know at the end of court."

"Thank you, Judge," Jesse added. "Don't know how to repay you for this."

"Just promise to keep a hold on that young 'un of yours while court is in session." He laughed. "I get the feeling that she is trouble in the making."

"That she can be." Jesse laughed as she lifted her arms up, swinging KC over her head to sit the baby on her shoulders. KC reached around Jesse's head and covered both eyes. "That she surely can be," Jesse repeated as she tried to move her daughter's hands.

As the judge walked toward the small path alongside Carpenter's store, Billie was walking toward the jails from the street.

"Morning, Judge," he greeted pleasantly.

"Morning, Sheriff."

"Jesse, Jennifer," Billie greeted his friends. "Your momma is worried sick about you," he told Jennifer.

Jennifer had stood and was again wrapped in Jesse's arms. "We had to stop and see Jesse."

"That's what I told 'em." He looked quizzically at the freed prisoner. "You ain't makin' a jail break, is ya?"

Jesse grinned. "Nope."

"The judge released Jesse into my custody," Jennifer proudly told their friend. "We have to be in court this afternoon but until then, she's all mine."

The sheriff grinned. "That sounds like it could be trouble."

"It surely does." Jesse laughed, yet in her heart she was hoping Jennifer would command her to bed. After all she had been through the last few days, she didn't have the energy to make love to her wife, but she would relish the opportunity to just hold her for the next several hours.

"I suppose we should let Mother and Thomas know what's happening," Jennifer said. "Then maybe we could go back to Leevie's for a while."

Jesse pulled Jennifer close, glad her wife had read her thoughts. "I'd like that."

"Don't leave Bannack," the marshal told the women as they walked toward the street.

"We'll see you this afternoon, Marshal," Jesse called back to the lawman. "I don't plan to leave this town until my name is cleared and you have to go back and tell the governor that Kensington played him for a jackass."

"You're free?" Mary asked.

"Not yet, Mother," Jennifer explained. "She's been released in my custody until the trial starts this afternoon."

Jesse, Jennifer, KC, Billie, and Leevie had walked to the Goodrich Hotel and found Mary and Thomas just finishing their breakfast. Since Jesse and Billie had yet to eat, they decided to stay and order a meal while Mary and Thomas were brought up to date on the morning's news.

"What's going to happen at the trial, Jennifer?" Thomas asked.

"I'm not sure." Jennifer looked to Billie for help.

"Hard to say." The sheriff handed a piece of toast to KC, who had been trying to snag it off his plate. "You said the judge sent out subpoenas for the marshal's supposed witnesses." Jesse and Jennifer nodded. "My guess would be that he plans to question them first and see if there's any reason to continue with a trial."

"You mean he might let Jesse go by the end of today?" Jennifer asked, incredulous.

"He could." Billie lifted his empty coffee cup and gestured for the waitress to bring more. "Or if he hears something that makes him think Jesse is guilty, he could continue the trial. But..." He stopped when the waitress appeared with a fresh pot of coffee. "Thank you," he said to the young girl. He was much more polite to waitresses since falling in love with one.

"But?" Thomas prodded.

"Since we don't know who or how many are on that list of witnesses, we don't know how long it'll take to question them. Could be the trial could stretch a couple of days just because of that."

"Hell, Billie," Jesse sputtered, then quickly apologized. "Sorry, darlin'. There can't be very many names on that list, since no one could have possibly seen me do anything."

"This whole thing is made up, sweetheart. They could have made up the witnesses, too."

Billie shook his head. "Hard to do that, Jennifer. They sent Jesse here for trial, so there have to be people on that list that are known to live here. They can't just make up some names and write them down. Someone would have to show up to testify."

"Oh, I never thought of that. Still, Jesse is right. It has to be a short list."

"I would think so."

Walks on the Wind watched as a young boy ran out of the brick courthouse with a fist full of papers. The boy worked his way down the length of one side of the street before reversing his course up the other side. Occasionally he would enter a store or office for a few moments before continuing on his way. The stack of papers grew smaller with each stop the lad made, until it had disappeared altogether before he returned to the courthouse.

One of the stops on the boy's route was the dressmaker's shop where Walk waited in the shadows. A few moments after the boy left the shop, Walk heard angry voices from inside the building, coming from an open window about a third of the way down the wall. He silently moved away from the street, down the narrow passage between the shop and the assay office next door. He knelt beneath the window to listen.

"I told you not to do this." The woman's voice was strident, scared.

"How did I know he would take it this far?" a man's voice huffed back.

"Because he's crazy when it comes to that woman. When you made up that story, did you really think he wouldn't use it against her?"

"We needed the money. You sure weren't making enough sewing dresses."

"If you weren't out gambling every night, we could have done without his blood money."

"It's too late now."

"I told you this would only lead to trouble, but you just had to send that telegram."

"Be quiet and let me think. I have to figure a way out of this."

"How? The subpoena says the marshal will arrest you and take you to court if you don't show up. How are you going to get out of that?"

"I'll think of something."

Walk remained where he was until the man had stomped out of the shop and down the boardwalk. Then he carefully made his way along the building, settling back in his original spot to watch.

As Jesse, Jennifer, and Leevie walked to the schoolteacher's cabin, Jesse saw Walks on the Wind shadowing them on the other side of the street. When they reached the cabin, she left the door unlatched and waited. A few moments after they entered, Walk slipped through the door.

Jesse smiled at her friend. "Howdy."

"Jesse." Walk smiled back. "You sure got yourself in one pile of horse—"

"Walk, don't say it," Jennifer warned as she came out of the sleeping area with KC after changing the baby.

"Sit, darlin'." Jesse took the baby and waited for her wife to get off her leg. "This is our friend, Leevie Temple."

"And this is Walks on the Wind," Jennifer supplied. "The friend I was telling you about this morning."

"It's a pleasure to meet you," Walk told Leevie.

"Oh, my, you speak—"

"Pretty good English for an Injun." Walk grinned. "Yes, I know."

Leevie grinned back, embarrassed but glad the man didn't seem to hold her tactlessness against her. "Please sit down. I can make coffee."

"No, thank you," Walk answered. "I just wanted to pass on some information to Jesse and Jennifer." He related the conversation he had overheard earlier.

"I should have known that bastard would be part of this," Jesse stewed. "I swear when this is over, my fist is goin' ta be sore from all the noses I plan to break."

At the mention of noses, KC reached up and tweaked her mother's. "Oonk." Jesse looked surprised, then burst out laughing.

Walk and Leevie looked to Jennifer for an explanation. "Jesse's been playing a game with her. She squeezes KC's nose and honks like a goose. She's been trying to get KC to do it, too. Today's the first time she has."

"Oonk." KC bopped her mother's nose again. "Oonk."

Jesse stilled the baby's hands and kissed them. "You pick the darnest times to say somethin'."

"I better get back and see if I hear anything else," Walk told the laughing group.

"Thank you, Walk," Jesse told her friend. "I'm glad you came." The Indian nodded and then was gone.

"Should we tell someone about this?" Jennifer asked.

Jesse looked thoughtful. "Let's wait and see if Thompson shows up in court. If he does, we can use the information against him. If he doesn't, we'll have Walk tell the judge what he heard. Either way, Thompson will have a lot of explaining to do. Now, if you don't mind, Leevie," Jesse said to the schoolteacher, "I'd like to lay down with my family. I didn't get a wink of sleep last night, and it doesn't look like you did either, darlin'. I think we'll probably need some rest before this afternoon."

"You go right ahead," Leevie told the women. "I have some lessons to prepare for when school resumes. I'll wake you in plenty of time to get something to eat and make it to court."

"Thanks," Jennifer said as Jesse helped her up.

Moments later, the Branson family was soundly, and happily, asleep in each other's arms.

CHAPTER TWENTY-NINE

Thomas and Mary were sitting in chairs on the boardwalk in front of the Goodrich Hotel. "Mother, I'm sorry this has turned out like it has. I thought I could control Father but...I guess it would have been better just to do what I had originally planned."

"And what was that, Thomas?"

"Alert the authorities here, and let them deal with him. As it turned out, that wouldn't have done much good either."

"Your father is a determined man when he wants something."

"Yes, I see that now." They sat in silence for a few moments before he cleared his throat and said, "We received your letter, Mother."

"Oh?" Mary looked at her son; it was the first she knew her letter describing Jennifer's new life, and the feelings she had about her old one, had reached her sons. "And how did it make you feel?"

"Sad. We talked about it. We hadn't realized how Jennifer felt. It wasn't intentional, our leaving her out of things; we were just busy—"

"With the company." Mary frowned. So much of their lives had been sacrificed to the success of her husband's company.

"Yes," Thomas agreed. "But that's going to change."

Mary remained silent, giving her son the time to elaborate.

"When I return East, I will speak with Howard and William about removing Father from the company. I think it's time. Many things are changing in the business world and Father has refused to change with them. And now, with his behavior here, I question if he is mentally stable enough to continue in the capacity of company president."

"And your brothers, how will they feel about that?" Mary was unfamiliar with any of the company's dealings; her husband had not seen fit to involve her in the business. That was an incongruity Mary never accepted as it had been her dowry that had provided the funds for the company to grow into the dominant enterprise it had become. She sighed. *No wonder he thought he could marry Jennifer off to the highest bidder.*

"They'll agree. William has been talking of leaving the business; working the ships is not how he wants to spend his life. And Howard has said that he may leave if Father doesn't start making changes to keep us competitive with the other shipping companies. You've seen how things move about here, Mother. You can't get to the frontier by ship."

"No." Mary smiled. "You cannot. And you, Thomas, will you stay with the company?"

"Yes. It's in my blood. I'll stay but I want to build for the future — railroads and freight lines."

"And your young woman?" Surprised when Thomas had told her he was engaged, she wanted to know more about his fiancée.

"She's beautiful, Mother," Thomas said proudly. "I met her just before you came to Montana. It was at one of the socials. We danced the first dance together, and I didn't let her out of my sight all night. We sat and talked, and laughed, and by the end of the evening, I was in love. I finally got up the courage to ask her to marry me, and you could have blown me over when she agreed."

"I am so happy for you, Thomas. Have you set a date?"

"No. I said we had to wait until you could be there. I'm hoping you'll come back with me. Howard and William want you to come home, too."

"I don't know." Determined to never again tolerate her husband's mistreatment of her or her children, she was hesitant to return to her home in the East.

"Things will be different, Mother," Thomas promised. "I'm buying a house for when we are married and there is room in it for you." He looked at his mother apprehensively. "If you'd like."

Mary felt the tears well in her eyes. "Thank you, Thomas." She barely squeezed the words out of her tight throat. "Let me think about it."

"Of course." He pulled a handkerchief from his pocket and handed it to his teary mother.

"No."

"Miss Temple, I want the child." Moments before, Reverend Tobias had knocked on the cabin door; as soon as it was opened, he insisted that KC be turned over to him.

Leevie stood squarely in front of the door to her cabin, blocking all attempts the man made to enter the building. "Reverend, you are not welcome in my home. Please leave."

"That child needs to be protected." The reverend tried again to push his way inside.

"*That* child, as you call her, is being protected. She has two mothers that love her very much and would do anything to make sure she doesn't face any harm. Including from you."

"Get out of my way, woman!" the preacher shouted. "Those women have no right to that child. Their union is an unholy one, and the child must be taken from them."

"You lay one hand on my daughter," Jesse growled from behind Leevie, "and I'll break it into a thousand pieces."

"You have no right to the child. You removed her from Bannack under false pretenses and you must return her."

"Who the hell do you think you are? You have no right coming here demanding KC. She is *our* daughter."

"You are to stand trial for—"

"You, of all people, know those charges are false," Jesse interrupted. "You know how we tried to locate any family of KC's. You were the one to tell us she had none. You do remember that, don't you?" Jesse clearly remembered the conversation she and Jennifer had had with the reverend in the dining room of the Goodrich Hotel when the man informed them KC's kin had been killed during an Indian attack.

Having been awakened by the loud voices, Jennifer appeared beside Jesse. "What's wrong?" She noted the visitor and frowned. "Reverend Tobias, what do you want?" she demanded remembering their last meeting with the self-righteous man. She and Jesse were preparing to leave Bannack and had ridden to the reverend's church to tell him they were going to raise KC themselves. The reverend had decided that KC must be raised in a home with both mother and father and had insisted the women not leave town with the child.

"He's come to take KC." Jesse scowled. "No doubt he has a family in need of another farmhand."

"How dare you talk to me like that when you have been accused of the ghastly crime of killing that poor child's parents!"

Before Jesse could grab the man by the neck, as Jennifer was sure the rancher wanted to do, Jennifer stepped in front of her wife. "Reverend, I have not been accused of any crime. And I can assure you that no matter what the court decides as to Jesse's innocence or guilt, KC will remain with me. Do I make myself clear?" Her eyes bored into those of the infuriating minister.

"We'll just see about that," the preacher threatened as he backed off the porch.

"We most certainly will," Jennifer called after him. "Now git." She growled loudly when the man didn't move away fast enough.

Jesse smirked, placing a comforting hand on Jennifer's back. "Down, tiger." The women watched the preacher beat a hasty retreat across the street to the safety of his church.

Leevie closed the door and latched it. "I'm sorry. I had no idea it was him or I wouldn't have opened the door."

Jesse was surprisingly calm after the upsetting encounter. "I kinda figured he would try something like this."

"You did?" The look on Jennifer's face echoed the surprise in her voice.

"You have to admit, darlin'," Jesse sat down and pulled Jennifer into her lap, "he wasn't exactly happy when we kept KC in the first place. It wouldn't surprise me to find out he's one of the marshal's witnesses."

"Darn." Jennifer leaned against her wife thinking. "Say, sweetheart?"

"Umm?"

"Do you think everyone named Tobias is a pain in the butt?"

Jesse reflected for a second, then laughed. "Now, darlin', that could explain Harrington, couldn't it?"

Ed Granger was pulling lumber off one of the piles of supplies stacked behind the store. He was starting his expansion project in the hopes that it would keep his mind off his missing friends. He picked up his hammer and a fistful of nails and started pounding boards together, his hammer blows blending in with the ones coming from next door where the new bank was taking shape. As he returned to the pile for more wood, Ed heard the distinctive sounds of the approaching stagecoach. He dropped his hammer and rushed back through his store. When he reached the boardwalk at the front of the store, he saw Thaddeus Newby hurrying across the street to the stage depot. The newspaperman squirted in front of the horses as they skidded to a stop at the station. Ed waited impatiently for Thaddeus to reappear.

Moments later, Thaddeus stepped back around the stage, waving an envelope in the air. He motioned for Ed to follow him down the street to the Silver Slipper where Bette Mae and Ruthie were anxiously waiting in the shade of its wide-covered porch.

"What's it say?" Bette Mae called out before the men reached the Slipper.

Thaddeus tore open the envelope and began to read it as he climbed the steps to the porch. "Marshal Morgan arrested Jesse at the Indian camp. He took her to Bannack where she's to stand trial."

"Damn," Ed grunted.

"Damn fool." Bette Mae shook her head in disgust. "Go git our things, Ruthie. Seems we'll be goin' ta Bannack." Ruthie ran back inside the Slipper.

"When was it sent, Thaddeus?" Ed asked.

"Yesterday. Billie had it sent special so it would get here today. He doesn't say when the trial is supposed to begin."

"Then we best git there as soon as possible," Bette Mae said.

"If we take the south route over the pass," Ed figured aloud, "and we ride all night, we could get there in three days."

"Git yer horse, Ed. We'll meet ya at the store as soon as I round up Nancy." Bette Mae disappeared inside.

"Are you coming, Thaddeus?" Ed asked the newspaperman.

"Wish I could but too much is happening in Sweetwater right now. I need to stay here."

"I'll send word when I know anything. I better go get my horse." Ed hurried down the porch steps and over to the livery. He knew Bette Mae was likely to leave without him if she thought he was taking too long to get ready.

Thaddeus watched him go, disappointed he couldn't travel to Bannack to support his friends. But being owner of the newspaper, he had a job to do in Sweetwater. And speaking of that, Frank Wilson was making his way to the mayor's office and by the look on the foreman's face, he wasn't happy. Thaddeus grinned. Time to get back to work.

They left Leevie's cabin in plenty of time to make a stop at the doctor's office so he could redress Jesse's wrists and they could still make it to court on time. Shortly before one o'clock, Jesse carried KC as she and Jennifer entered the impressive, two-story brick courthouse. Immediately inside the front door, Jesse and Jennifer turned right and faced the massive, hand-carved staircase that corkscrewed up to the second floor.

Jennifer's heart sank. She knew she would be unable to walk up the steep steps. "Um, Jesse?"

Jesse frowned at the obstacle. "Guess there's only one way to do this, darlin'."

"Jesse Branson, I will not have you carrying me up those stairs," Jennifer protested.

"You don't want to be late to court, now do you?"

"No, but those steps are too steep for you—"

Jesse bent forward and kissed Jennifer to stop her objections. "You hold KC," she handed the baby to her wife, "and I'll take you." She scooped Jennifer up in her arms. "And we'll get to court on time."

Jesse's strong legs made short work of the staircase and before Jennifer could say anything more, she was being set gently down on the second floor landing.

"Shall we?" Jesse took the baby and offered her arm to Jennifer, who laughed as she slipped her own arm around Jesse's. Arm-in-arm, they walked down the corridor to the courtroom.

Marshal Morgan was leaning against the enclosed judge's bench at the front of the courtroom when Jesse and Jennifer entered. He immediately walked toward them, his hand on the butt of his pistol.

"Is that really necessary, Marshal?" Jesse nodded toward his weapon. "I thought I made it clear that I wasn't going to do anything."

The marshal thought she should have spent the day locked safely away in the jail. "No matter what the judge says, Branson, you're still my prisoner and I'll do whatever I feel necessary to make sure you stay that way."

A man came out of a door to the side of the judge's bench and scanned the courtroom. Spotting Jesse and Jennifer, he scurried over to them. "Mrs. Branson?" The man addressed Jesse. "Um, Mrs. Branson..." He looked at Jennifer. "I'm Judge Henson's clerk."

Jennifer smiled at the befuddled man. "Why don't you call me Jennifer and her Jesse?" she offered. "It might be a little less confusing."

The clerk brightened. "Thank you. Miss Jennifer, if you would sit here, with the defendant." He led the women to a large table between the judge's bench and the gallery and set slightly off center to the left. Two oversized chairs had been placed behind the table, requiring their occupants to face the judge.

"Thank you." Jennifer sat in one of the chairs and found it quite comfortable. She wondered if the judge had purposely arranged that for them.

Jesse sat in the other chair and whispered something in the baby's ear. KC settled in the rancher's lap and cuddled against her, her eyes looking around the strange room. Jesse reached over and took hold of Jennifer's hand while Marshal Morgan took up his sentry post at the side of the room, next to the defendant's table.

Billie came into the courtroom along with Mary and Thomas. They took seats in the first row of gallery chairs directly behind Jesse and Jennifer. Leevie entered the courtroom and took the seat next to Billie. Residents of Bannack, eager to witness the proceedings, entered the courtroom and occupied the remaining chairs.

Jesse and Jennifer looked around to see who the people were. Most they didn't recognize, but a few they remembered from their first trip to Bannack. They saw the young woman who had served them their meal at the Chinese restaurant, and the gravedigger, and the boy from the stonemason's shop. Sitting in the back row of chairs was the desk clerk from the Goodrich Hotel and the waitress from its dining room. And on the far side of the room sat the clerk from Carpenter's Mercantile and the man from the livery where they had boarded their horses. As they made eye contact with the folks sitting behind them, many spoke words of encouragement or expressed outrage over the charges. The women were surprised by the outpouring of support and nodded their thanks.

Jesse's eyes hardened when the dressmaker entered the room and took a seat, but before she could say anything, the door marked "Judge Chambers" opened and the clerk came out. He looked around the courtroom, then went back through the door only to reappear a few moments later carrying some papers, which he put on the judge's bench.

"Must be the marshal's list of witnesses," Billie guessed.

"All rise," the clerk ordered.

Judge Henson entered the room and took a seat behind the elevated desk. "Good afternoon," he addressed the courtroom. "Please be seated." The judge reviewed the papers before him, occasionally looking for a face among the people sitting in the room. "Mrs. Thompson, I do not see your husband in the courtroom."

"No, I...um..."

"Do you know his whereabouts?"

"Not for sure."

"Mrs. Thompson, where might the marshal start looking for your husband?"

"He's likely in one of the saloons. Which one, I don't know."

"Marshal, would you kindly go find him and bring him to court?"

The marshal was startled to be ordered away from his prisoner. "But, Judge..."

"Oh, yes." The judge smiled humorlessly. "Your prisoner must be guarded." The marshal relaxed back against the wall. "Sheriff Monroe."

"Yes, sir."

"Would you be willing to stand in the marshal's stead and guard the prisoner in his absence?"

"It would be my pleasure."

"Very well. Marshal Morgan, please go find Mr. Thompson. Since he seems to be one of the most important witnesses you have listed, his absence could weigh heavily on the findings of this court."

The marshal stormed out of the courtroom as Billie took his place against the wall. Then Judge Henson nodded to his clerk. "Shall we get started?"

"Jesse Branson, please stand," Judge Henson commanded. "The clerk will read the indictment."

Jennifer squeezed Jesse's hand before releasing it. Jesse started to hand KC to Jennifer.

"That won't be necessary," the judge said.

"Jesse Marie Branson, a resident of, and business owner in, the town of Sweetwater, Montana Territory," the clerk read, his voice clear and strong, "is charged with having knowingly, and willfully, caused the following actions: the murders of Kenneth Williams and Katherine Williams; the kidnapping of a female child and the endangerment of said child's welfare; two counts of possessing a horse without the knowledge or permission of said owner; possessing a cow, dairy, without the knowledge or permission of said owner; purposely setting a fire with intent to destroy; removing personal property without the knowledge or permission of said owner; disturbing the peace; reckless disregard in the use of a firearm; theft; providing false information to an officer of the law; and failure to cooperate with an officer of the law in the investigation of said crimes."

Expecting only to be charged with the Williams murders and KC's kidnapping, Jesse shook her head in disbelief as the clerk continued to read. Several in the court chuckled, and soon the room was full of raucous laughter at the ridiculous list of charges.

"Ya forgot to charge her wit' stealin' the ground she buried them poor folks in," someone called out.

"Sure ya got the right piece of paper?" another person asked.

"Order." The judge rapped his gavel against the desk. "Order. Now I'll be the first to admit," he said as the courtroom quieted, "that is a mighty long list of wrongdoings for this defendant. But the charges have been brought, and we need to treat them seriously. Mrs. Branson, would you kindly tell this court how you plead?"

Jesse could not believe the absurdity of the situation as she answered, "Not guilty."

Judge Henson made a notation on the papers in front of him. "Do you wish a jury trial, or will you allow me to stand in judgment?"

Jesse wanted to get the trial over as quickly as possible and given that the judge had shown both her and Jennifer kindness since arriving in Bannack, she responded, "You'll do fine, Judge."

"You may be seated." The judge made another notation. "Call the first witness," he instructed the clerk.

As Jesse settled back down into her chair, KC snuggled against her. She could hear her mommy's heart beating hard and she pressed a small hand on top of the spot to help calm it.

Jennifer scooted her chair closer to Jesse's and took hold of her wife's hand, leaned over and whispered, "I love you, Jesse Marie Branson. And when this is all over, *I'll* break my father's nose." Jesse was chuckling as the first witness was sworn in.

"Mr. Tevey, did you see the defendant when she came to Bannack several months ago?" Judge Henson was asking the witness.

"Yes. She and the other young lady came into the Goodrich," the hotel clerk answered. He wore the same black vest over a smartly pressed white shirt that Jesse remembered from their first visit.

"Did she have a child with them?"

"Yes."

"Did she say how she came about having the child?"

"Said they had found the baby's parents on their way into town. They had been shot."

"What, if anything, else did she say?"

"They ask to rent a room. I only had one left, with one bed, and they said they could share. Them bein' sisters and all."

Jesse smirked at Jennifer, who shrugged as several in the courtroom tried unsuccessfully to repress laughter.

The desk clerk continued, understanding but not commenting on the amusement his comment had caused. "She asked where they could board their horses. I told them to go see Jasper; he'd take care of 'em."

"Anything else?"

"They asked where they could find the sheriff. I told 'em to check at Carpenter's."

"Is that all?"

The man thought for a moment. "Sheriff Logan did come looking for them one evening."

"What for?"

"He wouldn't say. Just asked if they were in their room. When I said no, he asked for the key and went upstairs."

"I knew someone had been in our room," Jesse said under her breath as she heard mutterings behind her.

"Did you inform Mrs. Branson that the sheriff had taken the key to her room?"

"No, sir. He told me not to."

"Step down. Call the next witness."

"Jasper Peabody, please step forward."

A grizzled man with one leg slightly shorter than the other stood and shuffled forward. Judge Henson added to his notes while the clerk swore the witness in.

"Mr. Peabody, did you see the defendant when she came to Bannack several months ago?"

"Yep, boarded two horses and a cow, dairy." He chuckled at repeating the language used in Jesse's indictment.

"Did you notice the brands on the horses?"

"Sure did, I always pay 'tention to those. Never know when sum horsethief will try to pass one over on ya."

"What was the brand?"

"Had a J with the cross bar looping round ta form a D. JD."

"Mrs. Branson," the judge looked at Jesse. "What is the name of your ranch, and what is the brand unique to your livestock?"

"At the time, sir, my brand was a JD."

"Thank you." He turned back to the witness. "Mr. Peabody, did the defendant tell you how she came to be in possession of the cow?"

"If ya mean how she found it?" He looked at the judge for verification.

"Yes." Judge Henson grinned. "That's what I mean."

"Said she found it when she found them folks dead. Said she figured they had it to feed the young 'un."

"Did she say anything else?"

"'Bout what?"

"Anything that would be relevant or have bearing on this case?"

"Paid to board the horses and cow, and left."

"Thank you, Jasper. Step down. The next witness, please."

"George Carpenter, please step forward."

"Mr. Carpenter," the judge said as the man took the witness chair after being sworn. "Did you see the defendant when she came to Bannack several months ago?"

"Yes. She and the other one came into my store."

"And?"

"They asked where they could find Sheriff Logan."

"Did she say why?"

"Said they had some trouble on the trail. Wouldn't say anymore. Just got uppity and said she'd rather discuss it with the sheriff. So I told 'em his office was out back."

It was rumored that Carpenter's store was more than just a building that housed the sheriff's office. Many in town believed Carpenter was not only aware of the sheriff's illegal activities, but also a part of them. So it came as no surprise to those in the courtroom that he would be a less than friendly witness.

"Is that all?"

"They bought sum baby bottles and linen while they was in the store."

"I see." The judge added to his notes. "Step down, Mr. Carpenter."

The storekeeper remained seated. "Wait. I saw them talking to Sheriff Logan the day they left town."

"And?"

"Logan had told them to check in with him before they left town. He caught them trying to leave without doing that."

"Mr. Carpenter, I am unaware of any law that requires people to check in with the sheriff before leaving Bannack. Why would Sheriff Logan tell anyone to do that?"

"He wanted to let folks know what roads were safe to travel." Several in the courtroom scoffed openly at the answer. "Logan also wanted to tell them what he had found when he went out to where them folks was killed."

"And what did he find?"

Everyone in the room was interested in the answer.

Carpenter realized he needed to keep his mouth shut or he might end up on trial. "Didn't say." He couldn't tell the judge that the sheriff had never gone out to where the Williamses had been shot because he already knew what he would find, having ordered their deaths. "But he did ask them why they wasn't leavin' the brat with Reverend Tobias."

Jennifer snarled at the mention of the preacher.

"Why would the sheriff be interested in that?" the judge wanted to know.

So did Jesse, now that she thought about it. The reverend had approached them almost immediately after they had talked to Logan. And Logan had questioned whether the preacher was agreeable to them keeping KC. Jesse wondered what connection, if any, there was between the two men.

"Mr. Carpenter?" Judge Henson asked when he received no answer from the witness.

"Don't rightly know," the storekeeper said truthfully.

"All right." The judge reviewed his notes. "Besides Sheriff Logan sticking his nose—"

Jesse reached down and grabbed KC's hands before the baby could repeat her trick of earlier in the day, but she wasn't fast enough. KC shouted loudly, "Oonk, oonk."

The judge chuckled. "Do I even want to know?"

"No," Jennifer said as Jesse whispered in the baby's ear.

Now that she had mastered it, KC thought the goose game was fun and wasn't happy when Jesse told her she couldn't play it. Her lower lip pushed out in a pout, and she dejectedly thumped down in Jesse's lap.

"I'll try again, if Miss KC will allow." The judge grinned at the adorable look on the baby's face. "Anyway, except for Sheriff Logan sticking his—" Before he could say the word, Jesse shook her head warning against it. "Except for Sheriff Logan," the judge tried again, "looking into business that he had no reason to, is there anything else you can offer on the case before this court?"

"No."

"Step down."

Jesse was starting to fidget more than KC. For two hours, they had listened as one after another witness was sworn in to testify that, several months before, they had seen Jesse come to Bannack. Some said they had seen her with a baby, others that they had seen her leading the dairy cow. All had testified that she had sought out Sheriff Logan to report what she and Jennifer had found on their way to Bannack and that she had repeatedly asked about any kin the baby might have.

After excusing the last witness, the judge pulled out his pocket watch and consulted it. "It appears the marshal is having trouble locating his star witness," the judge said as he deliberately wound the watch. "It also appears that, so far, most of the witnesses the marshal has provided have nothing to offer this court concerning the charges brought against Mrs. Branson. I could call one more witness before calling it a day." He looked at the baby squirming in Jesse's lap. "Think she'll sit for one more?"

"Probably better than I will," Jesse answered candidly.

The judge grinned at the restless woman. "So I've noticed." He banged his gavel a couple of times to quiet the snickers in the room.

The door to the courtroom opened, and Marshal Morgan entered, pushing another man before him. "Ah, I see our elusive Mr. Thompson has been found. Might I ask where?"

"Finney's saloon." The marshal pushed the reluctant witness to the front of the court. "He isn't in any shape to testify at the moment."

Marcus Thompson swayed on unsteady legs. He had gone to Finney's to think of a solution for his dilemma. Unfortunately, the only thing he had accomplished was downing half a bottle of whiskey.

Upon seeing the condition of the witness, the judge told the courtroom, "Due to the late hour, I will recess until tomorrow morning. Perhaps at that time Mr. Thompson will be able to throw some light on the charges against Mrs. Branson. Marshal, you will see that Mr. Thompson is kept in custody overnight. Court will resume at ten o'clock." The judge rapped his gavel once and stood up. "Oh, and Marshall, since you will have a male occupant in the jail, I will allow the defendant to remain in her wife's custody until court tomorrow."

It had been a long afternoon, and having to sit for so long had not helped, but at the moment, Jennifer was in heaven. "Ahhhhhhh." She moaned as Jesse's strong hands manipulated the kinks out of her tired muscles. Jennifer was naked and lying face down on the bed in Leevie's cabin. After returning to the cabin after court, Jesse had insisted her wife take a hot bath and receive a massage. Jennifer had not objected to either demand. Her only regret was that, for the sake of propriety, Jesse could not share the bath with her.

Jesse knelt on the end of the bed with her legs spread to straddle Jennifer as she carefully worked her hands up and down the injured leg. KC was sitting in the small of her momma's back, kneading Jennifer's skin with her little hands.

"Ohhhhhhh," Jennifer moaned again. "That feels sooooooooo gooooooddddddd."

Jesse gritted her teeth. Straddling her lover's naked body and listening to her moans, it was all she could do to keep herself from tearing off her own clothes and making love to her beautiful wife. It didn't help that they hadn't been intimate for several days.

"Darlin'," Jesse leaned down and whispered so Leevie wouldn't hear on the other side of the curtain, "you better stop that moaning or Leevie is going to be hearing a lot more than that."

Unsure what Jesse meant, Jennifer took a moment to think. "Oh." She grasped the meaning of her frustrated wife's words. "I'm sorry, sweetheart."

"Yeah," Jesse groaned. "So am I."

CHAPTER THIRTY

Jesse woke to the most wonderful feeling. KC was sprawled asleep on her chest, and Jennifer was pressed against her side, a leg draped possessively over her body. She lay still, content just to enjoy the loving contact with her family. She carefully turned her head just enough to plant a tender kiss on her wife's brow and was rewarded with a soft sigh from the sleeping woman. After several minutes, Jesse's eyes drifted shut, and she allowed sleep to reclaim her.

Walks on the Wind sat on the knoll overlooking Bannack as the sun started to lighten the sky. Completing his morning meal, he watched lamps begin to glow in many of the buildings in the town. The people of Bannack were rising for the coming day. The cabin where Jesse and Jennifer slept was still dark, and he decided to leave without disturbing them. He would make sure to return by nightfall to continue his vigil.

Mr. Glade, his face almost the same hue as his curly red hair, slammed his fist against the table before him. "What is the meaning of this?"

Moments before, a secretary had brought Frank Wilson's telegram into the company boardroom. Asked to read the paper aloud, the secretary did so and then quickly retreated as the men in the room reacted to the telegram's contents.

"How the hell could this happen?" demanded Mr. Weese, a bald man sucking deeply on a smelly cigar.

Another man stood to emphasize his words. "This is an outrage." He was joined by several other men around the table. "Did Harrington know about this?"

"Gentlemen," the elderly man at the head of the table spoke quietly, "please sit down." Daniel Prestly was the senior member of the board and the company's president.

"I can't believe he let this happen. Does he have any idea how much money this will cost us, if it's true?"

"Not to mention, we'll be the laughing stock of—"

"Gentlemen, please," Prestly tried again.

"...Why, I can just hear it now..."

"*Sit down!*" Prestly softened his voice to add, "Please." He picked up the telegram from the table in front of him and re-read it. "It appears that Mr. Wilson has uncovered what could potentially be a major problem with our investment in Sweetwater." Murmurs of agreement arose from around the table. "It is also suggested that Mr. Harrington may, or may not, be aware of this problem. If he is aware, then it is surely a matter of fraud on his part. And if he is not aware, then—"

"He's a bigger fool than we gave him credit for being," Glade finished.

"Yes, that is possible," Prestly agreed. "However, before we make any decisions, one way or the other, I believe that it would behoove us to have the situation checked out by someone with more knowledge in the area than we possess."

"What assayer provided the original report?" Mr. Weese's cigar bobbed up and down as he spoke.

Prestly opened a thick file on the table and searched through the papers. "It seems Mr. Harrington contracted the services of an assayer in one of the mining camps near Sweetwater."

"Why didn't he use our man in Denver?" the red-haired Glade asked. "That's what we have him on retainer for, isn't it?"

The president carefully closed the folder to insure no papers flew out of the overstuffed binder. "That will be a question you will ask Mr. Harrington when you arrive in Sweetwater."

"What?" He looked surprised as he realized he was being ordered west.

"I would like you, Mr. Glade, and you, Mr. Weese," Prestly addressed the man with the cigar, "to proceed immediately to Sweetwater and find out the truth behind Mr. Wilson's suspicions."

"But sir," Weese protested, "isn't it obvious that Harrington—"

"I expect you to be positive of your facts before any charges are made against any employee of this company," he said harshly.

Glade and Weese nodded. "Yes, sir," they responded simultaneously.

"Please make sure you are on the next train to Denver. You will telegraph me immediately once you have finished your investigation." The men nodded. The president studied them, hoping he hadn't made a mistake in his selection. "Don't make me wait too long."

Upon waking, Martin Kensington rolled onto his belly and gingerly pushed himself up by the arms, slowly pulling his legs under his body until he was balanced on his hands and knees. He remained in that position for several minutes before he was able to force his exhausted body upright. He had slept with his shoes on, not wanting a repeat of the previous morning when he was almost unable to cram his swollen feet back inside the leather bindings. As he balanced his full weight on his blistered feet and painful legs, he wondered if he would be able to walk at all. Then a vision of Jesse Branson floated in front of his eyes, and he had his answer. There was no way that woman was going to best him.

Kensington looked to the south. The hills he needed to cross were close enough that he could almost reach out and touch them. He took a step and bit back the cry of pain. He took another agonizing step, then another. He would cross into the next valley by the end of the day if it was the last thing he did.

The dark eyes watched, surprised that the man was continuing his trek. They followed Kensington as he began the climb up the first hillock, every step seemingly a struggle for the determined man. If Kensington could continue, he should make it through the band of hills and into the valley beyond by nightfall.

Dark eyes trailed their quarry for several more minutes before the watcher moved away from his hiding spot.

"Good morning, sweetheart," Jennifer murmured as Jesse's eyes fluttered open. The schoolteacher had awakened moments before and lay snuggled against her wife's side.

"Mornin', darlin'." Jesse smiled, awake for the second time this morning. "How'd ya sleep?"

"Wonderfully." Jennifer sighed as she snuggled even closer.

Jesse slipped an arm around Jennifer and held her tight. She turned her head and leaned in, running her tongue lightly around her wife's lips before kissing her. "I love you," Jesse whispered as she drew away.

Jennifer slipped a hand behind Jesse's neck and pulled her back. She pressed her lips to Jesse's and deepened the kiss. "I love you," Jennifer sighed, their mouths so close they were sharing the same air. "Jesse, when this is over," she looked into the eyes she adored, "I want to go back to Sweetwater and never leave."

Jesse smiled. "Me, too, darlin'."

KC's eyes opened when she heard her mothers' voices. The baby rolled over, slipped off Jesse's chest, and came to rest lodged between them. She pumped her arms and kicked her legs, struggling to get out of her self-created predicament. When it became apparent to the baby that she was firmly wedged between her mothers, she gave up her struggles. "Up," she demanded.

"Good morning, Sunshine." Jesse laughed as she gently pulled the baby free. "I do believe that someone," she tickled KC's tummy, "needs themselves a fresh set of britches."

KC giggled, slapping at Jesse's hands. She quickly worked herself onto her stomach and crawled up the solid body to wrap her arms around her mother's neck. "Wuv."

Tears forming in her eyes, Jesse rubbed the baby's back. "I love you, too, Sunshine."

"Guess I'm not the only one that hates sleeping without you." Jennifer laid her head on Jesse's shoulder.

Jesse smiled. "What about Momma, Sunshine?" Jesse asked the baby. "Do you love Momma?"

KC sat up on Jesse's chest, her head bobbing up and down. "Wuv Momma," she said as she threw her arms wide and launched herself toward Jennifer.

Jennifer barely got her arm up to catch the baby so she wouldn't fly over her and off the bed. "I love you, too, sweetie." She safely held onto KC.

The women remained in bed cuddling with KC until the smell emanating from her diaper finally forced them to get up and start the day.

Frank Wilson walked out of the tent being used as a dining hall for his work crew. The cook hired by Tobias Harrington had finally arrived and had prepared his first meal for the hungry workers.

"It ain't as good as the food at the Slipper," Wilson grumbled as he walked across the street to where the partially completed bank building stood.

"Good morning, Mr. Wilson."

The foreman groaned when he heard the voice of the man hurrying toward him. "Morning, Mayor." He kept walking.

"I see you have enjoyed your breakfast."

"Enjoyed isn't exactly the word I would have used," Wilson corrected.

"Oh?" The mayor looked toward the tent as more men exited after the morning meal. "Is the cook not to your liking?"

"He's all right," Wilson said. "He just ain't as good as what we've been eating at the Slipper."

"No, I suppose not." The mayor had enjoyed many a meal at the Slipper and felt that the cooking there was even better than his wife's, not that he would ever admit that to another living soul for fear of his wife's reaction.

"Was there something you needed?" Wilson wanted to be rid of the irritating man as quickly as possible. He had a lot of work to accomplish this day, especially since Harrington had sprung a complete redesign of one section of the hotel on him just the day before.

"Mr. Harrington asked me to have you provide the plans for the road to the Songbird. He would like to review them before you begin the work."

Wilson shook his head. Was there anything the little man didn't have to stick his nose into? "You can tell Wilson that ain't something you can write down and review. It's something that has to be done as you go, studying the terrain you have to work with. So if he wants to know where I plan to put the road, he can join us when we start the work. I'll even save a shovel for him to help."

The mayor was frustrated. The lack of cooperation between Harrington and Wilson was more than a nuisance, and he was tired of being in the middle of their animosity. "I'll tell Mr. Harrington that you'll be in later today with the information he has requested," the mayor said, turning on his heel and hurrying back to his office before the foreman could stop him.

"You do that," Wilson said to the mayor's back. "Come on, boys," he called to the men milling about in front of the cook's tent. "We got more than enough to keep us busy today."

Jesse carried KC as she and Jennifer made their way along the boardwalk to the doctor's office. Jennifer had insisted they stop there to have the dressings on Jesse's wrists changed before they went to the courthouse. The rancher had protested but finally gave in when she realized Jennifer wasn't going to relent. On the way, they passed a familiar Chinese restaurant.

Jennifer smiled, remembering the meal they had shared their first trip to Bannack. It had been her first experience with the foreign fare, and she had discovered she liked the exotic tastes. "Sweetheart?"

"Yes, darlin'."

"Do you think we could eat there again?" Jennifer tilted her head at the building beside them.

"Don't see why not," Jesse said. "Maybe Leevie would like to come with us. Be a way to pay her back for all the cooking she's done for us."

"That's a wonderful idea." Jennifer's attempts to help with the cooking chores had been firmly rebuffed by their friend.

"Let's see how long court goes today." Jesse had noticed Jennifer was limping more than usual and didn't want her walking on her damaged leg any more than necessary. She decided Jennifer would receive another massage at the end of the day, even though it would mean having to control her own desires. Just thinking about having her wife lying naked beneath her as her hands worked on the tired leg muscles was making Jesse hot, and she could feel a growing wetness between her legs. She had to stop for a moment to regain command of her ardor, which was running wild.

Jennifer saw the flush on Jesse's cheeks. "Are you okay?"

Jesse nodded as she stood, pressing her legs together to relieve the pressure building in her. "I'm fine," she said, but the words were strained.

"You don't look fine." Jennifer was really getting worried. "Maybe we need to have the doctor check you over."

"No." Jesse shook her head emphatically. "I'm okay. Just give me a minute."

Jennifer waited as Jesse took several deep breaths. Her color returned to normal, and she turned, unsteadily, to continue their walk. "Oh, no you don't." Jennifer grabbed Jesse's arm and pulled her back. "You tell me what that was all about."

"I was just thinkin'." She looked at her wife and smirked.

"Thinking? About what? You looked like you were going to pass out." Jennifer reached up and pressed the back of her hand against her lover's forehead.

Jesse grabbed the hand, gently kissing it. "I was thinking about last night, darlin'."

"Last night?" Jennifer asked, confused. Then she noticed the leering look Jesse was giving her and recalled how they'd had to refrain from making love in Leevie's cabin. "*That* made you almost pass out?"

Jesse leaned forward and kissed Jennifer on the lips, not caring if anyone saw them. "Darlin, I want to make love to you so bad I ache. And if this trial doesn't get over pretty soon so I can get you somewhere all to myself, I may just melt into a big, old puddle of mush from just thinkin' about it."

Jennifer sighed. "You say the nicest things."

"Good morning, Miss Jesse, Miss Jennifer," the court clerk greeted when they entered the courtroom.

"Good morning." Jennifer smiled at the man as she preceded Jesse to the defendant's table.

Jesse nodded to the clerk. "Mornin'." She pulled out Jennifer's chair and waited for her wife to settle into it before claiming her own seat, holding KC in her lap.

"Morning." Billie was standing off to the side of the room, prepared to serve as official impediment to any escape attempt Jesse might make.

"Morning, Billie. Still making sure I don't escape, I see." Jesse shared a laugh with her friend.

There were a few others seated in the courtroom, and more entered and took seats during the following minutes. Jennifer smiled when her mother and brother entered. "Good morning," she said cheerfully.

"You're in a good mood this morning," Thomas said as he helped Mary into a chair.

"I'm always in a good mood when I wake up with Jesse." Jennifer reached over and squeezed her wife's arm. Both of them had enjoyed their morning of snuggling together before they were forced from their bed.

Thomas looked away, embarrassed by his sister's words.

Jennifer noticed her brother's reaction and was about to apologize for making him uncomfortable but stopped herself. This was her life. And the reality was that she slept with and woke up with Jesse. If Thomas had a problem with that, then so be it. But it was his problem, and she would not apologize for loving her wife. She turned around to face the judge's bench.

"You all right?" Jesse asked when she saw the frown on Jennifer's face.

"Yes," she answered curtly.

Jesse ran her thumb lightly over the silky skin of Jennifer's arm. "Darlin'?"

Jennifer took a deep breath before turning to face her worried wife. She smiled to relieve the look of concern on Jesse's face. "I'm fine, sweetheart. I'll explain later. Okay?"

"Yes," Jesse agreed. "As long as you're okay."

"I am."

Leevie entered the courtroom and moved quickly to the defendant's table. "I found these." She placed a carved wooden horse and a couple of other objects on the table in front of KC, who happily grabbed at the toys. "I hope they're the right ones."

"Yes," Jennifer assured her friend. "These are just fine. Thank you."

At the doctor's office, Jennifer and Jesse realized they had left Leevie's cabin without taking any of the baby's toys. Not wanting KC to have to spend another day squirming restlessly in Jesse's lap, the women decided to chance her playing with some of her favorite toys during court. Leevie had happened by to make sure everything was all right with Jesse's injuries and volunteered to return to her cabin for the toys.

"Good." Leevie ruffled the baby's hair. "I'm glad I found the right ones, KC."

"Long as she's got her pony," Jesse told the woman, "she's happy with anything else."

"All rise," the clerk announced in a loud voice.

Jesse stood and assisted Jennifer to her feet as Judge Henson entered the room and took his seat behind the enclosed desk at the front of the room.

"Good morning, ladies." He nodded to Jesse and Jennifer. "And Miss KC. Please be seated." After watching Jesse help Jennifer back into her chair, he said, "Mrs. Branson, you are not required to stand if it creates a hardship."

"Thank you, Judge Henson. I'll take you up on that if it gets too bad."

The judge nodded. He had accepted soon after meeting the young woman that she asked for, and expected, no special considerations because of her leg. He respected her for that and would let her decide what adaptations she would require during court.

"I see Miss KC has brought herself some entertainment today," he commented as KC, standing in Jesse's lap, bounced her toy horse noisily across the table.

"I'm sorry, Judge." Jesse corralled the baby's hands. "We thought it would help keep her quiet, but we can put them away."

"No. These days get long for all of us. Just keep her corralled so I can hear the witnesses."

"Will do, Judge." Jesse leaned down and whispered something into KC's ear.

KC pulled the toy horse to the very edge of the table and softly bounced it in one spot. She looked up, questioning, at Jesse who smiled and nodded. KC smiled and went back to playing.

Judge Henson returned to the business that had brought them to court. "May I ask where Marshal Morgan and Mr. Thompson might be?" He had expected to see the marshal and his star witness in the room.

"The marshal sent word that Mr. Thompson is not yet sober enough to testify." The clerk handed a folded piece of paper to the judge. "He is staying at the jail with his prisoner."

"I see." Judge Henson did not appear happy at the news. "Then please call the next witness on the list."

"Leevie Temple."

"Miss Temple," Judge Henson addressed the schoolteacher as she took the witness chair, "did you have reason to speak with the defendant when she came to Bannack some months ago?"

"Yes, sir."

"Would you tell the court about that?"

"Jennifer and Jesse came to my cabin." Leevie smiled as she remembered the pair walking up to her door with a baby in Jesse's arms. "Jennifer is the schoolteacher in Sweetwater, and she asked if I'd be willing to talk with her, which I happily agreed to do."

"Did they have a child with them?"

"Yes. Jesse was carrying KC."

"Did she say how she came to have the child?"

"They told me they had found her parents on their way to town; they had been killed. They heard the baby crying from under what was left of a burned wagon."

"Did they say what they planned to do with the child?"

"They asked if I might know of any family KC might have in Bannack so they could return her to them."

"What did you tell them?"

"I said that I had only seen that poor young couple just the one time, that day they came through town with their Conestoga. That was really the only reason I paid any attention to them at all. We don't see many of those in town. And since I hadn't talked to them, I wasn't aware of any family they might have in Bannack. But I suggested they might want to talk to Reverend Tobias because I had seen him talking to the Williamses and I thought he might know of any kin they would have."

"How did the child seem with Mrs. Branson?"

"Jesse or Jennifer?"

"I'm sorry. With Jesse Branson."

"KC adored Jesse. She sat in her lap almost the whole time Jennifer and I were talking, which was most of the afternoon. In fact, I can remember saying that KC had already taken a liking to Jesse."

"Did the baby seem well cared for?"

"Oh, yes. They had brought diapers and milk with them to see to her needs. And Jesse rocked KC to sleep when it was time for her nap. Then she held the baby for the entire time she slept."

"Thank you, Miss Temple." The judge made several notations on his papers. "Is there anything else relevant to this case that you would like to say?"

"Yes." Leevie looked at the judge. "The morning that the Williamses left Bannack, I saw their wagon in front of Carpenter's store. Mrs. Williams was sitting in the wagon, and I assumed that Mr. Williams was inside the store."

"Do you know what Mr. Williams was doing in Carpenter's?"

"At the time, I just thought he was buying supplies. But after what happened, I believe that he was inside telling Sheriff Logan what road they planned to travel after leaving Bannack."

"But you don't know for sure?"

Leevie's shoulders slumped. "No."

"Thank you." Judge Henson made a final notation. "You may step down. Mr. Carpenter, please retake the stand."

The storeowner grumbled as he stood and made his way to the front of the courtroom. "You heard what Miss Temple said?" the judge asked the witness.

"Yes."

"What was Mr. Williams doing in your store that morning?"

"Buyin' supplies, I reckon."

"Sir, do not try my patience," Judge Henson warned the stubborn witness.

"He was talkin' to Logan," Carpenter grudgingly admitted.

"Was Mr. Williams telling Sheriff Logan the route he planned to follow after leaving Bannack?"

"Might have been."

"Mr. Carpenter, do you know what transpired between Mr. Williams and Sheriff Logan that morning in your store?" The judge glared at the witness. "I want the truth."

"I was waitin' on another customer so I couldn't hear what was said." Carpenter glared back. "And that's the truth."

The judge knew he wasn't going to get any more out of the man. "Call the next witness."

"Christopher Gaffney."

A young boy twelve or thirteen years of age hurried to the stand. He looked at the judge nervously as he waited to be questioned.

The judge smiled to relax the young witness. "Folks call you Gaff, don't they?"

"Yes, sir."

"Would it be all right if I called you Gaff?"

The boy nodded, his lips turning up slightly in a timid smile. "Yes, sir."

"Good. Gaff, can you tell me if the defendant, the lady sitting right there..." The judge pointed to Jesse when the boy looked at him quizzically. "Have you ever talked to her?"

The boy remembered the friendly women who had visited his father's shop. "Sure did."

"Can you tell me what she said to you, Gaff?"

"She and that other nice lady," the boy pointed at Jennifer, "they come in and askt ta have a stone made. She," he pointed at Jennifer again, "wrote down the name. Mighty pretty handwritin' it was. And she," this time he pointed at Jesse, "askt that pa put an angel on the stone."

"Whose headstone was it?"

"Mrs. Cassidy's. But they weren't puttin' that name on it. Said she didn' need ta be takin' it with her where she was goin', they said."

"Did they say anything else?"

"Said ta let Riley know when it was ready." Gaff named the town's gravedigger.

"Thank you, Gaff." The judge reached out his arm, offering to shake the boy's hand. "You've done yourself proud today."

The boy's chest puffed out as his hand was engulfed by the judge's much larger one. Then he jumped out of the chair and scampered back to his seat, a beaming smile spreading across his face.

Judge Henson looked to Jesse and Jennifer to amplify the boy's testimony. "Ladies?"

"The reason we came to town was to check on the sister of a friend. Didn't know until we talked with Logan that her husband had shot her. Figured the least we could do was give her a nice stone," Jesse explained.

"What name did you use?"

"Granger. It was her family name."

The judge wrote the information down, then he took out his watch and opened it. "I think we can all use a break. Court will adjourn until two o'clock. Please see if the marshal and his witness will be able to join us at that time," he told the clerk.

"All rise," the clerk said as the judge stood to leave.

Thomas stepped up behind Jesse and Jennifer. "I have a table waiting in the dining room at the Goodrich, if you'd like to join us for lunch, that is," he added tentatively. "Everyone is welcome," he said, to include Billie and Leevie.

Jesse looked to Jennifer. "Thank you, Thomas. We'll be there as soon as we get KC changed," Jennifer said.

"You can do that in my room, if you'd like," Thomas offered. "Save you from walking all the way back to Miss Temple's."

"Thanks," Jennifer smiled at her brother, "but we didn't bring any diapers with us."

"Come on, darlin'." Jesse took Jennifer's hand. "Let's get you downstairs, then I'll take KC for some fresh pants while you go with Thomas and your mother. I want you off that leg as much as possible."

In the dining room of the Goodrich Hotel, two tables had been pushed together to accommodate the large party. Jesse sat on one side of the combined tables with Jennifer just to her right, KC sitting in Jennifer's lap. Thomas sat at his sister's side, while Mary, Billie, and Leevie occupied the chairs on the opposite side of the long table. Their meal finished, they were preparing to leave.

Thomas leaned over to speak quietly to his sister. "Jennifer, since we have some time before we have to get back to court, I was wondering if we might speak for a few moments."

Jennifer didn't take long to consider. She turned to Jesse. "Would you mind, sweetheart?"

"No, darlin'." Jesse lifted the baby from Jennifer's lap and stood ready to help as the schoolteacher stood. "Just go somewhere you can sit, please." She winced as Jennifer leaned heavily on her cane, a silent indication of how much the leg was bothering her.

Jennifer leaned close to Jesse and kissed her. "We'll sit in the lobby."

"KC and I will wait for you outside on the boardwalk."

"I won't be long." Jennifer squeezed Jesse's arm as she kissed KC on top of the head. "You take care of Mommy for me," she told the baby.

"Otay."

Thomas offered his arm to Jennifer, and she accepted it. They walked out of the dining room and down the short hall to the lobby at the front of the building. Jesse followed but continued out of the building while Jennifer and Thomas crossed the small lobby to a pair of chairs near a window.

"Momma," KC cried when she saw her mother walking away.

"It's okay, Sunshine." Jesse patted the baby's back. "Your momma is just going to talk to your uncle for a bit, then she'll come find us."

KC stretched herself upward in Jesse's arms to be able to see over the tall rancher's shoulder. Her eyes followed Jennifer, and she smiled when Jennifer waved and blew her a kiss. "Wuv Momma."

"Yep, Sunshine," Jesse agreed, as she walked outside. "That we surely do."

"Thomas?" Jennifer prodded after they had sat in silence for several minutes.

"I'm not sure how to say what I want," he said nervously.

Jennifer sat back in the chair, willing to wait for her brother to gather his thoughts. She watched as Mary eased into a chair on the opposite side of the lobby and pretended to read a newspaper left on a side table. She wondered if her mother knew what was causing her brother's uneasiness.

Thomas looked at his sister. "I want to apologize, Jennifer, for myself and Howard and William. I guess when you were younger, we never gave much thought how our behavior must have seemed to you." His words rushed out. "We didn't do it to hurt you. Please believe that."

Unsure of exactly what her brother was referring to and somewhat fearful of the answer, Jennifer asked, "What did you do, Thomas?"

"The way we treated you. You were so much younger, and we really didn't know what to do with you. Considering you were a girl." He grinned sheepishly.

Jennifer began to understand. "So if I'd been a boy, you wouldn't have ignored me." Even though she smiled to lessen the sting of her words, she meant the truth behind them.

"Yes." Thomas nodded, then changed his mind. "No. I mean... Hell, Jennifer, to be honest, I don't know. By the time you were old enough for me to spend time with, Father had me working on the docks from morning to dark. I was just too tired at the end of the day to care much about anything except going to bed. Howard and William were working half days and going to school the other half, so they didn't have much time, either. It wasn't intentional, it just happened."

"It hurt," Jennifer whispered, remembering the many times she had tried to engage her brothers in a game or other activity, only to be rebuffed with a gruff word or, even worse, intentionally ignored. "I was so lonely."

"I know that now." Thomas reached for her hand, but unsure how she would respond, he pulled his hand back into his lap. "We all know that now. We really are sorry."

Jennifer was mystified as to how her brother could know of feelings she had never expressed to him. "How did you come to know, Thomas?"

"Mother wrote us."

Jennifer looked at Mary, who instantly became very interested in the paper she held. "I should have known."

"She told us how you didn't have much good to remember about us or your growing years. I can tell you, we didn't much care to read what she had written, but we did. And afterward, we talked about it. And the more we talked about those years, the more we came to see that you had good reason not to like us. But I can tell you, we missed you after you left, missed you a lot. And we'd very much like you to give us a second chance to show you that we do care." This time when he reached for his sister's hand, he didn't stop. "We do love you. Please let us prove that to you."

Jennifer studied her brother's larger hands wrapped tenderly around hers. Physically, Thomas looked like a younger version of their father, and Jennifer had to admit that was one of the reasons she had been avoiding him. She knew that she loved her brothers, as any sibling born into a family would, but she could honestly say she didn't like them. Of course, they had never given her much reason to. Maybe she should give her brother the second chance he was requesting, but it would come only under her terms. She glared at her brother, unsure of whether or not he was trying to accomplish what her father had been unable to.

"I'm not going back East." She pulled her hand free of her brother's grasp. "And I'm not leaving my family."

"I would never ask that of you." Thomas saw his sister for what she had become, a determined confident woman willing to fight for the life she had chosen. "Nor would I ever expect it. But I do hope you'll come home for a visit. And," he smiled, "bring your family."

Jennifer had never thought of taking Jesse back East, and she wasn't surprised that the thought of showing her wife where she had grown up did not carry much significance for her. That part of her life was buried too far in the past and, in truth, Jennifer Kensington was no longer who she was. She was Jennifer Branson now, and Montana was her home. There simply was no reason for her to ever leave it.

"I'm sorry, Thomas. I appreciate what you've told me. Although I'm not sure it will erase all the pain and loneliness I carry from those years, it does help to know that you care. As for giving you another chance, I wish I could, but I will never go back. My life is here. My home is, and always will be, with Jesse."

Thomas let Jennifer's words sink in before answering. "Maybe you'll let us come visit you, then. I've taken a liking to what I've seen of Montana and would like to come back when things aren't quite so..." He faltered, seeking the right word.

"Ridiculous. Bizarre. Outrageous. Disruptive. Crazy."

"Yes. All of that. I'm really sorry about all this, Jennifer. I wish I had stopped him from coming."

Jennifer looked out the window at Jesse waiting patiently for her. KC was standing in Jesse's lap, one hand resting on her mother's shoulder and the other pointing at something across the street that Jennifer couldn't see. The baby was talking non-stop, and Jesse was nodding animatedly at the child's gibberish. Jennifer used her cane to push herself up from the chair. "It's Jesse you should be apologizing to for that failure. She's the one paying the price for Father's behavior. Now if you'll excuse me, I'd like to spend some time with my wife and daughter before court starts."

"Of course." Thomas stood along with her. "Jennifer," he tentatively reached for her arm, "I do love you. We all do."

Jennifer studied her brother for a few moments. "I love you, too, Thomas, but I don't know where we go from here. Right now, my only concern is for Jesse and getting through this trial. Then I will do everything I can to make sure Father never has the opportunity to cause us any more trouble. I can't think past that."

"I understand. Perhaps when all this is over, we can talk some more."

"Perhaps."

CHAPTER THIRTY-ONE

Thaddeus Newby approached the guard stationed at the mouth of the Songbird mine, another man following a few steps behind him. Thaddeus took off his hat and wiped the sweat from his brow; it was a long, hot walk up to the Songbird in the heat of early afternoon. "Afternoon."

"Afternoon." The guard eyed his visitors warily. "What can I do for you gents?"

"We'd like to take a look inside the Songbird."

The guard recognized the Sweetwater newspaper editor, but the other man was a stranger to him. "Sorry, I'm not 'sposed to let anybody inside 'cept Mr. Wilson or Mr. Harrington."

"I understand your caution," Thaddeus replaced his hat, "but we will only be a moment. And I assure you we will not do anything but look. You're welcome to come with us."

"I don't know." The guard didn't like going into the dark, confining mine. "Mr. Harrington don' like folks nosin' around. Didn' even like it when Mr. Wilson come up here, and he's 'sposed to check on things."

"Oh?" The newspaperman's interest was instantly piqued. "When was Mr. Wilson here?"

"Couple days ago." The guard relaxed as he talked, not thinking the men posed much of a threat if they were just going to ask questions. "Said he wanted to check on things. Like I said, that bein' his job and all, I didn' think much about it. Then Mr. Harrington come up the next day and wanted to know what Wilson was checkin' on. Told him I didn' know, since I didn' go inside with him. Don' like goin' inside. Don' like bein' closed in like that."

"Can't say I blame you there." Thaddeus wasn't too fond of the idea of being inside the dark mine shaft himself. "But this gentlemen has come a long way at my request, and I'd really hate to have to tell him he wasted his trip."

The guard looked the pair over suspiciously. "What ya planning ta do in there?"

"Just look, like I said," Thaddeus said. "For a newspaper article I'm writing on all the changes the development of the Songbird is going to bring to Sweetwater and the valley."

"It sure will change things, won't it?"

"Yes. A new bank and hotel, even better roads, not to mention the jobs being provided to folks like yourself." Thaddeus felt he had the guard leaning toward letting them inside and decided to nudge him a little more. "Maybe I could even put in a mention about what a fine job you're doing up here."

"Me? In the *Gazette*?" The guard stood a little taller.

"Yep. I bet you've got someone you could send a copy to."

"Sure do."

"So, do you think we could go inside for a few minutes?"

The guard rubbed the stubble on his chin. "Don't see how it can hurt anythin'. Just don't cause any problems. I don't want to have to explain to Mr. Harrington that I let you inside."

"You have my word." Thaddeus shook the guard's hand. "We won't be but a few minutes, I promise."

Thaddeus started for the entrance, gesturing for his companion to follow. The men stopped long enough to light a couple of lanterns before entering the mine. Thaddeus quickly proceeded to the end of the shaft and held his lantern over his head to illuminate the rock wall.

"This is it, Cannan," Thaddeus said as the other man also raised the lantern he carried.

Leaning forward, Cannan carefully studied the golden vein running across the rock face. "Can you hold this for me?" He handed his lantern to Thaddeus.

"What do you think?"

"I'll know in a minute." Cannan pulled a pocketknife from his pocket and scraped across the rock, then he removed a small hammer from the waistband of his pants and rapped it against the stone. A sizeable chip fell from the deposit of ore. He bent down to pick it up, held it up in the lantern light, and turned it over in his hands. "I'd say your suspicions are right, Newby. This ain't nothin' but a vein of quartz with some fool's gold peppered into it."

"What's it worth?"

"Nothing."

Thaddeus Newby wasn't surprised to hear the assayer confirm the rumors he had heard in the mining camps that the Songbird mine had been salted by its previous owner. The question now was whether or not Tobias Harrington was aware of the deception, and that answer was not to be found in the dark tunnel. "Let's get out of here before that guard decides to come see what we're up to."

As if he had read the man's thoughts, the guard's voice echoed down the mine shaft, "You boys doin' okay?"

"Yes," Thaddeus called back. "We're coming out."

"What you planning on doing with this information?"

"As soon as you give me a written report, I plan to break the news in the *Gazette*. I don't know what Harrington is up to, but if it's all been a scam, it's best to put a stop to it before he goes any further."

"You could be making yourself some mighty powerful enemies, Thaddeus."

"I'm more concerned about my friends in Sweetwater." As they reached the entrance and stepped into the bright sunlight, the newspaperman blew out his lantern.

"I'll write you a report as soon as we get back to your office. No sense in me waiting until I get back to Garnet and having to send it to you."

"I'd appreciate that."

"Did you find what you wanted?" the guard asked as the men emerged.

"Yes. Thank you. I'll make sure you receive a copy of the *Gazette*. My compliments, of course."

Walks on the Wind dismounted in a small grove of trees next to a creek of fast-moving water. He let the horses drink before dipping his cupped hands into the water and bringing them up to his lips. The cold liquid felt good on his dry throat. He stood when he heard the call of a meadowlark. Holding one hand to the side of his mouth, he whistled, the high-pitched cry of an eagle. The meadowlark's call was repeated. Walk knelt to finish his drink. Moments later, one of his tribesmen entered the copse. Walk greeted his friend, and the two exchanged information in their native language, then the second man took the reins to one of the horses and disappeared in the direction from which he had come.

Walk mounted his horse and rode back to Bannack. His friend would make sure Kensington found the horse, just as he had been making sure that he survived his trek across the open plains. Though Jennifer's father would never know it, the only threats he had faced since leaving the Indian encampment were hunger and sore feet. Walk had made sure of that.

"Reverend Tobias," Judge Henson opened the afternoon session of Jesse's trial, "since it seems Mr. Thompson is still unable to appear before this court, would you please come forward?"

The reverend smiled primly as he passed the table where Jesse and Jennifer sat. The smile left his face when KC took notice of his passing. Her nose wrinkled as she stuck out her tongue and presented the reverend with a loud, "Pfttttt."

"That wasn't nice, Sunshine," Jesse admonished as she tried to maintain a straight face.

"Uck," KC told her mother as she wiped her hand across her mouth to dry the droplets of saliva left by her actions.

Several snickers were heard in the courtroom until the judge tapped his gavel for quiet. "Reverend Tobias, please take the stand," he directed the witness, who had stopped to stare disapprovingly.

"That child has no business at these proceedings."

"Miss KC is here at my request. Sit down and please refrain from telling me how to run my courtroom." Judge Henson could already tell he would not be pleased by the reverend's testimony. "Please tell the court if you had any contact with the defendant during her earlier visit to Bannack." His voice was sharp, as he was not in the mood for one of the reverend's tirades about Jesse.

Reverend Tobias ignored the unspoken warning. "That woman refused to give that child to me. I could have had a nice couple take it, good folks, who would have given it a decent home and been good parents. Would have taught it manners," the reverend sniffed in response to KC's recent outburst, "not let it run wild like them two."

"Reverend Tobias," the judge pressed his fingers against the bridge of his nose against the impending headache, "please answer the question. Did you have contact with the defendant, yes or no?"

"Yes. I told them I would take the child—"

"Reverend Tobias, you are to answer only the questions I ask. Do you understand?"

"But—"

"If you wish to testify before this court, you will do as you are told." Judge Henson glared at the witness. "Do you understand?"

"Yes."

"Good. Let's start again. Did you have contact with the defendant during her earlier trip to Bannack?"

"Yes." The reverend simmered as KC contentedly curled up in Jesse's arms, watching him.

"What was the nature of your contact?"

"Sheriff Logan told me they had brought an orphan to town. I went to get the child."

"Did Mrs. Branson say how she came to have the child?"

"Sheriff told me they'd found the parents dead on the trail."

"Did you ask the ladies where they had gotten the child?"

"Didn't need to." The reverend shrugged. "Already knew."

Judge Henson added to his notes before asking the next question. "Did Mrs. Branson say what she planned to do with the child?"

"She and her *sister*," the reverend mocked the women who, at the time had thought it best to hide their true relationship, "said they was looking for any kin. I told them there wasn't any and they should give the baby to me. I could find it a decent home with a mother *and* father. But they refused. Said they was keeping it to raise as their own. Said they could give it everything it needed."

"Reverend Tobias," the judge stopped the witness, "kindly stop referring to Miss KC as 'it'. I can't tell if you're talking about a baby or a stray dog."

"Being raised by them, there ain't much difference." The reverend sneered. "Look at her." He pointed at the defendant's table where the veins in Jesse's neck were standing out against tightly contracted muscles. "She's not much more than an animal herself."

Mindless of her leg, Jennifer was out of her chair, charging toward the witness stand. Only Billie's quick action saved the reverend from being attacked by the outraged mother and wife.

"He ain't worth it, Jennifer," Billie said as he struggled to maintain his grasp on her.

Jesse remained seated, not wanting to upset KC any more than she already was at seeing Jennifer storm from her chair.

"Come on." Billie fought Jennifer's attempts to break free. "You ain't gonna do Jesse much good if you get tossed in jail."

Jennifer let the sheriff pull her back to the defendant's table. She was still boiling mad, but Billie was right; she couldn't help Jesse from a jail cell.

"Momma," KC cried and promptly crawled into her momma's lap when Jennifer reclaimed her chair.

Jennifer wrapped her arms protectively around the baby, a clear message to the witness that he would never separate her from her child.

KC could feel her mother trembling and snuggled into her hug, looking up at her mother's angry face. "Wuv Momma," she said in a tiny voice.

Jennifer's anger melted away. "I love you, too, sweetie," she said, her voice breaking.

Jennifer was not the only one aghast at the reverend's comments. Mary had a firm grip on Thomas' arm to keep him in his seat. And Leevie's voice joined others in the courtroom in expressing their displeasure at the witness' remarks.

The judge rapped his gavel several times demanding quiet. Judge Henson turned to the witness when order had been re-established in the room. "Reverend Tobias, you will find yourself in jail if you make one more comment like that. Do I make myself clear?" When the reverend did not answer, the judge referred to the notes he had made during the reverend's testimony. Not seeing anything that required further questioning of the hostile witness, the judge said, "This witness is excused. Call the next witness."

"Just a minute," Reverend Tobias objected. "What's to be done with the child? You can't possibly be thinking of leaving it with those—"

"Don't say another word," Judge Henson warned. "I will determine the welfare of the child after I have heard all the testimony in this case. Until that time, Miss KC will remain with her mothers. You will not attempt to interfere with that again."

Reverend Tobias marched out of the courtroom as Judge Henson reshuffled his notes. "I think we could all use a few moments to calm ourselves after that."

Jesse reached over and tenderly rubbed the back of her hand against Jennifer's cheek. Jennifer smiled shyly. "Guess I got a little carried away."

Jesse leaned close so she could whisper and not be overheard. "I thought it was cute, you takin' after the preacher like that. Remind me never to get on your bad side."

Jennifer pressed her forehead against Jesse's. "I love you."

"I love you, darlin'." Jesse sighed. "Don't you fret, that man will never get his hands on our KC."

"Promise?"

"Promise."

The courtroom doors opened, and a man uneasily approached the judge. Words were quietly exchanged between the two men, and then the judge announced, "Cyrus Finney has asked to testify about the matters before this court. Clerk, swear in the witness."

Jesse and Jennifer had never seen the rough-looking man before and wondered how he could be involved with the charges against Jesse.

"Mr. Finney," the judge looked at the man squirming in the witness chair, "what do you wish to say?"

"Them two ain't killed nobody."

Judge Henson rapped his gavel several times to quiet the whoops and hollers that broke out in the courtroom. When quiet resumed, he asked, "And you know this how?"

"That fool Williams talked to Logan 'fore they left town. I heard Logan tell the boys to go after 'em. Said they'd be takin' the road through the Big Hole."

"Do you know why Sheriff Logan sent men after the Williams?"

"Williams told Logan their families had been killed by Injuns, and they was carryin' the only thing left of value to either one of 'em. Funny, considering..."

"Considering what?"

"'Cept for their horses, the boys didn't find nothin' of value when they went through the wagon, just clothes and some old furniture. Don't rightly know what Williams was talkin' 'bout."

Jesse and Jennifer looked at each other and then down at KC, now asleep in Jennifer's arms. They knew.

"Mr. Finney, how is it that you know this?"

"'Cause Logan talked to the boys in my bar." He loosened his collar; he could almost feel the noose around his neck. His only hope was that his testimony would save him from the hangman.

"Was it customary for Sheriff Logan to conduct his business in your saloon?"

The witness swiped at the beads of sweat gathering on his forehead. "The boys would be there drinkin' most times. So, if'n Logan had somethin' he wanted them to do, he'd come there lookin' for 'em."

"Was it usual for Sheriff Logan to order the death of a child?" the judge asked, knowing that by sending his henchmen after the Williamses, the sheriff had, in effect, sentenced their baby to die also.

"Nah, don't think he knew about the young 'un. Logan never would have sent the boys after anyone with a kid. He was funny 'bout that." Finney wiped at his brow again. "Fact is, only time I heard him tell the boys to kill a young 'un was when he sent 'em after them two."

Pandemonium exploded in the courtroom. This was the first time that folks in Bannack had heard that Jesse, Jennifer, and KC had been specifically targeted by their former sheriff.

"Told ya, ya had the wrong person on trial," a voice shouted.

"How the hell can you be trying her for a killing Logan ordered?" someone else asked loudly.

"Dammit, don' know why ya is wastin' our time with all this," another voice was heard. "Ain't it obvious that no good Logan is the one who killed them folks?"

Banging his gavel on the desk, Judge Henson tried to quiet the room enough so he could question the witness about this new development. Billie and the court clerk worked their way through the gallery, trying their best to calm and settle the outraged group. Only Jesse and Jennifer had failed to react to Finney's announcement, having already been very much aware of the events that Sheriff Logan had set in motion months prior.

Eventually, order was restored. "Mr. Finney," Judge Henson asked when the room quieted, "are you telling this court that Sheriff Logan ordered the death of the defendant?"

"Yeah. Both of 'em. He said he didn't trust 'em. He was afraid they'd go back to Sweetwater and talk to the law."

"Which is exactly what they did," Billie told the judge. "They came to me with what they had seen in Bannack and what had happened after they left. I wrote it up and sent it on to Virginia City."

The judge turned back to the witness. "What happened to the men Sheriff Logan sent after the defendant? It is apparent they failed to follow his instructions."

"Don't rightly know," Finney replied truthfully. "Never saw two of 'em again. Logan went out lookin' for 'em but came back without 'em. The third, Vince Packer, came in a few times after the vigilantes hanged Logan, but he always refused to talk about it."

Judge Henson looked to Jesse for an explanation. "Mrs. Branson?"

"They ambushed us near a stand of cottonwoods." Jesse looked at Jennifer and the baby sleeping in her arms and decided it would be better to have everything out in the open. "I killed two of them; the other one lit out on his horse." She was still haunted by nightmares over the men's deaths, yet if she hadn't defended her family that day, they would have been left dying in the hot sun instead of the bandits.

Jennifer placed a supportive hand on Jesse's thigh.

"Were you hurt?" the judge asked.

"Jennifer was thrown from her horse, had the wind knocked out of her. Took her some time to recover," Jesse answered. "Otherwise, we were okay."

"Except that we were all pretty scared, I didn't think KC would ever stop crying," Jennifer added furiously. "And Jesse still has nightmares about trying to save us from those monsters. Sorry, sweetheart," she gently told her wife, "but they should know that it did hurt us."

Jesse smiled ruefully; she wasn't the only one to suffer from nightmares. She scooted her chair closer to Jennifer's and wrapped a long arm around her, pulling their bodies together tightly. The judge could do what he wanted with the information. Right now, all she cared about was in her arms.

"I don't know about anyone else," Judge Henson looked at Jesse and Jennifer who were oblivious to what was going on around them, "but I need some time to consider what I have just heard. Court is recessed until ten o'clock tomorrow morning." He rapped his gavel on his desk and promptly left the room.

As he tied the horse to the tree, the brave hoped that Walks on the Wind knew what he was doing. It was almost dark, but once the horse was discovered, he knew Kensington would not let the darkness stop him from riding straight for Bannack, especially now that he would have a quicker mode of travel.

His task carried out, he began his return to camp near the buffalo herds.

Jesse was sitting on the porch of Leevie's cabin, KC playing at her feet. "What are you doing, sweetheart?" Jennifer asked, bringing two cups of hot coffee.

"Thanks." Jesse accepted one of the cups and took a sip. "Seems we'll be needin' a new house when we get back home, so I was tryin' to come up with one." She handed Jennifer the sketch she had been working on.

Jennifer studied the picture. Jesse had drawn a two-story ranch house with plenty of windows and a wide, wraparound porch, just like the one around the Silver Slipper. Tears welled in her eyes as she thought of the cabin they had shared since falling in love. "I'm so sorry."

"Hey." Jesse put down her cup of coffee and pulled Jennifer into her lap. "You didn't burn the house down, and I won't be having you apologize for what happened." Jesse tenderly wiped away her wife's tears. "Besides, it was getting a bit cramped. What with KC growing so fast, we would have needed to add on a room soon anyway. This way," she took the drawing from Jennifer and held it up for both of them to look at, "we get to start fresh.

It'll be ours, darlin'. A home we can raise KC in and live in until we're old and gray and she has to take care of us."

"Ours." Jennifer liked the sound of that. "We'll build it together?"

"Wouldn't have it any other way."

KC had pulled herself upright and was leaning against Jesse's leg. "Mommy."

"And you, Sunshine," Jesse managed to lift the baby, even with Jennifer in her lap, "will go right here." She pointed to a window in the corner of the upstairs level of the house. "That will be your room."

KC looked at the paper and tilted her head as she studied the picture. "Otay."

Martin Kensington could not believe his luck when he found the pony. He could not understand how his horse had made it so far from the Indian camp, but never having been one to unnecessarily question a fortunate windfall, Kensington pulled himself up into the saddle and kicked the horse into a gallop. He would ride hard through the night until he spotted tiny lights twinkling in the distance...Bannack.

CHAPTER THIRTY-TWO

"I don't understand why they didn't just let Jesse go after what that man said yesterday. Now there's evidence she didn't kill those people," Thomas said as he, Mary, and Billie entered the hotel dining room for breakfast.

"More charges against her than just the Williamses' deaths," Billie explained as they moved to an empty table. "You're right, it's pretty much proven that Jesse didn't kill them folks or steal their horses and burn their wagon, but I think Judge Henson is lookin' for more than that."

Mary sat in the chair Thomas was holding for her. "What else is there?"

"Who's behind the charges against Jesse," Billie sat in another chair at the table, "and why. Not to mention, what to do about KC."

"Oh, my," Mary gasped. "You don't think he'll take her away from Jennifer and Jesse?"

"Mother, the judge has seemed very friendly where KC is concerned," Thomas said. "I can't believe he'd take her from the only parents she knows. Do you, Billie?"

"Depends." Billie sipped coffee. "Don't know how much influence the reverend has in this town."

"That deplorable man," Mary said.

"Ya may not like his methods, but he does what few others will." Billie ordered, then waited as Mary and Thomas made their selections before he continued. "Mining camps are full of young 'uns that have no family. Reverend is doing his best ta find them places to grow up."

Thomas stirred sugar into his coffee. "But at what price? From what Jennifer says, they end up as cheap labor on some farm or ranch. What kind of way is that for a child to grow up?"

"Not saying I agree with it, but it does give them a chance. If they have ta fend for themselves, they could end up doing a lot worse." Billie thought sadly of the childhood his fiancée had suffered through. "At least, the reverend puts a roof over their heads and food in their bellies."

Mary sighed. "And not much else."

"The frontier can be rough on young 'uns, and growing up in a mining camp is even worse. Many don' live long, sickness and hunger see to that. Then there's accidents, like running in front of a horse or wagon or falling down an old mine shaft. Even if they survive, there ain't always a doctor around to see to their injuries. Then ya take into account something happenin' to their folks, and it just ain't easy for 'em. And there ain't many willing to foot the bill for children's homes or orphanages. So, much as I hate to say it, the reverend at least is tryin' ta help."

Mary thought about what the sheriff had said. "I guess we've forgotten what it's like to raise children in a wilderness since we don't face those challenges back East any more."

"Seems KC was very lucky to have Jennifer and Jesse find her when they did, for a lot of reasons," Thomas observed as the waitress returned with their breakfast.

"'Course, I'm not saying that the reverend shouldn't get the burr out from under his saddle when it comes to Jesse and Jennifer." Billie took a forkful of eggs from the plate the waitress set in front of him. "Love is love, even if he don't want to say so."

"We should get going." Though she spoke the words, Jennifer made no effort to leave her chair. She and Jesse had awakened early after a restless night full of troubling dreams. Leevie was already preparing breakfast.

KC had also slept fitfully and awakened in a very cranky mood. It had taken Jesse playfully teasing the baby almost the entire morning meal to get KC to smile. Once she had, the baby seemed to forget her reasons for being upset.

Jesse tilted a glass of milk for KC and let her finish the little bit remaining. "Don't want to be late to court," she said distractedly. After the testimony from the saloon owner the day before, she wondered what else could possibly be needed to prove her innocence. But she had to admit, she was also a little concerned over what the judge planned to do about her admitting to shooting the bandits that had been sent to kill her and Jennifer.

"It's almost over, sweetheart."

"I hope so." Jesse wiped a few drops of milk from the baby's chin. "Because all I want is to take you and KC and go home."

"I'd like that." Jennifer sighed as she leaned over and laid her head on Jesse's shoulder. "I love you."

Jesse softly rubbed the back of her knuckles on Jennifer's cheek. "I love you, too, darlin.'"

"Wuv?" KC looked up at her mothers.

Jennifer pulled the baby up to her chest. "Yes, sweetie. We love you, too."

Leevie quietly watched the exchange.

"We should get dressed, darlin.'" Jesse kissed her wife's forehead. Jennifer tilted her head, inviting Jesse to kiss her lips. The rancher didn't hesitate to accommodate her.

By the appointed time of the morning for the trial to reconvene, the courtroom was packed with citizens of Bannack, Yankee Flats, and the surrounding smaller camps. Word of the previous day's testimony by the saloon owner had spread to the miners working claims in the gullies and canyons. There wasn't an empty chair in the courtroom, and people were standing two to three deep by the back wall of the room, with more standing in the hallway outside.

"Mr. Thompson, don't bother," Judge Henson instructed the prisoner as he was escorted into the courtroom and Marshal Morgan looked for an empty chair in the gallery to seat him. "Since you've finally decided to make an appearance, I don't want to waste this opportunity. You can take the stand and be sworn in."

Jesse and Jennifer sat at the defendant's table, somewhat apprehensive at the large number of people in the room. KC stood in the rancher's lap, leaning on her hands braced against Jesse's chest. The wide-eyed baby peeked curiously over Jesse's shoulder; she had never seen so many people.

Jennifer glanced back and, seeing many friendly smiles and nods of support, relaxed a little bit. Turning back around in her chair, Jennifer patted Jesse on the thigh. "It's going to be all right, sweetheart. I can feel it."

Jesse looked at her wife and nodded nervously. "I hope so, darlin.'" She couldn't help feeling that some in the room must be friends of the men she had been forced to kill and worried that they might be there to settle the score.

"I see we have a few more folks interested in these proceedings today." Judge Henson looked around the crowded room. "Let me make it clear to everyone that I will not tolerate any outbursts of any kind," he told the spectators. "Marshal Morgan, Sheriff Monroe, you will remove anyone that speaks out or causes any disturbance." Both lawmen nodded as they took up their posts on opposite sides of the room.

The judge picked some papers up off his desk and, after scanning them, set all but one back. "Mr. Thompson, you are the owner of a dress shop in Bannack?"

"Yes." Marcus Thompson looked like a man who wished to be anywhere but where he found himself. He had spent the past two days trying to figure out a way to disentangle himself from the predicament his greed had landed him in. His introspection had revealed no solution, and now he was scared that the law would punish him in ways far outweighing the reward received from Martin Kensington.

"Did you have occasion to meet the defendant during her previous visit to Bannack?"

"No, sir."

"You did not meet the defendant?" Judge Henson was puzzled. This was supposed to be the key witness to Jesse's guilt.

Thompson swallowed nervously. "Not face to face."

"Care to explain?"

"She came into my shop with Jennifer Kensington."

"You knew Jennifer Branson?"

"Yes. No. Well, not exactly." Thompson wiped sweaty hands on his pants. He took a deep breath and tried to settle his nerves. It didn't help.

"Mr. Thompson, what exactly happened in your dress shop to make you accuse the defendant of murder?"

"I never accused her of murder." Thompson shook his head rapidly from side to side. "I didn't. I just told her father where he could find her, that's all, I swear."

"You told Jesse Branson's father?"

Jesse and Jennifer listened to the judge's perplexed question, already knowing the answer.

"No, the other one. Kensington. These two came into the shop and talked to my wife about having some dresses made. I was in the back room and thought I recognized her. I got to thinking about it and realized she looked like the daughter of an acquaintance of mine back East. And I remembered that just before we left to come West, I'd heard she had run away and her father was paying a reward for any information as to her whereabouts. So, we needing the money and all, I sent him a telegram and said she was living in Sweetwater."

"Is that all?"

"Yes."

"Mr. Thompson, do you expect me to believe that Jesse Branson has been brought before this court and charged with these contemptible crimes just because you reported a runaway?"

Thompson swallowed, the motion so exaggerated it was seen by those standing at the back of the room. "I ain't sure, but I may have led Kensington to believe—"

"Oh, tell him the truth, for god's sake," a woman's voice called out from the gallery. "You told him much more than that."

"Hush, woman!" Thompson shouted at his wife.

"Mrs. Thompson, come forward," the judge instructed the petite woman being restrained by the marshal. "Mrs. Thompson, what do you know of this matter?"

"Keep your mouth shut, woman," Thompson hissed.

"Marshal, silence the witness or have him gagged."

"Some time after my husband sent the first telegram to Mr. Kensington, he received a letter back. Mr. Kensington offered to pay him a substantial amount of money if he knew of anything that could put Jesse Branson in prison or...or get her hanged."

Judge Henson rapped his gavel on the bench as murmurs rumbled through the spectators. His look of warning was enough to quiet the grumbles. "What did your husband do?"

"Don't say anything, woman," Marcus Thompson pleaded.

"He wrote Mr. Kensington and told him that she had bragged about killing the Williamses so she could steal their baby and raise her as her own."

"*Nooo!*" Jennifer screamed. Slamming her hands against the table, she pushed herself up from the chair. It was happening all over again — her father trying to tear her family apart.

Jesse stood, attempting to wrap her free arm around Jennifer. She was angrily pushed away.

"Why?" Jennifer glared at Thompson, her eyes boring holes through the man. "Why would you do that to us?" Her voice held a deep, heart-wrenching sorrow.

Unable to bear the look of anguish on the woman's face, Thompson hung his head.

"Don't you understand? Don't you understand how much he's hurt us? Why would you help him to do that again?" Tears streamed down Jennifer's face.

Again Jesse reached for Jennifer. This time her comfort wasn't rebuffed as she pulled her distraught wife to her. Jesse kissed Jennifer's temple, hugging her tightly. KC whimpered, huddling between her wounded mothers.

"Why, Jesse?" Jennifer sobbed. "Why can't he just leave us alone?"

No one in the room was immune to the agony of Jennifer's cries, many feeling as if their own hearts were being broken as they listened to her sobs.

"I think we can all use a few minutes to compose ourselves," Judge Henson said. "Everyone is to remain in their seats. Court is recessed for fifteen minutes." The judge rapped his gavel and then motioned for Jesse to take Jennifer into his chambers.

"Darlin', come with me."

Jennifer nodded, allowing Jesse to guide her away from the table and into the sanctuary.

Mary and Thomas sat in their chairs, stunned by the revelation they had just heard about their husband and father.

"I had no idea," Thomas whispered, shaking his head. "I had no idea."

"Your father..." Mary stopped.

What was she going to say? What could she say? She had no understanding of who her husband had become or why he was trying so hard to ruin Jennifer's life. Could his only reason truly be that their daughter had somehow discovered the fortitude deep within herself to seek out her own destiny? Could a father really hold so much hatred for his own child over that one alleged act of defiance? Or was it simply because that by doing so, Jennifer had found a life that made her happy, a life that did not require her father's presence or guidance or dominance?

"Thomas," Mary said to her son, "I'm not sure why your father has done this, but I do know that it is time to put an end to it. When this trial is over, I want you to go find your father. Then we'll make sure he never does anything to Jennifer ever again."

"Here, sit." Jesse gently pushed Jennifer down onto a leather settee before sitting beside her.

"I'm sorry," Jennifer said in a voice so mournful Jesse had trouble holding back her own tears.

Jesse pulled a bandanna from her pocket and used it to dry her wife's cheeks. "You had good cause."

"Momma?" KC reached for Jennifer and was helped into her lap by Jesse.

"I love you, sweetie." Jennifer hugged the baby as if her life depended on it.

"Don't squash her, darlin'." Jesse smiled. "She's the only one we've got."

Jennifer laughed, thankful for Jesse's attempt to lighten the mood.

"Darlin'," Jesse leaned back and pulled Jennifer with her, "this will soon be all over, and we'll be back in Sweetwater. You'll be teaching school, and I'll be workin' the ranch."

"What about Father?"

"I have a feeling that the judge will have something to say about that." Jesse wiped away the few tears still trickling from her wife's eyes.

"I hate him, Jesse." Jennifer declared quietly.

Jesse tightened her hold on Jennifer, pulling their bodies together. "I know, darlin'." The women sat locked in each other's embrace for several minutes until a soft knock at the door interrupted their respite.

"We'll be out in a minute," Jesse called to the unseen knocker, guessing it was probably the judge's clerk. "Come on, darlin'." Jesse stood and offered her hand to Jennifer. "Let's get this over with so we can go home."

Once Jesse and Jennifer had resumed their seats at the defendant's table, Judge Henson addressed the witness. "Mr. Thompson, do you admit to conspiring with Martin Kensington to file false charges against the defendant?"

"No," Thompson said emphatically. "I didn't know what he planned to do with the information. I figured he was just going to use it to scare her, make her give up on his daughter. That's all, I swear. I never thought he would do this."

"So, you do admit that you provided Mr. Kensington with false information against the defendant?"

"But, I never—"

"Did you, or did you not, provide him the information?"

"Yes," the witness finally allowed.

"Mr. Thompson, I'm charging you with conspiracy and making false accusations. Due to your admission before this court, you are found guilty of said charges and are sentenced to serve ten years in the territorial prison for your despicable actions." Thompson gasped at the ruling. "Furthermore, Mr. Thompson, you will be escorted to Deer Lodge immediately upon the completion of this trial to begin your sentence. Marshal, please take the witness into custody."

Marcus Thompson sat dejectedly, resigned to his fate.

"Jesse Branson, please stand."

Jesse stood, and no one in the room was surprised when Jennifer stood defiantly alongside of her to hear the judge pronounce his verdict.

"I would suggest, most strongly," Judge Henson looked to the people sitting in the gallery, "that you withhold any reactions until the court's business is concluded."

Jesse smiled when Jennifer reached for her hand and entwined their fingers.

"Jesse Branson, as to the charges brought against you, I hereby find the following — on the charges of murder, I find you not guilty. On the charges of theft, arson, disturbing the peace, filing false charges, etcetera," he tossed the paper he had been reading onto his desk in disgust, "I find you not guilty."

No one said a word. Everyone, especially Jesse and Jennifer, was aware that he had not addressed two charges made against Jesse.

"Mrs. Branson, I wish to express my sincerest apologies for the grave injustices these charges have brought upon you. I do not know why the governor chose to believe the men responsible for this, but I can assure you that I will personally present my findings to him. And I will have some rather strong words to go along with them."

"Thank you," Jesse said, still apprehensive about what was to come. She felt Jennifer's body press against her and could feel her trembling.

KC, held in Jesse's strong but shaky arms, looked up at her mothers with worry.

Judge Henson smiled to reassure the women. "Before we get to the future of Miss KC, I would like to address a matter that came up during the testimony in this case. As to the men you killed, it is my belief that your response to their actions was a matter of self-defense, necessary to protect not only yourself but also your family. Therefore, it is my decision that you shall not face any charges for their deaths. I am adding that to my findings in this case." He winked at the women. "Just in case someone gets it in their fool head to try and use that against you."

Jennifer mouthed a silent *thank you* to the judge.

"Now for the remaining charges..." Judge Henson turned serious again. "I purposely asked that Miss KC be brought to these proceedings. I wished to observe how she interacted with the defendant. I also wished to monitor how the defendant and Mrs. Branson interacted with the child. I am very pleased to say that I have never seen a child cared for by more loving or devoted parents. Nor have I ever seen a child that so obviously adores her parents. Therefore, as to the charges of kidnapping and of endangering this child, I find the defendant, Jesse Branson, not guilty."

Jesse's knees started to shake, and she was sure she would have fallen if Jennifer hadn't had an arm around her. Several sighs of relief were heard from the people crowded into the gallery behind them.

"As for this child's future," the judge continued, "I find it impossible to imagine anyone providing a better home—"

"You can't be thinking of leaving that child with them!" Reverend Tobias howled from the rear of the room. "I most strongly object."

"Reverend Tobias, I have listened to your assertions against these women and find that the only reason you object to their caring for this child is the fact that they are, indeed, two women. Therefore, since you have provided this court with no reasonable or acceptable legal argument to what I am about to order, I am granting the Bransons full adoptive rights for the child. And to make sure that they have no further problems with you or anyone else, Reverend, I have put my decision in writing." He passed a sheet of parchment to his clerk. "Would you hand this to the Bransons?"

Jesse and Jennifer could barely read the paper through their tears.

> *It is hereby ordered that the infant daughter of Kenneth and Catherine Williams (deceased), having no known blood relatives to provide her a home, is to be placed in the care of Jesse and Jennifer Branson of Sweetwater, Montana Territory. The child shall be known from this day forward as KC Branson. It is further hereby ordered that this relationship is legally binding and shall not be questioned or challenged by any other party.*
> *By order of the honorable,*
> *Judge M.Q. Henson*
> *Bannack, Montana Territory*

"Reverend Tobias," the judge softened his voice as he again spoke to the incensed preacher, "it is hard enough to find good homes for children that are in need. That is a situation I'm sure you will have no trouble agreeing with. Might I suggest that you look into your heart and be glad for little KC? She will grow up having what many children can only hope for — the love of two adoring parents. This is something to be cherished, not attacked. Perhaps when you go back to your church and think about it, you'll see this matter with different eyes."

Without a word, the preacher turned and left the courtroom, his expression still outraged.

"How can we thank you?" Jennifer asked, tears streaming down her face.

"Just make sure you prove me right." Glad to finally have the travesty over, Judge Henson smiled as he lifted his gavel.

The door to the courtroom burst open, and Martin Kensington stormed in. Thomas immediately stood to block his father's entrance but was met with a fist to the face.

"That's for leaving me out there, you sorry excuse for a son," Kensington snapped as he stepped over his son's prone body.

"Martin!" Mary screamed.

"Good, you're here," Martin said to his wife. "Jennifer," he stepped toward his daughter, "it's time you stop your foolish games and start doing as you are told."

Jesse tried to hand KC to Jennifer as she moved her body between her wife and Kensington, but Jennifer was quicker and pushed Jesse out of the way.

"You sorry excuse for a father!" Jennifer roared as she pulled her arm back. Coiling into it all the strength that months of frustration, pain, anger, disappointment, and anguish had created, she unleashed a wicked roundhouse punch. Her fist caught her father on the chin, delivering a blow powerful enough to stop a surprised Martin Kensington in his tracks. He stared blankly at Jennifer for a second or two before dropping to the floor. Cheers erupted in the courtroom.

Billie stared dumbfounded. He, and many others in the room, had expected it would be Jesse who would flatten the large man if he made an appearance. "Damn."

Jesse casually draped her arm around Jennifer as they looked down at Kensington stretched out on the courtroom floor, too stunned to fully comprehend exactly what had hit him.

Jennifer leaned against Jesse. "I think I broke my hand."

"Should have let me do it." Jesse gently lifted the hand to examine it. A large black and purple bruise was already spreading across the fleshy part, and the knuckles were scraped and starting to swell. She tenderly cradled the hand against her body.

"Felt good."

"Yeah?"

"Yeah."

Martin Kensington tried to sit up. He raised a hand to the side of his face, wincing when he touched his bruised jaw.

"Arrest that man," Judge Henson ordered.

Marshal Morgan moved toward Kensington with Sheriff Monroe right behind him. Even with the prisoner stunned, it would likely take both lawmen to restrain the larger man.

"What the hell?" Kensington tried to shake free the grasp of the lawmen.

"You're under arrest," Billie happily informed him.

"You can't arrest me." Kensington continued to struggle as he was half pushed, half dragged to the front of the courtroom.

Forgotten with everyone's attention focused on the struggling men, Thomas sat up rubbing his jaw. Standing on shaky legs, he slowly returned to his mother's side.

"Martin Kensington, I am reinstating the prior order for your arrest in the event that you ever returned to Montana Territory. By your presence in this courtroom, it is obvious that you are in violation of the terms of your agreement."

Billie had thoughtfully provided his copy of the order to the judge before the start of the trial on the chance that things would turn out the way they had. He had also informed the judge about Kensington setting fire to Jesse and Jennifer's ranch house and of the other crimes he had committed after returning to the territory.

"I am also charging you with conspiracy, arson, and assault. And I'm sure there'll be more before we're done. Needless to say, Mr. Kensington, you will be spending the next several years behind the walls of the territorial prison. I hope you enjoy your stay. Remove him, Marshal."

"Now just a minute!" Kensington shouted as he was forced away from the judge. "That bitch is the one going to prison. Harrington assured me."

Jennifer pulled away from Jesse and advanced on her father. "Tobias Harrington?"

"Yes." Kensington fought to loosen the lawmen's grip. "He promised she would be sent to prison if I promised to sign over the Silver Slipper. It was all arranged. Her evil influence would be out of your life, and you would return East with me. Not to mention, I'd make a nice profit out of the deal," he added without forethought.

"You did all this just to get me back East, even after I told you I would *never, ever go back there*?"

"You belong there," Kensington insisted defiantly.

"And you thought you could just sell the Slipper and keep the money?" Jennifer's anger was rising again.

"And the ranch." Kensington smirked. "Women have no place in business."

"Why, you..." Jennifer pulled back her fist, ready to strike a second blow, determined to wipe the triumphant expression off his face.

Having passed a disgruntled KC to Mary, Jesse stepped between Jennifer and her father. "Don't, darlin'."

"Get out of my way, Jesse."

"He's not worth it."

"Get out of my way!"

"Please, darlin', if you hit him again, you *will* break your hand."

"I don't care." Jennifer's eyes narrowed as she took aim on the man being restrained behind Jesse.

Desperate to stop Jennifer from doing something she would later regret, Jesse looked directly into Jennifer's eyes and grinned. "I have plans for that hand when this is all over." Her eyebrows danced suggestively.

Jennifer deflated as the meaning of Jesse's words sank in, a blush steadily creeping up her neck and coloring her cheeks. "Jesse Marie Branson..." She lowered her fist and, opening her hand, swatted at her wife. When her injured fingers came in contact with Jesse's muscular arm, Jennifer pulled her hand back, hissing in pain. Jesse pulled Jennifer to her, cradling the injured hand. "I can't believe you said that," Jennifer groaned as she buried her face against Jesse's shoulder.

"Sorry, darlin'," Jesse kissed the top of her wife's head, "but I needed to get your attention."

Jennifer looked into Jesse's sparkling eyes. "I love you."

"I love you, too."

"Momma," KC cried, "Mommy."

Jesse and Jennifer looked to see their daughter struggling to free herself from her grandmother's arms. Jesse walked over and caught the baby as she launched herself toward her mothers. "I think we should get your momma to the doctor's. What do ya say?"

KC, happy to be reunited with her mommy, reached up and squeezed Jesse's nose. "Oonk, oonk." Laughter exploded in the courtroom.

Judge Henson joined in the laughter and rapped his gavel against his desk for the last time. "This trial is over."

Mary held Thomas back as a crowd of well-wishers converged on Jesse and Jennifer. "See if the judge has a moment to speak to me about your father," she directed.

Thomas looked at his mother and then at his father, who was being hauled out of the courtroom with a subdued Marcus Thompson following behind. "All right," he said as he turned back to his mother. "I'll be right back."

CHAPTER THIRTY-THREE

"Mr. Wilson," Thaddeus Newby approached the construction foreman at the site of Sweetwater's new bank. "I was wondering if you could spare a few moments of your time."

"What for?" Frank Wilson wiped the sweat off his face. He looked up into the cloudless sky and wondered if they would get any thunderstorms later in the day; he would sure welcome some rain.

"I have a few questions I'd like to ask you about the Songbird mine."

"Shouldn't you be asking Harrington?" Wilson strode to a bucket of water sitting in the shade of one of the partially completed walls.

Thaddeus followed the man into the shade. "I think I have a better chance of getting some honest answers from you."

"Not my job to answer questions." Wilson sank a dipper into the water, then lifted it to his mouth.

"Mr. Wilson," Thaddeus leaned against the unfinished wall, "I'm about to run an article in the *Gazette* exposing the Songbird as a fraud. And I have good reason to believe that you are aware that someone deliberately salted the mine by imbedding small amounts of gold ore into the rock. What I would like to know is what are you going to do about it before Sweetwater pays the price for the deception?"

Wilson dropped the dipper into the bucket; it rattled against the wooden side before disappearing beneath the water. He looked at Thaddeus. "I think you'd best be addressing your questions to Harrington. Perhaps it would serve your readers more to hear what he knows and what he is doing about it."

"Do you think he knows?"

"I'm sorry, Mr. Newby," Wilson retrieved the dipper and hooked it back onto the bucket's side, "but I've got work to do."

"Very well, Mr. Wilson, I shall address my questions to Mr. Harrington."

"You can't do this to me." Martin Kensington struggled to prevent shackles from being fastened around his ankles. "Do you have any idea who I am?"

The sheriff and marshal had brought their prisoners back to the jailhouse and shoved them inside. As soon as they were through the jail door, Billie slammed it shut and jammed the locking bolt in place to prevent Kensington from escaping. He and the marshal then set to the task of placing manacles on the belligerent prisoner.

"Yeah, I know who ya are." Billie fought to hold on to the man while the marshal completed the task of securing the leg irons. "Ye're an arrogant, pig-headed fool of a man who's got more money than brains," the lawman panted. "But now ye're the property of the Territory of Montana, and your money ain't goin' ta do ya much good where ye're goin."

While the lawmen grappled with Kensington, Marcus Thompson passively entered one of the two cells and stood patiently waiting. He saw no reason to fight the inevitable.

"Dammit, man," Marshal Morgan snapped when he was smacked in the head by one of Kensington's flailing knees. "Would you stop kicking me?" he barked.

"Hold still, Kensington," Billie grunted as he tried to control the thrashing man. "Ya ain't goin' ta change anything."

Marshal Morgan finally got the cuffs around Kensington's legs. "Let's get him in the cell and chain him down," he told Billie as he stood rubbing the side of his head.

Kensington was dragged into the same cell Jesse had been locked into only days before. But unlike during Jesse's confinement, a heavy chain was run through the iron ring in the middle of the floor and its ends were padlocked to each of the leg irons clasped around the prisoner's ankles. With Kensington's movement severely restricted, the lawmen had an easier time of placing similar restraints on his wrists.

"You can't do this to me!" Kensington screamed, pulling against the chains. "Harrington promised this couldn't happen."

"That was another mistake ya made," Billie muttered as he followed the marshal out of the cell. "Harrington ain't much better than a snake in the grass."

"Let me ouuuuuuttttttt of hhhhheeeeeeerrrrrrreeeeeee," was heard as the heavy, reinforced wooden cell door was slammed shut.

Marshal Morgan glared at his other prisoner. "I hope you don't plan to follow his example."

"No," Thompson said meekly.

"Good." Morgan slammed the door on Thompson's cell. He quickly slipped a chain through two rings bolted to the log walls that enclosed the cells and padlocked the end links together, preventing the cell doors from being opened.

"That takes care of that," Billie said as he heard the lock click shut.

"Guess it does." Morgan walked to the opposite end of the room and tossed the ring of keys on a hook in the wall. "Too bad these walls aren't thicker," he groaned as Kensington's unending screams of protest continued. "Not much reason for both of us to stay here." He dropped into a chair, worn out from his recent exertion. "Why don't you go back and spend some time with your friends?"

Billie studied the other lawman. Although he didn't approve of his methods, he knew the marshal had only been doing his job when he arrested Jesse. And that wasn't something he planned to hold against the man. Billie held out his hand. "I'll come back and spell you later tonight."

Marshal Morgan accepted Billie's gesture and shook the sheriff's hand. "No need, I can stay here tonight." The marshal smiled. "Be obliged if you'd have something sent over for supper, though."

"Consider it done." Billie unbolted the outside door and left. With the way Kensington was yelling, he figured he'd have some cotton sent over with the marshal's meal so he could stuff his ears. "Otherwise, he won't be gettin' any sleep tonight." Billie was chuckling as he walked away.

After enduring the jubilant celebration in the courtroom for almost an hour, Jesse and Jennifer begged out of any further congratulatory wishes, explaining that KC needed a nap and they wanted some time alone to absorb all that had happened that morning. They made their way through the crowd and, when confronted by the steep stairway to the ground floor, were flabbergasted to be lifted onto the shoulders of some of their well-wishers. The men carried them down the stairs, out the large double doors of the brick building, and down the outside steps before lowering them to the boardwalk.

Jennifer laughed as Jesse indignantly protested the entire time they were being manhandled, but she was grateful when the jostling came to an end and her own boots landed on solid ground.

KC thought the entire trip a wonderful adventure and jumped up and down in Jesse's arms trying to get her mother to do it all over again.

Jesse refused to indulge the child, grumbling under her breath when Jennifer teasingly echoed the baby's pleas. She thanked the men for their assistance and then, gently pushing Jennifer before her, walked away from the courthouse where the celebration continued.

"I can't believe all those people reacting that way." Jennifer eased closer to Jesse, laughing at the memory of the wild hooting, hollering, backslapping, and revelry that had taken place after Judge Henson declared the trial concluded.

Jesse shrugged, wrapping an arm around her wife's waist. "Guess it doesn't take much for folks to have a good time around here." But she too had been surprised at the overwhelming outpouring of support from the town's citizens, mostly total strangers to them.

"Aw, come on, sweetheart," Jennifer chided. "It has to be more than that."

"I suppose they were happy to have their doubts about Logan finally laid to rest."

"But the vigilantes hanged Logan." Jennifer's brow wrinkled in thought. "Wasn't that good enough for them?"

"It's one thing to have people accuse someone of wrongdoing and secretly talk about it; it's somethin' else to have someone involved come right out and say it happened."

"You mean like Finney did?"

"Yeah. My guess is that hearing him tell what he knew about Logan just gave folks the opportunity to let go of all the bottled-up fear and doubt they've been carrying around for some time."

"So it really didn't have that much to do with us, we just happened to be caught in the middle?"

"Yep." When Jennifer frowned, Jesse said, "What's wrong?"

"It kinda takes the fun out of it when you put it that way."

"Oh, I wouldn't go disclaiming all of it, darlin'." Jesse smiled. "I'm pretty sure some of that was because they'd gotten a real kick out of seeing you wallop your pop."

"Really?" Jennifer looked down at the swollen hand carefully cradled against her chest.

"Oh, yeah." Jesse smiled proudly. "Oh, yeah."

Mary smiled as she was met at the door to the judge's chambers. "Thank you for seeing me, Judge Henson."

"Your request intrigued me, Mrs. Kensington." The judge motioned to the settee. "I must say I was surprised that, under the circumstances, you would wish to speak to me about your husband." He pulled a chair across the floor and sat down.

"Yes, I'm sure it does seem a bit strange." Mary settled back. The events of the last several days were catching up to her, and she felt exhausted. "It is my understanding that you intend to send my husband to prison here in Montana." Judge Henson nodded. "I would like you to consider an alternative sentence for him."

"I see. And why would I do that?"

"Judge Henson, it is no secret the trouble my husband has caused my daughter and her family." He nodded again. "I can't bear to bring myself to think about the consequences of some of his actions." Mary blinked back tears as she thought of Jennifer screaming in agony, her leg ripped open by the mountain lion's claws. "I fear that should my husband remain in Montana, even though he would be confined to prison," Mary looked at the judge, her eyes conveying her desperation, "he will find some way to continue his persecution of Jennifer and Jesse."

The judge considered. Sadly, the woman's concerns about her husband were likely well founded. "You spoke of an alternative."

"Yes." Mary took a deep breath and reconsidered what she was about to suggest. She didn't take long to decide that it was the best option for everyone, especially Jennifer and Jesse. "I would like to have Martin transported to a facility back East."

"A prison?"

"I believe my husband needs what a prison cannot provide. I am acquainted with the director of one of the finest mental hospitals in the East. I can assure you that if Martin is placed under his care, never again will Jennifer or Jesse have to fear his actions. I can also assure you that he will never set foot outside the hospital walls. Ever," she stressed, leaning forward and locking eyes with the judge.

Judge Henson recognized the look in Mary's eyes for what it was — a declaration that she intended to have her husband committed for life. He stood and stepped to the window behind his desk. His eyes tracked the activity along the street below. He smiled when he saw two familiar figures walking arm-in-arm, a child happily riding on the shoulders of one. He thought about the women who were still so young themselves and yet had endured so much and somehow had become all the stronger for it. He felt that the Branson family deserved a real chance at life, a chance not constantly interrupted by a man whose aberrant behavior seemed to have no bounds.

"It would be expensive to transport him that far," Judge Henson commented as he watched Jesse and Jennifer. "An expense the territory could not afford, I'm afraid."

"I will pay all costs."

"Guards will need to be hired."

"Yes."

"He must be shackled and handcuffed at all times."

"I would expect no less."

"I will need to receive confirmation from your acquaintance that he will abide with all terms I specify for your husband's confinement."

"I will telegraph him today."

"Very well, Mrs. Kensington." Judge Henson turned away from the window. "As soon as I receive the confirmation, I will draft the order. Your husband will remain in jail here until then."

"Thank you." Mary stood and offered her hand to the judge.

"I am glad that your daughter has one parent with whom to share her life." Judge Henson clasped Mary's hand and lightly squeezed it. "You should be very proud of her."

"I'm proud of all three of them." Mary smiled. "I don't know many who could go through what they have and still be standing tall."

"They are quite remarkable."

"Yes," Mary released his hand, "they are."

After a stop at the doctor's office to check Jennifer's badly bruised hand, the women walked back to Leevie's cabin for some much needed time alone. As they approached, they spotted Walks on the Wind waiting for them, leaning against the fence that surrounded the cabin.

"Figured you'd be coming back here," Walk greeted his friends. "I'm glad it all worked out."

"Thanks." Jesse grasped the Indian's outstretched arm. "Appreciate you helpin' out."

"Doesn't appear you needed my help." Walk chuckled as Jennifer threw her arms around him and hugged him tight, not caring that it caused her hand to ache.

"Having you here helped," Jennifer said when she released him.

"Then I am glad I came."

"Will you be stickin' around?" Jesse asked.

"No. I must get back to the camp. They need me at the hunt."

"Oh." Jennifer was disappointed that their friend would be leaving so soon. They had barely had any time to spend with him.

"Maybe you can stop by on your way back to Sweetwater," Walk suggested as he mounted his horse.

"Can we, Jesse? I'd still like to see the large buffalo herds."

"Don't see why not, darlin'," Jesse agreed. "We'll see you in a few days then," she told Walk.

"I'll look forward to it." Walk waved as he rode away. "Take care of that hand, Jennifer. And Jesse," he called over his shoulder, "this time, leave the posse at home."

Jesse muttered as the Indian's laughter drifted back to them.

Billie was standing in front of the courthouse watching the celebration. Hearing his name being shouted, he turned to look down the street in the direction of the sound. A smile quickly spread across his face; Ed Granger, Bette Mae, and Ruthie were riding toward him.

"Ruth." Billie waved as he ran toward the riders. He pulled his fiancée off her horse and swung her around in a circle, hugging her. "What are you doing here?"

Billie's hug was so tight, Ruthie gasped for breath. "Let me go, honey," she said with a laugh. "I can't breathe."

"Sorry." Billie loosened his hold but kept the woman in his arms. "So, what are you doing here?"

"We came to help Miss Jesse."

"What's all the celebratin' fer?" Bette Mae asked as she dropped from her horse.

"Trial's over. Jesse was found innocent of all charges."

"Of course she was," Bette Mae said, exasperated. "That don' 'splain the celebratin'."

Billie grinned, unable to take his eyes off Ruthie. "It's so good to see you."

"It's good to see you, too," Ed teased the lovestruck sheriff as he joined the others. "Damn, that's a loud bunch." He raised his voice to be heard over the revelers.

"It sure is," Bette Mae agreed. "Where are Jesse and Jennifer?"

Billie looked back over his shoulder at the crowd that seemed to have grown in the last few minutes and was getting pretty wild, many of the celebrants having visited the numerous nearby saloons.

"Why don't we find someplace quiet?" Billie suggested. He helped Ed gather up the horses and tie them to a nearby hitching rail. Grabbing Ruthie's hand, he led the group across the street and down a narrow passage between two buildings. A short walk brought them to the banks of Grasshopper Creek, and they settled down in the shade of a large cottonwood tree to talk.

Jennifer tucked KC snugly into bed, bending to kiss the child's forehead. For a few moments, she stood beside the bed and simply watched the baby sleep. The sound of soft crying drew her attention to the other side of the cabin. The curtain that normally hung down the center of the one room building was pulled back, and she could see Jesse huddled on the floor at the base of the far wall, her face buried in her hands. The ragged movement of the hunched shoulders gave away her quiet sobbing. "Oh, sweetheart." Jennifer quickly crossed the room and slid down beside Jesse, gathering the weeping woman into her arms.

Jesse fell into Jennifer's embrace, her sobs deepening as she released her emotions, letting them drain out of her with her tears.

Jennifer held her grieving wife, tenderly stroking her hair and gently rocking their joined bodies. She wasn't sure what had precipitated Jesse's breakdown, but she was extremely grateful it had finally happened. It hadn't escaped her notice, the toll being taken by Jesse's need to maintain a brave front through all that was happening. It was quite amazing to Jennifer that her wife had managed to go as long as she had before breaking down.

After several minutes, Jesse wiped at her eyes with her shirtsleeve. The wet cloth did little to dry the moisture from her face. Jennifer pulled a napkin off the nearby table and handed it to Jesse. "Here, sweetheart."

"Thanks." Jesse's voice was shaky and raspy.

"Do you want to talk about it?" Jennifer asked softly, prepared to drop the subject if Jesse balked.

"Not much to talk about." Jesse raised her head; her eyes were red and puffy. "I was reading that paper again, the one the judge gave us, and..." She had to stop as her voice caught in her throat, a deep sob trembling through her. "I can't believe she's really ours," Jesse cried, fresh tears spilling from her eyes and tracking down her cheeks. "She's really ours."

Jennifer felt her own eyes fill with tears. KC was truly their daughter, the judge had seen to that. And no one, not even the Reverend Tobias, could ever question that again. "Yes, sweetheart," she whispered as tears streamed down her face, "KC is our daughter."

"Ours." Jesse smiled as she repeated the word.

"Yes." Jennifer returned the smile. "Ours."

Bette Mae wiped tears of laughter from her eyes. "I can't believe we missed that."

"I can't say that it surprises me." Ed laughed. "She's got a lot more fire than most give her credit for."

Billie had spent the better part of an hour filling in the new arrivals on the events of the trial. He had just finished telling them about Jennifer punching her father. Billie slapped his knee. "I sure didn't see it coming. When I saw Kensington throw that door open and strut into the courtroom, I expected Jesse would be the one to thump him. I can tell you, I wasn't the only one who was shocked when Jennifer beat her to the punch."

"In more ways than one, it seems." Bette Mae started laughing all over again.

"Then what happened, Billie?" Ruthie asked. She was sitting next to the sheriff, being careful to keep a respectable distance between them.

"The judge ordered Kensington arrested, and he refused to believe it was happening. Damn fool said that he couldn't be arrested because Harrington had promised Jesse would be the one to go to prison."

"What ta hell does that dandy have to do wit' all this?" Bette Mae asked.

"That's exactly what Jennifer asked her father. Seems the two of them made a deal that Harrington would have Jesse sent to prison, and in return, Kensington would sell him the Slipper."

"Why that..." Ed's hands clenched into fists. "I ought to go over to that jail and thump him myself."

"Won't do ya any good, Ed." Bette Mae tried to calm the big man. "His head is so damn thick, even yer big fists wouldn' have much effect on him. All you'd manage to do is break yer hands."

"I'd still like a chance to smack him," Ed grumbled, but he smiled, knowing Bette Mae was probably right.

"I wouldn't worry too much about Kensington." Billie chuckled. "I think Judge Henson plans to make sure he spends the next several years locked away at Deer Lodge."

"I would hope so!" Ruthie exclaimed. "All the things that man has done." She shook her head. "I can't imagine how anyone could be so mean."

"Some men just don' know how ta take 'no' fer an answer." Bette Mae patted the younger woman on the leg. "Ya remember tha' and make sure ya don' let Billie get away with anythin' after ya get hitched." She snickered as the lawman glowered at her.

Ed joined in the friendly teasing. "Bette Mae is right, Billie. Ruthie should know these things before you put the ring on her finger."

"How are you feeling?" Jennifer asked, squirming to get her leg into a more comfortable position.

Jesse immediately picked up on her wife's discomfort. "Damn, darlin'." Jesse jumped to her feet and helped Jennifer off the floor where they had been sitting for some time. "You shouldn't be sitting down there." She pulled a chair over and eased Jennifer into it. "Is that better?"

"Yes, thank you. But what would really be good is one of your massages."

Jesse grinned. "I'm pretty sure that can be arranged. Of course we are supposed to meet the others for dinner in a bit."

"Not for another couple of hours," Jennifer said hopefully.

Jesse tilted her head and pretended to contemplate. "KC is asleep in the bed."

"The floor isn't that uncomfortable." Jennifer tried to keep a straight face but failed. "Especially if I were to be lying on top of a nice soft blanket."

Jesse was suddenly overcome by the deep love she had for the woman smiling up at her. Dropping to her knees in front of Jennifer, she slowly reached up and captured Jennifer's face between her hands. Thumbs traced over smooth cheeks and around soft lips as she looked into the depths of Jennifer's eyes. "I love you so much."

Jennifer leaned forward, placing a hand behind Jesse's neck and gently pulling the rancher toward her. She sighed as their lips met.

The kiss began tenderly but quickly escalated into much more. Only their need to breathe eventually forced the women apart. "You stay right there." Jesse pushed up from the floor. "I'll be right back with that soft blanket."

"That was really somethin'," Bette Mae stretched her arms behind her and leaned back, "the judge puttin' it in writin' about my little angel."

"I'll say." Billie scratched his head. "You sure could have knocked Jesse over with a feather when he told them what he had done."

"Bet it didn't make that preacher too happy." Ed tossed a pebble into the creek.

"Nope. He left the room like a nest of bees had swarmed into his britches. Don't think they've seen the last of him yet."

"Let's hope he takes some notice of what the judge told him." Ed tossed another pebble and watched it disappeared into the murky water. "I doubt if Jesse will take much more off of him."

"I think he's got a lot more to worry about from Jennifer than Jesse." Billie laughed. "She sure took out after him during his testimony."

"I hate ta be the one ta break this up," Bette Mae sat up and dusted off her hands, "but we need ta be gettin' some rooms for the night. And I want ta be seein' Jesse and Jennifer and KC."

"We should be able to get you rooms at the Goodrich, and they've got a stable for your horses." Billie stood and held out his hands to help Ruthie up. "As for Jesse and Jennifer, they wanted some time to put KC down for a nap, but we made plans to meet up for dinner later. You can come along." He pulled Ruthie into a hug after tugging her to her feet. "Bet they'll be mighty glad to see ya."

"Bet they'll be mighty surprised, ya mean." Bette Mae laughed. "Come on. I could use a little nap myself."

Jesse carried KC as she and Jennifer walked into the Chinese restaurant where they were supposed to meet their family and friends. They were surprised to see Ed, Bette Mae, and Ruthie waiting with the others.

"Oh, my gosh, when did you get here?" Jennifer asked with a welcoming smile.

"They rode in 'bout an hour after you left the celebration," Billie said.

"Figured you'd be at the jail tonight, Billie," Jesse said. "Ruthie, you came, too?"

"I was worried about Billie," Ruthie explained shyly.

"We're glad you came." Jennifer hugged Ruthie. "And I know Billie is glad to see you," she teased.

"Marshal Morgan is stayin' there tonight. And you're right, Jennifer." He smiled at his fiancée. "I was mighty glad to see Ruth ride into town."

"Give me a hug 'fore I burst," Bette Mae cried. "You had me so worried." She sniffled as Jesse and Jennifer embraced her.

KC protested being squished by the hugging women. "Mommy, uck."

"Come here, my little angel." Bette Mae snatched the baby away from Jesse. KC was soon giggling under the barrage of kisses the older woman was placing all over her face.

"Guess we need to add a few folks to our reservation," Jesse said.

"It's all taken care of, Jesse." Ed happily gathered Jesse and Jennifer into one of his bear hugs as soon as Bette Mae released them. "We took over the entire restaurant for the night."

Jesse stared at her friend in amazement."

"Yep," Billie said. "It's all ours. We figured you could use some time without half the town watchin' your every move."

Jennifer laughed. "I'm not going to deny that."

"Jennifer?" Mary hesitantly approached her daughter, unsure of what kind of reception she would receive, given what her husband had been responsible for.

Jennifer was just as timid, unsure how her mother felt about her behavior in the courtroom. She hadn't been raised to strike her parents. "Mother?"

"I'm sorry, Jennifer. If I could have done something to stop him—"

"Oh, Mother." Jennifer closed the distance between them and hugged her tightly. "I don't blame you."

"I love you, Jennifer."

"I love you, too."

"Now that ya got that out of yer gizzards," Bette Mae muttered as Jennifer and her mother shared a tearful reunion, "what say we stop the cryin' and get ta eatin' this here fancy food Billie's been braggin' 'bout all afternoon. I ain't had a decent thing ta eat since we left Sweetwater."

Jesse moved close to Jennifer, ready to fulfill any need she might have during what appeared to be the start of a long and emotional night. "I agree. Let's eat, I'm starved."

"Yum." KC loudly let her feelings be known. "Yum, yum, yum."

"What's the matter, little angel?" Bette Mae clucked to the child. "Ain't yer mommas been feedin' ya?"

CHAPTER THIRTY-FOUR

"Good morning, darlin," Jesse whispered as Jennifer stretched in her arms.

"Morning, sweetheart." Jennifer squinted to block the bright sunlight filtering through the cabin's shaded window. "Seems we slept in this morning."

"Guess we must have needed it." Jesse tilted slightly to her side so she could slip her arm under Jennifer without waking KC, still sound asleep on top of her.

"Guess we did," Jennifer snuggled closer to Jesse's warm body, groaning when she couldn't get the skin to skin contact she craved. At home, they always slept in the nude, but here, in Leevie's bed, they wore nightshirts. She missed not being able to press against her wife's warm skin.

"What's wrong?" Jesse asked, concerned at the frustration she was noticing. "Does your hand hurt?"

"No." Jennifer grinned sheepishly. "I just miss not being able to feel you."

"Me, too. I can't wait until we're back home in our own bed." Both women flinched at the words as soon as they were spoken. "Sorry." Jesse frowned and sighed. "I keep forgetting it's all gone."

Jennifer slipped her uninjured hand out from under the blankets and tenderly touched Jesse's face, "I'm so sorry he—"

"No." Jesse took Jennifer's hand into her own. "I don't ever again want to hear you apologize for what your father has done. Not ever." She brought Jennifer's hand to her lips and lovingly kissed each finger. "You're not responsible for him, darlin', or for anything he's done."

"I know you're right." Jennifer's brow knitted in thought. "It's just—"

"No." Jesse pressed a finger against Jennifer's lips. "What's done is done. We can't change the past, but we have the chance to go forward, now that he's going where he can never hurt us again."

"What if he escapes?" Jennifer asked quietly.

"From what I've heard of the Deer Lodge prison, no one has ever escaped. I doubt if your father will be the first."

"He could pay somebody off."

"You heard Thomas last night," Jesse reminded Jennifer. "He's already taken steps to prevent your father's access to the family and company assets. Your father won't have anything to bribe anyone with."

Jennifer was quiet for a moment. Her brother had promised that he would make sure their father never again was able to bother her and Jesse, but she couldn't help feeling that he would never stop trying. "I don't like him being so close, Jesse. I just don't trust him."

"I know." Jesse curled her arm around Jennifer, pulling her tight. "I don't much care for him bein' so close either, but I guess there's not much we can do about it, except put our faith in the law to keep him inside the prison and away from us."

"I'm not sure I have that much faith," she grumbled, laying her head on Jesse's shoulder.

"One's thing for sure," Jesse said. "Once Judge Henson gets done with the territorial governor, I doubt if your father will ever talk his way out of prison."

"Let's hope not."

KC woke to the sound of her mothers' quiet voices. She lifted her head and looked first at Jesse, then at Jennifer, to make sure her mothers were both in bed with her.

Reassured, she smiled brightly and pushed herself upright to sit on Jesse's stomach. A frown replaced her smile as she reached back, patting her soiled diaper. "Uck," she proclaimed.

Jennifer laughed. "And good morning to you, too."

"Pftttt."

"I guess we better get up and dressed," Jesse said ruefully, loath to relinquish the feel of having her family together and safe. "I'm sure Bette Mae and your mother will be wantin' to spend time with us today." When Jennifer sighed deeply but didn't answer, Jesse hooked a finger under Jennifer's chin and gently tilted her face so she could look into her wife's eyes. "What's going on in your pretty head?"

"The truth?"

"Of course."

"I know that Bette Mae and Ed only arrived yesterday, and it probably isn't the best of manners considering they came so far..."

"But?"

"I'd really like to just pack up KC and head back to Sweetwater."

Jesse was relieved to hear Jennifer express the same desire she had about leaving Bannack as quickly as possible. "What about your mother and Thomas?"

"Thomas is going back East from here. As for Mother, maybe she could ride back with the others," Jennifer said quietly.

"Are you sure that's what you want?"

"What I want, sweetheart," Jennifer propped herself up on an elbow, her eyes never leaving Jesse's, "is to have some time alone with you and KC. I want to be someplace quiet where we can be a family again."

"I know what you mean. I feel like I've been in the center of a whirlwind ever since we got here."

"That's because you have." Jennifer caressed Jesse's face. "Can we just go, Jesse? Just us?"

"Of course we can, darlin'." Jesse leaned forward and kissed her wife's wrinkled forehead. "After breakfast, I'll talk to Bette Mae and explain what's going on. She'll be disappointed, but she'll understand. And I'm sure Ed and Billie will be glad to have Mary travel back to Sweetwater with them. We'll need to find a store, other than Carpenter's, to buy supplies. We'll leave as soon as we say our goodbyes."

"That sounds wonderful." Her voice husky with emotion, Jennifer said, "Take us home, sweetheart."

"I love you." Jesse pulled Jennifer back down to her and captured her lips for a long, lingering kiss.

After several moments of watching her mothers' kissing, KC bounced on Jesse. "Uck, uck, uck." The baby giggled loudly as Jesse's long arm swept her off her perch and she found herself buried under an avalanche of tickles and kisses.

Billie knocked on the jail door and called out, "Morning, Marshal." He waited patiently while Morgan unbolted the door. "I've got your breakfast," Billie said when the door was pulled open. "And some for the prisoners."

"Morning, Sheriff." Morgan pushed the door shut and slid the bolt back into place as Billie set the heavy tray down on the table in the corner of the room.

"Bit quieter in here this morning," Billie commented.

"Fool finally ran out of steam a few hours ago," Morgan grumbled as he sat at the table and removed the cloth covering the food on the tray. "Thanks for bringing this over." He poured himself a much-needed cup of coffee.

"Want me to spell ya for a while?" Billie asked as he filled a second cup with coffee and sipped at it. "You could go over to the Goodrich and get some sleep."

"Thanks, I could sure use some, but I'm leaving for Deer Lodge with Thompson as soon as I eat." Morgan lifted a forkful of eggs to his mouth.

"What about Kensington?"

"Judge Henson said to leave him here," Morgan answered around a mouthful of bacon. "Seems other arrangements been made for him."

"What arrangements?"

Morgan shrugged. "Guess you'll have to ask the judge. He didn't give me any details. I will need you to stay here and guard Kensington until I get back; shouldn't be more than three or four days. Sorry to delay your return to Sweetwater but I've got no choice. I can't leave him here without a guard, and the judge wants Thompson taken to Deer Lodge today."

Billie carried a plate of food to the cell occupied by Marcus Thompson and slid open the cover blocking the small slot beside the door. "Grab this if you want to eat," he told the despondent man inside. He handed the food over, slid the cover shut, and returned for the remaining plate. "Guess I don't mind staying. Just wish I knew what the judge had in mind," he said as he approached Kensington's cell.

Morgan stood and lifted the ring of keys from the hook on the wall. "Maybe he's sending him to another prison, one back East," he said as he crossed the room to unlock the chain securing the door to Kensington's cell. Unlike the other cell, the one occupied by Jennifer's father did not have a feeding slot. The plate of food would have to be placed inside the cell within reach of the chained prisoner.

"Maybe." Billie stepped inside the dark, windowless cell to find Kensington asleep on the floor. "No sense waking him up." He set the plate down, then backed out of the cell.

Jesse and Jennifer claimed their horses from the livery and left Dusty and Blaze tied to the hitching rail in front of the Goodrich Hotel, where they were to meet the others for a group meal before leaving Bannack.

KC rode atop Boy, her small hands clutching the horse's mane, while Jesse walked beside the big horse, keeping a close eye on the baby to make sure she didn't lose her balance. Jennifer walked alongside Jesse as they made their way to Yankee Flats at the end of town. Leevie had told them where to find a store so that they would not have to buy their supplies from Carpenter's.

"Mining camps aren't very pretty, are they, Jesse?" Jennifer commented as she looked at their surroundings.

The hillsides were spotted with exploratory pits dug by miners hoping to find their pot of gold, piles of discarded dirt and rock marking the mouth of each opening. Hastily thrown together shacks were packed closely on any available piece of open ground, with outhouses interspersed among them. There was very little vegetation along the town's streets or on the hillsides, as every usable piece of wood had been consumed for fuel or building material. Even the creek, running under the wooden bridge they were crossing, had little to offer, its waters uninvitingly murky while the surface was a rainbow of unnatural colors caused by the mining activity along its banks.

Jennifer was sure that this was one creek in which her talented wife would be unable to find any fish to catch, if she had an inclination to try.

"Something else to be said about Sweetwater," Jesse muttered as she surveyed the scene.

Jennifer was shocked at the thought of their small, picturesque valley being so mistreated. "Is this what Sweetwater will become when Harrington's mine begins operating? Jesse, we can't let that happen." The thought was so disheartening, she almost cried.

"If what Billie says is true, it won't."

"What did he say?"

"Told me last night that Thaddeus thinks the Songbird was salted." Jesse laughed at the perplexed look Jennifer was giving her. "It means that the miner who sold the claim to Harrington made it look as if it is rich in gold, but it really isn't."

"How could he do that?" Jennifer asked, hoping that it was true and Harrington wouldn't destroy the beautiful valley they called home.

"Many ways to do it, depending on the type of mine and what kind of ore it's supposed to have. Helps, too, if you can bribe an assayer to write up a report supporting your claims."

"Do you think Harrington did that?"

"Billie didn't know. Seems Thaddeus was going to do some pokin' around and see if he could find out any more. Don't think it matters much if Harrington was in on it or not," Jesse smirked at the thought, "since he'll surely end up having to answer for it, one way or another."

"If it's true, I bet his investors won't be too happy," Jennifer sniggered. "Oh, my. What about Mayor Perkins?"

"I doubt if he knew. Somehow I don't think Harrington would tell him much about his dealings. Perkins is just a convenience for him. When the time comes, Harrington will throw him to the dogs to save his own neck."

"Doesn't seem quite fair."

"Don't worry about Perkins, darlin'." Jesse smiled. "Everyone in Sweetwater knows he's a fool. Folks won't be too hard on him."

"Are you sure?" Jennifer didn't really like the pompous mayor, but she didn't dislike him either. He was more like that odd uncle every family has and simply tries to ignore at family functions, knowing that he will do something to embarrass himself and his relatives before the night is over.

"Yep. They'll give him a hard time about it for a while, but it'll be forgotten before long. That must be the store Leevie told us about." She nodded toward a large canvas tent several yards in front of them.

"What was your first clue?" Jennifer teased.

"Oh, I don't know," Jesse drawled. "Maybe that there big sign that says 'Mercantile'."

The women laughed as they led Boy to the tent and tied him to a hitching rail. Jesse reached up to lift KC off the horse's back. "Come on, Sunshine." She sat the baby in the crook of her arm. "Let's get our supplies so we can go home."

When Jesse and Jennifer returned from their walk to Yankee Flats, Mary asked to speak to them. Sensing that she really wanted to talk to Jennifer alone, Jesse encouraged her wife to accompany her mother inside. Now Mary and Jennifer were sitting in the lobby of the Goodrich Hotel.

"I've decided to return East with Thomas."

Jennifer wasn't surprised by her mother's comment, but it did sadden her. "I see."

"I've enjoyed my stay with you, Jennifer. And I think Jesse is a wonderful woman, and I'm so very glad that you found her. And KC is a delight. I'll miss not seeing her take her first steps. But we both know that the frontier is not where I belong. This isn't the kind of life I'm used to or comfortable with. My home is back East. That's where I am needed."

"I'll miss you, Mother, but I understand. I'll send your things to you," Jennifer offered, though there were few of her mother's belongings left at the ranch.

"No, keep them." Mary smiled. "It'll give me an excuse to come visit."

"You don't need an excuse."

"I know." Mary reached over and covered Jennifer's hands with her own. "I would very much like to come back and see how my granddaughter is growing."

"Jesse and I would love to see you, too."

"Jennifer, I want to tell you something about your father."

Jennifer felt her stomach lurch and then tighten into a knot.

"With Judge Henson's permission, I have made arrangements to have your father transported to a hospital in the East. It's run by a friend of mine."

"The hospital for the insane?" Jennifer asked, aware that her mother's long-time friend was the chief of staff at a major mental hospital.

"Yes. I believe that your father needs treatment for this sickness that has taken over his mind, treatment that he would not have access to in prison."

"But a hospital, Mother? That means he could be released." Much as she didn't want her father in Montana, Jennifer definitely didn't want him someplace he could just walk away from and be free to threaten her family again.

"No. Judge Henson has sent instructions such that, should your father ever be declared sane, he is to be returned to Montana to complete his prison term. But I am quite sure that day shall never come." She hoped Jennifer didn't realize the true import of her words.

"Mother, are you sure you want to do this?" Jennifer asked softly. "After all, he is your husband."

"Yes, dear." Mary sighed. "He is still my husband, but he is no longer the man I married. He has changed. I don't know what has caused him to become what he is today. I'm hoping the doctors will be able to discover the reason and can bring back the Martin Kensington I used to know. But, until then, my concern is for your safety, and for Jesse and KC. I could not bear to have your father cause your family any more pain, so I will accept what I must do."

"Does Thomas know?"

"Yes."

"Is he...?"

"It does not pleasure him any more than it does you or me, but he has agreed it is for the best."

"When will you leave?"

"We must wait until the official papers agreeing to the terms of his commitment are received and approved by Judge Henson. Then Thomas and I will accompany him East."

"You and Thomas can't take him back alone!"

"No." Mary patted her daughter's hand. "Judge Henson has offered Marshal Morgan's services, and deputies will be hired to assist him. Thomas and I will only travel with them. Your father will be Marshal Morgan's responsibility."

"I can't say that this news makes me unhappy. In fact, I'm relieved that Father won't be in Montana because I do fear he'll never give up hounding me or Jesse. I wish..."

"What?"

"I wish I knew why he hated me so."

Mary sighed. She had no answer. "I know there aren't many of them, Jennifer, but try to remember the good memories you have of your father. At one time, he loved you very much. Perhaps some day you will come to forgive him."

"I'm sorry, Mother. I might be able to forgive what he has done to me, but I'll never forgive him for what he has done to Jesse."

"I know."

Billie had carried the chairs out of the jail, and he and Ruthie were sitting in the shade behind Carpenter's Store. From their position, he could keep an eye on the jail yet not have to listen to Kensington's incessant ravings.

"Ya'd think he'd get tired of yelling at the walls," Billie muttered, rubbing his temples in a fruitless attempt to lessen the throbbing brought on by Kensington's howling. He had been listening to the prisoner's tirade since the marshal left with Thompson that morning. When his fiancée had knocked on the jail door, he wasn't about to have her sit inside the dark building and listen to the disturbed man.

"He must realize that you can't let him out."

"Don't think he realizes much about all the trouble he's in. He still thinks Harrington is going to get him out of this."

"Can he?"

"Nah." Billie gave up trying to get rid of his headache and decided, instead, to enjoy Ruthie's visit. He was going to be spending the next few days at the jail, and he didn't want to waste any time he had with the woman he loved. He smiled shyly as he scooted his chair closer to Ruthie's. "Harrington is going to be in as much trouble as Kensington if Thaddeus is right about the Songbird."

"Do you think he is, Billie?"

"Good bet that he is." Billie reached for Ruthie's hands. "I never saw that old miner with anything but holes in his pockets. Hard to believe he was working such a rich vein and never had anything to show for it."

"If it's true, what will happen to Sweetwater?"

"Reckon we'll have to wait and see, but we'll probably get a new hotel and bank out of it. Don't know who'll be staying in the hotel since the stage never brings more than a handful of folks to town each week and the Slipper has plenty of room for them. But we can sure use the bank. Folks don't like havin' ta travel to Bozeman all the time."

"What about all those men who came to work for Mr. Harrington?"

"They'll find other towns to go to. Won't be much use in staying in Sweetwater if there's no work for them."

"They could help Miss Jesse build a new house for her and Miss Jennifer."

"Honey, I think Jesse will be wantin' to build her family's new home all by herself."

"You're probably right." Ruthie smiled and shyly made her wishes known. "Maybe someday you can build us our own home."

"Ain't nothin' in the whole world I'd rather do, honey. And that's a fact."

Jesse walked down the narrow alley between Carpenter's store and the building next to it. She smiled when she came out at the back of the buildings and saw the couple staring into each other's eyes. How often had she and Jennifer done the same thing? She wondered, *How often do we still do it?* She chuckled to herself.

"See, I told ya your Uncle Billie would be here, Sunshine," Jesse said in a voice loud enough to warn Billie and Ruthie of her approach.

Ruthie tried to pull her hands free, but Billie held on to them. "Figured you'd be stoppin' by. Ruth saw your horses in front of the Goodrich. You plannin' on leavin' today?"

"Yep. Can't wait to put Bannack behind us." She lowered KC from her shoulders to let the baby sit in Billie's lap.

"Guess no one can blame you for that. Sure you want to travel alone?"

"We need some time, Billie." The last few days had taken a huge toll on her, and Jesse wasn't ashamed to admit it.

"Guess that's ta be expected."

"Will you be going straight back to Sweetwater, Miss Jesse?" Ruthie asked as she watched KC in her fiancé's lap. She smiled at the thought that one day he would be holding a child of their own.

"No. We'll be spending a few days at the buffalo camp with Walk. It'll give us time to get over what happened here."

KC lifted her arms to her mother. "Up."

"Sorry you can't join us at the Goodrich, Billie." Jesse lifted the baby back into her arms.

"Wish I could, Jesse." Billie stood. "Be nice to get away from Kensington's hollerin'."

"Big man, big mouth," Jesse muttered as she listened to the muffled shouting coming from the jail. "Will you be joining us, Ruthie?"

Ruthie turned a light shade of pink. "I was hopin' to stay here with Billie."

"Then that's what you should do." Jesse grinned at the shy woman. "If you love him, don't ever let him out of your sight."

"Thank you, Miss Jesse."

"Do me a favor on your ride back to Sweetwater, Billie?"

"Sure, Jesse."

"Work on getting her to drop the 'Miss'."

"I'll try, Jesse, but she's a might hard-headed when it comes to that."

"She must be hard-headed to put up with you." Jesse laughed and offered her hand to her friend.

Laughing at her good-natured teasing, Billie clasped the hand. "Have a safe trip home."

Jesse kept hold of her friend's hand. "I appreciate all you did for me, Billie."

"I just wish I could have done more."

"You did more than could have been expected. It could have cost you your job."

"Losing a friend would've been worse, Jesse."

"Thank you."

"You're welcome. Now you better be gettin' back to the Goodrich. Isn't Jennifer waiting for you?"

"She's talking to Mary." Jesse finally released her friend's hand. "But I did tell her I wouldn't be long."

"Then we'll see you in Sweetwater."

"Count on it." Jesse turned to walk away. "Seems like we'll be needin' to make some wedding plans when we all get back."

"I wouldn't do it without you, Jesse," Billie called after her. "And you can tell Jennifer that we expect her to stand up for Ruth when the day comes."

"She's already talking to Bette Mae about that," Jesse said as she disappeared back into the alley.

"Will they be all right?" Ruthie asked as Billie sat.

"They'll be fine. After what they've been through, nothin' and nobody will ever hurt them again. They've done paid their dues."

"I hope you're right, Billie."

"Me, too."

Jesse carried KC into the hotel lobby and saw the gloomy looks on Mary and Jennifer's faces. "Is something wrong?"

"No, everything is fine." Jennifer held out her arms when KC reached for her. "Mother was just telling me about some new developments concerning Father."

"Anything I need to know?"

"Yes, but why don't we talk while we get this cute little thing," Jennifer tickled KC, "some fresh britches before the others arrive."

"I think I'll freshen up, myself." Mary rose from her chair. "I'll meet you and the others in the dining room."

They took KC into the hotel office located in an alcove behind the lobby desk. The desk clerk let them use it whenever they needed to change KC's diaper so that Jennifer would not have to climb the stairs to her mother's room or walk the length of the town back to Leevie's cabin. Jesse remained quiet while Jennifer recounted her conversation with her mother.

With the baby changed, Jennifer sat in the desk chair and set KC on the floor. She looked over at her wife leaning against the office wall, her arms folded across her chest and a scowl on her face. "Sweetheart, what are you thinking?"

Jesse was watching KC crawling around the floor. The baby seemed to sense her mother's eyes and twisted around to grin at her before resuming her exploration of the room. Jesse was again amazed how much the ginger-haired, blue-eyed baby resembled Jennifer. It was hard most times to remember her wife hadn't actually given birth to their daughter.

Jesse lifted her eyes to gaze at her wife. "I'm thinking that having your father locked away back East where he can never hurt you again..." she took the few steps to where Jennifer sat and knelt down in front of her, "is the best news I've had since you agreed to become my wife."

Jennifer raised her hands to tenderly cup Jesse's face and gently pulled the rancher close. "Jesse Marie Branson, becoming your wife is the best thing that *ever* happened to me." She tugged Jesse forward, and their lips met.

With her mothers preoccupied, KC was free to investigate anything that looked interesting. The rows of shelves at the back of the room attracted the baby's curiosity, and she crawled toward them. The shelves were full of all kinds of different shaped and colored boxes, and KC couldn't wait to see what was inside each one. She found the boxes on the bottom shelf to be too heavy for her to move, so she pulled herself upright using the heavy boxes for support. On wobbling legs, she placed one hand on the shelf to steady herself while she reached into the nearest box on the shelf next up from the bottom and pulled out a handful of shiny objects. Thinking these looked like something she'd like to play with, KC opened her hand, dropping the items back into the box. To get the box off the shelf so she could get to its appealing contents, KC released the hand steadying her and reached as far back on the box as she could, and then, with a grunt, she pulled the box toward her.

Much to KC's delight, the box began to move. She was in the way of it coming completely off the shelf. But she didn't let that deter her as she continued to tug. Inching the container toward her until more of the box's weight was off the shelf than on, the box started to fall. Unable to do anything but go where the box took her, KC was forced over backward, falling to the floor. The box followed her down, crashing loudly as it spilled its contents.

"What the..." Jesse jerked away from Jennifer as the crash echoed about the room.

"KC?" Jennifer immediately began looking for the one she was sure was the source of the commotion.

Hearing the crash, the desk clerk hurried into the room. "Goodness, is everything all right?"

Jesse shook her head at the mess her daughter's curiosity had made. "What have you done now?"

"Ook." KC sat in the midst of a jumble of door keys. Holding up two hands full of the shiny metal objects, she proudly showed her new toys to her mother.

"Those aren't yours," Jennifer scolded the baby as Jesse picked her up and set her in her momma's lap.

KC sniffled when the keys were taken away from her. She ducked her head, cuddling against Jennifer, her lower lip poking out as she watched Jesse put the keys back into their box.

"Sorry 'bout this," Jesse apologized to the hotel clerk. "She's a bit curious when she's in new places."

"She can't hurt those keys. I'm just glad she didn't get hurt when they fell on her."

"She's got to learn not to go sticking her nose where it don't belong." Jesse reached over and tapped KC on the nose.

"Your mommy's right, KC." Jennifer spoke softly to the baby. "You shouldn't play with things that don't belong to you. Now look at the mess you made."

The clerk was having a hard time keeping a straight face, given the abject look of misery on the face of the disappointed baby. After Jesse replaced the box onto the shelf where KC had found it, the clerk reached inside and pulled out one brand new shiny room key. "Here ya go." He handed the key to KC. "A souvenir of your stay at the Goodrich Hotel."

KC snatched the key from his hand, a big smile replacing her pout. "Ook." She held up her prize so Jesse could see.

"It's a good thing you're as cute as your momma," she lifted the baby from Jennifer, "otherwise, I don't know what I'd do with you." She held out a hand to help Jennifer up.

"Thank you," Jennifer said to the desk clerk. "For letting us use this room and for being so nice to KC."

"Aw." The clerk grinned. "She's a cutie. Saw that the first time you carried her in here." He had been the first person Jesse and Jennifer had talked to when they came to Bannack after finding KC. "I'm just glad it's you having to keep track of her and not me," he teased.

"I'm just glad we only have one of her." Jesse laughed as she shook the man's hand. "Appreciate all you've done for us."

"Never much cared for Logan," the man said. "Least I can do for the ladies who finally rid this town of him."

"You could have done it yourself, you know." Jesse would never forget that she had been forced to kill two men because the citizens of Bannack had refused to stand up to their own sheriff.

The clerk took a deep breath. "I'm not proud of my actions. Fact is, I'm downright ashamed that I wasn't more forthcoming with you at the time. But I'm man enough to admit my mistakes. I know there isn't much I can say to make it up to you, but I truly regret what you had to go through."

"That means a lot," Jesse told him graciously.

CHAPTER THIRTY-FIVE

Jesse carried KC as she and Jennifer entered the dining room at the back of the Goodrich Hotel. Their friends and family were already seated at tables pushed together along one side of the room. The couple nodded to Judge Henson as they passed the table where he was enjoying his midday meal.

"'Bout time ya showed up," Bette Mae said by way of greeting. "We was beginnin' ta think ya took off without saying goodbye."

"We wouldn't do that, Bette Mae."

"I know that, Jennifer. I was just joshin' ya. Now, let me hold my little angel. Seems like it's been forever since I seen her." She held her arms out for the baby.

"Show Bette Mae where her nose is," Jesse whispered to KC before placing her in the older woman's waiting arms.

Doing as her mommy instructed, KC grabbed a hold of Bette Mae's nose. "Ooonnnkkk."

"Bless my soul," Bette Mae exclaimed, startled.

A huge grin on her face, KC looked to Jesse for assurance she had done as her mother wanted.

"That's my girl." Jesse laughed, winking at the baby.

Jennifer slapped Jesse's arm. "You shouldn't be teaching her to do that," she admonished, trying not to smile at the flabbergasted look on Bette Mae's face.

Ed guffawed. "First time I've known Bette Mae to be speechless."

Bette Mae tweaked the baby's nose. "I'm mighty embarrassed ta say that with this little one around, I bet it ain't the last." She joined the others in a good-natured laugh.

Two empty chairs sat between Mary and Bette Mae, and Jesse pulled one out for Jennifer. "Here ya go, darlin'."

"Thank you." Jennifer sat, then waited for Jesse to sit beside her. "I don't know about the rest of you, but I'm starving. Shall we order?"

"Yep." KC answered for everyone.

After their meal was completed and the dirty dishes removed from their table, Jesse talked a little more about the plans she and Jennifer had made to return to Sweetwater ahead of the others.

"I know that you all need to wait here for Billie for a bit longer, but Jennifer and I...well, we really want to get outta Bannack." Jesse grimaced. "This has all been mighty hard on us."

"I can't argue with that." Bette Mae frowned. "But I still think it would be better if'n we all went back ta Sweetwater together. Couldn' ya wait just a couple days?"

"She's right, Jesse," Ed said. "Considering all that's happened, it might be best."

"Jennifer," Mary turned to her daughter beside her, "I would feel better if you didn't go back alone. After all, you'll have plenty of time together when you get back to the ranch."

"We'll be fine, Mother." Jennifer spoke to her mother but was responding to the others as well. "I want some time with Jesse. We're going to have much to do when we get back to Sweetwater." Though she didn't say the words, everyone at the table knew she was referring to the loss of their home and the rebuilding of their lives.

"I understand, but there's so much that can happen, and you'll be alone."

"I have faith in Jesse." Jennifer reached for her wife's hand and squeezed it when she felt Jesse entwine their fingers. "She'll get us home safely."

"Besides," Jesse said to lighten the heavy mood that had descended over the group, "we plan to meet up with Walk and spend a few days with him. Jennifer wants some time to see the buffalo herds, and I promised we would."

"They're a sight to behold." Ed picked up on Jesse's intentions. "Hard to believe so many animals living together. You'd think they'd want more elbow room," he said with a chuckle.

"Must be like some of the cities in the East," Thomas added. "Thousands of people crowded into such a small area."

KC looked at her uncle who was sitting across the table from Bette Mae. The baby took notice of the similarities between the man and her momma and decided she wanted a closer look. Before Bette Mae knew what was happening, KC crawled onto the table and made her way to Thomas. She dropped into her uncle's lap, then pulled herself upright using his shirt for handholds. Leaning forward, the baby looked sharply at her uncle's face.

Thomas smiled and instinctively put a hand on the baby's back to steady her. The baby recognized the man's smile. "Momma?"

"Guess she must see the family resemblance," Jesse remarked. "You do look alike."

"Much more than Howard or William," Mary agreed. "They take after me."

"Oh, please don't say I look like Father," Jennifer groaned.

"No." Mary patted her daughter's hand. "You look like your brother, Thomas." But everyone at the table knew Thomas was the spitting image of his father.

"I'd take that as a compliment," Thomas teased.

"How about some dessert before you go?" Ed asked, motioning the waitress over.

A miner nervously approached the Goodrich Hotel. In his arms, he awkwardly held a crying baby, no more than three or four days old. The man hadn't shaved in several days, and a scruffy beard covered his face. His clothes were dirty and showed the wear of someone who toiled in the mines. He stopped to stomp his mud-caked boots on the boardwalk before reluctantly stepping through the doorway and into the building. He walked down the hallway to the restaurant at the rear of the building where he studied the occupants. Seeing the person that had been described to him, he made for their table.

"'Scuse me, ma'am." The miner removed his hat with his unencumbered hand. "But would ya be the lady that was on trial?"

"Yes," Jesse answered warily.

"They was talkin' in camp, and I heard what the judge said about you and yer missus. I'd be obliged if'n I could talk with ya. Won't take much of yer time."

"What a beautiful baby." Jennifer craned her neck to see the tiny infant who continued to wail. "Is he hungry?"

"Probably so, ma'am." The miner held the child as if he were afraid of it.

"May I?" Jennifer held out her arms.

"Yes, ma'am." Without hesitation, the miner passed her the child, sighing with relief at being rid of the screaming bundle.

"Oh, hungry and wet," Jennifer told Jesse.

"Do you have anything for him?" Jesse asked.

"No, ma'am." The miner shook his head. "Ran out of tinned milk this morning. That's what I'd be fixin' to talk with ya 'bout. Please, ma'am, if'n you could just give me a few minutes, I'd be mighty obliged ta ya."

Jesse could tell that whatever the man wanted to discuss didn't come easily for him. "We can't talk over his crying." She signaled for the waitress. "Do you think we could have some milk for the baby? In a bottle, if you have one."

The waitress nodded and rushed into the kitchen, as anxious as everyone else in the room to stop the infant's cries.

"Why don't you join us?" Jesse asked the miner.

"Thank you, ma'am, but I won't take but a minute of yer time." He fretfully shifted from one foot to the other.

The waitress returned and handed a bottle of milk to Jennifer. "Here you are, ma'am."

Jennifer shifted to hand the baby and bottle to the miner. He jumped back as if a hot poker had been jabbed at him. "Please ma'am, I'd be obliged if'n you'd keep him."

Thinking that the man meant only while they talked, Jennifer nodded and offered the bottle to the infant, who began to drink hungrily when the nipple of the bottle was placed in his mouth.

Jesse spoke to the man while she watched Jennifer with the baby. "Why don't you tell us what you want?"

"Ma'am..." he began, his nervous hands worrying the brim of his hat.

"Jesse," she corrected.

"Yes, ma'am," the miner continued, taking no notice, "like I said, I heard 'bout what the judge told the reverend 'bout you and your missus being good parents to that young 'un there you adopted." He nodded toward KC standing in her uncle's lap, curiously watching the tiny baby held by her momma. "I'd be obliged if'n you'd take my boy and raise him, too."

Taken aback by the unexpected request, Jennifer sputtered, "What about his mother?"

"His ma died givin' birth to him." The man looked down at his dirty hands, a look of extreme sadness on his face. "I buried her yesterday, out by our claim. She was a good woman, would've made a fine ma to the boy."

"What about you?" Jesse asked sympathetically. "You're his father."

Before he answered, he dug a dirty sleeve across his face to dry the tears in his eyes. "I work in the mines all day, ma'am, from dark to dark. Ain't no place for a baby even if'n I was ta know what ta do with him. Ain't never had no trainin' for carin' for young 'uns and with his ma gone, I got no one to look after him. Please, ma'am, I want ya to take him and raise him as if'n he was yer own. I even had this here paper writ up," the miner reached into his shirt pocket and pulled out a crumpled sheet of paper, "saying that the boy is yours, free and clear. I ain't askin' for nothin' in return, ma'am. Ain't needin' nothin' but ta be able ta tell his ma that he's in a good home. She'd be right pleased to know you and yer missus will be lookin' after him."

"Mister...?" Jesse asked.

"Finnigan, ma'am," the miner said, waiting anxiously for Jesse's answer.

"Mr. Finnigan, do you know what you're asking?" Though Jesse was stunned by the man's request, she was also intrigued by the prospect of a second child being added to her family. And by the way Jennifer was cooing at the infant, it was pretty clear how her wife felt about that possibility.

"So if'n you'll take the boy," the miner handed Jesse the paper, "I'd be obliged." Jesse accepted the paper. "Thank you, ma'am," the miner said, turning to leave the restaurant, secure in the knowledge that his son now had someone to care for him.

"Wait, if you change your mind..." Jesse called after the departing man.

"No, ma'am." The miner stopped and turned to take one last look at the baby. "Like I said, ain't got no place for the boy now with his ma gone." His voice was heavy with the pain of leaving his only child a day after burying his beloved wife.

"What's his name?" Jennifer asked.

"His ma didn' have a chance to name him; reckon you'll be wantin' to take care of that." The miner turned away from his son and quickly walked out of the dining room.

Jesse blew out a long breath. "Now what?"

"Don' rightly know what ta make of you two and Bannack." Bette Mae chuckled. "Seems like every time ya come ta this here town, ya come home with another young 'un."

Jennifer looked uncertainly at the paper Jesse had been given by the infant's father. "Is that paper legal?"

Judge Henson had been listening to the conversation and rose from his chair. "Let me see." He walked over to Jesse and reached for the paper. "May I?" Jesse nodded, handing him the document.

Judge Henson read the writing on the paper, then spread it on the table in front of Jesse and Jennifer and bent to add a few notations of his own before straightening up. "Do you want the boy?"

"What will happen to him if we don't take him?" Jesse asked, even though she already knew the answer.

"There aren't too many options. Most likely Reverend Tobias will be asked to find him a home."

"Darlin'?"

Jennifer looked up at her wife. "You know how I feel."

"We want him," Jesse told the judge.

"Well, then," Judge Henson returned the paper to Jesse, "say hello to your son. Congratulations."

Jesse grinned. "Thanks."

"He's a lucky boy." Judge Henson reached down and chucked the baby under his chin. "Two fine mothers to raise him and a big sister to help out." He smiled at KC, who was unsure what to make of the infant that seemed to be monopolizing everyone's attention.

"Thank you, Judge Henson," Jennifer said. "For everything."

"I'm glad I was here to help," he told them. "I wish you the best of luck. You have earned that much." He returned to his table to finish his meal.

Jesse looked at her wife and new son. "Darlin', if we're going to take him home, I think we best get back to that store and get us some tins of milk and more diapers."

"Sweetheart, let him say hello to his sister first."

Jesse retrieved KC from Thomas, then held her so she could get a close up look at the infant. KC pulled back when she got a whiff of his soiled britches and smelly gown. "Uck."

Jennifer had to agree with KC's assessment of the baby's condition. "I think we're also going to need some baby gowns. And he definitely needs a bath."

KC clapped when she heard a bath mentioned. She liked to play in the water.

Jesse chuckled. "We'll give both you stinkers a good washing before we leave town." She held a hand out to Jennifer and gently pulled her to her feet. "Looks like we've got ourselves the makin's of a family, darlin'," Jesse boasted.

"That it does, sweetheart."

CHAPTER THIRTY-SIX

"I have no intention of answering any of your questions," Tobias Harrington rudely responded to Thaddeus Newby.

"Don't you believe the citizens of Sweetwater deserve to know what is going on?" Thaddeus asked, unsurprised by the other's man reaction. "After all, it is the folks who call this valley home who will ultimately pay the price for any...shall we say dubious actions on the part of your company."

"Are you suggesting that we are somehow being deceitful in our business dealings?" Harrington challenged.

"I am questioning the truthfulness of some of your statements." Thaddeus smiled at the diminutive man. "And if they are not to be trusted, then I would suggest that the measures you are taking based on them must also be subject to enquiry."

"I don't know what you are suggesting." Harrington paced to the window and stared out at the dusty stretch of ground that made up Sweetwater's only street. Except for the sounds of construction coming from the building sites at the end of town, the street was devoid of all activity. He couldn't believe that he was standing there allowing the owner of a nothing newspaper in a nothing town question him. "Mr. Newby," he turned to face the newspapermen, "I am a law-abiding citizen, as is the company that employs me. And that is something you can't say about some of the citizens of this town."

"If you're talking about Jesse Branson, I'm sure she'll be acquitted of the charges against her. After all, there is no truth to them."

"Truth, ha." Harrington stomped back to the desk and dropped into the chair. "I don't think you are much of a judge of truth, Mr. Newby. You have defended that unnatural woman in your paper more than once. In fact, it seems that most folks in your fine town don't mind lying to the law to protect a kidnapper and murderer."

"Just a minute, Tobias." Mayor Perkins spoke for the first time. When Thaddeus entered his office, he had felt it in his best interest to let Harrington respond to the editor's questions, but now the good name of his town was being besmirched. "You know that no one knew where Jesse was when they told the marshal—"

"Shut up, Perkins," Harrington grunted. He leaned back in the chair, rested his elbows on its arms, and steepled his fingertips together. "If that is all you wish to talk about, Mr. Newby, I'll bid you a good day."

Thaddeus smiled shrewdly at the arrogant man. "Mr. Harrington, how much do you know about mining and about judging the true value of a mining claim?"

Caught off guard by the change in subject, Harrington answered. "I may not be a mining engineer, but I am qualified to hire competent men."

"So you believe that you are a good judge of men and their qualifications?"

"An excellent judge," Harrington bragged.

"And you stand behind the decisions these men make?"

"Of course. However, no decision is made without my final approval. So in essence, every decision is, effectively, my own," he said smugly.

"And the decision that the Songbird claim was one worth purchasing, was that one you made?"

"Yes."

Harrington had just admitted responsibility for purchasing a worthless mine. Now he needed to find out if the man knew of the Songbird's true worth at the time he made the decision. "Then you are aware that the Songbird is nothing more than a worthless hole in the side of a mountain?"

"I know no such thing," Harrington answered haughtily. "The Songbird's ore-bearing rock assayed out at one of the highest levels ever seen in these mountains."

"And that didn't make you suspicious?"

"Why would it?" Mayor Perkins asked, suddenly interested in the exchange.

"Because no one else had ever showed the least bit of interest in the Songbird, then Harrington comes along and the Songbird is the richest strike in the mountains."

"But the assay?" Perkins queried.

"The assay report was false."

"What the hell are you talking about?" Harrington exploded out of his chair, the veins in his neck standing out in anger.

Thaddeus thought Harrington looked like a man who had just seen his life flash before his eyes. "The previous owner of the Songbird gave you a false report."

If what Newby was saying was true, he would be responsible for his company becoming the laughingstock of the East. Not to mention the loss of the thousands of dollars that had been spent to purchase the Songbird. And the money already spent on the bank, hotel, wages, bribes... He would be ruined. Harrington pounded the desk. "He did no such thing." Harrington looked pleadingly at the newspaper editor. "It simply can't be true."

"I have a report here from an assayer I hired." Thaddeus pulled a copy of the report from his jacket pocket. "As you can read for yourself, the Songbird is worthless. Unless, of course, your plan is to mine quartz, because that is all that the Songbird's 'rich' vein is composed of."

Harrington snatched the paper out of the newspaperman's hand. "How did you get this?"

"I'd rather not say."

"Of course not, since it is as worthless as you claim the Songbird to be," Harrington huffed as he glanced at the report.

"Perhaps."

"You're making this up just to get me out of your precious town." He dug through the papers on top of the desk looking for his original assay report.

Thaddeus grinned. "I'm quite sure you will be leaving town. The only question is whether you'll be walking away or if you'll have the law chasing you. But either way, Sweetwater will be rid of you."

"Is this really true?" Perkins asked, hearing Harrington groan as he compared the two assay reports. "I had nothing to do with the purchase of the Songbird. That was all your doing," Perkins whined.

"Don't be an idiot," Harrington hissed at his business partner. "You're the one who said you knew of the perfect mine for my plans." The harried man didn't realize how his words sounded.

"May I quote you on that, Mr. Harrington?"

"No," Harrington barked. "And if you write one word of what you have just told me, I will have you sued for libel."

"It's not libel, Harrington, if it's true."

"I'll have you brought up on charges if you print a word of this."

"You seem to be very good at that. Perhaps it was you who precipitated the charges against Jesse?"

"Tobias, did you?" Perkins asked.

"Shut up."

Perkins wanted to know how much trouble Harrington had caused for him. "But if you lied to have her arrested—"

"I said shut up. There's more at stake here than that...that...deviate's reputation."

"Such as?" Thaddeus demanded.

Harrington had said all he was going to. "Get out!"

"What are you up to, Harrington?" Now more than ever, Thaddeus wanted to know what the Easterner had planned to accomplish in Sweetwater.

"Get out!"

"I'll find out eventually, and when I do, I'll splash it all over the *Gazette*. And I'll make sure my newspaper friends in Denver and St. Louis hear about it. Whatever you're playing at, Harrington, Sweetwater will be the last town you try to do it to. And Jesse will be the last person you try to destroy for your own gain. You can trust me on that."

"*Get out!*"

Jesse and Jennifer led the horses away from the Goodrich Hotel. Anxious to leave Bannack and the memories of the trial behind them, the women had changed their minds about bathing their new son in town. Instead, Jesse borrowed a pot of warm water from the kitchen and gave the infant a quick washing in the water bowl in Mary's room. He would be given a thorough cleaning when they made camp at the end of the day.

They turned to wave goodbye to their family and friends standing on the boardwalk. "Goodbye," Jennifer called. "Have a safe trip home, Mother, Thomas."

Bette Mae waved. "Ya be takin' good care of them young 'uns."

"We will," Jesse assured her. "You take care of yourselves."

"See you in Sweetwater," Ed added.

"Write us?" Jennifer asked her mother and brother.

"We will," Thomas called. "We'll be coming to visit, too."

"Love you." Jennifer waved one last time before joining Jesse.

With Jennifer at her side, Jesse carried the baby boy that had so recently joined their family while KC sat snugly in the carry sack on her back. The women were returning to the store in Yankee Flats to buy the additional supplies needed for the infant.

"I'll miss them." Jennifer sighed as she took one final look over her shoulder. Her mother was still standing on the boardwalk, waving at them. She waved back, blowing a kiss.

"We don't have to leave," Jesse offered, hoping Jennifer wouldn't change her mind.

"Yes, we do." Jennifer slipped her arm around Jesse's. She looked at the baby boy. "He's adorable."

"But tiny." Jesse smiled at the boy. "Smaller than KC was when we found her."

"He's a lot younger," Jennifer told her. "Jesse, why do you think Mr. Finnigan brought him to us?"

"Guess it was like he said — he must have heard about the trial and what Judge Henson said."

"I suppose." Jennifer looked at KC; the little girl was watching her parents intently. "But whatever the reason," she smiled at her daughter, "I'm glad he did. Now we have two wonderful children and a real family."

"You're all the family I ever needed, darlin'." Jesse smiled at her wife. "But I'm real proud to have been given the chance to raise these children with you. I love you."

"I love you, too."

It didn't take Jesse and Jennifer long to make their additional purchases. While Jesse added the items to their packs, Jennifer fashioned a sling from a piece of linen to carry the newborn in while they traveled. Jesse would undoubtedly make another carry sack when he was big enough to sit in one, but until then they could use the sling similar to the one they had used after finding KC.

With their packs secure on Boy's back, Jesse helped Jennifer slip the sling over her head and waited for her to mount Blaze. She handed the tiny boy up to Jennifer, who eased the baby inside the sling and made sure he was in a comfortable position. Jesse swung herself up into the saddle. "Ready?"

"Yes."

The women rode away from Yankee Flats, back across Grasshopper Creek and, upon reaching the wagon road, turned the horses west. With a mutual sigh of relief, they quickly put Bannack behind them.

They had been riding for a couple of hours when Jesse decided to call a halt for the day. KC was getting restless in her carry sack, and the baby boy was beginning to fuss.

"I know we haven't gone too far, darlin'," Jesse said as she surveyed the terrain surrounding them, "but what do you say we make camp and set up the tent over by that grove of cottonwoods?"

With the nights getting colder and the addition of their son, Jesse had decided it would be better for her family not to sleep in the open at night, so she had added a canvas tent to their purchases at the store in Yankee Flats.

"Sounds good." Jennifer guided Blaze to the trees Jesse had indicated. Between her leg and injured hand, she welcomed a short day in the saddle.

As soon as they reached the trees, Jesse slipped off Dusty's back. She stepped to Blaze's side and reached up to take the baby from Jennifer.

"He's hungry," Jennifer said as she swung her leg over the saddle and dropped down to join Jesse. "Bet you are, too, sweetie." She reached behind Jesse to ruffle KC's hair.

Jesse waited a moment while Jennifer settled down onto a grassy patch of ground near the bank of a small creek before handing the baby back. "You hold him while I get some diapers and open a tin of milk. KC, you stay right here and don't cause any trouble," Jesse cautioned her daughter as she helped her out of the carry sack.

"Otay." KC sat on the ground a few feet from where Jennifer held the baby, her head tilted to one side, curiously observing the baby.

Jesse pulled open the bundle that contained the supplies for their children. Pulling a tin of condensed milk from another bundle, she punched a hole in the top with an ice pick and poured the thick liquid into a bottle. She added a portion of water before handing it to Jennifer. Jesse pulled a clean diaper from the pack and returned to Jennifer and KC. "Let's get your britches changed while Momma feeds the baby." She spread a blanket on the ground and waited for KC to crawl on top of it.

"Otay." KC rolled unto her back so her mother could remove her soiled diaper.

"Jesse?" Jennifer watched the hungry baby drink.

"Hmm?" Jesse removed KC's soiled diaper, preparing to replace it with a fresh one.

"I think we should give him a name."

Jesse looked up to see Jennifer watching her expectantly. "What shall we call him?"

Jennifer lightly tickled the baby under his tiny chin. "Charley. Charley Branson."

"Charley?"

"Yes. I've always wanted a son named Charley."

Jesse finished redressing KC and sat beside Jennifer, with KC in her lap. "Charley, it is," she said, liking the sound of the name.

KC reached out and grabbed a tiny foot that hung down within her reach, giggling when Charley pulled his foot out of her reach.

"What do you think, Sunshine?" Jesse propped KC up so she could get a good look at her brother. "Cute, isn't he? Just like you."

"Yep."

It was the third night after Jesse and Jennifer had left Bannack, and the family was asleep inside their tent. The couple slept cuddled together in their bedroll, while KC and Charley slept within arm's reach in makeshift cradles that Jesse fashioned each night out of emptied supply packs. The regular contents of the packs were stacked neatly in one corner of the tent with their saddles and other supplies.

Two ethereal figures soundlessly flitted through the campsite and slipped through the canvas skin of the tent, then moved past the sleeping women to stand in front of the slumbering babies. The woman knelt beside KC, her hand slowly reaching out to lovingly brush a lock of hair away from the little girl's eyes. She smiled at the child sleeping so contentedly. Withdrawing her hand, she kissed her fingertips and gently pressed them against KC's cheek. After several moments, the woman held her arm up to the man so he could assist her up. He helped her stand, then, wrapping his arm around her waist, pulled her tight against his side. He smiled at the woman, placing a tender kiss on her temple.

Sensing the presence inside the tent, Jesse and Jennifer became restless in their sleep.

They moved to leave the tent, the woman turning back toward the sleeping women. "Thank you," she whispered. Then she and her husband slipped back through the canvas and disappeared into the night as quietly as they had appeared.

"Somebody better go get the sheriff."

"Who do you think did it?" asked one of the gathered crowd as a boy tore himself away from the grim discovery and rushed out the door to summon the law.

"Don' take much ta figure that." A grizzled miner strolled behind the bar that stretched the length of one side of the room. Pulling a bottle of whiskey and several glasses out from under the bar, he started filling the glasses.

"Can't say I'm too surprised." One of the drinkers set his empty glass on the bar. He didn't have to wait long before the impromptu bartender filled it.

"Me neither."

"Should hav' 'spected it after what he said in court."

"Man was a fool to say that 'bout Logan."

"You was a fool not ta stand up to 'im."

"Didn't see you bustin' down any doors in Virginia City."

Billie entered the building, the boy who had summoned him on his heels.

"Mornin', Sheriff." The miner behind the bar lifted the partially emptied whiskey bottle. "Care for a drink? It's on Finney." He laughed, and the others joined him.

"No, thanks." Billie scratched his cheek; the day-old growth of beard was itchy. "Who found him?"

"Came in like we does every mornin'," one of the men answered. "Found him like that."

"Bar's closed," Billie told the men crowding into the saloon. Word had spread quickly about the early morning discovery. "Everybody get out. Except you," he told the boy who had interrupted his morning shave. "You go find Judge Henson. Wake him up if you have to."

"He ain't goin' ta like that," the boy grumbled.

"Neither do I," Billie grunted. He went behind the bar and took the bottle of whiskey from the miner, who was still pouring free drinks. "Finish what you've got and get out." He shoved the cork back in the bottle and set it aside. Stepping to the end of the bar, he waited for the disgruntled men to leave, then turned to survey the scene.

The room was about twenty feet by forty feet, without any dividing walls. There was only one door and a single window at the front of the log building. Illumination came from several oil lamps hanging along the walls and from the ceiling beams. A few broken-down tables were situated about the room with various non-matching chairs haphazardly scattered around them. In the back corner of the opposite side of the room, a couple of cots were pushed against the walls to accommodate men too drunk to find their way home after a night of whiskey.

The only thing of any real value in the saloon was the bar itself. The elaborately hand-carved bar ran almost the entire length of the room. A border of scallop shells set off by a rope of flowers adorned the lip of the bar, which was supported by four ornate pillars carved in a circular motif. But it was the top of the bar that truly made it special. Shaped from a single piece of hardwood, the bar top was almost thirty feet long and three feet wide. Billie had heard stories of that bar being brought up the Missouri River to Fort Benton and then by wagon to Bannack. It had made Cyrus Finney the envy of saloon owners all over the territory. As he ran his hand along the opulently carved wood, Billie doubted if they would envy the man now.

Billie loosened the rope tied around one of the bar's pillars; the other end had been thrown over one of the crossbeams supporting the roof and at the end of the rope hung the lifeless body of Cyrus Finney.

"Figured the vigilantes would catch up to him," Judge Henson said as he entered the saloon. "Just didn't expect them to be so quick about it."

"Sure it was them?" Billie slowly lowered the body to the floor.

Judge Henson went to the body and bent over it. He pulled a piece of paper free from the pin that held it to the dead man's shirt. "This should answer your question." He stood upright and handed the paper to the sheriff.

Billie read the writing. "3-7-77."

"That's the message the vigilantes leave on all their victims. No one has unraveled what they mean by it, but everyone knows it serves as a warning for lawbreakers in the territory to leave Montana or suffer the consequences."

"Surprisin' he didn't leave after the trial." He handed the note back to the judge.

"Guess he had no place to go." Judge Henson slipped the paper into his pocket. "You best get back to the jail, Sheriff. There's not much else for you to do here."

Billie scratched his itchy cheek. "They caught me before I could shave this morning," he explained.

"You go on. I'll get the undertaker to take care of Finney."

"Go back to sleep, darlin'," Jesse told her half-asleep wife. "I'll take care of Charley."

The whimpering infant had awakened them. It wasn't the first time, and both women were exhausted from getting up several times during the night. KC had been many months older when they'd first found her and was already sleeping through the nights. But Charley was just a week old, and neither woman was used to getting up every few hours with a hungry baby. It didn't help that the tinned milk seemed to upset the infant's stomach.

Jesse rolled away from Jennifer and sat up, lifting Charley from his cradle and hugging him in her arms. "Shhhh." Jesse rubbed his back to calm him. "Don't want to be waking up your sister." In a way, she had welcomed Charley's cries. They had interrupted the disquieting dream she was having, and she was thankful for the chance to clear it from her mind.

"Come on, Charley," Jesse whispered to the tiny boy, "let's get some milk in your tummy. I know you don't like it much, but it's all we've got. When we get home, you can drink the milk we get from KC's cow. Bet you'll like that a whole lot better." She grabbed a can of milk, the ice pick, a canteen, and an empty bottle that had been left within easy reach for the nighttime feedings. Placing the baby on top of her crossed legs, Jesse opened the tin of milk and filled the bottle. "Here you go." She lifted the baby up, cuddling him in her arms as she fed him. Charley's eyes drooped in sleep as he suckled hungrily.

Jesse chuckled softly. "Guess you're not used to being up all night either."

Remembering her dream, Jesse looked to see if the flap of the tent had somehow come undone while they slept or whether any of their belongings had been disturbed. She was relieved to see the tent opening was still tied shut and nothing looked amiss. KC was sleeping soundly in her improvised bed, her toy horse clutched in her hand. Jesse was further comforted by the sounds of their horses moving about not far from the tent, knowing they would have alerted her and Jennifer to any danger. Shaking off the last fuzzy remnants of the dream, Jesse hummed softly as she rocked her new son.

"Where's Bette Mae?" Ed Granger asked Ruthie when she joined him in the dining room of the Goodrich Hotel.

"Said she had something to do this morning."

"What business could she have in Bannack?"

Before Ruthie could respond, Mary and Thomas entered the room to join them. "Good morning, Mary." Ed stood as Mary was assisted into a chair by her son. "Morning, Thomas."

"Good morning, Ed. Not too busy in here this morning," Thomas commented, seeing several empty tables.

Ed looked around the half empty room. "Guess folks have gone back to their business."

"Isn't Bette Mae joining us?" Mary enjoyed the other woman's company and was disappointed not to see her at the table.

"Seems she's got some of her own business to attend to," Ed explained. "Though I don't rightly know what that could be."

"She didn't tell me, Mr. Granger," Ruth said when she saw the questioning looks on the faces around her.

"Damn fool," one of the men was saying. "Was almost like he was just waitin' for it to happen. Ya think he'd have tried to get outta the territory."

"I'm sure as hell not going to shed any tears over him. I say he got exactly what he deserved. Surprised they didn't get around to him before now."

"Maybe so. But ya think they coulda at least drug him out of town ta string him up?"

"Gallows are still up where they hanged Logan. They could've used those, I s'pose."

"Or any number of other places."

"Excuse me." Thomas interrupted the men as they walked past their table. "May we ask what you are talking about?"

The men stopped and looked at Thomas and his tablemates. "Ain't you related to that fool they've got locked up in jail, the one that got knocked out by that woman?"

"Pretty good punch," the other man laughed, "ta put down a man as big as him. Did ya see the look on his face when she slugged him? Better than a lot of punches I've seen between the boys when they get ta goin' afta each other."

"Sir, please." Thomas tried to get the men to answer his question. "You're not saying that my father has been hanged?"

"Nah, though he maybe should be for what he done to those women. Vigilantes hanged Finney during the night, strung him up right inside his own saloon."

"My goodness!" Mary gasped. "Here in town?"

"Yeah, slick as a whistle. Just like they did with Logan." The men laughed as they walked to an empty table and sat down.

Ruthie sipped from her glass of water to ease the lump that had formed in her throat. She didn't think much of the saloon owner, but hearing that he had been hanged was disconcerting. "Billie said that might happen," she offered shyly.

Ed stirred sugar into his coffee. "I'd say he was lucky to survive the vigilantes as long as he did."

"If it's all the same to you," Mary asked the others, "I would very much like not to talk about this during breakfast."

"That would be nice," Ruthie agreed. "I don't think I can eat much as it is."

"You're right, enough has been said." To lighten the mood, Ed turned to her. "So, Ruthie, why don't you tell us what plans that sheriff of yours has made for getting the two of you hitched?"

CHAPTER THIRTY-SEVEN

"When did you find the time to catch these?" Jennifer indicated the fish frying in the pan over the fire.

"Couldn't sleep." Jesse patted KC on the rear after changing her diaper. "All nice and clean, Sunshine."

"Otay." KC smiled at her mother, then crawled over to the blanket where Charley was laying. She plopped down next to the baby, tilting her head as she scrutinized the newcomer.

"What do you think about your new brother?" Jennifer asked the curious little girl.

KC scratched her nose, then leaned over to get a closer look. Soon she was almost nose to nose with the infant. KC poked out a small finger at the baby's nose. "Oonk." She giggled.

"Be gentle," Jesse said as she sat next to KC. "He's not big enough to play with just yet."

KC pulled back her finger and crawled into Jesse's lap. "Mommy?" She looked up at Jesse.

"Yes, Sunshine."

"Go?" KC pointed at Charley, who was watching her with bright eyes.

"Yep." Jesse reached over and tenderly stroked the boy under his chin. Charley wrapped his tiny fingers around her much larger one. "We're going to take him home. Is that okay?" she asked, concerned that KC might feel like she was being replaced.

KC looked at the baby. "Yep."

Jesse hugged her daughter. "Good girl."

"Anybody hungry?" Jennifer had been watching and listening to the exchange between her wife and daughter and was pleased that KC didn't seem to mind the new addition to their family.

"I'm starving." Jesse smiled at Jennifer. "How about you?" She tickled KC, which made her giggle.

"Yum, yum, yum."

As Jesse helped Jennifer wash up after breakfast, she noticed her wife seemed preoccupied. "You okay, darlin'?"

Jennifer was frowning as she looked aimlessly at the children on the blanket a few feet from them, KC playing with her toy horse and Charley lying beside her.

"Darlin', is everything all right?"

"Huh?" Jennifer realized Jesse was talking to her. "What did you say?"

"I asked you if everything was okay. You seem to be someplace else this morning."

Jennifer turned to face Jesse. She reached out her hand and smiled when her wife instantly covered it with her own. "It's just that I had a strange dream last night. I can't seem to shake the feeling that—"

"Someone was in the tent watching us," Jesse finished.

"Yes." Jennifer looked quizzically at Jesse. "Was there?"

"Not that I could tell." Jesse tugged on Jennifer's arm, encouraging her to come closer. "But I had the same feeling. I thought it was a dream but it seemed—"

"So real."

"Yes." Jesse wrapped her arms around her wife, pleased to have her snuggling against her.

"Jesse?"

"Hmm?"

"Do you think..." Jennifer stopped, surprised at her own fanciful thoughts.

"That it was the Williamses? Could have been. What do you think?"

"I think they wanted to be sure KC is all right." Jennifer leaned back just enough to look into Jesse's eyes. "But why now, why here?"

"Maybe because they're buried not far from here."

"Oh?" Jennifer looked around at the sparsely vegetated hillocks surrounding them. She had paid little attention to the landmarks they passed after leaving Bannack, and she now realized she had no idea where they were.

"Yep, right on the other side of that rise." Jesse pointed at a hill about a half-mile behind them. "Maybe they thought it would be the last chance they'd have to check on her."

"Do you think they know how much we love her?" Jennifer asked as she remembered the graves she and Jesse had dug not that long ago.

Jesse hugged Jennifer tightly. "I'm sure of it."

"How?"

"Because just before she left the tent, Catherine thanked us."

"She did, didn't she?"

"Yep."

"I love you."

"Love you, too, darlin'." Jesse captured her wife's lips for a long, sensuous kiss.

KC stopped playing with her toy horse to watch her mothers kiss. "Uck, uck, uck," she told her brother, cackling when Charley, seemingly in response to her comment, blinked at her, his feet kicking wildly.

Bette Mae was walking along the road to the cemetery overlooking Bannack. This way would take longer, but the grade was not as steep or as rocky as the more direct path to the fenced hilltop graveyard. She had been putting off her visit, unsure how she would feel when she was finally faced with the reality of her friend's death. But she knew she would be returning home in another day or two, and she couldn't wait any longer to do what was needed. As she walked around the wide, sweeping curve the road took as it worked its way up to the graveyard, she thought back on the night many years before when she had met the woman who came to mean so much to her.

Bette Mae had been working in a Fort Benton saloon when she first saw the girl who would one day steal her heart. The girl had come into the saloon in search of her husband, a no good gambler who spent most nights in the company of the working girls. She had befriended the girl, who was not much younger than herself, and during one of the evenings they had spent talking, Bette Mae had fallen in love. She wasn't sure what she had expected of their friendship, but what she hadn't expected was how her heart ached after Elizabeth left Fort Benton with her husband. Now she was going to pay her last respects to the woman who would forever hold her heart.

"Seems I remember there being a hot springs 'bout where that line of trees starts." Jesse stretched her arms skyward, a giggling KC held high above her head.

Jennifer looked up from changing Charley's diaper and peered into the distance north of their campsite. "At the base of those hills?"

"Yep." Jesse tossed KC into the air, catching the squealing child as she dropped back toward the ground.

"Don't you drop her."

"Wouldn't dream of it. Would I, Sunshine?" Jesse tightened her arms around her daughter and rubbed noses with her.

KC giggled. "Mo."

Jesse let the girl fly again, being careful not to throw her too high.

"Mo," KC begged when Jesse set her on the ground.

"Not now, Sunshine." Jesse ruffled the girl's hair. "I need to help Momma finish packing. You stay here and keep an eye on Charley."

"Otay." KC looked at the baby, unsure what she was supposed to be keeping an eye on; the baby never moved except to wave his arms or kick his legs. He couldn't crawl like she could.

Jennifer finished with Charley and was picking up the last few items to put into the packs. Jesse waited for Jennifer to tie the pack flaps tight before making a final check on the ropes that secured the packs to their draft horse. "What do you say we head for that hot springs? Should be able to reach it by this afternoon."

"I'd like that." Jennifer sighed as she stretched her back and winced.

"Back sore, darlin'?"

"A little. I guess I'm still not used to carrying a baby."

"Why don't you let me carry him for a while?"

"You're already carrying KC."

"I can carry both."

"I know you can, sweetheart." Jennifer leaned against Jesse. "Maybe when we get to those hot springs, you can give me one of your special massages."

"You can count on that." Jesse worked her hands up and down Jennifer's back. She could feel the tight muscles under her wife's cotton shirt.

"In the meantime—"

"In the meantime, I'll carry Charley." Jesse gave Jennifer a look that said she would not entertain any protest. "It'll give your back a rest."

Knowing that arguing would be useless, Jennifer agreed. "All right. But if Charley gets restless, we switch back," she insisted.

"Agreed." Jesse turned to their children.

Jennifer turned to follow Jesse and ran smack into her wife's back. "What?"

"Shhh," Jesse whispered. "Look."

Jennifer peeked around Jesse and saw KC lying on her stomach right next to Charley. Her little body was pushed up and supported by her arms bent at the elbows. She was talking spiritedly to the infant, but few words were recognizable other than Momma and Mommy. Every so often KC would giggle and drop her head down to tease the baby in a game of peek-a-boo. Charley's eyes never left his sister. As Jesse and Jennifer watched, the infant's lips curled up into his first smile.

A smile quickly spread across KC's face when she saw the baby mimic her. She scooted around to sit up, pulling the baby partially into her lap. Leaning over, she kissed Charley's head.

Jesse sat down beside KC and rescued the baby from his precarious position, half in and half out of his sister's lap. KC pulled herself upright using her mommy's shirt for handholds.

"Wuv Wie," KC announced as she leaned against Jesse, her arms snaking around her mommy's neck.

"Charley loves you, too, Sunshine." Jesse smiled at the little girl.

Jennifer stood behind Jesse, her hands resting on her wife's shoulders. Tears welled in her eyes as she smiled down upon her family.

Bette Mae stood beside a grave marker. Etched on the polished face of the stone was the name *Elizabeth Granger* and under the name it said, *Beloved sister and friend.* At the top of the headstone floated an angel, symbolically protecting the person resting beneath.

"Might purty headstone Jesse and Jennifer bought ya," Bette Mae whispered as she ran her hand lightly over the cool surface.

Unlike most of the others in the cemetery, the grave was well cared for, another gift from Jesse and Jennifer, who had paid the town's gravedigger to take special care with Elizabeth's resting place. It was outlined by stones laid out in straight lines and the ground inside the stones had been picked free of weeds. Fresh flowers had been placed at the base of the headstone in a small hole lined with tin to keep its shape. A small bench made of a thick board placed atop two relatively flat stones of equal size sat invitingly alongside the grave.

Bette Mae took a seat on the bench. "Don' rightly know what I wan' ta say." Tears filled her eyes as she thought of what might have been. "Wish I'd had the nerve to speak my mind back in Fort Benton," she sniffled. "Don' know if it would have made much difference." She pulled a hankie from her sleeve to dab at her eyes. "I shoulda done better by ya, Lizzie. I shoulda insisted ya leave tha' bastard. We coulda gone some place where ya coulda been happy. I shoulda taken care of ya. I loved ya. Lizzie. I shoulda told ya tha'." Bette Mae allowed the years of secret feelings and emotions to wash out of her along with the tears streaming down her cheeks.

Mayor Perkins finished reading the lead story of the latest edition of the *Gazette* and then looked up at the newspaper editor. "Are you sure about this?"

"Yes." Thaddeus Newby had just finished typesetting what he had read in a letter from Ed Granger concerning the events since Marshal Morgan left Sweetwater to arrest Jesse, right up to the findings at her trial and Martin Kensington's admissions. As soon as the first copy of the paper came off the printing press, he carried it to the office of Sweetwater's mayor. "I thought you might want to know what kind of company you've been keeping."

"But to make up those lies about Jesse," the mayor tossed the newspaper onto his desk, "just so he could get the Slipper."

"There's more to it than that, Miles, and you know it." Thaddeus dropped wearily into the chair opposite the desk. "He's a man who will do anything to achieve what he wants. My question is: how much of this did you know about?"

"None," the mayor said emphatically. "I swear, I knew nothing."

Not surprised by the mayor's response, Thaddeus persisted. "Then what do you plan to do about Harrington and his company now that you do know?"

The man under discussion barged into the mayor's office in time to hear the last of the editor's query. "Know what?"

"That the Songbird is nothing but a hole in the ground." Angry, Thaddeus confronted the unwelcome man, ticking off on his fingers as he laid out the facts. "That you and Martin Kensington conspired to have Jesse arrested and imprisoned for crimes she did not commit. That you made a secret deal with Kensington for him to sign over ownership of the Silver Slipper for a percentage of the Songbird's profits."

Harrington glared at the newspaperman, surprised by the accuracy of his accusations. "You can't possible know that."

"I know that and much more."

"Tobias, why would you do such things?" Miles Perkins asked.

"I have done nothing wrong." Harrington sought to explain himself out of the tangled plots unraveling around him. "I was taken in by the owner of the Songbird." He looked to the mayor for help but received nothing but a blank stare in return. "I had no idea the mine was worthless. How am I going to make the investors understand? They will hold me responsible."

"What about Jesse and Jennifer?" Thaddeus exploded, caring little about the money the man had spent on the worthless mine. "Why would you do that to them? They never did anything to you, you sorry son of a bitch!" he bellowed at the man so concerned about himself.

"They laughed at me," Harrington said, his customary bravado gone.

"Dammit, Harrington." Mayor Perkins shook his head. "You did all this because they wouldn't sell the Slipper to you?"

In truth, he had been unable to forget the day he had approached the women about selling the Silver Slipper. "The investors were upset over having to spend money to build a hotel," he explained. "When I met Kensington on the stage, I thought it was too good to be true when he made me the offer for the Slipper."

"It was." Thaddeus sighed. He couldn't believe all that Jesse and Jennifer had gone through because this man's pride had been wounded.

"But it made sense. I would save my company money, and Kensington would get his daughter back. After all, he is an important man back East. He could make things right."

"You might be interested to know that Martin Kensington is currently awaiting Marshal Morgan's escort to prison. Seems the judge in Bannack wasn't too happy with your little conspiracy. In fact, I wouldn't be surprised if the territorial governor doesn't issue a warrant for your arrest once he's been told the kind of a fool you played him for."

"What?" Harrington gulped audibly. "That can't happen."

"Sounds like what Kensington has been saying since he was arrested and tossed into jail." Thaddeus frowned. "If I were you, Mr. Harrington, I'd be making plans to get far away from Sweetwater just as fast as I could. I don't think too many folks will be wanting you around once the *Gazette* hits the streets this afternoon."

"But..." Harrington opened his mouth, then closed it, unable to think of anything further to say.

"Miles, what do you plan to do about this?" Thaddeus asked.

Mayor Perkins finally found the courage to confront the man who had almost destroyed his town and some of its citizens. "Thaddeus, in the absence of Sheriff Monroe, I'm deputizing you. Would you please take Mr. Harrington to jail? I don't think he should be allowed to leave town until all of this is settled."

"Perkins, don't be a fool."

"You've been the fool, Harrington." Mayor Perkins stood. Stomping to within inches of the outsider, he poked a beefy finger into the smaller man's chest. "I can't believe you would do such a horrible thing to Jennifer and Jesse. After all that man Kensington has already done to them, you go and help him do even more just because they wouldn't sell you the Slipper." His jabbing finger drove Harrington back a step with each new poke. "You are a despicable human being, and I will make sure you do not get away with this. Thaddeus, lock this bastard up!"

Thaddeus chuckled at seeing a side of the mayor he never knew existed. "Damn, Miles," he said as he approached Harrington to comply with the mayor's instructions, "I didn't know you had that in you."

"Neither did I," Perkins replied honestly, collapsing back into his chair.

"Get your hands off me!" Harrington shouted, attempting to break free of the firm grasp. But years of operating a printing press had made the muscles in the newspaperman's arms as strong as steel cables, and the smaller man was unable to get loose.

"Come on, you worthless piece of horse pucky." Thaddeus pulled a screaming Harrington out of the mayor's office.

After breakfast, Ed decided to walk up and visit his sister's grave, something he had done every day since arriving in Bannack. Reaching the top of the rocky trail, he recognized the woman sitting on the small bench inside the fenced graveyard. Deep in concentration and with her back toward him, Bette Mae didn't hear his approach.

Not wanting to intrude and curious as to why Bette Mae would be at his sister's graveside, Ed leaned against the fence to wait. In the still morning air, he could hear the words spoken by the grieving woman.

"I was too young, Lizzie." Bette Mae wiped at her tears. "I was scared ya'd think less of me if I tol' ya the truth. But oh, how my heart ached afta ya left. I come lookin' for ya, did ya know that? Listen to me." She laughed sadly. "'Course ya didn' know. But I did. Followed ya to Bozeman, but that sorry excuse fer a husban' had already taken ya away from there. And by the time I made it ta Sweetwater, ya was gone again. Would have kep' lookin' for ya but I ran out a money. Took a job at the Slipper 'cause I figured ya'd come back someday, what with yer brother running the store and all. But ya never did. Guess I coulda asked Ed 'bout ya," she sighed deeply, "but I never did." For several minutes, Bette Mae sat silently looking at the final resting place of the only person she had ever loved.

"I loved ya, Lizzie." She spoke the words softly, and Ed, standing only a few feet away, had to strain to hear them. "It's the only thing in my life tha' I'm proud of." She stood to return to town. "Ya have a real pretty restin' spot, Lizzie. And someone is seeing ta ya, that's nice." She took a single step away, then stopped and looked back at the grave. "I won' be comin' back. I hope ya understand." She felt fresh tears rolling down her cheeks. "It hurts too much, my love. Goodbye."

Ed shifted from one foot to the other in uncertainty, knowing that Bette Mae would see him as soon as she turned completely away from the grave. He had never known about the feelings the woman held for his sister, and he now wondered how much different their lives might have turned out if the love had been mutual.

Bette Mae was startled to see the storekeeper standing so near. "Ed?"

"Sorry." Ed walked the few steps to wrap the brokenhearted woman in his arms. "Didn't mean to intrude, but I never expected to see you here."

"I..." Bette Mae welcomed the warm embrace. "I just wanted..."

"Let it go, Bette Mae." Ed could feel the woman's body shaking with bottled-up emotion. "You've got a right to grieve."

"But how..." Bette Mae asked between sobs.

"I heard enough to know you loved her."

Bette Mae was unsure how the big man would feel about what he had heard. "I'm sorry."

"Don't be." Ed gently rubbed her back. "It makes it easier knowing she had someone who cared."

"I did, Ed. I surely did." Protected in his strong arms, Bette Mae cried.

CHAPTER THIRTY-EIGHT

At the hot springs, they decided to set up camp for the night before enjoying the heated mineral waters. Jesse had chosen a small glade protected by trees to pitch the tent. Nearby, a creek of cold mountain water merged with the scalding water flowing out of the hot springs, creating a pool just the right size and temperature for the weary women to immerse themselves in the soothing water.

Now, moaning with pleasure, Jennifer dipped low into the steaming water of the hot spring. "This feels so good."

"You can say that again." Jesse held Charley and was using a cloth to bathe the baby in the warm water. "This will sure make it easy to sleep tonight."

"Be careful, sweetie," Jennifer told KC, who she held in her arms. KC was happily splashing water at Jesse. "Wait until Mommy is finished giving Charley his bath," she stilled the girl's hands, "then you can play with her."

"Otay." KC looked around for some other way to entertain herself. Her eyes followed the path of the creek as it flowed away from them into the valley. "Ook." She pointed excitedly at a doe drinking from the creek some distance downstream.

"A deer." Jennifer smiled. "Oh, sweetie, look." She lifted KC up so she could see better. "She has two babies." A pair of smaller animals stood beside the doe. They were no longer marked with the spotted coloring of fawns, but it was obvious by their size that they weren't yet yearlings.

"Ook, Mommy." Wanting to be sure everyone saw the deer family, KC poked Charley in the leg. "Ook," she commanded her tiny brother.

"He's a mite small to see them, Sunshine," Jesse said as she leaned back, slipping most of her body under the warm water. Charley lay between her breasts, securely held in place by her strong hands. She continually swept warm water over the washrag draped over the baby so he wouldn't get chilled.

Seeing that Jesse was finished with Charley's bath, KC forgot about the deer. She started bouncing in Jennifer's lap. "Mommy, Mommy, Mommy."

"I think it's time for you to play," Jennifer teased her relaxed wife.

"Ugh." Jesse playfully stretched out a long leg to tickle KC with a toe. "Don't want to play."

"Mommy, Mommy, Mommy."

Jennifer stood. "I think it's time for Charley and me to get some clothes on."

Jesse watched as water ran in rivulets from her wife's naked skin. "I can think of a reason not to do that." She smiled, twitching her eyebrows.

"I'm sure you can." Jennifer sloshed over to Jesse. "Maybe you should keep that thought until after the children are asleep," she said as she offered to trade KC for Charley.

Jesse held Charley up to her wife. "I will definitely keep it until then."

As soon as Jennifer set KC down on top of her mommy, the little girl splashed water at her, giggling when Jesse gave her a playful glare.

"Don't be too long," Jennifer said as she carried Charley out of the pool. "The stew should be ready soon."

"I won't be any longer than it takes to splash this little squirt silly."

Jennifer smiled as shrieks of laughter escaped from her daughter once Jesse began drenching her with a barrage of splashes.

Jennifer stirred the pot of stew while keeping a sharp eye on Charley, who was lying on a blanket a few feet away. She was getting ready to call Jesse and KC to supper when Jesse strode into camp with a squirming, wet daughter tucked under her arm.

KC giggled. "Mommy, dow."

"Not 'til you get some britches on." Jesse carried the laughing girl into the tent.

"Sweetheart?" Jennifer sat beside Charley. The baby's eyes were beginning to droop, and she knew it wouldn't be long before he was fast asleep.

"What?" Jesse called from inside the tent.

"How long do you think it will be before we reach Walk's camp?"

"Tomorrow or the next day. Why?"

"I'm thinking those tins of milk won't last us until we get home. Do you think they'll have a cow in Walk's camp."

Jesse chuckled. "No, darlin'. They don't have milk cows."

"Oh."

"But we can see if one of the women can wet nurse Charley while we're there. That will help stretch the tinned milk," Jesse said as she carried KC out of the tent. "It's probably a good thing KC refuses to drink it, or we would have already run out. Guess I didn't do very good at the buying in Yankee Flats."

"Well, it's not like either of us knew how much tinned milk a baby would drink. We had the cow for KC so we didn't have to worry about it." Jennifer started to rise in order to dish up the stew.

"Stay put." Jesse sat KC down on the blanket next to Jennifer. "I'll get supper. Looks like Charley will be asleep soon."

Jennifer pulled a corner of the blanket over to cover the boy, seeing her daughter's mouth open wide in a yawn. "I expect KC won't be too far behind."

"Here you go." Jesse handed Jennifer a bowl of stew and a chunk of bread to share before sitting next to her with her own bowl. "Come on, Sunshine." Jesse patted her thigh for KC to crawl into her lap. "Let's get you fed before you fall asleep on us."

Jennifer laughed as she remembered the many nights they had stayed up late with KC who refused to go to sleep. "Too bad we don't have a hot springs at home."

"Maybe we could make one." Jesse blew on a spoonful of stew before feeding it to KC. "But I think it's more likely the riding on the back of a horse all day than the hot water that's got her tuckered out."

"Probably." Jennifer tore off a piece of bread, offering it to Jesse.

"How're you doing?" Jesse asked, always concerned about Jennifer's damaged leg and the pain it caused her wife.

Jennifer smiled. "I wouldn't say no to a rubdown tonight."

"Good." Jesse smiled back. "I was planning on giving you one as soon as we put these two to bed."

"I hope Jennifer and Jesse are all right," Mary fretted as they walked down the stairs in the Goodrich Hotel on their way to the dining room for supper.

Thomas was following her down the steps. "I'm sure they're fine, Mother."

"I worry about them being alone with those babies."

"It seems they've done pretty well on their own so far. I wouldn't worry about them now."

Leevie walked into the lobby just as Mary and Thomas reached the bottom of the stairway. "Good evening."

"Good evening, Leevie." Mary smiled warmly at the schoolteacher. "I wasn't expecting to see you tonight."

"The cabin is kinda empty. I was hoping I could eat with you," Leevie explained sheepishly.

Mary understood how lonely an empty house could seem. "Of course you can."

The trio walked down the hallway leading to the dining room. Ed and Ruthie were already seated at a table, and they waved them over.

"Where's Bette Mae?" Mary was concerned that the woman had been absent all day. "Is she not feeling well?"

"She's fine," Ed assured Mary. Not wanting to give away Bette Mae's secret, he added, "She had some catchin' up to do with an old friend, and it tuckered her out. So she's making it an early night."

"I didn't know she had any friends in Bannack."

Anxious to change the subject, Ed said, "What shall we have tonight?" The others laughed, as they all knew the menu was limited, offering few choices. "I guess Billie is still stickin' close to the jail, huh?" Ed asked Ruthie.

"Yes." Ruthie had spent most of the day with her fiancé and would have preferred to stay and share the evening meal with him, but he had insisted she return to the hotel when the daylight began to fade. He didn't want her walking back to the Goodrich in the dark, his duties at the jail preventing him from escorting her back. "I wish the marshal would get back," she grumbled, then blushed when she realized how her comment might have sounded to the prisoner's wife and son.

"It's all right," Mary told the embarrassed girl. "I wish he would get back, too. I would like to put an end to this whole affair."

Ed knew how long the ride was to the territorial prison in Deer Lodge and that the marshal had had time to get there and back. "I expect he'll get back tomorrow."

"I guess we can last that long, can't we, Ruthie?" Mary smiled.

"Yes. We'll be leaving for Sweetwater as soon as he arrives, won't we, Ed?" Ruthie was eager to leave Bannack. After all, she had a wedding to prepare for.

"Far as I'm concerned, we can leave the minute the marshal gets back. I've got a store to get back to. Not to mention that I'd like to see what that Harrington fella has to say about all this. I sent a letter to Thaddeus a couple of days ago, laying out the details of the trial. Hopefully, he'll have some use for it."

"I'm sure if what you suspect is true about Mr. Harrington's dealings," Thomas said, "he'll have more than your newspaper editor to worry about. I've heard of the company he works for, and I'm quite sure the owner will not be pleased to hear his money has been wasted on a worthless mine."

"Maybe so, but my concern is more for Sweetwater than for Harrington. He's caused folks there a whole load of trouble, and I'm just hoping it ain't so bad the town can't recover."

"I'm sure Sweetwater will be fine, Ed," Thomas said. "Besides, your fine town now has a new hotel and bank to show for his efforts. Those you will have, and the business they bring, long after Harrington is gone."

"Bank we can use. Ain't so sure we need the hotel, especially since it'll take business away from the Slipper."

Thomas laughed. "The Slipper has the best cook in the territory in Bette Mae. Folks will still get their meals there."

"And," Mary added, "with Ruthie's new dress shop, there'll be plenty of reasons for people to continue staying at the Slipper. I think Thomas is right; a new hotel is not going to take away much business. As more people come to Sweetwater, the Slipper will have even more business. As will your store, Ed."

"I hope you're right."

Martin Kensington stood, indignant, as Billie set his plate of supper on the cell floor. "I demand you release me from these chains."

"Ain't gonna happen, Kensington," the sheriff muttered. He had heard the same demand every day since the man had been arrested.

"This is no way to treat a gentleman!" Kensington bellowed.

"Don' see no gentlemen 'round here." Billie backed out of the cell.

"At least give me a lamp." Kensington's tone changed, a mere hint of fear creeping into his words as he was about to be consumed by total darkness again.

"No." Billie pushed the solid wood door shut.

"A candle, then," Kensington begged.

Billie pulled the chain through the metal loops and secured the ends together with the padlock. He could feel sorry for the man shackled in the windowless cell. That is, he could if he didn't think about all the pain the man had caused his friends. He tossed the ring of keys back onto their hook and sat at the table preparing for another long night of listening to the prisoner's protestations and empty threats.

"How do you feel?" Jesse asked her wife, who was wrapped in her arms.

"Wonderful." Jennifer sighed. Jesse had just finished her promised massage, leaving her feeling almost boneless. They were lying atop their bedroll spread out on the floor of the tent. A lantern hanging overhead provided a dim light. KC and Charley were sleeping an arm's length away, snug in their makeshift beds. "I'm glad you bought this tent." Jennifer snuggled closer to Jesse.

"Does help keep out the cold." The rancher pulled the blanket, draped loosely over their naked bodies, up over Jennifer's shoulders to cover the goosebumps forming on her delicate skin.

Summer was ending, and the nights were getting longer and cooler. Many of the trees they passed were already showing the bright reds and yellows of fall.

"Not to mention it's not so embarrassing to be naked when I know no one can see us."

"Ain't nobody for miles, darlin'." Jesse chuckled. "Unless you're talkin' 'bout the animals."

"You know what I mean." Jennifer pinched Jesse's arm. "You never know when someone might happen by."

Jesse stretched leisurely, exposing her torso as the blanket fell away. "Having this tent does have a number of advantages." Usually she enjoyed sleeping under the stars, but she decided it was better to have the extra protection, especially now that they had KC and Charley to consider.

Charley gurgled in his sleep, and Jennifer glanced at him. "He'll be waking up hungry soon." Turning her attention back to her wife, she placed a hand on one of Jesse's bare breasts. Jesse put her own hand atop Jennifer's, encouraging the caress. Charley gurgled again, his eyes fluttering open, and Jennifer groaned. Feeling Jesse's firm nipple pressing into her palm had begun some equally pleasurable sensations between her own legs.

"I'll get the milk," Jesse said without moving. Jennifer shifted slightly, replacing her hand with her mouth to suck on the nipple.

"Darlin'," Jesse moaned. "I don't think this is a good time to be startin' that."

Charley was now awake and very hungry, his cries becoming more insistent.

Jennifer raked her teeth over Jesse's aroused nipple before releasing it.

"I'll get the milk," Jesse repeated, her voice shaky with the desire Jennifer had ignited within her. She pushed herself upright and reached for a tin of milk and a feeding bottle. "Darlin'," she took a deep breath to calm her racing heart, "that wasn't nice."

Jennifer giggled as she sat up and lifted Charley from his temporary cradle. "I'm sorry, sweetheart." She laid the baby on the bedroll. "Guess I have to work on my timing now that we have Charley."

"Oh, I don't think your timing is at fault." Jesse carefully poured milk into the feeding bottle and added some water to the thick condensed nourishment while Jennifer removed Charley's soiled diaper. "I think you just wanted to torture me," she said, handing over a clean diaper.

"Now why would I do that?"

"Because you're a tease."

"Ha. Guess I had a pretty good teacher." Jennifer finished the diapering and laid Charley in Jesse's arms. "Here, feed our son."

"Hi there, little man." Jesse settled the baby in her arms and offered him the bottle. "How long before you sleep through the night?" she asked the baby as he suckled.

Jennifer scooted over to sit beside Jesse, leaning her head against Jesse's bare shoulder. "He can't help it if he gets hungry."

"He ain't the only one hungry," Jesse said with a pout.

"Stop that. They'll be plenty of time when he goes back to sleep."

"What makes you think I'll still be in the mood?"

"Oh, somehow I think you will." Jennifer slipped her hand between Jesse's crossed legs and into the thatch of moist hair. She smiled when her wife pressed into her touch.

"That's not fair," Jesse growled.

"Just making my point." The hand was withdrawn. Wrapping her arm around Jesse's waist, Jennifer watched the baby. "He's adorable."

"Yeah," Jesse rested her head against Jennifer's, "he is. But he's so little. Guess I never figured they started out so small."

"He'll grow. Just like KC."

Jesse looked over at their sleeping daughter. "She has grown a bit, hasn't she?"

"Yes. And so will Charley. We just have to give him time."

Jesse nodded. Time was one thing she had plenty of when it came to her family.

"He has your coloring."

"What do you mean?"

"Look." Jennifer lovingly ran her fingers through the fine hair atop the infant's head. "It's going to be reddish brown, like yours. And he has brown eyes."

Jesse looked at the baby in the muted light. "He must have gotten that from his mother," she said, remembering that his father was sandy haired, with light blue eyes.

"Kinda funny, isn't it?"

"What is?"

"How much KC looks like me and, now, how much Charley looks like you."

"I think it's a little soon to be laying that on the boy," Jesse grumbled, but she wasn't really upset by the idea. She took great pleasure in the way KC favored Jennifer, and she was pleased that Jennifer thought the tiny boy favored her. "I'm just glad to have him. And KC." She turned to kiss her wife. "And I'm really glad to have you," she whispered as their lips met.

"Let's put him back to bed." Jennifer suggested when they broke apart several heartbeats later, Charley sound asleep in Jesse's arms.

It didn't take them long to tuck the baby back into his pack and to check on KC sleeping in her own pack beside him. Within minutes, they were back on the bedroll, wrapped in each other's arms.

Jesse sighed as she planted light kisses along Jennifer's chin line. "Have I told you today how much I love you?"

"Yes, but you can always tell me again." Jennifer allowed Jesse to roll her onto her back, liking the feeling of her wife's body pressing on top of her.

"I love you so much." Jesse's lips continued down her lover's neck, stopping only when she found a breast to explore. Jennifer moaned as Jesse ran her hand first down, then back up her leg, fingertips barely touching sensitive skin. "You are so beautiful," Jesse whispered as she planted a trail of kisses along the path her fingers had just sketched. Slipping her body between Jennifer's legs, Jesse gently spread them apart, revealing her wife to her. She breathed deeply, inhaling the sweet, musky scent of her lover's arousal. Dropping her head, she circled Jennifer's clit with her tongue. Enjoying the sensation, Jesse ran her tongue along her lover's nether lips, exploring every dip and fold along its silky path. She circled Jennifer's opening with teasing deliberation, her tongue pressing inside for a few seconds before retreating.

Jennifer moaned. Her body was on fire, and only Jesse could put out the blaze.

Jesse's tongue tracked slowly back to the waiting clit, exploring the silky softness as it moved. She placed her mouth over the hard nub, sucking it inside. At the same time, her hands moved up to claim Jennifer's firm breasts, kneading them rhythmically.

"Please." Jennifer tangled her hands in Jesse's thick hair, encouraging her downward to where she needed her wife the most.

After a moment of resistance, Jesse complied. Her tongue traveled back to the source of Jennifer's sweet nectar. Squeezing erect nipples between her thumbs and fingers, Jesse thrust her tongue inside her wife.

Jennifer's head tilted back as her heels dug into the rough material of their bedrolls, thrusting herself against her lover's tongue. Toes curling and back arching, she grabbed handfuls of blanket as Jesse bored into her, the building pressure finally exploding into powerful waves of orgasm that washed through her as she screamed Jesse's name.

Arriving at Walks on the Wind's camp that morning, the Bransons found him and the other hunters and their families preparing the bison killed during the hunt for transport back to their village. Knowing that Jennifer wanted to see the large animals up close, Walk offered to accompany the women to a spot where they would be able to observe the bison from safety. He guided them to a knoll several miles from his camp where they had sat watching the bison herd for the past few hours.

"This is amazing." Jennifer was gawking. "All these animals in one place."

"Yep." Jesse adjusted her position to be more comfortable. "Hard to believe the herds used to be a lot bigger."

Jennifer swept her arms across the scene playing out in front of her. "How could they get bigger than this?"

She, Jesse, and Walk were sitting high up the slope of a grass-covered hill. Before them, spread across the valley floor and dotting the surrounding hillsides, was a herd of bison numbering in the thousands. The air was rich with the sounds of their grunts and bellows and the ground vibrated with each passing hoof as it thudded against the hard earth. Here and there, clouds of dust swirled up from wallows being carved into the ground by animals rolling in the dirt, attempting to protect their sensitive skin from annoying flies and ticks. Occasionally, the crack of skulls butting would ricochet around the valley as two bulls fought for dominance, their deceivingly short, stubby legs driving their muscular bodies as the rivals battled.

Charley had been left in the Indian camp with the woman who had agreed to nurse him during their stay. KC was draped across Jennifer's legs, her attention switching between the large animals and the adults whose laps she crawled in and out of continuously.

"Ook, Momma." KC pulled on Jennifer's pant leg. She pointed as a bison bull pawed the ground, raising a large cloud of dust.

"I see, sweetie." Jennifer reached out a hand to steady KC as she rolled down off her lap to climb atop Walk's folded legs. "I can't believe the herds were bigger than this. What happened to them?"

"White men." Walk kept an eye on KC squirming around in his lap as she readied herself to stand, using his shirt for handholds. "They kill the bison for sport, not caring that we depend on them for our way of life."

Jennifer turned to look at her friend, a look of confusion on her face.

He smiled at KC when she accomplished her goal and stood on his legs, her arm encircling his neck for support. "They see all these animals and think that shooting a few won't have any effect. But they kill the cows as well as the bulls."

"Fewer cows mean fewer calves come spring," Jesse clarified.

"But they seem so docile," Jennifer said of the animals that walked so near yet showed them little notice, never making any move to threaten or charge.

"Ain't much of a challenge to shoot them if you have one of the new large bore rifles they're making back East. You can drop a bull with one well-placed shot."

"Don't the others run away?" Jennifer asked.

"No." Walk tickled KC's leg, eliciting a burst of giggles. "They're kind of stupid when it comes to that. They'll stick around a dead one to see if they can figure out what happened to it."

"By the time they do, someone shoots them," Jesse finished.

"What do the hunters do with them?" Jennifer asked.

"Most of the carcasses rot in the sun," Walk said, disgusted with the wasteful practice. "Some take the hides, some the tongues. The rest is left where the animal dies."

"Their tongues?"

"Yep. Seems it's a delicacy in Eastern restaurants," Jesse told her wife.

"Don't they know that the Indians depend on the bison to live?"

"Don't care."

"Ook." KC pointed to a pair of bulls jousting. "Boom, boom." She imitating the loud noise the animals' thick skulls made when they collided.

Jesse chuckled. "Think they'd give themselves a headache."

"Especially since their heads ain't half as thick as yours." Walk laughed at his own jest.

"Mommy." KC scooted out of Walk's lap, crawling over Jennifer's legs to Jesse's empty lap. "Boom, boom."

"Pretty loud, ain't they, Sunshine?" Jesse pulled the baby up and kissed her before turning her around to look at the milling herd. "Almost as loud as Charley when he wakes up hungry."

"Yep," the baby agreed.

Mention of the boy made Jesse wonder how he was doing. "Guess we probably should get back to camp."

"Thank you for bringing us here, Walk." Jennifer smiled. "It's a sight I'll never forget."

"Glad you got to see it. The bison probably won't be around much longer."

"What do you mean?"

"Some folks are starting to say that the bison should be wiped out." Jesse's voice was as sad as her friend's. "Say that they can force the Indians onto reservations if they don't have the bison for food."

Jennifer was shocked. "That's horrible."

"Yes, it is." Walk pushed himself up from his resting spot. "But unfortunately it's true. Without the bison to provide us meat, clothing, and shelter, we'd have little choice but to go onto the reservations."

Jennifer shook her head. The thought of the proud Indian people being forced to live confined to small reservations because of the wanton annihilation of their primary food source was appalling. "I hope it never comes to that. Hopefully, the soldiers will stop that from happening."

"Wouldn't put too much trust in them," Jesse said as she stood with KC. "They're some of the ones doing most of the talking."

Tears welling in her eyes, Jennifer scanned the valley and the dark shapes that filled it. Could these magnificent creatures really be destroyed so senselessly?

CHAPTER THIRTY-NINE

A bald, overweight man with a cigar hanging from the corner of his mouth entered Mayor Perkins' office. "Good day. I understand that we might find Mr. Tobias Harrington here."

"And who are you?" the mayor asked cautiously.

"My name is Weese and this," he stepped aside to expose a much thinner, red-haired man, "is Mr. Glade. We have been sent to check on the progress of Mr. Harrington's work. We came in on the afternoon stage, and one of the workmen over at the construction site directed us here."

"Not more of you people," Perkins groaned.

"Excuse me," Glade moved further into the room, "but I don't think I caught your name."

"Perkins. Mayor Perkins."

"Ah." Weese stepped forward and held out a beefy hand. "A pleasure to meet you, Mayor Perkins. I understand you have served our company well."

Perkins stared at the sweaty hand and decided he had no intention of touching it. "Harrington is in jail," he said bluntly, in hopes they would leave his office.

"You mean *at* the jail?"

"No." The mayor grimaced. "I mean he is *in* jail. I ordered him to be held until the sheriff gets back from Bannack."

Weese blew out a large cloud of cigar smoke. "Why on earth would you have him arrested?"

Perkins batted at the thick fog floating toward him. "Would you put that blasted thing out before you set my office on fire?"

"You haven't answered the question."

"Perhaps you should go ask Tobias what he's been up to." Perkins smirked. "Unless, of course, your company is already aware of the many laws he has broken since arriving in Sweetwater." Both men looked bewildered by the comment, so he embellished. "He has committed fraud, conspiracy, and attempted murder, just to name a few."

"What are you talking about?"

"Jail is two doors down. You can't miss it, it's the one with the bars on the windows," Mayor Perkins told the men between coughs. "Take that damn cigar and go ask him."

"Wilson, you have to get me out of here," Tobias Harrington told his foreman.

"Hell," Frank Wilson leaned against the wall opposite the cell bars, "your arrogance and stupidity got you in there. I say it's where you belong."

"Imbecile." Harrington paced in the small cell. "Can't you see I can't fix this from in here?"

"How you goin' to fix it?" Wilson chuckled. "Goin' ta make some more secret plans with Kensington?"

"How was I to know the man was crazy?"

"Should have been pretty obvious, if you ask me. Can't believe you thought he could, or would, just hand over the Slipper to you. Did you really think the Bransons would let all that happen without a fight? And isn't promising company stock to a complete outsider a little beyond your authority?"

"That's none of your business."

"But it is ours," Glade said as he walked through the door that separated the cells from the jail office, Weese right behind him.

Harrington stopped pacing, the color draining from his face when he saw the board members. "Mr. Glade, what are you doing here? And you, Mr. Weese?"

"We were sent to check up on you." Glade had never liked or trusted Harrington. "Though we were told your activities here seemed troubling, we weren't expecting to find you in jail."

"Oh damn." Harrington sank down onto the cot. "This can't be happening."

Wilson, Weese, and Glade left Harrington to his own thoughts and returned to the outer office. Weese sat in the chair behind the desk, his huge frame straining the furniture's limited strength, while Glade occupied the chair Billie kept for visitors. Wilson stood by the office window, keeping an eye on the workmen putting the finishing touches on the hotel across the street. Instead of trying to explain things to the other two men, he handed them copies of the most recent editions of the *Gazette*.

"I don't believe this," Weese said.

"Believe it," Wilson assured him. "It's all true."

"I don't understand." Weese tossed the paper on the desk. "If the Songbird is worthless, why would Harrington continue with the other projects?"

"You'll have to ask him," Wilson said. "But to be fair, he says he was taken in by the miner who sold the Songbird. So, as far as the mine goes, he was played for a sucker, and the company paid the price. As for the bank and hotel, maybe he thought he could sell them and recoup some of the loss."

"Maybe so, but what about the rest?"

"As for the rest of it, I haven't got a clue why he did it. Pride, I guess."

"Pride?"

"It seems he didn't take kindly to the Bransons saying no to him when he offered to buy the Silver Slipper."

"Because of that he conspired to send an innocent woman to prison?"

Wilson wanted to be sure the men understood the full severity of Harrington's plot. "Could have been hung."

"Oh, my," Weese stammered. "Do you realize what that would have done to the company's reputation?"

"Not to mention Jesse Branson's neck," Wilson said wryly.

Weese looked to Glade. "Now what?"

Glade frowned. "I guess we need the records Harrington was keeping. But before that, we need to get ourselves settled for the night. It looks to be a long one."

"Records should be in the mayor's office," Wilson told the men. "You can get rooms at the Silver Slipper."

"But isn't that the establishment Harrington tried to purchase?"

"Yes. But unless you want to sleep on a cot in the back of the stage depot, it's the only place in town you can rent a room and get a meal."

"I thought you said the hotel was finished?"

"Building is, but there ain't any furniture inside, so unless you plan to sleep on the floor, I suggest you get a room at the Slipper."

"Mr. Wilson," Glade stood, walking the few paces to stand beside the foreman, "how much longer before your work is done on those buildings?"

"Structures are basically finished," Wilson told the slender man. "Have a little more work on the hotel; should be done today or tomorrow. I was planning on paying off the men by the end of the day. 'Course, the insides aren't done, no furnishings or such. I put a hold on the orders. Figured you'd be wanting to save the money."

"Thank you, Mr. Wilson. I assure you your hard work will not be forgotten."

"Yeah, sure," Wilson said skeptically, having heard similar empty promises many times before.

Glade wasn't sure what to make of the foreman's attitude. "We will need you to take us to the Songbird tomorrow."

Frank Wilson removed his hat and wiped the sweat off his forehead. As he replaced the Stetson, he looked the two men over. One was average height and thin as a rail, his otherwise non-distinct form topped by a head framed in curly red hair and sideburns. The other man was of a similar height but much rounder, and a cloud of cigar smoke seemed to follow him. Wilson chuckled to himself. If he had a few drinks under his belt it would be easy to imagine Weese as one of the cigars he sucked on incessantly and Glade as the matchstick used to light it.

"It's a steep climb to the mine." Wilson looked at the rotund Weese. "Sure you can make it?"

"I thought you were constructing a road," Weese said, exhaling a puff of smoke.

"Never got started on it." Wilson waved his hand to clear the smoke that was beginning to fill the room. "After I found out about the mine, didn't think the company would want me to waste the money."

Weese stood to join the other men and let loose another puff. "Too bad Harrington didn't think like you."

"You want to go to the mine," Wilson waved at the smoke again, "you can hire horses at the livery behind the Oxbow. Find me when you're ready." Wilson pulled open the jailhouse door and stepped outside, inhaling deeply of the fresh air.

"Come on." Glade looked disgustedly at Weese and his cigar. "Let's go get us some rooms."

After returning from their day of watching the bison, Jesse took KC to explore a creek near the Indian camp. Jennifer remained at their tent with Charley, the baby needing a change of diapers. Walks on the Wind approached and sat beside Jennifer. "How's your hand?"

Jennifer paused to flex the injured fingers. "Still a little stiff, but that's better than having it broken." She finished with Charley's diaper, then lifted the baby into her arms and gently rocked the fussing infant. "Don't you go to sleep before your mommy and sister get back," Jennifer told the sleepy baby. "You know how much they like to say goodnight to you."

Walk stretched his hands behind him, leaning back on his braced arms. "Hope she's not looking for fish in that creek. We haven't found a single one big enough to eat."

Jennifer grinned. "No. She just wants an excuse to play with KC."

They watched as Jesse sat on the creek bank, removed her boots, and rolled up her pant legs. After saying something to KC, the rancher lifted the baby from the bank and held her over the creek so she could kick her feet in the water.

Jennifer was struck by the naturalness of the scene and the freedom it represented. She realized that the Indians had enjoyed such freedom for thousands of years to now find themselves threatened with the loss of it. She knew how she'd felt when her life with Jesse had been in jeopardy, and she wondered how her friend felt. She turned to look at the man who seemed relaxed. "Walk, don't you worry about what will happen?"

"When?"

"If the bison are killed, if your village is forced onto a reservation."

Walk sat up, brushing the dirt from his hands. "Worrying won't keep it from happening, Jennifer. My tribe has always tried to live in peace with the white man, but that didn't save my father."

"How did he die?" She didn't want to cause her friend pain but was curious as to the circumstances that had caused him as a young boy to lose his father.

"It was early spring, and a small herd of elk had been spotted not too far from my village. Father was part of the hunting party. A troop of soldiers on their way to Fort Walla Walla heard the sounds of gunfire and panicked. Thinking they were being attacked by a war party, they charged, firing as they rode." Walk sighed deeply. "None of the hunting party survived."

Jennifer placed a hand on his arm. "I'm so sorry."

"The soldiers were young and new to our lands. If they had only stopped to see what my father and the others were doing, they would have known they were in no danger. If they had approached in friendship, they would have been welcomed as brothers."

Jennifer frowned. "Before I came here, I read many descriptions of Indian attacks in the Eastern newspapers. They made it seem as if Indians tried to kill every white man and woman they saw. I'll admit I was afraid of what might happen if I saw an Indian."

"Yet you came anyway."

"Yes. Something seemed to draw me to the West."

Walk smiled. "Or someone?"

"I suppose so." Jennifer grinned. "It wasn't until I met Jesse that I saw the other side of the picture. She made me see that Indians are just people, with the same thoughts and worries and hopes as everyone else. I guess I never took the time to look at them that way."

"You are wrong, Jennifer. We are not the same. White men come into our lands, not to live as our brothers as we would ask, but to take away what has been ours for many generations. They fence our hunting grounds so their cattle can eat the tall grasses. They kill our braves because they are scared when they see them riding in hunting parties. Our elders and young children die from the diseases the white man carries. We offer them peace, but they give us death."

"Yet you are still friendly toward us. I don't know if I would be the same."

"You and Buffalo Heart have shown me only friendship; why would I show you anything less? I cannot judge a whole people by the actions of some."

"That's what Jesse says, too. It's sad that more people don't live that way."

"My mother's second husband said it is the way of the white man to conquer and control. They will not be happy until they take all the land between here and the great water to the west. I only hope that enough of my people survive to tell our stories to our children's children and their children." Walk looked at the baby now sound asleep in Jennifer's arms. "I still hope that one day our peoples will live together in peace."

"Do you really think you can lock me away and forget about me?" Martin Kensington shouted at his wife. "I have many friends that will see that I am freed."

"Father, please," Thomas pleaded, having listened to his father's ranting for the last few hours. "We can do nothing about this. Judge Henson has issued the order. Please stop taking it out on Mother."

"You weakling," Kensington spat. "I'll have you removed from the company. Your brothers will see to that."

Marshal Morgan wasn't about to listen to the man scream all the way to Denver and points beyond. "Kensington, either you shut up and keep quiet the remainder of the trip, or I will gag you."

"You will sit there and allow him to threaten me?" Kensington bellowed at his wife.

Mary stared out the coach window, doing her best to block out her husband's words. In a brief moment of weakness before they left Bannack, she had felt guilty over her plan to have her husband committed. But after listening to his ravings as the miles passed, she knew in her heart that she had made the right decision. Turning to face her husband who sat on the opposite side of the coach, she said, "Yes, Martin. I will let him threaten you. And if you continue in your ravings, I will sit by and let him gag you."

Kensington's face turned red with anger. The woman he had controlled since their wedding day had spoken back to him. "How dare you!"

Mary looked at the shackled, handcuffed man. Any resemblance to the man she had married was long gone and a stranger sat in his place. She turned back to the window, feeling no emotion whatsoever for the marshal's prisoner.

Glade and Weese were walking toward the Silver Slipper carrying their travel bags. "Mr. Newby, we cannot possibly respond to your questions at this time."

Ignoring their attempts to avoid his questions, Thaddeus had doggedly followed the men since they had exited the jail. "Mr. Glade, a simple comment as to why you and Mr. Weese are in Sweetwater is not too much to ask."

"As I have said," Glade was thankful to reach the steps to the Slipper's broad porch, "we are here to look into matters. That is all I am going to say at this time."

Thaddeus bounded up the steps behind him. "When can the people of Sweetwater expect more of an answer?"

"As soon as we have assessed the situation here." Glade entered the Slipper, leaving his associate to field the newspaperman's questions.

Thaddeus stood waiting on the porch as Weese lugged his travel bags up to the steps. The obese man stood in the dusty street, wheezing loudly as his tobacco-damaged lungs struggled to take in enough oxygen for the strenuous activity of climbing the stairs.

Taking pity on the rotund man, Thaddeus walked back down the steps and picked up the man's bags. "Come on, it'll be cooler inside," he said, leading the way up the stairs.

Crossing the porch, Thaddeus held open the door as Weese struggled to make it inside before collapsing from the exertion of walking the length of Sweetwater. Once inside the building, Weese headed straight for the nearest chair, slumping down into it. "Thank you," he gasped when Thaddeus set his bags down at his feet.

Glade shook two room keys at Weese, taking pleasure in telling his exhausted companion, "Our rooms are upstairs." When the other man only stared at him in response, Glade tossed one of the keys onto the table beside his fellow board member. "Guess you can make it up after you've had some rest. Don't answer any questions," he called out as he climbed the steps to the rooms.

Thaddeus dropped into a chair next to Weese.

"I'm sorry," Weese picked up a cloth napkin from the table, using it to wipe the sweat from his face and neck, "but I shouldn't say anything to you." He smiled apologetically.

Thaddeus smiled back. "But you will."

After checking to make sure Glade had disappeared from sight, Weese said, "We are here to look into Harrington's misuse of company assets."

"And?"

"I'm sorry, but I really can't say any more." Weese leaned over to pick up his bags.

"The citizens of Sweetwater will want more than that."

"And they shall have it. After," Weese stood, "we have finished our review. Until then, I'm sorry."

"But you can at least tell me what you plan to do while in Sweetwater."

"We will review Mr. Harrington's records first thing tomorrow, then we will examine the Songbird mine."

"I want to accompany you."

"I'll talk to Glade," Weese said, walking to the flight of steps he was already dreading having to climb every time he returned to his room. He hoped their stay in Sweetwater was a short one. "I can promise nothing."

Thaddeus watched the stout man labor up the stairs.

CHAPTER FORTY

When she limped back to camp from the small thicket of trees, Jennifer was surprised to see their horses still grazing near the creek. Walks on the Wind and the other hunters had left just after sunrise to return to their village far to the west. She and Jesse had decided to wait for KC and Charley to wake up and be fed before they broke down their own camp. She was expecting to find Jesse packing the tent and their other supplies onto Boy, but the tent was still standing and her wife and children were nowhere to be seen.

"Jesse?" Jennifer called out as she approached the campsite.

"In here, darlin'," Jesse answered from inside the tent.

Jennifer stepped through the opening made by the tied-back canvas flap. Jesse was laying on their bedroll, stretched out on her belly with her ankles crossed and her elbows tucked under her chest. KC was stretched out on Jesse's back, one arm wrapped around Jesse's neck, her head next to her mommy's. Both mother and daughter seemed to be enchanted by the sight of the diaper-clad infant lying on the bedroll before them.

"What are you doing?"

Jesse blew on the baby's tummy, her loose hair tickling his skin. "Playing," Jesse said.

"Playing?" Jennifer eased herself down on the bedroll on the opposite side of Charley.

"Yep."

KC giggled, watching Charley kick his tiny feet in response to Jesse's tickling.

"I thought you were going to start breaking camp, sweetheart." Jennifer slipped her pinkie finger under Charley's tiny hand, the baby's fingers instantly wrapping around it. She smiled as Jesse continued to tease smiles from their son and giggles from their daughter. It never ceased to amaze her how much Jesse was fascinated by the children. Her wife simply adored them. "Sweetheart?"

"Hmm?"

"Do you plan to play all day, or are we going home?"

Jesse cocked her head to one side, smiling at Jennifer. "Guess I kinda got carried away."

"Guess you did." Jennifer laughed as she lifted the baby into her arms.

KC slipped off Jesse's back, crawling to Jennifer's side and plopping down beside her.

Jennifer was amused when KC's head tilted to the side just as Jesse's had done moments before. "Now I know where she gets that."

"Gets what?" Jesse asked, pushing herself up from the bedroll.

"That." Jennifer pointed at their daughter, her head cocked to one side as she continued to watch her brother. "That's what you do when you're thinking."

"I do?"

"Yes."

Jesse scratched her head. "Never noticed."

Jennifer ruffled KC's hair. "You do."

"Okay, if you say so." Jesse surveyed the array of items needing to be packed and loaded on Boy. "I better get busy if we're going to start for home today."

"I'll get Charley dressed and these two settled where it's safe, while you get the horses saddled." Jennifer smiled as Jesse helped her to her feet. "If we both work at getting packed, it won't take too long."

"You've got yourself a deal."

"Ook. " KC pointed excitedly. "Ook."

"I see it, Sunshine." Jesse pulled Dusty to a stop.

The family was following a trail that paralleled a small river. At a point where the distance between riverbanks narrowed, a family of beaver had built a dam blocking the river's flow and causing the backed-up water to form a large pond. At the far side of the pond, a moose stood in hip-deep water, grazing on the plants he found growing under the surface of the water. The moose raised his head, water dripping off his antlers and shaggy head. A large brown eye scrutinized the riders as he chewed his mouthful of plants.

"Ook." KC bounced in the carry sack on Jesse's back. "Ook, Wie." She was disappointed that Charley was showing no interest in the large, gangly animal.

"Sweetie, he's too small to see." Jennifer nudged Blaze up alongside Dusty. "Funny looking, aren't they?" Since coming West, she had seen several moose and always thought they looked like someone had taken parts from different animals to put them together.

The moose had dark, thick hair covering its body. Large ears stood out on either side of a head that was fronted by a bulbous nose. Its round belly and lumpy hips were supported by long, skinny legs, all seeming to move independently of one another. A long clump of skin and hair hung under its neck and served no purpose that Jennifer could guess at.

"Oh, I don't know." Jesse reached for the canteen hanging from her saddle horn. "I think they're kinda cute."

"Really?" Jennifer lifted her own canteen and held it so KC could drink.

"Yep." Jesse smiled. "Kinda soft and cuddly like."

Jennifer took a drink as she watched the moose dunk its head back underwater in search of more watery plants. "They look like all legs and nose to me."

"But they have those big, brown eyes." Jesse urged Dusty forward. Even though they were next to the river, it was hot sitting in the sun. Before stopping for the day, she wanted to reach a small meadow just inside the forest they were nearing.

Jennifer took a firmer hold of her reins when Blaze moved to follow Dusty. She took one last look at the moose, its head again raised out of the water. "Jesse, why do you think it has that lump hanging under its neck?"

"My guess," Jesse led the horses off the main trail and onto a less used path that headed directly toward the forest, "is that it's for their protection."

"Protection?" Jennifer laughed. "How could that protect a moose?"

"When wolves attack, they go for the throat." As she explained, Jesse sadly recalled a similar conversation she'd once had with her father. She again wondered why her parents, after accepting an offer to move to the ranch, had not appeared in Sweetwater. "If they get hold of that lump instead, the moose can escape with only a minor injury."

Jennifer had never thought about such a large animal being attacked, but when she did, Jesse's explanation made sense.

"Gentlemen, it's late, and my wife is waiting dinner on me."

"Mayor Perkins," Glade did not look up from the papers he was studying, "I have told you before that you may leave. Your assistance is no longer required."

"I can't just leave you in my office."

"You afraid we're going to steal something?" Weese taunted, glancing around the sparsely furnished office.

"No, it's just that—"

"Either leave or be quiet," Glade growled. "I can't concentrate with all your babbling."

"Fine." Mayor Perkins grabbed his coat from the hook beside the door. He hadn't missed many meals in his life, and he wasn't about to start. Weese blew a puff of cigar smoke after the departing mayor.

Glade coughed as the sharp-tasting smoke entered his nose and mouth. "Do you ever not smoke those?"

"Only when I sleep." Weese deliberately took a long drag on the offensive cigar.

"Then why don't you go for a walk or go back to the Slipper and take a nap? You're not helping much here, anyway."

"Isn't much for me to do with you hovering over those papers like that." Weese leaned back in his chair, content to let the other man do all the work if he so chose.

"Damn." Glade pushed the papers aside and pulled a ledger book in front of him. "From what I can see, Harrington followed his instructions to the letter, with the exception of his dealings with Kensington."

"Seems I've heard that name." Weese puffed out a perfect ring of cigar smoke, watching it float to the ceiling before it broke apart.

"You should have." Glade shook his head, wondering not for the first time why the ignorant man was on the company's board of directors. "We've done business with his shipping company many times. Usually dealt with his son, though," he added, mostly to himself.

"Ah, yes, now I remember." Weese let loose another smoke ring. "What about the purchase of the Songbird?" he asked, addressing the true crux of the matter.

"The board approved the assay report before Harrington signed the papers."

Weese sat up, his movement so abrupt he almost spat his cigar at Glade. "How is that possible? I don't recall the board ever voting on that issue."

"The board didn't." Glade pushed a piece of paper across the desk. "One board member approved the purchase outright."

"That's not possible." Weese reached for the paper, rapidly reading it. "It's against board policy."

"That didn't keep someone from approving the assay report and signing an order authorizing Harrington to buy the Songbird."

"But whose signature is that?"

"That is a very good question?" Thaddeus Newby murmured to himself. He was sitting in the office of the *Gazette*, which shared a wall, a very thin wall, with the mayor's office. He wasn't officially eavesdropping, he told himself, but rather taking advantage of an opportunity that had so very fortuitously presented itself.

"I don't know." Glade scratched his cheek; it was time to trim his sideburns. "Wait a minute," he exclaimed, a thought floating up from the deep recesses of his memory. There just might be an answer to their question.

"What?"

"That assayer's report, where is it?"

"Which one, Harrington's or Newby's?"

"The first one."

"I think it's in that pile." Weese pointed to the desk. "We looked at it earlier."

Glade sorted through the mound of documents in questions. "Yes, here it is. Damn."

"What?"

"The name of the miner that sold the Songbird to Harrington?"

"Jackson, no," Weese scratched his bald head, "Jerkins, no."

"Jensen," Thaddeus whispered.

"Jensen!" Glade shouted at his companion's lack of memory. "Look at the signature on that order."

"Jensen."

"I'll be." Thaddeus chuckled. "Ol' Jensen made fools out of all of 'em."

"This doesn't make sense." Weese stubbed out his cigar on the mayor's desk. "Why wasn't the purchase questioned?"

"The board sent Harrington here to find a gold mine, one that showed promise of a rich vein. He received a follow-up order telling him the board has decided on the Songbird, based on an assay report the board ordered. Why would Harrington question it?"

"But he said nothing about this to the board?"

"We weren't asking him about the mine, only about the cost overruns caused by his failure to purchase the Silver Slipper."

"That's right."

"He had no reason to mention it, thinking we already knew. Clever," Glade slumped back in his chair, "don't you think?"

"Is Bette Mae, all right?" Ruthie asked as the older woman again took her plate and moved away from the others to eat her meal alone.

Since leaving Bannack, Bette Mae had been unusually quiet. She had said little while they rode, and when they stopped to camp, she had prepared their meals in silence, declining all offers of help. She answered inquiries about her well-being with polite but short responses that presented no opportunity for further inquiry.

Ed watched Bette Mae walk away from their camp to sit beside the creek flowing a short distance away. "Sometimes," he answered Ruthie's question, "the past comes back to you, bringing all the hurt you thought you'd left behind."

Ruthie and Billie looked quizzically at the storekeeper, but before they could ask for clarification of his statement, Ed picked up his own plate and moved to sit next to Bette Mae.

"Do you know what's goin' on?" Billie asked his fiancée.

"I don't." Ruthie shook her head. "She's been like this ever since the day she said she had business to attend to in Bannack."

"What business?"

"Don't know. She left the hotel one morning, and she's been like this ever since."

Billie watched Ed and Bette Mae speaking quietly, and he sensed they wanted their conversation to be private. "What would you say to a short walk? Looks like we're goin' have a clear night and a full moon." He smiled. "Perhaps we could do some courtin'?"

Ruthie blushed. "Billie, I've already agreed to marry you."

"Doesn't mean we can't do any courtin'." Billie stood, offering his hand to her. When she placed her hand in his, he gently pulled her upright. "Besides, I could do with a good stretch of my legs after being in that saddle the past few days."

Hearing movement, Ed turned to see Billie and Ruthie walking alongside the creek in a direction that took them away from where he sat with Bette Mae. Grateful for the added privacy, he turned back to his friend and gently broached the subject that had been on his mind for several days. "You can tell me it's none of my business, and I'll leave ya be."

"She was yer sister." Bette Mae sniffled. "Guessin' that makes it yer business."

"What went on between you ain't my business if you don't want it to be."

Bette Mae sat silently watching the water rippling over the rocks in the shallow creek. "I didn' do right by her," she said in a quiet voice.

"I don't believe that, Bette Mae." Ed was happy that the woman seemed to be willing to talk to him. "She had a strong will, did just what she wanted. Always had."

"I coulda spoke up, coulda tol' her how I felt."

"Don't think it would have made much difference," Ed said softly, not wanting to hurt Bette Mae more. "Don't know what she told you, but she loved Cassidy; would have stayed with him no matter what."

"Said she thought 'bout leavin' 'im, but she had no place ta go."

"I know, she told me that, too." Bette Mae looked up at him, her eyes questioning. "I tried to get her away from Cassidy many times." Ed tossed a pebble into the creek, watching it until it got lost among the other stones on the creek bed.

"She said yer momma thought the world of him, that you liked 'im, too."

"Oh, Momma liked him all right. Believed all his get-rich-quick claims, thought he'd buy her a big house with lots of servants. And I admit," Ed added as Bette Mae continued to look at him doubtfully, "for a while, I believed his boasts. But soon as I met up with them in Bozeman, it didn't take long to figure out he was all talk. He gambled away more money than their little store made. Wasn't long before he had bill collectors knocking on their door day and night. Then I woke up one day to find them gone. Bastard packed up the store and moved it to Sweetwater, leaving behind nothin' but promises that I'd clear his debts. I had to get me some jobs, and I stayed until I had."

"Lizzie left you there to pay off *their* debts?"

Ed tossed another pebble. "She had a real blind spot when it came to Cassidy. No matter what that bastard did, she stuck up for him. When I finally made it to Sweetwater, he had taken off again, only he left the store behind that time. I tried to get her to leave him, but she wouldn't. Just kept telling me that he was going to strike it rich in the gold camps. Over the years, I gave up. I kept track of her by the towns he left owing money. I'd get the bills at the store; they came from just about every mining camp in the territory. Garnet, Coloma, Granite, Pony, Elkhorn, Boulder, Nevada City, Alder Gulch, Marysville, Last Chance — you name it and Cassidy owed somebody money there."

"But she was so..."

"Smart? I thought so, too, until she met him. I know you're thinking that you could have made a difference. And I truly wish that she could have had the same feelings for you that you had for her. But the truth is, she loved him, Bette Mae. And no matter how rough it got or how poorly he treated her, she was determined to stick by him."

"She was mighty pretty, Ed. I do believe she took my heart tha' first night we met. I woulda done anythin' to save her from the pain he gave her."

"I know you would have. Just sometimes, we can't be saved from ourselves."

"She's the only one I ever loved." Bette Mae leaned against Ed's strong shoulder. "The only one I ever will."

"I know," Ed whispered, hoping it wasn't true. It was sad to think of his sister with a man who never really loved her when she could have had so much more.

"Beautiful night," Jennifer said, leaning back on her arms braced behind her, her head tilted back as she scanned the cloudless sky.

"Sure is." Jesse's head rested on Jennifer's thigh, her legs stretched out with booted feet crossed at the ankles.

KC and Charley were asleep in the tent, which had been set up on the opposite side of the fire. The tent flap was tied open so the mothers could keep watch on their sleeping children.

"You've been quiet tonight." Jennifer lifted one hand, brushing it free of earth before running it though Jesse's hair. "Anything wrong?"

"No."

"Sweetheart?"

"No."

"They're going to come, Jesse."

Jesse rolled her head to look at Jennifer. "How do you know what I'm thinking?"

"I'm your wife." Jennifer smiled. "And I love you."

"That doesn't explain it."

"Sweetheart." Jennifer looked down at her wife. Her hair hung over Jesse's face as she tenderly caressed it. "You've had this on your mind since we left Bozeman. I don't think a day has gone by that you haven't thought about it at least once. There's a reason it's taking so long, and when they get to Sweetwater, they'll let us know what it was."

"They could send us a letter," Jesse groused.

"Oh, Jesse." Jennifer chuckled. "You are a very proud woman, do you know that?"

Jesse looked at Jennifer, unsure where she was heading.

"Have you ever thought to ask where you get that from?"

"Pop?" Jesse offered after a few moments.

Jennifer playfully tapped the end of Jesse's nose. "That's right."

"You think Pop's ashamed to come to the ranch?"

"No, I think he just has to do it in his way."

"Just like I would."

"Yes."

"How'd you get so smart?"

"I spent my youth in a library."

"Ugh." Jesse smirked. "How awful for you."

Jennifer laughed, smacking Jesse's arm. "You're rotten."

"Come here." Jesse held out her arm, waiting as her wife scooted around to snuggle against her.

"This is nice," Jennifer sighed.

"Very nice."

The women looked up at the sky they knew so well. It was a practice they'd started on the first night they had spent sleeping under the familiar blanket of stars. At the time they were tired, dirty, and being chased by a posse, but it hadn't stopped them from falling in love.

"Jesse, do you remember that night I broke you out of jail?"

"Kinda hard to forget somethin' like that, darlin'."

"It was just like this. We were looking up at the stars, and you said you had feelings for me."

"That I did."

"When did you know?"

Jesse smiled as she remembered the day the new schoolteacher had arrived in Sweetwater. "I fell for you the minute you stepped off the stage."

"Really?"

"Yep. I took one look at you, and my heart starting racing so fast, I thought I was goin' ta pass out. I think Ed thought I was, too, but he probably thought it was from the sun."

"It was hot that day."

"Darlin'?" Jesse asked. "You tired?"

"No."

"Want ta go to bed?"

"Yes."

The couple walked for some time before deciding to sit. They chose a sandy beach carved by the creek in times of high water. It was now dry, providing a pleasant spot to sit and enjoy each other's company. Billie sat with his back against a small boulder while Ruthie was nestled between his legs and wrapped in his embrace, half-turned in his arms. He tenderly held her face between his hands as he kissed her. With the full moon highlighting her face in its soft glow, he thought she was the most beautiful woman on earth.

"I love you," he whispered as their lips parted. His eyes never leaving his fiancée's face, he said, "It's a beautiful night."

"Yes, very beautiful." Ruthie tilted her head back to gaze at the millions of stars twinkling above them. She smiled as one shot across the sky, a sign of good luck. "Billie?"

"Yes, honey."

"If I asked you to do something, would you think about it?"

"What is it, Ruth?" he asked, concerned she might be changing her mind about the marriage. When he received no answer, he gently turned her face back toward him. "Tell me what's wrong."

"I don't want you to..."

"Don't want me to what?"

Ruthie dropped her eyes, unable to look into Billie's when she said, "I don't want you to be sheriff after we get married."

Billie let out a breath. "Why not?"

"I don't want anything happening to you, Billie."

Billie laughed in an attempt to lessen Ruthie's fears. "What could happen to me in Sweetwater?"

"You've already been shot, Billie," she cried. "I don't want it to happen again."

Billie hadn't forgotten that Ruthie was in the Slipper the night he faced down the lynch mob. How could he forget? That was the night he fell in love with the shy girl as she helped to dress his wounds.

Normally Sweetwater's sheriff had little to do but lock up the occasional drunken cowboy until he sobered up and could return to whatever ranch employed him. But the night he had had to face down an angry group of men he thought of as his friends taught Billie that even in his usually quiet town, the sheriff was vulnerable to violence.

"Don't know what else I could do."

Sure that Billie was going to refuse her request, Ruthie felt her heart drop.

"But I'll find something." He smiled as she looked up at him.

"Thank you." She leaned against him.

Billie stroked Ruthie's cheek. "Fact is, I've been thinking of finding somethin' else to do."

"You have?"

"Yeah. That night at the Slipper kinda got me thinking. I was plannin' on asking Jesse if she needed help at the Slipper or out at the ranch, but all this stuff with Kensington kinda got in the way."

"You could still ask."

"I will, honey. Soon as all this is over."

"What do you mean?" Ruthie pushed away from Billie just enough to see his face.

"Something tells me there's gonna be some trouble in Sweetwater to deal with when we get back."

"What kind of trouble?"

"Harrington."

CHAPTER FORTY-ONE

KC craned her neck to see around Jennifer, who was dressing Charley.

"What are you looking at, sweetie?" Jennifer asked, sitting with her back to the tent's doorway. Jesse had tied open the canvas door flap moments before.

"Dat." KC pointed outside.

Jennifer turned to look over her shoulder. "It looks like snow," she said, astounded to see everything outside the tent covered in a light dusting of white. "But it can't be."

"Sure it can," Jesse said, stomping her boots free of the wet powder before re-entering the tent.

"Jesse, it's too soon for snow. Isn't it?" Jennifer picked up Charley, wrapping him in a blanket to protect the newborn against the morning's frostiness.

"Never too early to snow in Montana." Jesse was gathering up the loose items in the tent, packing them as she went.

"Guess it's a good thing we're heading home." Jennifer settled Charley on the tent floor next to his sister, freeing herself to help Jesse pack.

KC crawled to the tent opening, reaching out and scooping up a handful of snow. When the cold snow started melting in her hand, she laughed and offered the melting scoop to Charley.

"Oh no, you don't," Jennifer intercepted her daughter's hand, "I just got him dressed."

"Come on, Sunshine." Carrying a pack outside, Jesse lifted KC up and tucked her under her arm. "You can play in the snow out here," she told the giggling baby.

"Sweetheart," Jennifer called after her wife, "I don't want her getting cold."

"Sun's already warming things up out here." Steam was rising from the cold ground wherever the sun's rays fell on it. One advantage of waiting to break camp until KC and Charley woke up was that the sun was up and its warming beams were already at work. "Snow won't last very long, let her play while she has the chance." Jesse set the pack down on a clear spot of dirt, depositing her daughter on top of it.

"But it's cold out there."

"She'll be fine." Jesse walked the few steps back to the tent.

KC slapped her hands at the small mound of snow Jesse had dumped between her legs. Reaching for the rapidly melting snow, KC grabbed a handful. Happy to discover the snow formed a ball in her fist, she drew her arm back and threw as hard as she could. Giggling, KC watched the snowball strike the ground a foot in front of the pack where she sat. Reaching back into the pile of snow, she pulled out another snowball.

"It's not that cold," Jesse told Jennifer as she bent over to pick up the other pack. "But the temperature has dropped a bit from yesterday. I'm surprised you weren't cold last night, darlin'."

"Sweetheart," Jennifer grinned, "I'm never cold when I sleep with you."

"Glad to be of service." Jesse paused to plant a kiss on Jennifer's lips before carrying the second pack outside.

Whistling for Boy, Jesse carried the pack toward KC. The horse trotted up. Stopping near the baby, he dropped his head to continue grazing while Jesse loaded their gear. With a convenient target so close, KC let her snowball fly. It smacked into the ground at Boy's nose, startling the large draft horse. Laughing, KC clapped her hands enthusiastically as Boy pranced about, vigorously shaking his head to free the cold snow from his muzzle.

"Whoa, there." Dropping the pack to the ground, Jesse rubbed Boy's neck to calm him. "It's just a little snow. No reason for you to get so riled up." She brushed the offending snow off the horse's nose. Seeing KC forming another snowball to fire at the annoyed horse, Jesse warned, "Nope."

Dropping her handful, KC looked sadly up at her mommy. Her lower lip quivered. "Praa?"

With Boy settled, Jesse turned her attention to her daughter. "Playing is when everyone is having fun, Sunshine." She knelt in front of KC, putting herself at eye level with the sad girl. "Boy wasn't having fun, was he?" Jesse stood up, lifting KC as she did. "I think you owe Boy an apology for spooking him like that."

With her mother holding her, KC leaned her head against Boy's neck and patted the large horse. Boy twitched the muscle under KC's head, causing the baby to laugh. Apology accepted.

"Now," Jesse kissed KC's nose, "let's get you into your carry sack and load this stuff on Boy so we can get your momma and brother home."

"Otay." KC brightened, glad that her mommy didn't seem upset with her. She let Jesse slip her into her carry sack, sitting quietly as her mommy slipped her arms through the shoulder straps and adjusted the weight on her back.

"Everything okay out here?" Jennifer asked softly, having watched the events from inside the tent. She carried their bedrolls out to Jesse, carefully laying them on top of the packs so they wouldn't roll off.

"Yep." Jesse swung the harness onto Boy that she would secure their packs to. "I'll get the packs taken care of, then we can take down the tent. Give ya someplace dry to keep Charley until then."

Jennifer reached up and tweaked KC's nose. "Did you like playing with the snow, sweetie?" KC smiled, her head bobbing up and down. "But you're not going to throw it again, are you?" KC's lower lip thrust forward as she reluctantly shook her head from side to side.

"Good girl." Jennifer smiled at her daughter and waited until KC smiled back. "I love you, sweetie."

KC leaned forward, wrapping her arms around Jesse's neck. "Wuv."

"I love you, too, Sunshine." Jesse reached back and patted KC on the head. "Now let's get going, or we might as well spend another night here."

"Oh, no." Jennifer hurried back to the tent. "I want to get home and back to a nice warm bed at the Slipper, with a solid roof over my head if it's going to be snowing."

"Easterner," Jesse teased.

"It snows in the East, sweetheart," Jennifer called back, "just not in the summer."

"Ain't much left of summer." Jesse lifted a pack into place and tightened the ropes securing it.

"There's enough left that it shouldn't be snowing."

The two women were sitting in the shade of a pine tree, the babies napping on a blanket next to them. "I can't believe we had snow this morning," Jennifer said, fanning her face with her Stetson.

Jesse smirked. "Told ya we weren't done with summer yet."

Jennifer longingly eyed the small lake a few feet from where they sat. "That water sure looks nice and cool."

"Sure does."

"Last one in has to wash diapers tonight," Jennifer challenged, already unbuttoning her shirt.

"Oh, no." Jesse began tugging off her boots. "You're not sticking me with that again."

Both of them rushed to remove their clothing, then Jesse paused in her disrobing to kneel in front of Jennifer and tug off her boots, knowing how difficult it was for her wife to twist her damaged leg into position to do so herself. "Come on." Jesse stood, offering a hand to Jennifer.

Jennifer scooted past her, hurrying to the lake and splashing into the water up to her knees before coming to an abrupt stop. She screamed, "Jesse, this is cold!"

Jesse ambled to the edge of the lake, stepping in only enough to get her ankles wet. "But the best way to get used to it is just to jump in." She took a couple of steps before diving under the surface, reappearing moments later in the center of the small lake. "Ya have ta admit, it sure does cool ya off," she said with a grin.

"You could have warned me," Jennifer groused playfully as she swam out to Jesse.

"Now, darlin'," Jesse easily treaded water until her wife reached her, "where would be the fun in that?"

Jennifer slapped the water, spraying Jesse with cold droplets. Rolling over unto her back, Jesse floated. "Does feel better than sitting in the shade and sweating, doesn't it?"

"Yes." Jennifer rolled over to float beside her wife. "I still can't believe there was snow on the ground this morning."

"That's Montana for ya, darlin'." Turning her head, Jesse smiled at Jennifer. "Don't like the weather, just stick around for an hour or so; it'll change."

"I'm finding that out." Jennifer held out a hand that was instantly taken by Jesse. After a few minutes, she started to feel chilled from the cold water of the mountain lake. "Jesse, I think I'll head back."

"Yeah, it sure ain't warm enough to stay in too long." Jesse flipped over to swim to shore with Jennifer.

They emerged from the lake at a small, sandy beach. Jesse walked to a couple of large boulders that had been soaking up the sun. "Here, darlin'," she sat on the largest rock, "we can sit here in the sun to dry off."

Jennifer stretched out on the stony surface. Exposing as much of her wet skin to the sun's warm rays as possible, she shivered a little. "Think I may still need a towel, sweetheart."

"Be right back." Jesse scooted off the boulder to where Boy was grazing, their packs still secured on his back. After pulling out a towel, she checked on the babies, then picked up their clothes on the way back to Jennifer. Kneeling beside her wife, Jesse lovingly wiped the water from her body. "You are so beautiful." She dropped down next to Jennifer, enjoying the sight of her naked lover.

Jennifer smiled at Jesse. Normally she would have been embarrassed to be unclothed where anyone could see her, but sitting there with Jesse admiring her body seemed so natural. Of course, being able to gaze at her wife's nude body wasn't bad, either.

Jesse's smile disappeared as she placed her fingers on Jennifer's ankle, then ran them lightly up her damaged leg. Leaning down, she kissed the ugly scars. As she thought of the pain her wife endured every day, tears fell from her eyes and dropped onto Jennifer's skin.

"Sweetheart, what's wrong?"

"I'm so sorry," Jesse cried.

"Sorry for what?" Jennifer sat up and opened her arms, encouraging Jesse to move inside them.

Jesse didn't move, her head hanging down so Jennifer couldn't see her face. "I'm so sorry."

"Sweetheart, please tell me what's wrong." Jennifer moved closer to Jesse, embracing her. "Please, tell me," Jennifer whispered.

"If I had been there sooner, it wouldn't have happened," Jesse sobbed.

"What wouldn't have happened?"

Jesse couldn't say the words. Instead, she pointed at Jennifer's leg and the damage done by the mountain lion's claws.

Jennifer tightened her arms around her tormented wife. "What happened to my leg is not your fault."

"But—"

"No, Jesse." Jennifer lifted Jesse's chin so she could look into the eyes she loved. "You cannot blame yourself for this. You did all you could, sweetheart, and by killing the cougar when you did, you saved my life."

Jesse shook her head. "I should have been there sooner."

"Oh, sweetheart." The grief in Jesse's voice was heart wrenching. "Please don't blame yourself. I don't."

Jesse looked into Jennifer's eyes. "I just wish…"

"So do I, but it happened, and I won't let you blame yourself." She kissed the tears off Jesse's cheeks. "I love you, Jesse Branson. Don't you ever again tell me that you should have been able to prevent this, not ever."

"I love you so much. I want to protect you…"

Slowly, Jennifer lay back down on the boulder, pulling Jesse with her. "Let it out, sweetheart." She stroked Jesse's head, running her fingers through wet hair. "You've been holding on to this hurt way too long. Just let it out," she murmured as her wife cried in her arms.

"Sorry," Jesse said when her sobs finally stopped and the tears abated.

Jennifer kissed her forehead. "For what?"

"I'm not the one who should be crying about this."

Jesse tried to sit up, but Jennifer held her tight. "Why not?"

"Because it's not me who has to suffer 'cause of it."

"Don't be an idiot," Jennifer said, more harshly than she intended. "I've seen the pain in your eyes when you have to watch me struggle to do something that used to come easily. I may carry the physical scars, sweetheart, but you carry scars in here." She tapped Jesse's head. "And here." She pressed her hand over Jesse's heart. "We both have to live with it for the rest of our lives," her voice softened, "but we will live, Jesse. And that's all that's important to me. And should be to you."

Jennifer reached down and felt her leg. What had once been a symmetrically shaped limb was now uneven and misshapen, the flesh stretched and pulled together to cover the gashes carved out by the sharp claws. Chunks of flesh were missing from her thigh and above her knee and would never be replaced. The scars would eventually fade, but for now their bright reds and purples stood out against her otherwise tanned skin.

"Does seeing it bother you, Jesse?" Jennifer asked. She still found it hard to look at the deformed leg and accept it as her own.

"No, darlin'." Jesse placed a hand on the leg in question. "It only makes me hurt for you."

"It's so ugly."

"No, darlin'." It was Jesse's turn to comfort Jennifer. She rearranged their bodies so she could hold her wife. "There's nothin' ugly about you. You are the most beautiful woman I have ever seen. Those scars just remind me how much I love you and how lucky I am to still have you."

Jennifer sighed, resting her head on Jesse's shoulder. They remained wrapped in each other's embrace for several minutes until their daughter unexpectedly interrupted the much-needed interlude.

"Momma," KC called to her mothers after being awakened by her brother's whimpers.

"Uh, oh." Raising her head, Jesse looked to where they had left the children. "Sounds like someone is awake."

"And hungry." Jennifer pushed herself up when she heard Charley start to cry. "Guess we'd better get dressed."

Jesse rubbed at her eyes, red and itchy from crying. "I'll take care of them," Jennifer said as she pulled on her shirt; she'd leave the pants and boots for later. "You take a few minutes to wash the tears from your face. You know how KC gets if she thinks we're upset."

Jesse kissed Jennifer. "You are much too good for me, darlin'."

"I love you, too."

Wheezing heavily, Weese stumbled onto the plateau where the entrance to the Songbird mine was located. Once back on level ground, the stout man braced his hands on his knees, trying to draw air into his laboring lungs. His rubbery legs barely supported him, and he felt lightheaded.

Glade had crested the top of trail several minutes before and was already talking to the young man hired to guard the mine.

"Is he okay?" the guard asked when he spied the rotund man gasping, his face as red as one of the apples he had eaten for breakfast.

"Too many cigars." Glade sent a lazy glance in the direction of the suffering man. "He'll be fine in a few minutes."

"I would suggest that you sit for a while," Thaddeus observed as he appeared over the crest of the trail, having followed the two men since they'd left their horses tied at the bottom of the path. "You could have killed yourself trying to climb up here."

Glade glowered at the newspaperman. "Newby, what the hell are you doing here?"

"Thought it would be interesting to see your face when you got a look inside the Songbird," Thaddeus said as he handed a canteen to Weese, now sitting in the shade of a ponderosa pine.

Glade shook his head. "Light a couple of lanterns," he told the guard. "You can keep an eye on him," he nodded toward Weese, "while we're inside."

"Anything in particular you're looking for?" Thaddeus asked as they walked to the entrance. "Ah, I see you're still not answering questions," he said when he received no reply. "Maybe after you see the nice empty hole in the ground Harrington purchased with your company's money, you'll change your mind."

Glade accepted a lantern from the guard and stepped into the dark mine tunnel. "Might I ask a question of you?"

"Fire away." Thaddeus accepted the second lantern and followed Glade inside.

"How did you come to find out about the Songbird's false assay report?"

"Like any good reporter," Thaddeus boasted, "I followed the leads."

"And those would be?" Glade studied the rock walls as he slowly made his way down the tunnel.

"To be honest, Mr. Glade," Thaddeus held his lantern so it would cast light where the other man was looking, "I took an instant dislike to Harrington." Glade grunted. "And I decided to check on his background. Then when Miles got involved and starting making promises he shouldn't have, I really began to wonder about Harrington and the company he represented."

"Hmph."

"But it was when Billie mentioned that he had doubts about Jensen that I decided to visit the mining camps and see what I could find out."

"Doubts?"

"He wondered how a miner that never seemed to have enough gold dust to pay off his balance at the general store could be sitting on a claim as rich as Harrington made it out to be."

"I see."

"It was in one of the mining camps that I discovered the assayer was related to Jensen and that he had packed up and moved back East about the same time Jensen did. Seemed a little odd to me, don't you think?" Thaddeus' smirk was lost on the other man in the dark mine.

"What are these flakes?" Glade had reached the end of the tunnel and was examining the vein of quartz running through the rock.

"Fool's gold." Thaddeus leaned against the cool stone face. "Probably shot into the quartz with a shotgun."

Glade dug one of the flakes out with his fingernail and rubbed the tiny chip between his fingers. "Is this common practice in the West?"

"It's been known to happen a time or two."

"To sell a worthless claim to an unsuspecting fool, no doubt."

"No doubt."

Glade turned back toward the entrance. "Is there a reason, Mr. Newby, that you chose not to make your suspicions known to my company?"

"The *Gazette* doesn't serve your company, Mr. Glade. My concern was for Sweetwater and how Harrington's activities were going to affect the town and the folks that live around here. Harrington refused to cooperate. So..."

"Fair enough." Glade stepped out of the mine, shading his eyes against the harsh sunlight.

"I've answered your questions, Mr. Glade." Thaddeus blew out his lantern and handed it back to the guard. "How about answering mine?"

"I'm sorry, but I have yet to question Harrington about this. I must insist that you wait until I have done that."

"I'm trying to be fair to you and your company, Mr. Glade, but I must say you aren't making it easy. Folks want to know what is going to happen now that you no longer have a reason to be in Sweetwater. I'd say it's only fair you tell them."

"I shall, Mr. Newby, but not until I have sent my report back to Mr. Prestly and receive his instructions in return."

"Harrington," Glade pulled a chair from the sheriff's office into the area in front of the cells, "we've been to the Songbird, and we've looked at your records." He dragged the chair opposite the occupied cell and sat. "Now I want to hear what you have to say."

"Where's Weese?" Harrington asked when the other man did not appear.

"The climb up to the Songbird was too much for him. He's at the Slipper, resting in his room."

"He ought to give up his cigars," Harrington mumbled.

Glade drew the conversation back to its original purpose. "You want to tell me your side of all this?"

Harrington sat on the bunk in his cell, his usually neat appearance significantly deteriorated. He had several days' worth of stubble on his face, and his clothes were rumpled from being slept in. He ran a hand through his disheveled hair. "I did what I was told to do. I was just following my instructions."

Glade settled in for a long afternoon. "Let's start with the fact that you were sent to Montana to find a suitable mine for us to purchase. How did you go about that?"

"I visited many of the mining camps, listening to what people said, talking to several assayers to find out what areas showed the most promise." Harrington was proud of the detail work he had done, and his tone reflected that pride. "I had narrowed it down to a half dozen possibilities before I made the deal on the Songbird."

"Why the Songbird?"

"Why ask me? The board made that decision."

"Did we?"

"Of course you did." Harrington didn't like the way Glade was watching him, seeming to study his every word and movement. "I received a letter telling me the board had decided on the Songbird. I was instructed to meet with the miner that held the claim and buy it from him."

"Did those instructions come from the entire board?"

"No." Harrington didn't have to think about his answer; it had bothered him at the time that only one board member had signed the letter. But he wasn't being paid to question his instructions, only to carry them out.

"Who signed it?"

"Robert Jensen."

"In all the years you have worked for us, Harrington, how often did you receive instructions from a single board member?"

"Just the once."

"Have you ever known any member of the board to make a decision that was not sanctioned by the president of our company?"

"No."

"Have you ever received an instruction or order not signed by the president?"

"No."

"Yet you chose to follow instructions that were sent to you by a single board member and not signed by the president."

Harrington remained silent; there was nothing for him to say.

"Have you met all of the board members?" Glade was beginning to pity the man sitting so dejectedly in the cell.

"I believe so."

"Yet you do not know all their names, do you?" Glade asked, guessing that was the reason Harrington had unquestioningly accepted the signature on his instructions. And if so, the board really couldn't blame the man for what he had done. After all, weren't the board members accountable for having such arrogant attitudes that they had never even introduced themselves to their employee? "Would it surprise you to learn that we do not have a board member named Jensen?"

Harrington stared at Glade, his stomach dropping as he suddenly realized the impact of the assertion. "You don't?"

"No."

Harrington slumped against the cell wall, knowing he had spent thousands of dollars on a project that had been doomed from the start.

"Is there a reason you chose not to listen to both Mr. Newby and Mr. Wilson's warnings about the Songbird?" Again, Harrington had nothing to say.

"I'll take your silence to mean that your ego once again got in the way of your responsibilities. Would it not have been prudent for you, at the very least, to let the board know that inconsistencies had been noticed concerning the Songbird's true value? After all, you could have saved the company a great deal of money if you had done so."

Glade paused a few moments to let Harrington respond, but he remained silent. "Would you care to explain your arrangement with Martin Kensington? It is most unusual for company stock to be bandied about so offhandedly, especially to a complete outsider. I can see no reason for you to take such action except for your own personal gain. Ownership of the Silver Slipper would have been most beneficial to you, isn't that true?"

"Do with me as you will." Harrington reclined on the cot. He knew he had no future with the company and could, in all likelihood be facing criminal charges for his dealings with Martin Kensington. He saw no reason to discuss either situation with the man questioning him. "I have nothing left to say."

Glade sat back, gathering his thoughts in the heavy silence that hung over the room. "Much to my regret, Harrington," he shrugged his shoulders, "I feel that I must report to the board that I am unable to hold you responsible for this situation. Though I have never liked you or your methods, I am forced to admit that, if nothing else, you have always been a loyal employee. Even here in Sweetwater, you simply carried out your instructions. We told you to find a town that we could invest in, and you did that, Sweetwater being ideal for our plans. Unfortunately, we failed to make certain that the Songbird was the mine that you had been led to believe it was. And for that, it will be my opinion that the board must take full responsibility and bear the cost of our own negligence."

Harrington looked at Glade hopefully; maybe he would survive the debacle after all.

"However, as for Kensington and the Branson woman," Glade said, making Harrington's hope short lived, "I can only imagine why you did what you did. And I'm sure that, as you look back on it, you, yourself, must admit that it was a rather foolish road to travel. But as it stands, I will report that the company bears no responsibility in those particular matters, and you alone must face whatever judgment the law chooses to make against you."

Glade stood to leave Harrington to his fate. "Mr. Harrington, I suggest that you prepare yourself for the very real possibility that any action from the board and Mr. Prestly will result in the company no longer requiring your services. Before I go, I do have one more question."

"What?"

"Why did you not notice the name of the board member and the owner of the Songbird were the same?"

Harrington thought for a moment. That was a very good question; why hadn't he noticed? He had a reputation for catching such details, but this time he had failed to do so. His memory replayed the meeting he had had with the Songbird's owner, and slowly he realized that he had never once asked the man his name. Unhappy at being sent to the territory and upset with having to deal with people he believed to be quite crude, he had only asked if the man was the legal owner of the mine. With the deed signed over to the investment group and the miner paid off, he had never even bothered to look at the paper bearing the man's signature. Harrington groaned as he realized he could have stopped everything from happening if he had just asked the miner his name. He rolled over to face the wall, leaving Glade to stare at his back.

Realizing that he was not going to receive an answer to his question, Glade left the jail.

CHAPTER FORTY-TWO

Ed, Bette Mae, Billie, and Ruthie rode up to the Silver Slipper. Thaddeus rushed to meet them, having seen the riders approaching town. "Where's Jesse and Jennifer?" he asked.

"They'll be along." Ed dismounted and stretched his back. "They needed time for themselves and the young 'uns before they come back." He turned to help Bette Mae off her horse.

"Young 'uns?"

"Yep." Billie slipped out of his saddle, turning immediately to help Ruthie to the ground. "Got themselves a baby boy."

Thaddeus looked incredulous. "I can't wait to hear that story."

"You're gonna have to wait," Ed told the newspaperman. "We've been in the saddle for too many days, and all I want is a nice, long hot bath. I'm sure the ladies will agree."

"That sounds wonderful," Ruthie sighed as she rubbed her sore back.

"Sure does, honey," Billie said as he pulled saddlebags off the horses. "I'll take the horses back to the livery. You and Bette Mae go on inside." He set their bags on the Slipper's porch. "I'll come by when I've cleaned up."

"May be a little later than that," Thaddeus told the sheriff. "You've got a prisoner over at the jail."

"Who?"

"Harrington. Mayor Perkins ordered his arrest."

"Why?"

"Figured Harrington would have some legal problems to deal with after hearing about Jesse's trial. Not to mention he may have some problems here in Sweetwater."

"Why's that?"

"Two big shots from his company are in town looking into his activities."

"What do they plan to do with him?" Ed asked.

"Don't know. They refuse to say anything."

"I'll be back as soon as I can, honey." Billie gave Ruthie a peck on the cheek, then gathered the reins to the horses. "They know about the Songbird?"

"Whole town does." Thaddeus dropped into step with Billie as he made his way to the livery.

"I figured there'd be more to deal with when we got back. Let's hope we can get it taken care of before Jesse and Jennifer get here. Hate to have them step back in the middle of it."

Thaddeus slapped Billie on the back. "So, tell me about this new baby of theirs."

The wagon bounced over the ruts in the road, jostling the man and woman on the bench seat. The bed of the wagon was covered with a tarp to protect their meager belongings from the dust raised by the team of horses. The man leaned over the edge of the wagon to check on the status of the rear wheel, relieved to see that the patched axle seemed to be holding. Forced to stop for several hours to make necessary repairs, they had only recently been able to continue their journey. The old wagon had served many hard years on rough mountain roads, and the worn wood was finally giving up after being jarred one too many times. The man hoped he could nurse the wagon as far as Sweetwater.

"When do you think we'll get back to Sweetwater?" Jennifer asked as she relaxed next to the fire. They were camped in a small meadow with a spring bubbling up nearby.

"Day after tomorrow." Jesse deposited another armload of wood near the fire. "How do you feel?"

"Tired." Jennifer flexed her legs under the towels Jesse had soaked in heated water before wrapping them around her limbs. "But this feels good."

"Probably gettin' cool by now." Jesse knelt beside Jennifer. "Let me re-soak 'em."

"Mommy, praa?" KC looked up at Jesse, her eyes full of hope. She had been trying to engage Charley in playing with her toy horse, but, to her great disappointment, her brother just gurgled at her.

"In a minute, Sunshine." Jesse smiled at the girl. "Let me get Momma taken care of first."

"Otay." KC resumed her efforts with Charley.

Wringing out the towels, Jesse moved back to Jennifer's side. "Wish we had a way to give you a hot bath, darlin'." Jesse gently wrapped the towels around Jennifer's legs.

"It's okay." Jennifer smiled. "This really does help. Give me a few more minutes, and I'll start supper."

"KC and I will cook supper. Won't we, Sunshine?"

KC grinned at her mommy. "Otay." She handed her horse to Charley before crawling to Jesse and pulling herself upright on the rancher's arm.

"Are you sure?" Jennifer knew that her wife could do just about anything but cook.

"Sure." Jesse shrugged her shoulders. "How hard can it be?"

"Jesse?"

"Tell ya what, you tell me what to do, and I'll do it."

Jennifer grinned. "That sounds like a better plan."

"Come on, Sunshine." Jesse circled the baby with a strong arm, lifting her as she stood. "Let's see what we have for supper. I bet you're hungry." KC giggled as Jesse tickled her tummy.

Jennifer laughed as she watched Jesse carry the baby inside the tent to their packs. "I think there's enough of the dried meat Walk gave us to make stew," she called. "Should still be some bread left, too. Charley," Jennifer reached over to rub the infant's belly, "supper ought to be interesting tonight."

Smiling, Charley looked back at her, his legs kicking and arms waving in response to his momma's attention.

"I heard that." Jesse reappeared with her hands full of food, pots, utensils, and KC. She set the items and baby down next to Jennifer before carrying a cooking pot to the spring. After filling it with water, she walked back to her family and sat cross-legged next to the fire, waiting for her instructions. It didn't take long before she had cut up the meat and the few vegetables remaining from their purchases in Yankee Flats, adding them to the pot.

As their supper simmered, Jesse lay on the blanket next to Jennifer and waited for KC to climb atop her. The baby's shouts of laughter soon echoed around the meadow as Jesse held her at arm's length, swooping and swinging the baby above her head.

"Mo'," KC giggled.

Grunting, Jesse dropped KC onto her chest, her arms too tired to keep the child aloft any longer. "Ya ain't as tiny as ya used ta be." She tickled the growing girl.

KC squirmed about until she could sit straddling her mommy, her legs hanging at Jesse's sides. She grinned as her little hands dug into Jesse's ribs, tickling her.

"Hey." Jesse laughed, playfully batting at KC's hands. "You're not supposed to do that."

KC's fingers worked harder as she screamed with laughter.

"So, ol' Jensen hoodwinked all of 'em," Billie said as he and Thaddeus walked to the jail. He wasn't surprised to see Ed already sweeping the boardwalk in front of his store; the big man had become more and more concerned with his business as the days away from town had passed.

"Seems so."

"Wonder how he figured it."

"Don't know all the details, but I did find out that Jensen worked for a company in St. Louis that made its money by investing, like Harrington's company did."

"Now what? Do they go after Jensen and try to get back their money?"

"Won't do them much good. I tried to contact him," Thaddeus said. "Seems he's left for the gold fields in California."

"You'd think he'd have enough money already."

"When you've got gold fever, there's never enough."

"So it's over?"

"Except for their plans for Sweetwater."

"Wouldn't think they'd have any more plans, considering the Songbird doesn't have any gold in it." Billie stepped onto the boardwalk, stomping the dust off his boots. Nodding at Ed, he opened the door to the jail.

"They've still got the hotel and bank," Thaddeus reminded him.

Billie had noticed that both buildings had been completed during their absence. "Doesn't make much sense that they'd want to run them now. Probably just sell them off, if you ask me."

"Nobody around here has the money to buy them." Thaddeus followed the sheriff inside.

Billie crossed his office to the door leading to the cells. "Afternoon, Harrington. Looks like you've had a rough few days." Harrington lay on the cot. He remained silent. Billie wrapped a hand around one of the bars and peered in at the dispirited prisoner. "I expect we'll receive word from the governor after Judge Henson talks to him. And Jesse may have a thing or two to say about your future. If she doesn't, I'm sure Jennifer will." Harrington rolled his head to stare at the sheriff.

"Looks like hitchin' ya horse to Kensington's cart wasn't the best of ideas."

"What do you plan to do, Billie?" Thaddeus asked.

"Not much to do tonight." The sheriff sniffed the air. "'Cept maybe get a bath for Harrington, here."

"What about Perkins?"

"Right now, I want a hot bath and a hot meal. But first, I want to check on Ruth. Everything else can wait until tomorrow." Billie turned on his heel, walking out of the room and leaving the building without another word.

"Don't suppose you'd have anything to say?" Thaddeus asked the prisoner. Harrington rolled over to face the wall, putting his back to the newspaperman. "Didn't figure you would."

"This stew's pretty tasty." Jesse refilled her bowl from the pot.

Jennifer wiped her last bite of bread around the inside of her bowl, then popped it into her mouth. "For your first attempt at real cooking," she grinned, "you did pretty well."

"Didn't do much but cut the stuff up," Jesse said around a mouthful of stew. "You told me what spices to put in."

"Still, I think you did a good job. Don't you?" she asked KC, wiping crumbs off the girl's chin.

"Yep." KC nodded. "Mo'?"

"My, you are the hungry one tonight." Jennifer laughed. "Must have been all that playing you and Mommy did before supper."

"You plumb wore me out," Jesse groaned, causing KC to giggle. She couldn't imagine what it would be like to keep the girl entertained when she started walking. "You sure it's a good idea to feed her so much?"

"Sweetheart," Jennifer fed KC another spoonful of stew, "not feeding her won't stop her from growing. Besides, I think it's good for you."

"How's that?" Jesse emptied her bowl, setting it aside to be washed later.

"It'll keep you in shape for when Charley gets big enough to play with the two of you."

Jesse grunted. "Don't remind me."

"You'll be just fine." Jennifer chuckled, patting Jesse on the head. "You are a wonderful mother."

"Think so?"

"Yep," Jennifer and KC answered together.

Jesse laughed. "I better get the dishes scrubbed up, so we can get to bed."

"It's a little early, isn't it?"

Jesse scratched her head. "I was kinda hopin' we could get an early start in the morning."

"In a hurry to get home?" Jennifer teased, though she shared Jesse's feelings.

"Yeah."

"Me, too, sweetheart." Jennifer sighed. "Me, too."

Billie followed Ed as he drove a wagon from the livery to the back of general store. "What ya doing?"

"Figured Jesse and Jennifer could use this wood to build them a new house." Ed jumped down from the wagon seat.

"Thought you were plannin' on adding on to the store?"

"I am." Ed picked up an armful of cut lumber and loaded it into the wagon. "I put in another order this morning. Store can wait until it arrives, but they'll be needin' a new house right soon, before winter. Once Jesse gets here, we can sort out any differences."

"Want a hand?"

"Sure."

The men drove the wagonload of lumber out to the ranch where they planned to unload it, leaving it ready for Jesse to use in building a new house for her family. It had been the first time Ed had seen the blackened hulk of what once had been Jesse and Jennifer's home.

"Damn." Billie shook his head. "I still can't believe that fool burned it down."

"Nasty sight, that's for sure," Ed blew out a long breath. "And to do it to your own daughter's home."

"Yeah."

"Think we should clean it up for them?" Ed asked.

"No. Jesse will be wantin' to see what happened. Best we leave it to her." It was the way his friend was, and though he didn't understand, he would respect her feelings.

Ed knew the sheriff was right, and there was no point in arguing. "Where should we leave this?"

Looking around the ranch yard, Billie saw several suitable spots, but without knowing where Jesse planned to locate the new ranch house, he didn't want to put the pile of lumber where it would be in her way. "Over by the barn," he decided. "Only place for sure it'll be out of the way."

Slapping the reins on the horses' flanks, Ed maneuvered the wagon next to the barn. "Let's get this done," Billie said as he jumped down from the wagon.

"It's beautiful up here," Jennifer said as they rode along a mountain trail.

"It sure is." Jesse smiled as she looked around.

"How come more people don't live in the mountains, Jesse?"

"Winters are hard. Lots of snow, wind, and cold. Even the animals move south when that time of year comes around."

They were up high enough that the majority of trees were below them, and they had an unobstructed view of the surrounding mountain peaks, many topped with a fresh covering of snow. On a bare hillside about a half mile away, a small herd of elk grazed on late summer grasses and wildflowers. Soon they would be driven to lower hillsides and meadows by winter snowfalls. High above their heads, an eagle flew in lazy circles, hoping they would stir up a gopher or rabbit that would provide him an early lunch. He too would soon be heading south to spend the winter in a more hospitable location.

"So nobody lives in the mountains over the winter?"

"Few do. Mostly fur trappers or the occasional miner looking for his next strike. But even they don't do it more than a year or two. If they survive, that is."

"What do you mean?"

"Either you'll freeze, starve, or meet with an accident. It's no place to be if you're not prepared."

"You make it sound horrible."

"It would be if you were stuck up here, darlin'."

"But it's so beautiful now."

"Yep. And come winter, it'll look beautiful from a distance."

Jennifer tried to imagine the passing scenery covered in snow. "I think it would look beautiful close up, too. That is, as long as you had a nice warm cabin with a great big fire."

"And who would be going out to collect the firewood to keep that great big fire burning?"

"You would, sweetheart." Jennifer smiled winningly. "Because you love me so much."

"Don't know if I love you that much, darlin'." Jesse edged Dusty away from Blaze before her wife could swat her.

The women stopped a short time later, setting up their camp near a small creek. Deciding it was too early for supper and wanting to stretch out her legs, Jennifer suggested a short walk. They were exploring the woods around their campsite. With Jennifer relying heavily on her cane, Jesse carried Charley while KC rode on her shoulders.

"Sweetheart?"

"Yes."

"What's that?"

Jesse looked in the direction Jennifer pointed. "Looks like an old cabin. Want to take a look?"

"Sure."

"Who do you think built it?" Jennifer asked as they neared the roughly constructed log structure.

The roof and one wall had collapsed, leaving the interior of the cabin exposed to the elements. The other walls looked ready to follow. Inside, what once had been someone's home was buried in branches and other debris blown in by the wind.

"Hard to say, darlin'." Jesse peered through a window; if it ever held glass, it was long gone. "It's been here a while so I'm guessing a fur trapper. But it's a good distance to any rivers big enough for beaver, so it could have been a prospector or someone who thought 'bout makin' a go of it up here."

Jennifer moved to the open wall of the structure to get a closer look inside. "Careful, darlin'," Jesse warned. "You never know what the ground is like near these old cabins. If it was a miner, he could have dug holes all around it." Jennifer carefully stepped back to Jesse's side.

"Ook." KC pointed to a squirrel sitting on a branch that hung over the cabin. The animal seemed to be as curious about them as they were about the cabin.

As Jennifer looked up, the squirrel chattered. "Isn't it cute?"

"Make a good stew for supper." Jesse eyed the noisy squirrel as it scampered higher into the tree and out of her range.

"Jesse, that's awful."

Jesse laughed. "What say we get back to camp?"

"Good idea. Maybe instead of eating the cute squirrel, you can find us some trout in that creek."

"Already spotted a pair. Nice and fat, too," Jesse led them away from the cabin and the chattering squirrel.

"We'll be sleeping in a nice, comfy bed tomorrow night, darlin'," Jesse said as Jennifer snuggled against her.

"Hmmm, can't wait."

"'Course it'll mean staying at the Slipper."

Jennifer draped a leg over Jesse's. "Sweetheart, how long will it take to build the new house?"

"Hard to say." Jesse turned her head to kiss Jennifer. "Have to order the wood from Bozeman. Could take a while for the mill to send it."

"You don't think we'll have to wait until spring, do you?" Jennifer had gotten used to being alone with Jesse out at the ranch, where they were free to be themselves.

"Sure hope not, darlin'." Jesse adjusted her position to pull Jennifer on top of her. "Don't think I'd much care to stay in town that long."

"Me neither." Jennifer rested her head on Jesse's chest.

Jesse had been amazed at how Jennifer had taken to living on the ranch. She'd just assumed that being used to living in a city, the schoolteacher would prefer to live in town. But once they'd professed their love for each other, Jennifer insisted on moving to the ranch and had never shown any regret over her decision. Jesse had grown up on a ranch and fondly remembered the years she had spent exploring the land her father worked: playing make-believe among the big rocks in the boulder fields; tracking animals through the woods; galloping across the plains on the back of her pony. To her, it was the best way for a child to grow up, but she wondered if Jennifer felt differently.

"Do you still think that, now that we have the babies?"

"Especially now that we have the babies."

Jennifer's answer was surprising. "What do you mean?"

"The city is no place to grow up. You have nowhere to play but your own yard, and you can't play there because it would ruin the grass Father paid so much to nurture and care for. There were a few parks scattered about. I remember Mother used to take me to them until he refused to allow her to go any longer. I longed to run barefoot in the grass or play in a cool stream. I felt so constrained, forced to play in my room so I wouldn't get dirty. I never want our children to feel like I did Jesse. Promise me they never will."

Jesse tightened her hold on Jennifer. "I promise, darlin'."

Breaking camp as soon as it was light, Jesse and Jennifer led the horses back to the trail. It wasn't long before their path crossed the stage road from Bozeman. Leaving the narrow trail, they followed the road as it made its way down the western slope of the mountains and into the open valleys that would have to be crossed before they reached the last forested pass before Sweetwater.

As they rode, Jesse kept looking to a range of low mountain peaks to their left.

"What's wrong?" Jennifer asked after Jesse again looked south.

"Mommy, dow'?" KC was already tired of sitting in her carry sack; it had been a long journey from Bannack for her.

Jesse pulled Dusty to a stop beside a small creek that snaked its way alongside the road. She swung herself out of the saddle, "This is as good a place as any to take a break."

"You didn't answer my question," Jennifer said, slipping off Blaze, careful to protect the newborn in the sling around her shoulders.

"Just thinkin'." Jesse set the carry sack on the ground. "Bet you need some fresh britches." She smiled as KC struggled to free herself from the confining sack.

"Charley does, too." Jennifer chucked the baby under the chin, receiving a smile in response. "Bet you'd like some milk, too."

"Praa?" KC asked, pointing at the creek and its inviting water.

"Sorry, Sunshine." Jesse walked back to Boy, digging through the packs for clean diapers, a tin of milk, and a feeding bottle. "What say we wait to play until we get home?" KC frowned.

"Thanks, sweetheart." Jennifer accepted a clean diaper for Charley as Jesse spread a blanket on the ground. Sitting on the blanket, Jennifer spread her legs to lay the infant between them before removing his soiled diaper.

Jennifer was pretty sure she knew the reason behind Jesse's distraction. They weren't far from Sweetwater, the town being less than a few hours ride by the stage road. But that also meant they weren't too far from the ranch. She guessed that her wife was anxious to get to their ranch and see for herself the damage caused to the home they had worked so hard to create.

Still not familiar with the area's landmarks, Jennifer thought the ranch lay somewhere southwest of their present location. To reach it, they could ride south through the forest and shave a few hours off the end of their travels. "Sweetheart, why don't we head for the ranch?"

"Hmm?" Jesse murmured, working on KC's diaper.

Jennifer sat back and stretched her legs, enjoying the sight of the smiling infant's legs kicking and arms swinging now that he was unrestrained. "We can go into town tomorrow and let everyone know we've arrived, but I would really like to go home first."

Helping a freshly diapered KC sit up, Jesse plopped down on the blanket facing Jennifer. "You sure?" she asked, even though that was exactly what she had been thinking.

"Yes."

Jesse smiled at Jennifer, grateful that her wife seemed to have read her thoughts. "Might not be a pretty sight."

"We have to see it sometime." Jennifer sighed. "I think I'd rather see it when we can be alone." She knew if they went to Sweetwater first, several of their friends would insist on accompanying them to the ranch.

Jesse laid a hand on Jennifer's thigh and rubbed it tenderly. "From what Billie told me, most everything's gone."

"Except our memories." Jennifer looked at Jesse. "No matter what, Father hasn't destroyed those."

"No." Jesse smiled, thinking back to all the days of hard work she and Jennifer shared making the rough log cabin into their home and how much those days had meant to the love growing between them.

"So we feed our little ones and head home?"

"Yep."

KC looked up at Jesse. "Yum?"

"You eat too much," Jesse tickled KC in the ribs, "and too often."

"Mommy," KC squealed.

"Come on." Jesse draped the baby over her shoulder as she stood. "Let's see what we have left to feed you."

"I cooked up the last of the bacon this morning." Jennifer was recalling what was left in their larder. "And there should be some biscuits from last night and those apples we found yesterday."

"Not much." Jesse pulled the mentioned items out of the packs. KC, now sitting on her shoulders and wearing Jesse's Stetson, peered over her head curiously. "Sure you don't want to stop in town? Might not be much at the ranch to eat."

"There was some food in Mother's cabin, and the vegetables we put in the barn before we left. Won't be much but it should get us through a couple of meals. And we have the milk cow for Charley."

"Moo?" KC asked hopefully.

Jesse carried the baby and food back to the blanket. "You can have some of Charley's milk, Sunshine."

"Uck." KC wrinkled up her nose and shook her head violently. She steadfastly refused to drink the overly sweet and thick condensed milk purchased in Bannack for her brother. "Moo." She much preferred the fresh milk from their dairy cow.

"You'll have to wait until we get home for that. I could use a nice big, glass myself." Jesse liked the real thing as much as KC.

"Otay." With her mother now re-seated on the blanket, KC saw no need to remain on Jesse's shoulders. Grabbing a fistful of hair for support, she squirmed around until both legs hung over Jesse's chest. Then, using the convenient breasts for stepping-stones, the baby climbed down to sit between her mother's legs.

"Damn good thing she doesn't wear boots," Jesse grumbled as the baby descended.

"Jesse," Jennifer scowled, trying to hide her amusement at the baby's antics, "you shouldn't talk like that in front of her."

"Humpft."

Unconcerned with her mother's recent discomfort, KC smiled at Jesse and held out her little hands. "Pease."

"Good thing you look like yer momma." Jesse put a piece of biscuit in the baby's hands.

"Yep." KC nodded as she shoved the food into her mouth. "Mo'."

Chuckling, Jennifer filled a bottle for Charley.

"Here," Jesse held out her arms, "let me feed him. You can feed this little rascal."

Jennifer handed the bottle, then the hungry infant to her wife. "Come on, sweetie," she told KC, "let's make some bacon sandwiches."

"Otay." KC crawled over Jesse's legs to sit beside Jennifer.

Trudging doggedly, the tired horses pulled the old buckboard along the stage road. Emerging from the forest, the man and woman smiled when they spotted a scattering of buildings in the distance — the town of Sweetwater.

"Shouldn't be too bad," Jesse said as they rode back into the thick forest. They would be making their own trail as they traveled a direct route back to their ranch. "We have one ridge to cross, but it won't be much of a climb, and we'll drop down the other side at the north end of the ranch property.

"I'm ready." Jennifer adjusted Charley in his sling so the baby was more comfortable.

"You ready, KC?" Jesse reached back, patting the girl on the bottom. When she received no answer, she looked back over her shoulder.

"She's asleep, sweetheart." Jennifer told Jesse what she couldn't see for herself.

"Been tough on her," Jesse sighed, "all this traveling."

"It's been tough on all of us." Jennifer nudged Blaze up alongside Dusty. "But I wouldn't trade it for the world."

"You wouldn't?"

"No." Jennifer reached over and took her wife's hand, bringing it up to her face and tenderly rubbing it against her cheek. "The past few days have been good for us, Jesse. We've become a family."

"Thought we already was a family." Jesse slipped her hand from Jennifer's grasp, moving it behind her wife's neck to gently pull her close.

"You know what I mean." Jennifer sighed as their lips met. Several heartbeats later, the women separated just enough to breathe.

With their lips almost touching, Jennifer caressed Jesse's face. "Let's get home."

"I love you." Jesse closed the distance to kiss her wife, again and more deeply.

Broom in hand, Ed stepped out of the general store to sweep the wide boardwalk as he did every morning. He looked at the new bank building that occupied the lot next to his store. It was probably the only good thing to come out of the whole affair with Harrington and his company.

Billie stepped out of the jail, taking a deep breath of the late morning air. "Morning, Ed."

"Morning. How's your prisoner?"

"Quiet, as always." Billie walked toward the storekeeper. "Wish Kensington had been as quiet."

"Kinda makes you feel sorry for Marshal Morgan, doesn't it?"

"Better him than me."

"What do you think Kensington will do once he figures out where he's headed?" Ed asked as he finished his chore.

"He'll throw a fit, that's for sure," Billie leaned against one of the columns that supported the roof over the boardwalk. "After that, who knows? I just hope Mary's plan works, for Jesse and Jennifer's sakes."

Ed leaned his broom against the side of the building before dropping into one of the chairs he had carried out to the boardwalk earlier. "What d'ya think will happen to those?" He looked at the two new buildings.

"Bank probably won't be a problem; town's been needin' one for a while now." Billie moved a few paces along the boardwalk and dropped into the other chair. "Gonna be harder for the hotel. Don't really need it, seeing as we already have the Slipper. Figure they'll try to sell it."

"Hmm?"

"Ain't gonna be too many takers, I'm afraid."

"Hmm?"

"What you thinkin' 'bout, Ed?"

"Just considering some possibilities."

"Any you want to share?"

"Not really."

Billie leaned back in the chair, pushing his Stetson off his forehead. He had no need to push his friend. He knew Ed would talk when he was ready.

"Saw Ruthie leavin' the jail earlier."

The sheriff nodded. "Brought over breakfast."

"She seems awfully happy," Ed teased.

Billie beamed a wide smile of his own. "I hope so."

"Hear you told Miles you was turning in your badge."

"Yep. Ruth asked me to, and I'd already been thinkin' of doing it. Don't think I want to face any more bullets."

"Can't say I blame you. Know what you plan to do?"

"Thought I'd ask Jesse for a job, maybe help out at the Slipper or the ranch."

Ed scratched his head. Billie chuckled at the look on his friend's face. "Whatever you're thinking, it sure must be something."

"Might be, but I need to do some more thinking before I'm sure."

"All right." Billie pushed himself up out of the chair.

"Dat?"

KC had become so restless in her carry sack that Jesse had taken pity on the baby and was letting her ride on Dusty in front of her. The child had been asking the same question for the last several miles. Rather than get angry or frustrated with her inquisitive daughter, Jesse patiently answered the question every time it was posed.

"That, Sunshine, is a magpie," Jesse watched the black and white bird hop across the forest floor in front of the horses.

Satisfied, KC looked around for something else to question.

Jennifer was enjoying the exchange as Blaze trailed behind Dusty. She was learning more about her adopted home every mile they rode.

"Dat?"

Dusty whinnied, shying away from the forest in the direction KC was pointing. The horse's sudden agitation concerned Jesse. She peered into the forest as a sudden movement caught her attention. "Darlin', come up here."

"What is it?" Jennifer rode Blaze around Dusty, putting her wife's larger horse between herself and whatever danger the forest hid.

"Bear." Jesse lifted KC up. "Sit with Momma," she said, placing the baby on Blaze. Jennifer immediately wrapped a protective arm around the girl while Jesse pulled her rifle out of the saddle scabbard. "Let's keep moving." She nudged Dusty forward, Blaze matching his steps.

KC excitedly pointed again. "Ook, Momma."

Jennifer spotted a dark shadow moving in the trees some distance from them.

"Damn, she's got good eyes," Jesse muttered.

"Dat?" KC looked up at Jennifer.

"Jesse, are we in danger?"

"No," Jesse said, even as she kept her rifle cocked and ready for use. "It's going in the opposite direction."

"Dat?" KC scowled, her question yet to be answered.

"That, my little eagle-eyed daughter," Jesse turned away from the bear just long enough to ruffle the baby's hair, "was a bear."

"Ber?"

"Yes, sweetie." Jennifer tightened her hold on the baby. Jesse might think the animal posed no danger, but she wasn't taking any chances. "A big, furry bear."

"Can't believe she saw it back in those shadows," Jesse murmured as she watched the bear disappear deeper into the forest. "Even saw it before Dusty noticed."

KC reached for Jesse, wanting to resume her seat in front of the rancher. Jesse returned the rifle to the scabbard before urging Dusty close enough to Blaze to retrieve the baby. "The bear's probably more interested in finding some berries than eating you, anyway."

"They eat berries?" Jennifer asked.

"Yep."

"I thought they ate meat."

"They do," Jesse told her, "but they also eat lots of grasses and berries. And fish, if they can catch them. This time of year, they eat whatever they come across. They want to fatten up for the winter."

"What do they do in the winter?"

"Sleep, mostly."

"Sleep?"

"Yep. They'll find a cozy cave or dig a hole in the side of a hill and curl up inside and go to sleep. That's why they eat as much as they can before then."

"Oh. Guess that's good to know I won't have to worry about them in the winter."

"I wouldn't go that far," Jesse told the schoolteacher.

"But you said they go to sleep."

"Most do. Always one or two that might not. And if it's warmer than usual with lighter snowfall, they'll wake up thinkin' it's already spring."

"Oh."

"Never pays to forget they're out there, darlin'."

"Guess not." Jennifer turned to look back in the direction the bear had disappeared.

CHAPTER FORTY-THREE

The tired horses were standing impatiently at the crossroads waiting for their driver to make a decision. "What do you think?" Stanley Branson asked his wife.

Marie Branson could see the buildings of Sweetwater in the distance. She knew there was a chance her daughter might be in town. Her eyes followed the less used path that led away from the road and toward the ranch. She was tired of riding on the hard seat as the wagon bounced over obstacles in the dusty road. Her husband was tired. The horses were tired. And the old wagon was almost falling apart beneath them. Even though it would mean a slightly longer distance to travel, she easily made her decision. "The ranch."

Stanley nodded as he flipped the reins over the horses' rumps, urging them to move in the desired direction. "Hope the wagon makes it that far."

"If it doesn't, we'll at least be close enough to walk the rest of the way."

Stanley leaned over the side of the wagon, taking a long look at the back wheel as the wagon started down the road to his daughter's ranch. "Should be okay," he said as he straightened up, "if we don't hit a lot of bumps."

Marie laughed. "Stan, do you know of any road in Montana that isn't mainly potholes and rocks?"

"Nope."

Frank Wilson walked into the general store and greeted the proprietor. "Good afternoon."

"Afternoon, Wilson," Ed cordially greeted the foreman. "Something I can do for you?"

"I was thinking that I might be able to do something for you."

"I see..."

"I hear that you are adding onto the building," Wilson explained. "And I was wondering if you'd be needing someone to help you with the work."

"Thought you had a job," Ed said, curious.

"I figure it might be best to move on."

"Well..." Ed took a moment to consider the man's offer. "I could use the help. It's a mite hard to keep an eye on the store and do the work. Won't be able to pay you much."

"That's okay," Wilson smiled. "Looking more for an excuse to tell Glade and Weese I'll be stayin' in Sweetwater than for pay."

"Thought you liked workin' for them?"

"Liked the pay, never liked the men."

"So why quit?"

"Let's just say that recent events have changed my feelings."

"Fair enough." Ed wasn't a stranger to the frontier's custom of asking few questions about someone's past. If the man didn't want to say more, he wasn't going to pry. "Don't know when you'll be able to start working," the storekeeper told his new employee. "Had to send to Bozeman for the lumber."

Wilson was sure he had seen a stack of building supplies behind the general store. "I thought you already had it."

"Took what I had out to Jesse and Jennifer's. Figured they'd be needin' it as soon as they got back. More important for them to get a house built before winter than for me to get some extra room at the back of the store."

Wilson wasn't surprised at the big man's generosity; it was something he had come to appreciate about the citizens of Sweetwater.

"But if you're willin'," Ed grinned, "I can always use help around here, unloading the freight wagons and making deliveries. I can give you a dollar a day."

Wilson was used to being paid much more, but at this point in his life, money wasn't the real issue. He extended his hand to the storekeeper. "Sounds fair. Where do you want me to start?"

The stage rolled to a stop in front of the adobe station, a cloud of dust announcing its arrival.

"Only one passenger today," the driver informed the stationmaster as he came out of the building. "And a mail pouch." He tossed the leather bag into the man's waiting hands as the door to the stage opened and a man in a dust-covered suit stepped out. A canvas travel bag was dropped at his feet, raising a fresh cloud of dust.

"Thank you," the passenger sarcastically told the stage driver.

"Aim ta please," the driver said as he climbed down from the top of the coach. "Silver Slipper, at the end of the street, has the best food in town. And you can get a room there or stay at the depot."

The newcomer's eyes surveyed the dilapidated adobe that served as the stage station. Considering the outside condition of the small structure, he had no wish to view the interior. He would get a room at the recommended establishment, but first he had business to attend to. "I have business with the sheriff. Where might I find him?"

"'Cross the street at his office, I 'spect," the driver said as he slapped the dust from his clothes. "If he ain't there, look around. Town ain't big 'nough ta git lost in."

KC laughed wildly as Jesse pranced around beneath her. The baby sat on her mommy's shoulders, her hands grasped firmly by Jesse who was running, jumping, twisting, and leaping around the small clearing where they had stopped to rest.

Jennifer sat on a large boulder with Charley in her lap. She laughed as she watched her wife and daughter play. "Look, Charley," she held the infant up to see, "look at them. Aren't they funny?"

"Mo'," KC screamed when Jesse slowed down.

Jesse lifted the baby over her head, hanging her upside down as she walked back to Jennifer. "I'm tired."

"Mo', Mommy," KC demanded between giggles.

"More, more, more." Jesse let the baby's legs slip through her hands, grabbing her by the ankles before she hit the ground. "You need to learn a different word."

KC hung her hands down, letting her fingertips drag along the ground. "Mo', mo', mo'."

Jesse laughed as her daughter mimicked her. She stepped onto the boulder, sitting beside Jennifer. "Here, play with your brother," she said, setting KC down on the stone's surface between her legs.

KC pushed onto her knees, propping her elbows on Jesse's thigh so she could make faces at Charley lying in Jennifer's lap. She laughed loudly when the baby smiled, gurgling and kicking his legs.

"Here." Jennifer handed Jesse a canteen.

"Thanks." Jesse took a long drink. "You want some, Sunshine." KC shook her head.

"'Course not." Jesse tickled the baby. "I was doin' all the work. All you did was laugh."

"Mommy," KC protested loudly, rolling onto her side to slap at Jesse's hand.

"Sweetheart, don't pick on the baby."

Jesse glared at her wife, but her eyes twinkled with amusement.

With her mother's hands stilled, KC took the opportunity to climb up Jesse's shirt and look her in the eye. "Mo', mo', mo', mo', mo', mo'." The baby's words dissolved into shrieks of laughter as Jesse renewed her tickling.

Charley smiled as he bounced in Jennifer's arms, her body shaking with laughter.

The man newly arrived on the stage walked into the sheriff's office and announced, "I'm looking for Sheriff Monroe."

"You found him." Billie finished filling his coffee cup from the pot on the wood stove. "What can I do for you?"

"I have a letter from the governor instructing you to arrest Mr. Tobias Harrington."

"Already done." Billie stepped back to his desk. "He's in there." He gestured at the door to the cells as he sat down. "Figured I'd be hearing from the governor."

The man laid a sealed envelope on the desk in front of the sheriff. "Those are the governor's instructions regarding Mr. Harrington."

Billie reached for the envelope. "You taking him back with you?"

"I don't know."

"You're just the messenger, huh?" Billie slipped a knife under the flap of the envelope, neatly slicing it open and pulling out the papers inside. "Damn," he muttered, reading them.

"Excuse me?"

"I'm getting married in a few weeks; I don't have time to take Harrington to Virginia City." Billie threw the papers back onto his desk. He had thought the governor's message would mark the end of his involvement with Harrington and the whole sordid affair. He studied the man standing opposite his desk. "You work for the governor, right?"

"Yes."

"You're a fine, upstanding, law-abiding citizen of the Territory of Montana, ain't ya?"

"Yes," the suited man slowly answered, not sure what the sheriff was asking or why.

"Good." Billie pulled open a drawer at the side of his desk, searching around until he found what he was looking for. "Hold up your right hand," he instructed.

"Why?"

"Just do it," Billie commanded as he stood. As soon as the other man complied, he continued, "Do you swear to uphold the laws of the Territory of Montana to the best of your ability?"

"Y...ye...yes."

"Good." Billie flipped a deputy badge at him. "Put that on. You are now a duly sworn deputy sheriff."

"But..."

"Stage leaves in an hour. I expect you and your prisoner to be on it."

"But..."

"Once you turn him over to the sheriff in Virginia City, you can hand in your badge. Unless, of course, you want to return here and take over the sheriff job."

"But..."

"Because I quit." Billie pulled off his own badge and slapped it down on the desk. "Cell keys are in the drawer." He walked around the desk, grabbed his hat from the peg on the wall, and opened the door. With one final look around, he left the jailhouse for the last time.

"But..."

"Hope we don't have much further to go," Stanley Branson knelt in the dirt beside the wagon. He carefully ran his hand along the patchwork on the rear axle.

"The map Jennifer sent doesn't give any distance from the stage road to the ranch." Marie studied the piece of paper for the hundredth time. It had surprised her to receive the letter from her daughter's wife. During Jennifer's recovery from the mountain lion attack, she had observed the love shared by the two young women, but she had never realized the depth of that love until Jennifer's letter arrived. In it, their daughter-in-law expressed how much she wanted them to come to the ranch to live. It was Jennifer's way of giving Jesse a chance to heal the wounds with her own father, a chance she, herself, would never have. Marie never showed the actual letter to her husband, choosing instead to only tell him of the map it contained. Marie would always hold Jennifer's gracious act near to her heart.

"Talking about it sure ain't gonna get us there any quicker." Stanley stood, brushing dirt off his pants. "Might as well just keep goin' 'til the damn thing falls apart," he said, climbing back up into the wagon.

"Let's hope that doesn't happen." Marie folded the map and tucked it into her pocket.

"Git up."

"Shouldn't be too far now, darlin'," Jesse could see that the trees were starting to thin and more daylight was making its way to the forest floor, a sure sign they were approaching the basin where the ranch buildings were nestled.

Jennifer didn't reply. The closer they got to their home, the more she didn't want to face what her father had done. Her stomach was tied up in knots, and just the thought of what lay ahead made her feel sick.

"Darlin'?" Jesse slowed Dusty's progress to ride beside Jennifer. "You okay?"

"No."

"It'll be all right." Jesse, glad that KC was asleep in her carry sack, reached over and took Jennifer's hand, entwining their fingers. They continued in silence, each afraid of what they were about to discover but thankful to be facing it together.

Ed walked across the street to see if the stage carried any mail for him. "Whatever came of the talk about a new stage depot?" he asked the stationmaster.

"Nothin' much," the man said, handing him one envelope. "They say they want a new building, but don't think they want to spend the money."

Ed looked at the return address on the envelope he had been given; the letter was from the bank in Bozeman where he kept an account. He smiled to himself; maybe this was a sign his idea wasn't as outlandish as he first thought. Turning his attention back to the stationmaster, he asked, "If there was something available, think they'd be willing to make a change?"

"Don't know." The stationmaster scratched his bearded chin. "You got somethin' in mind?"

"I might." Ed proceeded to share his idea.

Holding KC, Jesse stood with an arm wrapped around Jennifer, who held Charley in her arms. Each needed the comfort of the other as they stood in front of the blackened ruin of what once had been their home. Tears welled in their eyes at the depth of Martin Kensington's hatred.

"Should we try to go inside?" Jennifer asked.

Jesse saw no point in attempting to enter what was left of the burned structure. "No, darlin'." She turned to kiss her wife's brow. "Ain't nothing worth saving in there. No sense in us gettin' hurt tryin'."

"Why, Jesse? Why would he do this?"

Jesse tightened her embrace; she had no answer. She looked around the yard to see what else had been damaged by what must have been an intense fire. The corner of the cabin used by her mother-in-law was scarred by flames but otherwise unharmed. She was thankful to see the rest of the buildings seemed untouched. The garden fence was gone, and most of the plants were wilted from their exposure to the extreme heat. The fence could be replaced, and the garden could be replanted in the spring. As her eyes swept over the barn and corrals, Jesse spied the pile of lumber. "Wonder where that came from?"

"What?"

"That." Jesse pointed at the barn.

"Ed?"

"Doubt he'd know what we needed to rebuild." Jesse started walking toward the lumber, her hand firmly grasped in Jennifer's.

"Might be what he had on hand," Jennifer offered.

"He was usin' that for the store." Jesse studied the pile. "But it'd be just like him, wouldn't it?"

"Yes."

Jesse took a deep breath, blowing it out noisily, which caused KC to giggle. The baby's laughter helped relieve the tension building in her mothers. "What say we spend tonight in town and start building us a new home in the morning?"

"I'd rather not stay in town."

"You want to stay here?"

"Yes."

Jesse looked around the ranch yard. "The cabin is too small for all of us. Guess it's the barn."

"What about the tent?" Jennifer asked, not relishing the thought of sharing the barn with their horses. "We could set it up in the yard."

"Gettin' too cold at night," Jesse told her. "But it's plenty big enough in the barn to set up the tent. It's not much, but it'll give us someplace to sleep and keep stuff. Otherwise, it'll have to be the Slipper."

"The barn it is." Jennifer smiled at Jesse, her mind flooding with tasks that needed to be done. "What do we do first?"

"First, we find a place for you and the little ones to sit while I unpack the horses." Jesse went to Boy to retrieve a blanket.

"We could wait in the cabin."

Jesse turned and shyly smiled at Jennifer. "I'd rather have ya someplace I can see ya."

Jennifer smiled knowingly. "I'd like that, too."

"Ook." KC pointed toward the road coming from town.

Jesse and Jennifer were bewildered to see a buckboard slowly making its way over the crest of the hillock to cross under the arch marking the entrance to their ranch.

"Who can that be?" Jennifer asked as Jesse rejoined her.

Jesse peered at the couple sitting at the front of the wagon. "Poppa?"

Jennifer looked at Jesse. By the shocked but hopeful look on her wife's face, she knew it was true. Approaching in the wagon must be Stanley and Marie Branson, Jesse's parents. She turned and waved.

Marie returned Jennifer's wave. "They're here."

"Wonder what happened," Stanley said as he saw the burned ruins.

"We'll know soon enough."

Jesse and Jennifer started walking toward the wagon, its back wheel wobbling precariously as the buckboard closed the distance.

Excited to see her daughters and granddaughter, Marie urged, "Can't you go any faster?"

"If I do, this old wagon will fall apart under us for sure," Stanley grumbled.

"Hi," Jennifer called as the wagon neared.

"Hello, yourself." Marie laughed, quickly climbing down from the wagon as soon as her husband pulled the horses to a stop. "Give me a hug," she told Jesse.

"It's good to see you again, Marie," Jennifer said as the woman hugged her daughter. KC recognized her grandmother. "Grmm."

"My goodness." Marie stared at the baby Jesse held. "Is this our little KC?"

Stanley joined the women. "She ain't so little any more."

"No, she's grown some." Jennifer laughed as she tried to settle Charley, hungry, wet, and whimpering, in her arms.

"Who's this?" Marie asked as she peered at the infant.

"This is Charley," Jennifer announced proudly. "Your grandson."

"My," Marie gushed, "seems you have a lot to tell us."

"You don't know the half of it." Jennifer let Marie take the baby from her.

"You plan to say anything?" Stanley asked the silent Jesse.

"I didn't think you'd come," the rancher whispered.

"If you've changed your mind, we can leave."

"No." Jesse reached out, grabbing her father's arm. "No, I'm glad you're here."

"Good." Stanley smiled at his daughter. "Now let me say hello to my granddaughter." KC happily wrapped her arms around her grandfather's neck. "Grump."

"That," Stanley sternly told the child as the women laughed, "will have to change."

"I'm sorry, Jennifer," Marie was saying. "If we'd known..."

"I know." Jennifer sighed. "But there wasn't much you could have done, even if you had."

The women were sitting in the shade of the barn on a pair of chairs pulled from the back of the buckboard. The tired babies slept on a blanket spread at their feet. Jesse had taken time to milk the cow, providing a meal for the hungry newborn, while KC had been fed from the food her grandparents had brought.

Jennifer had recounted the recent events to Marie as they watched Jesse and Stanley unload the buckboard they had managed to get to the barn without losing its wheel. The horses were relieved of their burden and set free in the corral.

"But to be locked up like that must have been awful for Jesse," Marie said sadly.

"It was." Jennifer rubbed at the tears on her cheeks. "But the worst part was when she couldn't hold KC. It broke my heart to see how much they both suffered from that. I'll forever be thankful that Judge Henson ordered her released as quickly as he did. I think Jesse would have died if she'd had to stay in that cell any longer. One night was almost more than she could take."

"She's always been that way. Many a night, I'd find she'd climbed out her bedroom window to sleep under the stars. She'd always tell me her bed was too confining."

"Thank goodness she outgrew that." Jennifer spoke without thinking, then blushed as her mother-in-law chuckled.

"I think you might have a bit more to do with that than any growing up she's done." Marie winked at the embarrassed woman.

Jesse glanced at Jennifer and her mother as she carried another armload into the barn. She wondered what the two women were talking about and hoped her mother wasn't filling her wife with stories of her as a little girl.

"That's the last of it," Stanley said as he entered the barn. "Good thing this place is so big. You still plan on staying here 'til your house is built?"

"We do, Poppa." Jesse added her load to the items that had been neatly stacked in a corner of the structure. The tent had been set up in another corner, and the food had been placed inside to protect it. Their bedrolls and blankets had been laid out on a layer of fresh hay spread in front of the tent.

"Still think you should stay with your young 'uns in that cabin instead of your ma and me."

"It's too small for all of us." Jesse had insisted her parents stay in the cabin Mary had used. "We'll be fine in here. Besides, with your help," she smiled at her father, "it won't take any time to build us a house. I'm really glad you're here, Poppa." Jesse gingerly wrapped her arms around him.

"It'll take some gettin' used to." Stanley's voice was gruff, but when he returned her hug, Jesse knew he didn't mean it. Suddenly self-conscious of the intimate contact, Stanley stepped back. "Let's go see what those women are up to."

"Finished?" Jennifer asked as Jesse and Stanley emerged from the barn and walked toward her and Marie.

"Yep." Jesse smiled. "Except for putting that buckboard someplace."

"Use it for firewood," Stanley said. "'Bout all it's good for any more."

"Rather keep it around for spare parts for our buckboard. Be cheaper than havin' to buy them in town."

"Guess we could push it out of the way." Stanley turned back to the wagon.

Jesse stopped him. "Tomorrow."

"Suit yourself."

"We should get a fire started." Jesse looked to the west. "It'll be dark soon, and since we'll be cookin' outside for a while..."

"Guess it's too late for you to go fishing," Jennifer said, disappointed.

"Nope." Jesse leaned down to kiss her wife. "I'll be back in a few minutes. You and Poppa can get the fire going. One thing we're not short of is firewood," she said as she walked toward the river.

"How 'bout I whip up some cornbread to go along with that fish?" Marie offered.

Jennifer smiled. "I'd love it."

"Grump'?" KC pointed at her grandfather's plate that still held a portion of trout.

"Come here, Sunshine." Jesse chuckled. "Let your grandpa eat his own fish, you have some over here."

"Otay." KC crawled back to where Jesse sat beside Jennifer.

"Don't know of anyone else he'd let call him that." Marie laughed as her husband scowled. "Maybe it'll be good for him to be around KC."

Stanley grunted. "Sounds just like Jesse," Jennifer giggled.

"They're so much alike, it's scary," Marie whispered loudly.

"Stop it, woman," Stanley growled as Jennifer and Marie burst into laughter.

Jesse glared at Jennifer. "I think this may have been a mistake, Poppa."

"Too late," Marie teased.

"I need some fresh air," Stanley said, even though the group was sitting in the open around the campfire. He stood and stalked toward the river.

"Think I'll go with him." Jesse quickly stood and followed her father.

"Think we hurt their feelings?" Jennifer asked as she watched Jesse leave.

"No." Marie pulled KC into her lap, letting the baby eat the fish and cornbread that remained on her plate. "They need to talk, that's all."

Jennifer was concerned that the teasing had crossed a line with the pair. "But we were kind of hard on them."

"They know there's truth behind our words." Marie sighed. "It feels good to finally say it, and, if we're all going to live here, it's best they come to terms with it right off."

Jesse walked to a rise overlooking the river where her father stood. "Nice night," she said, looking up at the clear sky.

"Your mother—"

"Was speaking the truth, Poppa. We are alike."

"Is that bad?"

"No." They stood quietly for several minutes. "What took you so long to come, Poppa?"

"Had business to attend to. Couldn't just pack up and come."

"What business?"

"Damn, girl," Stanley paced a few steps away, "ain't it good enough I'm here?"

"Yes." Jesse moved to stand beside her father. "But I'd like to know."

"You're stubborn, always have been."

Jesse grinned. "Jennifer would agree with you."

"Smart woman."

"She also says I'm proud, Poppa. Sometimes too proud, just like you."

"Humpft."

"You don't have to tell me." Jesse turned back toward the campfire and her family.

"Needed to earn me some money," Stanley said softly. "Couldn't just come with my hat in my hand. I had to be able to pay my way."

Jesse understood. She would have felt the same if their roles were reversed. "You're here. That's all I care about. What say we go back...Grump?"

"*That*, daughter, has to change."

"You'll have to talk to KC about that." Jesse laughed. "I suggest you do it soon, before she teaches it to Charley."

Stanley groaned as he followed Jesse back to the campfire.

Frank Wilson made his way up the rocky trail that led to the Songbird mine. Slung over his shoulder was a saddlebag, one of its pockets filled with carefully packed sticks of dynamite while the other contained extra long fuses. He was about to perform his final official duty for the company that had recently employed him, having been ordered by Glade and Weese to seal off the Songbird mine. Cresting the top of the trail, Wilson walked to the opening of the mine. He pulled a small pick from the saddlebag and then gently placed the bag on the cool ground, just inside the shaft's entrance.

Moving a few feet deeper into the tunnel, Wilson dug several holes along the base of the rock walls. Returning to the saddlebag, he removed the sticks of dynamite, inserting the fuses he had cut earlier, making sure they were longer than usual to give him plenty of time to get off the mountain plateau before the blast shook the hillside. He carefully slid one stick of the explosive in each of the holes, then, walking backward, strung the fuses back to the entrance.

With a final look down the worthless tunnel, Wilson struck a match and lit the bundle of fuses. He grabbed his saddlebag, running for the trail and the safety it would provide. Moments later, the mountain rumbled beneath his boots as the dynamite ignited and collapsed the tunnel.

Along the length of the shaft, the stone was split apart as the rock walls exploded. At the end of the tunnel, a large rift was created in the stone ceiling. A chunk of mountain, the size of a small buggy dropped from where it had moments before been securely anchored, crashing to the tunnel floor. In the gaping abscess, sparkling in the deepening darkness, ran a vein of gold as thick as a miner's fist and longer than a muleskinner's bullwhip.

EPILOGUE

Wearing a new, store-bought suit, Billie twitched nervously as he stood in the late morning sunlight. At his side stood Ruthie, just as nervous in her white wedding dress. Neither of them would remember most of what Mayor Perkins had said.

"By the authority of the Governor of the Territory of Montana, I am honored to present Mr. and Mrs. William Monroe." When neither of the newlyweds moved, Mayor Perkins whispered, "Go on, boy. Kiss her."

Billie turned to Ruthie, thinking anew that she was the most beautiful woman he had ever seen. Bending his head, he placed a chaste kiss on her cheek.

"Go on, Billie," Jesse teased. "You can do better than that."

Jennifer poked her wife in the ribs. "Leave them be, sweetheart."

She and Jesse were standing behind the couple, serving as official witnesses to the marriage. KC and Charley were in the arms of their grandparents, who stood off to the side with Bette Mae and Ed and Thaddeus.

"If tha's all he can do," Bette Mae laughed, "it's gonna be a mighty long time afore they has any young 'uns of theirs own."

"Hush, Bette Mae." Marie grinned. "They're just shy in front of all of us."

"There ain't nobody here ta be shy in front of." She had not been happy when Jesse and Jennifer had supported Billie and Ruthie's request for a small wedding ceremony at the ranch, as she had been planning a big wedding in town for the couple. Her disappointment had been somewhat appeased when Jesse had insisted the reception and dance be held at the ranch, on the grounds that it would be easier to fit everyone in the ranch yard than in the dining room at the Silver Slipper.

"Congratulations." Jennifer moved forward to hug Ruthie. "I'm so happy for you."

Ruthie beamed. "Thank you, Miss Jennifer."

"Unh, uh." Jennifer shook her finger at the bride. "You promised." She and Jesse had made the shy woman promise to drop the "miss", now that they were in business together in the dress shop.

"Jennifer." Ruthie blushed.

Jesse stepped up to the groom, her hand outstretched. "I'm happy for ya, Billie."

"Thanks, Jesse." The former sheriff grabbed his friend's hand and pulled her into a hug. "And thanks for letting us have the weddin' here."

"Wouldn't have let you have it anywhere else."

In the lull between the late morning wedding and early afternoon reception, Jesse stood on the porch of the new ranch house. Looking around the yard, she smiled at all the changes.

After deciding to build the new house in a different location, one that would provide a better view of the valley and surrounding mountains, they had set to work. The burned hulk of the old cabin had been cleared away, making room for an enlarged garden, encircled by a new picket fence. And a new well had been dug, the pump conveniently located inside the kitchen of the new ranch house.

With the help of her father, Billie, Ed, and Frank Wilson, the house was almost complete. It was a simple, square, two-story structure with a covered porch wrapping around all four sides. The upstairs was divided into three bedrooms, one for Jesse and Jennifer and one for each of the children when they got older. For the time being, their cribs remained in their mothers' bedroom. The first floor consisted of an office, a small parlor, a dining room, and a kitchen, with a small bathing room enclosed on the back porch. Jesse had wanted to put the bathtub upstairs between the bedrooms, but Jennifer insisted that with the way Jesse and KC got dirty, she wanted the tub as close to the outdoors as possible so they wouldn't track dirt all through the house.

Jennifer had furnished the house with the barest of necessities. The rest would have to wait until they had the money to spend. But they had protection from the coming winter, and for now, that was enough.

Stanley and Marie had turned down an offer of one of the bedrooms, deciding instead to enlarge the separate cabin into more livable space.

Changes had also taken place in Sweetwater. Mayor Perkins had refused to have his name removed from the bank's charter, so the investment company had been unable to sell it to a third party, and Glade and Weese had grudgingly turned the bank over to the town. The two men returned back East with little more than a hole in the side of the mountain to show for their company's planned investment in the town of Sweetwater.

Ed had astounded everyone by buying the new hotel and moving his general store onto the ground floor of the larger structure, explaining it gave him more room and ended up being less expensive than expanding the existing store. To help pay for the purchase, he had signed a contract with the stage line to use a corner of the ground floor for a new stage depot. The top floor had been split into two parts: the smaller end was made into living quarters for Ed, and the larger end had been converted into an apartment for Billie and Ruthie to rent.

Jesse's old office at the Silver Slipper now housed a busy dress shop run by Ruthie. The first dresses to be sewn by the new businesswoman were her own wedding dress and Jennifer's maid-of-honor dress. Ruthie had also sewn a matching dress for KC and a small suit for Charley that matched the one Jesse wore for the ceremony.

Tobias Harrington had been taken to Virginia City to stand trial for his part in the conspiracy against Jesse. Even without the testimony of the Branson women, who refused all attempts by the governor to get them to travel to the territory's capital to testify, Harrington was found guilty. He was serving the first of many years in the territorial prison at Deer Lodge in a cell not too far from the one occupied by Marcus Thompson.

Word had arrived from Mary Kensington that her husband had been committed to a mental hospital, as arranged with Judge Henson. Unfortunately for Kensington, his behavior after being told of the arrangement had only reinforced the claim of his diminished mental capacity. It was unlikely he would ever convince anyone he had been unjustly committed.

Jennifer's brothers had taken over the family business and welcomed their mother's interest in its operation. Thomas was planning his own marriage, as was their youngest brother William, and Mary was looking forward to lots of grandchildren to spoil.

Jesse's thoughts returned to her immediate surroundings when she heard the door behind her open. She turned to see Jennifer emerge from the house, dressed in a beautiful pale blue gown.

Jennifer smiled as Jesse stepped forward to meet her. "I love that suit on you."

Jesse was dressed in the same suit of soft buckskin she had worn for her own wedding. Miraculously, it and Jennifer's own wedding dress, stored in an old trunk, had survived the fire.

"Looks like the guests are starting to arrive," Jennifer said as she saw a buggy crest the hillock to the north of the ranch house.

Jesse pulled Jennifer to her, not bothering to look at the approaching buggy. "Don't let Ruthie know, but I think you were the most beautiful woman at the wedding this morning. I love you, darlin."

Jennifer laid her head against Jesse's shoulder. "I love you, too."

"Come on, you two." Bette Mae pushed her way out the door and past the women, her arms full of baskets holding freshly baked breads and biscuits. "We got lots ta do b'fore folks start arrivin'. You can snuggle up wit' one 'nother afterwards."

"Yes, Bette Mae." Jesse chuckled as she watched the woman carry her load to the tables set up in the yard. "Where are our little ones?"

"Sleeping upstairs. Billie and Ruthie are watching them; they wanted some time together."

"I'd best get to work helping Bette Mae carry all that food outside."

"I'll help, too."

"Don't overdo it," Jesse warned. "I want to enjoy some dancing with you later."

"I promise." Jennifer rested her head against Jesse's. "Thank you."

"For what?"

"For loving me. Despite everything that we have been through, this past year has been the best part of my life."

"Plenty more years in front of us, darlin'." Jesse pulled Jennifer to her, kissing her soundly.

Mickey was born and raised in Southern California. She has lived in New Mexico and Washington state and, for the past several years, in Western Montana. A lifelong history and nature enthusiast, Mickey has explored many of the locations she uses in her stories. She is also an amateur photographer and enjoys photographing the natural beauty of Montana as well as recording remnants of life in the frontier.

Mickey has plans for several more books and looks forward to the day she can spend all her time writing. Visit Mickey's website at mickeyminner.com

Printed in the United States
200407BV00004B/88-93/A